THE LITERARY WEST

THE
LITERARY
WEST

$\blacktriangleright\!\!\blacksquare\!\!\blacklozenge\!\!\blacksquare\!\!\blacktriangleleft$

An Anthology
of
Western American Literature

edited by Thomas J. Lyon

New York   Oxford
Oxford University Press
1999

Oxford University Press

Oxford   New York
Athens   Auckland   Bangkok   Bogotá   Buenos Aires   Calcutta
Cape Town   Chennai   Dar es Salaam   Delhi   Florence   Hong Kong   Istanbul
Karachi   Kuala Lumpur   Madrid   Melbourne   Mexico City   Mumbai
Nairobi   Paris   São Paulo   Singapore   Taipei   Tokyo   Toronto   Warsaw

and associated companies in

Berlin   Ibadan

Copyright © 1999 by Thomas J. Lyon

Published by Oxford University Press, Inc.,
198 Madison Avenue, New York, New York 10016

Oxford is a registered trademark of Oxford University Press

Library of Congress Cataloging-in-Publication Data
The literary west : an anthology of western American literature /
edited by Thomas J. Lyon
        p.   cm.
Includes bibliographical references (p. 425) and index.
ISBN 0-19-512460-X (acid-free paper). -- ISBN 0-19-512461-8 (pbk.)
1.American literature--West (U.S.) 2.West (U.S.)--Literary
collections.   I. Lyon,Thomas J. (Thomas Jefferson), 1937-   .
PS561.L58   1999
810.8'03278--dc21   99-10579

1 3 5 7 9 8 6 4 2
Printed in the United States of America
on acid-free paper

for Max, who loved the stories

CONTENTS

Ultimately, much of this book originates in the sense of place inhering in the human mind, and in people's experiences of place in the American West. A simple enough idea, perhaps, but one that bucks a present trend. There is abroad today a notion that the world is becoming an electronic village and that we are headed toward a universal, market-centered monoculture. Where you're from or where you live is supposed to be pretty much interchangeable with other places, both in the mind and on the ground. Global electronic consumerism may actually be our future, of course, but if so, I think we would stand to lose something very close to the bone. The shape of the world—what the Utah writer Edward Geary once called "the proper edge of the sky" and Edith Cobb referred to as the "good gestalt"—comes to us, after all, in the form of particular surroundings and helps make the furniture of our minds. To trade this rooting for a life of marketplace globalism would be to forfeit a lot of the sharpness and reality of unmediated, personal perception.

On the other side, from a sophisticated, world-spanning point of view, place is too obvious a theme and tends to be the source of nostalgia, one of the more banal emotions.

But place is close to the heart of western writing. (And up until very recently, this sense for surroundings was part of what brought western literature condescension in the term "regional.") Now, as the political and economic drums beat for a world economy and culture, we may ask if there are more significant virtues in emplaced literature than we have noticed. The writing that is coming out of the West today leans strongly toward what is distinctive in that region ecologically, topographically, climatically, culturally—in short, toward the specifics of *place*. Through western writers, we may collectively be asking if allegiances and connections to our surroundings are not only nostalgic but somehow integral, and not to be discarded lightly.

Several helpful and friendly people put their marks, sometimes unknowingly, on this book. At Utah State University, my colleagues, Barre Toelken, Morlyn Seamons, David Lewis, Clyde A. Milner II, Roberta Stearman, and Jane Reilly allowed me to interrupt their work and gave unstintingly of their considerable expertise. Writer and scholar Gerald Haslam helped me into his specialty, California literature. At the University of California, San Diego, Linda Claasen, Director of the Mandeville Special Collections of the Geisel Library, and Bradley D. Westbrook, Manuscripts Librarian, were especially helpful. Elda Rotor, at Oxford University Press, furthered the project at every turn with unfailing insight and efficiency. My wife Jan, a native Westerner and a reader of uncommon attention, has studied every aspect of this book, saving me from several errors and making the whole project a pleasure.

THE LITERARY WEST

INTRODUCTION
The Conquistador, the Lone Ranger, and Beyond

There are two Wests. One is a mostly mental place, a projection. Wild and open, this West is everything the over-civilized East, or Europe, is not. It's a ticket to freedom. Here, "a man's a man, and the women love it." In the big new space, you create a new life, a liberation from the past. The very soil is untapped, so even being a farmer is a kind of adventure. Plant seed and jump back.

We came into the West in the early years of our culture's worldwide blaze of expansionary triumph, a "frontier" era that would last for something more than 400 years, and from the start (for example, Coronado's trek in search of the supposedly golden "Seven Cities of Cibola" in 1540), our image of the West was prone to a certain dreaminess. The region seemed to be a natural repository for fantasy. As the unknown quarter, it might really harbor the legendary Queen Califia and her Amazonian tribe, or, later, the hypothetically easy portage to Pacific waters that Thomas Jefferson believed in, or any number of El Dorados, or, indeed (and into our own time), an endless supply of trees for lumber. It became the "territory" that Huck Finn naturally gravitated toward, and sixty-odd years later it was where Holden Caulfield thought he might, perhaps, find work on a ranch. The amazing durability of the western image as a treasure trove, an exotic land of wonders, or simply an "out," as in "out West," is good evidence of dualistic and projective consciousness, a bit out of touch.

As the scholar Walter Prescott Webb pointed out almost a half century ago, the American West was only one of several frontiers to feel the effects of the Euro-American, post-Renaissance energy. South America, Africa, India, Australia, and New Zealand, among other regions, became scenes of adventure, accumulation, and the peculiar reinforcement of identity that borderlands, as meeting-places with the unknown, tend to generate. But the West offered a persuasive set of images—the rider and his horse, the wide-brimmed hat, the sea of grass, the long, wild view to the far mesa, the war-bonneted Indian, to name some basics—and it came into our consciousness just when romance and individualism were flowering, and thus it became the dominant iconic frontier for an entire culture. Shortly after the development of the steam-powered printing press (the industrialization of literature, one might call it), the mass media would come close to solidifying the American-western construct. Over a few

decades in the latter part of the nineteenth century and the early twentieth, the West became totally familiar as a set of expectations and images—
it became "stock." The Wild West.

But fly over the region today (say, from Denver to San Francisco, a
journey of about two and a half hours) and you will see below you not
only the beautiful natural matrix—the jagged peaks and dark sweeps of
forest in Rocky Mountain National Park, for example, and later on the
chasms of the canyon country of Utah, the long stretches of the "sage-
brush ocean" of the Great Basin, and finally the dramatically clean-cut
granite of the Sierra Nevada and Yosemite National Park—but also, un-
avoidably, you will see a perhaps surprising number of other things not
so classically beautiful. Early in the flight you will look down on cattle
feedlots covering hundreds, perhaps thousands of acres; then, shortly, an
astonishing number of drillpads and working oil and gas wells in western
Colorado and eastern Utah, speckled across the pinyon-juniper landscape
and connected by a network of roads; open-pit mines of huge scale in
Utah and northeastern Nevada; cities along the way (Denver, Salt Lake
City, Reno, Sacramento) spaghettied with freeways; hundreds of square
miles of center-pivot-irrigated cropland (wherever there is soil and
enough water to keep the circles green); reservoirs, canals, and aqueducts,
particularly sizable and numerous as you fly over California; interstate
highways, of course, and a maze of lesser roads, most surprising, perhaps,
in the Great Basin. And several airplanes will pass below you, many of
them in the service of commuter airlines, further threading together this
well-developed region. What isn't seen, except for the telltale bristle of
repeater towers on mountaintops, is the network of electronic communi-
cations that smoothly integrates the American West into the global life-
way. This below you, in short, is a second West: ordinary ground, less
densely populated than better-watered regions, more fragile than they,
more easily abused and taking longer to recover. (A roadcut here is not
going to melt back into the humid woods, as in Vermont or Pennsylvania;
it is going to stand out as a scar for decades, perhaps centuries.) This
West where people actually live and have effects on the landscape isn't
the stock one.

The real West has been written about since first contact in the sixteenth
century, initially in certain explorers' reports and journals, fitfully in the
mid–nineteenth century by realists and satirists like Mark Twain, very
precisely in the writings of naturalists like John Muir and Mary Austin
working at the close of the frontier era, and in more recent times by such
novelists as Willa Cather, Harvey Fergusson, Frederick Manfred, Wallace
Stegner, and Larry McMurtry. But until quite recently, the last thirty years
or so, this "higher" or more serious kind of western literature has been a

minor tradition. Until the late 1960s, it was hardly given scholarly and historical attention even as a regional voice, so overwhelming was the literary presence of the first, projective West. The story of western literature, then, is the story of two Wests, the one immediately and deeply persuasive, the second more complex in its intentions and effects. The second has been gaining ground, more rapidly since about 1970, with the general expansion of environmental awareness in America and a beginning recognition of minority and alternative views.

Before there were any written western literatures, there was long-term, profoundly rooted cultural expression in the West. The Indian tribes, whose history in the region goes back perhaps thirty thousand years, declared their allegiance to honored homelands through origin and migration stories, cemented family and tribal bonds in community-oriented narratives, and commented on human psychology and morality in instructive, symbol-laden myths. Speaking generally, of course, for we are summarizing several hundred local cultures, the consciousness behind this literature appears to have been focused in a manner different from that of the later-coming Western civilization. What is valued is communitarian rather than individualistic; right living is founded in reciprocity. Indians shared basic human consciousness, of course, but the balance appears to have tipped in the opposite direction from that of Euro-American culture, toward relational awareness—a crucial difference. Another significant difference is that for Indians, their literature seems to have *mattered tremendously*. Story was central as a means of education and community. Countless Indian tales dramatize the temptations of individualism and the rightness of dedication to community. Along the environmental line, many tribes had a stock of stories describing the area they lived in, telling why they had come to fit just there, and what was required of them to continue to live in the home place. Animals were depicted as having full consciousness and sensitivity. In short, the relational matrix of human life was deeply honored. Unfortunately, much of this literature, elaborated over thousands of years, was lost after contact, when large numbers of Indians were subjugated, relocated, or killed. Very few groups were able to hold on to a significant percentage of their former traditions and to live according to their lights.

In the late nineteenth century, the Smithsonian Institution, the Bureau of American Ethnology, and various academic anthropologists began what must have seemed an emergency effort to collect Indian stories and to understand the Native American outlooks. The Bureau of American Ethnology's Annual Reports, beginning in 1879, opened up some of the first cracks in the façade of the frontier mind. Sympathetic observers like Frank Hamilton Cushing (1857–1900) and Franz Boas (1858–1942) showed their readers native cultures that were sophisticated and philosophically interesting. About this same time, Indian writers themselves were breaking into print. The Piute woman Sarah Winnemucca (1844?–1891) was one of the first (1883) to demonstrate command of a bicultural point of view and flexible, effective English prose.

The first western writing—in fact the only western writing until San Francisco became established as a city and literary center in the 1850s—consisted of travel accounts and diaries kept during explorations. The earliest records were made by Spaniards, the first of whom, Álvar Núñez Cabeza de Vaca (c.1490–c.1557), straggled into the West after a shipwreck on the Florida coast in 1528 and left an interesting account describing eight years of travail and apparent transformation from would-be conqueror of Indians to near-insider in native culture. The other early Spanish diarists came northward from Mexico, seeking gold, converts to Christianity, or, beginning in the later sixteenth century, opportunities for settlement. Pedro de Castañeda's record of the Coronado expedition of 1540, Juan de Oñate's description of a successful settlement in New Mexico in 1598, and Diego de Vargas's account of his punishment of rebellious Pueblo Indians a century later illustrate the limited range of most of this early literature: All three accounts deal primarily with what kind of treasure at what level of abundance the West offers, how useful or dangerous or open to conversion the native people are, and what heroic frontiersmanship will be required in order to take possession of the new land. One of the better early accounts, remarkable in its author's recognizable humanity and depiction of human relations during his journey, is that of Pedro Font (1738–1781), a Franciscan missionary who accompanied Juan Bautista de Anza's second northward expedition in 1776. This trek covered a long stretch of country between north-central Mexico and San Francisco Bay and resulted in the planting of a colony at San Francisco. Only a few months later in 1776, two more Spanish missionaries, Francisco Atanasio Dominguez and Silvestre Vélez de Escalante, made a remarkable journey from Santa Fe northward to what is now central Utah, looking for a good route to the Pacific Coast from the New Mexico settlements. Giving up on getting to California, they returned home by crossing a good deal of the canyon country of the Colorado Plateau. Escalante's journal describes some of the most difficult terrain on the planet in matter-of-fact fashion and displays a fair-minded attitude toward the Indians the explorers encountered.

That the early Spanish narratives have not loomed large in western literary history is a function of who, mainly, has written that history. The commanding image of the West is indeed that it is the West, and not the North, El Norte. The typical understanding behind the "we" of America is that "we" landed on the East coast, developed seaboard colonies, achieved independence through revolution, found a way through the Appalachian mountain barrier, crossed the Great Plains in wagon trains, fought the Indians, crossed the Rocky Mountains and the deserts to the west of them, finally to stand on the shores of Oregon and California. From sea to shining sea. This westward movement, as the familiar phrase has it, is the ruling plot. But beginning with the scholarly work of Herbert Eugene Bolton early in the twentieth century and continuing now under the impact of the western reality, which is increasingly and undeniably polyglot, the dominant narrative has started showing signs of wear and tear. Perhaps future literary histories will have different emphases.

In the mainstream story, the first major reference point is the expedition of Lewis and Clark, 1804–1806. It hardly matters, and is hardly known, that Alexander Mackenzie preceded Lewis and Clark to the Pacific (indeed, they carried his account with them), or that John Ledyard, Peter Pond, and others had made far-western journeys before them: Lewis and Clark are first in our hearts. They were official, having been sent by President Thomas Jefferson, and they carried our young nation's territorial ambitions. In truth they accomplished an almost miraculously successful exploration, along the way keeping detailed journals that gave reality to the Louisiana Purchase, our biggest leap until then toward continental closure. Many pages of the journals, particularly those written by Meriwether Lewis (1774–1809), have depth of reflection and show consciousness of the historical momentousness of the trek, but it is the sheer fact of what they saw that compels modern attention. Their descriptions of vast herds of wild game in what is now North Dakota or of numbers of grizzly bears near the present Great Falls, Montana, for example, give the journals an Edenic flavor and our present-day reading of them a certain very American, nostalgic-tragic dimension.

Other travelers, among them some rather good writers like Robert Stuart of the "Astoria" expedition of 1810–1812 and the naturalists Thomas Nuttall (1786–1859) and John Kirk Townsend (1809–1851) in the 1820s and 1830s, followed Lewis and Clark into the West as the fur trade began to open up the country. And some of the fur trappers, or "mountain men," themselves kept journals, which are still very much worth reading. Two in particular, Osborne Russell (1814–1892) and Warren Angus Ferris (1810–1873), responded sensitively to the wild landscapes they worked in. Russell's *Journal of a Trapper* (1855; reprint 1921) and Ferris's *Life In the Rocky Mountains* (1843–1844; reprint 1940) offer more than antiquarian interest because the authors reveal their personalities and dramatize the aesthetic rapture that in later times became known as the "wilderness experience." In 1838, the Army Corps of Topographical Engineers was created and became the sponsor of several survey expeditions. Two of the early surveyors, John Charles Fremont and Howard Stansbury, during expeditions of 1842 and 1843–1844 in Fremont's case and 1849 in Stansbury's, left records of some literary quality. These men responded positively to the wildness and solitude they found in the West. Despite their relatively late arrival in the region, their journals and reports convey at times the magical note of first-seeing.

But it was not until the 1850s, when enough talent had gathered in San Francisco (the first major urban area to develop in the West, and the region's first literary center), that a wider range of writing began to develop. In the decade of the Civil War, sophisticated journalists like Bret Harte, poets such as Ada Clare and Adah Menken (who had been advised by Walt Whitman to go west and find greater scope for their talent), and young Samuel Clemens had found work in the city by the bay and were contributing "local color" sketches, poetry, and satire to the *Golden Era* and the more literary *The Californian*. By 1868, there was sufficient good local writing and a felt need for a nationally distributed magazine based in San Francisco, and the *Overland Monthly* was founded, with Bret Harte as editor. The *Overland* cast itself as a western peer of the eastern establishment's *Atlantic* and did earn a national reputation, publishing a diverse array of writing that included some of Harte's mining-camp parables, the poetry of Californians Ina Coolbrith and Charles Warren Stoddard, economic essays by Henry George, and, in the 1870s, John Muir's series of articles on the glacial origins of Yosemite.

Literary life in San Francisco and the Bay area has continued to thrive. Merely listing a few names, among many possible, suggests the richness of the locale through the decades: Ambrose Bierce, Frank Norris, Gertrude Atherton, Jack London, Wallace Stegner, Kenneth Rexroth, Gary Snyder, Maxine Hong Kingston. Yet another development of the 1860s would come to overshadow not only San Francisco but the entire West and threaten to lock the region into a set of fixed frontier images. The mass-market dime novels and their successors, originating with the New York publisher House of Beadle and Adams in 1860, became, by both sheer quantity and compelling subject matter, the main literary activity drawing on the West. Valuing individual heroism, the rightness of progress, decisive action, and showing a bit of sentimental regard for the fated natives and the glorious wilderness, the dime novels and their inheritors settled into certain plots and character types. Soon the stories became programmatic, but the reading public did not become bored. On the contrary, as civilization spread and real-life opportunities for individual heroism and decisive action dwindled and as the Indians and the wilderness presented less and less and, finally, no significant challenge, the Western prospered.

Literary quality was never an issue. Readers did not appear to be seeking complexity or self-examination, and certainly not a reading experience involving indeterminacy or discovery; rather, they seemed to prefer the repetition of a formula in which, in the words of the scholar Daryl Jones in *The Dime Novel Western* (1978), "conflicts irresolvable in the real world could find swift and clear-cut solutions." For a long time, a simplified and heroic West would hold sway in the public imagination. During this time, for example, the 121 Buffalo Bill novels—nine in 1892 alone—by Prentiss Ingraham (1843–1904), Owen Wister's (1860–1938) *The Virginian* (1902), Zane Grey's (1875–1939) *Riders of the Purple Sage* (1912), countless short stories from the 1920s onward in "pulps" like *Western Story* and "slicks" like the *Saturday Evening Post*, and (after World War II) several million copies of the novels of Louis L'Amour (1908–1988) all appeared and were read avidly. Those stories offered something priceless to the American people, as well as to a very large readership in Europe: The opportunity to revel in the spacious freedom of the wild frontier and to identify with a hero who can somehow live beautifully in both the wild world and the civilized one to come. (The nameless Virginian, at the end of the novel, has gotten into coal and is becoming a capitalist; Shane, in Jack Schaefer's 1949 classic, is minutely aware of ladies' fashions back East and passes on the information to Marian Starrett in her Wyoming log cabin.) The essential centerpoint is the hero. It is no accident that *Shane* begins in the resonant key of mythology, with the simple masculine pronoun "he": "He rode into our valley in the summer of '89." The hero not only manages a dual world but carries within him unerring morality; he "knows what he has to do" and does it, even if the job involves violence. In one form or another (including, in their slant way, take-offs and anti-Westerns), the Western offers a hero who will in some way make us feel that our history, by virtue of culminating in such a product, has not been all that bad. It seems safe to predict that the genre will be around for some time to come.

John Muir, born in Scotland in 1838, raised on a pioneer farm in Wisconsin, and resident in California since the spring of 1868, became in the 1870s the first western writer to transcend the frontier mentality and its dualistic frame of reference. This emergence was arguably the source of Muir's charisma and rather amazing public-policy success, and it began in his intense experience of wild nature. He became a hero of a different kind, a hero of the contemplative, nature-oriented life. During the early heyday of the Western, Muir provided an alternative way of responding to the much-talked-about closing of the frontier: To cultivate attentiveness and reverence so that nature's sacred vitality flooded one's being, carrying one into a frontierless world in which no "petty personal hope or experience," as Muir wrote, "has room to be." When Muir described the landscape as "beaming with consciousness" or wrote of glaciers that "blend with the snow and the snow blends with the thin invisible breath of the sky" or of trees feeling the "sting" of squirrels' claws, he was inviting his readers to see the world nondualistically, a grand system that included human life as just one of its manifestations—nothing separate. Where the contemporaneous popular Western solved the fragmented mental landscape of our culture by creating and identifying with a kind of superself, the hero, Muir dissolved the dualistic attitude that creates a separate self in the first place. He stands at the beginning of a line of western nature-writers, only a few of whom have recorded eco-mystical experience with such intensity but all of whom write within the world of discourse he legitimatized. The Muir revival, with first stirrings in the 1960s, coincides with the growth of ecological awareness in the modern industrial world. A high percentage of the most important writing done in the American West over the past thirty years shares Muir's basic values.

Among the more important western nature writers who immediately succeeded Muir, Enos Mills (1870–1922) of the Colorado Rockies and Mary Austin (1868–1934) of the "land of little rain," the Southwest, honored him explicitly. The next generation of natural historians—such as the ecologists Aldo Leopold (1886–1948) and Olaus Murie (1889–1963), the Texans J. Frank Dobie (1888–1964) and Roy Bedichek (1878–1959), and the influential student of the Sonoran Desert, Joseph Wood Krutch (1893–1970)—all followed the Muir example by emphasizing the ways in which the bewildering diversity of flora and fauna comes together to make a system—the ecosystem. They saw the world ecologically, and they paid tribute to wildness as the source of insight and the standard of health. Two of them, Leopold and Krutch, ventured sweeping statements on the importance of wilderness that have become touchstones for the modern environmental movement. Krutch also explored issues of consciousness (influencing in this regard another western writer of significance, Edward Abbey), and though he eschewed mysticism, he did question the adequacy of the received Cartesian dualistic outlook.

Besides ecology, a critique of the nation's economic system also called into question the mainstream triumphalist reading of western history. It was also galvanizing, for example, to become cognizant of inequalities in money and power—the fundamental unfairness that capitalism can exhibit. In the early part of his career, when he wrote in a realistic style he called "veritism," Hamlin Garland (1860–1940) drew great energy from the awareness of inequity, something that he had recognized as a boy on Iowa farms. American farm life, that great and good way honored by Crèvecoeur and Jefferson, had become something else by the 1880s. Garland's *Main-Travelled Roads* (1891) was the first collection of fiction to take a frank look at the money powers making for rural desperation. *McTeague* (1899), *The Octopus* (1901), and *The Pit* (1902), by the tragically short-lived San Franciscan Frank Norris (1870–1902), all showed a keen sensitivity to greed, an awareness that it not only could ruin individual lives but was, in the bigger picture, a driving force behind American economic life. One of the intellectual touchstones for the self-taught Californian Jack London (1876–1916) was the socialist critique of capitalism; he had earned many of his insights growing up on the wrong side of the tracks in Oakland, and crossing the country as a "hobo"; he subsequently recorded his analysis in *The Iron Heel* (1908) and in the nonfiction collection *Revolution and Other Essays* (1910). Two decades after London's death, John Steinbeck (1902–1968) researched the migrant and displaced farmworker camps of Depression-era central California, published a series of hard-hitting newspaper exposés, and eventually transmuted his understanding into great art in *Of Mice and Men* (1937) and *The Grapes of Wrath* (1939). During the Depression, young Tillie Olsen wrote scathingly, out of her own experience, of economic unfairness and the grinding life of poverty in Omaha in *Yonnondio*, a powerful novel not published until 1974. Meridel Le Sueur (1901–1996), like Olsen a radical and activist, recorded her dissenting analysis in *North Star Country* (1945), a history that includes what might be called the darker side of the Upper Midwest past. In more recent time, the New Mexico novelist John Nichols (b. 1940) has continued the generally "left" perspective on American economic practice and its imperialist weight on disadvantaged western groups, with his novels *The Milagro Beanfield War* (1974) and *The Magic Journey* (1978). It has become clear in the literature of the past century that the West, with its spaciousness and seeming opportunity, and simply its newness, had once appeared to offer a last chance for something different, politically and economically. Perhaps this was only another western fantasy; what is certain is that disillusionment with the eventuating historical reality has energized much western writing. The new land has been clear-cut and overgrazed, minorities and the working class have been exploited in exactly the traditional manner, the alternating fevers of fear and desire so well known to the stock markets have destabilized the economic life of the West right along with everyone else's. The inchoate but once strongly felt dreams of a new start have dwindled. Thus a certain tragic vision of history has become a core element in serious western literature.

The view of life set forth by perhaps the best-known western novelist, Nebraska's Willa Cather (1873–1947), was, economically, not dissenting or radical, and she was not an environmentalist in the political sense, but she had a penetrating ethical critique of modern civilization. It was rooted in her western experience. The old ways of the first pioneer generation—hard work and sacrifice and a certain nobly simple if repressed morality—and the even older ways of the cliff-dwelling Anasazi of the Southwest, who seemed to build and live in graceful harmony with their environment, endured as references for Cather. In *The Professor's House* (1925), she describes a well-off modern midwestern family whose very affluence has only damaged their relationships with each other and smoothed their way into an affectless consumerism. The father of the family, the professor, has contact with the older, lost world through his memories of a former student, Tom Outland, who had discovered a "Cliff City" high on a mesa in the Southwest and while exploring the ruins had experienced a profound, life-changing epiphany. Tom's Blue Mesa becomes the locus of the old, better way in the novel, a quiet contrast to contemporary reality. The professor, at midlife, is caught between the two worlds.

In her first successful novel, *O Pioneers!* (1913), and in *My Ántonia* (1918), Cather had honored the courage and immensely hard work of the pioneers of the Nebraska plains but had not whitewashed them. Psychological blindness on the part of a pioneer heroine, portrayed as part of her perhaps necessarily narrow emotional life, helps generate a tragedy in *O Pioneers!*, and in *My Ántonia* there is a suicide and a climate of stifling village conformity to darken and round out the picture of earlier times.

There has, in fact, been a tremendous drive in western fiction over the past century to reveal the real West. At the popular or "grade B" level of western writing, the urge toward truth (as in *True Frontier, True West*, etc.) has been largely antiquarian and empirical: how many bullets, what kind of rifle, what kind of saddle, and so forth. In more "serious" or literary hands, the ambition is to cut through mythology. Cather, for instance, refused to simplify and stereotype her honored Indians. She had a realist's allegiance to psychological complexity—her artistic, ancient cliff-dwellers in *The Professor's House* left evidence, for example, of violent breaks in family relationships. Other writers in the West's realistic and modernist lineage, novelists like New Mexican Harvey Fergusson (1890–1971), Idaho native Vardis Fisher (1895–1968), Montana's A. B. Guthrie Jr. (1901–1991), Nebraskan Mari Sandoz (1896–1966), Iowa and "Siouxland" chronicler Frederick Manfred (1912–1994), Nevadan Walter Van Tilburg Clark (1909–1971), Southwesterner Frank Waters (1902–1995), and the "dean" of western writers, Wallace Stegner (1909–1993), were all determined to get underneath the dominant imagery and portray life in the West in its human conflict, paradox, and sometimes sheer perversity. It is worth noting that each of these writers wrote unsparingly in the autobiographical mode. Vardis Fisher typified this quest when in searching his own background, he discovered and wrote frankly about a number of what he called "evasions" both in his family and himself—attempts to gloss over contradictions and align family history with the nominal codes of western culture. Stegner (who was a student of Fisher's at the University of Utah) also attempted to look objectively at his own family, and like Fisher he extrapolated insights from his background onto the more general level of western history. To Stegner, his father typified the "boomer," a rootless Westerner who had an eye only for quick fortune. His mother, temperamentally, was a "sticker," who above all wanted family stability in a good place. These are the two main western types, according to Stegner. In addition, the persistence and dominance of the cowboy myth seems to have bothered Stegner more than a little, for he was writing about it into the 1990s. (Fictionally speaking, Walter Van Tilburg Clark had undermined the cowboy monolith back in 1940, with *The Ox-Bow Incident*.) A. B. Guthrie Jr. created realistic characters out of "mountain men" in *The Big Sky* (1947)—that is, he showed their normal human potential for greed, arrogance, and unconsciousness, qualities co-existing with their innocent reveling in wilderness freedom. Frank Waters took some of the gilt off the western mining tradition in *Below Grass Roots* (1937) and *The Dust within the Rock* (1940); Harvey Fergusson, who had been influenced in youth by H. L. Mencken, went behind the mellow adobe of the Spanish grantees and their successors in *The Blood of the Conquerors* (1921) and *Grant of Kingdom* (1950). Mari Sandoz (1896–1966) honored the Native American perspective in *Crazy Horse* (1942) and *Cheyenne Autumn* (1953), and in *Old Jules* (1935) and *Slogum House* (1937), she delved into western violence at the family level. Frederick Manfred (1912–1994) wrote boldly of the gritty side of midwestern farm life in *The Chokecherry Tree* (1948), *Eden Prairie* (1968), and the autobiographical *Green Earth* (1977). One by one, subregion by subregion and character type by character type, from mountain man to pioneer to cowboy, these writers established an ambitious and serious literary West, a kind of shadow country to the frontier that ruled so brightly in popular imagination.

Other important fiction writers in the generation that built a realistic western canon include Sinclair Lewis (1885–1951), Dorothy Scarborough (1878–1935), and Ole E. Rølvaag (1876–1931). Collectively, the realists established truth-telling as normative for serious western fiction. They were the foundation-layers. In the past twenty-five years or so, we have seen a flowering of serious western fiction in which any and all themes, characters, and techniques can be and are used, and the new freedom owes much to the pioneer generation. At the literary level now, a western novelist doesn't need to debunk mythology or prove anything; the territory has been won, and its materials can be played with in any way the writer sees fit. The maturity is readily seen in the works of such writers as Larry

McMurtry (b. 1936), Tony Hillerman (b. 1925), Richard Ford (b. 1944), Barbara Kingsolver (b. 1955), Jim Harrison (b. 1937), Levi Peterson (b. 1933), Raymond Carver (1938–1988), Joan Didion (b. 1934), Cormac McCarthy (b. 1933), Gerald Haslam (b. 1937), and Norman Maclean (1902–1990), to name only a few of the West's leading spirits in fiction.

Another sign that the western literary terrain has been freed up is the recent rise and acceptance of writing coming from ethnic minorities. (Under current demographic trends, "minorities" may one day be an inaccurate term; see the Chronology entry for 1994.) Chinese newspapers in San Francisco were publishing lyric poetry in the 1860s, black novelists Sutton E. Griggs (1872–1930) of Texas (*Unfettered*, 1902) and Oscar Micheaux (1884–1951) of South Dakota (*The Conquest*, 1913) published novels well before our time, and the narrative ballads called *corridos* had flourished in the Mexican-American population since the mid–nineteenth century. But it has only been since the late 1950s that writing of ethnic or minority origin has broken into the larger literary marketplace and begun to be appreciated widely for its quality. John Okada's (1923–1971) *No-No Boy* (1957) and José Antonio Villarreal's (b. 1924) *Pocho* (1959), two uncompromising novels detailing life in minority situations, started to open things up, followed by Ishmael Reed's (b. 1938) *The Free-Lance Pallbearers* in 1967 and Ernest J. Gaines's (b. 1933) collection of stories *Bloodline* in 1968 and his celebrated novel, *The Autobiography of Miss Jane Pittman*, in 1971. Luis Valdez (b. 1940)—first by organizing the Teatro Campesino to support Cesar Chavez and the United Farm Workers and then with his play *Zoot Suit* (premiered in Los Angeles in 1978)—contributed greatly to what is perhaps the strongest ethnic minority literary tradition in the West, the Mexican-American. Rolando Hinojosa (b. 1929), with his chronicles of south Texas life such as *Estampas del valle y otras obras* (1973), New Mexico's Rudolfo Anaya (b. 1937), with his widely celebrated novel *Bless Me, Ultima* (1972), and Californian Richard Rodriguez (b. 1944), with his autobiography *Hunger of Memory* (1982), showed early on the broad reach of the Hispanic contribution; all three continue to expand and deepen the content of that ever freer and larger literary range. Maxine Hong Kingston's (b. 1940) *Woman Warrior* (1976) and Amy Tan's (b. 1952) *The Joy Luck Club* (1989) have been recent examples of nationwide success and critical esteem. Expectably perhaps, and rightly so, a major focus in minority fiction coming out of the West has been on race relations and the seemingly impenetrable system of discrimination practiced by the white majority. Ethnic writers are not necessarily interested in, say, the Euro-American dialectic of civilization and wilderness; their West is culturally different from that of Anglo writers. But over the last forty years their writing has come forward insistently and earned its standing. It has helped bring the real, diverse West to light.

The story of poetry in the West shows a somewhat similar plotline to fiction's. There were romantic beginnings (Joaquin Miller [1837–1913], for example, and later John G. Neihardt [1881–1973], much more thorough and accurate in his researches), a realistic or "major phase," embodied best in the heavyweight, much-written-about work of Robinson Jeffers (1887–1962), and most recently a tremendous creative proliferation after World War II. Meanwhile, a less literary verse analogous to the Western's position in fiction has flourished from the beginning, culminating in recent times in the popular "cowboy" poetry. The major figures in serious western poetry have been Neihardt and Jeffers, with the ironic retrospecter Thomas Hornsby Ferril (1896–1988) of Colorado occupying approximately the same time frame as Jeffers; since midcentury, Theodore Roethke (1908–1963), for whom a move to the Northwest in 1947 meant poetic rejuvenation and who planned an epic treatment of Indian history before his untimely death; William Stafford (1914–1993) of Kansas and Oregon, whose poetic voice is quietly but thoroughly subversive of the frontier myth, the knowledge-is-power myth, the personal-self myth, and in fact every favorite self-congratulation; Richard Hugo (1923–1982), who helped make Montana a literary center through both poetry and teaching; David Wagoner (b. 1926), also a significant novelist, who has been described as "the Pacific Northwest's Robert Frost" for his deep connection with his adopted region; William Everson (1912–1994), one of the great, many-careered, intense writers to have grown up in California; and Gary Snyder (b. 1930), the most accomplished and influential poet of the San Francisco renaissance. The westernness of these poets is found in their critical attitude toward expansionary "frontier" culture, their allegiance to nature and more specifically to particular western places, and their descriptions of transcendent personal experience. From Neihardt onward, this combination of characteristics has essentially described western poetry's outlines. It continues in the work of Pattiann Rogers (b. 1940) of Texas, Richard Shelton (b. 1933) of Arizona, Keith Wilson (b. 1927) of New Mexico, David Lee (b. 1944) and Kenneth Brewer (b. 1941) of Utah, Linda Hasselstrom (b. 1943) of South Dakota, Garrett Hongo (b. 1951) of Hawaii, and Gary Soto (b. 1952), Robert Hass (b. 1941), and Diane Wakoski (b. 1937) of California, perhaps the present-day western poets of greatest note.

Truth-telling and accuracy have been notoriously difficult for Euro-American writers when the subject is the American Indian. The brute fact is that an invading culture expropriated, killed, and/or culturally dispossessed nearly all of the Indians. This made understanding at a significant literary level very rare and difficult for the conquerors. Certain persistent stereotypes smothered the potential for insight. It has been uphill work for Euro-American writers to get beyond "savagism," the curious blend of "pity and censure," as Roy Harvey Pearce put it, that has been the mainstream American view. In general, Otherness rules. Even the Indians in the novels of realists like Harvey Fergusson and Vardis Fisher were viewed at a seemingly irreducible distance and tended to fall into familiar grooves of character-type. Several important writers of the West, including John Muir, Robinson Jeffers, and the otherwise comprehensive Wallace Stegner, seemed hardly to notice the Indians. Among exceptions to the general trend, the significant naturalist-novelist-playwright-folklorist Mary Austin, Frederick Manfred in several historical novels, and especially Frank Waters, over a long career, departed from the mainstream to take Native Americans seriously on their own terms. Waters's insight into the difference in worldview between Euro-American and Indian cultures fueled novels such as *The Man Who Killed the Deer* (1942) and *The Woman At Otowi Crossing* (1966) and gave depth to his nonfiction studies *Masked Gods* (1950) and *Book of the Hopi* (1963).

Over the past thirty years Native American authors themselves have been immensely prolific and have provided the materials for a wider vision of humanity and the West. Before this recent renaissance and going back as far as 1854 to the Cherokee John Rollin Ridge's novel *The Life and Adventures of Joaquin Murieta, the Celebrated California Bandit*, a book carrying a strong indictment of race prejudice, there was a fair amount of Indian writing from the West, including a number of autobiographies. In 1936, the Montana native D'Arcy McNickle (1904–1977), son of a part-Cree mother and an Irish father, published *The Surrounded*, a novel whose themes and general "map" have proved to be characteristic: there is disorder within the soul of McNickle's mixed-blood protagonist, microcosmic to the larger societal conflicts around him, and he must try to overcome this seemingly intractable problem. In short, he has to deal with a world that is fragmented inside and out. This is the general situation of modern civilization, it could be argued, but for an Indian, fragmentation can work on life with a daily, insistent, terrible weight.

The contemporary Native renaissance in fiction is usually said to have begun with *House Made of Dawn* (1968) by the Kiowa artist, writer, poet, and professor N. Scott Momaday (b. 1934). Abel, its protagonist, is stalled under the heavy burdens general to modern-day Indians, but his story begins to move when he starts to awaken to ancient traditions of harmony—including, perhaps most instructively, ritual acts reconnecting with and re-respecting the earth. Momaday's novel thus harks back to literary conventions and values thousands of years old in Native American life. But his telling of the story is up-to-date indeed; the voice and the fictional techniques employed are as sophisticated as those of any post–World War II American or European novel. James Welch (b. 1940), a Montanan of Blackfeet, Gros Ventre, and European background, and Laguna Pueblo Leslie Marmon Silko (b. 1948), along with Momaday the most-studied and perhaps most influential contemporary Indian fiction writers, also write with command of contemporary techniques. Welch's breakthrough novel, *Winter in the Blood* (1974), portrays tragic situations with accuracy and poetic economy (and occasional dark humor), so that the poetic flexibility of the nameless narrator's mind becomes as important as his turn toward healing tradition, in showing a possible way out of the contemporary bleakness. Silko's *Ceremony* (1977) looms as large as *House Made of Dawn* and *Winter in the Blood* and shares with them a traumatized protagonist, an affirmation of the power of story and the possibility of healing, as well as technical virtuosity. But her long novel *Almanac of the Dead* (1991), in its thorough and angry-seeming catalog of the ills and injustices of contemporary life, may shock even more readers into recognition of the nature of our moment in history, as seen through Indian eyes.

Across the West, coming from a diversity of tribes and situations, other Indian writers contributing vitally to the new wave include most prominently Simon Ortiz of Acoma Pueblo (b. 1941), Gerald Vizenor (Anishinabe, b. 1934), Sherman Alexie (Spokane/Coeur d'Alene, b. 1966), Louise Erdrich (Turtle Mountain Chippewa, b. 1954), and Linda Hogan (Chickasaw, b. 1947). The great undercurrent in these contemporary writers' work is that any resource, any story technique, any relevant cultural memory can and should be brought to bear in the struggle to heal the broken world. Broadly speaking, the motivation is similar to that which moved Native literature for thousands of years.

Parallel and akin to the new Indian writing, a great emphasis on place and nature has developed in western literature over the past three decades, beginning with Edward Abbey (1927–1989) and his influential *Desert Solitaire* (1968). The close attention that is being paid to writers' home localities represents a change of paradigm from that of the frontier mind, which has its eyes, so to speak, on the far horizon. The rise of nature writing, together with personal reminiscences about nature that are not predominantly natural-historical in intent, dovetails with the revived Indian perspective. Common to these two now-predominant trends is the search for community—in family, society, and with the natural world surroundings. The signs coming from these movements indicate that, collectively, we might be preparing to awaken from the egoistic, separatist fantasies of the frontier mythology.

Abbey, a central figure in the western literature of the outdoors, did not consider himself a nature writer—that was a type much closer to "naturalist" in his mind, someone who described biology. He was more interested in narrating his experiences and moments of perception in wild places, and reflecting on their possible meanings. He was a brilliant dissecter of his culture's shibboleths and its money-driven, mechanical disregard for nature, and his talent for caricature was prodigious. In *Desert Solitaire* he described working as a ranger in Arches National Monument in Utah and going on adventures in places like the Grand Canyon, Glen Canyon, and the Maze, now part of Canyonlands National Park. His allegiance to this silent wilderness of slickrock and slot canyon was so pure that its designation as "Abbey Country" by himself and his enthusiastic readers has not been argued. In *Desert Solitaire* and several succeeding essay collections, as well as in his novels, especially *The Monkey Wrench Gang* (1975), Abbey helped make defense of wilderness both literarily legitimate and culturally urgent.

Social criticism and allegiance to wilderness mark the work of one of Abbey's chief southwestern inheritors, the Arizona writer Charles Bowden. Like Abbey, Bowden (b. 1945?) is a fearless denouncer of bloat (see *Blue Desert* [1986] and *Frog Mountain Blues* [1987]) and a candid self-revealer (see *Blood Orchid* [1996]), and like Abbey, his understanding of wilderness allegiance also ranges to confession to complicity in civilization. In both these writers, self-inclusive humor saves the social criticism from too much righteousness.

Contemporary western literature of the wild records, often quite explicitly, a search for some quality of mind and experience on which to rethink and perhaps build a new community. The drive is toward reconstituting community and morality on a broader basis than the solely human: In the experience of the deep order of nature, something instructive might be found. Oregon resident Barry Lopez (b. 1945), for example, describes trips to many far fields, returning repeatedly to the theme that a strong sense of respect—more precisely, reverence—would be a crucial precondition for any sort of redemption. His writing in *Of Wolves and Men* (1978), *Crossing Open Ground* (1988), and *The Rediscovery of North America* (1990) typifies the deeply moral intention of modern-day western "green" literature. Lopez also conveys the humbling notion that we cannot *know* enough for the purpose—we will have to learn to respect the essential mysteriousness of existence. There is a point of view here that is beyond old-style progressivism, in which a problem was simply seen and then simply solved.

In the essays and stories of William Kittredge (b. 1932), of Oregon and Montana, there is again a recognition of the recalcitrant perverseness of life, the way we often act against our better knowledge. Kittredge grew up on a ranch in southeastern Oregon, where the frontier-macho ethos of manipulating nature ruled without question. He has examined the assumptions, values, and psyche behind that practice and found them wanting, but he has also recognized the seductiveness of the old way and the degree of his own participation in it. His *Owning It All* (1987), *Hole in the Sky* (1992), and *Who Owns the West?* (1996) are important texts in the new western literature of mind and place. The ambiguousness of the modern situation is acknowledged in these books, but a clear moral intention still comes across. Kittredge's comment to interviewer Gregory Morris, in *Talking Up a Storm* (1994), could serve as a credo for a movement: "... the *culture* should ... stop trying to be the Lone Ranger. There's nothing left to conquer, there's nothing left to take over, there's nothing left to make subservient to us, and what we have to do is stop and figure out how to stay where we are, live where we are, and take care of what we've got."

Terry Tempest Williams (b. 1955) of Utah, probably the best-known contemporary writer from the Great Basin, would share those sentiments. Williams's important book, *Refuge* (1991), is decidedly postfrontier in its sense of the interrelatedness of life, its sacred rage over such events as atom-bomb testing in Nevada and the fallout over Utah, and its particular dedication to learn and accurately describe the natural history of the Great Salt Lake. A yearning for a true, nature-embracing community is almost palpable. *Refuge's* high achievement is to have juxtaposed the rise of the lake in the early 1980s, which flooded out hundreds of square miles of productive marsh, with the process of the terminal illness of Williams's mother, dramatizing a perspective from which the natural world and the human house are seen as continuous. *Refuge* gives a full ecological dimension to the word "family."

In both fiction and nonfiction, the work of Rick Bass (b. 1958) of Montana practically vibrates with the vitality and moral urgency of the ecological point of view. Houston-raised, Bass came to Montana several years ago and is apparently keenly conscientious about fitting in, being a good citizen, a good animal in place. He has become a knowledgeable defender of his home ground, the Yaak Valley, where the lumber giants threaten a remarkable diversity and wildness. *The Book of Yaak* (1996), *The Ninemile Wolves* (1992), and his first Montana book, *Winter* (1991), all show the fire of green allegiance, the release of energy coming from love of place. Bass writes freely, confidingly, making idiomatic contact with his reader, in effect forging the very start of a community; this is not the scenic nature-writing of earlier, more genteel times, but a serious enterprise in which together we are trying, before the necessary parts are destroyed, somehow to find the means of right living.

The same kind of seriousness underpins the contemporary writing of Arizona and Montana's Douglas Peacock (b. 1942), Montana's David Quammen (b. 1948), Mary Clearman Blew (b. 1939) of Idaho, Gary Paul Nabhan (b. 1952) of Arizona, Gretel Ehrlich (b. 1946) of Wyoming and California, Jack Turner (b. 1942) and C. L. Rawlins (b. 1949) of Wyoming, David Petersen (b. 1946) of Colorado, Robert Michael Pyle (b. 1947) and Brenda Peterson (b. 1950) of Washington, Kim Stafford (b. 1949) and George Venn (b. 1943) of Oregon, Stephen Trimble (b. 1950) of Utah, Richard Nelson (b. 1941) of Alaska, New Mexico's John Nichols (b. 1940), the Colorado natural historian Ann Zwinger (b. 1925), and a host of other western authors who write essays in cognizance of nature. A mere list (all that space allows here) proves little, it might be argued; but these are the writers who, along with the Indians, are giving clear voice to today's West. They are speaking to the state of the world out of a certain experience and affirmation—a sense of home. Coming from a level of awareness beyond that of the frontier mind, their writing begins to suggest a new western identity, something broader and more open than the simple "he" of the traditional West. Perhaps it will not be too much to say that in western literature of today, a sensibility of historical significance is being formed.

A WESTERN CHRONOLOGY, WITH 200 SIGNIFICANT TITLES

25,000–30,000 B.C.	Approximate era of first settlement in western North America.
10,000 B.C.	"Clovis" Paleo-Indian culture (presumably small bands of hunter-gatherers) flourishes in the West, hunting woolly and imperial mammoths.
10,000–8,000 B.C.	Extinction of several large mammalian species, through overkill or climate change or both.
6500 B.C.	Paleo-Indians conduct bison slaughter at "Olsen-Chubbuck" site, east-central Colorado.
A.D. 500	Anasazi culture widespread in Four Corners area. Approximately five hundred specialized small tribes are living in California's extraordinarily diverse environment.
500–1400	Hohokam culture brings large areas in southern Arizona under irrigation, with canals up to sixteen miles long.
950+	Mesa Verde cliff dwellings constructed.
950–1300	Chaco culture flowers in New Mexico; includes 125 planned towns.
1000	Pueblo and Hopi villages flourishing in their present locations.
c.1150	Oraibi (Arizona) established.
1200–1400	Navahos, coming from the north, arrive in the Southwest.
1276–1299	Severe drought in the Southwest.
1528	Álvar Núñez Cabeza de Vaca shipwrecked on Gulf Coast; begins eight-year trek to Mexico.
1540	Francisco Vásquez de Coronado begins an exploration from Arizona; over the next two years, travels as far northeast as Kansas. One of his officers, Don Garcia Lopez de Cardenas, takes a side trip with twelve men and sees the Grand Canyon, the first European to do so.
1598	Juan de Oñate colonizes northern New Mexico.
1609–1610	Santa Fe founded; "Palace of the Governors" built.

1680	Pueblo Indians revolt, drive Spanish from New Mexico.
1692	Don Diego de Vargas reconquers New Mexico.
1769	Father Junípero Serra founds mission at San Diego; in the next thirteen years, establishes nine of the twenty-one Franciscan missions in California.
1774–1776	Juan Bautista de Anza leads exploring and colonizing parties from Mexico to the San Francisco Bay area.
1776	Fathers Dominguez and Escalante traverse much of Colorado and Utah.
1783	Treaty of Paris concludes Revolutionary War, sets U.S. boundary at Mississippi River.
1803	Thomas Jefferson buys "Louisiana" from France, doubling the size of the United States.
1804–1806	Lewis and Clark cross the Louisiana Purchase and go on to the mouth of the Columbia River; return with information about the West. Their *Journals* become an American benchmark.
1805–1807	Zebulon Pike explores in Colorado and New Mexico.
1810–1812	J. J. Astor sends a party overland to the Pacific, to gain control of the western fur market. The expedition fails in its main purpose. Returning "Astorian" Robert Stuart crosses through South Pass in Wyoming, documented in *On the Oregon Trail; Robert Stuart's Journey of Discovery*, ed. Kenneth Spaulding (Norman, 1953).
1819	Naturalist Thomas Nuttall makes a solo trek up the Arkansas River drainage onto the plains; describes the trip in *A Journal of Travels into the Arkansa Territory, During the Year 1819* (Philadelphia, 1821).
1821	Mexico gains independence; assumes control of the Southwest.
1824	Jedediah Smith, Jim Bridger, and other trappers cross South Pass; enter Great Basin and "discover" the Great Salt Lake. Mountain-man heyday begins.
1826–1827	Jedediah Smith accomplishes immense explorations through Great Basin, California, and Oregon. Records these trips in his journal, *The Southwest Expedition of Jedediah S. Smith: His Personal Account of the Journey to California, 1826–1827*, ed. George R. Brooks (Glendale, Calif., 1977).

1832	Washington Irving tours a portion of Oklahoma; describes journey in *A Tour on the Prairies* (1835). Capt. Benjamin Bonneville, on leave from U.S. Army, begins three years' stay in the West as a would-be mountain man; keeps a detailed journal used by Washington Irving for *The Adventures of Capt. Bonneville U.S.A.* (1837), but subsequently lost to history. Painter George Catlin tours the West. In *Letters and Notes on the Manners, Customs, and Condition of the North American Indians* (1841), suggests a huge "nation's park," covering much of the High Plains, in which Indians and wildlife would be left undisturbed.
1834	Mountain man Joe Walker leads a group across the Great Basin to California; sees Yosemite Valley, the first Euro-American to do so.
1835	Washington Irving meets J. J. Astor; working from Astor's documents, writes *Astoria* (1836). Thomas Nuttall conducts natural-history studies in California.
1836	Washington Irving meets Capt. Benjamin Bonneville, buys his journal, and writes *The Adventures of Capt. Bonneville U.S.A.* (1837), the first account of the western fur trade. Republic of Texas founded (21 April); lasts until July 1845, when Texas becomes a state.
1839	John K. Townsend, *Narrative of a Journey Across the Rocky Mountains, to the Columbia River, and a Visit to the Sandwich Islands, Chili, & c.*
1841	Last mountain-man rendezvous.
1842–1844	John Charles Fremont surveys the West for the government; writes *Report of the Exploring Expedition to the Rocky Mountains in the Year 1842 and to Oregon and North California in the Years 1843–'44* (1845).
1844	James Clyman, former mountain man and now a wagon-train guide, notes in his journal that buffalo are now "seldom seen beyond the Sweetwater [River, central Wyoming]."
1845	Journalist John L. O'Sullivan coins phrase, "Manifest Destiny."
1846	Francis Parkman takes post-college tour into eastern Wyoming; writes *The Oregon Trail* (1849). Thousands of emigrants travel the Oregon and Cal-

ifornia trails; Donner party becomes trapped by Sierra Nevada snows.

1846–1848   Mexican-American War. Treaty of Guadalupe-Hidalgo transfers control of Southwest to United States.

1847   Mormons cross from Nebraska to Salt Lake Valley.

1848–1849   Discovery of gold at Sutter's Mill on the American River inspires fortune hunters and others to enter California.

1850   California admitted to statehood.

1852   An estimated one hundred thousand prospectors and miners are at work in the foothills of the Sierra Nevada.

            Howard Stansbury, *Exploration and Survey of the Valley of the Great Salt Lake of Utah.*

1853   Gadsden Purchase sets border with Mexico along its present lines.

1854   John Rollin Ridge [Cherokee], *The Life and Adventures of Joaquin Murieta, the Celebrated California Bandit*, the first novel published by a Native American.

1857   Mountain Meadows Massacre in southwest Utah; Mormon settlers, with Piute accomplices, kill somewhere between 90 and 115 members of a wagon train bound for California.

1858–1860   Gold rushes in Nevada, Colorado, and Idaho add to the western population. San Francisco flourishes as the West's first literary center.

1860   House of Beadle and Adams, New York, begins publication of popular fiction with frontier and western themes.

1861   Telegraph connects East and West.

1862   Homestead Act facilitates western settlement.

1864   The "Colorado Volunteers" destroy a village of Cheyenne Indians at Sand Creek.

            President Lincoln sets aside Yosemite Valley as a protected reserve.

            Majority of Navaho tribe is captured in Arizona and taken to New Mexico, where they are held until 1868.

1867   Appointment of General Philip Sheridan as commander of the Department of the Missouri signals increased militarization of U.S. policy toward western Indians.

1868	Lieutenant Colonel George A. Custer leads the 7th Cavalry in massacre of a Cheyenne village on the Washita River in Oklahoma.
	The *Overland Monthly* begins publication in San Francisco, under editorship of Bret Harte.
1869	"Golden Spike" driven at Promontory, Utah, completing the transcontinental railroad.
	American locomotives are estimated to burn nineteen thousand cords of wood per day nationwide.
	John Muir's first summer in the Sierra Nevada.
	John Wesley Powell and party descend the Green and Colorado rivers, make the last "discoveries" of a mountain range (the Henry Mountains) and river (the Escalante) in the continental United States.
1872	Clarence King, *Mountaineering in the Sierra Nevada.*
	Mark Twain, *Roughing It.*
	Yellowstone National Park created; world's first such reserve.
1874	Barbed wire patented; "open range" days numbered.
	George A. Custer, *My Life on the Plains.*
	John Wesley Powell, *The Exploration of the Colorado River and Its Tributaries.*
1876	George A. Custer leads 7th Cavalry into disaster near Little Bighorn River, Montana.
1881	Helen Hunt Jackson, *A Century of Dishonor,* exposé of Indian policy.
	Isabella Bird, *A Lady's Life in the Rocky Mountains*
1882	Clarence Dutton, *Tertiary History of the Grand Cañon District.*
1883	Sarah Winnemucca (Northern Piute), *Life Among the Piutes.*
1884	Last significant shipment of buffalo hides from the Plains.
	First of some 350 western dude ranches established in Wyoming.
1887	541 buffalo remain alive in the United States; of these, an estimated 85 are living in the wild.
1890	Ghost Dance takes place, followed by massacre of Indian village at Wounded Knee, South Dakota, conducted by the 7th Cavalry; 102 Lakota men, 44 women, and 18 children are killed.

Yosemite National Park is created, along lines suggested by John Muir.

U.S. Census Bureau declares frontier closed.

Mormon leader Wilford Woodruff issues manifesto against polygamy; in succeeding decades, Mormon society becomes increasingly "mainstream."

1891   Hamlin Garland, *Main-Travelled Roads*.

President Harrison creates Forest Reserves.

1893   Frederick Jackson Turner promulgates "frontier thesis."

1894   John Muir, *The Mountains of California*.

1897   Klondike gold rush.

1899   Frank Norris, *McTeague*.

1900   First motor vehicle reaches south rim of Grand Canyon.

1901   Frank Norris, *The Octopus*.

1902   Owen Wister, *The Virginian*.

Newlands Act establishes Bureau of Reclamation, inaugurating era of large, federally sponsored water projects that will affect much of the West.

1903   Mary Austin, *The Land of Little Rain*.

Jack London, *The Call of the Wild*.

1904–1907   Reuben G. Thwaites, ed., *Early Western Travels*, a thirty-two-volume set of narratives by explorers and early travelers.

1905   Los Angeles voters approve bonds for an aqueduct that will supply the city by appropriating the Owens River, 250 miles distant.

1906   Much of San Francisco destroyed by earthquake and fire.

1911   Enos Mills, *The Spell of the Rockies*.

1912   Zane Grey, *Riders of the Purple Sage*.

John Muir, *The Yosemite*.

1913   Congress authorizes reservoir in Hetch Hetchy, within Yosemite National Park.

Willa Cather, *O Pioneers!*

1915   Rocky Mountain National Park established.

Taos Society of Artists founded.

1916   National Park Service created.

Jeanette Rankin of Montana becomes first woman elected to Congress.

Federal Aid Highway Act authorizes government

road subsidies; in time, federal highway building will have a major effect on the West.

1918	Willa Cather, *My Ántonia.*
1920	Sinclair Lewis, *Main Street.*
1922	Willa Cather, *One of Ours* (Pulitzer Prize, 1923).

Colorado River Compact apportions that stream's flow among Wyoming, Colorado, Utah, New Mexico, Nevada, Arizona, and California, solidifies federal role in western natural-resource development.

1923–1924	Teapot Dome oil scandal.
1924	Mary Austin, *The Land of Journeys' Ending.*
1925	Willa Cather, *The Professor's House.*

Dorothy Scarborough, *The Wind.*

Robinson Jeffers, *Roan Stallion, Tamar, and Other Poems.*

Cougars eliminated from Yellowstone National Park, in Park Service's predator eradication program.

1927	Ole Rølvaag, *Giants in the Earth.*

Mourning Dove [Okanogan], *Co-ge-we-a,* the first novel by an Indian woman.

Harvey Fergusson, *Wolf Song.*

1929	Oliver LaFarge, *Laughing Boy.*
1930s	Depression era enlarges federal presence in the West. In per capita assistance received through the New Deal, fourteen western states lead the nation. Farm support and work relief programs contribute significantly to western survival.
1931	Vardis Fisher, *Dark Bridwell.*
1932	Mary Austin, *Earth Horizon.*

Black Elk, *Black Elk Speaks.*

Bernard DeVoto, *Mark Twain's America.*

Vardis Fisher, *In Tragic Life.*

1933	The Lone Ranger debuts on station WXYZ, Detroit.
1934	Thomas Hornsby Ferril, *Westering.*

Taylor Grazing Act effectively sets aside public domain for federal management, not sale to the public.

1935	H. L. Davis, *Honey in the Horn.*

Frank Waters, *The Wild Earth's Nobility.*

1936	D'Arcy McNickle [Cree/Irish], *The Surrounded.*

Boulder Dam completed, largest federal project to date.

Averell Harriman creates Sun Valley, a ski resort in

	central Idaho. In years to follow, skiing becomes a major factor in the economics of western recreation.
1937	John Steinbeck, *Of Mice and Men*.
1938	Norm Nevills, of Mexican Hat, Utah, initiates commercial river-running in the Grand Canyon. The first women to go through the canyon, botanist Elzada Clover and her assistant Lois Jotter, accompany Nevills.
1939	John Steinbeck, *The Grapes of Wrath*.
	Vardis Fisher, *Children of God*.
	Franklin Walker, *San Francisco's Literary Frontier*.
	Nathanael West, *The Day of the Locust*.
1940	Walter Van Tilburg Clark, *The Ox-Bow Incident*.
1941	Entrance of United States into World War II. By 1943, the federal government has become the largest single employer in the West.
	Maurine Whipple, *The Giant Joshua*.
1942	110,000 Americans of Japanese descent are removed from the West Coast and placed in camps in the interior.
	Frank Waters, *The Man Who Killed the Deer*.
1943	Wallace Stegner, *The Big Rock Candy Mountain*.
	First instances of smog in Los Angeles.
1943–1945	Atomic bombs are developed in a secret project at Los Alamos, New Mexico.
1944	Adolph Murie, *The Wolves of Mount McKinley*.
1945	Walter Van Tilburg Clark, *The City of Trembling Leaves*.
1947	A. B. Guthrie Jr., *The Big Sky*.
	Bernard DeVoto, *Across the Wide Missouri*.
1949	Jack Schaefer, *Shane*.
	A. B. Guthrie Jr., *The Way West*.
	Walter Van Tilburg Clark, *The Track of the Cat*.
1950s	Military presence in the West and defense industries lead to increasing dependence of the area on Cold War spending. Atomic-bomb testing in Nevada rains fallout on surrounding states and beyond. Uranium prospecting becomes last great western "rush."
1950	Frank Waters, *Masked Gods*.
	Harvey Fergusson, *Grant of Kingdom*.
1952	Walter Prescott Webb, *The Great Frontier*.
1954	Frederick Manfred, *Lord Grizzly*.

Joseph Wood Krutch, *The Voice of the Desert.*
Wallace Stegner, *Beyond the Hundredth Meridian.*

1955   Poetry reading at the Six Gallery in San Francisco inaugurates public consciousness of the "Beat Generation."

1956   Wright Morris, *The Field of Vision.*
Edward Abbey, *The Brave Cowboy.*
Construction begins on Glen Canyon Dam.

1957   John Okada, *No-No Boy.*

1958   First ascent of Yosemite's El Capitan. In years to follow, rock climbing and mountaineering become significant in western recreation.

1960s–1990s   Flourishing electronics and aerospace industries, along with growing Pacific trade, verify the West's increasing economic importance.

1960   John Graves, *Goodbye to a River.*
Vardis Fisher, *Orphans in Gethsemane.*

1962   John Steinbeck wins Nobel Prize for Literature.
California becomes the most populous state.
William Stafford, *Traveling Through the Dark.*
Theodora Kroeber, *Ishi in Two Worlds.*
Cesar Chavez organizes National Farm Workers Organization.

1963   Frank Waters, *Book of the Hopi.*

1965   Luis Valdez organizes El Teatro Campesino in support of Cesar Chavez and the California farm workers.
Vardis Fisher, *Mountain Man.*

1966   Frank Waters, *The Woman at Otowi Crossing.*
Theodore Roethke, *The Collected Poems of Theodore Roethke.*
Larry McMurtry, *The Last Picture Show.*

1967   Gary Snyder, *The Back Country.*
"Summer of Love" in San Francisco heightens public awareness of counterculture and "hippies."

1968   Edward Abbey, *Desert Solitaire.*
Leslie Fiedler, *The Return of the Vanishing American.*
N. Scott Momaday, *House Made of Dawn.*
Larry McMurtry, *In a Narrow Grave.*

1969   Gary Snyder, *Earth House Hold.*
Wallace Stegner, *The Sound of Mountain Water.*
N. Scott Momaday, *The Way to Rainy Mountain.*

	Indians occupy Alcatraz in protest against federal policies.
1970	John G. Cawelti, *The Six-Gun Mystique.*
1971	Wallace Stegner, *Angle of Repose.*
	Frank Waters, *Pike's Peak.*
1972	Rudolfo Anaya, *Bless Me, Ultima.*
1973	Indians and FBI endure lengthy armed standoff at Wounded Knee, South Dakota. Two FBI agents are killed.
1974	Gary Snyder, *Turtle Island.*
	John Nichols, *The Milagro Beanfield War.*
	James Welch, *Winter in the Blood.*
	Ann Zwinger, *Run, River, Run.*
1975	Edward Abbey, *The Monkey Wrench Gang.*
1976	Wallace Stegner, *The Spectator Bird.*
	David Wagoner, *Collected Poems.*
	William Everson, *Archetype West.*
	Norman Maclean, *A River Runs Through It.*
1977	William Stafford, *Stories That Could Be True: New and Collected Poems.*
	Gary Soto, *The Elements of San Joaquin.*
	Leslie Silko, *Ceremony.*
	Howard Lamar, ed., *Reader's Encyclopedia of the American West.*
	Frederick Manfred, *Green Earth.*
	Richard Hugo, *31 Letters and 13 Dreams.*
1978	Luis Valdez, *Zoot Suit.*
	Barry Lopez, *Of Wolves and Men.*
1979	Wallace Stegner, *Recapitulation.*
1980	Sam Shepard, *True West.*
	Census Bureau reports that 27% of the Los Angeles population is foreign-born.
1981	Frank Waters, *Mountain Dialogues.*
1983	Gerard Haslam, *Hawk Flights: Visions of the West.*
	Raymond Carver, *Cathedral.*
1984	Louise Erdrich, *Love Medicine.*
1985	Cormac McCarthy, *Blood Meridian.*
	Donald Worster, *Rivers of Empire: Water, Aridity, and the Growth of the American West.*
	Marc Reisner, *Cadillac Desert.*
	Ursula LeGuin, *Always Coming Home.*

	Larry McMurtry, *Lonesome Dove.*
	Gretel Ehrlich, *The Solace of Open Spaces.*
1986	James Welch, *Fools Crow.*
	Barry Lopez, *Arctic Dreams.*
	Louis L'Amour, *Last of the Breed.*
1987	Frank and Deborah Popper, in the journal *Planning,* call for re-establishment of a "Buffalo Commons" on the High Plains, which would require de-fencing and encouragement of native vegetation.
	Patricia Nelson Limerick, *Legacy of Conquest.*
	Western Literature Association, *A Literary History of the American West.*
	William Kittredge, *Owning It All.*
	Charles Bowden, *Frog Mountain Blues.*
	Vera Norwood and Janice Monk, *The Desert Is No Lady.*
1989	John Haines, *The Stars, the Snow, the Fire.*
	Amy Tan, *The Joy Luck Club.*
	Richard Nelson, *The Island Within.*
1990s	Increasing migration of upper economic class and celebrities to the interior West creates localized booms, consolidating parts of Aspen, Vail, Jackson, Ketchum, Telluride, Sedona, and Santa Fe as islands of wealth. In early 1998, the average price of a single-family dwelling in Aspen reaches $1.8 million.
1990	Ted Turner buys a large ranch in Montana, begins stocking it with buffalo.
	William DeBuys, *River of Traps.*
	Gary Snyder, *The Practice of the Wild.*
	Linda Hogan, *Mean Spirit.*
	James Welch, *The Indian Lawyer.*
	Gerald Haslam, *The Other California: The Great Central Valley in Life and Letters.*
	Douglas Peacock, *Grizzly Years.*
1991	Terry Tempest Williams, *Refuge.*
	Rick Bass, *Winter.*
	Leslie Silko, *Almanac of the Dead.*
	Charles Bowden, *Desierto.*
1992	First captivity-bred California condors are released into the wild.

James Galvin, *The Meadow.*
William Kittredge, *Hole in the Sky.*
Rick Bass, *The Ninemile Wolves.*
Jane Tompkins, *West of Everything: The Inner Life of Westerns.*
Wallace Stegner, *Where the Bluebird Sings to the Lemonade Springs: Living and Writing in the West.*

1993   Linda Hogan, *The Book of Medicines.*
C. L. Rawlins, *Sky's Witness.*

1994   Cormac McCarthy, *The Crossing.*
Gerald Haslam, *Condor Dreams.*
James Welch, *Killing Custer.*
Clyde Milner II, Carol O'Connor, and Martha A. Sandweiss, eds., *The Oxford History of the American West.*
California Department of Finance estimates ethnic backgrounds of the state's present population as follows:
52.8% white
31% Hispanic
9.3% Asian
5.9% black
California Almanac projects ethnic makeup of the state in 2040 as follows:
50% Hispanic
32% white
12% Asian
6% black

1995   Wolves are re-established in Yellowstone National Park.
Ann Zwinger, *Downcanyon: A Naturalist Explores the Colorado River Through the Grand Canyon.*
Linda Hogan, *Dwellings: Reflections on the Natural World.*
Rick Bass, *In the Loyal Mountains.*

1996   Gary Snyder, *Mountains and Rivers Without End.*
Jack Turner, *The Abstract Wild.*
Rick Bass, *The Book of Yaak.*

1997   Rick Bass, *The Sky, the Stars, the Wilderness.*
Western Literature Association, *Updating the Literary West.*

KATHLAMET CHINOOK
(ORAL TRADITION)

ranz Boas (1858–1942), a German scholar self-trained in anthropology, was one of the shapers of that discipline in America. A fifteen-month stay with Eskimos in the early 1880s helped establish in him a profoundly sympathetic attitude toward indigenous people and a sense that "the idea of a 'cultured' individual is merely relative." He labored assiduously to gather tales from several Northwest tribes while the holders of the traditional stories were still alive. Charles Cultee, a Kathlamet Chinook from the lower Columbia River region and one of the last speakers of his dialect, told "The Sun's Myth" to Boas in the summer of 1891. The version here is a modern retranslation by Dell Hymes, one of the foremost contemporary translators and interpreters of Indian texts. As Hymes points out in his introduction (in *Coming to Light: Contemporary Translations of the Native Literatures of North America* [New York, 1994], ed. Brian Swann), the myth is a powerful dramatization of human hubris.

"The Sun's Myth" (transcribed 1891)

They live there, those people of a town.
Five the towns of his relatives, that chief.

In the early light,
  now he used to go out,
  and outside,
  now he used to stay;
    now he used to see that sun:
    she would nearly come out, that sun.
Now he told his wife,
  "What would you think,
    if I went to look for that sun?"
She told him, his wife,
  "You think it is near?
  And you will wish to go to that sun?"

Another day,
  again in the early light,
  he went out;

now again he saw that sun:
she did nearly come out there, that sun.
He told his wife,
"You shall make ten pairs of moccasins,
you shall make me leggings,
leggings for ten people."
Now she made them for him, his wife,
moccasins for ten people,
the leggings of as many.

Again it became dawn,
now he went,
far he went.
He used up his moccasins;
he used up his leggings;
he put on others of his moccasins and leggings.
Five months he went;
five of his moccasins he used up;
five of his leggings he used up.
Ten months he went—
now she would rise nearby, that sun—
he used up his moccasins.
Now he reached a house,
a large house;
he opened the door,
now some young girl is there;
he entered the house,
he stayed.

Now he saw there on the side of that house:
arrows are hanging on it,
quivers full of arrows are hanging on it,
armors of elk skin are hanging on it,
armors of wood are hanging on it,
shields are hanging on it,
axes are hanging on it,
war clubs are hanging on it,
feathered regalia are hanging on it—
all men's property there on the side of that house.
There on the other side of that house:
mountain goat blankets are hanging on it,
painted elk-skin blankets are hanging on it,
buffalo skins are hanging on it,

dressed buckskins are hanging on it,
long dentalia are hanging on it,
shell beads are hanging on it,
short dentalia are hanging on it—
Now, near the door, some large thing hangs over there;
he did not recognize it.

Then he asked the young girl,
"Whose property are those quivers?"
    "Her property, my father's mother,
    she saves them for my maturity."
"Whose property are those elk-skin armors?"
    "Our property, my father's mother [and I],
    she saves them for my maturity."
"Whose property are those arrows?"
    "Our property, my father's mother [and I],
    she saves them for my maturity."

"Whose property are those wooden armors?"
    "Our property, my father's mother [and I],
    she saves them for my maturity."
"Whose property are those shields,
    and those bone war clubs?"
    "Our property, my father's mother [and I]."
"Whose property are those stone axes?"
    "Our property, my father's mother [and I]."

Then again on the other side of that house:
"Whose property are those buffalo skins?"
    "Our buffalo skins, my father's mother [and I],
    she saves them for my maturity."
"Whose property are those mountain goat blankets?"
    "Our property, my father's mother [and I],
    she saves them for my maturity."
"Whose property are those dressed buckskins?"
    "Our property, my father's mother [and I],
    she saves them for my maturity."

"Whose property are those deerskin blankets?"
    "Our property, my father's mother [and I],
    she saves them for my maturity."
"Whose property are those shell beads?"
    "Our property, my father's mother [and I],
    she saves them for my maturity."

"Whose property are those long dentalia?
Whose property are those short dentalia?"
　"Her property, my father's mother,
　　she saves them for my maturity."

He asked her about all those things.
　He thought,
　　"I will take her."

At dark,
　now that old woman came home.
Now again she hung up one [thing],
　that which he wanted,
　　that thing shining all over.
He stayed there.

A long time he stayed there;
　now he took that young girl.
They stayed there.
In the early light,
　already that old woman was gone.
In the evening,
　　she would come home;
she would bring things,
　she would bring arrows;
　sometimes mountain goat blankets she would bring,
　sometimes elk-skin armors she would bring.
Every day like this.

A long time he stayed.
Now he felt homesick.
Twice he slept,
　he did not get up.
That old woman said to her grandchild,
　"Did you scold him,
　　and he is angry?"
[—]*"No, I did not scold him,
　he feels homesick."

Now she told her son-in-law,
　"What will you carry when you go home?
　Will you carry those buffalo skins?"
He told her,

*A dash in brackets indicates a change in speaker.

"No."
"Will you carry those mountain goat blankets?"
He told her,
"No."
"Will you carry all those elk-skin armors?"
He told her,
"No."

She tried in vain to show him all that on one side of the house.
    Next all those [other] things.
        She tried in vain to show him all, *everything*.
He wants only that,
    that thing that is large,
        that [thing] put up away.
When it would sway,
    that thing put up away,
        it would become turned around,
        at once his eyes would be extinguished;
            that thing [is] shining all over,
            now he wants only that thing there.

He told his wife,
    "She shall give me one [thing],
        that blanket of hers, that old woman."
His wife told him,
    "She will never give it to you.
    In vain people continue to try to trade it from her;
    she will never do it."
Now again he became angry.

Several times he slept.
        Now again she would ask him,
    "Will you carry that?"
        she would tell him.
She would try in vain to show him all those things of hers;
    she would try in vain to show him those men's things;
        she would try in vain to show him all.
She would reach that [thing] put up away,
    now she would become silent.
When she would reach that [thing] put away,
    now her heart became tired.
Now she told him:
    "You must carry it then!
    Take care! if you carry it.

It is you who choose.
I try to love you,
indeed I do love you."

She hung it on him,
    she hung it all on him.
Now she gave him a stone ax.
She told him:
    "Go home now!"

He went out,
    now he went,
        he went home;
        he did not see a land;
            he arrived near his father's brother's town.
Now that which he had taken throbbed,
    now that which he had taken said,
        "We two shall strike your town,
        we two shall strike your town,"
            said that which he had taken.}*
His reason became nothing,
    he did it to his father's brother's town,
        he crushed, crushed, crushed it,
            he killed all the people.
He recovered—
    all those houses are crushed,
        his hands are full of blood.}
He thought,
    "O I am a fool!
    See, that is what it is like, this thing!
    Why was I made to love this?"
In vain he tried to begin shaking it off,
    and his flesh would be pulled.}

Now again he went,
    and he went a little while—
Now again his reason became nothing—
    he arrived near another father's brother's town.
Now again it said,
    "We two shall strike your town,
    we two shall strike your town."

*A closed brace indicates the end point of a pair of units. There are three pairs of stanzas
in this scene.

In vain he would try to still it,
  it was never still.
In vain he would try to throw it away,
  always those fingers of his would cramp.

Now again his reason became nothing,
  now again he did it to his father's brother's town,
  he crushed it all.
He recovered:
  his father's brother's town [is] nothing,
    the people all are dead.
Now he cried.
In vain he tried in the fork of a tree,
  there in vain he would try squeezing through it;
in vain he would try to shake it off,
  it would not come off,
  and his flesh would be pulled;
in vain he would keep beating what he had taken on rocks,
  it would never be crushed.

Again he would go,
  he would arrive near another father's brother's town.

Now again that which he had taken would shake:
  "We two shall strike your town,
  we two shall strike your town."
His reason would become nothing,
  he would do it to his father's brother's town,
    crush, crush, crush, crush;
  all his father's brother's town he would destroy,
    and he would destroy the people.
He would recover;
  he would cry out;
  he would grieve for his relatives.

In vain he would try diving into water;
  in vain he would try to shake it off,
    and his flesh would be pulled.
In vain he would try rolling in a thicket;
  in vain he would keep beating what he had taken on rocks;
  he would abandon hope.
Now he would cry out.

Again he would go.
Now again he would arrive at another town,

a father's brother's town.
Now again what he had taken would shake:
"We two shall strike your town,
we two shall strike your town."

His reason would become nothing,
  he would do it to the town,
    crush, crush, crush, crush,
      and the people.
He would recover:
  all the people and the town [are] no more;
    his hands and arms [are] only blood.
He would become
  "Qa! qa! qa! qa!"
    he would cry out.

In vain he would try to beat it on the rocks,
  what he had taken would not be crushed.
In vain he would try to throw away what he had taken,
  always his fingers stick to it.

Again he would go.
Now his too, his town,
  he would be near his town.
In vain he would try to stand, that one;
  see, something would pull his feet.

His reason would become nothing,
  he would do it to his town,
    crush, crush, crush, crush;
    all his town he would destroy,
      and he would destroy his relatives.
He would recover:
  his town is nothing;
    the dead fill the ground.
He would become
  "Qa! qa! qa! qa!"
    he would cry out.

In vain he would try to bathe;
  in vain he would try to shake off what he wears,
    and his flesh would be pulled.
Sometimes he would roll about on rocks;
  he would think,

"Perhaps it will break apart";
 he would abandon hope.
Now again he would cry out,
 and he wept.

He looked back.
Now she is standing near him, that old woman.
"You,"
 she told him,
 "You.
In vain I try to love you,
 in vain I try to love your relatives.
Why do you weep?
 It is you who choose;
 now you carried that blanket of mine."
Now she took it,
 she lifted off what he had taken;
 now she left him,
 she went home.
He stayed there;
 he went a little distance;
 there he built a house,
 a small house.

PEDRO FONT

Catalan Father Pedro Font (1738–1781), a Franciscan missionary working in Mexico, was asked in 1775 by the explorer Juan Bautista de Anza to serve as chaplain and chronicler for an expedition planning to travel overland from Sonora northwestward to San Francisco Bay. The nearly two-thousand-mile trek, undertaken in the autumn of 1775 and bearing fruit in June of the next year with the planting of a small colony at San Francisco, is one of the great resettlement sagas in North American history. Much of the way had been laid out earlier (some of it by de Anza in 1774), and the several tribes of Native Americans along the new trail had already had contact with Europeans, but Font's account—"the greatest of all California diaries," according to his translator Herbert Eugene Bolton—nevertheless conveys the excitement of discovery. In this passage, Font describes the party's route along the California coast from approximately present-day Ventura to the vicinity of Santa Barbara.

[Ventura to Santa Barbara in 1776], from *Pedro Font's Diary* (1776)

75. Saturday, February 24 [1776]—We set out from the Santa Clara River at half past nine in the morning, and at half past three in the afternoon halted on a small elevation on the shore of the sea near the village of La Rinconada, having traveled some nine leagues. After starting we went three to the west, reaching the sea beach and the village called La Carpintería, situated near the Rio de la Asumpta, the first village of the Channel of Santa Barbara, unless one counts as the first one that of the Santa Clara River. The rest of the way was west by north, with some minor turns to the west at the headlands along the coast, which are numerous.[1]— Nine leagues.

After going three leagues, all the way over level country, we came to the sea beach and the village of La Carpintería, so-called because the first expedition saw them building launches there. Two leagues beyond is the

---

[1]The route was from the Santa Clara to the Ventura River (Rio de la Asumpta) where Carpintería was situated. Font's Carpintería was further east than that so-named by the Portolá expedition. Los Pitos was at Pitas Point. La Rinconada, where camp was made, was at Rincón Creek, near Rincón Point, on the western boundary of Ventura County. The day's march was close to the beach where the highway now runs.

village of Los Pitos, so-called because of the whistle which the men of the first expedition of Commander Portolá heard blown there all night. For this reason Señor Ribera, who then was going in the vanguard, fearful of some trick on the part of the Indians, kept the men on their arms all night, only to discover in the morning that it was a very small village of four little huts and without people.

All this road as far as the camp site runs along the sea beach, almost touching the waves. For this reason it is a very diverting way, and it would have been more so if the day had been clear and good, and not so murky from the fog. The people of the expedition who had never seen the sea found many things to marvel at. The Channel of Santa Barbara, which is very long, is so-called because out in the sea at a distance of some six or eight leagues there are several islands which with the mainland form a strait. And I would say that it also might be called a channel because the road runs all along the beach between the sea and the land; for there the land ends in very steep cliffs, as if they had been sliced off, so that it is almost impossible to climb up them because they are so high and broken, although they are not rocky but are composed of land well grown with good pasturage. In places there is no other way except along the beach, and in other stretches although there is a road which they call "along the heights," it runs on the edge of the sliced-off part of the hills, with great precipices over the sea, which is visible there below.

The Indians of the Channel are of the Quabajay tribe.[1] They and the Beñeme have commerce with the Jamajab and others of the Colorado River, with their cuentas or beads, consisting of flat, round, and small shells which they hunt for in the sands of the beach, and of which they have long strings hung around the neck and on the head. The dress of the men is total nakedness. For adornment only they are in the habit of wearing around the waist a string or other gewgaw which covers nothing. For a head dress they are accustomed to tie in the hair a cord, as I said of the Gileños on November 7, in which they put a little stick or feather, and especially the *cuchillo*. This is a thin stick about two inches wide and a third of a vara long, at the end of which they fix with pitch a rather long flint, pointed and sharpened to cut on both sides, or a knife blade,

---

[1]The Quabajay and Beñemé, and the Jeniguechis mentioned below, are all identified with the Serranos. The Jamajab were the Mohaves. Fages wrote of these Channel people: "The Indians of all these villages are of good disposition and average figure; they are inclined to work, and much more to self-interest. They show with great covetousness a certain inclination to traffic and barter, and it may be said in a way that they are the Chinese of California. In matters concerning their possessions, they will not yield or concede the smallest point. They receive the Spaniards well and make them welcome; but they are very warlike among themselves, living at almost incessant war, village against village" (Fages, *Historical, Political and Natural Description of California*).

or some similar piece of iron if they are able to obtain one. This *cuchillo* they all wear across the head, fastening it with the hair.

They are also accustomed to carry a sweat stick, which is a long and somewhat sharp bone or similar thing, with which they scrape the body when they are perspiring, to remove the perspiration. They say that this is a very good thing because by doing so they cease to be tired. Some of them have the cartilage of the nose pierced, and all have the ears perforated with two large holes, in which they wear little canes which look like two horns, as thick as the little finger and more than half a palm long, in which they are accustomed to carry powder made of their wild tobacco, or some other gewgaw.

Their language is entirely distinct from the others. The captain whom they recognize in the villages they call Temí, just as the Jeniguechis and Benyemé call him Tomiár. The women cover themselves with a deer skin hung round the waist, and with some sort of a beaver skin cape over their backs, yet I saw very few women close at hand, for as soon as they saw us they all hastily hid in their huts, especially the girls, the men remaining outside blocking the doors and taking care that nobody should go inside. Once I went near a hut which I saw open, to examine its structure, for among all the huts which I saw in all the journey these are the best. They are round in form, like a half orange, very spacious, large and high. In the middle of the top they have an aperture to afford light and to serve as a chimney, through which emerges the smoke of the fire which they make in the middle of the hut. Some of them also have two or three holes like little windows. The frames of all of them consist of arched and very strong poles, and the walls are of very thick grass interwoven. At the doors there is a mat which swings toward the inside like a screen, and another one toward the outside which they ordinarily bar with a whalebone or a stick.

I went to the door, and although I did not ask permission to go in, knowing their dislike for it, nevertheless two minutes could not have passed when they shut the inner door on me and I withdrew unenlightened. This is the result of the extortions and outrages which the soldiers have perpetrated when in their journeys they have passed along the Channel, especially in the beginning. Among them a certain Camacho was outrageous, and his fame became so wide among the Indians that they call every soldier *Camacho*. In fact, they all kept asking us for Camacho, and where was Camacho, and if Camacho was coming. Among the men I saw a few with a little cape like a doublet reaching to the waist and made of bear skin, and by this mark of distinction I learned that these were the owners or masters of the launches.

The Indians are great fishermen and very ingenious. They make baskets of various shapes, and other things very well formed, such as wooden trays and boxes, and things made of stone. Above all, they build launches with which they navigate. They are very carefully made of several planks which they work with no other tools than their shells and flints. They join them at the seams by sewing them with very strong thread which they have, and fit the joints with pitch, by which they are made very strong and secure. Some of the launches are decorated with little shells and all are painted red with hematite. In shape they are like a little boat without ribs, ending in two points somewhat elevated and arched above, the two arcs not closing but remaining open at the points like a V. In the middle there is a somewhat elevated plank laid across from side to side to serve as a seat and to preserve the convexity of the frame. Each launch is composed of some twenty long and narrow pieces. I measured one and found it to be thirty-six palms long and somewhat more than three palms high. In each launch, when they navigate or go to fish, according to what I saw, ordinarily not more than two Indians ride in each end. They carry some poles about two varas long which end in blades, these being the oars with which they row alternately, putting the ends of the poles into the water, now on one side and now on the other side of the launch. In this way they guide the launch wherever they wish, sailing through rough seas with much boldness. In this place of La Rinconada I counted nine launches, besides one that was to be mended, and I concluded that with some instruction those Indians would become fine sailors.

All the settlements or rancherías of the Channel have a community place for playing, consisting of a very smooth and level ground, like a bowling green, with low walls around it, in which they play, rolling a little half-round stick. Likewise, near the villages they have a place which we called the cemetery, where they bury their dead. It is made of several poles and planks painted with various colors, white, black, and red, and set up in the ground. And on some very tall, straight and slim poles which we called the towers, because we saw them from some distance, they place baskets which belonged to the deceased, and other things which perhaps were esteemed by them, such as little skirts, shells, and likewise in places some arrows. Over the deceased they place the ribs or other large bones of the whales which are customarily stranded on those coasts.

They also have a common temescal. This is a hot, closed room for sweating, made somewhat subterranean and very firm with poles and earth, and having at the top, in the middle, an opening like a scuttle, to afford air and to serve as a door, through which they go down inside by a ladder consisting of straight poles set in the ground and joined together, one being shorter than the other. I peeped into a temescal and perceived a strong heat coming up from it. In the middle of them they make a fire.

The Indians enter to perspire, seated all around, and as soon as they perspire freely and wet the ground with their sweat, they run out and jump into the sea, which is close by, to bathe themselves.

These Indians are well formed and of good body, although not very corpulent, on account of their sweating, as I judge. The women are fairly good looking. They wear pendants in their ears and have the front hair short and banged like a tupé, the rest falling over the shoulders. The arms used by these Indians are the bow and arrow, like all the rest, but their arrows are of wood and very well and carefully made, and not of reeds like those commonly used by the Apaches, Pimas, and the others. Their bows are small, being only about a vara long, but very strong, and all are wound with tendons and are graceful in form. Their customs are the same as those of the others. They live without law or king, and especially without knowledge of God, so far as I was able to ascertain. They devote themselves to fishing, by means of which, together with the seeds of grass, they maintain themselves with much misery and hunger. They are also clever and not very dull, as it appeared to me; for although we did not have an interpreter through whom to talk to them, we were able to understand them by signs like those used by mutes, with which they explained themselves well.

But they are very thievish, a characteristic of all Indians. On passing through the village of La Carpintería we stopped for a while because it was the first one, to see the launches, cemetery, etc. Señor Ansa, I, and others dismounted, and right there in front of so many people an Indian was clever enough to take from the saddle of Señor Ansa a linen suncloth which he left on it when he dismounted. We remounted and a little after we started Señor Ansa missed the cloth. A servant of his went back to the village to look for it. He asked for the cloth, and they denied knowledge of it, but told him to go to a certain hut where he might find it. From there they sent him to another hut, and from this one to still another. Seeing that they did not intend to give it to him, and were hiding it, the servant took his musket and told them that if they did not give him the cloth he would kill them. This was only a threat, but immediately an Indian, frightened, told him that he would look for the cloth, and without delay he found it and gave it to him.

Everywhere they appeared to us to be gentle and friendly, and they did not seem to be very warlike. But it will not be easy to reduce them, for they are displeased with the Spaniards because of what they have done to them, now taking away their fish and their food to provision themselves when they pass along the Channel, now stealing their women and abusing them, as well as because they are very much attached to living on the coast. In all this coast, although there are more than thirty arroyos, there is no place to establish a good mission[1] because of the small amount of water which the arroyos carry, for many dry up in the course of the year, and especially for lack of sufficient level lands suitable for crops, although as for pasturage, in all places it is plentiful and good, and in some places there is an abundance of timber and trees.

Finally, the tribe which occupies the Channel is very large, and the land is the most thickly settled of all that I saw, judging from what could be gathered from the villages which I shall proceed to name. But I do not agree with the estimate of the population which was made at first, putting it at more than twenty thousand souls; for although it is true that there are villages which may exceed a thousand persons, most of them, I judged, contain less than a thousand, and there are some small ones which I think do not reach five hundred souls.

At this place of La Rinconada there is an arroyo in the very ravine where the village is located.[2] Having crossed it we halted on a little elevation very close to the sea, with a very extensive view, although the fog prevented us from seeing the islands which were in front of us. Among the Indians who came to the camp I saw one who wore a cotton blanket like those made by the Gila Pimas, and I inferred that he must have acquired it from that great distance by means of the commerce which they have with others. They pointed out and showed me an Indian who was there, saying that he was from the large island of the Channel called Santa Cruz, and that he had just come for pleasure; for it is a marvel to see how they navigate those seas. Although his hair was reddish he looked to me very much like the Indians of the Channel.

The island of Santa Cruz is nearly triangular, and must be some twenty leagues long, and they say that it is very thickly settled and very well wooded, but because of the fog I was scarcely able to make it out. The fathers told me that the viceroy had instructed and ordered the officials to see to it that these islands should not be depopulated, especially this one, and that efforts should not be made to have the Indians leave it for the purpose of their reduction and conversion to Christianity.

---

[1] Two fine missions were founded on the coast, San Buenaventura and Santa Barbara.
[2] Rincón Creek.

LEWIS AND CLARK

For most Americans, western history begins with Meriwether Lewis (1774–1809) and William Clark (1770–1838). President Thomas Jefferson had gone to Congress for $1,500 (in 1803 dollars) to supply the expedition and had given the twenty-nine-year-old Lewis, formerly his personal secretary, a set of detailed instructions. The "Corps of Discovery" were to take notes and keep journals every mile of the way to the Pacific. And they did, creating a record of the "virgin land" that for poignancy in the retrospect has no equal. These are the golden pages of the West. In 1933, in his caustic poem, the ironically titled "Empire Builders," Archibald MacLeish used the journals as counterpoint to dramatize the exploitation behind the big American fortunes. In 1964, the documentary film-maker Ted Yates mounted a realistic reenactment of the expedition, dressing his actors in authentic period wear and having them carry only 1804-vintage tools and arms. To Yates's intense disappointment, the film crew and actors had to travel 1,500 miles up the Missouri from St. Louis before the cameras could be turned on. The text here is Bernard DeVoto's edited version of 1953. The expedition is just leaving the Mandan village where they had spent the winter of 1804–1805. Over the next four months, they would see no other human beings.

[North Dakota journals from the spring of 1805], from *The Journals of Lewis and Clark* (1805)

[Lewis]   FORT MANDAN APRIL 7TH. 1805.

Having on this day at 4. P.M. completed every arrangement necessary for our departure, we dismissed the barge and crew with orders to return without loss of time to St. Louis,   a small canoe with two French hunters accompanyed the barge; these men had assended the missouri with us the last year as engages. The barge crew consisted of six soldiers and two [blank space in MS.] Frenchmen; two Frenchmen and a Ricara Indian also take their passage in her as far as the Ricara Vilages, at which place we expect Mr. Tiebeau to embark with his peltry who in that case will make an addition of two, perhaps four men to the crew of the barge. We gave Richard Warfington, a discharged Corpl., the charge of the Barge and crew, and confided to his care likewise our dispatches to the government, letters to our private friends and a number of articles to the President of the United States. One of the Frenchmen by the Name of Gravline an honest discrete man and an excellent boat-man is imployed to conduct the barge as a pilot; we have therefore every hope that the barge and with her our dispatches will arrive safe at St. Louis. Mr. Gravlin who speaks the Ricara language extreemly well, has been imployed to conduct a few of the Recara Chiefs to the seat of government who have promised us to decend in the barge to St: Liwis with that view.

At the same moment that the Barge departed from Fort Mandan, Capt. Clark emba[r]ked with our party and proceeded up the River. as I had used no exercise for several weeks, I determined to walk on shore as far as our encampment of this evening.

Our vessels consisted of six small canoes, and two large perogues. This little fleet altho' not quite so rispectable as those of Columbus or Capt. Cook, were still viewed by us with as much pleasure as those deservedly famed adventurers ever beheld theirs; and I dare say with quite as much anxiety for their safety and preservation. we were now about to penetrate a country at least two thousand miles in width, on which the foot of civilized man had never trodden; the good or evil it had in store for us was for experiment yet to determine, and these little vessells contained every article by which we were to expect to subsist or defend ourselves. however, as the state of mind in which we are, generally gives the colouring to events, when the immagination is suffered to wander into futurity, the picture which now presented itself to me was a most pleasing one. enterta[in]ing as I do, the most confident hope of succeeding in a voyage which had formed a da[r]ing project of mine for the last ten years, I could but esteem this moment of my departure as among the most happy of my life. The party are in excellent health and sperits, zealously attached to the enterprise, and anxious to proceed; not a whisper of murmur or discontent to be heard among them, but all act in unison, and with the most perfict harmony. Capt. Clark myself the two Interpretters and the woman and child sleep in a tent of dressed skins.[1] this tent is in the Indian stile, formed of a number of dressed Buffaloe skins sewed together with sinues. it is cut in such manner that when foalded double it forms the quarter of a circle, and is left open at one side here it may be attached or loosened at pleasure by strings which are sewed to its sides for the purpose.

[Clark]   FORT MANDAN APRIL TH 7TH 1805

Sunday, at 4 oClock PM, the Boat, in which was 6 Soldiers 2 frenchmen & an Indian, all under the command of a corporal who had the charge of dispatches, &c.—and a canoe with 2 french men, Set out down the river

[1]Drewyer, Charbonneau, Sacajawea, and her baby, who was not yet two months old.

for St. Louis. at the same time we Sout out on our voyage up the river in 2 perogues and 6 canoes, and proceded on to the 1st villag. of Mandans & camped on the S.S. our party consisting of Sergts. Nathaniel Pryor, John Ordway, Patrick Gass, Pvts. William Bratton, John Colter, Joseph and Reuben Fields, John Shields, George Gibson, George Shannon, John Potts, John Collins, Joseph Whitehouse, Richard Windsor, Alexander Willard, Hugh Hall, Silas Goodrich, Robert Frazier, Peter Cruzatte, Baptiste Lepage, Francis Labiche, Hugh McNeal, William Werner, Thomas P. Howard, Peter Wiser, John B. Thompson and my servent York, George Drewyer who acts as a hunter & interpreter, Charbonneau and his *Indian Squar* to act as an Interpreter & interpretress for the snake Indians—one Mandan & Charbonneau's infant.

[Lewis]   TUESDAY APRIL 9TH
    when we halted for dinner the squaw busied herself in serching for the wild artichokes which the mice collect and deposit in large hoards. this operation she performed by penetrating the earth with a sharp stick about some small collections of drift wood. her labour soon proved successful, and she procured a good quantity of these roots. the flavor of this root resembles that of the Jerusalem Artichoke, and the stalk of the weed which produces it is also similar,

[Clark]   9TH OF APRIL TUESDAY 1805.—
    I saw a Musquetor to day   great numbers of Brant flying up the river, the Maple, & Elm has buded & cotton and arrow wood beginning to bud. But fiew resident birds or water fowls which I have Seen as yet   Saw Great numbers of Gees feedin in the Praries on the young grass,   I saw flowers in the praries to day, juniper grows on the Sides of the hills, & runs on the ground

[Lewis]   WEDNESDAY APRIL 10TH 1805.
    at the distance of 12 miles from our encampment of last night we arrived at the lower point of a bluff on the Lard side; about 1½ miles down this bluff from this point, the bluff is now on fire and throws out considerable quantities of smoke which has a strong sulphurious smell. at 1. P.M. we overtook three french hunters who had set out a few days before us with a view of traping beaver; they had taken 12 since they left Fort Mandan. these people avail themselves of the protection which our numbers will enable us to give them against the Assinniboins who sometimes hunt on the Missouri; and intend ascending with us as far as the mouth of the Yellow stone river and continue there hunt up that river.

this is the first essay of a beaver hunter of any discription on this river [above the villages]. the beaver these people have already taken is by far the best I have ever seen.

[Lewis]   SATURDAY APRIL 13TH
    The wind was in our favour after 9 A.M. and continued favourable until three 3. P.M.   we therefore hoisted both the sails in the White Perogue, consisting of a small squar sail, and spritsail, which carried her at a pretty good gate, until about 2 in the afternoon when a sudden squall of wind struck us and turned the perogue so much on the side as to allarm Sharbono who was steering at the time,   in this state of alarm he threw the perogue with her side to the wind, when the spritsail gibing was as near overseting the perogue as it was possible to have missed. the wind however abating for an instant I ordered Drewyer to the helm and the sails to be taken in, which was instant executed and the perogue being steered before the wind was agin plased in a state of security. this accedent was very near costing us dearly. beleiving this vessell to be the most steady and safe, we had embarked on board of it our instruments, Papers, medicine and the most valuable part of the merchandize which we had still in reserve as presents for the Indians. we had also embarked on board ourselves, with three men who could not swim and the squaw with the young child, all of whom, had the perogue overset, would most probably have perished, as the waves were high, and the perogue upwards of 200 yards from the nearest shore;   just above the entrance of the little Missouri the great Missouri is upwards of a mile in width, tho' immediately at the entrance of the former it is not more than 200 yards wide and so shallow that the canoes passed it with seting poles.
    we found a number of carcases of the Buffaloe lying along shore, which had been drowned by falling through the ice in winter and lodged on shore by the high water when the river broke up about the first of this month. we saw also many tracks of the white bear of enormous size, along the river shore and about the carcases of the Buffaloe, on which I presume they feed. we have not as yet seen one of these anamals, tho' their tracks are so abundant and recent. the men as well as ourselves are anxious to meet with some of these bear. the Indians give a very formidable account of the strength and ferocity of this anamal, which they never dare to attack but in parties of six eight or ten persons; and are even then frequently defeated with the loss of one or more of their party. the savages attack this anamal with their bows and arrows and the indifferent guns with which the traders furnish them,   with these they shoot with such uncertainty and at so short a distance, that (*unless shot thro' head or heart wound not mortal*) they frequently mis their aim & fall a sacrefice to the

bear. this anamall is said more frequently to attack a man on meeting with him, than to flee from him. When the Indians are about to go in quest of the white bear, previous to their departure, they paint themselves and perform all those supersticious rights commonly observed when they are about to make war uppon a neighbouring nation. Oserved more bald eagles on this part of the Missouri than we have previously seen. saw the small hawk, frequently called the sparrow hawk, which is common to most parts of the U. States. great quantities of gees are seen feeding in the praries. saw a large flock of white brant or gees with black wings pass up the river;   there were a number of gray brant with them.

SUNDAY APRIL 14TH 1805.
     where the land is level, it is uniformly fertile consisting of a dark loam intermixed with a proportion of fine sand. it is generally covered with a short grass resembling very much the blue grass. the miniral appearances still continue; considerable quantities of bitumenous water, about the colour of strong lye trickles down the sides of the hills; this water partakes of the taste of glauber salts and slightly of allumn. while the party halted to take dinner today Capt. Clark killed a buffaloe bull; it was meagre, and we therefore took the marrow bones and a small proportion of the meat only. passed an Island, above which two small creeks fall in on Lard. side; the upper creek largest, which we called Sharbono's Creek, after our interpreter who encamped several weeks on it with a hunting party of Indians. this was the highest point to which any whiteman had ever ascended, except two Frenchmen (*one of whom Lapage was now with us*) who having lost their way had straggled a few miles further tho' to what place precisely I could not learn.

[Clark]   18TH OF APRIL THURSDAY 1805
     after brackfast I assended a hill and observed that the river made a great bend to the South, I concluded to walk thro' the point about 2 miles and take Shabono, with me, he had taken a dost of Salts &c.   his squar followed on with her child,   when I struck the next bend of the [river] could see nothing of the Party, left this man & his wife & child on the river bank and went out to hunt,   Killed a young Buck Elk, & a Deer, the Elk was tolerable meat, the Deer verry pore, Butchered the meat and continued untill near Sunset before Capt Lewis and the party came up,   they were detained by the wind, which rose soon after I left the boat from the NW. & blew verry hard untill verry late in the evening. Saw several old Indian camps,   the game, such as Buffalow Elk, antelopes & Deer verry plenty

19TH OF APRIL FRIDAY 1805

the wind so hard from the N.W. that we were fearful of ventering our Canoes in the river, lay by all day on the S. Side in a good harber, the Praries appear to Green, the cotton trees bigin to leave, Saw some plumb bushes in full bloom, The beaver of this river is much larger than usial, Great deal of Sign of the large Bear,

20TH OF APRIL SATTURDAY 1805

we set out at 7 oClock proceeded on, soon after we set out a Bank fell in near one of the canoes which like to have filled her with water, the wind became hard and waves so rough that we proceeded with our little canoes with much risque, our situation was such after setting out that we were obliged to pass round the 1st Point or lay exposed to the blustering winds & waves, in passing round the Point several canoes took in water as also our large Perogue but without injuring our stores &c. much a short distance below our Camp I saw some rafts on the S. S. near which, an Indian woman was scaffeled in the Indian form of Deposing their Dead and fallen down She was or had been raised about 6 feet, inclosed in Several robes tightly laced around her, with her dog Slays, her bag of Different coloured earths paint small bones of animals beaver nales and Several other little trinkets, also a blue jay, her dog was killed and lay near her. Capt. Lewis joined me soon after I landed & informed me he had walked several miles higher, & in his walk killed 2 Deer & wounded an Elk & a Deer, our party shot in the river four beaver & cought two, which were verry fat and much admired by the men, after we landed they killed 3 Elk 4 Gees & 2 Deer we had some of our Provisions &c. which got a little wet aired, the wind continued so hard that we were compelled to delay all day. Saw several buffalow lodged in the drift wood which had been drouned in the winter in passing the river.

[Lewis]   MONDAY APRIL 22ND 1805.

Set out at an early hour this morning; proceeded pretty well untill breakfast, when the wind became so hard a head that we proceeded with difficulty even with the assistance of our toe lines. the party halted and Cpt. Clark and myself walked to the white earth river which approaches the Missouri very near at this place, being about 4 miles above it's entrance. we found that it contained more water than streams of it's size generally do at this season. the water is much clearer than that of the Missouri. the banks of the river are steep and not more than ten or twelve feet high; the bed seems to be composed of mud altogether. the salts [alkali] which have been before mentioned as common on the Missouri, appears in great quantities along the banks of this river, which are in many places so thickly covered with it that they appear perfectly white. perhaps it has been from this white appearance of it's banks that the river has derived it's name. this river is said to be navigable nearly to it's source, which is at no great distance from the Saskashawan, and I think from it's size the direction wich it seems to take, and the latitude of it's mouth, that there is very good ground to believe that it extends as far North as latitude 50°   this stream passes through an open country generally.

Coal or carbonated wood pumice stone lava and other mineral apearances still continue. the coal appears to be of better quality; I exposed a specimen of it to the fire and found that it birnt tolerably well, it afforded but little flame or smoke, but produced a hot and lasting fire. I asscended to the top of the cutt bluff this morning, from whence I had a most delightful view of the country, the whole of which except the vally formed by the Missouri is void of timber or underbrush, exposing to the first glance of the spectator immence herds of Buffaloe, Elk, deer, & Antelopes feeding in one common and boundless pasture. we saw a number of bever feeding on the bark of the trees alonge the verge of the river, several of which we shot, found them large and fat. walking on shore this evening I met with a buffaloe calf which attatched itself to me and continued to follow close at my heels untill I embarked and left it. it appeared allarmed at my dog which was probably the cause of it's so readily attatching itself to me. Capt Clark informed me that he saw a large drove of buffaloe pursued by wolves today, that they at length caught a calf which was unable to keep up with the herd. the cows only defend their young so long as they are able to keep up with the herd, and seldom return any distance in surch of them.

THURSDAY APRIL 25TH 1805.
    the water friezed on the oars this morning as the men rowed. about 10 oclock A.M. the wind began to blow so violently that we were obliged to lye too. my dog had been absent during the last night, and I was fearfull we had lost him altogether, however, much to my satisfaction he joined us at 8 oclock this morning. Knowing that the river was crooked, from the report of the hunters who were out yesterday, and beleiving that we were at no very great distance from the Yellow stone River; I determined, in order as much as possible to avoid detention, to proceed by land with a few men to the entrance of that river and make the necessary observations to determine its position; accordingly I set out at 11 OCk. on the

Lard. side, accompanyed by four men. when we had proceeded about four miles, I ascended the hills from whence I had a most pleasing view of the country, particularly of the wide and fertile vallies formed by the missouri and the yellowstone rivers, which occasionally unmasked by the wood on their borders disclose their meanderings for many miles in their passage through these delightful tracts of country. I determined to en-camp on the bank of the Yellow stone river which made it's appearance about 2 miles South of me. the whol face of the country was covered with herds of Buffaloe, Elk & Antelopes; deer are also abundant, but keep themselves more concealed in the woodland. the buffaloe Elk and Ante-lope are so gentle that we pass near them while feeding, without appear-ing to excite any alarm among them; and when we attract their attention, they frequently approach us more nearly to discover what we are, and in some instances pursue us a considerable distance apparently with that view. we encamped on the bank of the yellow stone river, 2 miles South of it's confluence with the Missouri.

FRIDAY APRIL 26TH 1805.

This morning I dispatched Joseph Fields up the yellowstone river with orders to examine it as far as he could conveniently and return the same evening; while I proceeded down the river with one man in order to take a view of the confluence of this great river with the Missouri, which we found to be two miles distant on a direct line N.W. from our encampment. the bottom land on the lower side of the yellowstone river near it's mouth, for about one mile in width appears to be subject to inundation; while that on the opposite side of the Missouri and the point formed by the junction of these rivers is of the common elivation, say from twelve to 18 feet above the level of the water, and of course not liable to be overflown except in extreem high water, which dose not appear to be very frequent. there is more timber in the neighbourhood of the junction of these rivers, and on the Missouri as far below as the White-earth river, than there is on any part of the Missouri above the entrance of the Chyenne river to this place.

about 12 O[c]lock I heard the discharge of several guns at the junction of the rivers, which announced to me the arrival of the pa[r]ty with Capt Clark; I afterwards learnt that they had fired on some buffaloe which they met with at that place, and of which they killed a cow and several Calves; the latter are now fine veal. after I had completed my observations in the evening I walked down and joined the party at their encampment on the point of land formed by the junction of the rivers; found them all in good health, and much pleased at having arrived at this long wished for spot, and in order to add in some measure to the general pleasure which seemed to pervade our little community, we ordered a dram to be issued to each person; this soon produced the fiddle, and they spent the evening with much hilarity, singing & dancing, and seemed as perfectly to forget their past toils, as they appeared regardless of those to come.

JOHN MUIR

Patrick Delaney, a San Joaquin Valley rancher, deserves great credit for presci-
ence and insight into character. He saw something in John Muir (1838–1914),
who in the early months of 1869 had done some work for him but was (at age
thirty-one) essentially careerless, and he hired the young man to supervise his
summer sheep operation in the Sierra Nevada. Muir would have plenty of time
for exploration, writing, and sketching, Delaney assured him. In effect, Patrick
Delaney turned Muir loose in the promised land. Over the summer, Muir discovered the glacier-borne boulders called "erratics," thus launching his maverick geological interpretation of the range, made the acquaintance of his totem bird, the
stream-loving water ouzel, crawled to the edge of Yosemite Falls in an adventure
that disturbed his dreams for several nights, had a strange, clairvoyant experience
that probably indicated the degree to which his consciousness was loosening and
deepening, hiked across the entire range to the dry, Great Basin side and back,
withal becoming intextricably enmeshed, body and soul, in the wild beauty of the
mountains. After this summer, Muir knew exactly where the lines of his life
pointed.

"Through the Foothills with a Flock of Sheep," from *My First Summer in the Sierra* (1869)

June 5. This morning a few hours after setting out with the crawling
sheep-cloud, we gained the summit of the first well-defined bench on the
mountain-flank at Pino Blanco. The Sabine pines interest me greatly. They
are so airy and strangely palm-like I was eager to sketch them, and was
in a fever of excitement without accomplishing much. I managed to halt
long enough, however, to make a tolerably fair sketch of Pino Blanco peak
from the southwest side, where there is a small field and vineyard irrigated by a stream that makes a pretty fall on its way down a gorge by
the roadside.

After gaining the open summit of this first bench, feeling the natural
exhilaration due to the slight elevation of a thousand feet or so, and the
hopes excited concerning the outlook to be obtained, a magnificent section
of the Merced Valley at what is called Horseshoe Bend came full in
sight—a glorious wilderness that seemed to be calling with a thousand
songful voices. Bold, down-sweeping slopes, feathered with pines and

clumps of manzanita with sunny, open spaces between them, make up most of the foreground; the middle and background present fold beyond fold of finely modeled hills and ridges rising into mountain-like masses in the distance, all covered with a shaggy growth of chaparral, mostly adenostoma, planted so marvelously close and even that it looks like soft, rich plush without a single tree or bare spot. As far as the eye can reach it extends, a heaving, swelling sea of green as regular and continuous as that produced by the heaths of Scotland. The sculpture of the landscape is as striking in its main lines as in its lavish richness of detail; a grand congregation of massive heights with the river shining between, each carved into smooth, graceful folds without leaving a single rocky angle exposed, as if the delicate fluting and ridging fashioned out of metamorphic slates had been carefully sandpapered. The whole landscape showed design, like man's noblest sculptures. How wonderful the power of its beauty! Gazing awe-stricken, I might have left everything for it. Glad, endless work would then be mine tracing the forces that have brought forth its features, its rocks and plants and animals and glorious weather. Beauty beyond thought everywhere, beneath, above, made and being made forever. I gazed and gazed and longed and admired until the dusty sheep and packs were far out of sight, made hurried notes and a sketch, though there was no need of either, for the colors and lines and expression of this divine landscape-countenance are so burned into mind and heart they surely can never grow dim.

The evening of this charmed day is cool, calm, cloudless, and full of a kind of lightning I have never seen before—white glowing cloud-shaped masses down among the trees and bushes, like quick-throbbing fireflies in the Wisconsin meadows rather than the so-called "wild fire." The spreading hairs of the horses' tails and sparks from our blankets show how highly charged the air is.

June 6. We are now on what may be called the second bench or plateau of the Range, after making many small ups and downs over belts of hill-waves, with, of course, corresponding changes in the vegetation. In open spots many of the lowland compositæ are still to be found, and some of the Mariposa tulips and other conspicuous members of the lily family; but the characteristic blue oak of the foothills is left below, and its place is taken by a fine large species (*Quercus Californica*) with deeply lobed deciduous leaves, picturesquely divided trunk, and broad, massy, finely lobed and modeled head. Here also at a height of about twenty-five hundred feet we come to the edge of the great coniferous forest, made up mostly of yellow pine with just a few sugar pines. We are now in the mountains and they are in us, kindling enthusiasm, making every nerve quiver, filling every pore and cell of us. Our flesh-and-bone tabernacle seems transparent as glass to the beauty about us, as if truly an inseparable part of it, thrilling with the air and trees, streams and rocks, in the waves of the sun,—a part of all nature, neither old nor young, sick nor well, but immortal. Just now I can hardly conceive of any bodily condition dependent on food or breath any more than the ground or the sky. How glorious a conversion, so complete and wholesome it is, scarce memory enough of old bondage days left as a standpoint to view it from! In this newness of life we seem to have been so always.

Through a meadow opening in the pine woods I see snowy peaks about the head-waters of the Merced above Yosemite. How near they seem and how clear their outlines on the blue air, or rather *in* the blue air; for they seem to be saturated with it. How consuming strong the invitation they extend! Shall I be allowed to go to them? Night and day I'll pray that I may, but it seems too good to be true. Some one worthy will go, able for the Godful work, yet as far as I can I must drift about these love-monument mountains, glad to be a servant of servants in so holy a wilderness.

Found a lovely lily (*Calochortus albus*) in a shady adenostoma thicket near Coulterville, in company with *Adiantum Chilense*. It is white with a faint purplish tinge inside at the base of the petals, a most impressive plant, pure as a snow crystal, one of the plant saints that all must love and be made so much the purer by it every time it is seen. It puts the roughest mountaineer on his good behavior. With this plant the whole world would seem rich though none other existed. It is not easy to keep on with the camp cloud while such plant people are standing preaching by the wayside.

During the afternoon we passed a fine meadow bounded by stately pines, mostly the arrowy yellow pine, with here and there are a noble sugar pine, its feathery arms outspread above the spires of its companion species in marked contrast; a glorious tree, its cones fifteen to twenty inches long, swinging like tassels at the ends of the branches with superb ornamental effect. Saw some logs of this species at the Greeley Mill. They are round and regular as if turned in a lathe, excepting the butt cuts, which have a few buttressing projections. The fragrance of the sugary sap is delicious and scents the mill and lumber yard. How beautiful the ground beneath this pine thickly strewn with slender needles and grand cones, and the piles of cone-scales, seed-wings and shells around the instep of each tree where the squirrels have been feasting! They get the seeds by cutting off the scales at the base in regular order, following their spiral arrangement, and the two seeds at the base of each scale, a hundred or two in a cone, must make a good meal. The yellow pine cones and those of most other species and genera are held upside down on the ground by the Douglas squirrel, and turned around gradually until stripped, while he sits usually with his back to a tree, probably for safety. Strange to say, he never seems to get himself smeared with gum, not even his paws or whiskers—and how cleanly and beautiful in color the cone-litter kitchen-middens he makes.

We are now approaching the region of clouds and cool streams. Magnificent white cumuli appeared about noon above the Yosemite region,—floating fountains refreshing the glorious wilderness,—sky mountains in whose pearly hills and dales the streams take their rise,—blessing with cooling shadows and rain. No rock landscape is more varied in sculpture, none more delicately modeled than these landscapes of the sky; domes and peaks rising, swelling, white as finest marble and firmly outlined, a most impressive manifestation of world building. Every rain-cloud, however fleeting, leaves its mark, not only on trees and flowers whose pulses are quickened, and on the replenished streams and lakes, but also on the rocks are its marks engraved whether we can see them or not.

I have been examining the curious and influential shrub *Adenostoma fasciculata*, first noticed about Horseshoe Bend. It is very abundant on the lower slopes of the second plateau near Coulterville, forming a dense, almost impenetrable growth that looks dark in the distance. It belongs to the rose family, is about six or eight feet high, has small white flowers in racemes eight to twelve inches long, round needle-like leaves, and reddish bark that becomes shreddy when old. It grows on sun-beaten slopes, and like grass is often swept away by running fires, but is quickly renewed from the roots. Any trees that may have established themselves in its midst are at length killed by these fires, and this no doubt is the secret of the unbroken character of its broad belts. A few manzanitas, which also rise again from the root after consuming fires, make out to dwell with it, also a few bush compositæ—baccharis and linosyris, and some liliaceous plants, mostly calochortus and brodiæa, with deepset bulbs safe from fire. A multitude of birds and "wee, sleekit, cow'rin', tim'rous beasties" find good homes in its deepest thickets, and the open bays and lanes that fringe the margins of its main belts offer shelter and food to the deer when winter storms drive them down from their high mountain pastures. A most admirable plant! It is now in bloom, and I like to wear its pretty fragrant racemes in my buttonhole.

Azalea occidentalis, another charming shrub, grows beside cool streams hereabouts and much higher in the Yosemite region. We found it this evening in bloom a few miles above Greeley's Mill, where we are camped for the night. It is closely related to the rhododendrons, is very showy and fragrant, and everybody must like it not only for itself but for the shady alders and willows, ferny meadows, and living water associated with it.

Another conifer was met to-day—incense cedar (*Libocedrus decurrens*), a large tree with warm yellow-green foliage in flat plumes like those of arborvitæ, bark cinnamon-colored, and as the boles of the old trees are without limbs they make striking pillars in the woods where the sun chances to shine on them—a worthy companion of the kingly sugar and yellow pines. I feel strangely attracted to this tree. The brown close-grained wood, as well as the small scale-like leaves, is fragrant, and the flat over-lapping plumes make fine beds, and must shed the rain well. It would be delightful to be storm-bound beneath one of these noble, hospitable, inviting old trees, its broad sheltering arms bent down like a tent, incense rising from the fire made from its dry fallen branches, and a hearty wind chanting overhead. But the weather is calm to-night, and our camp is only a sheep camp. We are near the North Fork of the Merced. The night wind is telling the wonders of the upper mountains, their snow fountains and gardens, forests and groves; even their topography is in its tones. And the stars, the everlasting sky lilies, how bright they are now that we have climbed above the lowland dust! The horizon is bounded and adorned by a spiry wall of pines, every tree harmoniously related to every other; definite symbols, divine hieroglyphics written with sunbeams. Would I could understand them! The stream flowing past the camp through ferns and lilies and alders makes sweet music to the ear, but the pines marshaled around the edge of the sky make a yet sweeter music to the eye. Divine beauty all. Here I could stay tethered forever with just bread and water, nor would I be lonely; loved friends and neighbors, as love for everything increased, would seem all the nearer however many the miles and mountains between us.

CLARENCE DUTTON

Captain of Ordnance in the U.S. Army when he made his great geological surveys of the Four Corners and Grand Canyon region, Clarence Dutton (1841–1912) wrote some of the most stylish, evocative, and excited prose ever included in a government document. A native of Connecticut, graduate of Yale at age nineteen, and a Civil War veteran, he came to know Spencer Fullerton Baird and John Wesley Powell in Washington after the war. Powell sent him west, where he was deeply affected by the bare-rock drama of the landscape in what is now southern Utah and northern Arizona. He became convinced that a wholly new frame of mind was needed, for people such as himself, simply to see the West accurately. And a long time of immersion would be required: "Forms so new to the culture of civilized races and so strongly contrasted with those which have been the ideals of thirty generations of white men cannot indeed be appreciated after the study of a single hour or day," he wrote. So deep was Dutton's appreciation that, reportedly, he had little need to refer to his notes in composing his formal accounts. In the following passage, excerpted from *Tertiary History of the Grand Cañon District* (Washington, D.C.: U.S. Government, 1882), Dutton and his party approach Zion Canyon, today part of Zion National Park.

"The Valley of the Virgen," from *Tertiary History of the Grand Cañon District* (1882)

As we moved northward from Short Creek, we had frequent opportunities to admire these cliffs and buttes; with the conviction that they were revealed to us in their real magnitudes and in their true relations. They awakened an enthusiasm more vivid than we had anticipated, and one which the recollection of far grander scenes did not dispel. At length the trail descended into a shallow basin where a low ledge of sandstones, immediately upon the right, shut them out from view; but as we mounted the opposite rim a new scene, grander and more beautiful than before, suddenly broke upon us. The cliff again appeared, presenting the heavy sandstone member in a sheer wall nearly a thousand feet high, with a steep talus beneath it of eleven or twelve hundred feet more. Wide alcoves receded far back into the mass, and in their depths the clouds floated.

Long, sharp spurs plunged swiftly down, thrusting their monstrous buttresses into the plain below, and sending up pinnacles and towers along the knife edges.

But the controlling object was a great butte which sprang into view immediately before us, and which the salient of the wall had hitherto masked. Upon a pedestal two miles long and 1,000 feet high, richly decorated with horizontal moldings, rose four towers highly suggestive of cathedral architecture. Their altitude above the plain was estimated at about 1,800 feet. They were separated by vertical clefts made by the enlargement of the joints, and many smaller clefts extending from the summits to the pedestal carved the turrets into tapering buttresses, which gave a graceful aspiring effect with a remarkable definiteness to the forms. We named it Smithsonian Butte, and it was decided that a sketch should be made of it; but in a few moments the plan was abandoned or forgotten. For over a notch or saddle formed by a low isthmus which connected the butte with the principal mesa there sailed slowly and majestically into view, as we rode along, a wonderful object. Deeply moved, we paused a moment to contemplate it, and then abandoning the trail we rode rapidly towards the notch, beyond which it soon sank out of sight. In an hour's time we reached the crest of the isthmus, and in an instant there flashed before us a scene never to be forgotten. In coming time it will, I believe, take rank with a very small number of spectacles each of which will, in its own way, be regarded as the most exquisite of its kind which the world discloses. The scene before us was

The Temples and Towers of the Virgen

At our feet the surface drops down by cliff and talus 1,200 feet upon a broad and rugged plan cut by narrow cañons. The slopes, the winding ledges, the bosses of projecting rock, the naked, scanty soil, display colors which are truly amazing. Chocolate, maroon, purple, lavender, magenta, with broad bands of toned white, are laid in horizontal belts, strongly contrasting with each other, and the ever-varying slope of the surface cuts across them capriciously, so that the sharply defined belts wind about like the contours of a map. From right to left across the further foreground of the picture stretches the inner cañon of the Virgen, about 700 feet in depth, and here of considerable width. Its bottom is for the most part unseen, but in one place is disclosed by a turn in its course, showing the vivid green of vegetation. Across the cañon, and rather more than a mile and a half beyond it, stands the central and commanding object of the picture, the western temple, rising 4,000 feet above the river. Its glorious summit was the object we had seen an hour before, and now the matchless beauty and majesty of its vast mass is all before us. Yet it is only the central object of a mighty throng of structures wrought up to the same exalted style, and filling up the entire panorama. Right opposite us are the two principal forks of the Virgen, the Parúnuweap coming from the right or east, and the Mukúntuweap or Little Zion Valley, descending towards us from the north. The Parúnuweap is seen emerging on the extreme right through a stupendous gateway and chasm in the Triassic terrace, nearly 3,000 feet in depth. The further wall of this cañon, at the opening of the gateway, quickly swings northward at a right angle and becomes the eastern wall of Little Zion Valley. As it sweeps down the Parúnuweap it breaks into great pediments, covered all over with the richest carving. The effect is much like that which the architect of the Milan Cathedral appears to have designed, though here it is vividly suggested rather than fully realized— as an artist painting in the "broad style" suggests many things without actually drawing them. The sumptuous, bewildering, mazy effect is all there, but when we attempt to analyze it in detail it eludes us. The flank of the wall receding up the Mukúntuweap is for a mile or two similarly decorated, but soon breaks into new forms much more impressive and wonderful. A row of towers half a mile high is quarried out of the palisade, and stands well advanced from its face. There is an eloquence to their forms which stirs the imagination with a singular power, and kindles in the mind of the dullest observer a glowing response. Just behind them, rising a thousand feet higher, is the eastern temple, crowned with a cylindric dome of white sandstone; but since it is, in many respects, a repetition of the nearer western temple, we may turn our attention to the latter. Directly in front of us a complex group of white towers, springing from a central pile, mounts upwards to the clouds. Out of their midst, and high over all, rises a dome-like mass, which dominates the entire landscape. It is almost pure white, with brilliant streaks of carmine descending its vertical walls. At the summit it is truncated, and a flat tablet is laid upon the top, showing its edge of deep red. It is impossible to liken this object to any familiar shape, for it resembles none. Yet its shape is far from being indefinite; on the contrary, it has a definiteness and individuality which extort an exclamation of surprise when first beheld. There is no name provided for such an object, nor is it worth while to invent one. Call it a dome; not because it has the ordinary shape of such a structure, but because it performs the function of a dome.

The towers which surround it are of inferior mass and altitude, but each of them is a study of fine form and architectural effect. They are white above, and change to a strong, rich red below. Dome and towers are planted upon a substructure no less admirable. Its plan is indefinite, but its profiles are perfectly systematic. A curtain wall 1,400 feet high descends vertically from the eaves of the temples and is succeeded by a steep slope of ever-widening base courses leading down to the esplanade below. The curtain-wall is decorated with a lavish display of vertical moldings, and the ridges, eaves, and mitered angles are fretted with serrated cusps. This ornamentation is suggestive rather than precise, but it is none the less effective. It is repetitive, not symmetrical. But though exact symmetry is wanting, nature has here brought home to us the truth that symmetry is only one of an infinite range of devices by which beauty can be materialized.

> And finer forms are in the quarry
> Than ever Angelo evoked.

Reverting to the twin temple across Little Zion Valley, its upper mass is a repetition of the one which crowns the western pile. It has the same elliptical contour, and a similar red tablet above. In its effect upon the imagination it is much the same. But from the point from which we first viewed them—and it is by far the best one accessible—it was too distant to be seen to the fullest advantage, and the western temple by its greater proximity overpowered its neighbor.

Nothing can exceed the wondrous beauty of Little Zion Valley, which separates the two temples and their respective groups of towers. Nor are these the only sublime structures which look down into its depths, for similar ones are seen on either hand along its receding vista until a turn in the course carries the valley out of sight. In its proportions it is about equal to Yo Semite, but in the nobility and beauty of the sculptures there is no comparison. It is Hyperion to a satyr. No wonder the fierce Mormon zealot, who named it, was reminded of the Great Zion, on which his fervid thoughts were bent—"of houses not built with hands, eternal in the heavens."

From those highly wrought groups in the center of the picture the eye escapes to the westward along a mass of cliffs and buttes covered with the same profuse decoration as the walls of the temples and of the Parúnuweap. Their color is brilliant red. Much animation is imparted to this part of the scene by the wandering courses of the mural fronts which have little continuity and no definite trend. The Triassic terrace out of which they have been carved is cut into by broad amphitheaters and slashed in all directions by wide cañon valleys. The resulting escarpments stretch their courses in every direction, here fronting towards us, there averted; now receding behind a nearer mass, and again emerging from an unseen alcove. Far to the westward, twenty miles away, is seen the last palisade lifting its imposing front behind a mass of towers and domes to an altitude of probably near 3,000 feet and with a grandeur which the distance cannot dispel. Beyond it the scenery changes almost instantly, for it passes at once into the Great Basin, which, to this region, is as another world.

SARAH WINNEMUCCA

ccording to Peter Farb's categorization in *Man's Rise to Civilization* (1968), the Great Basin tribes had some of the least complex cultures in North America. Sarah Winnemucca's (1844?–1891) group, the Northern Piutes, had first contact with Euro-Americans in about 1848, when Thocmetony (Sarah's original name—"Shell Flower" in English) was a girl of four. Her fleeing parents, hearing stories of the whites' cannibalism, buried her in the sand temporarily for safety. From this background, and as a member of a family who came to believe in peaceful coexistence with the whites, Sarah Winnemucca dedicated her life to developing liaison between the cultures, while never downplaying the wrongs done to hers. Educated by missionary nuns, she became fluent and creative in English and used her talent courageously. She gave her first public address in San Francisco in 1879 (first of some three hundred such efforts, coast to coast) with a forthright description of the Piutes' situation, published an essay describing her tribe in 1882 in *The Californian*, and in the following year she became the first Indian woman to write a book of personal and tribal history. The selection here is from "Domestic and Social Moralities," Chapter 2 of *Life Among the Piutes* (New York: G. P. Putnam's, 1883).

From *Life Among the Piutes: Their Wrongs and Claims* (1883)

Domestic and Social Moralities

Our children are very carefully taught to be good. Their parents tell them stories, traditions of old times, even of the first mother of the human race; and love stories, stories of giants, and fables; and when they ask if these last stories are true, they answer, "Oh, it is only coyote," which means that they are make-believe stories. Coyote is the name of a mean, crafty little animal, half wolf, half dog, and stands for everything low. It is the greatest term of reproach one Indian has for another. Indians do not swear,—they have no words for swearing till they learn them of white men. The worst they call each is bad or coyote; but they are very sincere with one another, and if they think each other in the wrong they say so.

We are taught to love everybody. We don't need to be taught to love our fathers and mothers. We love them without being told to. Our tenth cousin is as near to us as our first cousin; and we don't marry into our relations. Our young women are not allowed to talk to any young man that is not their cousin, except at the festive dances, when both are dressed in their best clothes, adorned with beads, feathers or shells, and stand alternately in the ring and take hold of hands. These are very pleasant occasions to all the young people.

Many years ago, when my people were happier than they are now, they used to celebrate the Festival of Flowers in the spring. I have been to three of them only in the course of my life.

Oh, with what eagerness we girls used to watch every spring for the time when we could meet with our hearts' delight, the young men, whom in civilized life you call beaux. We would all go in company to see if the flowers we were named for were yet in bloom, for almost all the girls are named for flowers. We talked about them in our wigwams, as if we were the flowers, saying, "Oh, I saw myself today in full bloom!" We would talk all the evening in this way in our families with such delight, and such beautiful thoughts of the happy day when we should meet with those who admired us and would help us to sing our flower-songs which we made up as we sang. But we were always sorry for those that were not named after some flower, because we knew they could not join in the flower-songs like ourselves, who were named for flowers of all kinds.

At last one evening came a beautiful voice, which made every girl's heart throb with happiness. It was the chief, and every one hushed to hear what he said to-day.

"My dear daughters, we are told that you have seen yourselves in the hills and in the valleys, in full bloom. Five days from to-day your festival day will come. I know every young man's heart stops beating while I am talking. I know how it was with me many years ago. I used to wish the Flower Festival would come every day. Dear young men and young women, you are saying, 'Why put it off five days?' But you all know that is our rule. It gives you time to think, and to show your sweetheart your flower."

All the girls who have flower-names dance along together, and those who have not go together also. Our fathers and mothers and grandfathers and grandmothers make a place for us where we can dance. Each one gathers the flower she is named for, and then all weave them into wreaths and crowns and scarfs, and dress up in them.

Some girls are named for rocks and are called rock-girls, and they find some pretty rocks which they carry; each one such a rock as she is named for, or whatever she is named for. If she cannot, she can take a branch of sage-brush, or a bunch of rye-grass, which have no flower.

They all go marching along, each girl in turn singing of herself; but she is not a girl any more,—she is a flower singing. She sings of herself, and her sweetheart, dancing along by her side, helps her sing the song she makes.

I will repeat what we say of ourselves. "I, Sarah Winnemucca, am a shell-flower, such as I wear on my dress. My name is Thocmetony. I am so beautiful! Who will come and dance with me while I am so beautiful? Oh, come and be happy with me! I shall be beautiful while the earth lasts. Somebody will always admire me; and who will come and be happy with me in the Spirit-land? I shall be beautiful forever there. Yes, I shall be more beautiful than my shell-flower, my Thocmetony! Then, come, oh come, and dance and be happy with me!" The young men sing with us as they dance beside us.

Our parents are waiting for us somewhere to welcome us home. And then we praise the sage-brush and the rye-grass that have no flower, and the pretty rocks that some are named for; and then we present our beautiful flowers to these companions who could carry none. And so all are happy; and that closes the beautiful day.

My people have been so unhappy for a long time they wish now to *disincrease*, instead of multiply. The mothers are afraid to have more children, for fear they shall have daughters, who are not safe even in their mother's presence.

The grandmothers have the special care of the daughters just before and after they come to womanhood. The girls are not allowed to get married until they have come to womanhood; and that period is recognized as a very sacred thing, and is the subject of a festival, and has peculiar customs. The young woman is set apart under the care of two of her friends, somewhat older, and a little wigwam, called a teepee, just big enough for the three, is made for them, to which they retire. She goes through certain labors which are thought to be strengthening, and these last twenty-five days. Every day, three times a day, she must gather, and pile up as high as she can, five stacks of wood. This makes fifteen stacks a day. At the end of every five days the attendants take her to a river to bathe. She fasts from all flesh-meat during these twenty-five days, and continues to do this for five days in every month all her life. At the end of the twenty-five days she returns to the family lodge, and gives all her clothing to her attendants in payment for their care. Sometimes the wardrobe is quite extensive.

It is thus publicly known that there is another marriageable woman, and any young man interested in her, or wishing to form an alliance, comes forward. But the courting is very different from the courting of the white people. He never speaks to her, or visits the family, but endeavors to attract her attention by showing his horsemanship, etc. As he knows that she sleeps next to her grandmother in the lodge, he enters in full dress after the family has retired for the night, and seats himself at her feet. If she is not awake, her grandmother wakes her. He does not speak to either young woman or grandmother, but when the young woman wishes him to go away, she rises and goes and lies down by the side of her mother. He then leaves as silently as he came in. This goes on sometimes for a year or longer, if the young woman has not made up her mind. She is never forced by her parents to marry against her wishes. When she knows her own mind, she makes a confidant of her grandmother, and then the young man is summoned by the father of the girl, who asks him in her presence, if he really loves his daughter, and reminds him, if he says he does, of all the duties of a husband. He then asks his daughter the same question, and sets before her minutely all her duties. And these duties are not slight. She is to dress the game, prepare the food, clean the buckskins, make his moccasins, dress his hair, bring all the wood,—in short, do all the household work. She promises to "be himself," and she fulfils her promise. Then he is invited to a feast and all his relatives with him. But after the betrothal, a teepee is erected for the presents that pour in from both sides.

At the wedding feast, all the food is prepared in baskets. The young woman sits by the young man, and hands him the basket of food prepared for him with her own hands. He does not take it with his right hand; but seizes her wrist, and takes it with the left hand. This constitutes the marriage ceremony, and the father pronounces them man and wife. They go to a wigwam of their own, where they live till the first child is born. This event also is celebrated. Both father and mother fast from all flesh, and the father goes through the labor of piling the wood for twenty-five days, and assumes all his wife's household work during that time. If he does not do his part in the care of the child, he is considered an outcast. Every five days his child's basket is changed for a new one, and the five are all carefully put away at the end of the days, the last one containing the navel-string, carefully wrapped up, and all are put up into a tree, and the child put into a new and ornamented basket. All this respect shown to the mother and child makes the parents feel their responsibility, and makes the tie between parents and children very strong. The young mothers often get together and exchange their experiences about the attentions of their husbands; and inquire of each other if the fathers did their duty to their children, and were careful of their wives' health. When they are married they give away all the clothing they have ever worn, and dress themselves anew. The poor people have the same ceremonies, but do not make a feast of it, for want of means.

Our boys are introduced to manhood by their hunting of deer and mountain-sheep. Before they are fifteen or sixteen, they hunt only small game, like rabbits, hares, fowls, etc. They never eat what they kill themselves, but only what their father or elder brothers kill. When a boy becomes strong enough to use larger bows made of sinew, and arrows that are ornamented with eagle-feathers, for the first time, he kills game that is large, a deer or an antelope, or a mountain-sheep. Then he brings home the hide, and his father cuts it into a long coil which is wound into a loop, and the boy takes his quiver and throws it on his back as if he was going on a hunt, and takes his bow and arrows in his hand. Then his father throws the loop over him, and he jumps through it. This he does five times. Now for the first time he eats the flesh of the animal he has killed, and from that time he eats whatever he kills but he has always been faithful to his parents' command not to eat what he has killed before. He can now do whatever he likes, for now he is a man, and no longer considered a boy. If there is a war he can go to it; but the Piutes, and other tribes west of the Rocky Mountains, are not fond of going to war. I never saw a war-dance but once. It is always the whites that begin the wars, for their own selfish purposes. The government does not take care to send the good men; there are a plenty who would take pains to see and understand the chiefs and learn their characters, and their good will to the whites. But the whites have not waited to find out how good the Indians were, and what ideas they had of God, just like those of Jesus, who called him Father, just as my people do, and told men to do to others as they would be done by, just as my people teach their children to do. My people teach their children never to make fun of anyone, no matter how they look. If you see your brother or sister doing something wrong, look away, or go away from them. If you make fun of bad persons, you make yourself beneath them. Be kind to all, both poor and rich, and feed all that come to your wigwam, and your name can be spoken of by every one far and near. In this way you will make many friends for yourself. Be kind both to bad and good, for you don't know your own heart. This is the way my people teach their children. It was handed down from father to son for many generations. I never in my life saw our children rude as I have seen white children and grown people in the streets.

HAMLIN GARLAND

ector St. John de Crèvecoeur, the eighteenth century's great celebrator of the hearth and the home fields, saw a deep contradiction between the American agrarian hope and the flat realities of a money-driven culture. A century later, by the time of Hamlin Garland (1860–1940), industrial capital was clearly in the ascendant, clearly the "lion's paw." Already in his growing-up years on northern Iowa farms, Garland had noticed that the product of the farmer's toil often became a chip parlayed into riches for others, while the actual worker of the ground stayed poor and plowing. The six stories in his first book *Main-Travelled Roads*, consistently emphasizing reality as he saw it, undercut both agrarian and American-dream mythology. He dedicated the book to "my father and mother, whose half-century pilgrimage on the main-travelled road of life has brought them only toil and deprivation." Later in his career, now a success as a writer, Garland slipped into a kind of Rocky Mountain romanticism seemingly at variance with his early "veritism," but at the same time he wrote against discriminatory Indian policies and in favor of forest and range conversation. A fundamental sympathy and democracy of outlook remained constant.

"Under the Lion's Paw," from *Main Travelled Roads* (1891)

"Along this main-travelled road trailed an endless line of prairie-schooners, coming into sight at the east, and passing out of sight over the swell to the west. We children used to wonder where they were going and why they went."

1

It was the last of autumn and first day of winter coming together. All day long the ploughmen on their prairie farms had moved to and fro in their wide level fields through the falling snow, which melted as it fell, wetting them to the skin—all day, notwithstanding the frequent squalls of snow, the dripping, desolate clouds, and the muck of the furrows, black and tenacious as tar.

Under their dripping harness the horses swung to and fro silently, with that marvellous uncomplaining patience which marks the horse. All day the wild geese, honking wildly, as they sprawled sidewise down the wind, seemed to be fleeing from an enemy behind, and with neck outthrust and wings extended, sailed down the wind, soon lost to sight.

Yet the ploughman behind his plough, though the snow lay on his ragged great-coat, and the cold clinging mud rose on his heavy boots, fettering him like gyves, whistled in the very beard of the gale. As day passed, the snow, ceasing to melt, lay along the ploughed land, and lodged in the depth of the stubble, till on each slow round the last furrow stood out black and shining as jet between the ploughed land and the gray stubble.

When night began to fall, and the geese, flying low, began to alight invisibly in the near corn-field, Stephen Council was still at work "finishing a land." He rode on his sulky plough when going with the wind, but walked when facing it. Sitting bent and cold but cheery under his slouch hat, he talked encouragingly to his four-in-hand.

"Come round there, boys!—Round agin! We got t' finish this land. Come in there, Dan! *Stiddy*, Kate,—stiddy! None o' y'r tantrums, Kittie. It's purty tuff, but got a be did. *Tchk! tchk!* Step along, Pete! Don't let Kate git y'r single-tree on the wheel. *Once* more!"

They seemed to know what he meant, and that this was the last round, for they worked with greater vigor than before.

"Once more, boys, an' then, sez I, oats an' a nice warm stall, an' sleep f'r all."

By the time the last furrow was turned on the land it was too dark to see the house, and the snow was changing to rain again. The tired and hungry man could see the light from the kitchen shining through the leafless hedge, and lifting a great shout, he yelled, "Supper f'r a half a dozen!"

It was nearly eight o'clock by the time he had finished his chores and started for supper. He was picking his way carefully through the mud, when the tall form of a man loomed up before him with a premonitory cough.

"Waddy ye want?" was the rather startled question of the farmer.

"Well, ye see," began the stranger, in a deprecating tone, "we'd like t' git in f'r the night. We've tried every house f'r the last two miles, but they hadn't any room f'r us. My wife's jest about sick, 'n' the children are cold and hungry—"

"Oh, y' want a stay all night, eh?"

"Yes, sir; it 'ud be a great accom——"

"Waal, I don't make it a practice t' turn anybody way hungry, not on sech nights as this. Drive right in. We ain't got much, but sech as it is——"

But the stranger had disappeared. And soon his steaming, weary team, with drooping heads and swinging single-trees, moved past the well to the block beside the path. Council stood at the side of the "schooner" and helped the children out—two little half-sleeping children—and then a small woman with a babe in her arms.

"There ye go!" he shouted jovially, to the children. "Now we're all right! Run right along to the house there, an' tell Mam' Council you wants sumpthin' t' eat. Right this way, Mis'—keep right off t' the right there. I'll go an' git a lantern. Come," he said to the dazed and silent group at his side.

"Mother," he shouted, as he neared the fragrant and warmly lighted kitchen, "here are some wayfarers an' folks who need sumpin' t' eat an' a place t' snooze." He ended by pushing them all in.

Mrs. Council, a large, jolly, rather coarse-looking woman, took the children in her arms. "Come right in, you little rabbits. 'Most asleep, hey? Now here's a drink o' milk f'r each o' ye. I'll have s'm tea in a minute. Take off y'r things and set up t' the fire."

While she set the children to drinking milk, Council got out his lantern and went out to the barn to help the stranger about his team, where his loud, hearty voice could be heard as it came and went between the hay-mow and the stalls.

The woman came to light as a small, timid, and discouraged-looking woman, but still pretty, in a thin and sorrowful way.

"Land sakes! An' you've travelled all the way from Clear Lake t'-day in this mud! Waal! waal! No wonder you're all tired out. Don't wait f'r the men, Mis'———" She hesitated, waiting for the name.

"Haskins."

"Mis' Haskins, set right up to the table an' take a good swig o' tea whilst I make y' s'm toast. It's green tea, an' it's good. I tell Council as I git older I don't seem to enjoy Young Hyson n'r Gunpowder. I want the reel green tea, jest as it comes off'n the vines. Seems t' have more heart in it, some way. Don't s'pose it has. Council says it's all in m' eye."

Going on in this easy way, she soon had the children filled with bread and milk and the woman thoroughly at home, eating some toast and sweet-melon pickles, and sipping the tea.

"See the little rats!" she laughed at the children. "They're full as they can stick now, and they want to go to bed. Now, don't git up, Mis' Haskins; set right where you are an' let me look after 'em. I know all about young ones, though I'm all alone now. Jane went an' married last fall. But, as I tell Council, it's lucky we keep our health. Set right there, Mis' Haskins; I won't have you stir a finger."

It was an unmeasured pleasure to sit there in the warm, homely kitchen, the jovial chatter of the housewife driving out and holding at bay the growl of the impotent, cheated wind.

The little woman's eyes filled with tears which fell down upon the sleeping baby in her arms. The world was not so desolate and cold and hopeless, after all.

"Now I hope Council won't stop out there and talk politics all night. He's the greatest man to talk politics an' read the *Tribune*. How old is it?" She broke off and peered down at the face of the babe.

"Two months 'n' five days," said the mother, with a mother's exactness.

"Ye don't say! I want 'o know! The dear little pudzy-wudzy!" she went on, stirring it up in the neighborhood of the ribs with her fat forefinger.

"Pooty tough on 'oo to go gallivant'n' 'cross lots this way———"

"Yes, that's so; a man can't lift a mountain," said Council, entering the door. "Mother, this is Mr. Haskins, from Kansas. He's been eat up 'n' drove out by grasshoppers."

"Glad t' see yeh!—Pa, empty that wash-basin 'n' give him a chance t' wash."

Haskins was a tall man, with a thin, gloomy face. His hair was a reddish brown, like his coat, and seemed equally faded by the wind and sun. And his sallow face, though hard and set, was pathetic somehow. You would have felt that he had suffered much by the line of his mouth showing under his thin, yellow mustache.

"Hain't Ike got home yet, Sairy?"

"Hain't seen 'im."

"W-a-a-l, set right up, Mr. Haskins; wade right into what we've got; 'taint much, but we manage to live on it—she gits fat on it," laughed Council, pointing his thumb at his wife.

After supper, while the women put the children to bed, Haskins and Council talked on, seated near the huge cooking-stove, the steam rising from their wet clothing. In the Western fashion Council told as much of his own life as he drew from his guest. He asked but few questions; but by and by the story of Haskins' struggles and defeat came out. The story was a terrible one, but he told it quietly, seated with his elbows on his knees, gazing most of the time at the hearth.

"I didn't like the looks of the country, anyhow," Haskins said, partly rising and glancing at his wife. "I was ust t' northern Ingyannie, where we have lots o' timber 'n' lots o' rain, 'n' I didn't like the looks o' that dry prairie. What galled me the worst was goin' s' far away acrosst so much fine land layin' all through here vacant."

"And the 'hoppers eat ye four years hand runnin', did they?"

"Eat! They wiped us out. They chawed everything that was green. They jest set around waitin' f'r us to die t' eat us, too. My God! I ust t' dream of 'em sittin' 'round on the bedpost, six feet long, workin' their jaws. They eet the fork-handles. They got worse 'n' worse till they jest rolled on one another, piled up like snow in winter. Well, it ain't no use. If I was t' talk all winter I couldn't tell nawthin'. But all the while I couldn't help thinkin' of all that land back here that nobuddy was usin' that I ought 'o had 'stead o' bein' out there in that cussed country."

"Wall, why didn't ye stop an' settle here?" asked Ike, who had come in and was eating his supper.

"Fer the simple reason that you fellers wantid ten 'r fifteen dollars an acre fer the bare land, and I hadn't no money fer that kind o' thing."

"Yes, I do my own work," Mrs. Council was heard to say in the pause which followed. "I'm a gettin' purty heavy t' be on m' laigs all day, but we can't afford t' hire, so I keep rackin' around somehow, like a foundered horse. S' lame—I tell Council he can't tell how lame I am, f'r I'm jest as lame in one laig as t' other." And the good soul laughed at the joke on herself as she took a handful of flour and dusted the biscuit-board to keep the dough from sticking.

"Well, I hain't *never* been very strong," said Mrs. Haskins. "Our folks was Canadians an' small-boned, and then since my last child I hain't got up again fairly. I don't like t' complain. Tim has about all he can bear now—but they was days this week when I jest wanted to lay right down an' die."

"Waal, now, I'll tell ye," said Council, from his side of the stove, silencing everybody with his good-natured roar, "I'd go down and *see* Butler, *anyway*, if I was you. I guess he'd let you have his place purty cheap; the farm's all run down. He's ben anxious t' let t' somebuddy next year. It 'ud be a good chance fer you. Anyhow, you go to bed and sleep like a babe. I've got some ploughing t' do, anyhow, an' we'll see if somethin' can't be done about your case. Ike, you go out an' see if the horses is all right, an' I'll show the folks t' bed."

When the tired husband and wife were lying under the generous quilts of the spare bed, Haskins listened a moment to the wind in the eaves, and then said with a slow and solemn tone:

"There are people in this world who are good enough t' be angels, an' only haff t' die to *be* angels."

2

Jim Butler was one of those men called in the West "land poor." Early in the history of Rock River he had come into the town and started in the grocery business in a small way, occupying a small building in a mean part of the town. At this period of his life he earned all he got, and was up early and late sorting beans, working over butter, and carting his goods to and from the station. But a change came over him at the end of the second year, when he sold a lot of land for four times what he paid for it. From that time forward he believed in land speculation as the surest way of getting rich. Every cent he could save or spare from his trade he put into land at forced sale, or mortgages on land, which were "just as good as the wheat," he was accustomed to say.

Farm after farm fell into his hands, until he was recognized as one of the leading landowners of the county. His mortgages were scattered all over Cedar County, and as they slowly but surely fell in he sought usually to retain the former owner as tenant.

He was not ready to foreclose; indeed, he had the name of being one of the "easiest" men in the town. He let the debtor off again and again, extending the time whenever possible.

"I don't want y'r land," he said. "All I'm after is the int'rest on my money—that's all. Now, if y' want 'o stay on the farm, why, I'll give y' a good chance. I can't have the land layin' vacant." And in many cases the owner remained as tenant.

In the meantime he had sold his store; he couldn't spend time in it; he was mainly occupied now with sitting around town on rainy days smoking and "gassin' with the boys," or in riding to and from his farms. In fishing-time he fished a good deal. Doc Grimes, Ben Ashley, and Cal Cheatham were his cronies on these fishing excursions or hunting trips in the time of chickens or partridges. In winter they went to Northern Wisconsin to shoot deer.

In spite of all these signs of easy life Butler persisted in saying he "hadn't enough money to pay taxes on his land," and was careful to convey the impression that he was poor in spite of his twenty farms. At one time he was said to be worth fifty thousand dollars, but land had been a little slow of sale of late, so that he was not worth so much. A fine farm, known as the Higley place, had fallen into his hands in the usual way the previous year, and he had not been able to find a tenant for it. Poor Higley, after working himself nearly to death on it in the attempt to lift the mortgage, had gone off to Dakota, leaving the farm and his curse to Butler.

This was the farm which Council advised Haskins to apply for; and the next day Council hitched up his team and drove down to see Butler.

"You jest let *me* do the talkin'," he said. "We'll find him wearin' out his pants on some salt barrel somew'ers; and if he thought you *wanted* the place he'd sock it to you hot and heavy. You jest keep quiet; I'll fix 'im."

Butler was seated in Ben Ashley's store telling fish yarns when Council sauntered in casually.

"Hello, But; lyin' agin, hey?"

"Hello, Steve! How goes it?"

"Oh, so-so. Too dang much rain these days. I thought it was gon' t' freeze up f'r good last night. Tight squeak if I get m' ploughin' done. How's farmin' with *you* these days?"

"Bad. Ploughin' ain't half done."

"It 'ud be a religious idee f'r you t' go out an' take a hand y'rself."

"I don't haff to," said Butler, with a wink.

"Got anybody on the Higley place?"

"No. Know of anybody?"

"Waal, no; not eggsackly. I've got a relation back t' Michigan who's ben hot an' cold on the idee o' comin' West f'r some time. *Might* come if he could get a good lay-out. What do you talk on the farm?"

"Well, I d' know. I'll rent it on shares or I'll rent it money rent."

"Wall, how much money, say?"

"Well, say ten per cent, on the price—two-fifty."

"Wall, that ain't bad. Wait on 'im till 'e thrashes?"

Haskins listened eagerly to this important question, but Council was coolly eating a dried apple which he had speared out of a barrel with his knife. Butler studied him carefully.

"Well, knocks me out of twenty-five dollars interest."

"My relation'll need all he's got t' git his crops in," said Council, in the same, indifferent way.

"Well, all right; *say* wait," concluded Butler.

"All right; this is the man. Haskins, this is Mr. Butler—no relation to Ben—the hardest-working man in Cedar County."

On the way home Haskins said: "I ain't much better off. I'd like that farm; it's a good farm, but it's all run down, an' so 'm I. I could make a good farm of it if I had half a show. But I can't stock it n'r seed it."

"Waal, now, don't you worry," roared Council in his ear. "We'll pull y' through somehow till next harvest. He's agreed t' hire it ploughed, an' you can earn a hundred dollars ploughin' an' y' c'n git the seed o' me, an' pay me back when y' can."

Haskins was silent with emotion, but at last he said, "I ain't got nothin' t' live on."

"Now, don't you worry 'bout that. You jest make your headquarters at ol' Steve Council's. Mother'll take a pile o' comfort in havin' y'r wife an' children 'round. Y' see, Jane's married off lately, an' Ike's away a good 'eal, so we'll be darn glad t' have y' stop with us this winter. Nex' spring we'll see if y' can't git a start agin." And he chirruped to the team, which sprang forward with the rumbling, clattering wagon.

"Say, looky here, Council, you can't do this. I never saw———" shouted Haskins in his neighbor's ear.

Council moved about uneasily in his seat and stopped his stammering gratitude by saying: "Hold on, now; don't make such a fuss over a little thing. When I see a man down, an' things all on top of 'm, I jest like t' kick 'em off an' help 'm up. That's the kind of religion I got, an' it's about the *only* kind."

They rode the rest of the way home in silence. And when the red light of the lamp shone out into the darkness of the cold and windy night, and he thought of this refuge for his children and wife, Haskins could have put his arm around the neck of his burly companion and squeezed him like a lover. But he contented himself with saying, "Steve Council, you'll git y'r pay f'r this some day."

"Don't want any pay. My religion ain't run on such business principles."

The wind was growing colder, and the ground was covered with a white frost, as they turned into the gate of the Council farm, and the children came rushing out, shouting, "Papa's come!" They hardly looked like the same children who had sat at the table the night before. Their torpidity, under the influence of sunshine and Mother Council, had given way to a sort of spasmodic cheerfulness, as insects in winter revive when laid on the hearth.

3

Haskins worked like a fiend, and his wife, like the heroic woman that she was, bore also uncomplainingly the most terrible burdens. They rose early and toiled without intermission till the darkness fell on the plain, then tumbled into bed, every bone and muscle aching with fatigue, to rise with the sun next morning to the same round of the same ferocity of labor.

The eldest boy, now nine years old, drove a team all through the spring, ploughing and seeding, milked the cows, and did chores innumerable, in most ways taking the place of a man; an infinitely pathetic but common figure—this boy—on the American farm, where there is no law against child labor. To see him in his coarse clothing, his huge boots, and his ragged cap, as he staggered with a pail of water from the well, or trudged in the cold and cheerless dawn out into the frosty field behind his team, gave the city-bred visitor a sharp pang of sympathetic pain. Yet Haskins loved his boy, and would have saved him from this if he could, but he could not.

By June the first year the result of such Herculean toil began to show on the farm. The yard was cleaned up and sown to grass, the garden ploughed and planted, and the house mended. Council had given them four of his cows.

"Take 'em an' run 'em on shares. I don't want a milk s' many. Ike's away s' much now, Sat'd'ys an' Sund'ys, I can't stand the bother any-how."

Other men, seeing the confidence of Council in the newcomer, had sold him tools on time; and as he was really an able farmer, he soon had round him many evidences of his care and thrift. At the advice of Council he had taken the farm for three years, with the privilege of re-renting or buying at the end of the term.

"It's a good bargain, an' y' want 'o nail it," said Council. "If you have any kind ov a crop, you c'n pay y'r debts, an' keep seed an' bread."

The new hope which now sprang up in the heart of Haskins and his wife grew almost as a pain by the time the wide field of wheat began to wave and rustle and swirl in the winds of July. Day after day he would snatch a few moments after supper to go and look at it.

"Have ye seen the wheat t'-day, Nettie?" he asked one night as he rose from supper.

"No, Tim, I ain't had time."

"Well, take time now. Let's go look at it."

She threw an old hat on her head—Tommy's hat—and looking almost pretty in her thin, sad way, went out with her husband to the hedge.

"Ain't it grand, Nettie? Just look at it."

It was grand. Level, russet here and there, heavy-headed, wide as a lake, and full of multitudinous whispers and gleams of wealth, it stretched away before the gazers like the fabled field of the cloth of gold.

"Oh, I think—I *hope* we'll have a good crop, Tim; and oh, how good the people have been to us!"

"Yes; I don't know where we'd be t'-day if it hadn't ben f'r Council and his wife."

"They're the best people in the world," said the little woman, with a great sob of gratitude.

"We'll be in the field on Monday, sure," said Haskins, gripping the rail on the fences as if already at the work of the harvest.

The harvest came, bounteous, glorious, but the winds came and blew it into tangles, and the rain matted it here and there close to the ground, increasing the work of gathering it threefold.

Oh, how they toiled in those glorious days! Clothing dripping with sweat, arms aching, filled with briers, fingers raw and bleeding, backs broken with the weight of heavy bundles, Haskins and his man toiled on.

Tommy drove the harvester, while his father and a hired man bound on the machine. In this way they cut ten acres every day, and almost every night after supper, when the hand went to bed, Haskins returned to the field shocking the bound grain in the light of the moon. Many a night he worked till his anxious wife came out at ten o'clock to call him in to rest and lunch.

At the same time she cooked for the men, took care of the children, washed and ironed, milked the cows at night, made the butter, and sometimes fed the horses and watered them while her husband kept at the shocking. No slave in the Roman galleys could have toiled so frightfully and lived, for this man thought himself a free man, and that he was working for his wife and babes.

When he sank into his bed with a deep groan of relief, too tired to change his grimy, dripping clothing, he felt that he was getting nearer and nearer to a home of his own, and pushing the wolf of want a little farther from his door.

There is no despair so deep as the despair of a homeless man or woman. To roam the roads of the country or the streets of the city, to feel there is no rood of ground on which the feet can rest, to halt weary and hungry outside lighted windows and hear laughter and song within— these are the hungers and rebellions that drive men to crime and women to shame.

It was the memory of this homelessness, and the fear of its coming again, that spurred Timothy Haskins and Nettie, his wife, to such ferocious labor during that first year.

4

" 'M, yes; 'm, yes; first-rate," said Butler, as his eye took in the neat garden, the pig-pen, and the well-filled barnyard. "You're gitt'n quite a stock around yeh. Done well, eh?"

Haskins was showing Butler around the place. He had not seen it for a year, having spent the year in Washington and Boston with Ashley, his brother-in-law, who had been elected to Congress.

"Yes, I've laid out a good deal of money durin' the last three years. I've paid out three hundred dollars f'r fencin'."

"Um—h'm! I see, I see," said Butler, while Haskins went on.

"The kitchen there cost two hundred; the barn ain't cost much in money, but I've put a lot o' time on it. I've dug a new well, and I——"

"Yes, yes, I see. You've done well. Stock worth a thousand dollars," said Butler, picking his teeth with a straw.

"About that," said Haskins, modestly. "We begin to feel's if we was gitt'n' a home f'r ourselves; but we've worked hard. I tell ye we begin to feel it, Mr. Butler, and we're goin' t' begin to ease up purty soon. We've been kind o' plannin' a trip back t' her folks after the fall ploughin's done."

"*Eggs*-actly!" said Butler, who was evidently thinking of something else. "I suppose you've kine o' kalklated on stayin' here three years more?"

"Well, yes. Fact is, I think I c'n buy the farm this fall, if you'll give me a reasonable show."

"Um—m! What do you call a reasonable show?"

"Waal; say a quarter down and three years' time."

Butler looked at the huge stacks of wheat which filled the yard, over which the chickens were fluttering and crawling, catching grasshoppers, and out of which the crickets were singing innumerably. He smiled in a peculiar way as he said, "Oh, I won't be hard on yer. But what did you expect to pay f'r the place?"

"Why, about what you offered it for before, two thousand five hundred, or *possibly* three thousand dollars," he added quickly, as he saw the owner shake his head.

"This farm is worth five thousand and five hundred dollars," said Butler, in a careless and decided voice.

"*What!*" almost shrieked the astounded Haskins. "What's that? Five thousand? Why, that's double what you offered it for three years ago."

"Of course, and it's worth it. It was all run down then; now it's in good shape. You've laid out fifteen hundred dollars in improvements, according to your own story."

"But *you* had nothin' t' do about that. It's my work an' my money."

"You bet it was; but it's my land."

"But what's to pay me for all my———"

"Ain't you had the use of 'em?" replied Butler, smiling calmly into his face.

Haskins was like a man struck on the head with a sand-bag; he couldn't think; he stammered as he tried to say: "But—I never'd git the use—You'd rob me! More'n that: you agreed—you promised that I could buy or rent at the end of three years at———"

"That's all right. But I didn't say I'd let you carry off the improvements, nor that I'd go on renting the farm at two-fifty. The land is doubled in value, it don't matter how; it don't enter into the question; an' now you can pay me five hundred dollars a year rent, or take it on your own terms at fifty-five hundred, or—git out."

He was turning away when Haskins, the sweat pouring from his face, fronted him, saying again:

"But *you've* done nothing to make it so. You hain't added a cent. I put

it all there myself, expectin' to buy. I worked an' sweat to improve it. I
was workin' for myself an' babes————"

"Well, why didn't you buy when I offered to sell? What y' kickin'
about?"

"I'm kickin' about payin' you twice f'r my own things,—my own
fences, my own kitchen, my own garden."

Butler laughed. "You're too green t' eat, young feller. *Your* improvements! The law will sing another tune."

"But I trusted your word."

"Never trust anybody, my friend. Besides, I didn't promise not to do
this thing. Why, man, don't look at me like that. Don't take me for a thief.
It's the law. The reg'lar thing. Everybody does it."

"I don't care if they do. It's stealin' jest the same. You take three thousand dollars of my money. The work o' my hands and my wife's." He
broke down at this point. He was not a strong man mentally. He could
face hardship, ceaseless toil, but he could not face the cold and sneering
face of Butler.

"But I don't take it," said Butler, coolly. "All you've got to do is to
go on jest as you've been a-doin', or give me a thousand dollars down,
and a mortgage at ten per cent on the rest."

Haskins sat down blindly on a bundle of oats near by, and with staring
eyes and drooping head went over the situation. He was under the lion's
paw. He felt a horrible numbness in his heart and limbs. He was hid in
a mist, and there was no path out.

Butler walked about, looking at the huge stacks of grain, and pulling
now and again a few handfuls out, shelling the heads in his hands and
blowing the chaff away. He hummed a little tune as he did so. He had
an accommodating air of waiting.

Haskins was in the midst of the terrible toil of the last year. He was
walking again in the rain and the mud behind his plough; he felt the dust
and dirt of the threshing. The ferocious husking-time, with its cutting
wind and biting, clinging snows, lay hard upon him. Then he thought of
his wife, how she had cheerfully cooked and baked, without holiday and
without rest.

"Well, what do you think of it?" inquired the cool, mocking, insinu-
ating voice of Butler.

"I think you're a thief and a liar!" shouted Haskins, leaping up. "A
black-hearted houn'?" Butler's smile maddened him; with a sudden leap
he caught a fork in his hands, and whirled it in the air. "You'll never rob
another man, damn ye!" he grated through his teeth, a look of pitiless
ferocity in his accusing eyes.

Butler shrank and quivered, expecting the blow; stood, held hypno-
tized by the eyes of the man he had a moment before despised—a man
transformed into an avenging demon. But in the deadly hush between
the lift of the weapon and its fall there came a gush of faint, childish
laughter and then across the range of his vision, far away and dim, he
saw the sun-bright head of his baby girl, as, with the pretty, tottering run
of a two-year-old, she moved across the grass of the dooryard. His hands
relaxed; the fork fell to the ground; his head lowered.

"Make out y'r deed an' morgige, an' git off'n my land, an' don't ye
never cross my line agin; if y' do, I'll kill ye."

Butler backed away from the man in the wild haste, and climbing into
his buggy with trembling limbs, drove off down the road, leaving Haskins
seated dumbly on the sunny pile of sheaves, his head sunk into his hands.

OWEN WISTER

A s a twenty-four-year-old bank clerk in Boston, trained in the law, doing what his father wanted him to do rather than following his own star (becoming a pianist and composer), Owen Wister (1860–1938) suffered from neuralgia and severe depression. In early 1885, hardly enduring the misery, he was ready for the family doctor's advice to go west for the summer and take a rest cure on a Wyoming ranch. This time out became the transforming event of Wister's life, and might even be said to underlie a major American industry—the Western. Out under the blue sky, breathing the bracing air of the Wyoming steppe, hearing workingmen's folk speech, doing physical activity, Wister was made whole. One of his notebook entries that summer speaks of a transformation from being "all varnished over with Europe" to joining the company of "real Americans." (He did retain one part of the European varnish, a passion for Wagnerian spectacle, emotion, and mythic romance, confirmed in the devotee's visit to Bayreuth in 1882.) After Wyoming, he developed a theory of real Americanism based on what seemed to him the western essence—rugged individualism, physical beauty and courage, and casual directness, combined with a natural, non-effete refinement. All of these qualities inhered in his cowboy hero, and in 1902 his "Virginian" leaped instantly to American iconhood. The novel sold 50,000 copies in its first two months.

"Enter the Man," from *The Virginian* (1902)

Some notable sight was drawing the passengers, both men and women, to the window; and therefore I rose and crossed the car to see what it was. I saw near the track an enclosure, and round it some laughing men, and inside it some whirling dust, and amid the dust some horses, plunging, huddling, and dodging. They were cow ponies in a corral, and one of them would not be caught, no matter who threw the rope. We had plenty of time to watch this sport, for our train had stopped that the engine might take water at the tank before it pulled us up beside the station platform of Medicine Bow. We were also six hours late, and starving for entertainment. The pony in the corral was wise, and rapid of limb. Have you seen a skilful boxer watch his antagonist with a quiet, incessant eye? Such an eye as this did the pony keep upon whatever man took the rope. The man might pretend to look at the weather, which was fine; or he might affect earnest conversation with a bystander; it was bootless. The pony saw through it. No feint hoodwinked him. This animal was thoroughly a man of the world. His undistracted eye stayed fixed upon the dissembling foe, and the gravity of his horse expression made the matter one of high comedy. Then the rope would sail out at him, but he was already elsewhere; and if horses laugh, gayety must have abounded in that corral. Sometimes the pony took a turn alone; next he had slid in a flash among his brothers, and the whole of them like a school of playful fish whipped round the corral, kicking up the fine dust, and (I take it) roaring with laughter. Through the window-glass of our Pullman the thud of their mischievous hoofs reached us, and the strong, humorous curses of the cow-boys. Then for the first time I noticed a man who sat on the high gate of the corral, looking on. For he now climbed down with the undulations of a tiger, smooth and easy, as if his muscles flowed beneath his skin. The others had all visibly whirled the rope, some of them even shoulder high. I did not see his arm lift or move. He appeared to hold the rope down low, by his leg. But like a sudden snake I saw the noose go out its length and fall true; and the thing was done. As the captured pony walked in with a sweet, church-door expression, our train moved slowly on to the station, and a passenger remarked, "That man knows his business."

But the passenger's dissertation upon roping I was obliged to lose, for Medicine Bow was my station. I bade my fellow-travellers good-by, and descended, a stranger, into the great cattle land. And here in less than ten minutes I learned news which made me feel a stranger indeed.

My baggage was lost; it had not come on my train; it was adrift somewhere back in the two thousand miles that lay behind me. And by way of comfort, the baggage-man remarked that passengers often got astray from their trunks, but the trunks mostly found them after a while. Having offered me this encouragement, be turned whistling to his affairs and left me planted in the baggage-room at Medicine Bow. I stood deserted among crates and boxes, blankly holding my check, furious and forlorn. I stared out through the door at the sky and the plains; but I did not see the antelope shining among the sage-brush, nor the great sunset light of Wyoming. Annoyance blinded my eyes to all things save my grievance: I saw only a lost trunk. And I was muttering half aloud, "What a forsaken hole this is!" when suddenly from outside on the platform came a slow voice:—

"Off to get married *again*? Oh, don't!"

The voice was Southern and gentle and drawling; and a second voice came in immediate answer, cracked and querulous:—

"It ain't again. Who says it's again? Who told you, anyway?"

And the first voice responded caressingly:—

"Why, your Sunday clothes told me, Uncle Hughey. They are speakin' mighty loud o' nuptials."

"You don't worry me!" snapped Uncle Hughey, with shrill heat.

And the other gently continued, "Ain't them gloves the same yu' wore to your last weddin'?"

"You don't worry me! You don't worry me!" now screamed Uncle Hughey.

Already I had forgotten my trunk; care had left me; I was aware of the sunset, and had no desire but for more of this conversation. For it resembled none that I had heard in my life so far. I stepped to the door and looked out upon the station platform.

Lounging there at ease against the wall was a slim young giant, more beautiful than pictures. His broad, soft hat was pushed back; a loose-knotted, dull-scarlet handkerchief sagged from his throat, and one casual thumb was hooked in the cartridge-belt that slanted across his hips. He had plainly come many miles from somewhere across the vast horizon, as the dust upon him showed. His boots were white with it. His overalls were gray with it. The weather-beaten bloom of his face shone through it duskily, as the ripe peaches look upon their trees in a dry season. But no dinginess of travel or shabbiness of attire could tarnish the splendor that radiated from his youth and strength. The old man upon whose temper his remarks were doing such deadly work was combed and curried to a finish, a bridegroom swept and garnished; but alas for age! Had I been the bride, I should have taken the giant, dust and all.

He had by no means done with the old man.

"Why, yu've hung weddin' gyarments on every limb!" he now drawled, with admiration. "Who is the lucky lady this trip?"

The old man seemed to vibrate. "Tell you there ain't been no other! Call me a Mormon, would you?"

"Why, that—"

"Call me a Mormon? Then name some of my wives. Name two. Name one. Dare you!"

"—that Laramie wido' promised you—"

"Shucks!"

"—only her docter suddenly ordered Southern climate and—"

"Shucks! You're a false alarm."

"—so nothing but her lungs came between you. And next you'd most got united with Cattle Kate, only—"

"Tell you you're a false alarm!"

"—only she got hung."

"Where's the wives in all this? Show the wives! Come now!"

"That corn-fed biscuit-shooter at Rawlins yu' gave the canary—"

"Never married her. Never did marry—"

"But yu' come so near, uncle! She was the one left yu' that letter explaining how she'd got married to a young cyard-player the very day before her ceremony with you was due, and—"

"Oh, you're nothing; you're a kid; you don't amount to—"

"—and how she'd never, never forgot to feed the canary."

"This country's getting full of kids," stated the old man, witheringly. "It's doomed." This crushing assertion plainly satisfied him. And he blinked his eyes with renewed anticipation. His tall tormentor continued with a face of unchanging gravity, and a voice of gentle solicitude:—

"How is the health of that unfortunate—"

"That's right! Pour your insults! Pour 'em on a sick, afflicted woman!" The eyes blinked with combative relish.

"Insults? Oh, no, Uncle Hughey!"

"That's all right! Insults goes!"

"Why, I was mighty relieved when she began to recover her mem'ry. Las' time I heard, they told me she'd got it pretty near all back. Remembered her father, and her mother, and her sisters and brothers, and her friends, and her happy childhood, and all her doin's except only your face. The boys was bettin' she'd get that far too, give her time. But I reckon afteh such a turrable sickness as she had, that would be expectin' most too much."

At this Uncle Hughey jerked out a small parcel. "Shows how much you know!" he cackled. "There! See that! That's my ring she sent me back, being too unstrung for marriage. So she don't remember me, don't she? Ha-ha! Always said you were a false alarm."

The Southerner put more anxiety into his tone. "And so you're a-takin' the ring right on to the next one!" he exclaimed. "Oh, don't go to get married again, Uncle Hughey! What's the use o' being married?"

"What's the use?" echoed the bridegroom, with scorn. "Hm! When you grow up you'll think different."

"Course I expect to think different when my age is different. I'm havin' the thoughts proper to twenty-four, and you're havin' the thoughts proper to sixty."

"Fifty!" shrieked Uncle Hughey, jumping in the air.

The Southerner took a tone of self-reproach. "Now, how could I forget you was fifty," he murmured, "when you have been telling it to the boys so careful for the last ten years!"

Have you ever seen a cockatoo—the white kind with the top-knot—enraged by insult? The bird erects every available feather upon its person. So did Uncle Hughey seem to swell, clothes, mustache, and woolly white beard; and without further speech he took himself on board the East-bound train, which now arrived from its siding in time to deliver him. Yet this was not why he had not gone away before. At any time he could have escaped into the baggage-room or withdrawn to a dignified distance until his train should come up. But the old man had evidently got a sort of joy from this teasing. He had reached that inevitable age when we are tickled to be linked with affairs of gallantry, no matter how.

With him now the East-bound departed slowly into that distance whence I had come. I stared after it as it went its way to the far shores of civilization. It grew small in the unending gulf of space, until all sign of its presence was gone save a faint skein of smoke against the evening sky. And now my lost trunk came back into my thoughts, and Medicine Bow seemed a lonely spot. A sort of ship had left me marooned in a foreign ocean; the Pullman was comfortably steaming home to port, while I—how was I to find Judge Henry's ranch? Where in this unfeatured wilderness was Sunk Creek? No creek or any water at all flowed here that I could perceive. My host had written he should meet me at the station and drive me to his ranch. This was all that I knew. He was not here. The baggage-man had not seen him lately. The ranch was almost certain to be too far to walk to, to-night. My trunk—I discovered myself still staring dolefully after the vanished East-bound; and at the same instant I became aware that the tall man was looking gravely at me,—as gravely as he had looked at Uncle Hughey throughout their remarkable conversation.

To see his eye thus fixing me and his thumb still hooked in his cartridge-belt, certain tales of travellers from these parts forced themselves disquietingly into my recollection. Now that Uncle Hughey was gone, was I to take his place and be, for instance, invited to dance on the platform to the music of shots nicely aimed?

"I reckon I am looking for you, seh," the tall man now observed.

MARY AUSTIN

"The secret of learning the mesa life," Mary Austin (1868–1934) wrote in *California, the Land of the Sun* (1914), "is to sit still, and to sit still, and to keep on sitting still"—the very opposite of the activism of a manifest-destinarian. She had come to the stillness method during years of apprenticeship as a writer (in the 1890s), living in the Owens Valley in remote eastern California. Having grown up in Illinois, she needed time and quietness to learn the new, dry-land plants and animals; then it took a certain Indian quality of attention to go beyond fact-accumulation and begin to see the ecological patterns—the knit of the place. For example, heightened perception would be required before a seemingly barren field could come to life on the page. Austin said she gained the needed wisdom from her new friends, certain Piutes camped at the edge of the little town of Independence. She explained that over their long history, they had seen how to connect the surface, factual mind with the more profound awareness emanating from the deep-self. "Learning that," she said in her third-person way, "she learned how to write." In her urge toward synthesis and her reverence for the mystical, unifying center of experience ("the one abiding reality of my life"), she transcended the dichotomous frame of reference of her culture. The following essay is from her first book, *The Land of Little Rain* (Boston: Houghton Mifflin, 1903).

"My Neighbor's Field," from *The Land of Little Rain* (1903)

It is one of those places God must have meant for a field from all time, lying very level at the foot of the slope that crowds up against Kearsarge, falling slightly toward the town. North and south it is fenced by low old glacial ridges, boulder strewn and untenable. Eastward it butts on orchard closes and the village gardens, brimming over into them by wild brier and creeping grass. The village street, with its double row of unlike houses, breaks off abruptly at the edge of the field in a footpath that goes up the streamside, beyond it, to the source of waters.

The field is not greatly esteemed of the town, not being put to the plough nor affording firewood, but breeding all manner of wild seeds that go down in the irrigating ditches to come up as weeds in the gardens and grass plots. But when I had no more than seen it in the charm of its spring smiling, I knew I should have no peace until I had bought ground and built me a house beside it, with a little wicket to go in and out at all hours, as afterward came about.

Edswick, Roeder, Connor, and Ruffin owned the field before it fell to my neighbor. But before that the Paiutes, mesne lords of the soil, made a campoodie by the rill of Pine Creek; and after, contesting the soil with them, cattle-men, who found its foodful pastures greatly to their advantage; and bands of blethering flocks shepherded by wild, hairy men of little speech, who attested their rights to the feeding ground with their long staves upon each other's skulls. Edswick homesteaded the field about the time the wild tide of mining life was roaring and rioting up Kearsarge, and where the village now stands built a stone hut, with loopholes to make good his claim against cattle-men or Indians. But Edswick died and Roeder became master of the field. Roeder owned cattle on a thousand hills, and made it a recruiting ground for his bellowing herds before beginning the long drive to market across a shifty desert. He kept the field fifteen years, and afterward falling into difficulties, put it out as security against certain sums. Connor, who held the securities, was cleverer than Roeder and not so busy. The money fell due the winter of the Big Snow, when all the trails were forty feet under drifts, and Roeder was away in San Francisco selling his cattle. At the set time Connor took the law by the forelock and was adjudged possession of the field. Eighteen days later Roeder arrived on snowshoes, both feet frozen, and the money in his pack. In the long suit at law ensuing, the field fell to Ruffin, that clever one-armed lawyer with the tongue to wile a bird out of the bush, Connor's counsel, and was sold by him to my neighbor, whom from envying his possession I call Naboth.

Curiously, all this human occupancy of greed and mischief left no mark on the field, but the Indians did, and the unthinking sheep. Round its corners children pick up chipped arrow points of obsidian, scattered through it are kitchen middens and pits of old sweat-houses. By the south corner, where the campoodie stood, is a single shrub of "hoopee" (*Lycium andersonii*), maintaining itself hardly among alien shrubs, and near by, three low rakish trees of hackberry, so far from home that no prying of mine has been able to find another in any cañon east or west. But the berries of both were food for the Paiutes, eagerly sought and traded for as far south as Shoshone Land. By the fork of the creek where the shepherds camp is a single clump of mesquite of the variety called "screw bean." The seed must have shaken there from some sheep's coat, for this is not the habitat of mesquite, and except for other single shrubs at sheep camps, none grows freely for a hundred and fifty miles south or east.

Naboth has put a fence about the best of the field, but neither the Indians nor the shepherds can quite forego it. They make camp and build their wattled huts about the borders of it, and no doubt they have some sense of home in its familiar aspect.

As I have said, it is a low-lying field, between the mesa and the town, with no hillocks in it, but a gentle swale where the waste water of the creek goes down to certain farms, and the hackberry-trees, of which the tallest might be three times the height of a man, are the tallest things in it. A mile up from the water gate that turns the creek into supply pipes for the town, begins a row of long-leaved pines, threading the watercourse to the foot of Kearsarge. These are the pines that puzzle the local botanist, not easily determined, and unrelated to other conifers of the Sierra slope; the same pines of which the Indians relate a legend mixed of brotherliness and the retribution of God. Once the pines possessed the field, as the worn stumps of them along the streamside show, and it would seem their secret purpose to regain their old footing. Now and then some seedling escapes the devastating sheep a rod or two down-stream. Since I came to live by the field one of these has tiptoed above the gully of the creek, beckoning the procession from the hills, as if in fact they would make back toward that skyward-pointing finger of granite on the opposite range, from which, according to the legend, when they were bad Indians and it a great chief, they ran away. This year the summer floods brought the round, brown, fruitful cones to my very door, and I look, if I live long enough, to see them come up greenly in my neighbor's field.

It is interesting to watch this retaking of old ground by the wild plants, banished by human use. Since Naboth drew his fence about the field and restricted it to a few wild-eyed steers, halting between the hills and the shambles, many old habitués of the field have come back to their haunts. The willow and brown birch, long ago cut off by the Indians for wattles, have come back to the streamside, slender and virginal in their spring greenness, and leaving long stretches of the brown water open to the sky. In stony places where no grass grows, wild olives sprawl; close-twigged, blue-gray patches in winter, more translucent greenish gold in spring than any aureole. Along with willow and birch and brier, the clematis, that shyest plant of water borders, slips down season by season to within a hundred yards of the village street. Convinced after three years that it would come no nearer, we spent time fruitlessly pulling up roots to plant in the garden. All this while, when no coaxing or care prevailed upon any transplanted slip to grow, one was coming up silently outside the fence near the wicket, coiling so secretly in the rabbit-brush that its presence was never suspected until it flowered delicately along its twining length. The horehound comes through the fence and under it, shouldering the pickets off the railings; the brier rose mines under the horehound; and no care, though I own I am not a close weeder, keeps the small pale moons of the primrose from rising to the night moth under my apple-trees. The first summer in the new place, a clump of cypripediums came up by the irrigating ditch at the bottom of the lawn. But the clematis will not come inside, nor the wild almond.

I have forgotten to find out, though I meant to, whether the wild almond grew in that country where Moses kept the flocks of his father-in-law, but if so one can account for the burning bush. It comes upon one with a flame-burst as of revelation; little hard red buds on leafless twigs, swelling unnoticeably, then one, two, or three strong suns, and from tip to tip one soft fiery glow, whispering with bees as a singing flame. A twig of finger size will be furred to the thickness of one's wrist by pink five-petaled bloom, so close that only the blunt-faced wild bees find their way in it. In this latitude late frosts cut off the hope of fruit too often for the wild almond to multiply greatly, but the spiny, taprooted shrubs are resistant to most plant evils.

It is not easy always to be attentive to the maturing of wild fruit. Plants are so unobtrusive in their material processes, and always at the significant moment some other bloom has reached its perfect hour. One can never fix the precise moment when the rosy tint the field has from the wild almond passes into the inspiring blue of lupines. One notices here and there a spike of bloom, and a day later the whole field royal and ruffling lightly to the wind. Part of the charm of the lupine is the continual stir of its plumes to airs not suspected otherwise. Go and stand by any crown of bloom and the tall stalks do but rock a little as for drowsiness, but look off across the field, and on the stillest days there is always a trepidation in the purple patches.

From midsummer until frost the prevailing note of the field is clear gold, passing into the rusty tone of bigelovia going into a decline, a succession of color schemes more admirably managed than the transformation scene at the theatre. Under my window a colony of cleome made a soft web of bloom that drew me every morning for a long still time; and one day I discovered that I was looking into a rare fretwork of fawn and straw colored twigs from which both bloom and leaf had gone, and I could not say if it had been for a matter of weeks or days. The time to plant cucumbers and set out cabbages may be set down in the almanac, but never seed-time nor blossom in Naboth's field.

Certain winged and mailed denizens of the field seem to reach their heyday along with the plants they most affect. In June the leaning towers of the white milkweed are jeweled over with red and gold beetles, climbing dizzily. This is that milkweed from whose stems the Indians flayed fibre to make snares for small game, but what use the beetles put it to except for a displaying ground for their gay coats, I could never discover.

The white butterfly crop comes on with the bigelovia bloom, and on warm mornings makes an airy twinkling all across the field. In September young linnets grow out of the rabbit-brush in the night. All the nests discoverable in the neighboring orchards will not account for the numbers of them. Somewhere, by the same secret process by which the field matures a million more seeds than it needs, it is maturing red-hooded linnets for their devouring. All the purlieus of bigelovia and artemisia are noisy with them for a month. Suddenly as they come as suddenly go the fly-by-nights, that pitch and toss on dusky barred wings above the field of summer twilights. Never one of these nighthawks will you see after linnet time, though the hurtle of their wings makes a pleasant sound across the dusk in their season.

For two summers a great red-tailed hawk has visited the field every afternoon between three and four o'clock, swooping and soaring with the airs of a gentleman adventurer. What he finds there is chiefly conjectured, so secretive are the little people of Naboth's field. Only when leaves fall and the light is low and slant, one sees the long clean flanks of the jack-rabbits, leaping like small deer, and of late afternoons little cotton-tails scamper in the runways. But the most one sees of the burrowers, gophers, and mice is the fresh earthwork of their newly opened doors, or the pitiful small shreds the butcher-bird hangs on spiny shrubs.

It is a still field, this of my neighbor's, though so busy, and admirably compounded for variety and pleasantness,—a little sand, a little loam, a grassy plot, a stony rise or two, a full brown stream, a little touch of humanness, a footpath trodden out by moccasins. Naboth expects to make town lots of it and his fortune in one and the same day; but when I take the trail to talk with old Seyavi at the campoodie, it occurs to me that though the field may serve a good turn in those days it will hardly be happier. No, certainly not happier.

JACK LONDON

A fter a working childhood, during which he was stimulated to read (and undoubtedly to write) by conversations with librarian Ina Coolbrith at the Oakland Public Library, Jack London (1876–1916) emerged into a full and famous life: "hobo"-ing across the country at eighteen, joining the Klondike gold rush at twenty-one, hitting the best-seller list with *The Call of the Wild* (1903), producing almost fifty books and eight plays in a blaze of creative effort sixteen years long (in the process becoming the first writer ever to realize a million dollars from his work), building up and managing a 1,400-acre ranch in California, setting out to sail around the world with his wife Charmian, and dying at just forty, back on the ranch, of a mysterious combination of ailments. All of this brought him celebrity, and his enormous international popularity may have contributed to a longtime slighting by academic critics. But good writing eventually prevails, and now London is being looked at for psychological subtlety, a strong sense of life as an adventure more than physical (though it is certainly that, too), and an agrarian-ecological sophistication, among other themes. He is particularly good, as readers of the following story will note, at describing experience—and even mechanical process—at a pitch of intensity that reveals a character's innermost life.

"All Gold Canyon," from *Moon-face and Other Stories* (1906)

It was the green heart of the canyon, where the walls swerved back from the rigid plan and relieved their harshness of line by making a little sheltered nook and filling it to the brim with sweetness and roundness and softness. Here all things rested. Even the narrow stream ceased its turbulent down-rush long enough to form a quiet pool. Knee-deep in the water, with drooping head and half-shut eyes, drowsed a red-coated, many-antlered buck.

On one side, beginning at the very lip of the pool, was a tiny meadow, a cool, resilient surface of green that extended to the base of the frowning wall. Beyond the pool a gentle slope of earth ran up and up to meet the opposing wall. Fine grass covered the slope—grass that was spangled with flowers, with here and there patches of color, orange and purple and golden. Below, the canyon was shut in. There was no view. The walls leaned together abruptly and the canyon ended in a chaos of rocks, moss-covered and hidden by a green screen of vines and creepers and boughs of trees. Up the canyon rose far hills and peaks, the big foot-hills, pine-covered and remote. And far beyond, like clouds upon the border of the sky, towered minarets of white, where the Sierra's eternal snows flashed austerely the blazes of the sun.

There was no dust in the canyon. The leaves and flowers were clean and virginal. The grass was young velvet. Over the pool three cotton-woods sent their snowy fluffs fluttering down the quiet air. On the slope the blossoms of the wine-wooded manzanita filled the air with springtime odors, while the leaves, wise with experience, were already beginning their vertical twist against the coming aridity of summer. In the open spaces on the slope, beyond the farthest shadow-reach of the manzanita, poised the mariposa lilies, like so many flights of jewelled moths suddenly arrested and on the verge of trembling into flight again. Here and there that woods harlequin, the madrone, permitting itself to be caught in the act of changing its pea-green trunk to madder-red, breathed its fragrance into the air from great clusters of waxen bells. Creamy white were these bells, shaped like lilies-of-the-valley, with the sweetness of perfume that is of the springtime.

There was not a sigh of wind. The air was drowsy with its weight of perfume. It was a sweetness that would have been cloying had the air been heavy and humid. But the air was sharp and thin. It was as starlight transmuted into atmosphere, shot through and warmed by sunshine, and flower-drenched with sweetness.

An occasional butterfly drifted in and out through the patches of light and shade. And from all about rose the low and sleepy hum of mountain bees—feasting Sybarites that jostled one another good-naturedly at the board, nor found time for rough discourtesy. So quietly did the little stream drip and ripple its way through the canyon that it spoke only in faint and occasional gurgles. The voice of the stream was as a drowsy whisper, ever interrupted by dozings and silences, ever lifted again in the awakenings.

The motion of all things was a drifting in the heart of the canyon. Sunshine and butterflies drifted in and out among the trees. The hum of the bees and the whisper of the stream were a drifting of sound. And the drifting sound and drifting color seemed to weave together in the making of a delicate and intangible fabric which was the spirit of the place. It was a spirit of peace that was not of death, but of smooth-pulsing life, of quietude that was not silence, of movement that was not action, of repose that was quick with existence without being violent with struggle and travail. The spirit of the place was the spirit of the peace of the living, somnolent with the easement and content of prosperity, and undisturbed by rumors of far wars.

The red-coated, many-antlered buck acknowledged the lordship of the spirit of the place and dozed knee-deep in the cool, shaded pool. There seemed no flies to vex him and he was languid with rest. Sometimes his ears moved when the stream awoke and whispered; but they moved lazily, with foreknowledge that it was merely the stream grown garrulous at discovery that it had slept.

But there came a time when the buck's ears lifted and tensed with swift eagerness for sound. His head was turned down the canyon. His sensitive, quivering nostrils scented the air. His eyes could not pierce the green screen through which the stream rippled away, but to his ears came the voice of a man. It was a steady, monotonous, singsong voice. Once the buck heard the harsh clash of metal upon rock. At the sound he snorted with a sudden start that jerked him through the air from water to meadow, and his feet sank into the young velvet, while he pricked his ears and again scented the air. Then he stole across the tiny meadow, pausing once and again to listen, and faded away out of the canyon like a wraith, soft-footed and without sound.

The clash of steel-shod soles against the rocks began to be heard, and the man's voice grew louder. It was raised in a sort of chant and became distinct with nearness, so that the words could be heard:

"Tu'n around an' tu'n yo' face
Untoe them sweet hills of grace
(D' pow'rs of sin yo' am scornin'!).
Look about an' look aroun',
Fling yo' sin-pack on d' groun'
(Yo' will meet wid d' Lord in d' mornin'!)."

A sound of scrambling accompanied the song, and the spirit of the place fled away on the heels of the red-coated buck. The green screen was burst asunder, and a man peered out at the meadow and the pool and the sloping side-hill. He was a deliberate sort of man. He took in the scene with one embracing glance, then ran his eyes over the details to verify the general impression. Then, and not until then, did he open his mouth in vivid and solemn approval:

"Smoke of life an' snakes of purgatory! Will you just look at that! Wood an' water an' grass an' a side-hill! A pocket-hunter's delight an' a cayuse's paradise! Cool green for tired eyes! Pink pills for pale people ain't in it. A secret pasture for prospectors and a resting-place for tired burros, by damn!"

He was a sandy-complexioned man in whose face geniality and humor seemed the salient characteristics. It was a mobile face, quick-changing to inward mood and thought. Thinking was in him a visible process. Ideas chased across his face like wind-flaws across the surface of a lake. His hair, sparse and unkempt of growth, was as indeterminate and colorless as his complexion. It would seem that all the color of his frame had gone into his eyes, for they were startlingly blue. Also, they were laughing and merry eyes, within them much of the naïveté and wonder of the child; and yet, in an unassertive way, they contained much of calm self-reliance and strength of purpose founded upon self-experience and experience of the world.

From out the screen of vines and creepers he flung ahead of him a miner's pick and shovel and gold-pan. Then he crawled out himself into the open. He was clad in faded overalls and black cotton shirt, with hobnailed brogans on his feet, and on his head a hat whose shapelessness and stains advertised the rough usage of wind and rain and sun and camp-smoke. He stood erect, seeing wide-eyed the secrecy of the scene and sensuously inhaling the warm, sweet breath of the canyon-garden through nostrils that dilated and quivered with delight. His eyes narrowed to laughing slits of blue, his face wreathed itself in joy, and his mouth curled in a smile as he cried aloud:

"Jumping dandelions and happy hollyhocks, but that smells good to me! Talk about your attar o' roses an' cologne factories! They ain't in it!"

He had the habit of soliloquy. His quick-changing facial expressions might tell every thought and mood, but the tongue, perforce, ran hard after, repeating, like a second Boswell.

The man lay down on the lip of the pool and drank long and deep of its water. "Tastes good to me," he murmured, lifting his head and gazing across the pool at the side-hill, while he wiped his mouth with the back of his hand. The side-hill attracted his attention. Still lying on his stomach, he studied the hill formation long and carefully. It was a practised eye that travelled up the slope to the crumbling canyon-wall and back and down again to the edge of the pool. He scrambled to his feet and favored the side-hill with a second survey.

"Looks good to me," he concluded, picking up his pick and shovel and gold-pan.

He crossed the stream below the pool, stepping agilely from stone to stone. Where the side-hill touched the water he dug up a shovelful of dirt and put it into the gold-pan. He squatted down, holding the pan in his two hands, and partly immersing it in the stream. Then he imparted to the pan a deft circular motion that sent the water sluicing in and out through the dirt and gravel. The larger and the lighter particles worked to the surface, and these, by a skilful dipping movement of the pan, he spilled out and over the edge. Occasionally, to expedite matters, he rested the pan and with his fingers raked out the large pebbles and pieces of rock.

The contents of the pan diminished rapidly until only fine dirt and the smallest bits of gravel remained. At this stage he began to work very deliberately and carefully. It was fine washing, and he washed fine and finer, with a keen scrutiny and delicate and fastidious touch. At last the pan seemed empty of everything but water; but with a quick semicircular flirt that sent the water flying over the shallow rim into the stream, he disclosed a layer of black sand on the bottom of the pan. So thin was this layer that it was like a streak of paint. He examined it closely. In the midst of it was a tiny golden speck. He dribbled a little water in over the depressed edge of the pan. With a quick flirt he sent the water sluicing across the bottom, turning the grains of black sand over and over. A second tiny golden speck rewarded his effort.

The washing had now become very fine—fine beyond all need of ordinary placer-mining. He worked the black sand, a small portion at a time, up the shallow rim of the pan. Each small portion he examined sharply, so that his eyes saw every grain of it before he allowed it to slide over the edge and away. Jealously, bit by bit, he let the black sand slip away. A golden speck, no larger than a pin-point, appeared on the rim, and by his manipulation of the water it returned to the bottom of the pan. And in such fashion another speck was disclosed, and another. Great was his care of them. Like a shepherd he herded his flock of golden specks so that not one should be lost. At last, of the pan of dirt nothing remained but his golden herd. He counted it, and then, after all his labor, sent it flying out of the pan with one final swirl of water.

But his blue eyes were shining with desire as he rose to his feet. "Seven," he muttered aloud, asserting the sum of the specks for which he had toiled so hard and which he had so wantonly thrown away. "Seven," he repeated, with the emphasis of one trying to impress a number on his memory.

He stood still a long while, surveying the hillside. In his eyes was a curiosity, new-aroused and burning. There was an exultance about his bearing and a keenness like that of a hunting animal catching the fresh scent of game.

He moved down the stream a few steps and took a second panful of dirt.

Again came the careful washing, the jealous herding of the golden specks, and the wantonness with which he sent them flying into the stream when he had counted their number.

"Five," he muttered, and repeated, "five."

He could not forbear another survey of the hill before filling the pan farther down the stream. His golden herds diminished. "Four, three, two, two, one," were his memory-tabulations as he moved down the stream. When but one speck of gold rewarded his washing, he stopped and built a fire of dry twigs. Into this he thrust the gold-pan and burned it till it was blue-black. He held up the pan and examined it critically. Then he nodded approbation. Against such a color-background he could defy the tiniest yellow speck to elude him.

Still moving down the stream, he panned again. A single speck was his reward. A third pan contained no gold at all. Not satisfied with this, he panned three times again, taking his shovels of dirt within a foot of one another. Each pan proved empty of gold, and the fact, instead of discouraging him, seemed to give him satisfaction. His elation increased with each barren washing, until he arose, exclaiming jubilantly:

"If it ain't the real thing, may God knock off my head with sour apples!"

Returning to where he had started operations, he began to pan up the stream. At first his golden herds increased—increased prodigiously. "Fourteen, eighteen, twenty-one, twenty-six," ran his memory tabulations. Just above the pool he struck his richest pan—thirty-five colors.

"Almost enough to save," he remarked regretfully as he allowed the water to sweep them away.

The sun climbed to the top of the sky. The man worked on. Pan by pan, he went up the stream, the tally of results steadily decreasing.

"It's just booful, the way it peters out," he exulted when a shovelful of dirt contained no more than a single speck of gold.

And when no specks at all were found in several pans, he straightened up and favored the hillside with a confident glance.

"Ah, ha! Mr. Pocket!" he cried out, as though to an auditor hidden somewhere above him beneath the surface of the slope. "Ah, ha! Mr. Pocket! I'm a-comin', I'm a-comin', an' I'm shorely gwine to get yer! You heah me, Mr. Pocket? I'm gwine to get yer as shore as punkins ain't cauliflowers!"

He turned and flung a measuring glance at the sun poised above him in the azure of the cloudless sky. Then he went down the canyon, following the line of shovel-holes he had made in filling the pans. He crossed the stream below the pool and disappeared through the green screen. There was little opportunity for the spirit of the place to return with its quietude and repose, for the man's voice, raised in ragtime song, still dominated the canyon with possession.

After a time, with a greater clashing of steel-shod feet on rock, he returned. The green screen was tremendously agitated. It surged back and forth in the throes of a struggle. There was a loud grating and clanging of metal. The man's voice leaped to a higher pitch and was sharp with imperativeness. A large body plunged and panted. There was a snapping and ripping and rending, and amid a shower of falling leaves a horse burst through the screen. On its back was a pack, and from this trailed broken vines and torn creepers. The animal gazed with astonished eyes at the scene into which it had been precipitated, then dropped its head to the grass and began contentedly to graze. A second horse scrambled into view, slipping once on the mossy rocks and regaining equilibrium when its hoofs sank into the yielding surface of the meadow. It was riderless, though on its back was a high-horned Mexican saddle, scarred and discolored by long usage.

The man brought up the rear. He threw off pack and saddle, with an eye to camp location, and gave the animals their freedom to graze. He unpacked his food and got out frying-pan and coffee-pot. He gathered an armful of dry wood, and with a few stones made a place for his fire.

"My!" he said, "but I've got an appetite. I could scoff iron-filings an' horseshoe nails an' thank you kindly, ma'am, for a second helpin'."

He straightened up, and, while he reached for matches in the pocket of his overalls, his eyes travelled across the pool to the side-hill. His fingers had clutched the match-box, but they relaxed their hold and the hand came out empty. The man wavered perceptibly. He looked at his preparations for cooking and he looked at the hill.

"Guess I'll take another whack at her," he concluded, starting to cross the stream.

"They ain't no sense in it, I know," he mumbled, apologetically. "But keepin' grub back an hour ain't goin' to hurt none, I reckon."

A few feet back from his first line of test-pans he started a second line. The sun dropped down the western sky, the shadows lengthened, but the man worked on. He began a third line of test-pans. He was cross-cutting the hillside, line by line, as he ascended. The centre of each line produced the richest pans, while the ends came where no colors showed in the pan. And as he ascended the hillside the lines grew perceptibly shorter. The regularity with which their length diminished served to indicate that somewhere up the slope the last line would be so short as to have scarcely length at all, and that beyond could come only a point. The design was growing into an inverted "V." The converging sides of this "V" marked the boundaries of the gold-bearing dirt.

The apex of the "V" was evidently the man's goal. Often he ran his eye along the converging sides and on up the hill, trying to divine the apex, the point where the gold-bearing dirt must cease. Here resided "Mr. Pocket"—for so the man familiarly addressed the imaginary point above him on the slope, crying out:

"Come down out o' that, Mr. Pocket! Be right smart an' agreeable, an' come down!"

"All right," he would add later, in a voice resigned to determination. "All right, Mr. Pocket. It's plain to me I got to come right up an' snatch you out bald-headed. An' I'll do it! I'll do it!" he would threaten still later.

Each pan he carried down to the water to wash, and as he went higher up the hill the pans grew richer, until he began to save the gold in an empty baking-powder can which he carried carelessly in his hip-pocket. So engrossed was he in his toil that he did not notice the long twilight of oncoming night. It was not until he tried vainly to see the gold colors in the bottom of the pan that he realized the passage of time. He straightened up abruptly. An expression of whimsical wonderment and awe overspread his face as he drawled:

"Gosh darn my buttons! if I didn't plumb forget dinner!"

He stumbled across the stream in the darkness and lighted his long-delayed fire. Flapjacks and bacon and warmed-over beans constituted his supper. Then he smoked a pipe by the smouldering coals, listening to the night noises and watching the moonlight stream through the canyon. After that he unrolled his bed, took off his heavy shoes, and pulled the blankets up to his chin. His face showed white in the moonlight, like the face of a corpse. But it was a corpse that knew its resurrection, for the man rose suddenly on one elbow and gazed across at his hillside.

"Good night, Mr. Pocket," he called sleepily. "Good night."

He slept through the early gray of morning until the direct rays of the sun smote his closed eyelids, when he awoke with a start and looked about him until he had established the continuity of his existence and identified his present self with the days previously lived.

To dress, he had merely to buckle on his shoes. He glanced at his fireplace and at his hillside, wavered, but fought down the temptation and started the fire.

"Keep yer shirt on, Bill; keep yer shirt on," he admonished himself. "What's the good of rushin'? No use in gettin' all het up an' sweaty. Mr. Pocket'll wait for you. He ain't a-runnin' away before you can get yer breakfast. Now, what you want, Bill, is something fresh in yer bill o' fare. So it's up to you to go an' get it."

He cut a short pole at the water's edge and drew from one of his pockets a bit of line and a draggled fly that had once been a royal coachman.

"Mebbe they'll bite in the early morning," he muttered, as he made his first cast into the pool. And a moment later he was gleefully crying: "What 'd I tell you, eh? What 'd I tell you?"

He had no reel, nor any inclination to waste time, and by main strength, and swiftly, he drew out of the water a flashing ten-inch trout. Three more, caught in rapid succession, furnished his breakfast. When he came to the stepping-stones on his way to his hillside, he was struck by a sudden thought, and paused.

"I'd just better take a hike down-stream a ways," he said. "There's no tellin' what cuss may be snoopin' around."

But he crossed over on the stones, and with a "I really oughter take that hike," the need of the precaution passed out of his mind and he fell to work.

At nightfall he straightened up. The small of his back was stiff from stooping toil, and as he put his hand behind him to soothe the protesting muscles, he said:

"Now what d'ye think of that, by damn? I clean forgot my dinner again! If I don't watch out, I'll sure be degeneratin' into a two-meal-a-day crank."

"Pockets is the damnedest things I ever see for makin' a man absent-minded," he communed that night, as he crawled into his blankets. Nor did he forget to call up the hillside, "Good night, Mr. Pocket! Good night!"

Rising with the sun, and snatching a hasty breakfast, he was early at work. A fever seemed to be growing in him, nor did the increasing richness of the test-pans allay this fever. There was a flush in his cheek other than that made by the heat of the sun, and he was oblivious to fatigue and the passage of time. When he filled a pan with dirt, he ran down the hill to wash it; nor could he forbear running up the hill again, panting and stumbling profanely, to refill the pan.

He was now a hundred yards from the water, and the inverted "V" was assuming definite proportions. The width of the pay-dirt steadily decreased, and the man extended in his mind's eye the sides of the "V" to their meeting-place far up the hill. This was his goal, the apex of the "V," and he panned many times to locate it.

"Just about two yards above that manzanita bush an' a yard to the right," he finally concluded.

Then the temptation seized him. "As plain as the nose on your face," he said, as he abandoned his laborious cross-cutting and climbed to the indicated apex. He filled a pan and carried it down the hill to wash. It contained no trace of gold. He dug deep, and he dug shallow, filling and washing a dozen pans, and was unrewarded even by the tiniest golden speck. He was enraged at having yielded to the temptation, and cursed himself blasphemously and pridelessly. Then he went down the hill and took up the cross-cutting.

"Slow an' certain, Bill; slow an' certain," he crooned. "Short-cuts to fortune ain't in your line, an' it's about time you know it. Get wise, Bill; get wise. Slow an' certain's the only hand you can play; so go to it, an' keep to it, too."

As the cross-cuts decreased, showing that the sides of the "V" were converging, the depth of the "V" increased. The gold-trace was dipping into the hill. It was only at thirty inches beneath the surface that he could get colors in his pan. The dirt he found at twenty-five inches from the surface, and at thirty-five inches, yielded barren pans. At the base of the "V," by the water's edge, he had found the gold colors at the grass roots. The higher he went up the hill, the deeper the gold dipped. To dig a hole three feet deep in order to get one test-pan was a task of no mean magnitude; while between the man and the apex intervened an untold number of such holes to be dug. "An' there's no tellin' how much deeper it 'll pitch," he sighed, in a moment's pause, while his fingers soothed his aching back.

Feverish with desire, with aching back and stiffening muscles, with pick and shovel gouging and mauling the soft brown earth, the man toiled up the hill. Before him was the smooth slope, spangled with flowers and made sweet with their breath. Behind him was devastation. It looked like some terrible eruption breaking out on the smooth skin of the hill. His slow progress was like that of a slug, befouling beauty with a monstrous trail.

Though the dipping gold-trace increased the man's work, he found consolation in the increasing richness of the pans. Twenty cents, thirty cents, fifty cents, sixty cents, were the values of the gold found in the pans, and at nightfall he washed his banner pan, which gave him a dollar's worth of gold-dust from a shovelful of dirt.

"I'll just bet it's my luck to have some inquisitive cuss come buttin' in here on my pasture," he mumbled sleepily that night as he pulled the blankets up to his chin.

Suddenly he sat upright. "Bill!" he called sharply. "Now, listen to me, Bill; d'ye hear! It's up to you, to-morrow mornin', to mosey round an' see what you can see. Understand? To-morrow morning, an' don't you forget it!"

He yawned and glanced across at his side-hill. "Good night, Mr. Pocket," he called.

In the morning he stole a march on the sun, for he had finished breakfast when its first rays caught him, and he was climbing the wall of the canyon where it crumbled away and gave footing. From the outlook at the top he found himself in the midst of loneliness. As far as he could see, chain after chain of mountains heaved themselves into his vision. To the east his eyes, leaping the miles between range and range and between many ranges, brought up at last against the white-peaked Sierras—the main crest, where the backbone of the Western world reared itself against the sky. To the north and south he could see more distinctly the cross-systems that broke through the main trend of the sea of mountains. To the west the ranges fell away, one behind the other, diminishing and fading into the gentle foothills that, in turn, descended into the great valley which he could not see.

And in all that mighty sweep of earth he saw no sign of man nor of the handiwork of man—save only the torn bosom of the hillside at his feet. The man looked long and carefully. Once, far down his own canyon, he thought he saw in the air a faint hint of smoke. He looked again and decided that it was the purple haze of the hills made dark by a convolution of the canyon wall at its back.

"Hey, you, Mr. Pocket!" he called down into the canyon. "Stand out from under! I'm a-comin', Mr. Pocket! I'm a-comin'!"

The heavy brogans on the man's feet made him appear clumsy-footed, but he swung down from the giddy height as lightly and airily as a mountain goat. A rock, turning under his foot on the edge of the precipice, did not disconcert him. He seemed to know the precise time required for the turn to culminate in disaster, and in the meantime he utilized the false footing itself for the momentary earth-contact necessary to carry him on into safety. Where the earth sloped so steeply that it was impossible to stand for a second upright, the man did not hesitate. His foot pressed the impossible surface for but a fraction of the fatal second and gave him the bound that carried him onward. Again, where even the fraction of a second's footing was out of the question, he would swing his body past by a moment's hand-grip on a jutting knob of rock, a crevice, or a precariously rooted shrub. At last, with a wild leap and yell, he exchanged the face of the wall for an earth-slide and finished the descent in the midst of several tons of sliding earth and gravel.

His first pan of the morning washed out over two dollars in coarse gold. It was from the centre of the "V." To either side the diminution in the values of the pans was swift. His lines of cross-cutting holes were growing very short. The converging sides of the inverted "V" were only a few yards apart. Their meeting-point was only a few yards above him. But the pay-streak was dipping deeper and deeper into the earth. By early afternoon he was sinking the test-holes five feet before the pans could show the gold-trace.

For that matter, the gold-trace had become something more than a trace; it was a placer mine in itself, and the man resolved to come back after he had found the pocket and work over the ground. But the increasing richness of the pans began to worry him. By late afternoon the worth of the pans had grown to three and four dollars. The man scratched his head perplexedly and looked a few feet up the hill at the manzanita bush that marked approximately the apex of the "V." He nodded his head and said oracularly:

"It's one o' two things, Bill; one o' two things. Either Mr. Pocket's spilled himself all out an' down the hill, or else Mr. Pocket's that damned rich you maybe won't be able to carry him all away with you. And that 'd be hell, wouldn't it, now?" He chuckled at contemplation of so pleasant a dilemma.

Nightfall found him by the edge of the stream, his eyes wrestling with the gathering darkness over the washing of a five-dollar pan.

"Wisht I had an electric light to go on working," he said.

He found sleep difficult that night. Many times he composed himself and closed his eyes for slumber to overtake him; but his blood pounded with too strong desire, and as many times his eyes opened and he murmured wearily, "Wisht it was sun-up."

Sleep came to him in the end, but his eyes were open with the first paling of the stars, and the gray of dawn caught him with breakfast finished and climbing the hillside in the direction of the secret abiding-place of Mr. Pocket.

The first cross-cut the man made, there was space for only three holes, so narrow had become the pay-streak and so close was he to the fountainhead of the golden stream he had been following for four days.

"Be ca'm, Bill; be ca'm," he admonished himself, as he broke ground for the final hole where the sides of the "V" had at last come together in a point.

"I've got the almighty cinch on you, Mr. Pocket, an' you can't lose me," he said many times as he sank the hole deeper and deeper.

Four feet, five feet, six feet, he dug his way down into the earth. The digging grew harder. His pick grated on broken rock. He examined the rock.

"Rotten quartz," was his conclusion as, with the shovel, he cleared the bottom of the hole of loose dirt. He attacked the crumbling quartz with the pick, bursting the disintegrating rock asunder with every stroke.

He thrust his shovel into the loose mass. His eye caught a gleam of yellow. He dropped the shovel and squatted suddenly on his heels. As a farmer rubs the clinging earth from fresh-dug potatoes, so the man, a piece of rotten quartz held in both hands, rubbed the dirt away.

"Sufferin' Sardanopolis!" he cried. "Lumps an' chunks of it! Lumps an' chunks of it!"

It was only half rock he held in his hand. The other half was virgin gold. He dropped it into his pan and examined another piece. Little yellow was to be seen, but with his strong fingers he crumbled the rotten quartz away till both hands were filled with glowing yellow. He rubbed the dirt away from fragment after fragment, tossing them into the gold-pan. It was a treasure-hole. So much had the quartz rotted away that there was less of it than there was of gold. Now and again he found a piece to which no rock clung—a piece that was all gold. A chunk, where the pick had laid open the heart of the gold, glittered like a handful of yellow jewels, and he cocked his head at it and slowly turned it around and over to observe the rich play of the light upon it.

"Talk about yer Too Much Gold diggin's!" the man snorted contemptuously. "Why, this diggin' 'd make it look like thirty cents. This diggin' is All Gold. An' right here an' now I name this yere canyon 'All Gold Canyon,' b' gosh!"

Still squatting on his heels, he continued examining the fragments and tossing them into the pan. Suddenly there came to him a premonition of danger. It seemed a shadow had fallen upon him. But there was no shadow. His heart had given a great jump up into his throat and was choking him. Then his blood slowly chilled and he felt the sweat of his shirt cold against his flesh.

He did not spring up nor look around. He did not move. He was considering the nature of the premonition he had received, trying to locate the source of the mysterious force that had warned him, striving to sense the imperative presence of the unseen thing that threatened him. There is an aura of things hostile, made manifest by messengers too refined for the senses to know; and this aura he felt, but knew not how he felt it. His was the feeling as when a cloud passes over the sun. It seemed that between him and life had passed something dark and smothering and menacing; a gloom, as it were, that swallowed up life and made for death—his death.

Every force of his being impelled him to spring up and confront the unseen danger, but his soul dominated the panic, and he remained squatting on his heels, in his hands a chunk of gold. He did not dare to look around, but he knew by now that there was something behind him and above him. He made believe to be interested in the gold in his hand. He examined it critically, turned it over and over, and rubbed the dirt from it. And all the time he knew that something behind him was looking at the gold over his shoulder.

Still feigning interest in the chunk of gold in his hand, he listened intently and he heard the breathing of the thing behind him. His eyes searched the ground in front of him for a weapon, but they saw only the uprooted gold, worthless to him now in his extremity. There was his pick, a handy weapon on occasion; but this was not such an occasion. The man realized his predicament. He was in a narrow hole that was seven feet deep. His head did not come to the surface of the ground. He was in a trap.

He remained squatting on his heels. He was quite cool and collected; but his mind, considering every factor, showed him only his helplessness. He continued rubbing the dirt from the quartz fragments and throwing the gold into the pan. There was nothing else for him to do. Yet he knew that he would have to rise up, sooner or later, and face the danger that breathed at his back. The minutes passed, and with the passage of each minute he knew that by so much he was nearer the time when he must stand up, or else—and his wet shirt went cold against his flesh again at the thought—or else he might receive death as he stooped there over his treasure.

Still he squatted on his heels, rubbing dirt from gold and debating in just what manner he should rise up. He might rise up with a rush and claw his way out of the hole to meet whatever threatened on the even footing above ground. Or he might rise up slowly and carelessly, and feign casually to discover the thing that breathed at his back. His instinct and every fighting fibre of his body favored the mad, clawing rush to the surface. His intellect, and the craft thereof, favored the slow and cautious meeting with the thing that menaced and which he could not see. And while he debated, a loud, crashing noise burst on his ear. At the same instant he received a stunning blow on the left side of the back, and from the point of impact felt a rush of flame through his flesh. He sprang up in the air, but halfway to his feet collapsed. His body crumpled in like a leaf withered in sudden heat, and he came down, his chest across his pan of gold, his face in the dirt and rock, his legs tangled and twisted because of the restricted space at the bottom of the hole. His legs twitched convulsively several times. His body was shaken as with a mighty ague. There was a slow expansion of the lungs, accompanied by a deep sigh. Then the air was slowly, very slowly, exhaled, and his body as slowly flattened itself down into inertness.

Above, revolver in hand, a man was peering down over the edge of the hole. He peered for a long time at the prone and motionless body beneath him. After a while the stranger sat down on the edge of the hole so that he could see into it, and rested the revolver on his knee. Reaching his hand into a pocket, he drew out a wisp of brown paper. Into this he dropped a few crumbs of tobacco. The combination became a cigarette, brown and squat, with the ends turned in. Not once did he take his eyes from the body at the bottom of the hole. He lighted the cigarette and drew its smoke into his lungs with a caressing intake of the breath. He smoked slowly. Once the cigarette went out and he relighted it. And all the while he studied the body beneath him.

In the end he tossed the cigarette stub away and rose to his feet. He moved to the edge of the hole. Spanning it, a hand resting on each edge, and with the revolver still in the right hand, he muscled his body down into the hole. While his feet were yet a yard from the bottom he released his hands and dropped down.

At the instant his feet struck bottom he saw the pocket-miner's arm leap out, and his own legs knew a swift, jerking grip that overthrew him. In the nature of the jump his revolver-hand was above his head. Swiftly as the grip had flashed about his legs, just as swiftly he brought the revolver down. He was still in the air, his fall in process of completion, when he pulled the trigger. The explosion was deafening in the confined space. The smoke filled the hole so that he could see nothing. He struck the bottom on his back, and like a cat's the pocket-miner's body was on top of him. Even as the miner's body passed on top, the stranger crooked in his right arm to fire; and even in that instant the miner, with a quick thrust of elbow, struck his wrist. The muzzle was thrown up and the bullet thudded into the dirt of the side of the hole.

The next instant the stranger felt the miner's hand grip his wrist. The struggle was now for the revolver. Each man strove to turn it against the other's body. The smoke in the hole was clearing. The stranger, lying on his back, was beginning to see dimly. But suddenly he was blinded by a handful of dirt deliberately flung into his eyes by his antagonist. In that moment of shock his grip on the revolver was broken. In the next moment he felt a smashing darkness descend upon his brain, and in the midst of the darkness even the darkness ceased.

But the pocket-miner fired again and again, until the revolver was empty. Then he tossed it from him and, breathing heavily, sat down on the dead man's legs.

The miner was sobbing and struggling for breath. "Measly skunk!" he panted; "a-campin' on my trail an' lettin' me do the work, an' then shootin' me in the back!"

He was half crying from anger and exhaustion. He peered at the face of the dead man. It was sprinkled with loose dirt and gravel, and it was difficult to distinguish the features.

"Never laid eyes on him before," the miner concluded his scrutiny. "Just a common an' ordinary thief, damn him! An' he shot me in the back! He shot me in the back!"

He opened his shirt and felt himself, front and back, on his left side. "Went clean through, and no harm done!" he cried jubilantly. "I'll bet he aimed all right all right; but he drew the gun over when he pulled the trigger—the cuss! But I fixed 'm! Oh, I fixed 'm!"

His fingers were investigating the bullet-hole in his side, and a shade of regret passed over his face. "It's goin' to be stiffer'n hell," he said. "An' it's up to me to get mended an' get out o' here."

He crawled out of the hole and went down the hill to his camp. Half an hour later he returned, leading his pack-horse. His open shirt disclosed the rude bandages with which he had dressed his wound. He was slow and awkward with his left-hand movements, but that did not prevent his using the arm.

The bight of the pack-rope under the dead man's shoulders enabled him to heave the body out of the hole. Then he set to work gathering up his gold. He worked steadily for several hours, pausing often to rest his stiffening shoulder and to exclaim:

"He shot me in the back, the measly skunk! He shot me in the back!"

When his treasure was quite cleaned up and wrapped securely into a number of blanket-covered parcels, he made an estimate of its value.

"Four hundred pounds, or I'm a Hottentot," he concluded. "Say two hundred in quartz an' dirt—that leaves two hundred pounds of gold. Bill! Wake up! Two hundred pounds of gold! Forty thousand dollars! An' it's yourn—all yourn!"

He scratched his head delightedly and his fingers blundered into an unfamiliar groove. They quested along it for several inches. It was a crease through his scalp where the second bullet had ploughed.

He walked angrily over to the dead man. "You would, would you?" he bullied. "You would, eh? Well, I fixed you good an' plenty, an' I'll give you decent burial, too. That's more'n you'd have done for me."

He dragged the body to the edge of the hole and toppled it in. It struck the bottom with a dull crash, on its side, the face twisted up to the light. The miner peered down at it.

"An' you shot me in the back!" he said accusingly.

With pick and shovel he filled the hole. Then he loaded the gold on his horse. It was too great a load for the animal, and when he had gained his camp he transferred part of it to his saddle-horse. Even so, he was compelled to abandon a portion of his outfit—pick and shovel and gold-pan, extra food and cooking utensils, and divers odds and ends.

The sun was at the zenith when the man forced the horses at the screen of vines and creepers. To climb the huge boulders the animals were compelled to uprear and struggle blindly through the tangled mass of vegetation. Once the saddle-horse fell heavily and the man removed the pack to get the animal on its feet. After it started on its way again the man thrust his head out from among the leaves and peered up at the hillside.

"The measly skunk!" he said, and disappeared.

There was a ripping and tearing of vines and boughs. The trees surged back and forth, marking the passage of the animals through the midst of them. There was a clashing of steel-shod hoofs on stone, and now and again an oath or a sharp cry of command. Then the voice of the man was raised in song:—

> "Tu'n around an' tu'n yo' face
> Untoe them sweet hills of grace
> (D' pow'rs of sin yo' am scornin'!).
> Look about an' look aroun',
> Fling yo' sin-pack on d' groun'
> (Yo' will meet wid d' Lord in d' mornin'!)."

The song grew faint and fainter, and through the silence crept back the spirit of the place. The stream once more drowsed and whispered; the hum of the mountain bees rose sleepily. Down through the perfume-weighted air fluttered the snowy fluffs of the cottonwoods. The butterflies drifted in and out among the trees, and over all blazed the quiet sunshine. Only remained the hoof-marks in the meadow and the torn hillside to mark the boisterous trail of the life that had broken the peace of the place and passed on.

ZANE GREY

■ ike Owen Wister, Zane Grey (1875–1939) was a frustrated easterner rejuve-
■ nated by a western trip (in his case it was the sight of the wild Grand Canyon,
■ visited in 1907, that opened life up), and as with Wister his most popular writing
offered a fantasy alternative to the narrowing, overcivilized twentieth century. "In
Grey's world," writes the scholar Franz Blaha in an essay in *Updating the Literary
West* (1997), "the male protagonists are protectors and providers, exposing themselves willingly to the cruel Darwinian forces in nature to create a safe environment for their women. Surviving by courage, resourcefulness, determination, and
measured violence, they successfully resist natural disasters, outlaws, and efforts
to domesticate them by the women they love." Grey's world is also a beautifully
endless wilderness, depicted in the light of the author's love (a late afternoon or
evening light, golden, deep-shadowed, and sublime), a landscape whose nobility is
internalized by the better characters. His Lassiter is easily the equal of Wister's
Virginian in heroism—and darker, more mysterious. After achieving success in the
formula mode, Grey tried to deepen his stories and make them more complex,
venturing even an Indian-white marriage (censored by his publishers) in the original
draft of *The Vanishing American* (1925). Like Louis L'Amour later, he chafed under
dismissive criticism. But the world he built early from the heart, heroic and rev-
elatory in its solitude and wildness, has stayed firmly in place. Here is Chapter
One of Grey's initial success.

"Lassiter," from *Riders of the Purple Sage* (1912)

Chapter 1

A sharp clip-clop of iron-shod hoofs deadened and died away, and clouds
of yellow dust drifted from under the cottonwoods out over the sage.

Jane Withersteen gazed down the wide purple slope with dreamy and
troubled eyes. A rider had just left her and it was his message that held
her thoughtful and almost sad, awaiting the churchmen who were coming
to resent and attack her right to befriend a Gentile.

She wondered if the unrest and strife that had lately come to the little
village of Cottonwoods was to involve her. And then she sighed, remembering that her father had founded this remotest border settlement of
southern Utah and that he had left it to her. She owned all the ground

and many of the cottages. Withersteen House was hers, and the great ranch, with its thousands of cattle, and the swiftest horses of the sage. To her belonged Amber Spring, the water which gave verdure and beauty to the village and made living possible on that wild purple upland waste. She could not escape being involved by whatever befell Cottonwoods.

That year, 1871, had marked a change which had been gradually coming in the lives of the peace-loving Mormons of the border. Glaze—Stone Bridge—Sterling, villages to the north, had risen against the invasion of Gentile settlers and the forays of rustlers. There had been opposition to the one and fighting with the other. And now Cottonwoods had begun to wake and bestir itself and grow hard.

Jane prayed that the tranquility and sweetness of her life would not be permanently disrupted. She meant to do so much more for her people than she had done. She wanted the sleepy quiet pastoral days to last always. Trouble between the Mormons and the Gentiles of the community would make her unhappy. She was Mormonborn, and she was a friend to poor and unfortunate Gentiles. She wished only to go on doing good and being happy. And she thought of what that great ranch meant to her. She loved it all—the grove of cottonwoods, the old stone house, the amber-tinted water, and the droves of shaggy, dusty horses and mustangs, the sleek, clean-limbed, blooded racers, and the browsing herds of cattle and the lean, sun-browned riders of the sage.

While she waited there she forgot the prospect of untoward change. The bray of a lazy burro broke the afternoon quiet, and it was comfortingly suggestive of the drowsy farmyard, and the open corrals, and the green alfalfa fields. Her clear sight intensified the purple sage-slope as it rolled before her. Low swells of prairie-like ground sloped up to the west. Dark, lonely cedar-trees, few and far between, stood out strikingly, and at long distances ruins of red rocks. Farther on, up the gradual slope, rose a broken wall, a huge monument, looming dark purple and stretching its solitary mystic way, a wavering line that faded in the north. Here to the westward was the light and color and beauty. Northward the slope descended to a dim line of cañons from which rose an up-flinging of the earth, not mountainous, but a vast heave of purple uplands, with ribbed and fan-shaped walls, castle-crowned cliffs, and gray escarpments. Over it all crept the lengthening, waning afternoon shadows.

The rapid beat of hoofs recalled Jane Withersteen to the question at hand. A group of riders cantered up the lane, dismounted, and threw their bridles. They were seven in number, and Tull, the leader, a tall, dark man, was an elder of Jane's church.

"Did you get my message?" he asked, curtly.

"Yes," replied Jane.

"I sent word I'd give that rider Venters half an hour to come down to the village. He didn't come."

"He knows nothing of it," said Jane. "I didn't tell him. I've been waiting here for you."

"Where is Venters?"

"I left him in the courtyard."

"Here, Jerry," called Tull, turning to his men, "take the gang and fetch Venters out here if you have to rope him."

The dusty-booted and long-spurred riders clanked noisily into the grove of cottonwoods and disappeared in the shade.

"Elder Tull, what do you mean by this?" demanded Jane. "If you must arrest Venters you might have the courtesy to wait till he leaves my home. And if you do arrest him it will be adding insult to injury. It's absurd to accuse Venters of being mixed up in that shooting fray in the village last night. He was with me at the time. Besides, he let me take charge of his guns. You're only using this as a pretext. What do you mean to do to Venters?"

"I'll tell you presently," replied Tull. "But first tell me why you defend this worthless rider?"

"Worthless!" exclaimed Jane, indignantly. "He's nothing of the kind. He was the best rider I ever had. There's not a reason why I shouldn't champion him and every reason why I should. It's no little shame to me, Elder Tull, that through my friendship he has roused the enmity of my people and become an outcast. Besides, I owe him eternal gratitude for saving the life of little Fay."

"I've heard of your love for Fay Larkin and that you intend to adopt her. But—Jane Withersteen, the child is a Gentile!"

"Yes. But, Elder, I don't love the Mormon children any less because I love a Gentile child. I shall adopt Fay if her mother will give her to me."

"I'm not so much against that. You can give the child Mormon teaching," said Tull. "But I'm sick of seeing this fellow Venters hang around you. I'm going to put a stop to it. You've so much love to throw away on these beggars of Gentiles that I've an idea you might love Venters."

Tull spoke with the arrogance of a Mormon whose power could not be brooked and with the passion of a man in whom jealousy had kindled a consuming fire.

"Maybe I do love him," said Jane. She felt both fear and anger stir her heart. "I'd never thought of that. Poor fellow! he certainly needs some one to love him."

"This'll be a bad day for Venters unless you deny that," returned Tull, grimly.

Tull's men appeared under the cottonwoods and led a young man out into the lane. His ragged clothes were those of an outcast. But he stood tall and straight, his wide shoulders flung back, with the muscles of his bound arms rippling and a blue flame of defiance in the gaze he bent on Tull.

For the first time Jane Withersteen felt Venters's real spirit. She wondered if she would love this splendid youth. Then her emotion cooled to the sobering sense of the issue at stake.

"Venters, will you leave Cottonwoods at once and forever?" asked Tull, tensely.

"Why?" rejoined the rider.

"Because I order it."

Venters laughed in cool disdain.

The red leaped to Tull's dark cheek.

"If you don't go it means your ruin," he said, sharply.

"Ruin!" exclaimed Venters, passionately. "Haven't you already ruined me? What do you call ruin? A year ago I was a rider. I had horses and cattle of my own. I had a good name in Cottonwoods. And now when I come into the village to see this woman you set your men on me. You hound me. You trail me as if I were a rustler. I've no more to lose—except my life."

"Will you leave Utah?"

"Oh! I know," went on Venters, tauntingly, "it galls you, the idea of beautiful Jane Withersteen being friendly to a poor Gentile. You want her all yourself. You're a wiving Mormon. You have use for her—and Withersteen House and Amber Spring and seven thousand head of cattle!"

Tull's hard jaw protruded, and rioting blood corded the veins of his neck.

"Once more. Will you go?"

"No!"

"Then I'll have you whipped within an inch of your life," replied Tull, harshly. "I'll turn you out in the sage. And if you ever come back you'll get worse."

Venters's agitated face grew coldly set and the bronze changed to gray.

Jane impulsively stepped forward. "Oh! Elder Tull!" she cried. "You won't do that!"

Tull lifted a shaking finger toward her.

"That'll do from you. Understand, you'll not be allowed to hold this boy to a friendship that's offensive to your Bishop. Jane Withersteen, your father left you wealth and power. It has turned your head. You haven't yet come to see the place of Mormon women. We've reasoned with you, borne with you. We've patiently waited. We've let you have your fling, which is more than I ever saw granted to a Mormon woman. But you haven't come to your senses. Now, once for all, you can't have any further friendship with Venters. He's going to be whipped, and he's got to leave Utah!"

"Oh! Don't whip him! It would be dastardly!" implored Jane, with slow certainty of her failing courage.

Tull always blunted her spirit, and she grew conscious that she had feigned a boldness which she did not possess. He loomed up now in different guise, not as a jealous suitor, but embodying the mysterious despotism she had known from childhood—the power of her creed.

"Venters, will you take your whipping here or would you rather go out in the sage?" asked Tull. He smiled a flinty smile that was more than inhuman, yet seemed to give out of its dark aloofness a gleam of right-eousness.

"I'll take it here—if I must," said Venters. "But by God!—Tull, you'd better kill me outright. That'll be a dear whipping for you and your pray-ing Mormons. You'll make me another Lassiter!"

The strange glow, the austere light which radiated from Tull's face, might have been a holy joy at the spiritual conception of exalted duty. But there was something more in him, barely hidden, a something per-sonal and sinister, a deep of himself, an engulfing abyss. As his religious mood was fanatical and inexorable, so would his physical hate be mer-ciless.

"Elder, I—I repent my words," Jane faltered. The religion in her, the long habit of obedience, of humility, as well as agony of fear, spoke in her voice. "Spare the boy!" she whispered.

"You can't save him now," replied Tull, stridently.

Her head was bowing to the inevitable. She was grasping the truth, when suddenly there came, in inward constriction, a hardening of gentle forces within her breast. Like a steel bar it was, stiffening all that had been soft and weak in her. She felt a birth in her of something new and unintelligible. Once more her strained gaze sought the sage-slopes. Jane Withersteen loved that wild and purple wilderness. In times of sorrow it had been her strength, in happiness its beauty was her continual delight. In her extremity she found herself murmuring, "Whence cometh my help!" It was a prayer, as if forth from those lonely purple reaches and walls of red and clefts of blue might ride a fearless man, neither creed-bound nor creed-mad, who would hold up a restraining hand in the faces of her ruthless people.

The restless movements of Tull's men suddenly quieted down. Then followed a low whisper, a rustle, a sharp exclamation.

"Look!" said one, pointing to the west.

"A rider!"

Jane Withersteen wheeled and saw a horseman, silhouetted against the western sky, coming riding out of the sage. He had ridden down from the left, in the golden glare of the sun, and had been unobserved till close at hand. An answer to her prayer!

"Do you know him? Does any one know him?" questioned Tull, hurriedly.

His men looked and looked, and one by one shook their heads.

"He's come from far," said one.

"Thet's a fine hoss," said another.

"A strange rider."

"Huh! he wears black leather," added a fourth.

With a wave of his hand, enjoining silence, Tull stepped forward in such a way that he concealed Venters.

The rider reined in his mount, and with a lithe forward-slipping action appeared to reach the ground in one long step. It was a peculiar movement in its quickness and inasmuch that while performing it the rider did not swerve in the slightest from a square front to the group before him.

"Look!" hoarsely whispered one of Tull's companions. "He packs two black-butted guns—low down—they're hard to see—black agin them black chaps."

"A gun-man!" whispered another. "Fellers, careful now about movin' your hands."

The stranger's slow approach might have been a mere leisurely manner of gait or the cramped short steps of a rider unused to walking; yet, as well, it could have been the guarded advance of one who took no chances with men.

"Hello, stranger!" called Tull. No welcome was in this greeting, only a gruff curiosity.

The rider responded with a curt nod. The wide brim of a black sombrero cast a dark shade over his face. For a moment he closely regarded Tull and his comrades, and then, halting in his slow walk, he seemed to relax.

"Evenin', ma'am," he said to Jane, and removed his sombrero with quaint grace.

Jane, greeting him, looked up into a face that she trusted instinctively and which riveted her attention. It had all the characteristics of the range rider's—the leanness, the red burn of the sun, and the set changelessness that came from years of silence and solitude. But it was not these which held her; rather the intensity of his gaze, a strained weariness, a piercing wistfulness of keen, gray sight, as if the man was forever looking for that which he never found. Jane's subtle woman's intuition, even in that brief instant, felt a sadness, a hungering, a secret.

"Jane Withersteen, ma'am?" he inquired.

"Yes," she replied.

"The water here is yours?"

"Yes."

"May I water my horse?"

"Certainly. There's the trough."

"But mebbe if you knew who I was—" He hesitated, with his glance on the listening men. "Mebbe you wouldn't let me water him—though I ain't askin' none for myself."

"Stranger, it doesn't matter who you are. Water your horse. And if you are thirsty and hungry come into my house."

"Thanks, ma'am. I can't accept for myself—but for my tired horse—"

Trampling of hoofs interrupted the rider. More restless movements on the part of Tull's men broke up the little circle, exposing the prisoner Venters.

"Mebbe I've kind of hindered somethin'—for a few moments, perhaps?" inquired the rider.

"Yes," replied Jane Withersteen, with a throb in her voice.

She felt the drawing power of his eyes; and then she saw him look at the bound Venters, and at the men who held him, and their leader.

"In this here country all the rustlers an' thieves an' cut-throats an' gun-throwers an' all-round no-good men jest happen to be Gentiles. Ma'am, which of the no-good class does that young feller belong to?"

"He belongs to none of them. He's an honest boy."

"You *know* that, ma'am?"

"Yes—yes."

"Then what has he done to get tied up that way?"

His clear and distinct question, meant for Tull as well as for Jane Withersteen, stilled the restlessness and brought a momentary silence.

"Ask him," replied Jane, her voice rising high.

The rider stepped away from her, moving out with the same slow, measured stride in which he had approached; and the fact that his action placed her wholly to one side, and him no nearer to Tull and his men, had a penetrating significance.

"Young feller, speak up," he said to Venters.

"Here, stranger, this's none of your mix," began Tull. "Don't try any interference. You've been asked to drink and eat. That's more than you'd have got in any other village on the Utah border. Water your horse and be on your way."

"Easy—easy—I ain't interferin' yet," replied the rider. The tone of his voice had undergone a change. A different man had spoken. Where, in addressing Jane, he had been mild and gentle, now, with his first speech to Tull, he was dry, cool, biting. "I've jest stumbled onto a queer deal. Seven Mormons all packin' guns, an' a Gentile tied with a rope, an' a woman who swears by his honesty! Queer, ain't that?"

"Queer or not, it's none of your business," retorted Tull.

"Where I was raised a woman's word was law. I 'ain't quite outgrowed that yet."

Tull fumed between amaze and anger.

"Meddler, we have a law here something different from woman's whim—Mormon law! . . . Take care you don't transgress it."

"To hell with your Mormon law!"

The deliberate speech marked the rider's further change, this time from kindly interest to an awakening menace. It produced a transformation in Tull and his companions. The leader gasped and staggered backward at a blasphemous affront to an institution he held most sacred. The man Jerry, holding the horses, dropped the bridles and froze in his tracks. Like posts the other men stood, watchful-eyed, arms hanging rigid, all waiting.

"Speak up now, young man. What have you done to be roped that way?"

"It's a damned outrage!" burst out Venters. "I've done no wrong. I've offended this Mormon Elder by being a friend to that woman."

"Ma'am, is it true—what he says?" asked the rider of Jane; but his quiveringly alert eyes never left the little knot of quiet men.

"True? Yes, perfectly true," she answered.

"Well, young man, it seems to me that bein' a friend of such a woman would be what you wouldn't want to help an' couldn't help. . . . What's to be done to you for it?"

"They intend to whip me. You know what that means—in Utah!"

"I reckon," replied the rider, slowly.

With his gray glance cold on the Mormons, with the restive bit-champing of the horses, with Jane failing to repress her mounting agitation, with Venters standing pale and still, the tension of the moment tightened. Tull broke the spell with a laugh, a laugh without mirth, a laugh that was only a sound betraying fear.

"Come on, men!" he called.

Jane Withersteen turned again to the rider.

"Stranger, can you do nothing to save Venters?"

"Ma'am, you ask me to save him—from your own people?"

"Ask you? I beg of you!"

"But you don't dream who you're askin'."

"Oh, sir, I pray you—save him!"

"These are Mormons, an' I . . ."

"At—at any cost—save him. For I—I care for him!"

Tull snarled. "You love-sick fool! Tell your secrets. There'll be a way to teach you what you've never learned. . . . Come men, out of here!"

"Mormon, the young man stays," said the rider.

Like a shot his voice halted Tull.

"What!"

"He stays."

"Who'll keep him? He's my prisoner!" cried Tull, hotly. "Stranger, again I tell you—don't mix here. You've meddled enough. Go your way now or—"

"Listen! . . . He stays."

Absolute certainty, beyond any shadow of doubt breathed in the rider's low voice.

"Who are you? We are seven here."

The rider dropped his sombrero and made a rapid movement, singular in that it left him somewhat crouched, arms bent and stiff, with the big black gun-sheaths swung round to the fore.

"*Lassiter!*"

It was Venter's wondering, thrilling cry that bridged the fateful connection between the rider's singular position and the dreaded name.

Tull put out a groping hand. The life of his eyes dulled to the gloom with which men of his fear saw the approach of death. But death, while it hovered over him, did not descend, for the rider waited for the twitching fingers, the downward flash of hand that did not come. Tull, gathering himself together, turned to the horses, attended by his pale comrades.

WILLA CATHER

Imprinted on the grand trees, green grass, and old family usages of a Virginia country life, then suddenly uprooted at age nine and taken to barren-seeming Nebraska, Willa Cather (1873–1947) had an ambivalence about the West all her life. It was the source of some of her most deeply felt writing, yet in adulthood she herself never went back for more than visits, and not at all after her mother's death in 1931. She lived in New York City, summered on Grand Manan Island, and is buried in New Hampshire. Speaking of her first year on the plains, she said the landscape looked "as naked as the back of your hand," and added, "So the country and I had it out together and by the end of the first autumn, that shaggy grass country had gripped me with a passion I have never been able to shake. It has been the happiness and the curse of my life." Part of the happiness came from the rich diversity of immigrant society, the stories told within the sharp hearing of young "Willie" Cather, who wanted to be a doctor, and, at least in retrospect, there was also joy in the land, the sky, the weather. Not so good, as she grew older, was the smallness of midwestern village life. She escaped to Lincoln, then Pittsburgh, then New York, but it was only after she came back west, a successful magazine editor and beginning fiction writer, that something clicked, something came back to her. It was 1912, and the place she visited was Arizona, one of what she later called the "bright edges of the world," as Nebraska had been thirty years earlier. Something in the air, or the landforms, or the Anasazi ruins, reawakened her creativity. Now she could look again at her Nebraska, taking in the country and the people with fresh eyes, looking deeply and nonjudgmentally, as a great-hearted novelist. In the following selections from O Pioneers! and My Ántonia, Cather writes of the earth with incantatory power and of the people with profound compassion, a complex emotion not without humor. In the first, we meet young Emil Bergson, whose older sister Alexandra has become a heroine of the land, the first to tap its native but hidden fertility, and we see Cather's sense of the generations: young Emil is one of the successors, the advantaged ones. Pioneers like the unmarried Alexandra were too busy, their lives too hard, to imagine that ease for those coming after could be anything but good; and their emotional lives perhaps too narrow to see certain kinds of trouble coming. My Ántonia, of which we have here Chapters 13 and 14, is narrated by Cather's alter ego, Jim Burden, who is looking back at early Nebraska with tenderness and wonder.

From *O Pioneers!* (1913)

1

It is sixteen years since John Bergson died. His wife now lies beside him, and the white shaft that marks their graves gleams across the wheat-fields. Could he rise from beneath it, he would not know the country under which he has been asleep. The shaggy coat of the prairie, which they lifted to make him a bed, has vanished forever. From the Norwegian graveyard one looks out over a vast checker-board, marked off in squares of wheat and corn; light and dark, dark and light. Telephone wires hum along the white roads, which always run at right angles. From the graveyard gate one can count a dozen gayly painted farmhouses; the gilded weather-vanes on the big red barns wink at each other across the green and brown and yellow fields. The light steel windmills tremble throughout their frames and tug at their moorings, as they vibrate in the wind that often blows from one week's end to another across that high, active, resolute stretch of country.

The Divide is now thickly populated. The rich soil yields heavy harvests; the dry, bracing climate and the smoothness of the land make labor easy for men and beasts. There are few scenes more gratifying than a spring plowing in that country, where the furrows of a single field often lie a mile in length, and the brown earth, with such a strong, clean smell, and such a power of growth and fertility in it, yields itself eagerly to the plow; rolls away from the shear, not even dimming the brightness of the metal, with a soft, deep sigh of happiness. The wheat-cutting sometimes goes on all night as well as all day, and in good seasons there are scarcely men and horses enough to do the harvesting. The grain is so heavy that it bends toward the blade and cuts like velvet.

There is something frank and joyous and young in the open face of the country. It gives itself ungrudgingly to the moods of the season, holding nothing back. Like the plains of Lombardy, it seems to rise a little to meet the sun. The air and the earth are curiously mated and intermingled, as if the one were the breath of the other. You feel in the atmosphere the same tonic, puissant quality that is in the tilth, the same strength and resoluteness.

One June morning a young man stood at the gate of the Norwegian graveyard, sharpening his scythe in strokes unconsciously timed to the tune he was whistling. He wore a flannel cap and duck trousers, and the sleeves of his white flannel shirt were rolled back to the elbow. When he was satisfied with the edge of his blade, he slipped the whetstone into his hip pocket and began to swing his scythe, still whistling, but softly, out of respect to the quiet folk about him. Unconscious respect, probably, for he seemed intent upon his own thoughts, and, like the Gladiator's, they were far away. He was a splendid figure of a boy, tall and straight as a young pine tree, with a handsome head, and stormy gray eyes, deeply set under a serious brow. The space between his two front teeth, which were unusually far apart, gave him the proficiency in whistling for which he was distinguished at college. (He also played the cornet in the University band.)

When the grass required his close attention, or when he had to stoop to cut about a headstone, he paused in his lively air,—the "Jewel" song,— taking it up where he had left it when his scythe swung free again. He was not thinking about the tired pioneers over whom his blade glittered. The old wild country, the struggle in which his sister was destined to succeed while so many men broke their hearts and died, he can scarcely remember. That is all among the dim things of childhood and has been forgotten in the brighter pattern life weaves to-day, in the bright facts of being captain of the track team, and holding the interstate record for the high jump, in the all-suffusing brightness of being twenty-one. Yet sometimes, in the pauses of his work, the young man frowned and looked at the ground with an intentness which suggested that even twenty-one might have its problems.

When he had been mowing the better part of an hour, he heard the rattle of a light cart on the road behind him. Supposing that it was his sister coming back from one of her farms, he kept on with his work. The cart stopped at the gate and a merry contralto voice called, "Almost through, Emil?" He dropped his scythe and went toward the fence, wiping his face and neck with his handkerchief. In the cart sat a young woman who wore driving gauntlets and a wide shade hat, trimmed with red poppies. Her face, too, was rather like a poppy, round and brown, with rich color in her cheeks and lips, and her dancing yellow-brown eyes bubbled with gayety. The wind was flapping her big hat and teasing a curl of her chestnut-colored hair. She shook her head at the tall youth.

"What time did you get over here? That's not much of a job for an athlete. Here I've been to town and back. Alexandra lets you sleep late. Oh, I know! Lou's wife was telling me about the way she spoils you. I was going to give you a lift, if you were done." She gathered up her reins.

"But I will be, in a minute. Please wait for me, Marie," Emil coaxed. "Alexandra sent me to mow our lot, but I've done half a dozen others, you see. Just wait till I finish off the Kourdnas'. By the way, they were Bohemians. Why are n't they up in the Catholic grave-yard?"

"Free-thinkers," replied the young woman laconically.

"Lots of the Bohemian boys at the University are," said Emil, taking up his scythe again. "What did you ever burn John Huss for, anyway? It's made an awful row. They still jaw about it in history classes." "We'd do it right over again, most of us," said the young woman hotly. "Don't they ever teach you in your history classes that you'd all be heathen Turks if it had n't been for the Bohemians?"

Emil had fallen to mowing. "Oh, there's no denying you're a spunky little bunch, you Czechs," he called back over his shoulder.

Marie Shabata settled herself in her seat and watched the rhythmical movement of the young man's long arms, swinging her foot as if in time to some air that was going through her mind. The minutes passed. Emil mowed vigorously and Marie sat sunning herself and watching the long grass fall. She sat with the ease that belongs to persons of an essentially happy nature, who can find a comfortable spot almost anywhere; who are supple, and quick in adapting themselves to circumstances. After a final swish, Emil snapped the gate and sprang into the cart, holding his scythe well out over the wheel. "There," he sighed. "I gave old man Lee a cut or so, too. Lou's wife need n't talk. I never see Lou's scythe over here."

Marie clucked to her horse. "Oh, you know Annie!" She looked at the young man's bare arms. "How brown you've got since you came home. I wish I had an athlete to mow my orchard. I get wet to my knees when I go down to pick cherries."

"You can have one, any time you want him. Better wait until after it rains." Emil squinted off at the horizon as if he were looking for clouds.

"Will you? Oh, there's a good boy!" She turned her head to him with a quick, bright smile. He felt it rather than saw it. Indeed, he had looked away with the purpose of not seeing it. "I've been up looking at Angé-lique's wedding clothes," Marie went on, "and I'm so excited I can hardly wait until Sunday. Amédée will be a handsome bridegroom. Is anybody but you going to stand up with him? Well, then it will be a handsome wedding party." She made a droll face at Emil, who flushed. "Frank," Marie continued, flicking her horse, "is cranky at me because I loaned his saddle to Jan Smirka, and I'm terribly afraid he won't take me to the dance in the evening. Maybe the supper will tempt him. All Angélique's folks are baking for it, and all Amédée's twenty cousins. There will be barrels of beer. If once I get Frank to the supper, I'll see that I stay for the dance. And by the way, Emil, you must n't dance with me but once or twice. You must dance with all the French girls. It hurts their feelings if you don't. They think you're proud because you've been away to school or something."

Emil sniffed. "How do you know they think that?"

"Well, you did n't dance with them much at Raoul Marcel's party, and I could tell how they took it by the way they looked at you—and at me."

"All right," said Emil shortly, studying the glittering blade of his scythe.

They drove westward toward Norway Creek, and toward a big white house that stood on a hill, several miles across the fields. There were so many sheds and outbuildings grouped about it that the place looked not unlike a tiny village. A stranger, approaching it, could not help noticing the beauty and fruitfulness of the outlying fields. There was something individual about the great farm, a most unusual trimness and care for detail. On either side of the road, for a mile before you reached the foot of the hill, stood tall osage orange hedges, their glossy green marking off the yellow fields. South of the hill, in a low, sheltered swale, surrounded by a mulberry hedge, was the orchard, its fruit trees knee-deep in timothy grass. Any one there-abouts would have told you that this was one of the richest farms on the Divide, and that the farmer was a woman, Alexandra Bergson.

If you go up the hill and enter Alexandra's big house, you will find that it is curiously unfinished and uneven in comfort. One room is papered, carpeted, over-furnished; the next is almost bare. The pleasantest rooms in the house are the kitchen—where Alexandra's three young Swedish girls chatter and cook and pickle and preserve all summer long—and the sitting-room, in which Alexandra has brought together the old homely furniture that the Bergsons used in their first log house, the family portraits, and the few things her mother brought from Sweden.

When you go out of the house into the flower garden, there you feel again the order and fine arrangement manifest all over the great farm; in the fencing and hedging, in the windbreaks and sheds, in the symmetrical pasture ponds, planted with scrub willows to give shade to the cattle in fly-time. There is even a white row of beehives in the orchard, under the walnut trees. You feel that, properly, Alexandra's house is the big out-of-doors, and that it is in the soil that she expresses herself best.

From *My Ántonia* (1918)

13

The week following Christmas brought in a thaw, and by New Year's Day all the world about us was a broth of gray slush, and the guttered slope between the windmill and the barn was running black water. The soft black earth stood out in patches along the roadsides. I resumed all my chores, carried in the cobs and wood and water, and spent the afternoons at the barn, watching Jake shell corn with a hand-sheller.

One morning, during this interval of fine weather, Ántonia and her mother rode over on one of their shaggy old horses to pay us a visit. It was the first time Mrs. Shimerda had been to our house, and she ran about examining our carpets and curtains and furniture, all the while commenting upon them to her daughter in an envious, complaining tone. In the kitchen she caught up an iron pot that stood on the back of the stove and said: "You got many, Shimerdas no got." I thought it weak-minded of grandmother to give the pot to her.

After dinner, when she was helping to wash the dishes, she said, tossing her head: "You got many things for cook. If I got all things like you, I make much better."

She was a conceited, boastful old thing, and even misfortune could not humble her. I was so annoyed that I felt coldly even toward Ántonia and listened unsympathetically when she told me her father was not well.

"My papa sad for the old country. He not look good. He never make music any more. At home he play violin all the time; for weddings and for dance. Here never. When I beg him for play, he shake his head no. Some days he take his violin out of his box and make with his fingers on the strings, like this, but never he make the music. He don't like this kawn-tree."

"People who don't like this country ought to stay at home," I said severely. "We don't make them come here."

"He not want to come, nev-er!" she burst out. "My *maminka* make him come. All the time she say: 'America big country; much money, much land for my boys, much husband for my girls.' My papa, he cry for leave his old friends what make music with him. He love very much the man what play the long horn like this"—she indicated a slide trombone. "They go to school together and are friends from boys. But my mama, she want Ambrosch for be rich, with many cattle."

"Your mama," I said angrily, "wants other people's things."

"Your grandfather is rich," she retorted fiercely. "Why he not help my papa? Ambrosch be rich, too, after while, and he pay back. He is very smart boy. For Ambrosch my mama come here."

Ambrosch was considered the important person in the family. Mrs. Shimerda and Ántonia always deferred to him, though he was often surly with them and contemptuous toward his father. Ambrosch and his mother had everything their own way. Though Ántonia loved her father more than she did any one else, she stood in awe of her elder brother.

After I watched Ántonia and her mother go over the hill on their miserable horse, carrying our iron pot with them, I turned to grand-mother, who had taken up her darning, and said I hoped that snooping old woman would n't come to see us any more.

Grandmother chuckled and drove her bright needle across a hole in Otto's sock. "She's not old, Jim, though I expect she seems old to you. No, I would n't mourn if she never came again. But, you see, a body never knows what traits poverty might bring out in 'em. It makes a woman grasping to see her children want for things. Now read me a chapter in 'The Prince of the House of David.' Let's forget the Bohemi-ans."

We had three weeks of this mild, open weather. The cattle in the corral ate corn almost as fast as the men could shell it for them, and we hoped they would be ready for an early market. One morning the two big bulls, Gladstone and Brigham Young, thought spring had come, and they began to tease and butt at each other across the barbed wire that separated them. Soon they got angry. They bellowed and pawed up the soft earth with their hoofs, rolling their eyes and tossing their heads. Each withdrew to a far corner of his own corral, and then they made for each other at a gallop. Thud, thud, we could hear the impact of their great heads, and their bellowing shook the pans on the kitchen shelves. Had they not been dehorned, they would have torn each other to pieces. Pretty soon the fat steers took it up and began butting and horning each other. Clearly, the affair had to be stopped. We all stood by and watched admiringly while Fuchs rode into the corral with a pitchfork and prodded the bulls again and again, finally driving them apart.

The big storm of the winter began on my eleventh birthday, the 20th of January. When I went down to breakfast that morning, Jake and Otto came in white as snow-men, beating their hands and stamping their feet. They began to laugh boisterously when they saw me, calling:—

"You've got a birthday present this time, Jim, and no mistake. They was a full-grown blizzard ordered for you."

All day the storm went on. The snow did not fall this time, it simply spilled out of heaven, like thousands of feather-beds being emptied. That afternoon the kitchen was a carpenter-shop; the men brought in their tools and made two great wooden shovels with long handles. Neither grand-mother nor I could go out in the storm, so Jake fed the chickens and brought in a pitiful contribution of eggs.

Next day our men had to shovel until noon to reach the barn—and the snow was still falling! There had not been such a storm in the ten years my grandfather had lived in Nebraska. He said at dinner that we would not try to reach the cattle—they were fat enough to go without their corn for a day or two; but to-morrow we must feed them and thaw out their water-tap so that they could drink. We could not so much as see the corrals, but we knew the steers were over there, huddled together under the north bank. Our ferocious bulls, subdued enough by this time, were probably warming each other's backs. "This'll take the bile out of 'em!" Fuchs remarked gleefully.

At noon that day the hens had not been heard from. After dinner Jake and Otto, their damp clothes now dried on them, stretched their stiff arms and plunged again into the drifts. They made a tunnel under the snow to the henhouse, with walls so solid that grandmother and I could walk back and forth in it. We found the chickens asleep; perhaps they thought night had come to stay. One old rooster was stirring about, pecking at the solid lump of ice in their water-tin. When we flashed the lantern in their eyes, the hens set up a great cackling and flew about clumsily, scattering down-feathers. The mottled, pin-headed guinea-hens, always resentful of captivity, ran screeching out into the tunnel and tried to poke their ugly, painted faces through the snow walls. By five o'clock the chores were done—just when it was time to begin them all over again! That was a strange, unnatural sort of day.

14

On the morning of the 22nd I wakened with a start. Before I opened my eyes, I seemed to know that something had happened. I heard excited voices in the kitchen—grandmother's was so shrill that I knew she must be almost beside herself. I looked forward to any new crisis with delight. What could it be, I wondered, as I hurried into my clothes. Perhaps the barn had burned; perhaps the cattle had frozen to death; perhaps a neighbor was lost in the storm.

Down in the kitchen grandfather was standing before the stove with his hands behind him. Jake and Otto had taken off their boots and were rubbing their woolen socks. Their clothes and boots were steaming, and they both looked exhausted. On the bench behind the stove lay a man, covered up with a blanket. Grandmother motioned me to the dining-room. I obeyed reluctantly. I watched her as she came and went, carrying dishes. Her lips were tightly compressed and she kept whispering to herself: "Oh, dear Saviour!" "Lord, Thou knowest!"

Presently grandfather came in and spoke to me: "Jimmy, we will not have prayers this morning, because we have a great deal to do. Old Mr. Shimerda is dead, and his family are in great distress. Ambrosch came over here in the middle of the night, and Jake and Otto went back with him. The boys have had a hard night, and you must not bother them with questions. That is Ambrosch, asleep on the bench. Come in to breakfast, boys."

After Jake and Otto had swallowed their first cup of coffee, they began to talk excitedly, disregarding grandmother's warning glances. I held my tongue, but I listened with all my ears.

"No, sir," Fuchs said in answer to a question from grandfather, "nobody heard the gun go off. Ambrosch was out with the ox team, trying to break a road, and the women folks was shut up tight in their cave. When Ambrosch come in it was dark and he did n't see nothing, but the oxen acted kind of queer. One of 'em ripped around and got away from him—bolted clean out of the stable. His hands is blistered where the rope run through. He got a lantern and went back and found the old man, just as we seen him."

"Poor soul, poor soul!" grandmother groaned. "I'd like to think he never done it. He was always considerate and un-wishful to give trouble. How could he forget himself and bring this on us!"

"I don't think he was out of his head for a minute, Mrs. Burden," Fuchs declared. "He done everything natural. You know he was always sort of fixy, and fixy he was to the last. He shaved after dinner, and washed hisself all over after the girls was done the dishes. Ántonia heated the water for him. Then he put on a clean shirt and clean socks, and after he was dressed he kissed her and the little one and took his gun and said he was going out to hunt rabbits. He must have gone right down to the barn and done it then. He layed down on that bunk-bed, close to the ox stalls, where he always slept. When we found him, everything was decent except,"—Fuchs wrinkled his brow and hesitated,—"except what he could n't nowise foresee. His coat was hung on a peg, and his boots was under the bed. He'd took off that silk neckcloth he always wore, and folded it smooth and stuck his pin through it. He turned back his shirt at the neck and rolled up his sleeves."

"I don't see how he could do it!" grandmother kept saying.

Otto misunderstood her. "Why, mam, it was simple enough; he pulled the trigger with his big toe. He layed over on his side and put the end of the barrel in his mouth, then he drew up one foot and felt for the trigger. He found it all right!"

"Maybe he did," said Jake grimly. "There's something mighty queer about it."

"Now what do you mean, Jake?" grandmother asked sharply.

"Well, mam, I found Krajiek's axe under the manger, and I picks it up and carries it over to the corpse, and I take my oath it just fit the gash in the front of the old man's face. That there Krajiek had been sneakin' round, pale and quiet, and when he seen me examinin' the axe, he begun whimperin', 'My God, man, don't do that!' 'I reckon I'm a-goin' to look into this,' says I. Then he begun to squeal like a rat and run about wringin' his hands. 'They'll hang me!' says he. 'My God, they'll hang me sure!' "

Fuchs spoke up impatiently. "Krajiek's gone silly, Jake, and so have you. The old man would n't have made all them preparations for Krajiek to murder him, would he? It don't hang together. The gun was right beside him when Ambrosch found him."

"Krajiek could 'a' put it there, could n't he?" Jake demanded.

Grandmother broke in excitedly: "See here, Jake Marpole, don't you go trying to add murder to suicide. We're deep enough in trouble. Otto reads you too many of them detective stories."

"It will be easy to decide all that, Emmaline," said grandfather quietly. "If he shot himself in the way they think, the gash will be torn from the inside outward."

"Just so it is, Mr. Burden," Otto affirmed. "I seen bunches of hair and stuff sticking to the poles and straw along the roof. They was blown up there by gunshot, no question."

Grandmother told grandfather she meant to go over to the Shimerdas with him.

"There is nothing you can do," he said doubtfully. "The body can't be touched until we get the coroner here from Black Hawk, and that will be a matter of several days, this weather."

"Well, I can take them some victuals, anyway, and say a word of comfort to them poor little girls. The oldest one was his darling, and was like a right hand to him. He might have thought of her. He's left her alone in a hard world." She glanced distrustfully at Ambrosch, who was now eating his breakfast at the kitchen table.

Fuchs, although he had been up in the cold nearly all night, was going to make the long ride to Black Hawk to fetch the priest and the coroner. On the gray gelding, our best horse, he would try to pick his way across the country with no roads to guide him.

"Don't you worry about me, Mrs. Burden," he said cheerfully, as he put on a second pair of socks. "I've got a good nose for directions, and I never did need much sleep. It's the gray I'm worried about. I'll save him what I can, but it'll strain him, as sure as I'm telling you!"

"This is no time to be over-considerate of animals, Otto; do the best you can for yourself. Stop at the Widow Steavens's for dinner. She's a good woman, and she'll do well by you."

After Fuchs rode away, I was left with Ambrosch. I saw a side of him I had not seen before. He was deeply, even slavishly, devout. He did not say a word all morning, but sat with his rosary in his hands, praying, now silently, now aloud. He never looked away from his beads, nor lifted his hands except to cross himself. Several times the poor boy fell asleep where he sat, wakened with a start, and began to pray again.

No wagon could be got to the Shimerdas' until a road was broken, and that would be a day's job. Grandfather came from the barn on one of our big black horses, and Jake lifted grandmother up behind him. She wore her black hood and was bundled up in shawls. Grandfather tucked his bushy white beard inside his overcoat. They looked very Biblical as they set off, I thought. Jake and Ambrosch followed them, riding the other black and my pony, carrying bundles of clothes that we had got together for Mrs. Shimerda. I watched them go past the pond and over the hill by the drifted cornfield. Then, for the first time, I realized that I was alone in the house.

I felt a considerable extension of power and authority, and was anxious to acquit myself creditably. I carried in cobs and wood from the long cellar, and filled both the stoves. I remembered that in the hurry and excitement of the morning nobody had thought of the chickens, and the eggs had not been gathered. Going out through the tunnel, I gave the hens their corn, emptied the ice from their drinking-pan, and filled it with water. After the cat had had his milk, I could think of nothing else to do, and I sat down to get warm. The quiet was delightful, and the ticking clock was the most pleasant of companions. I got "Robinson Crusoe" and tried to read, but his life on the island seemed dull compared with ours. Presently, as I looked with satisfaction about our comfortable sitting-room, it flashed upon me that if Mr. Shimerda's soul were lingering about in this world at all, it would be here, in our house, which had been more to his liking than any other in the neighborhood. I remembered his contented face when he was with us on Christmas Day. If he could have lived with us, this terrible thing would never have happened.

I knew it was homesickness that had killed Mr. Shimerda, and I wondered whether his released spirit would not eventually find its way back to his own country. I thought of how far it was to Chicago, and then to Virginia, to Baltimore,—and then the great wintry ocean. No, he would not at once set out upon that long journey. Surely, his exhausted spirit, so tired of cold and crowding and the struggle with the ever-falling snow, was resting now in this quiet house.

I was not frightened, but I made no noise. I did not wish to disturb him. I went softly down to the kitchen which, tucked away so snugly underground, always seemed to me the heart and center of the house. There, on the bench behind the stove, I thought and thought about Mr. Shimerda. Outside I could hear the wind singing over hundreds of miles of snow. It was as if I had let the old man in out of the tormenting winter, and were sitting there with him. I went over all that Ántonia had ever told me about his life before he came to this country; how he used to play the fiddle at weddings and dances. I thought about the friends he had mourned to leave, the trombone-player, the great forest full of game,—belonging, as Ántonia said, to the "nobles,"—from which she and her mother used to steal wood on moonlight nights. There was a white hart that lived in that forest, and if any one killed it, he would be hanged, she said. Such vivid pictures came to me that they might have been Mr. Shimerda's memories, not yet faded out from the air in which they had haunted him.

It had begun to grow dark when my household returned, and grandmother was so tired that she went at once to bed. Jake and I got supper, and while we were washing the dishes he told me in loud whispers about the state of things over at the Shimerdas'. Nobody could touch the body until the coroner came. If any one did, something terrible would happen, apparently. The dead man was frozen through, "just as stiff as a dressed turkey you hang out to freeze," Jake said. The horses and oxen would not go into the barn until he was frozen so hard that there was no longer any smell of blood. They were stabled there now, with the dead man, because there was no other place to keep them. A lighted lantern was kept hanging over Mr. Shimerda's head. Ántonia and Ambrosch and the mother took turns going down to pray beside him. The crazy boy went with them, because he did not feel the cold. I believed he felt cold as much as any one else, but he liked to be thought insensible to it. He was always coveting distinction, poor Marek!

Ambrosch, Jake said, showed more human feeling than he would have supposed him capable of; but he was chiefly concerned about getting a priest, and about his father's soul, which he believed was in a place of torment and would remain there until his family and the priest had prayed a great deal for him. "As I understand it," Jake concluded, "it will be a matter of years to pray his soul out of Purgatory, and right now he's in torment."

"I don't believe it," I said stoutly. "I almost know it is n't true." I did not, of course, say that I believed he had been in that very kitchen all afternoon, on his way back to his own country. Nevertheless, after I went to bed, this idea of punishment and Purgatory came back on me crushingly. I remembered the account of Dives in torment, and shuddered. But Mr. Shimerda had not been rich and selfish; he had only been so unhappy that he could not live any longer.

DOROTHY SCARBOROUGH

Born and raised in West Texas, Dorothy Scarborough knew something about wind and dryness, and she had heard at her mother's knee stories of the "savage isolation of the past," the era of widely separated cattle operations and infrequent society for lonely ranch wives. The Wind's realistic portrayal of the 1880s, leading up to the catastrophic drought years of 1886–1887, was so strong, so unrelieved, that it proved too realistic for some Texas readers. She had published the novel anonymously, partly as a marketing gimmick, but the book's authorship was soon "out," and in the next year the second edition had her name on it. A pioneering female faculty member at Columbia University (having been educated at Baylor, Chicago, Oxford, and Columbia), and already a scholar and fiction author of some standing, she defended her accuracy and her West Texas patriotic spirit forthrightly. She succeeded in making a dent in the aura of romance surrounding the longhorn cattle days, and opened the door for further realistic literary treatments of Texas life. (The movie version of The Wind, however, substituted a happy ending for Scarborough's bleak conclusion.) In this selection from Chapter 10, we see the sensitive, nervous heroine, Virginia-raised Letty Mason, in her hot kitchen and out on the open range.

From *The Wind* (1925)

After Wirt Roddy's visit, Letty's nervous lethargy deepened. It was as if some long-anticipated event had taken place, leaving a queer emptiness in the world, because now nothing was to be expected. Ever since Letty had said good-bye to him that night at the station in Sweetwater, and watched the train vanish in a swirl of wind, she had looked for him to return. Consciously or unconsciously she had expected him. Up to the time of her marriage, she had counted on his dashing up as a figure of romance, to relieve her of the unhappiness that Cora's tyranny imposed on her. Somehow, he would change things. Would he not have power even over the wind? She had not definitely thought of him as a wooer, had not pictured marriage, but had merely dazzled her dull environment with romantic imagery of rescue and change. He would open the door of her prison and show her a way of flight.

Since her marriage she had been too inert to be actively interested in him, or in anything, but she had made an effort, according to her ideals of wifehood that must be dutiful, even though unwilling, to put him out of her conscious mind. A married woman shouldn't be thinking of any other man.

But he had not gone, for frequently he had risen to the surface of her languid musings, electrifying them to life, had given a tingling color to hours that otherwise were as empty as the gray sand.

He was a man that would not be forgotten. The very thought of him seemed, with casual insolence, to dare one to ignore him. She could see his lip curl with amused scorn at the idea, could catch the flicker of his black eyelashes over ironic eyes as he challenged her to forget him, if she could. He was always aware of himself, in much the same way that Cora was of herself, though with more subtlety, more suavity, more worldly poise instead of her forthright methods. His egoism was a rapier thrust while Cora's knocked you down with a stick of stove-wood if you got in her way.

Well, she hadn't forgotten him, but she must, she told herself. Thinking about him upset her. That was bad enough, but the thought of him might cause disturbance between her and Lige, or between him and Lige, or between her husband and his partner. The situation held a danger, any way you looked at it. Thinking was a mental ferment that might lead to explosions—and wreckage, if you didn't watch out. She would forget him, if she had to remember to remind herself every hour of the day!

She spoke no more to her husband, nor he to her, of Wirt Roddy or his visit, but often as she looked at Lige she wondered what was in his thought. She scarcely knew this calm and quiet man she lived with. She didn't know him, she was only married to him. She realized the steady strength of him, his sure wisdom, in every day practicality, his sane justice; but she felt that there might be passions, swift and vehement, to which he could be roused that as yet she knew nothing about. She had never heard his voice raised in anger or impatience, yet she dimly comprehended that there were in his nature possibilities of wrath as resistless as a cyclone. Only some extraordinary occasion would call forth rage in him, she felt sure, as he probably would live his placid life out without any such disturbance. He would never seek trouble.

She watched him often, as the spring days passed into summer. He might be good-looking if he shaved oftener, and took better care of himself and of his clothes, like the men she had known in Virginia. But his hard life made him too careless. She shivered with repulsion when she saw him unshaved, with a dirty shirt on, covered with dust from the range, with his heavy boots that scarcely knew what a polishing meant. And the repulsion deepened when she had to wash his dirty shirts—she, who had never had to wash so much as a pocket handkerchief in her girlhood at home. . . .

And he seemed to take her drudgery too much for granted, as if it were natural that a woman should wash and cook and clean up for her man. Such things were expected of pioneer wives—but she wasn't a pioneer, and she hadn't wanted to be a wife. Life had compelled her against her will—life and Cora and the relentless wind. . . .

One Sunday Bev and Cora and the children drove over to spend the day with her. She hadn't seen Cora since her marriage, and had almost hoped never to see her again. She knew, with a woman's sure intuitiveness, that Cora still blamed her for her quarrel with Bev, and she on her side had felt too bitterly resentful to make any advances toward reconciliation. The fact that she was not happy had shut a door between them. If hers had been a love marriage, if she had been happy and content, she could joyously have gone all the way to be friends again. But when she remembered how Cora's hardness and fiery jealousy without cause had driven her into this uncongenial environment, this blind alley from which she could not hope to escape, she felt a surge of anger, almost of hatred. If Cora had not in her selfish egotism misjudged her, she might have had time to find herself, to work out a better way from her problems.

She had seen Bev a few times for brief glimpses since her marriage, when neither had dared speak of what was in their hearts, or do more than hint sympathy and encouragement.

Now, she told herself, she must be more distant to him, for fear Cora would misunderstand and be jealous again.

"I'm so glad to see you all," she said. "But, Cora, I'm ashamed for you to see my house so cluttered up."

Cora's housewifely eye swept the shack and passed judgment on the sand and disorder she saw, but her tongue withheld criticism. "Oh, with this terrible wind blowing sand everywhere, nobody can keep a clean house," she said formally.

But Letty read in her look, "You ought to do better than this."

And the truth hurt, for she realized her shortcomings as a housekeeper. She couldn't put any heart into the work, and then, too she had never had any training to fit her for it. At home Mammy had treated her like a child that couldn't even wait on herself properly, for she dearly loved to wait on her "baby." If Mammy could see her in her present life, cooking and washing and scrubbing, even picking up cow-chips from the prairies sometimes to use as fuel—and cooking in that stingy way, without the things to do with, or the food to cook! How Mammy would curl her lip in pitying scorn at her baby's Sunday dinner—and company come in, too !

As she bustled about preparing dinner for her guests, Letty told herself for the hundredth time that girls ought to be trained to work, to support themselves, so that misfortune couldn't overwhelm them as it had her. To be expected to be a competent pioneer heroine and wife without warning or preparation was like being drowned suddenly, or smothered in an avalanche of sand!

Little Alice shyly trotted everywhere after Letty, but with cautious glances at her mother, obviously realizing her fiery jealousy and fearful of kindling it, but adoring Letty as ever.

"I don't like you to be married," the child said to Letty, as she stood by the stove frying ham.

Letty almost flashed back, "Neither do I!" but she caught her words in time, horrified at the instinctive impulse of revelation.

She smiled at Alice and said, "I miss you little folks a lot."

"Since you been gone, I don't have nobody to play with," mourned Alice.

Ironically Letty thought, "Neither do I." She held up her hand to protect her face from the sputtering hot grease, and it served as a shield for her eyes as well, to hide them from the child.

"The boys think they're smarter'n me an' they don't let me know how to play their games."

"Boys don't know much about girls, do they, little Alice?" asked Letty, with a twisting, fugitive smile.

"Not much," said Alice, proudly passing the fork for her to turn the ham with, her face lighted with love, so that for a moment it was actually pretty.

Letty felt a sudden ache of pity for the child. Some day she would be a woman, with her sensitive soul athrill with dreams, with ideals of life and love that perhaps the plain face would render futile. What would life do to little Alice? Would it fling her unready into the arms of a husband she didn't love? Would it break her heart in loneliness, or send her to serve as a patient drudge in some other woman's house?

If only she could snatch little Alice in her arms, and run away from the cruel world with her!

"Papa used to play with me, but he's mos' gen'rally too tired now of nights," went on Alice.

"Don't he feel well?" asked Letty, with quick anxiety.

"I dunno. He's just tired, I reckon. Mother says he's mopey."

"Maybe he's worried about the drought," suggested Letty. "Men have a lot of things to worry them, come to think of it. They've got the living to make, you know."

"I'm goin' to make a living myself when I'm grown," boasted the child.

"That'll be fine. I hope you will."

"Big Buddy says I ain't pretty, so nobody'll ever want to marry me. Do you think I ain't pretty—a bit?" She peered wistfully at the woman.

Letty gave her a quick hug. "To me you're the sweetest, prettiest little girl I know! And all sorts of lovely things are going to happen to you when you're grown. You can make them happen, little Alice, if only you don't get in a hurry about life—or let anybody push you too fast. Take your time!"

The small face brightened as if some one had lighted rose candles within her breast. "I will—I won't," she declared joyously.

Letty sent a defiant adjuration to fate to be kind to little Alice. For a moment she felt that it didn't matter what happened to her, if only little Alice could be happy. And ordinary happiness wouldn't do for Alice, any more than for herself. Each was an idealist, sensitive, too easily hurt. . . .

From the other room came the sound of high, boyish laughter and Cora's chatter with Sourdough.

Lige poked a face in the doorway. "Chuck most ready?"

"Pretty soon," she said.

"I'll set the table for you."

"No—me!" cut in Alice.

"All right. '*Sta bueno*—but get a shove on, 'cause I'm most ready to pass out with hunger."

He withdrew to the other room to talk with Bev.

Presently Letty summoned them in to dinner. It was a tight squeeze to get them all seated round the table in the small kitchen, but the feat was accomplished with laughter which helped to ease the social strain. Letty, her face flushed from the heat of the stove, presided, and urged upon her guests the plain fare, fried ham, grits, the eternal frijoles, biscuit that had too much soda in them, and canned peaches for dessert.

Even if she had known the guests were coming, she told herself, she had no materials to serve a better meal—but, oh, she might have had her house shining clean! She writhed as she read Cora's contemptuous thoughts.

The men chatted on, unaware of what the women were thinking.

"How your cattle holding out in the drought?" Lige asked Bev.

Cora rushed in to answer for him. "I got my brothers to drive most of his herd to free lands northeast when they took theirs."

"That was a good hunch," said Lige soberly. "Sourdough is aimin' to start right soon with as many of ours as can stand the trip. But there's a lot of 'em that are so poor they couldn't make it. They'll have to take their chances here. Slim chances they are, too, with feed so high, and costing so much to haul it that it would break a man to try to do it."

"Bev wanted to go long with his cattle, but I knew he wasn't strong enough to stand the trip," said Cora. "Hard ridin' an' campin' out nights is no job for a man that's had lung trouble. You never know when you'll start something again."

"He looks well now," said Letty. She felt that perhaps Bev was sensitive about his ailment—his disability—and resented Cora's lack of tact in parading it.

Bev smiled indulgently. "Cora keeps a sharp eye out for me, and a good thing that she does, too, I guess."

"Yep, I watch him like a hawk. I ain't ambitious to be a widow, for I don't think crepe would be becomin' to my style of beauty at all," said his wife emphatically.

"When are you goin' to start your bunch off, Lige?" asked Bev.

"Sourdough is aimin' to go with 'em in a couple o' days now. I'll start with him, an' go a little piece, and then I'll come back to stay with Letty an' look after the ones that are left here."

It was, in fact, the next day that Lige and Sourdough began to round up the cattle in preparation for taking them to the free lands in sections where rain had fallen and where there was grazing. The plan was for him to go, in company with two other men, to drive the cattle to the neighborhood of Devil's River, about one hundred fifty miles southwest of them, and try their chances there. The other man who had gone scouting had reported that the grass was better there, and there was water for the cattle.

It was a hard task to gather the cattle together, scattered as they were over the vast, unfenced pastures, mixed in with cattle of many other ranchmen. The creatures were not only wild, according to their nature, but they were nervous and frightened and high-strung on account of their famished condition.

They seemed to realize that this round-up was unusual, out of time, not a regular affair like the spring and fall round-up, and so they were suspicious and hard to manage. Lige and Sourdough "worked the range" for miles and miles, closing in on groups of cattle here and there, and heading them toward a central point not far from the ranch house, from which they planned to make a start for the drive to Devil's River. But the animals would break away from their control, and scatter, to run back in all directions. Full of tricky impulses, nervous from fear, and wild and intractable as well as stubborn, they made the task of collecting them very hard for the two men.

From the window, as she watched, Letty tried to see what was happening, since the day was clear and windless, so that no sand was blown to obscure the vision, and the extraordinary clearness of the atmosphere made it possible to see objects on the rolling plains for long distances. She was moved with pity alike for the struggling men and for the scared beasts that could not understand what was being attempted.

Two days they worked at the seemingly hopeless task, but by nightfall of the second day, they had succeeded in bunching about half of the herd, and would start the drive next morning.

Lige came in exhausted.

"We've had a hell of a time gettin' these cow brutes herded," he said, as he slumped down into a chair and leaned his arms on the table. "They been starved so long, that they're more'n half mad. We didn't get more'n half of 'em together, work as hard as we could. I'm wore out."

His face was streaked with dirt and sweat, his hair disheveled, his attitude one of fatigue and dejection.

He went on to explain the situation to her. "I got to stand night guard over the bunch tonight, so Sourdough can be fresh to start tomorrow morning early. Would you be scared to stay here at the house by yourself?"

"Oh, yes, I would!" she quavered.

"I could get old Pedro to sleep in the kitchen, though I was aimin' to have him help me with the cattle," he offered.

"I'd rather go with you. Let me do that, Lige."

He smiled a tired smile. "You never sat up all night on the plains with a bunch of wild cattle that's liable to stampede any time. Don't take nothin' to start a bunch when it's restless an' suspicious as these are now."

"Let me try it this once," she pleaded. "I'm afraid to stay here without you. An' I wouldn't be so scared on the plains tonight, because the wind's not blowing. Please, Lige!"

"All right," he said slowly, too tired to argue with her. "I reckon there ain't no real danger with me an' Pedro both on the job. It'll be something different from anything you've ever done."

And so it was, she found out. It was an experience that she would never forget, she told herself often during the night. Lige made a fire on the ground to keep her warm, and spread a bed of blankets for her, a little distance away from the cattle which he had at last succeeded in "bedding down," or getting settled to rest and sleep. He and old Pedro took turns staying with her and circling round and round the herd on horseback, to keep them in place. It was a weird and impressive picture, the flaring firelight, where she sat huddled in blankets, the vast empty plains silver-gray with the unearthly radiance of moonlight, the cattle bunched together in a mass of dark bodies and long horns like polished spears in the moonlight.

At the least sign of restlessness in the cattle, Lige would begin to circle round them, singing to them, some cowboy song, dolorous, monotonous, soothing in its sad strains.

The cattle, tired from their two days' struggle, at last became quiet and slept. Then Letty rested, too, with Pedro keeping guard over her, and Lige a silent watcher by the cattle. She felt like some being in another world, in a life alien to anything she had ever known, as she lay, half awake, half asleep, there on the hard ground, under the white tent of the sky, with the wind blowing on her face. Would the wild cattle stampede suddenly and trample her to death? But Lige was watching over her and them. . . . And so she slept.

The next morning by daybreak Lige and Sourdough were making preparations for the start for their "drive." Letty gave them breakfast by lamplight and watched them mount their horses before the first streak of color came in the sky, and called out her "good-bye and good luck" to them.

But the cattle, rested from the night's sleep, were more active than ever, and seemed suspicious of danger. As the dark, moving mass came nearer the ranch house, when the drive begun, they were showing signs of panic. Would the men be able to control them? Would they stampede in spite of what could be done?

Long horns tossed wildly in the air, bodies lunged and plunged against each other, and the brutes began a mad bellowing. The fear of each intensified the fear of the others, and the mass surged forward, uncontrollable with rage and fright.

The stampede that Lige had been afraid of had come!

Thrilled by the sight, so novel and strange to her, yet terrified of what might happen to the two men, Letty watched from the door. Lige and Sourdough were riding desperately to try to keep the herd together, to keep the cattle from scattering all over the range again, and rendering their hard toil of no avail. She could see them circling round and round the lunging, plunging mass, and above the lowing and bellowing of the beasts their voices rose in shouts and calls to quiet them.

The stampede swept on, till the dark mass was hid in the cloud of sand it raised about it, so that the woman, waiting at the door, could not see what was happening. Would the men be able to hold the herd? And turn them, circle them till they wore them out and get them under control again? Or would the maddened beasts trample them underfoot to their death?

All day Letty walked the floor in a fever of fear. She pictured the bodies of the men lying face downward in the sand, while the avalanche of cattle that had swept over them passed on. Who would be left to bear her the news? She felt as never before the desolation of this lonely land, where human habitations, human faces were so few, so few, so far away. What would happen to her there helpless, if Lige and Sourdough never came back? She could not walk the ten miles to the nearest ranch. Perhaps no passerby might come for days on days. . . .

Perhaps the men had not been killed, but were lying wounded and helpless, in need of aid, with no one nigh to give it! . . .

Night came, and Lige had not returned. Would he ever come back? Letty lighted the lamp and set it in the window, so that he could see its glimmer from afar if he should be on his way home. She had supper ready, in case he should be there to eat it. . . . Then she folded her hands in an agony of helplessness, and waited. . . .

The wind was mercifully still, so that she did not suffer tortures of fear of it, as she had that night of the storm at Bev's house, but she imagined that it was quiet with some purpose in view. Was it stealing up on tiptoe, to peer into the window at her? to listen to hear if she cried aloud, to eavesdrop her heartbeats and her thoughts? That would be just like the evil, treacherous wind. . . .

As her terror began to mount unbearably because of the wind's crafty stillness, she heard the sound of galloping hoofs in the sand, and she hushed her very breathing.

Then the door sprang open and Lige staggered in, dropping with fatigue. She had never seen a man look so worn out, so completely used up. His eyes were bleared and bloodshot, and half closed for lack of sleep, his face was lined with exhaustion and covered with dirt and sweat, and his whole body sagged as if the backbone had been taken from it.

He dropped into a chair, too spent to speak at first. She ran to him, brought water to bathe his face, eased off his heavy boots from his swollen feet, and held a cup of coffee to his parched lips. "Poor fellow, so tired!" she murmured, with tears in her eyes for his sufferings.

When he had recovered enough so that he could eat the food she had prepared for him, she waited on him with eager solicitude for his every wish, and then turned the covers of the bed back for him so that he might drag himself to rest.

"How did you stop the stampede?" she asked.

"Oh, we kept circlin' round an' round 'em till we got 'em wore out, but it pretty nigh wore us out first. But we caught up with the rest o' the bunch that are goin' an' Sourdough ought not have any more trouble much with 'em now."

"How long will it take Sourdough to get to where they're going?"

"About ten days or so to get to Devil's River. The critters are so weak they can't travel more'n about a dozen miles a day. Trail drivers usually can make fifteen, but these beasts are too feeble."

After that, for a time, from day to day would come rumors to Lige that some of the cattle were in various places. He would go out and work the range to bring them in, in the effort to collect them near the last water hole that had any water in it. That was near the ranch house. Gradually he got a fair number of them rounded up, almost as many as the herd that Sourdough had driven away with him. Some had died from starvation and thirst, and some were so weak that they seemed on their last legs, but maybe they could hold out till it rained, Lige said. But rain would have to come soon.

The weeks that should have been late spring passed into summer, and still no rain came—a strange cycle of days that mocked their name—May! . . .

ROBINSON JEFFERS

erhaps more consistently than any other major American poet, Robinson Jeffers (1887–1962) applied himself to themes of cosmic scale: the nature and
ways of God; the small, odd place of humans and their works in the greater
scheme; evolution; the cooling planet and the apparently expanding universe; good
and evil. His intentions were that classical and serious—indeed, he had imbibed
the great Greeks and Romans and Hebrews as a youth, under the heavy tutelage
of his professor-cleric father. A prophet-poet standing symbolically on the final,
California shore, Jeffers spoke to his comparatively frivolous fellow humans critically and unabashedly. In flush times like the 1920s, he was regarded virtually as a
seer. In more nervous eras like the Cold War period, he began to slip from the
anthologies. What seems inarguable is that his verse in its rhythms and images,
and behind it perhaps his very reach of mind, are founded in a deep experience
of place. It was no small thing that he helped build his house, yards from the surf,
handling the granite boulders that were anchored to whaleback-shaped bedrock
tors. No American writer is more tightly identified with a locale than is Jeffers
with the rocky, central California coast, from Carmel south to Point Sur. Almost
invariably, his expression of ideas grows from moments of perception in specific,
described, often locatable places along that beautiful coastline. Few have contem-
plated the wild more steadily and acceptingly.

"Granite and Cypress," from *Roan Stallion, Tamar, and Other Poems* (1925)

White-maned, wide-throated, the heavy-shouldered children of
    the wind leap at the sea-cliff.
The invisible falcon
Brooded on water and bred them in wide waste places, in a bride-
    chamber wide to the stars' eyes
In the center of the ocean,
Where no prows pass nor island is lifted . . . the sea beyond Lobos is
    whitened with the falcon's
Passage, he is here now,
The sky is one cloud, his wing-feathers hiss in the white grass, my
    sapling cypresses writhing
In the fury of his passage

Dare not dream of their centuries of future endurance of tempest.
    (I have granite and cypress,
Both long-lasting,
Planted in the earth; but the granite sea-boulders are prey to no
    hawk's wing, they have taken worse pounding,
Like me they remember
Old wars and are quiet; for we think that the future is one piece
    with the past, we wonder why tree-tops
And people are so shaken.)

"Tor House," from *Cawdor and Other Poems* (1928)

If you should look for this place after a handful of lifetimes:
Perhaps of my planted forest a few
May stand yet, dark-leaved Australians or the coast cypress,
    haggard
With storm-drift; but fire and the axe are devils.
Look for foundations of sea-worn granite, my fingers had the
    art
To make stone love stone, you will find some remnant.
But if you should look in your idleness after ten thousand years:
It is the granite knoll on the granite
And lava tongue in the midst of the bay, by the mouth of the
    Carmel
River-valley, these four will remain
In the change of names. You will know it by the wild sea-
    fragrance of wind
Though the ocean may have climbed or retired a little;
You will know it by the valley inland that our sun and our moon
    were born from
Before the poles changed; and Orion in December
Evenings was strung in the throat of the valley like a lamp-
    lighted bridge.
Come in the morning you will see white gulls
Weaving a dance over blue water, the wane of the moon
Their dance-companion, a ghost walking
By daylight, but wider and whiter than any bird in the world.
My ghost you needn't look for; it is probably
Here, but a dark one, deep in the granite, not dancing on wind
With the mad wings and the day moon.

"November Surf," from *Thurso's Landing* (1932)

Some lucky day each November great waves awake and are drawn
Like smoking mountains bright from the west
And come and cover the cliff with white violent cleanness: then
   suddenly
The old granite forgets half a year's filth:
The orange-peel, eggshells, papers, pieces of clothing, the clots
Of dung in corners of the rock, and used
Sheaths that make light love safe in the evenings: all the droppings
   of the summer
Idlers washed off in a winter ecstasy:
I think this cumbered continent envies its cliff then. . . . But all seasons
The earth, in her childlike prophetic sleep,
Keeps dreaming of the bath of a storm that prepares up the long coast
Of the future to scour more than her sea-lines:
The cities gone down, the people fewer and the hawks more
   numerous,
The rivers mouth to source pure; when the two-footed
Mammal, being someways one of the nobler animals, regains
The dignity of room, the value of rareness.

"Gray Weather," from *Solstice* (1935)

It is true that, older than man and ages to outlast him, the Pacific surf
Still cheerfully pounds the worn granite drum;
But there's no storm; and the birds are still, no song; no kind of excess;
Nothing that shines, nothing is dark;
There is neither joy nor grief nor a person, the sun's tooth
   sheathed in cloud,
And life has no more desires than a stone.
The stormy conditions of time and change are all abrogated, the
   essential
Violences of survival, pleasure,
Love, wrath and pain, and the curious desire of knowing, all per-
   fectly suspended.
In the cloudy light, in the timeless quietness,
One explores deeper than the nerves or heart of nature, the womb
   or soul,
To the bone, the careless white bone, the excellence.

"Signpost," from *Solstice* (1935)

Civilized, crying how to be human again: this will tell you how.
  Turn outward, love things, not men, turn right away from hu-
  manity,
Let that doll lie. Consider if you like how the lilies grow,
Lean on the silent rock until you feel its divinity
Make your veins cold, look at the silent stars, let your eyes
Climb the great ladder out of the pit of yourself and man.
Things are so beautiful, your love will follow your eyes;
Things are the God, you will love God, and not in vain,
For what we love, we grow to it, we share its nature. At length
You will look back along the stars' rays and see that even
The poor doll humanity has a place under heaven.
Its qualities repair their mosaic around you, the chips of strength
And sickness; but now you are free, even to become human,
But born of the rock and the air, not of a woman.

"The Answer," from *Such Counsels You Gave to Me* (1937)

Then what is the answer?—Not to be deluded by dreams.
To know that great civilizations have broken down into violence,
  and their tyrants come, many times before.
When open violence appears, to avoid it with honor or choose
  the least ugly faction; these evils are essential.
To keep one's own integrity, be merciful and uncorrupted and
  not wish for evil; and not be duped
By dreams of universal justice or happiness. These dreams will
  not be fulfilled.
To know this, and know that however ugly the parts appear the
  whole remains beautiful. A severed hand
Is an ugly thing, and man dissevered from the earth and stars
  and his history . . . for contemplation or in fact . . .
Often appears atrociously ugly. Integrity is wholeness, the greatest beauty is
Organic wholeness, the wholeness of life and things, the divine
  beauty of the universe. Love that, not man
Apart from that, or else you will share man's pitiful confusions,
  or drown in despair when his days darken.

LUTHER STANDING BEAR

S ome interesting elements in the Indian-white relationship are bound up in the
life of Luther Standing Bear (1868–1939). A Teton, or western Sioux, he was
born just as the War Department began its domination of U.S. Indian policy on
the plains. Thus, although he had a traditional upbringing, his culture was under
harassment and attack. In 1879, after the "Indian Wars" had died down, he was
enrolled in the first class at the Carlisle Indian School in Pennsylvania; there he
was a quick study, but the ethos of the place is shown clearly in the fact that when
his father came to visit, they had to have permission to speak in their native
language. After schooling, Standing Bear returned to the Lakota reservation in
South Dakota but left when reservation policy became too stifling. "I was a bad
Indian, and the agent and I never got on," he later wrote. He joined William F.
Cody's "Wild West Show" in 1902, eventually moved to California and found
work as a lecturer and movie actor, and finally, late in life, wrote My People the
Sioux (1928), My Indian Boyhood (1931), Land of the Spotted Eagle (1933), and Stories
of the Sioux (1934). Standing Bear thought Land of the Spotted Eagle, from which
the following is excerpted, his best book.

"Nature," part of chapter 7, "Indian Wisdom," from Land of the Spotted Eagle (1933)

The Lakota was a true naturist—a lover of Nature. He loved the earth
and all things of the earth, the attachment growing with age. The old
people came literally to love the soil and they sat or reclined on the
ground with a feeling of being close to a mothering power. It was good
for the skin to touch the earth and the old people liked to remove their
moccasins and walk with bare feet on the sacred earth. Their tipis were
built upon the earth and their altars were made of earth. The birds that
flew in the air came to rest upon the earth and it was the final abiding
place of all things that lived and grew. The soil was soothing, strengthening, cleansing, and healing.

This is why the old Indian still sits upon the earth instead of propping
himself up and away from its life-giving forces. For him, to sit or lie upon
the ground is to be able to think more deeply and to feel more keenly;
he can see more clearly into the mysteries of life and come closer in kinship to other lives about him.

The earth was full of sounds which the old-time Indian could hear, sometimes putting his ear to it so as to hear more clearly. The forefathers of the Lakotas had done this for long ages until there had come to them real understanding of earth ways. It was almost as if the man were still a part of the earth as he was in the beginning, according to the legend of the tribe. This beautiful story of the genesis of the Lakota people furnished the foundation for the love they bore for earth and all things of the earth. Wherever the Lakota went, he was with Mother Earth. No matter where he roamed by day or slept by night, he was safe with her. This thought comforted and sustained the Lakota and he was eternally filled with gratitude.

From Wakan Tanka there came a great unifying life force that flowed in and through all things—the flowers of the plains, blowing winds, rocks, trees, birds, animals—and was the same force that had been breathed into the first man. Thus all things were kindred and brought together by the same Great Mystery.

Kinship with all creatures of the earth, sky, and water was a real and active principle. For the animal and bird world there existed a brotherly feeling that kept the Lakota safe among them. And so close did some of the Lakotas come to their feathered and furred friends that in true brotherhood they spoke a common tongue.

The animal had rights—the right of man's protection, the right to live, the right to multiply, the right to freedom, and the right to man's indebtedness—and in recognition of these rights the Lakota never enslaved the animal, and spared all life that was not needed for food and clothing.

This concept of life and its relations was humanizing and gave to the Lakota an abiding love. It filled his being with the joy and mystery of living; it gave him reverence for all life; it made a place for all things in the scheme of existence with equal importance to all. The Lakota could despise no creature, for all were of one blood, made by the same hand, and filled with the essence of the Great Mystery. In spirit the Lakota was humble and meek. 'Blessed are the meek: for they shall inherit the earth,' was true for the Lakota, and from the earth he inherited secrets long since forgotten. His religion was sane, normal, and human.

Reflection upon life and its meaning, consideration of its wonders, and observation of the world of creatures, began with childhood. The earth, which was called *Maka*, and the sun, called *Anpetuwi*, represented two functions somewhat analogous to those of male and female. The earth brought forth life, but the warming, enticing rays of the sun coaxed it into being. The earth yielded, the sun engendered.

In talking to children, the old Lakota would place a hand on the ground and explain: 'We sit in the lap of our Mother. From her we, and all other living things, come. We shall soon pass, but the place where we now rest will last forever.' So we, too, learned to sit or lie on the ground and become conscious of life about us in its multitude of forms. Sometimes we boys would sit motionless and watch the swallow, the tiny ants, or perhaps some small animal at its work and ponder on its industry and ingenuity; or we lay on our backs and looked long at the sky and when the stars came out made shapes from the various groups. The morning and evening star always attracted attention, and the Milky Way was a path which was traveled by the ghosts. The old people told us to heed *wa maka skan*, which were the 'moving things of earth.' This meant, of course, the animals that lived and moved about, and the stories they told of *wa maka skan* increased our interest and delight. The wolf, duck, eagle, hawk, spider, bear, and other creatures, had marvelous powers, and each one was useful and helpful to us. Then there were the warriors who lived in the sky and dashed about on their spirited horses during a thunder storm, their lances clashing with the thunder and glittering with the lightning. There was *wiwila*, the living spirit of the spring, and the stones that flew like a bird and talked like a man. Everything was possessed of personality, only differing with us in form. Knowledge was inherent in all things. The world was a library and its books were the stones, leaves, grass, brooks, and the birds and animals that shared, alike with us, the storms and blessings of earth. We learned to do what only the student of nature ever learns, and that was to feel beauty. We never railed at the storms, the furious winds, and the biting frosts and snows. To do so intensified human futility, so whatever came we adjusted ourselves, by more effort and energy if necessary, but without complaint. Even the lightning did us no harm, for whenever it came too close, mothers and grandmothers in every tipi put cedar leaves on the coals and their magic kept danger away. Bright days and dark days were both expressions of the Great Mystery, and the Indian reveled in being close to the Big Holy. His worship was unalloyed, free from the fears of civilization.

I have come to know that the white mind does not feel toward nature as does the Indian mind, and it is because, I believe, of the difference in childhood instruction. I have often noticed white boys gathered in a city by-street or alley jostling and pushing one another in a foolish manner. They spend much time in this aimless fashion, their natural faculties neither seeing, hearing, nor feeling the varied life that surrounds them. There is about them no awareness, no acuteness, and it is this dullness that gives ugly mannerisms full play; it takes from them natural poise and stimulation. In contrast, Indian boys, who are naturally reared, are alert to their surroundings; their senses are not narrowed to observing only one another, and they cannot spend hours seeing nothing, hearing nothing, and thinking nothing in particular. Observation was certain in its rewards; interest, wonder, admiration grew, and the fact was appreciated that life was more than mere human manifestation; that it was expressed in a multitude of forms. This appreciation enriched Lakota existence. Life was vivid and pulsing; nothing was casual and commonplace. The Indian lived—lived in every sense of the word—from his first to his last breath.

The character of the Indian's emotion left little room in his heart for antagonism toward his fellow creatures, this attitude giving him what is sometimes referred to as 'the Indian point of view.' Every true student, every lover of nature has 'the Indian point of view,' but there are few such students, for few white men approach nature in the Indian manner. The Indian and the white man sense things differently because the white man has put distance between himself and nature; and assuming a lofty place in the scheme of order of things has lost for him both reverence and understanding. Consequently the white man finds Indian philosophy obscure—wrapped, as he says, in a maze of ideas and symbols which he does not understand. A writer friend, a white man whose knowledge of 'Injuns' is far more profound and sympathetic than the average, once said that he had been privileged, on two occasions, to see the contents of an Indian medicine-man's bag in which were bits of earth, feathers, stones, and various other articles of symbolic nature; that a 'collector' showed him one and laughed, but a great and world-famous archeologist showed him the other with admiration and wonder. Many times the Indian is embarrassed and baffled by the white man's allusions to nature in such terms as crude, primitive, wild, rude, untamed, and savage. For the Lakota, mountains, lakes, rivers, springs, valleys, and woods were all finished beauty; winds, rain, snow, sunshine, day, night, and change of seasons brought interests; birds, insects, and animals filled the world with knowledge that defied the discernment of man.

But nothing the Great Mystery placed in the land of the Indian pleased the white man, and nothing escaped his transforming hand. Wherever forests have not been mowed down; wherever the animal is recessed in their quiet protection; wherever the earth is not bereft of four-footed life— that to him is an 'unbroken wilderness.' But since for the Lakota there was no wilderness; since nature was not dangerous but hospitable; not forbidding but friendly, Lakota philosophy was healthy—free from fear and dogmatism. And here I find the great distinction between the faith of the Indian and the white man. Indian faith sought the harmony of man with his surroundings; the other sought the dominance of surroundings. In sharing, in loving all and everything, one people naturally found a measure of the thing they sought; while, in fearing, the other found need of conquest. For one man the world was full of beauty; for the other it was a place of sin and ugliness to be endured until he went to another world, there to become a creature of wings, half-man and half-bird. Forever one man directed his Mystery to change the world He had made; forever this man pleaded with Him to chastise His wicked ones; and forever he implored his Wakan Tanka to send His light to earth. Small wonder this man could not understand the other.

But the old Lakota was wise. He knew that man's heart, away from nature, becomes hard; he knew that lack of respect for growing, living things soon led to lack of respect for humans too. So he kept his youth close to its softening influence.

JOHN STEINBECK

It fell to John Steinbeck (1902–1968) to record the final breakdown of the agrarian dream—its poignant improbability under corporate America. The little place that Lennie and George dream of in *Of Mice and Men* (1937), where they can work together and "live off the fatta the lan'," is gone now—or is it? The Joads, in *The Grapes of Wrath*, flee the Dust Bowl and hope to have, or at least work in, one of the abundant fruit orchards of California. The dream peters out in a Depression migrant labor camp, but some members of the family make an important step: They begin to see that they are part of a greater family. With that realization, this book says that the dream of community is still alive. In the writing of one of the great American novels, Steinbeck was much influenced by two friends, the biologist Edward Ricketts and the farm-labor organizer Tom Collins. Ricketts, whom he had known since 1930, taught Steinbeck a great deal about patient, objective observation; Collins, whose brave experience in the migrant camps Steinbeck deeply respected, provided facts and an interpretation behind the farmland scenes Steinbeck observed as he toured the San Joaquin Valley gathering material for a newspaper series. But the synthesis of eye and heart, the making of the novel, was all the author's. He wrote the final draft of the book in an exhausting six months, on fire with the truth of it.

Chapters 1, 2, and 3, from *The Grapes of Wrath* (1939)

Chapter 1

To the red country and part of the gray country of Oklahoma, the last rains came gently, and they did not cut the scarred earth. The plows crossed and recrossed the rivulet marks. The last rains lifted the corn quickly and scattered weed colonies and grass along the sides of the roads so that the gray country and the dark red country began to disappear under a green cover. In the last part of May the sky grew pale and the clouds that had hung in high puffs for so long in the spring were dissipated. The sun flared down on the growing corn day after day until a line of brown spread along the edge of each green bayonet. The clouds appeared, and went away, and in a while they did not try anymore. The weeds grew darker green to protect themselves, and they did not spread anymore. The surface of the earth crusted, a thin hard crust, and as the sky became pale, so the earth became pale, pink in the red country and white in the gray country.

In the water-cut gullies the earth dusted down in dry little streams. Gophers and ant lions started small avalanches. And as the sharp sun struck day after day, the leaves of the young corn became less stiff and erect; they bent in a curve at first, and then, as the central ribs of strength grew weak, each leaf tilted downward. Then it was June, and the sun shone more fiercely. The brown lines on the corn leaves widened and moved in on the central ribs. The weeds frayed and edged back toward their roots. The air was thin and the sky more pale; and every day the earth paled.

In the roads where the teams moved, where the wheels milled the ground and the hooves of the horses beat the ground, the dirt crust broke and the dust formed. Every moving thing lifted the dust into the air: a walking man lifted a thin layer as high as his waist, and a wagon lifted the dust as high as the fence tops, and an automobile boiled a cloud behind it. The dust was long in settling back again.

When June was half-gone, the big clouds moved up out of Texas and the Gulf, high heavy clouds, rain heads. The men in the fields looked up at the clouds and sniffed at them and held wet fingers up to sense the wind. And the horses were nervous while the clouds were up. The rain heads dropped a little spattering and hurried on to some other country. Behind them the sky was pale again and the sun flared. In the dust there were drop craters where the rain had fallen, and there were clean splashes on the corn, and that was all.

A gentle wind followed the rain clouds, driving them on northward, a wind that softly clashed the drying corn. A day went by and the wind increased, steady, unbroken by gusts. The dust from the roads fluffed up and spread out and fell on the weeds beside the fields, and fell into the fields a little way. Now the wind grew strong and hard and it worked at the rain crust in the cornfields. Little by little the sky was darkened by the mixing dust, and the wind felt over the earth, loosened the dust, and carried it away. The wind grew stronger. The rain crust broke and the dust lifted up out of the fields and drove gray plumes into the air like sluggish smoke. The corn threshed the wind and made a dry, rushing sound. The finest dust did not settle back to earth now, but disappeared into the darkening sky.

The wind grew stronger, whisked under stones, carried up straws and old leaves, and even little clods, marking its course as it sailed across the fields. The air and the sky darkened and through them the sun shone redly, and there was a raw sting in the air. During a night the wind raced faster over the land, dug cunningly among the rootlets of the corn, and the corn fought the wind with its weakened leaves until the roots were freed by the prying wind and then each stalk settled wearily sideways toward the earth and pointed the direction of the wind.

The dawn came, but no day. In the gray sky a red sun appeared, a dim red circle that gave a little light, like dusk; and as that day advanced, the dusk slipped back toward darkness, and the wind cried and whimpered over the fallen corn.

Men and women huddled in their houses, and they tied handkerchiefs over their noses when they went out, and wore goggles to protect their eyes.

When the night came again it was black night, for the stars could not pierce the dust to get down, and the window lights could not even spread beyond their own yards. Now the dust was evenly mixed with the air, an emulsion of dust and air. Houses were shut tight, and cloth wedged around doors and windows, but the dust came in so thinly that it could not be seen in the air, and it settled like pollen on the chairs and tables, on the dishes. The people brushed it from their shoulders. Little lines of dust lay at the doorsills.

In the middle of that night the wind passed on and left the land quiet. The dust-filled air muffled sound more completely than fog does. The people, lying in their beds, heard the wind stop. They awakened when the rushing wind was gone. They lay quietly and listened deep into the stillness. Then the roosters crowed, and their voices were muffled, and the people stirred restlessly in their beds and wanted the morning. They knew it would take a long time for the dust to settle out of the air. In the morning the dust hung like fog, and the sun was as red as ripe new blood. All day the dust sifted down from the sky, and the next day it sifted down. An even blanket covered the earth. It settled on the corn, piled up on the tops of the fence posts, piled up on the wires; it settled on roofs, blanketed the weeds and trees.

The people came out of their houses and smelled the hot stinging air and covered their noses from it. And the children came out of the houses, but they did not run or shout as they would have done after a rain. Men stood by their fences and looked at the ruined corn, drying fast now, only a little green showing through the film of dust. The men were silent and they did not move often. And the women came out of the houses to stand beside their men—to feel whether this time the men would break. The women studied the men's faces secretly, for the corn could go, as long as something else remained. The children stood nearby, drawing figures in the dust with bare toes, and the children sent exploring senses out to see whether men and women would break. The children peeked at the faces of the men and women, and then drew careful lines in the dust with their toes. Horses came to the watering troughs and nuzzled the water to clear the surface dust. After a while the faces of the watching men lost their bemused perplexity and became hard and angry and resistant. Then the women knew that they were safe and that there was no break. Then they asked, What'll we do? And the men replied, I don't know. But it was all right. The women knew it was all right, and the watching children knew it was all right. Women and children knew deep in themselves that no misfortune was too great to bear if their men were whole. The women went into the houses to their work, and the children began to play, but cautiously at first. As the day went forward the sun became less red. It flared down on the dust-blanketed land. The men sat in the doorways of their houses; their hands were busy with sticks and little rocks. The men sat still—thinking—figuring.

Chapter 2

A huge red transport truck stood in front of the little roadside restaurant. The vertical exhaust pipe muttered softly, and an almost invisible haze of steel-blue smoke hovered over its end. It was a new truck, shining red, and in twelve-inch letters on its sides—OKLAHOMA CITY TRANSPORT COMPANY. Its double tires were new, and a brass padlock stood straight out from the hasp on the big back doors. Inside the screened restaurant a radio played, quiet dance music turned low the way it is when no one is listening. A small outlet fan turned silently in its circular hole over the entrance, and flies buzzed excitedly about the doors and windows, butting the screens. Inside, one man, the truck driver, sat on a stool and rested his elbows on the counter and looked over his coffee at the lean and lonely waitress. He talked the smart listless language of the roadsides to her. "I seen him about three months ago. He had a operation. Cut somepin out. I forget what." And she—"Doesn't seem no longer ago than a week I seen him myself. Looked fine then. He's a nice sort of a guy when he ain't stinko." Now and then the flies roared softly at the screen door. The coffee machine spurted steam, and the waitress, without looking, reached behind her and shut it off.

Outside, a man walking along the edge of the highway crossed over and approached the truck. He walked slowly to the front of it, put his hand on the shiny fender, and looked at the *No Riders* sticker on the windshield. For a moment he was about to walk on down the road, but instead he sat on the running board on the side away from the restaurant. He was not over thirty. His eyes were very dark brown and there was a hint of brown pigment in his eyeballs. His cheekbones were high and wide, and strong deep lines cut down his cheeks, in curves beside his mouth. His upper lip was long, and since his teeth protruded, the lips stretched to cover them, for this man kept his lips closed. His hands were hard, with broad fingers and nails as thick and ridged as little clamshells. The space between thumb and forefinger and the hams of his hands were shiny with callus.

The man's clothes were new—all of them, cheap and new. His gray cap was so new that the visor was still stiff and the button still on, not shapeless and bulged as it would be when it had served for a while all the various purposes of a cap—carrying sack, towel, handkerchief. His suit was of cheap gray hardcloth and so new that there were creases in the trousers. His blue chambray shirt was stiff and smooth with filler. The coat was too big, the trousers too short, for he was a tall man. The coat shoulder peaks hung down on his arms, and even then the sleeves were too short and the front of the coat flapped loosely over his stomach. He wore a pair of new tan shoes of the kind called "army last," hobnailed and with half-circles like horseshoes to protect the edges of the heels from wear. This man sat on the running board and took off his cap and mopped his face with it. Then he put on the cap, and by pulling started the future ruin of the visor. His feet caught his attention. He leaned down and loosened the shoelaces, and did not tie the ends again. Over his head the exhaust of the diesel engine whispered in quick puffs of blue smoke.

The music stopped in the restaurant and a man's voice spoke from the loudspeaker, but the waitress did not turn him off, for she didn't know the music had stopped. Her exploring fingers had found a lump under her ear. She was trying to see it in a mirror behind the counter without letting the truck driver know, and so she pretended to push a bit of hair to neatness. The truck driver said, "They was a big dance in Shawnee. I heard somebody got killed or somepin. You hear anything?" "No," said the waitress, and she lovingly fingered the lump under her ear.

Outside, the seated man stood up and looked over the cowl of the truck and watched the restaurant for a moment. Then he settled back on the running board, pulled a sack of tobacco and a book of papers from his side pocket. He rolled his cigarette slowly and perfectly, studied it, smoothed it. At last he lighted it and pushed the burning match into the dust at his feet. The sun cut into the shade of the truck as noon approached.

In the restaurant the truck driver paid his bill and put his two nickels' change in a slot machine. The whirling cylinders gave him no score. "They fix 'em so you can't win nothing," he said to the waitress.

And she replied, "Guy took the jackpot not two hours ago. Three-eighty he got. How soon you gonna be back by?"

He held the screen door a little open. "Week-ten days," he said. "Got to make a run to Tulsa, an' I never get back soon as I think."

She said crossly, "Don't let the flies in. Either go out or come in."

"So long," he said, and pushed his way out. The screen door banged behind him. He stood in the sun, peeling the wrapper from a piece of gum. He was a heavy man, broad in the shoulders, thick in the stomach. His face was red and his blue eyes long and slitted from having squinted always at sharp light. He wore army trousers and high laced boots. Holding the stick of gum in front of his lips he called through the screen, "Well, don't do nothing you don't want me to hear about." The waitress was turned toward a mirror on the back wall. She grunted a reply. The truck driver gnawed down the stick of gum slowly, opening his jaws and lips wide with each bite. He shaped the gum in his mouth, rolled it under his tongue while he walked to the big red truck.

The hitchhiker stood up and looked across through the windows. "Could ya give me a lift, Mister?"

The driver looked quickly back at the restaurant for a second. "Didn't you see the *No Riders* sticker on the win'shield?"

"Sure—I seen it. But sometimes a guy'll be a good guy even if some rich bastard makes him carry a sticker."

The driver, getting slowly into the truck, considered the parts of this answer. If he refused now, not only was he not a good guy, but he was forced to carry a sticker, was not allowed to have company. If he took in the hitchhiker he was automatically a good guy and also he was not one whom any rich bastard could kick around. He knew he was being trapped, but he couldn't see a way out. And he wanted to be a good guy. He glanced again at the restaurant. "Scrunch down on the running board till we get around the bend," he said.

The hitchhiker flopped down out of sight and clung to the door handle. The motor roared up for a moment, the gears clicked in, and the great truck moved away, first gear, second gear, third gear, and then a high whining pickup and fourth gear. Under the clinging man the highway blurred dizzily by. It was a mile to the first turn in the road, then the truck slowed down. The hitchhiker stood up, eased the door open, and slipped into the seat. The driver looked over at him, slitting his eyes, and he chewed as though thoughts and impressions were being sorted and arranged by his jaws before they were finally filed away in his brain. His eyes began at the new cap, moved down the new clothes to the new shoes. The hitchhiker squirmed his back against the seat in comfort, took off his cap, and swabbed his sweating forehead and chin with it. "Thanks, buddy," he said. "My dogs was pooped out."

"New shoes," said the driver. His voice had the same quality of secrecy and insinuation his eyes had. "You oughtn' to take no walk in new shoes—hot weather."

The hiker looked down at the dusty yellow shoes. "Didn't have no other shoes," he said. "Guy got to wear 'em if he got no others."

The driver squinted judiciously ahead and built up the speed of the truck a little. "Goin' far?"

"Uh-uh! I'd a walked her if my dogs wasn't pooped out."

The questions of the driver had the tone of a subtle examination. He seemed to spread nets, to set traps with his questions. "Lookin' for a job?" he asked.

"No, my old man got a place, forty acres. He's a cropper, but we been there a long time."

The driver looked significantly at the fields along the road where the corn was fallen sideways and the dust was piled on it. Little flints shoved through the dusty soil. The driver said, as though to himself, "A forty-acre cropper and he ain't been dusted out and he ain't been tractored out?"

" 'Course I ain't heard lately," said the hitchhiker.

"Long time," said the driver. A bee flew into the cab and buzzed in back of the windshield. The driver put out his hand and carefully drove the bee into an airstream that blew in out of the window. "Croppers going fast now," he said. "One cat' takes and shoves ten families out. Cat's all over hell now. Tear in and shove the croppers out. How's your old man hold on?" His tongue and his jaws became busy with the neglected gum, turned it and chewed it. With each opening of his mouth his tongue could be seen flipping the gum over.

"Well, I ain't heard lately. I never was no hand to write, nor my old man neither." He added quickly, "But the both of us can, if we want."

"Been doing a job?" Again the secret investigating casualness. He looked out over the fields, at the shimmering air, and gathering his gum into his cheek, out of the way, he spat out the window.

"Sure have," said the hitchhiker.

"Thought so. I seen your hands. Been swingin' a pick or an ax or a sledge. That shines up your hands. I notice all stuff like that. Take a pride in it."

The hitchhiker stared at him. The truck tires sang on the road. "Like to know anything else? I'll tell you. You ain't got to guess."

"Now don't get sore. I wasn't gettin' nosy."

"I'll tell you anything. I ain't hidin' nothin'."

"Now don't get sore. I just like to notice things. Makes the time pass."

"I'll tell you anything. Name's Joad, Tom Joad. Old man is ol' Tom Joad." His eyes rested broodingly on the driver.

"Don't get sore. I didn't mean nothin'."

"I don't mean nothin' neither," said Joad. "I'm just tryin' to get along without shovin' nobody around." He stopped and looked out at the dry fields, at the starved tree clumps hanging uneasily in the heated distance. From his side pocket he brought out his tobacco and papers. He rolled his cigarette down between his knees, where the wind could not get at it.

The driver chewed as rhythmically, as thoughtfully, as a cow. He waited to let the whole emphasis of the preceding passage disappear and be forgotten. At last, when the air seemed neutral again, he said, "A guy that never been a truck skinner don't know nothin' what it's like. Owners don't want us to pick up nobody. So we got to set here an' just skin her along 'less we want to take a chance of gettin' fired like I just done with you."

" 'Preciate it," said Joad.

"I've knew guys that done screwy things while they're drivin' trucks. I remember a guy use' to make up poetry. It passed the time." He looked over secretly to see whether Joad was interested or amazed. Joad was silent, looking into the distance ahead, along the road, along the white road that waved gently, like a ground swell. The driver went on at last, "I remember a piece of poetry this here guy wrote down. It was about him an' a couple other guys goin' all over the world drinkin' and raisin' hell and screwin' around. I wisht I could remember how that piece went. This guy had words in it that Jesus H. Christ wouldn't know what they meant. Part was like this: 'An' there we spied a nigger, with a trigger that was bigger than a elephant's proboscis or the whanger of a whale.' That proboscis is a nose-like. With a elephant it's his trunk. Guy showed me in a dictionary. Carried that dictionary all over hell with him. He'd look in it while he's pulled up gettin' his pie an' coffee." He stopped, feeling lonely in the long speech. His secret eyes turned on his passenger. Joad remained silent. Nervously the driver tried to force him into participation. "Ever know a guy that said big words like that?"

"Preacher," said Joad.

"Well, it makes you mad to hear a guy use big words. 'Course with a preacher it's all right because nobody would fool around with a preacher anyway. But this guy was funny. You didn't give a damn when he said a big word 'cause he just done it for ducks. He wasn't puttin' on no dog." The driver was reassured. He knew at least that Joad was listening. He swung the great truck viciously around a bend and the tires shrilled. "Like I was sayin'," he continued, "guy that drives a truck does

screwy things. He got to. He'd go nuts just settin' here an' the road
sneakin' under the wheels. Fella says once that truck skinners eats all the
time—all the time in hamburger joints along the road."

"Sure seem to live there," Joad agreed.

"Sure they stop, but it ain't to eat. They ain't hardly ever hungry.
They're just goddamn sick of goin'—get sick of it. Joints is the only place
you can pull up, an' when you stop you got to buy somepin so you can
sling the bull with the broad behind the counter. So you get a cup a coffee
and a piece pie. Kind of gives a guy a little rest." He chewed his gum
slowly and turned it with his tongue.

"Must be tough," said Joad with no emphasis.

The driver glanced quickly at him, looking for satire. "Well, it ain't
no goddamn cinch," he said testily. "Looks easy, jus' settin' here till you
put in your eight or maybe your ten or fourteen hours. But the road gets
into a guy. He's got to do somepin. Some sings an' some whistles. Company won't let us have no radio. A few takes a pint along, but them kind
don't stick long." He said the last smugly. "I don't never take a drink till
I'm through."

"Yeah?" Joad asked.

"Yeah! A guy got to get ahead. Why, I'm thinkin' of takin' one of
them correspondence school courses. Mechanical engineering. It's easy.
Just study a few easy lessons at home. I'm thinkin' of it. Then I won't
drive no truck. Then I'll tell other guys to drive trucks."

Joad took a pint of whiskey from his side coat pocket. "Sure you won't
have a snort?" His voice was teasing.

"No, by God. I won't touch it. A guy can't drink liquor all the time
and study like I'm goin' to."

Joad uncorked the bottle, took two quick swallows, recorked it,
and put it back in his pocket. The spicy hot smell of the whiskey filled
the cab. "You're all wound up," said Joad. "What's the matter—got a
girl?"

"Well, sure. But I want to get ahead anyway. I been training my mind
for a hell of a long time."

The whiskey seemed to loosen Joad up. He rolled another cigarette
and lighted it. "I ain't got a hell of a lot further to go," he said.

The driver went on quickly. "I don't need no shot," he said. "I train
my mind all the time. I took a course in that two years ago." He patted
the steering wheel with his right hand. "Suppose I pass a guy on the
road. I look at him, an' after I'm past I try to remember ever'thing about
him, kind a clothes an' shoes an' hat, an' how he walked an' maybe how
tall an' what weight an' any scars. I do it pretty good. I can jus' make a
whole picture in my head. Sometimes I think I ought to take a course to

be a fingerprint expert. You'd be su'prised how much a guy can remember."

Joad took a quick drink from the flask. He dragged the last smoke from his raveling cigarette and then, with callused thumb and forefinger, crushed out the glowing end. He rubbed the butt to a pulp and put it out the window, letting the breeze suck it from his fingers. The big tires sang a high note on the pavement. Joad's dark quiet eyes became amused as he stared along the road. The driver waited and glanced uneasily over. At last Joad's long upper lip grinned up from his teeth and he chuckled silently, his chest jerked with the chuckles. "You sure took a hell of a long time to get to it, buddy."

The driver did not look over. "Get to what? How do you mean?"

Joad's lips stretched tight over his long teeth for a moment, and he licked his lips like a dog, two licks, one in each direction from the middle. His voice became harsh. "You know what I mean. You give me a goin'-over when I first got in. I seen you." The driver looked straight ahead, gripped the wheel so tightly that the pads of his palms bulged, and the backs of his hands paled. Joad continued, "You know where I come from." The driver was silent. "Don't you?" Joad insisted.

"Well—sure. That is—maybe. But it ain't none of my business. I mind my own yard. It ain't nothing to me." The words tumbled out now. "I don't stick my nose in nobody's business." And suddenly he was silent and waiting. And his hands were still white on the wheel. A grasshopper flipped through the window and lighted on top of the instrument panel, where it sat and began to scrape its wings with its angled jumping legs. Joad reached forward and crushed its hard skull-like head with his fingers, and he let it into the wind stream out the window. Joad chuckled again while he brushed the bits of broken insect from his fingertips. "You got me wrong, Mister," he said. "I ain't keepin' quiet about it. Sure I been in McAlester. Been there four years. Sure these is the clothes they give me when I come out. I don't give a damn who knows it. An' I'm goin' to my ole man's place so I don't have to lie to get a job."

The driver said, "Well—that ain't none of my business. I ain't a nosy guy."

"The hell you ain't," said Joad. "That big old nose of yours been stickin' out eight miles ahead of your face. You had that big nose goin' over me like a sheep in a vegetable patch."

The driver's face tightened. "You got me all wrong—" he began weakly.

Joad laughed at him. "You been a good guy. You give me a lift. Well, hell! I done time. So what! You want to know what I done time for, don't you?"

"That ain't none of my affair."

"Nothin' ain't none of your affair except skinnin' this here bull bitch along, an' that's the least thing you work at. Now look. See that road up ahead?"

"Yeah."

"Well, I get off there. Sure, I know you're wettin' your pants to know what I done. I ain't a guy to let you down." The high hum of the motor dulled and the song of the tires dropped in pitch. Joad got out his pint and took another short drink. The truck drifted to a stop where a dirt road opened at right angles to the highway. Joad got out and stood beside the cab window. The vertical exhaust pipe puttered up its barely visible blue smoke. Joad leaned toward the driver. "Homicide," he said quickly. "That's a big word—means I killed a guy. Seven years. I'm sprung in four for keepin' my nose clean."

The driver's eyes slipped over Joad's face to memorize it. "I never asked you nothin' about it," he said. "I mind my own yard."

"You can tell about it in every joint from here to Texola." He smiled. "So long, fella. You been a good guy. But look, when you been in stir a little while, you can smell a question comin' from hell to breakfast. You telegraphed yours the first time you opened your trap." He spatted the metal door with the palm of his hand. "Thanks for the lift," he said. "So long." He turned away and walked into the dirt road.

For a moment the driver stared after him, and then he called, "Luck!" Joad waved his hand without looking around. Then the motor roared up and the gears clicked and the great red truck rolled heavily away.

Chapter 3

The concrete highway was edged with a mat of tangled, broken, dry grass, and the grass heads were heavy with oat beards to catch on a dog's coat, and foxtails to tangle in a horse's fetlocks, and clover burrs to fasten in sheep's wool; sleeping life waiting to be spread and dispersed, every seed armed with an appliance of dispersal, twisting darts and parachutes for the wind, little spears and balls of tiny thorns, and all waiting for animals and for the wind, for a man's trouser cuff or the hem of a woman's skirt, all passive but armed with appliances of activity, still, but each possessed of the anlage of movement.

The sun lay on the grass and warmed it, and in the shade under the grass the insects moved, ants and ant lions to set traps for them, grasshoppers to jump into the air and flick their yellow wings for a second, sow bugs like little armadillos, plodding restlessly on many tender feet. And over the grass at the roadside a land turtle crawled, turning aside for nothing, dragging his high-domed shell over the grass. His hard legs and yellow-nailed feet threshed slowly through the grass, not really walking, but boosting and dragging his shell along. The barley beards slid off his shell, and the clover burrs fell on him and rolled to the ground. His horny beak was partly open, and his fierce, humorous eyes, under brows like fingernails, stared straight ahead. He came over the grass leaving a beaten trail behind him, and the hill, which was the highway embankment, reared up ahead of him. For a moment he stopped, his head held high. He blinked and looked up and down. At last he started to climb the embankment. Front clawed feet reached forward but did not touch. The hind feet kicked his shell along, and it scraped on the grass, and on the gravel. As the embankment grew steeper and steeper, the more frantic were the efforts of the land turtle. Pushing hind legs strained and slipped, boosting the shell along, and the horny head protruded as far as the neck could stretch. Little by little the shell slid up the embankment until at last a parapet cut straight across its line of march, the shoulder of the road, a concrete wall four inches high. As though they worked independently the hind legs pushed the shell against the wall. The head upraised and peered over the wall to the broad smooth plain of cement. Now the hands, braced on top of the wall, strained and lifted, and the shell came slowly up and rested its front end on the wall. For a moment the turtle rested. A red ant ran into the shell, into the soft skin inside the shell, and suddenly head and legs snapped in, and the armored tail clamped in sideways. The red ant was crushed between body and legs. And one head of wild oats was clamped into the shell by a front leg. For a long moment the turtle lay still, and then the neck crept out and the old humorous frowning eyes looked about and the legs and tail came out. The back legs went to work, straining like elephant legs, and the shell tipped to an angle so that the front legs could not reach the level cement plain. But higher and higher the hind legs boosted it, until at last the center of balance was reached, the front tipped down, the front legs scratched at the pavement, and it was up. But the head of wild oats was held by its stem around the front legs.

Now the going was easy, and all the legs worked, and the shell boosted along, waggling from side to side. A sedan driven by a forty-year-old woman approached. She saw the turtle and swung to the right, off the highway, the wheels screamed and a cloud of dust boiled up. Two wheels lifted for a moment and then settled. The car skidded back onto the road, and went on, but more slowly. The turtle had jerked into its shell, but now it hurried on, for the highway was burning hot.

And now a light truck approached, and as it came near, the driver saw the turtle and swerved to hit it. His front wheel struck the edge of the shell, flipped the turtle like a tiddlywink, spun it like a coin, and rolled it off the highway. The truck went back to its course along the right side. Lying on its back, the turtle was tight in its shell for a long time. But at last its legs waved in the air, reaching for something to pull it over. Its front foot caught a piece of quartz and little by little the shell pulled over and flopped upright. The wild oat head fell out and three spearhead seeds stuck in the ground. And as the turtle crawled on down the embankment, its shell dragged dirt over the seeds. The turtle entered a dust road and jerked itself along, drawing a wavy shallow trench in the dust with its shell. The old humorous eyes looked ahead, and the horny beak opened a little. His yellow toenails slipped a fraction in the dust.

A. B. GUTHRIE JR.

he "Mountain Man" is a temptingly heroic figure. Historically he lived in freedom and danger and under a requirement of absolute self-reliance that altogether shrink the cowboy's much written-about wage-earner's life. About half
of the mountain men (beaver trappers, in prose) met violent ends in the wilderness; some were writers and even sort-of philosophers. Their day was short,
roughly 1822 to 1845 or so, though a few held on for more years of solo adventure. With the beaver trapped out, they became guides for safari hunters and
wagon trains; a few became prospectors; or they went back east and took up a
farm. Their course is somehow very American, spanning the nineteenth century,
and there is no missing the resonance in Guthrie's name for his protagonist: Boone.
The temptation in the mountain man story is to glory in the bright romance of
life in the wilderness, to the exclusion of the shadows and contradictions that are
in real life and that are gone into in great fiction. So careful a novelist as Vardis
Fisher, as recently as his *Mountain Man* (New York, 1965), made his title character
a non-credible romance hero. A. B. Guthrie Jr. (1901–1991), a Montanan who'd
had years of Kentucky newspaper work and a Neiman Fellowship to Harvard
under his belt, refused the easy road. He had a theme, he wrote later: Each man
kills the thing he loves. Here we see his character Boone Caudill at a crucial,
character-revealing time of decision.

Chapters 31 and 32, from *The Big Sky* (1947)

Chapter 31

A man could sit and let time run on while he smoked or cut on a stick
with nothing nagging him and the squaws going about their business and
the young ones playing, making out that they warred on the Assiniboines.
He could let time run on, Boone thought while he sat and let it run, and
feel his skin drink the sunshine in and watch the breeze skipping in the
grass and see the moon like a bright horn in the sky by night. One day
and another it was pretty much the same, and it was all good. The sun
came up big in the fall mornings and climbed warm and small and got
bigger again as it dropped, and the slow clouds sailed red after it had
gone from sight. There was meat to spare, and beaver still to trap if a
man wanted to put himself out. In the summer the Piegans went to buffalo

and later pitched camp close to Fort McKenzie and traded for whisky and tobacco and blankets and cloth and moved on to the Marias or the Teton or the Sun or the Three Forks for a little trapping and the long, lazy winter.

If the beaver were few, buffalo still were plenty, for all that the Piegans slaughtered more and more of them just so's to have hides to trade. Boone had seen regular herds of them chased over the steep bluffs that the Indians called *pishkuns* and lying at the bottom afterwards with broken necks or standing or lunging on three legs while the hunters rode among them with battleaxes and bows and arrows, and then the squaws, chattering and happy, following up with their knives and getting bloody and not caring, and everybody taking a mouth of raw meat now and then and all feeling good because they had something to set by for winter.

Boone drew slow on his pipe while his eye took in the meat drying on the racks and the squaws working with the skins and the lodges pitched around. A dog came up and got a whiff of his tobacco and made a nose and backed up and by and by went on. Off a little piece Heavy Runner lay in front of his lodge with his head in his squaw's lap. The squaw was going through his hair with her fingers, looking for lice and cracking them between her teeth when she found any. In other lodges medicine men thumped on drums and shook buffalo-bladder rattles to drive the evil spirits out of the sick. They made a noise that a man got so used to that he hardly took notice of it.

It was a good life, the Piegan's life was. There were buffalo hunts and sometimes skirmishes with the Crows and Sioux, or the Nepercy who came from across the mountains to hunt Blackfoot buffalo, being as they didn't have any of their own; the sun heated a man in the summer and the winter put a chill in his bones, so that he kept close by his fire and ate jerked meat and pemmican if need be and looked often to the western sky for the low bank of clouds that would mean a warm wind was coming. Life went along one day after another as it had for five seasons now, and the days went together and lost themselves in one another. Looking back, it was as if time ran into itself and flowed over, running forward from past times and running back from now so that yesterday and today were the same. Or maybe time didn't flow at all but just stood still while a body moved around in it. A man hunted or fought, and sat smoking and talking at night, and after a while the camp went silent except for the dogs taking a notion to answer to the wolves, and so then he went in and lay with his woman, and it was all he could ask, just to be living like this, with his belly satisfied and himself free and his mind peaceful and in his lodge a woman to suit him.

Boone didn't guess, though, that Jim ever would be shut of fret the way he was, maybe because Jim never had found a squaw that wore good with him. Jim was forever pulling up and going somewhere, to Union or Pierre or St. Louis. Boone had traveled a considerable himself, but not to places where people were; he went into the mountains or across to British country or north into Canada where the Gros Ventres lived when they weren't on the move. He liked free country, with no more than some Indians about, and his squaw.

When Jim came back from a trip he was full of talk about new forts along the river and new people moving out from the settlements and the farmers in Missouri palavering about Oregon and California, as if the mountains were a prime place for plows and pigs and corn. When Jim went on too long that way, Boone cut him off, not wanting to be bothered with fool talk that stirred a man up inside.

Jim always seemed glad to be back, even if he was always setting out again. His face would light up when he saw Boone, and his hand was warm and strong and his mouth smiling. When he looked at Teal Eye it was as if he wished her double was around somewhere. Boone would catch just a gleam in his blue eye sometimes, or a kind of long, slow look that would make a man flare up if he didn't know Teal Eye so well, that maybe would put blood in his eye if Jim wasn't his friend.

Teal Eye was the woman for Boone. He reckoned he never would take a second woman in his lodge, and never have to cut Teal Eye's nose off, either, the way a Piegan did when he found his woman had lain in secret with another man. It was a sight, the squaws you saw with no end to their noses. Cut-nose women, they were called. They went around like nigger slaves, not having a man any longer or any proper home.

Teal Eye suited him all right. There wasn't any sense in a man nosing around like a bull, or wanting to cover every new woman just from being curious. One woman was enough, if she was the right one. Teal Eye never whined or scolded or tried to make a man something else than what he was by nature, but just took him and did her work and was happy. She had got a little heavier lately but was still well-turned in her body, with sharp, full breasts and a flat stomach and legs slim and quick as a deer's. Most squaws aged early, looking pretty just when the first bloom was on them and then drying up or going all to flesh, but not Teal Eye, maybe because she never had caught herself a baby. Looking at her, Boone couldn't tell much difference from five seasons back when he had found her on the Teton with Red Horn. He couldn't tell much difference, even, from the *Mandan* time, except that she was a woman now and rounded out as a woman ought to be. Her face was still slim and delicate, and her eyes melting and her spirit quick and cheerful and her body graceful. What she cared about most was to please him. She watched while he ate the meat or tried a new pair of moccasins and showed pleasure in her face when he grunted an all right. And she was always ready for him when his body was hungry, not lying still and spraddled, either, like a shot doe, but joining in, unashamed, her legs smooth and warm and strong and her breath whispering in his ear.

Boone uncrossed one leg and stretched it out before him and studied the moccasin he wore. Teal Eye had put a decoration of colored porcupine quills on it, arranging them neat and in a nice pattern. She had tanned the leather for this foot white and for the right foot yellow, so that a person not knowing Piegan ways would think the moccasins didn't match. They were slick shoes, he thought, while his mind went to wishing that Jim would come back soon from St. Louis. He felt better with Jim around. There was more spirit in him, and he laughed oftener. There wasn't anyone could find fun like Jim, or set a man's head to working so. When he thought of it, it was as if Jim was a part of all the life he liked, as if he always had been ever since they had met up on the road between Frankfort and Louisville, and Jim uneasy with the dead body in his wagon. Take Jim away and Boone felt there was something wanting, though he still wouldn't trade his way of living for any he ever knew or heard tell of. When Jim came back, it was as if all was well again. A man went with the feeling inside him that everything was right and just about as he would order it if it was his to order. Jim ought to be back soon, Boone figured, from going down the river with a boat of furs. It could be he had made up his mind to stay the winter in the settlements and to come back in the spring when the flood water would float steamboats to Fort Union and farther. Boone reckoned not, though. Jim never stayed away for a long stretch. Likely he would come overland, maybe with a party of mountain men who had spent their beaver. For all his traipsing around, Jim was a true mountain man, with the life showing in his face and in the set of his shoulders and legs and the way of his walk.

The wind was moving out of the west, as it nearly always did, sometimes hard and sometimes easy but nearly always moving. A shadow fell on the land, and lightning flickered and thunder sounded, and a big splash of rain fell on the hand Boone held his pipe with. The Piegans spent a heap of time inside their lodges. He liked to sit outside where the sun could hit him and the breeze get at him. Sometimes he put himself in mind of the menfolk back in Kentucky, sitting around the door while the day turned by, only he didn't have a hickory chair and wouldn't sit in it if he had. A man got so he didn't feel right unless seated crosslegged. The rain wouldn't be but a drop or two. Already the cloud was sailing over him, passing on east.

Boone knocked out his pipe and sat still, letting time run by. Each part of time was good in itself, if a man knew to enjoy it and didn't press for it to pass so as to get ahead to something different.

By and by Red Horn came along and sat down by him, not speaking until he got his pipe going. Red Horn's eyes seemed to get sharper with the years, and his nose higher and more hooked. The wrinkles were like cuts at the side of his mouth though he wasn't old yet. He made Boone think of an eagle, except he didn't bite or claw any more. The hand he held the pipe with lacked the joint of one finger. He had cut it off, along with his hair, when old Heavy Otter died of the smallpox.

"We have meat enough, and hides," said Red Horn, speaking the Blackfoot tongue that Boone knew almost as well as white men's talk.

"More hides than meat."

Red Horn puffed on his pipe.

"The buffalo die fast, Red Horn."

"They are plenty."

"They die fast, with hunters killing them for hides alone."

Red Horn hunched his shoulders. "They are more now than before the big sickness. We need robes to trade."

"I hope we never want for meat."

The lines in Red Horn's face deepened. He spread his hands, as if there was no use in anything. "The buffalo will last while the Indian lasts. Then we do not care. The buffalo cannot die faster than the Indian."

"We do well enough."

"The white Piegan does not know. He did not see the Piegans when their lodges were many and their warriors strong. We are a few now, and we are weak and tired, and our men drink the strong water and will not go far from the white man's trading house. They quarrel with one another. The white man's sickness kills them. We are like Sheepeaters. We are poor and sick and afraid."

"The nation will grow strong. The white man will leave us. We shall be many and have buffalo and beaver and live as the old ones lived."

Red Horn grunted and took the pipe from his lips to speak. "Strong Arm is a paleface. He will go back to his brothers when the Piegans go to the spirit land."

"No!" Boone answered in English. "Damn if ever I go back—not for good, anyways!" He switched to Blackfoot. "Strong Arm is a Piegan though his face is white."

"Already," said Red Horn, "the white hunters make ready to trap our rivers again."

"They have no right. It is Piegan land."

"We are weak. We cannot fight the Long Knives. Red Horn will not fight. He tells his people to keep the arrow from the bow and their hands from the medicine iron."

It was no use arguing with Red Horn. The spirit was dead in him, except for a sadness and an old anger that fanned up sometimes like a coal touched by wind. He couldn't see ahead. Already the white hunter was getting scarce in the mountains, finding beaver too few and too cheap and the life too risky now that the big parties were gone and he had to travel small. It would be the same with the other white men, with the traders who crowded the river and with those who figured to settle and make crops where crops wouldn't grow. Things came and went and came again.

"Red Hair should be back soon," Boone said, watching Teal Eye come toward the lodge with water from the stream and stoop and go in while the edge of her eye looked at him and her face told him he was her man. He heard her freshening the fire. The days were getting shorter. Already the sun was dipping behind the mountain rim, well to the south of its summer setting place. The breeze began to quiet, as if it couldn't blow without the sun shining on it.

"Red Hair waits at the trading house?" Red Horn asked.

"Maybe Jim is there."

"Two suns, and we go to trade."

"Good."

Red Horn got up and looked around the village, the lines cutting into his face, as if he could see how far the Piegan lodges would stand if the big sickness hadn't come along.

Boone smoked another pipe after Red Horn had gone. From inside there came the little noises that told him Teal Eye was readying the pot for him. The smell of wood smoke was in the air and of good meat cooking. A man's stomach answered to it. The water came into his mouth. High in the sky Boone could hear the whimper of nighthawks. Looking close, he spied one of them, diving crazy and crooked and whimpering as it dived.

He knocked the ash from his pipe and got up, stretching, and ducked under his medicine bundle that hung over the entrance and went in—to his lodge, to his meat, to his woman.

Chapter 32

The first snow had fallen before Jim came back. It was a wet and heavy snow that weighted the branches down and dropped from them onto a man's shoulders and down his neck as he poked through the brush along the Musselshell looking for beaver-setting. The first flight of ducks from the north came with it, their wings whistling in the gray dusk. The water in the beaver ponds stood dark and still against the whitened banks. Deep down, the trout lay slow as suckers. In a day the snow slushed off. The sun came again and the wind swung back to the west and the ground dried, but the country wasn't the same; it looked brown and tired, with no life in it, lying ready for winter, lying poor and quiet while the wind tore at it one day after another. A trapper making his lift heard the wind in the brush and the last stubborn leaves ticking dead against the limbs; he looked up and saw the sky deep and cold and a torn cloud in it, and when he sniffed he got the smell of winter in his nose—the sharp and lonesome smell of winter, of cured grass and fallen leaves and blown grit and cold a-coming on. His legs cramped in the water and his fingers stiffened with his traps, and he felt good inside that his meat was made and berries gathered against the time ahead. Now was a time to hunt, and to think forward to lodge fires and long, fat days and a full stomach and talk like Jim knew how to make.

One beaver from six settings. A poor lift, but a man couldn't expect better, not while he traveled with a parcel of other folks and trapped waters that trappers before him had worn paths along. A plew wouldn't buy much from Chardon, the new bourgeois at McKenzie. A man could put one beaver of whisky in his eye and never wink, and a beaver of red cotton for Teal Eye wouldn't much more than flag an antelope. It was good a man needed but a little of boughten things. The buffalo gave him meat and clothing and a bed and a roof over his head, and what the buffalo didn't give him the deer or sheep did, except for tobacco and powder and lead and whisky, and cloth and fixings for his squaw.

Boone picked up the beaver by a leg and went to his horse and mounted and rode back toward camp. Teal Eye would skin out the beaver and cook the tail. Her hands worked fast and sure for all they were so small. And she hardly needed to look what they were doing. She could watch him or laugh or talk, and they never missed a lick and never lagged. His lodge was kept as well as anybody's, no matter if they had half a dozen wives, and it didn't crawl with lice, either, like some did. Maybe that was because of the winter she had spent in St. Louis with the whites; more likely it was just because she was Teal Eye and neat by nature and knew how to keep a lodge right and how to fix herself pretty, using red beads in her black hair, where they looked good, and blue or white beads against her brown skin, where they looked good, too.

Near his tepee Boone saw two horses standing gaunt and hip-shot and heard voices coming from inside. He checked his own horse and listened and knew that Jim had come home. Teal Eye's laugh floated out to him. He jumped off and dropped the beaver by the door and stooped and went in.

Jim yelled, "How! How, Boone!" He scrambled to his feet, holding a joint of meat in one hand. He spoke through a mouthful of it. "Gimme your paw, Boone. I reckon I'm plumb glad to be back."

Boone looked at the red hair and the face wrinkling into a smile and the white teeth showing and felt Jim's hand hard and strong in his own. "Goddam you, Jim," he said. "What kep' you? Ought to hobble you or put you on a rope. And damn if you didn't get your hair cut! Like an egg with a fuzz on it, your head looks."

Jim ran a hand through the short crop on his skull. "Done it to keep people from askin' questions back in the States. Wisht I could grow it back as quick as I cut it off."

In Blackfoot Teal Eye said, "We thought Red Hair had taken a white squaw."

"Not me," said Jim. "Too fofaraw, them bourgeways are. I got things to do besides waitin' on a woman." He changed to Blackfoot talk. "The white men in their big villages do not have squaws like you. The women are weak and lazy. They do not dress skins and cut wood and pitch and break camp. They are not like Teal Eye."

Boone could see Teal Eye was pleased. He sat down by the fire and put out his wet feet and lighted his pipe. Teal Eye came and took off his wet moccasins and brought dry ones. Jim sat down and lit up, too.

It was good, this was, this having Jim here and winter edging close and a pot of meat fretting and the fire coming out and warming a man's feet and tobacco smoke sweet in his mouth. It made Boone feel snug inside and satified. He wished it could be that the Piegan men wouldn't come visiting until he and Jim had had their own visit out. "You didn't beat winter but by a hair, Jim."

"I look for open weather for a while."

"Red Horn says no. Says it'll be cold as all hell."

"Some thinks one way, some another; God Hisself only knows. I look for an easy winter."

"How'd you travel—boat or horse or how?"

"Horse mostly. Steamboat to the Platte, and then traded two horses away from the Grand Pawnees and follered my nose to McKenzie. Chardon told me where you was."

"Any Indian doin's?"

"Cheyennes was all. A hunting party. I got one fair through my sights after he taken a shot at me, and give the others the slip. They pounded around a right smart, tryin' to get wind of me, but it weren't so much. Not like the old Blackfeet was. Not like them hornets."

"Cheyennes?"

"That was it, now. A man wouldn't expect it."

Sitting there in the dark of the lodge with the fire warming his feet and Jim's voice coming to his ears and reminding him of old things, Boone thought back to times he and Summers and Jim had had with the Blackfeet. They had killed more than a few, the three of them had, and come close to being killed more than once. There was no one fought like the old Blackfeet did, so fierce and unforgiving, until the smallpox came along and made good Indians of them. Put together all the Indians he and Summers and Jim had rubbed out, and it would make a fair village. "See Dick?" he asked.

"Married! Damn if he ain't! And to a white woman! He's farmin'. Corn and pigs and some tobacco."

"Pigs?"

"Pigs."

"I mind when he didn't like the notion of hog meat."

"Nor white women neither, for that part."

"How's he?"

"Good enough, I reckon. He 'lows it's better'n bein' dead, but of course he don't know about that. I allus figgured that bein' dead would save a man a sight of trouble."

"You never acted that way. Keen to keep your hair, you was."

"On account of maybe a man's got to go to hell yet. But if he don't, I mean if when he's dead he's dead and no more to it, why, then, bein' dead could be better than bein' deviled."

Teal Eye had fed the fire and seen there was plenty of meat in the pot and had sat down to work on a shirt. Boone saw her eyes go from one to the other of them as they talked, and quick understanding showing in them. She followed most things that a man might say in English, though she didn't use it much.

"The Piegan knows that he goes to the spirit land," she put in. "He does not fear dying like the white man does, because he knows."

Jim gave her a quick smile. "Some Indians think different. Some believe in the Great Medicine of the white man."

"The Flatheads," she said, "and the Pierced Noses. They have the black robes and the Book of Heaven. They are not warriors like the Piegans. They are not a great people."

Jim took a wooden bowl and filled it from the pot with a horn spoon and got his knife out and began eating again. After a while he said, "I went clean to Kentucky, Boone. Seed the place I was brung up and all."

Boone grunted.

"I left word to get to your kin, figurin' you wouldn't mind. Someone said your pap was ailin'."

"Dead now and gone to hell I hope."

"It's a poor way of doin' back there, it is."

"Looks like you wouldn't always be a-goin', then."

"A man likes to get around." Jim wiped his mouth with the back of his hand while a little frown came over his eyes as if he was studying what to say. "It's a sight, Boone, how people are pointin' west."

"Just talk, I reckon."

"A body wouldn't know the river any more, with the new forts on her and the Mandans all dead and the Rees gone. You wouldn't know her, Boone."

Boone grunted again. A grunt was a handy thing, saying much with little.

"And steamboats! Damn if ever you seed such boats, Boone, so many of 'em and so white and fancy."

"A heap get wrecked."

"That don't stop the building of 'em."

"In time it will, I'm thinkin'."

"Folks everywhere talk about Oregon and California. They aim to make up parties."

"What for?"

"To get to new land, Boone. To get where there's room to breathe, I reckon. To get away from the fever. Y'ever stop to think about the fever, Boone? How many's got ager and such? Nigh half has the shakes."

"They'll shake worse, time they hear a war whoop."

"The Piegans have sickness," Teal Eye put in, looking up from her awl. It was as if her eye didn't see them but looked into other lodges and watched the children that had caught fevers and cramps in the belly lately and had died, some of them, while the medicine men had made a racket over them trying to scare the bad spirits out. It was as if, for a little while, her ear heard only the shake of a rattle and the pound of a drum.

"It ain't nothin', the Piegans' sickness ain't," Jim answered, smiling into her still face. He got up. "I brung you a present," he said as if he had just thought of it, and went to the old trap sack he had laid inside the lodge and brought out a looking glass with a wooden back and a wooden handle. Teal Eye made a little noise in her throat as she took it.

Boone caught Teal Eye's glance and made a gesture with his head. "I left a beaver outside."

Jim had turned back to the trap sack. He brought a bottle of whisky out of it and handed it to Boone. "Just so's you can wet your dry."

Teal Eye got up and went outside to skin the beaver.

"Huntin' ain't much?" Jim asked.

"I catch a few." Boone took a drink and offered the bottle to Jim. It was sure-enough whisky, not the alcohol and water that mostly passed for whisky. He felt Jim's mind studying him, as if there was something hadn't been brought to sight yet.

"There's better ways of making money."

"Could be ways of makin' more, but not better ways."

"Easier, anyhow."

Boone drank again and passed the bottle and refired his pipe.

"Teal Eye looks slick," Jim said, as if he was just making talk while his mind worked. Before he could go on, the entrance to the lodge was darkened and Red Horn came in, and after him Heavy Runner and Big Shield. They sat down, not speaking, and seeing it was a solemn visit, Boone passed around a bowl of dried meat and berries and got out his best pipe, which had the red head of a woodpecker fastened to the long stem and a big fan of feathers above the head. He loaded it and set the bowl on a chunk of dirt and blew up to the sun and down to the earth and passed it to Red Horn on his left.

Red Horn had dressed himself up for the meeting with Jim. He wore a scarlet uniform with blue facings on it that Chardon had given him and had a company medal hanging from his neck. There was red on his eyelids and red stripes on his cheeks and beads hanging from his ears, and he carried a swan's wing in his hand. Before he smoked he spit to the north and south because that was his medicine.

Boone started the half-empty bottle around then and sat back, waiting. Heavy Runner grunted the sting of the whisky from his throat and patted his bare belly with his hand. He was one Indian wouldn't dress up for anything, but would wear his old leggings and his dirty robe no matter what. He had let the robe drop around his hams, leaving the upper part of him naked and showing the two old scars he had cut crosswise on each arm. Boone guessed his squaw hadn't done such a good job on the lice; he could see one climbing out on a hair. After a while old Heavy Runner felt it moving and lifted one scarred arm and picked it off and put it in his mouth.

Big Shield let the whisky trickle slow into his mouth. His face, raised to the bottle, was red with vermilion mixed with grease. The light of the fire glistened on it and shone white on the new bighorn shirt he wore. The bottle had just a drop in it when it came back to Boone.

It was a time before they got their palavering done and even then the three stayed on looking at Jim and asking a question now and then while he took up his talk with Boone, though none of them, except for Red Horn, could follow a white man's words.

"A man runs on to some queer hosses," Jim said. "I met up with one aims to learn every pass across the mountains."

"Ain't so queer. We l'arn't a few ourselves."

"That was for beaver."

Boone used a grunt again.

"This man ain't no trapper. I can't figure what he is, exactly. Says he's goin' to be ready when people really start to move. Maybe he aims to set up trading posts along the way or hire out to take people from the settlements. I don't guess he knows, himself, yet, but he's certain sure there'll be a galore of chances for a man as knows his way in the mountains. He's an educated man, he is, educated so high and fine a man can't make out more'n half he says."

"It's fool talk all the same."

"If there's a pass as'll do, he looks for steamboats to bring a pile of settlers and traders and such to Union, from where they'll head acrost to the Columbia. He's got a flock of notions flyin' around in his head."

Boone drew on his pipe and blew the smoke out in a thin jet while he looked at Jim. "When you startin'?"

Jim's eyelids flicked. "I didn't say nothin' about startin'."

"No need to."

"He's been south and's headin' up this way. Lookin' for a couple of mountain men to show him a north pass. Dollar and a half a day he'll pay."

"It's a fool thing, a damn fool thing."

"Maybe so, maybe not. If people are bound to get to Oregon seems like a good way is from one boat to another, across the mountains. Anyhow, it's bein' a fool thing wouldn't make no difference to us."

"No," Boone said, turning the thing over in his mind.

"We get our money and he gits his l'arnin'."

"Where at you aim to take him?"

"Up the Medicine, maybe, and over. You know best."

"Best is up the Marias and yan way to the Flathead. The snow'll catch him, though, and the cold."

Heavy Runner scratched his head, and Big Shield picked at the ground with a stick. Red Horn sat quiet. Only his eyes moved. It was as if he followed the talk with his eyes.

Jim said, "It ain't such a big party, just him and a couple of pork eaters to help out, and us, if you throw in."

"And a pile of stuff to tote."

"Some."

"How far does he want us?"

"I ain't sure as to that. Boat Encampment, maybe."

"Christ! When'll he be ready?"

"Aims to get to McKenzie in about a moon."

"Late. Red Horn says it will be a mean winter."

Red Horn turned his deep eyes on Jim. "Heap cold. Heap snow."

"I ain't never knowed Boone Caudill to back away from a thing on account of weather or whatever," Jim said.

"On account it's a goddam fool thing." Boone felt the whisky giving a bite to his words. "You're bad as any greenhorn yourself, talkin' about people comin', people comin', people comin'. You seen enough to know the mountains ain't farmin' country, any of it, let alone this Piegan land. A farmer'd have frost on his whiskers before the dust settled from plowin'."

"It ain't Piegan land the man's pointin' to, except to get acrost. And I ain't sayin' it's farm country. I'm sayin' we can get us a dollar and a half a day, easy."

"I mind the time such money weren't nothin'."

"There ain't no money in rememberin'."

"A man don't need money so much."

"It don't hurt him. Look, Boone, it ain't money alone, nor anything alone. It's money and movin' around and havin' fun. It's a time since me and you had us some fun together—some new fun, anyhow—you been sittin' in Blackfoot country so much."

Red Horn had been waiting to speak. There was a steady, hard look under his red eyelids. He hunched forward and started slow, speaking in Blackfoot. "Our old ones fought to keep the white trader away from our enemies beyond the mountains. They watched the pass that leads along the waters the Long Knife calls Maria. They met the Flatheads there, and the Kootenai. They met the Hanging Ears and the Pierced Noses and the Snakes. They were brave. They fought many battles. They took many scalps. They drove the enemies back. The enemies no more tried to travel the pass. To go to the hunting grounds they had to turn south and travel by the River of the Road to the Buffalo and come down the Medicine River to the plains. The old ones kept the white trader away. They made him travel far to the north to get to the country of the Flatheads and Snakes. Our old ones were wise. They did not want the palefaces to give medicine irons and powder and lead to our enemies."

Red Horn stopped, as if to let the words sink in. His nose pointed at Jim like a beak, and then at Boone. Heavy Runner had quit his scratching to listen.

"The old ones were wise," Jim agreed, and added, "for their time."

"No one travels where the old ones fought," Red Horn went on. "The white man does not know the trail. The Flatheads and the Snakes have forgotten what they knew. Only the Piegan remembers—the Piegan and the people that are his brothers, the Bloods and Big Bellies."

"The old ones are dead," Jim said. "The nation comes to a new time."

"The faces of the Flatheads and the Snakes are still blacked toward us. It is not wise to let our enemies be armed."

Boone said, "It is not a trading party. The white men will not carry rifles and powder and ball across the mountains."

"The white trader goes to our enemies by other ways," Jim argued. "He travels the Southern Pass and the trail from the Athabasca."

Red Horn smoothed his uniform over his chest, his eye not looking at what he was doing but fixed sharp as an awl on Boone. The lines were so deep in his cheeks they seemed to set the mouth off by itself. "My young men will not like it. My young men will get mad. They will feel blood in their eyes, and Red Horn will have no power over them."

"Red Horn will not fight the Long Knife. He has said so himself." Boone felt anger stirring in him. Red Horn was a man right enough, no matter if he looked silly in his red suit, but there wasn't any man going to scare him off a thing or tell him what to do.

"My young men will get mad."

Boone held the anger back. "We are Piegans, Red Horn. We are your brothers."

"The young warriors will say that a Piegan would not show the secret of the pass."

"You can keep power over your young men if you want to."

"The white brother who goes to the enemy is not a brother."

Big Shield was nodding. The shine of the fire on his red face went up and down his cheeks as his head moved.

"Goddam it! Have it that way, then! I reckon I'll do as I please."

Red Horn sat straight in his scarlet uniform, holding the swan's wing idle in both his hands, while his mind seemed working at the English Boone had used.

"No cause to git r'iled," Jim put in. "You don't even know you're goin' yet, Boone."

Teal Eye came back into the lodge, came back noiselessly and went to work again on the shirt. From the trouble in her face Boone could tell she had been listening. Christ, even a squaw cramped a man some, or anyhow wanted to!

He turned to Jim. "I been settin' on my ass quite a spell, all right."

JACK SCHAEFER

The "camera angle" in *Shane* is set in the book's second sentence: we'll see everything, pretty much, as young Bob Starrett did—we'll look up, literally, to the hero who has just entered our western valley. And what a man he is. A past churns in him just below the surface, but he wants to put it down, put it away along with his gun in the barn, start over. He changes into farmer's clothes, having instinctively made his choice for the underdogs, the good-hearted settlers, when barely into the valley. But peace and farming and a family are not in Shane's future. He seems somehow to be fated to sacrifice himself for us and for progress. In the end he will ride away wounded, never to be seen again. Jack Schaefer (1907–1991), an Ohio newspaperman at the time he wrote *Shane*, went on to other projects, other concerns, including a beautiful novella of pre–white man times, *The Canyon* (1967), and the ecological sermon *An American Bestiary* (1975). From the vantage point of the latter study, Schaefer wrote that he could never create another Shane. He had fallen out of sympathy with hero-worship, and with the related notion of humanity's singularity and predominance on the globe. He was more than a little pessimistic about the future. But *Shane* came out of a different sensibility, perhaps a different world. It represents the up-curve.

Chapter 1, from *Shane* (1949)

1

He rode into our valley in the summer of '89. I was a kid then, barely topping the backboard of father's old chuck-wagon. I was on the upper rail of our small corral, soaking in the late afternoon sun, when I saw him far down the road where it swung into the valley from the open plain beyond.

In that clear Wyoming air I could see him plainly, though he was still several miles away. There seemed nothing remarkable about him, just another stray horseman riding up the road toward the cluster of frame buildings that was our town. Then I saw a pair of cowhands, loping past him, stop and stare after him with a curious intentness.

He came steadily on, straight through the town without slackening pace, until he reached the fork a half-mile below our place. One branch turned left across the river ford and on to Luke Fletcher's big spread. The other bore ahead along the right bank where we homesteaders had pegged our claims in a row up the valley. He hesitated briefly, studying the choice, and moved again steadily on our side.

As he came near, what impressed me first was his clothes. He wore dark trousers of some serge material tucked into tall boots and held at the waist by a wide belt, both of a soft black leather tooled in intricate design. A coat of the same dark material as the trousers was neatly folded and strapped to his saddle-roll. His shirt was finespun linen, rich brown in color. The handkerchief knotted loosely around his throat was black silk. His hat was not the familiar Stetson, not the familiar gray or muddy tan. It was a plain black, soft in texture, unlike any hat I had ever seen, with a creased crown and a wide curling brim swept down in front to shield the face.

All trace of newness was long since gone from these things. The dust of distance was beaten into them. They were worn and stained and several neat patches showed on the shirt. Yet a kind of magnificence remained and with it a hint of men and manners alien to my limited boy's experience.

Then I forgot the clothes in the impact of the man himself. He was not much above medium height, almost slight in build. He would have looked frail alongside father's square, solid bulk. But even I could read the endurance in the lines of that dark figure and the quiet power in its effortless, unthinking adjustment to every movement of the tired horse.

He was clean-shaven and his face was lean and hard and burned from high forehead to firm, tapering chin. His eyes seemed hooded in the shadow of the hat's brim. He came closer, and I could see that this was because the brows were drawn in a frown of fixed and habitual alertness. Beneath them the eyes were endlessly searching from side to side and forward, checking off every item in view, missing nothing. As I noticed this, a sudden chill, I could not have told why, struck through me there in the warm and open sun.

He rode easily, relaxed in the saddle, leaning his weight lazily into the stirrups. Yet even in this easiness was a suggestion of tension. It was the easiness of a coiled spring, of a trap set.

He drew rein not twenty feet from me. His glance hit me, dismissed me, flicked over our place. This was not much, if you were thinking in terms of size and scope. But what there was was good. You could trust father for that. The corral, big enough for about thirty head if you crowded them in, was railed right to true sunk posts. The pasture behind, taking in nearly half of our claim, was fenced tight. The barn was small, but it was solid, and we were raising a loft at one end for the alfalfa growing green in the north forty. We had a fair-sized field in potatoes that year and father was trying a new corn he had sent all the way to Washington for and they were showing properly in weedless rows.

Behind the house mother's kitchen garden was a brave sight. The house itself was three rooms—two really, the big kitchen where we spent most of our time indoors and the bedroom beside it. My little lean-to room was added back of the kitchen. Father was planning, when he could get around to it, to build mother the parlor she wanted.

We had wooden floors and a nice porch across the front. The house was painted too, white with green trim, rare thing in all that region, to remind her, mother said when she made father do it, of her native New England. Even rarer, the roof was shingled. I knew what that meant. I had helped father split those shingles. Few places so spruce and well worked could be found so deep in the Territory in those days.

The stranger took it all in, sitting there easily in the saddle. I saw his eyes slow on the flowers mother had planted by the porch steps, then come to rest on our shiny new pump and the trough beside it. They shifted back to me, and again, without knowing why, I felt that sudden chill. But his voice was gentle and he spoke like a man schooled to patience.

"I'd appreciate a chance at the pump for myself and the horse."

I was trying to frame a reply and choking on it, when I realized that he was not speaking to me but past me. Father had come up behind me and was leaning against the gate to the corral.

"Use all the water you want, stranger."

Father and I watched him dismount in a single flowing tilt of his body and lead the horse over to the trough. He pumped it almost full and let the horse sink its nose in the cool water before he picked up the dipper for himself.

He took off his hat and slapped the dust out of it and hung it on a corner of the trough. With his hands he brushed the dust from his clothes. With a piece of rag pulled from his saddle-roll he carefully wiped his boots. He untied the handkerchief from around his neck and rolled his sleeves and dipped his arms in the trough, rubbing thoroughly and splashing water over his face. He shook his hands dry and used the handkerchief to remove the last drops from his face. Taking a comb from his shirt pocket, he smoothed back his long dark hair. All his movements were deft and sure, and with a quick precision he flipped down his sleeves, reknotted the handkerchief, and picked up his hat.

Then, holding it in his hand, he spun about and strode directly toward the house. He bent low and snapped the stem of one of mother's petunias and tucked this into the hatband. In another moment the hat was on his head, brim swept down in swift, unconscious gesture, and he was swinging gracefully into the saddle and starting toward the road.

I was fascinated. None of the men I knew were proud like that about their appearance. In that short time the kind of magnificence I had noticed had emerged into plainer view. It was in the very air of him. Everything about him showed the effects of long use and hard use, but showed too the strength of quality and competence. There was no chill on me now. Already I was imagining myself in hat and belt and boots like those.

He stopped the horse and looked down at us. He was refreshed and I would have sworn the tiny wrinkles around his eyes were what with him would be a smile. His eyes were not restless when he looked at you like this. They were still and steady and you knew the man's whole attention was concentrated on you even in the casual glance.

"Thank you," he said in his gentle voice and was turning into the road, back to us, before father spoke in his slow, deliberate way.

"Don't be in such a hurry, stranger."

I had to hold tight to the rail or I would have fallen backwards into the corral. At the first sound of father's voice, the man and the horse, like a single being, had wheeled to face us, the man's eyes boring at father, bright and deep in the shadow of the hat's brim. I was shivering, struck through once more. Something intangible and cold and terrifying was there in the air between us.

I stared in wonder as father and the stranger looked at each other a long moment, measuring each other in an unspoken fraternity of adult knowledge beyond my reach. Then the warm sunlight was flooding over us, for father was smiling and he was speaking with the drawling emphasis that meant he had made up his mind.

"I said don't be in such a hurry, stranger. Food will be on the table soon and you can bed down here tonight."

The stranger nodded quietly as if he too had made up his mind. "That's mighty thoughtful of you," he said and swung down and came toward us, leading his horse. Father slipped into step beside him and we all headed for the barn.

"My name's Starrett," said father. "Joe Starrett. This here," waving at me, "is Robert MacPherson Starrett. Too much name for a boy. I make it Bob."

The stranger nodded again. "Call me Shane," he said. Then to me: "Bob it is. You were watching me for quite a spell coming up the road." It was not a question. It was a simple statement. "Yes ..." I stammered. "Yes. I was."

"Right," he said. "I like that. A man who watches what's going on around him will make his mark."

A man who watches . . . For all his dark appearance and lean, hard look, this Shane knew what would please a boy. The glow of it held me as he took care of his horse, and I fussed around, hanging up his saddle, forking over some hay, getting in his way and my own in my eagerness. He let me slip the bridle off and the horse, bigger and more powerful than I had thought now that I was close beside it, put its head down patiently for me and stood quietly while I helped him curry away the caked dust. Only once did he stop me. That was when I reached for his saddle-roll to put it to one side. In the instant my fingers touched it, he was taking it from me and he put it on a shelf with a finality that indicated no interference.

When the three of us went up to the house, mother was waiting and four places were set at the table. "I saw you through the window," she said and came to shake our visitor's hand. She was a slender, lively woman with a fair complexion even our weather never seemed to affect and a mass of light brown hair she wore piled high to bring her, she used to say, closer to father's size.

"Marian," father said, "I'd like you to meet Mr. Shane."

"Good evening, ma'am," said our visitor. He took her hand and bowed over it. Mother stepped back and, to my surprise, dropped in a dainty curtsy. I had never seen her do that before. She was an unpredictable woman. Father and I would have painted the house three times over and in rainbow colors to please her.

"And a good evening to you, Mr. Shane. If Joe hadn't called you back, I would have done it myself. You'd never find a decent meal up the valley."

She was proud of her cooking, was mother. That was one thing she learned back home, she would often say, that was of some use out in this raw land. As long as she could still prepare a proper dinner, she would tell father when things were not going right, she knew she was still civilized and there was hope of getting ahead. Then she would tighten her lips and whisk together her special most delicious biscuits and father would watch her bustling about and eat them to the last little crumb and stand up and wipe his eyes and stretch his big frame and stomp out to his always unfinished work like daring anything to stop him now.

We sat down to supper and a good one. Mother's eyes sparkled as our visitor kept pace with father and me. Then we all leaned back and while I listened the talk ran on almost like old friends around a familiar table. But I could sense that it was following a pattern. Father was trying, with mother helping and both of them avoiding direct questions, to get hold of facts about this Shane and he was dodging at every turn. He was aware of their purpose and not in the least annoyed by it. He was mild and courteous and spoke readily enough. But always he put them off with words that gave no real information.

He must have been riding many days, for he was full of news from towns along his back trail as far as Cheyenne and even Dodge City and others beyond I had never heard of before. But he had no news about himself. His past was fenced as tightly as our pasture. All they could learn was that he was riding through, taking each day as it came, with nothing particular in mind except maybe seeing a part of the country he had not been in before.

Afterwards mother washed the dishes and I dried and the two men sat on the porch, their voices carrying through the open door. Our visitor was guiding the conversation now and in no time at all he had father talking about his own plans. That was no trick. Father was ever one to argue his ideas whenever he could find a listener. This time he was going strong.

"Yes, Shane, the boys I used to ride with don't see it yet. They will some day. The open range can't last forever. The fence lines are closing in. Running cattle in big lots is good business only for the top ranchers and it's really a poor business at that. Poor in terms of the resources going into it. Too much space for too little results. It's certain to be crowded out."

"Well, now," said Shane, "that's mighty interesting. I've been hearing the same quite a lot lately and from men with pretty clear heads. Maybe there's something to it."

"By Godfrey, there's plenty to it. Listen to me, Shane. The thing to do is pick your spot, get your land, your own land. Put in enough crops to carry you and make your money play with a small herd, not all horns and bone, but bred for meat and fenced in and fed right. I haven't been at it long, but already I've raised stock that averages three hundred pounds more than that long-legged stuff Fletcher runs on the other side of the river and it's better beef, and that's only a beginning.

"Sure, his outfit sprawls over most of this valley and it looks big. But he's got range rights on a lot more acres than he has cows and he won't even have those acres as more homesteaders move in. His way is wasteful. Too much land for what he gets out of it. He can't see that. He thinks we small fellows are nothing but nuisances."

"You are," said Shane mildly. "From his point of view, you are."

"Yes, I guess you're right. I'll have to admit that. Those of us here now would make it tough for him if he wanted to use the range behind us on this side of the river as he used to. Altogether we cut some pretty good slices out of it. Worse still, we block off part of the river, shut the range off from the water. He's been grumbling about that off and on ever since we've been here. He's worried that more of us will keep coming and settle on the other side too, and then he will be in a fix."

The dishes were done and I was edging to the door. Mother nailed me as she usually did and shunted me off to bed. After she had left me in my little back room and went to join the men on the porch, I tried to catch more of the words. The voices were too low. Then I must have dozed, for with a start I realized that father and mother were again in the kitchen. By now, I gathered, our visitor was out in the barn in the bunk father had built there for the hired man who had been with us for a few weeks in the spring.

"Wasn't it peculiar," I heard mother say, "how he wouldn't talk about himself?"

"Peculiar?" said father. "Well, yes. In a way."

"Everything about him is peculiar." Mother sounded as if she was stirred up and interested. "I never saw a man quite like him before."

"You wouldn't have. Not where you come from. He's a special brand we sometimes get out here in the grass country. I've come across a few. A bad one's poison. A good one's straight grain clear through."

"How can you be so sure about him? Why, he wouldn't even tell where he was raised."

"Born back east a ways would be my guess. And pretty far south. Tennessee maybe. But he's been around plenty."

"I like him." Mother's voice was serious. "He's so nice and polite and sort of gentle. Not like most men I've met out here. But there's something about him. Something underneath the gentleness . . . Something . . ." Her voice trailed away.

"Mysterious?" suggested father.

"Yes, of course. Mysterious. But more than that. Dangerous."

"He's dangerous all right." Father said it in a musing way. Then he chuckled. "But not to us, my dear." And then he said what seemed to me a curious thing. "In fact, I don't think you ever had a safer man in your house."

FRANK WATERS

A s he described himself in several books, Frank Waters (1902–1995) was the child of a not altogether happy marriage between a white Colorado Springs woman and a man from an Indian background on the Great Plains. Perhaps not surprisingly, his chief subject as a writer is the two consciousnesses: the "white"— rational, superficial, verbal, linear—and the "red"—intuitive, profound, mysteriously comprehensive. This is not too different from what Mary Austin wrote about, or D. H. Lawrence, or C. G. Jung, but what makes Waters distinctive is his own sense of place, the American Southwest with its sweeping scale and dramatic feel of the bare-rock authentic. Waters writes with an inner feel for the landscape and the light, the quietness, the entire natural ambience out of which, for the natives of the region, ceremonies and ceremony-imbued daily life grew. He studied the same subjects as the anthropologist Elsie Clews Parsons (1875–1941)—mentioned in the following selection—but had his own methods. Always he looked for the inward dimensions, the mind within the outward forms. Always he looked for hints on what could link the two sides of human consciousness and make a whole. His interpretations of Pueblo and Navaho ceremonialism leaped over anthropological convention, frightening the publications committee at the University of New Mexico. They would publish *Masked Gods* only if it contained a foreword by a recognized academic authority, Dr. Clyde Kluckhohn of Harvard. To his credit, Kluckhohn saw merit in Waters's idiosyncratic, intuitive approach—saw, perhaps, that this writer was after a bigger picture than could be put together out of footnoted fragments.

"Hopi Ceremonialism," from *Masked Gods* (1950)

The ripe richness, grotesque imagery, and barbaric beauty of Hopi ceremonials are almost unbelievable and certainly indescribable. They fill the calendar year. The *Soyal* at the winter solstice turning back the sun to summer. The fire ritual of *Wuwuchim*. The *Powamu* and *Niman Kachina*. The women's ceremonials of *Marau, Lakon,* and *Oazol*. The Flute ceremonial observing the Emergence. The Snake-Antelope ceremonial. The Summer Solstice ceremonial turning back the sun to winter. The War and Stick Swallowing ceremonies. The spring races, the kachina races. The many dances—kachina dances, masked and unmasked, the women's beautiful Buffalo Dance and delicate Butterfly Dance. With all their perpetual prayer stick planting. Their dry paintings of sand, meal, and pollen, on the altar, in front of it, or around the *sipapu*. The kiva withdrawals, initiation of children, ritual songs, prayers, and myths, the directional color systems, the symbolism of stone, animal, plant . . . All these parallel those we have already observed in other Pueblo and Navaho ceremonials.

Like the Navaho sings, the major Hopi ceremonials are of nine nights' duration, but measured by the intervening and overlapping eight or ten days. They too are healing ceremonials. The *Powamu* for rheumatism, the *Flute* for lightning shock, the Snake-Antelope for swellings, the War for bronchial trouble, the *Lakon* for eczema, the *Maru* for venereal diseases. Like Pueblo ceremonials their last days end in great public dances. Like both Navaho and Pueblo ceremonials they are myth-dramas, mystery plays. They are, in a sense, a recapitulation of all Navaho and Pueblo ceremonialism. They stem back, as the symbolism of the Navaho Flint Way derives from the Mesa Verde Sun Temple, to the earliest cliff dwellers. They parallel the meanings and often the exact rituals of the ancient Aztecs, Toltecs, and Mayas. And their extraordinary richness and complexity is the despair of all ethnological and anthropological study.

Their specific functions are to heal, bring rain, fertilize crops, recount myths, preach sermons, afford fiestas, perpetuate tradition. But above all they are structured to maintain the harmony of the universe. Everything else is partial. Hence their ultimate meanings are rooted in the same old, familiar premise that the unplumbed universe within individual man is indivisibly linked with the immeasurable universe. Whatever distorts the whole warps the part; what can happen within the psyche can take place in the cosmos.

This truth is stated nowhere more clearly than in the ceremonial which is at once the chief goal of all tourists, the most fascinating and repulsive, and the least understood: the so-called Hopi Snake Dance.

The Snake-Antelope Ceremonial

This nine-night, ten-day ceremonial begins four days after the ten-day *Niman Kachina* which is given ten days after the summer solstice—which places it usually sometime in early August if you figure it out. Alternating with the Flute ceremonial, it is given on First Mesa on the odd years and on Second and Third Mesas in the even years.

So now, blinded by the sun and choked with dust, we are crawling westward from Keam's Canyon around the high rocky rampart of First Mesa. To sleep for the night at its foot. Below Tom Pavatea's trading post, where we can get water and groceries. In the ancient peach orchard on the soft sand. That is, if we don't spread our bed rolls in the dark right over the ant hills as Doc Harlin and I did late one night in 1932. The

dance this year of course is not in Walpi, high above. It's in Hotevilla on
the far end of Third Mesa. But there's no hurry to get there. The folks
concerned are still busy in the kivas, tending to those rattlesnakes. Let's
let Dr. Elsie Clews Parsons give us the horrible secret details. Being invited into a kiva is no fun. Sitting there hours on end is work; stuffy,
smelly work. Let her do it while we loaf around the post.

"Howdy," says Tom. "How's tricks?"

"Hi," we say. "Good crop this summer?"

"Fair to middling," says Tom. "But they ask too many questions and
don't buy enough souvenirs. Mebbe the bunch comin' in for the dance
will be better. Don't know why I think so."

The dance is a Butterfly Dance late this afternoon up above. So off we
go, leaving Pavatea to harvest his crop of tourists and Mrs. Parsons her
crop of notes in the kiva, where she has been a week already.

On the first day of the ceremonial, she notes, the Antelope Chief sets
up his standard on the kiva. Then he goes in for a smoke. The Snake
Chief, in his kiva, smokes, sprinkles meal, prays, then begins to make
snake whips—little wooden stems decorated with eagle feathers. They're
in no hurry either.

Next day Antelope Chief spreads a mound of sand marked in corn
meal with the lines of the six directions. On this he sets the *tiponi*, about
two feet long, made of eagle wing feathers and decorated with feathers
of the birds of the cardinal directions: oriole of the north, bluebird of the
west, parrot of the south, magpie of the east; all bound in buckskin and
tied with red thongs. Snake Chief receives more members of his kiva. He
gives them some root of the beetle plant so if they are bit by snakes they
can chew a little and spread it on the fang puncture. They go out and
gather the first few snakes in a snake bag, returning at sunset.

In the morning the snakes are taken carefully out of the bag, being
held in back of the head so that they cannot strike, and inserted in a large
bottle. Then the Snake priests go out after more snakes. To the north, the
west, the south, the east. Every day it is the same. Each man stripped to
a loin cloth, his face painted red, his body marked with a red stripe, a
red feather tied in his crown lock. Each carries a digging whip to dig
snakes out of the ground if necessary, and a snake whip of eagle feathers
to make them straighten so they can be grabbed.

In the Antelope kiva—But no. No more running back and forth between kivas, old Sikyapiki tells Mrs. Parsons gently but firmly. She must
choose to observe the ceremonies in either kiva, and not enter the other.
Only he can and must visit the Antelope kiva each day. So she stays in
the Snake kiva.

But we know what is going on in the Antelope this fourth day. The altar is being made and set with bowls of water from the sacred springs, green cornstalks and vines of squash and beans. Then the dry painting is laid with colored sand. It is about five feet square. At the four corners are built the cloud-mountains—yellow, black, red, and white—each with a hawk feather thrust into its apex. On these the clouds perch, and in them the four chiefs of the directions live. The outer lines are similarly colored, and the whole makes the rainbow house.

Next day in the Snake kiva the snakes are fed with pollen, sprinkled with meal. Songs and prayers are given. It is an elaborate ceremony. Mrs. Parsons is busy making notes. She has to sharpen her pencil and is about to throw the shavings in the fire. No, no! Cedar charcoal is associated with Masawu. She must deposit the shavings on the floor under the ladder.

So the days crawl by, the sixth and seventh. The complexity, the intensity is mounting. Prayer sticks are being made. Set after set. For the cardinal directions, the Cloud Chiefs, who sit at those four corners of space, the sun, the moon. For that of the sun a journey food packet is made with meal, pollen, honey taken in the mouth and mixed with saliva. Systole and diastole, the songs rise and fall. Pale light steals down the ladder opening upon the naked backs of the painted priests, the jars of coiled serpents. Smoke blown to the directions drifts upward. The long myth chant continues.

In this cabalistic maze the snakes are taken out of their jars and loosed on the clean mound of sand. Bull snakes, rattle-snakes, whip snakes, snakes mottled, streaked, and patterned: a coiled, interlocked maze of sinewy serpents. The priests do not hesitate to pick them up while in coil. They stroke their heads with the feathers of the whip to make them uncoil, believing that only when a snake is coiled can it strike. The movements of their hands are "slow and gentle but sure and unhesitating." There is no snake drugging, extraction of fangs, nor inducing them to strike until they empty their sacs of poison. Even so a man is bit twice on arm and leg. He calmly rubs the wound with sand or the beetle-root. The dark stripe constrictors rear up five feet high, a monstrous sight. Some rattle-snakes wriggle toward Mrs. Parson's flinching body. One lunges into her very lap—

"God, how they make me creep!"

Why, Dr. Elsie! Imagine that in the middle of a scientific ethnological report! There she is, the cold, objective, analytical scientist immersed in her research. Suddenly shaken smack-dab into the role of a mere woman.

> Dear Dr. Elsie. I can't see you there at all. I remember you as I saw you during my first trip to New York, so generously and thoughtfully

calling me to ask, "Have you ever been to Grand Opera at the Met? Wonderful! Friday night then."

How beautiful, strange and remote it all seems—the Metropolitan, that gaunt old stone kiva, the revered sanctum sanctorum of a culture ritual of a whole civilization. Like the Snake Antelope ceremonial, it is a ceremonial of a vanished culture, observed by a civilization itself swiftly vanishing. Now indeed the Diamond Horseshoe is already gone. The deep canyons of New York with their crowded cliff dwellers are losing vitality as the tides of change beat upon the shores. The tall towers are shaking. But there, while the hour was still unspent, we sat as guests of our thoughtful and generous hostess. A gracious lady in brocaded scarlet, perfectly at home in her family box, held for years.

But now squatting in a dingy, stuffy hole full of crawling rattlesnakes while far overhead the clouds begin to form.

We can see them late this seventh afternoon, tenuous wisps of white gathering in the blue, as we jolt westward to camp tonight on Third Mesa. Thirty miles of grey sand, grey cliffs and a single old windmill and water tank, a dismal oasis.

We boil up the steep slope of the mesa. Past Oraibi, on the near edge, a clump of dreary stone and adobe huts that looks like a ruin. Across the wind swept tableland to Hotevilla, on the far edge. It doesn't look much better. None of them look like much, compared to Zuñi and Taos. Nothing seems alive. Everything seems to have retreated underground from the sun and wind. For us it is another dry camp outside the pueblo.

Before dawn we are awakened by a faint jingle. A file of shadows slips across the horizon. That other year when we slept at the foot of First Mesa it was the same. The Snake priests, palely outlined by white breech clouts, were moving by us to the spring. We could hear their low voices in prayer. And next morning when we went there we saw the planted prayer sticks and the ground white with sprinkled meal. Every morning of the last four they do so, a different spring each day. Sleepily we turn over. The clouds still hang threateningly above us, a little thicker and a little whiter in the black.

At dawn they are still there. Underneath them, on top of both kivas, are tiny figures laying bands of sand across the roof in all directions. On each band is sprinkled a line of prayer meal. These kivas are now the All Directions Altars, the cloud road markers, for over these roads the clouds will travel.

It is the eighth day. The intensity is spreading outside the kivas. A restrained air of excitement permeates the dusty, squalid village. Outside, everybody gathers for the Antelope Race. The prize is a bunch of prayer sticks and a bottle of water taken from a sacred spring. The winner will

pour the water on his field and plant the prayer sticks. Along the course
are deposited prayer sticks and prayer meal. The racers are urged along
by kiva members whirling their whizzers or bull roarers, a stick whirled
on a string to make the roaring sound of low thunder; and shooting their
lightning frames, a jointed wooden frame which is shot out in a long
zigzag like lightning.

Formerly racers ran naked, hair flowing loose like rain. Now the boys
are short-haired, wear shorts, and their feet are daubed with mud. So
they race across the plain at sunrise, forty brown bodies straining and
panting. To be met by more men and boys carrying cornstalks and squash
blossoms, with women and girls scrambling for these trophies when the
race is over.

In the early afternoon a burro loaded with cottonwood branches is
driven into the plaza. A leafy green bower is built; the *kisi*, the shrine, to
hold the snakes. In front of it a shallow hole is dug, perhaps two feet
deep. Over it is laid a board smoothed over with sand: the *sipapu*.

A few people are coming in by now. A band of Navaho horsemen,
some visiting Pueblos in an old flivver, a sprinkle of Anglos with a case
of soda pop which they generously pass around before the ice is melted.
Everything is restrained and easy; everybody loafing quietly in the shadows. Till late in the afternoon, when the kivas suddenly begin to empty.

The Antelope Dance

The Antelope dancers appear first, led by the Antelope Chief carrying the
feather *tiponi* on his left arm. All twelve are decorated alike. The chin is
outlined by a white line from ear to ear. The lower leg from foot to knee,
and the lower arm from hand to elbow are painted white. There are zigzag lines of lightning on the upper arm and leg, and white clouds painted
on both shoulders. Each wears a white kirtle and embroidered sash, a fox
skin hung in back, feathers in his hair, and beaded anklets. One carries
gourd and prayer sticks; another a rattle; another wears a cottonwood
wreath and carries a medicine bowl of water.

As they file silently across the plaza and around the bower, the Snake
dancers come out. In contrast to the greyish-white Antelopes, the Snakes
are reddish brown. Their faces are smeared dark red, with a splotch of
white clay on the hair over the right eye. Their dark-brown bodies are
spotted with white. Each man wears a fringed kirtle, a fringed deerskin
garter on the left leg, a turtleshell rattle below the right knee. All wear
necklaces of turquoise, shell, and coral, and carry a fringed bag of meal
in the left hand and a snake whip in the right. The chief carries his bow
standard.

They too encircle the green bower four times, each casting a pinch of meal. Each man too on reaching the *sipapu* stamps hard with one foot on the plank resonator, the foot drum. Then they line up facing the Antelopes.

Two opposite lines. The greyish white and the forbidding reddish brown. All held in a moment of suspense, a theatrical pause. Then suddenly it begins.

The Antelopes shaking their rattles, dancing their stamping dance, singing their deep voiced chant. The Snakes bending over, stamping their dance steps, shaking their leg rattles, waving their snake whips.

The lines dance forward and back. Up and down between the lines dances the Antelope Chief, followed by the Snake Chief stroking his back with his snake whip.

Then, in pairs, each Antelope and each Snake dance up between the lines, Snake's left arm resting on Antelope's shoulder.

Now the Antelope darts into the bower and grabs a bunch of cornstalks and bean vines. This he carries in his mouth while resuming dancing. The Snake helps to support it with one hand. When it is dropped he picks it up deftly as he would a snake and restores it to his partner's mouth.

Back in line again the Snakes wheel in unison, circling the *kisi* four times and stamping on the *sipapu* as before, every circle larger in radius, and then file back to the kiva. The Antelopes leave with the same ceremony . . .

It is over. It is sunset, and dark, and the eighth night of the ceremonial. Poor Mrs. Parsons! So busy still taking notes in her Hopi Diamond-back Horseshoe. Endless ritual, ceremony, costume, prayer, chant, song, and paraphernalia. Imagine trying to record a Grand Opera in similar detail without a convenient place to put your pencil shavings! Now she must fast for the busiest twenty-four hours of all.

The whirling whizzer will seem to whirl inside her empty stomach. The rattlesnakes will rattle inside her aching head. Near cockcrow the singing will commence. At daylight sixty or more prayer sticks will be planted outside at different shrines. Two of the Snakes will go to the roof of the Antelope kiva, whirling their whizzers and shooting their lightning frames to the four directions. Inside, perhaps, there begins the same ceremony as is held in other pueblos when a young boy and girl come in. The Antelope Youth painted and holding a rattlesnake in his hand. The Snake Maid ceremonially dressed in white, holding a jar of bean and melon vines, her hair whorled in squash blossoms. Both standing on the sand-painting during the ceremony. Mrs. Parsons must have her head washed. All Snake priests have their heads washed. The snakes must be washed too. Those snakes!

No. It is better to be a tourist. My earliest ambition in life was to be a tourist. To travel and see the sights, to travel on and see still more sights. A forever stepping out of Fred Harvey dining rooms, toothpick in mouth, with an air of smug satisfaction. A never-ending trail of indulgence requiring no work, no worry, no effort to understand such fuss and fol-de-rol on the part of such ignorant, heathenish savages as these.

So here for once we lie in our bedrolls while Mrs. Parsons does the work. Watching the clouds gather thicker and heavier around the morning star. Listening to the Crier on the kiva roof giving that resonant call which floats over the pueblo, across the mesa and out over the lightening plain. A call, like a muezzin's call to prayer; one of the most beautiful sounds on earth.

He is arousing the young men for the sunrise Snake Race which duplicates the Antelope Race of yesterday morning. Another fine sight to see.

There are more tourists to help us enjoy the day. We can see them beginning to come in already as we cook breakfast afterward. Like tiny black beetles far down on the immeasurable plain they look, crawling sixty, seventy miles along the rutted dirt road, puffing up the grade, disgorging. Fred Harvey tourist busses with uniformed drivers. Dudes in droves from guest ranches, all in elaborate, colored cowboy boots. Old jalopies. New Chevies. Long sleek limousines hunting vainly for a "Reserved" parking lot. Trucks and pickups jammed with laughing Spanish-American families. Ranchers. Casual visitors detouring off Highway 66. Station-wagons loaded with boys and girls from summer camps and schools. Government Indian Service agents, looking very important. Forest Service rangers in green whipcord. A group of bifocalled scientists. Mystified foreigners perpetually slapping the thick talcum dust off their shiny black suits. Wagon loads of Navahos of course, one after another. Pueblos springing up from nowhere. A movie star in dark glasses. Yes she is! Look!

All day long they keep coming. The whole American melting pot. Decorated with Tiffany diamonds, costume jewelry by Woolworth, turquoise and heavy silver from the Navahos. Under felts, stiff straws, scarlet head bands, Lily Daché creations, black umbrellas and colored parasols. Carrying fans, thermos bottles, sandwiches, and little black notebooks— no cameras please.

All broiling and perspiring under the blinding sun and the sultry clouds lowering over the kivas. Fighting for a place on the flat Hopi roofs. Swarming the terraces. Massing the plaza. Peering in the squalid doorways. Bargaining for Navaho jewelry and Hopi pottery at twice the price. Flocking everywhere like sheep.

But, on the whole, a tolerant and well-behaved mob. For all are drawn here to see only one thing. Native Indians dancing with live rattlesnakes in their mouths. If there is one thing that evokes the most shivering horror, the worst agony of tingling suspense, this must be it. The United States Indian Office has threatened to stop it as a "loathsome practice." La Junta, Colorado, Boy Scouts, calling themselves *"Koshares,"* imitate it yearly with $100,000 worth of costumes. Business men of Prescott, Arizona, annually calling themselves "Smokis," have tried to exploit it in the most derisive, cheap, and vulgar parody yet attempted. And still it goes on, year after year. So from the four corners of the world everybody comes here to the ancient wilderness heart, the nerve center of America. To see Indians dance with rattlesnakes in their mouths.

It is more than that. Though they may not know it, it is the oldest rite in all America, stemming unbroken from the earliest prehistoric cliff dwellers, deriving from the first era of human life on this continent. It is more than that. Although they do not realize it, it is an evocation of that dormant and stifled other component of all our lives, that intuition of the dark self which lies hidden deep within us. Towards this invisible, irrational, and unadmitted fourth-dimension they stand reaching out, hour after hour, with a confused sense of irritation and unbelievable patience, repugnance and longing, angry denial and intolerable suspense. And over them all, the thousands of tourists and the hundreds of Hopis, the squalid village and the majestic plain, the mystery lies heavy as upon the first naked prehistoric cliff dwellers who waited here watching the lowering, darkening clouds . . . Lies heavy upon the same mankind, the same earth, that are still dependent upon the same ancient verities of above and below for survival . . . Waiting till almost sunset for the concluding ceremony on this ninth day.

The Snake Dance

It always seems sudden and unlooked for when at last they come. And it is always new, though it is essentially a duplicate of the Antelope Dance of the day before.

First come the Antelopes. Twelve men, a pair like prayer sticks for each of the six directions. But today more somber grey with black hands and feet, black chins, and a white line across their upper lips, their bodies dirty ash grey.

Then the Snakes. Today their faces are blackened with charcoal, with smears of red-brown on the cheeks, their black and red-brown bodies covered only with black kirtles.

Grotesque and horrible they file somberly around the plaza, their loose black hair flowing in the breeze. Short, heavy, powerfully built, as if compressed to the ground.

Ash grey and reddish black, they each in turn encircle the bower and cast their pinches of meal. Bend forward, shaking their rattles. Then stoop and stamp powerfully upon the plank resonator or foot drum, the *sipapu*. All call softly with a deep, somber, wordless chant.

This is the one supreme moment of mystery. Here, now, at the mouth of the cavern world where the power gushes up on call. Everything later is an anticlimax, even the snakes.

So it begins. The dull resonant stamp like distant thunder, like a faint rumble underground, sounds in the silent sunlit square. It is echoed by that deep, somber, thunderous chant. The sound is one we never hear, so deep and powerful it is. And it reveals how deep these men are in the mystery of its making. Calling to the deep cavern world below. Summoning the serpent power. Calling up the creative life force to the underground streams, to the roots of the corn, to the feet, the loins, the mind of man.

And the power does gush up. It shakes the two opposite lines of Snakes and Antelopes into motion, into dance. And now it begins—what the crowd has been waiting for.

A Snake stoops down into the *kisi* and emerges with a snake in his mouth. He holds it gently but firmly between his teeth, just below the head. It is a rattlesnake. The flat birdlike head with its unmoving eyes flattened against his cheek, its spangled body dangling like a long thick cord. Immediately another Snake steps up beside him, a little behind, stroking the rattlesnake with his snake whip with intense concentration. Up and down they commence dancing, while another Snake emerges with a giant bull snake between his teeth. At the end of the circle the Snake dancer gently drops his snake upon the ground and goes after another. The snake raises its sensitive head, darts out its small tongue like antennae, then wriggles like lightning towards the massed spectators. Now the yells and screams and scramble! But a third man, the snake watcher, is waiting. He rushes up. Deftly he grabs the escaping snake, waves the long undulating body over his head, and carries it to the Antelopes. They smooth it with their feathers and lay it down on a circle of cornmeal.

Soon it is all confusion. The whole plaza is filled with Snake dancers dancing with snakes in their mouths. Rattlesnakes, huge bull snakes almost too heavy to carry, little whip, racer, and garter snakes curling in a frenzy about one's ears. A loosely held rattler strikes a man on the jowl and dangles there a moment before it is gently disengaged. The dance goes on. Snakes wriggling on the ground, darting toward the spectators.

Brought back by the snake watchers, an armful at a time. Until all of the snakes have been danced with and deposited in a great wriggling mound by the ash-grey Antelopes.

Suddenly it is over. Two Hopi girls dressed in ceremonial mantles sprinkle the writhing mass with baskets of meal. Then Snake priests grab up the snakes in armfuls, like loose disjointed sticks of kindling, and run out of the plaza. Down the trails into the stark Arizona desert to four shrines where the snakes are freed. Released at last, after giving up their dark potency, to carry the meal prayers sprinkled upon them, the feather breaths of life, the ceremonial commands laid upon them, back to the deep spinal core of the dark source.

The setting sun spreads its effulgence over the mesa, the farther mesas, and distant buttes. The whole arid rock wilderness floods with twilight. The clouds hang heavy, dark and somber. A few drops of rain sprinkle the crowds. They hurry away swiftly. The motorcars start buzzing, filing in a funeral cortege down the slope. Quickly, to "cross the wash," to escape the coming flood.

The ash-grey Antelopes and the brown-black Snakes file ceremoniously back to their kivas. Each drinks a large bowl of emetic medicine concocted out of the root medicine and handsful of beetles and stinking tumblebugs. They go out to the edge of the cliff and vomit. If they didn't their bellies would swell up with the power like clouds and burst. Then they may eat and wash. But the dark power called up for nine nights and days is still within them. So tomorrow morning they must wash again; heads, bodies, necklaces, planting sticks. And again they must rub with the dry root medicine, must chew it and spit it in their hands and rub themselves. While the Snake Chief touches each with his snake whip, the last strike of the serpent, comes the vivid flame stroke of lightning which at last releases the sweet smelling rain, the torrential swishing floods.

JOSÉ ANTONIO VILLARREAL

P ocho (1959) demonstrates that an identity crisis and a minority childhood can, for a fortunately creative nature, bring about rich opportunities for understanding. "Richard Rubio," the protagonist of the story, grows up in California in the 1930s, caught between cultures and generations, disadvantaged in any number of ways. He emerges from a childhood and adolescence that are marked by unexpected physical sophistication, immense variety of experience despite limited outward circumstances, at times danger, and above all interesting chances to learn something. Richard endures racist conditions, but his response to life is affirmation. In the 1960s, some Chicano activists, while respecting the novel's trailbreaking, thought Pocho too accommodating. "For the most part, I was attacked for my posture," Villarreal (b. 1924) has said. Describing his upbringing in a migrant worker family, "following crops throughout California," he once said that he grew up "living almost always in tents outdoors—for me, a most bucolic life which I loved. The only diversion for the men after twelve hours of labor in the fields or orchards was to sit around a campfire after supper and tell stories of their homelands, different parts of Mexico. As I recall, I was usually the only child who listened." Villarreal's other books include The Fifth Horseman: A Novel of the Mexican Revolution (1974) and Clemente Chacon (1984). In the following excerpt from Pocho, young Richard is tempted toward the gang life of the pachuco.

From *Pocho* (1959)

It was not until the following year that Richard knew that his town was changing as much as his family was. It was 1940 in Santa Clara, and, among other things, the Conscription Act had done its part in bringing about a change. It was not unusual now to see soldiers walking downtown or to see someone of the town in uniform. He was aware that people liked soldiers now, and could still remember the old days, when a detachment of cavalry camped outside the town for a few days or a unit of field artillery stayed at the university, and the worst thing one's sister could do was associate with a soldier. Soldiers were common, were drunkards, thieves, and rapers of girls, or something, to the people of Santa Clara, and the only uniforms with prestige in the town had been those of the CCC boys or of the American Legion during the Fourth of

July celebration and the Easter-egg hunt. But now everybody loved a soldier, and he wondered how this had come about.

There were the soldiers, and there were also the Mexicans in ever-increasing numbers. The Mexican people Richard had known until now were those he saw only during the summer, and they were migrant families who seldom remained in Santa Clara longer than a month or two. The orbit of his existence was limited to the town, and actually to his immediate neighborhood, thereby preventing his association with the Mexican family which lived on the other side of town, across the tracks. In his wanderings into San Jose, he began to see more of what he called "the race." Many of the migrant workers who came up from southern California in the late spring and early summer now settled down in the valley. They bought two hundred pounds of flour and a hundred pounds of beans, and if they weathered the first winter, which was the most difficult, because the rains stopped agricultural workers from earning a living, they were settled for good.

As the Mexican population increased, Richard began to attend their dances and fiestas, and, in general, sought their company as much as possible, for these people were a strange lot to him. He was obsessed with a hunger to learn about them and from them. They had a burning contempt for people of different ancestry, whom they called Americans, and a marked hauteur toward México and toward their parents for their old-country ways. The former feeling came from a sense of inferiority that is a prominent characteristic in any Mexican reared in southern California; and the latter was an inexplicable compensation for that feeling. They needed to feel superior to something, which is a natural thing. The result was that they attempted to segregate themselves from both their cultures, and became truly a lost race. In their frantic desire to become different, they adopted a new mode of dress, a new manner, and even a new language. They used a polyglot speech made up of English and Spanish syllables, words, and sounds. This they incorporated into phrases and words that were unintelligible to anyone but themselves. Their Spanish became limited and their English more so. Their dress was unique to the point of being ludicrous. The black motif was predominant. The tight-fitting cuffs on trouserlegs that billowed at the knees made Richard think of some longforgotten pasha in the faraway past, and the fingertip coat and highly lustrous shoes gave the wearer, when walking, the appearance of a strutting cock. Their hair was long and swept up to meet in the back, forming a ducktail. They spent hours training it to remain that way.

The girls were characterized by the extreme shortness of their skirts, which stopped well above the knees. Their jackets, too, were fingertip in length, coming to within an inch of the skirt hem. Their hair reached below the shoulder in the back, and it was usually worn piled in front to form a huge pompadour.

The pachuco was born in El Paso, had gone west to Los Angeles, and was now moving north. To society, these zootsuiters were a menace, and the name alone classified them as undesirables, but Richard learned that there was much more to it than a mere group with a name. That in spite of their behavior, which was sensational at times and violent at others, they were simply a portion of a confused humanity, employing their self-segregation as a means of expression. And because theirs was a spontaneous, and not a planned, retaliation, he saw it as a vicissitude of society, obvious only because of its nature and comparative suddenness.

From the leggy, short-skirted girls, he learned that their mores were no different from those of what he considered good girls. What was under the scant covering was as inaccessible as it would be under the more conventional dress. He felt, in fact, that these girls were more difficult to reach. And from the boys he learned that their bitterness and hostile attitude toward "whites" was not merely a lark. They had learned hate through actual experience, with everything the word implied. They had not been as lucky as he, and showed the scars to prove it. And, later on, Richard saw in retrospect that what happened to him in the city jail in San Jose was due more to the character of a handful of men than to the wide, almost organized attitude of a society, for just as the zoot-suiters were blamed en masse for the actions of a few, they, in turn, blamed the other side for the very same reason.

As happens in most such groups, there were misunderstandings and disagreements over trivia. Pachucos fought among themselves, for the most part, and they fought hard. It was not unusual that a quarrel born on the streets or backalleys of a Los Angeles slum was settled in the Santa Clara Valley. Richard understood them and partly sympathized, but their way of life was not entirely justified in his mind, for he felt that they were somehow reneging on life; this was the easiest thing for them to do. They, like his father, were defeated—only more so, because they really never started to live. They, too, were but making a show of resistance.

Of the new friends Richard made, those who were native to San Jose were relegated to become casual acquaintances, for they were as Americanized as he, and did not interest him. The newcomers became the object of his explorations. He was avidly hungry to learn the ways of these people. It was not easy for him to approach them at first, because his clothes labeled him as an outsider, and, too, he had trouble understanding their speech. He must not ask questions, for fear of offending them; his deductions as to their character and makeup must come from close association. He was careful not to be patronizing or in any way act superior.

And, most important, they must never suspect what he was doing. The most difficult moments for him were when he was doing the talking, for he was conscious that his Spanish was better than theirs. He learned enough of their vernacular to get along; he did not learn more, because he was always in a hurry about knowledge. Soon he counted a few boys as friends, but had a much harder time of it with the girls, because they considered him a traitor to his "race." Before he knew it, he found that he almost never spoke to them in English, and no longer defended the "whites," but, rather, spoke disparagingly of them whenever possible. He also bought a suit to wear when in their company, not with such an extreme cut as those they wore, but removed enough from the conservative so he would not be considered a square. And he found himself a girl, who refused to dance the faster pieces with him, because he still jittered in the American manner. So they danced only to soft music while they kissed in the dimmed light, and that was the extent of their lovemaking. Or he stood behind her at the bar, with his arms around her as she sipped a Nehi, and felt strange because she was a Mexican and everyone around them was also Mexican, and felt strange still from the knowledge that he felt strange. When the dance was over, he took her to where her parents were sitting and said goodnight to the entire family.

Whenever his new friends saw him in the company of his school acquaintances, they were courteously polite, but they later chastised him for fraternizing with what they called the enemy. Then Richard had misgivings, because he knew that his desire to become one of them was not a sincere one in that respect, yet upon reflection he realized that in truth he enjoyed their company and valued their friendship, and his sense of guilt was gone. He went along with everything they did, being careful only to keep away from serious trouble with no loss of prestige. Twice he entered the dreamworld induced by marihuana, and after the effect of the drug was expended, he was surprised to discover that he did not crave it, and was glad, for he could not afford a kick like that. As it was, life was too short for him to be able to do the many things he knew he still must do. The youths understood that he did not want it, and never pressed him.

Now the time came to withdraw a little. He thought it would be a painful thing, but they liked him, and their friendliness made everything natural. He, in his gratefulness, loved them for it.

I can be a part of everything, he thought, because I am the only one capable of controlling my destiny. . . . Never—no, never—will I allow myself to become a part of a group—to become classified, to lose my individuality. . . . I will not become a follower, nor will I allow myself to become a leader, because I must be myself and accept for myself only that which I value, and not what is being valued by everyone else these days . . . like a Goddamn suit of clothes they're wearing this season or Cuban heels . . . a style in ethics. What shall we do to liven up the season this year of Our Lord 1940, you from the North, and you from the South, and you from the East, and you from the West? Be original, and for Chrissake speak up! Shall we make it a vogue to sacrifice virgins—but, no, that's been done. . . . What do you think of matricide or motherrape? No? Well—wish we could deal with more personal things, such as prolonging the gestation period in the Homo sapiens; that would keep the married men hopping, no?

He thought this and other things, because the young are like that, and for them nothing is impossible; no, nothing is impossible, and this truism gives impetus to the impulse to laugh at abstract bonds. This night he thought this, and could laugh at the simplicity with which he could render powerless obstacles in his search for life, he had returned to the Mexican dancehall for the first time in weeks, and the dance was fast coming to a close. The orchestra had blared out a jazzedup version of "Home, Sweet Home" and was going through it again at a much slower tempo, giving the couples on the dancefloor one last chance for the sensual embraces that would have to last them a week. Richard was dancing with his girl, leading with his leg and holding her slight body close against his, when one of his friends tapped him on the shoulder.

"We need some help," he said. "Will you meet us by the door after the dance?" The question was more of a command, and the speaker did not wait for an answer. The dance was over, and Richard kissed the girl goodbye and joined the group that was gathering conspicuously as the people poured out through the only exit.

"What goes?" he asked.

"We're going to get some guys tonight," answered the youth who had spoken to him earlier. He was twenty years old and was called the Rooster.

The Mexican people have an affinity for incongruous nicknames. In this group, there was Tuerto, who was not blind; Cacarizo, who was not pockmarked; Zurdo, who was not lefthanded; and a drab little fellow who was called Slick. Only Chango was appropriately named. There was indeed something anthropoidal about him.

The Rooster said, "They beat hell out of my brother last night, because he was jiving with one of their girls. I just got the word that they'll be around tonight if we want trouble."

"Man," said Chango, "we want a mess of trouble."

"Know who they are?" asked the Tuerto.

"Yeah. It was those bastards from Ontario," said the Rooster. "We had trouble with them before."

"Where they going to be?" asked Richard.

"That's what makes it good. Man, it's going to be real good," said the Rooster. "In the Orchard. No cops, no nothing. Only us."

"And the mud," said the Tuerto. The Orchard was a twelve-acre cherry grove in the new industrial district on the north side of the city.

"It'll be just as muddy for them," said the Rooster. "Let's go!"

They walked out and hurriedly got into the car. There were eight of them in Zurdo's sedan, and another three were to follow in a coupé. Richard sat in the back on Slick's lap. He was silent, afraid that they might discover the growing terror inside him. The Rooster took objects out of a gunnysack.

"Here, man, this is for you. Don't lose it," he said. It was a doubledup bicycle chain, one end bound tightly with leather thongs to form a grip.

Richard held it in his hands and, for an unaccountable reason, said, "Thank you." Goddamn! he thought. What the hell did I get into? He wished they would get to their destination quickly, before his fear turned to panic. He had no idea who it was they were going to meet. Would there be three or thirty against them? He looked at the bludgeon in his hand and thought, Christ! Somebody could get killed!

The Tuerto passed a pint of whiskey back to them. Richard drank thirstily, then passed the bottle on.

"You want some, Chango?" asked the Rooster.

"That stuff's not for me, man. I stick to yesca," he answered. Four jerky rasps came from him as he inhaled, reluctant to allow the least bit of smoke to escape him, receiving the full force of the drug in a hurry. He offered the cigarette, but they all refused it. Then he carefully put it out, and placed the butt in a small match-box.

It seemed to Richard that they had been riding for hours when finally they arrived at the Orchard. They backed the car under the trees, leaving the motor idling because they might have to leave in a hurry. The rest of the gang did not arrive; the Rooster said, "Those sons of bitches aren't coming!"

"Let's wait a few minutes," said the Tuerto. "Maybe they'll show up."

"No, they won't come," said the Rooster, in a calm voice now. He unzipped his pants legs and rolled them up to the knees. "Goddamn mud," he said, almost good-naturedly. "Come on!" They followed him into the Orchard. When they were approximately in the center of the tract, they stopped. "Here they come," whispered the Rooster.

Richard could not hear a thing. He was more afraid, but had stopped shaking. In spite of his fear, his mind was alert. He strained every sense, in order not to miss any part of this experience. He wanted to retain everything that was about to happen. He was surprised at the way the Rooster had taken command from the moment they left the dancehall. Richard had never thought of any one of the boys being considered a leader, and now they were all following the Rooster, and Richard fell naturally in line. The guy's like ice, he thought. Like a Goddamn piece of ice!

Suddenly forms took shape in the darkness before him.

And just as suddenly he was in the kaleidoscopic swirl of the fight. He felt blows on his face and body, as if from a distance, and he flayed viciously with the chain. There was a deadly quietness to the struggle. He was conscious that some of the fallen were moaning, and a voice screamed, "The son of a bitch broke my arm!" And that was all he heard for a while, because he was lying on the ground with his face in the mud.

They halfdragged, halfcarried him to the car. It had bogged down in the mud, and they put him in the back while they tried to make it move. They could see headlights behind them, beyond the trees.

"We have to get the hell out of here," said the Rooster. "They got help. Push! Push!" Richard opened the door and fell out of the car. He got up and stumbled crazily in the darkness. He was grabbed and violently thrown in again. They could hear the sound of a large group coming toward them from the Orchard.

"Let's cut out!" shouted the Tuerto. "Leave it here!"

"No!" said the Rooster. "They'll tear it apart!" The car slithered onto the sidewalk and the wheels finally got traction. In a moment, they were moving down the street.

Richard held his hands to his head. "Jesus!" he exclaimed. "The cabrón threw me with the shithouse."

"It was a bat," said the Rooster.

"What?"

"He hit you with a Goddamn baseball bat!"

They took Richard home, and the Rooster helped him to his door. "Better rub some lard on your head," he told him.

"All right. Say, you were right, Rooster. Those other cats didn't show at all."

"You have to expect at least a couple of guys to chicken out on a deal like this," said the Rooster. "You did real good, man. I knew you'd do good."

Richard looked at his friend thoughtfully for a moment. In the dim light, his dark hair, Medusalike, curled from his collar in back almost to his eyebrows. He wondered what errant knight from Castile had traveled four thousand miles to mate with a daughter of Cuahtémoc to produce this strain. "How did you know?" he asked.

"Because I could tell it meant so much to you," said the Rooster.

"When I saw them coming, it looked like there were a hundred of them."

"There were only about fifteen. You're okay, Richard. Any time you want something, just let me know."

Richard felt humble in his gratification. He understood the friendship that was being offered. "I'll tell you, Rooster," he said. "I've never been afraid as much as I was tonight." He thought, If he knows this, perhaps he won't feel the sense of obligation.

"Hell, that's no news. We all were."

"Did we beat them?" asked Richard.

"Yeah, we beat them," answered the Rooster. "We beat them real good!"

And that, for Richard Rubio, was the finest moment of a most happy night.

WILLIAM STAFFORD

William Stafford's poems seem to come from about four o'clock in the morning, the time of very first awakening when, as Thoreau put it, the unconscious mind is still available. We can still feel the real weight and soul of things. Stafford (1914–1993) said that his habit was to awaken before the other members of his family, get dressed, and then lie down again on the living room couch. Words and thoughts would arrive, whole poems might arrive. In *Writing the Australian Crawl* (1978), his book on how poetry is made, there is much about trust. In effect, you are to lie back down again, relaxing into whatever happens. There is a suspension of willfullness—what you mainly do is listen. The language that arises will more likely be connected to the world, because you, listening rather than imposing, are better connected. The words can be trusted. Stafford grew up in Kansas, spent World War II up and down the West Coast in work camps as a conscientious objector, a life described in *Down in My Heart* (1948), and worked many years as a teacher and mentor at Lewis and Clark College in Portland, Oregon. These biographical details are indicative, perhaps, but not entirely explanatory. The poems seem to have come on their own; Stafford seems merely to have nudged them, as it were, into our common space.

"In Response to a Question," from *Traveling Through the Dark* (1962)

The earth says have a place, be what that place
requires; hear the sound the birds imply
and see as deep as ridges go behind
each other. (Some people call their scenery flat,
their only picture framed by what they know:
I think around them rise a riches and a loss
too equal for their chart—but absolutely tall.)

The earth says every summer have a ranch
that's minimum: one tree, one well, a landscape
that proclaims a universe—sermon
of the hills, hallelujah mountain,
highway guided by the way the world is tilted,

reduplication of mirage, flat evening:
a kind of ritual for the wavering.

The earth says where you live wear the kind
of color that your life is (gray shirt for me)
and by listening with the same bowed head that sings
draw all into one song, join
the sparrow on the lawn, and row that easy
way, the rage without met by the wings
within that guide you anywhere the wind blows.

Listening, I think that's what the earth says.

"Speaking Frankly," from *Someday, Maybe* (1973)

It isn't your claim, or mine, or
what we do or don't do, or how
we feel, or our gain or loss—it's something
other, and across our whole country a fine
soft rain comes, the wide gray clouds
and a sigh in the wind for us all.

Those endless experiments in woods and
grass go on, get ready to pay; the whole
world clenches itself, and quietly
shouts: it waves the days forward.
On the edge of each moment a little
voice tells the scenario, "Come."

And you feel it come down: the end,
the beginning, the part between, light
as a dance that draws near in the big
expanse maintained for us by the sky.
We go wandering out. And at the end we sense
here none of you, none of us—no one.

"Representing Far Places," from *Traveling Through the Dark* (1962)

In the canoe wilderness branches wait for winter;
every leaf concentrates; a drop from the paddle falls.
Up through water at the dip of a falling leaf

to the sky's drop of light or the smell of another star
fish in the lake leap arcs of realization,
hard fins prying out from the dark below.

Often in society when the talk turns witty
you think of that place, and can't polarize at all:
it would be a kind of treason. The land fans in your head
canyon by canyon; steep roads diverge.
Representing far places you stand in the room,
all that you know merely a weight in the weather.
It is all right to be simply the way you have to be,
among contradictory ridges in some crescendo of knowing.

"Montana Eclogue," from *Allegiances* (1970)

1

After the fall drive, the last
horseman humps down the trail south;
High Valley turns into a remote, still cathedral.
Stone Creek in its low bank turns calmly
through the trampled meadow. The one scouting
thunderhead above Long Top hangs to watch,
ready for its reinforcement due in October.

Logue, the man who always closes down the camp,
is left all alone at Clear Lake, where
he is leisurely but busy, pausing to glance across
the water toward Winter Peak. The bunkhouse
will be boarded up, the cookshack barricaded
against bears, the corral gates lashed shut.
Whatever winter needs, it will have to find
for itself, all the slow months the wind owns.

From that shore below the mountain the water
darkens; the whole surface of the lake livens,
and, upward, high miles of pine tops bend where a storm
walks the country. Deeper and deeper, autumn
floods in. Nothing can hold against that current
the aspens feel. And Logue, by being there, suddenly
carries for us everything that we can load on him,
we who have stopped indoors and let our faces
forget how storms come: that lonely man works for us.

2

Far from where we are, air owns those ranches
our trees hardly hear of, open places
braced against cold hills. Mornings, that
news hits the leaves like rain, and we
stop everything time brings, and freeze that one,
open, great, real thing—the world's gift: day.

Up there, air like an axe chops, near timberline,
the clear-cut miles the marmots own. We
try to know, all deep, all sharp, even while
busy here, that other: gripped in a job,
aimed steady at a page, or riffled by distractions,
we break free into that world of the farthest coat—air.

We glimpse that last storm when the wolves
get the mountains back, when our homes will flicker
bright, then dull, then old; and the trees
will advance, knuckling their roots or lying in
windrows to match the years. We glimpse
a crack that begins to run down the wall,
and like a blanket over the window at night
that world is with us and those wolves are here.

3

Up there, ready to be part of what comes, the high lakes
lie in their magnificent beds; but men,
great as their heroes are, live by their deeds
only as a pin of shadow in a cavern their thought
gets lost in. We pause; we stand where
we are meant to be, waver as foolish as
we are, tell our lies with all the beautiful grace
an animal has when it runs—

Citizen, step back from the fire and let night
have your head: suddenly you more than hear
what is true so abruptly that God is cold:—
winter is here. What no one saw, has
come. Then everything the sun approved could
really fail? Shed from your back, the years
fall one by one, and nothing that comes
will be your fault. You breathe a few breaths
free at the thought: things can come so great

that your part is too small to count,
if winter can come.

Logue brings us all that. Earth took
the old saints, who battered their hearts,
met arrows, or died by the germs God sent;
but Logue, by being alone and occurring to us,
carries us forward a little,
and on his way out for the year will
stand by the shore and see winter in,
the great, repeated lesson every year.

A storm bends by that shore and
one flake at a time teaches grace,
even to stone.

N. SCOTT MOMADAY

The last thirty years or so have seen a great renaissance in writing about place—personal place, family place, place that has gotten into the genes and has helped shape the foot, the hand, the eye, and not least the heart. This is true east and west, but in the West there is special significance to an expression of roots because the West is so strongly associated with free roaming, always being ready to head for the next strike at a moment's notice. Beginning with the following piece, first published in *The Reporter* in 1967, and with Edward Abbey's *Desert Solitaire* in the next year, the recent western literature of place has been subverting a large habit of restlessness. The new writing is about being somewhere and really paying attention. In *The Way to Rainy Mountain*, which as title and theme could very easily be translated as "the way to the world" or "the way to life," N. Scott Momaday (b. 1934) combines historical scholarship, traditional Kiowa stories, and his own personal narrative (together with his father's drawings) into a montage-like presentation. The mixedness and the somewhat experimental or postmodernist surface of the text, however, create no barriers at all. The feel for place, plainly the heart of the matter, makes everything clear and close as a dream of home.

"Introduction" to *The Way to Rainy Mountain* (1968)

A single knoll rises out of the plain in Oklahoma, north and west of the Wichita Range. For my people, the Kiowas, it is an old landmark, and they gave it the name Rainy Mountain. The hardest weather in the world is there. Winter brings blizzards, hot tornadic winds arise in the spring, and in summer the prairie is an anvil's edge. The grass turns brittle and brown, and it cracks beneath your feet. There are green belts along the rivers and creeks, linear groves of hickory and pecan, willow and witch hazel. At a distance in July or August the steaming foliage seems almost to writhe in fire. Great green and yellow grasshoppers are everywhere in the tall grass, popping up like corn to sting the flesh, and tortoises crawl about on the red earth, going nowhere in the plenty of time. Loneliness is an aspect of the land. All things in the plain are isolate; there is no confusion of objects in the eye, but *one* hill or *one* tree or *one* man. To look upon that landscape in the early morning, with the sun at your back, is to lose the sense of proportion. Your imagination comes to life, and this, you think, is where Creation was begun.

I returned to Rainy Mountain in July. My grandmother had died in the spring, and I wanted to be at her grave. She had lived to be very old and at last infirm. Her only living daughter was with her when she died, and I was told that in death her face was that of a child.

I like to think of her as a child. When she was born, the Kiowas were living the last great moment of their history. For more than a hundred years they had controlled the open range from the Smoky Hill River to the Red, from the headwaters of the Canadian to the fork of the Arkansas and Cimarron. In alliance with the Comanches, they had ruled the whole of the southern Plains. War was their sacred business, and they were among the finest horsemen the world has ever known. But warfare for the Kiowas was preeminently a matter of disposition rather than of survival, and they never understood the grim, unrelenting advance of the U.S. Cavalry. When at last, divided and ill-provisioned, they were driven onto the Staked Plains in the cold rains of autumn, they fell into panic. In Palo Duro Canyon they abandoned their crucial stores to pillage and had nothing then but their lives. In order to save themselves, they surrendered to the soldiers at Fort Sill and were imprisoned in the old stone corral that now stands as a military museum. My grandmother was spared the humiliation of those high gray walls by eight or ten years, but she must have known from birth the affliction of defeat, the dark brooding of old warriors.

Her name was Aho, and she belonged to the last culture to evolve in North America. Her forebears came down from the high country in western Montana nearly three centuries ago. They were a mountain people, a mysterious tribe of hunters whose language has never been positively classified in any major group. In the late seventeenth century they began a long migration to the south and east. It was a journey toward the dawn, and it led to a golden age. Along the way the Kiowas were befriended by the Crows, who gave them the culture and religion of the Plains. They acquired horses, and their ancient nomadic spirit was suddenly free of the ground. They acquired Tai-me, the sacred Sun Dance doll, from that moment the object and symbol of their worship, and so shared in the divinity of the sun. Not least, they acquired the sense of destiny, therefore courage and pride. When they entered upon the southern Plains they had been transformed. No longer were they slaves to the simple necessity of survival; they were a lordly and dangerous society of fighters and thieves, hunters and priests of the sun. According to their origin myth, they entered the world through a hollow log. From one point of view, their migration was the fruit of an old prophecy, for indeed they emerged from a sunless world.

Although my grandmother lived out her long life in the shadow of

Rainy Mountain, the immense landscape of the continental interior lay like memory in her blood. She could tell of the Crows, whom she had never seen, and of the Black Hills, where she had never been. I wanted to see in reality what she had seen more perfectly in the mind's eye, and traveled fifteen hundred miles to begin my pilgrimage.

Yellowstone, it seemed to me, was the top of the world, a region of deep lakes and dark timber, canyons and waterfalls. But, beautiful as it is, one might have the sense of confinement there. The skyline in all directions is close at hand, the high wall of the woods and deep cleavages of shade. There is a perfect freedom in the mountains, but it belongs to the eagle and the elk, the badger and the bear. The Kiowas reckoned their stature by the distance they could see, and they were bent and blind in the wilderness.

Descending eastward, the highland meadows are a stairway to the plain. In July the inland scope of the Rockies is luxuriant with flax and buckwheat, stonecrop and larkspur. The earth unfolds and the limit of the land recedes. Clusters of trees, and animals grazing far in the distance, cause the vision to reach away and wonder to build upon the mind. The sun follows a longer course in the day, and the sky is immense beyond all comparison. The great billowing clouds that sail upon it are shadows that move upon the grain like water, dividing light. Farther down, in the land of the Crows and Blackfeet, the plain is yellow. Sweet clover takes hold of the hills and bends upon itself to cover and seal the soil. There the Kiowas paused on their way; they had come to the place where they must change their lives. The sun is at home on the plains. Precisely there does it have the certain character of a god. When the Kiowas came to the land of the Crows, they could see the dark lees of the hills at dawn across the Bighorn River, the profusion of light on the grain shelves, the oldest deity ranging after the solstices. Not yet would they veer southward to the caldron of the land that lay below; they must wean their blood from the northern winter and hold the mountains a while longer in their view. They bore Tai-me in procession to the east.

A dark mist lay over the Black Hills, and the land was like iron. At the top of a ridge I caught sight of Devil's Tower upthrust against the gray sky as if in the birth of time the core of the earth had broken through its crust and the motion of the world was begun. There are things in nature that engender an awful quiet in the heart of man; Devil's Tower is one of them. Two centuries ago, because they could not do otherwise, the Kiowas made a legend at the base of the rock. My grandmother said: *Eight children were there at play, seven sisters and their brother. Suddenly the boy was struck dumb; he trembled and began to run upon his hands and feet. His fingers became claws, and his body was covered with fur. Directly there was a bear where the boy had been. The sisters were terrified; they ran, and the bear after them. They came to the stump of a great tree, and the tree spoke to them. It bade them climb upon it, and as they did so it began to rise into the air. The bear came to kill them, but they were just beyond its reach. It reared against the tree and scored the bark all around with its claws. The seven sisters were borne into the sky, and they became the stars of the Big Dipper.*

From that moment, and so long as the legend lives, the Kiowas have kinsmen in the night sky. Whatever they were in the mountains, they could be no more. However tenuous their well-being, however much they had suffered and would suffer again, they had found a way out of the wilderness.

My grandmother had a reverence for the sun, a holy regard that now is all but gone out of mankind. There was a wariness in her, and an ancient awe. She was a Christian in her later years, but she had come a long way about, and she never forgot her birthright. As a child she had been to the Sun Dances; she had taken part in those annual rites, and by then she had learned the restoration of her people in the presence of Tai-me. She was about seven when the last Kiowa Sun Dance was held in 1887 on the Washita River above Rainy Mountain Creek. The buffalo were gone. In order to consummate the ancient sacrifice—to impale the head of a buffalo bull upon the medicine tree—a delegation of old men journeyed into Texas, there to beg and barter for an animal from the Goodnight herd. She was ten when the Kiowas came together for the last time as a living Sun Dance culture. They could find no buffalo; they had to hang an old hide from the sacred tree. Before the dance could begin, a company of soldiers rode out from Fort Sill under orders to disperse the tribe. Forbidden without cause the essential act of their faith, having seen the wild herds slaughtered and left to rot upon the ground, the Kiowas backed away forever from the medicine tree. That was July 20, 1890, at the great bend of the Washita. My grandmother was there. Without bitterness, and for as long as she lived, she bore a vision of deicide.

Now that I can have her only in memory, I see my grandmother in the several postures that were peculiar to her: standing at the wood stove on a winter morning and turning meat in a great iron skillet; sitting at the south window, bent above her beadwork, and afterwards, when her vision failed, looking down for a long time into the fold of her hands; going out upon a cane, very slowly as she did when the weight of age came upon her; praying. I remember her most often at prayer. She made long, rambling prayers out of suffering and hope, having seen many things. I was never sure that I had the right to hear, so exclusive were they of all mere custom and company. The last time I saw her she prayed standing by the side of her bed at night, naked to the waist, the light of a kerosene lamp moving upon her dark skin. Her long, black hair, always drawn and braided in the day, lay upon her shoulders and against her breasts like a shawl. I do not speak Kiowa, and I never understood her prayers, but there was something inherently sad in the sound, some merest hesitation upon the syllables of sorrow. She began in a high and descending pitch, exhausting her breath to silence; then again and again— and always the same intensity of effort, of something that is, and is not, like urgency in the human voice. Transported so in the dancing light among the shadows of her room, she seemed beyond the reach of time. But that was illusion; I think I knew then that I should not see her again.

Houses are like sentinels in the plain, old keepers of the weather watch. There, in a very little while, wood takes on the appearance of great age. All colors wear soon away in the wind and rain, and then the wood is burned gray and the grain appears and the nails turn red with rust. The windowpanes are black and opaque; you imagine there is nothing within, and indeed there are many ghosts, bones given up to the land. They stand here and there against the sky, and you approach them for a longer time than you expect. They belong in the distance; it is their domain.

Once there was a lot of sound in my grandmother's house, a lot of coming and going, feasting and talk. The summers there were full of excitement and reunion. The Kiowas are a summer people; they abide the cold and keep to themselves, but when the season turns and the land becomes warm and vital they cannot hold still; an old love of going returns upon them. The aged visitors who came to my grandmother's house when I was a child were made of lean and leather, and they bore themselves upright. They wore great black hats and bright ample shirts that shook in the wind. They rubbed fat upon their hair and wound their braids with strips of colored cloth. Some of them painted their faces and carried the scars of old and cherished enmities. They were an old council of warlords, come to remind and be reminded of who they were. Their wives and daughters served them well. The women might indulge themselves; gossip was at once the mark and compensation of their servitude. They made loud and elaborate talk among themselves, full of jest and gesture, fright and false alarm. They went abroad in fringed and flowered shawls, bright beadwork and German silver. They were at home in the kitchen, and they prepared meals that were banquets.

There were frequent prayer meetings, and great nocturnal feasts. When I was a child I played with my cousins outside, where the lamplight fell upon the ground and the singing of the old people rose up around us and carried away into the darkness. There were a lot of good things to eat, a lot of laughter and surprise. And afterwards, when the quiet returned, I lay down with my grandmother and could hear the frogs away by the river and feel the motion of the air.

Now there is a funeral silence in the rooms, the endless wake of some final word. The walls have closed in upon my grandmother's house. When I returned to it in mourning, I saw for the first time in my life how small it was. It was late at night, and there was a white moon, nearly full. I sat for a long time on the stone steps by the kitchen door. From there I could see out across the land; I could see the long row of trees by the creek, the low light upon the rolling plains, and the stars of the Big Dipper. Once I looked at the moon and caught sight of a strange thing. A cricket had perched upon the handrail, only a few inches away from me. My line of vision was such that the creature filled the moon like a fossil. It had gone there, I thought, to live and die, for there, of all places, was its small definition made whole and eternal. A warm wind rose up and purled like the longing within me.

The next morning I awoke at dawn and went out on the dirt road to Rainy Mountain. It was already hot, and the grasshoppers began to fill the air. Still, it was early in the morning, and the birds sang out of the shadows. The long yellow grass on the mountain shone in the bright light, and a scissortail hied above the land. There, where it ought to be, at the end of a long and legendary way, was my grandmother's grave. Here and there on the dark stones were ancestral names. Looking back once, I saw the mountain and came away.

AL YOUNG

erhaps it is his background in music (guitar and flute, professionally, and a memorable stint as a disc jockey on the San Francisco Bay Area's KJAZ) that lends the easy, vernacular ride to Al Young's poetic line—and a certain scope to his outlook. Clearly, jazz and dancing are important metaphors for a stance and a way through life. Among many other significant western writers, Young (b. 1939) was a Wallace Stegner Fellow at Stanford University before taking his B.A. at the University of California, Berkeley, in 1969. He returned to Stanford to teach creative writing for several years in the early seventies, and has lectured widely at universities throughout the United States. He earned praise for the novel *Snakes* (1970), a bildungsroman, and was hailed by the *New Yorker* for being "cool and objective." That magazine's reviewer continued, "The restraint makes it all the more necessary for us to read him...." Young's work radiates a strong love of life and sees freedom not as an attainment but an ongoing process. The feel for movement and the bigger, always changing picture tends to make his comments on injustice seem undeniable. His books include *The Blues Don't Change: New and Selected Poems* (1982) and *Kinds of Blue: Musical Memoirs* (1984). Following is the title poem from *Dancing* (1969).

"Dancing" from *Dancing* (1969)

1

Yes the simplicity of my life
is so complicated,
on & on it goes,
my lady is gone,
she's at work by now
pulling that 4 to midnight shift.
The hours pass,
I make passes at sumptuous shapes
(typewritten you know)
& rediscover that the Muse is a bitch,
any muse,
music
comes into the picture.
I should be out having adventures

like all the other authors
chasing down dialogue
in the fashionable ghettos,
spearing the bizarre,
everything but falling deeper & deeper
into bad habits
into debt
into traps
in to love
in love
in love with strangers.
I couldve been a trench-coated pusher
& dealt heroin to diplomats
or stood around looking innocent enough
& landed up in the dexamil chewinggum nights
with some of the Go-Go girls who really know
Sun Frun Cisco,
like the time you had to lead me around like a sister
& buy me hangover sandwiches;
I went banging into one pay phone after another
& emptied out musta been a good 6 bucks in coins
all toll
& we did a little laughing of our own
on the benches.

But getting by in Never-Never Land is never enough.
Life *is* more than fun & games.
The thought
after all
that either of us is capable of being assassinated
at any moment
for absolutely nothing
& relatively little
is of course unnerving.
The clouds of blue summer
keep getting whiter & thicker
by the afternoon
especially up around the mountains
but nobody cares
in California
nobody dares.

Ladies & gentlemen keep sitting down
at the same old exquisite harpsichords;
bluesmen keep hanging around recording studios
for 3 days in a row
trying to get a hit out of there;
blurry-eyed filipinos
with matching wives or irish girlfriends
keep having a go at pizza
in dim lit parlors run by greeks
served up by lackadaisical she-slavs
from the middlewests,
shy wasps out of Bakersfield.

Kids who werent even born
when I first got on to
how completely the Word can kill
& restore
keep practicing up to tangle with the Man;
drunks & soberer citizens
keep trying to sneak free looks
up inside the topless shoeshine stand
on Columbus Ave,
more post-colonial amuricana;
dogs & cats keep checking out pet food commercials
& running up more in vet bills
than my late grayed grandfather
ever earned,
he was a farmer all right
but who isnt
nowadays
we all keep farming one another
into the ground
& steady losing.

Ahhhhhmerica!
you old happy whore
you miserable trigger-happy cowboy
as bound to death as an overweight film harlot
whose asset's begun to drag
& whose hollywood prophets have to put
the bad mouth out
to gentlemen of the board backeast—
"It's all over dolling

it's *been* all over."
Pity
how fast the deal can go down
when there's nothing
even speculative
to hold it up.

    2

In the end there are only beautiful things to say.
Never mind how dirty the floor was
or the mind of the cuban lady across the street
who suspects you of being a filthy drug addict
who heaves stones at his wife every night
& if his house burned down this evening
it wouldnt be any big thing.
There is all this.
There are friends who'll never know
who you really are
& care less;
sick powerful men
in high dizzying places
who do not operate under the influence of music
who would just as soon assassinate
as make a hero of you
once youre no longer capable of
impeding their selfish proposals.
Their children wear sweatshirts
with your face
your hallowed face shines promiscuously
from the fronts of their sweatless children's
T-shirts
& there will be talk of a 6-hour TV spectacular
the combined effort of all the net-
works.
        20th Century Fox is going to do the picture.
The donations come rolling in.

    ●

It keeps coming back tho.
Children keep getting themselves born,
the soil that once was sweet to taste
draws up & hardens like cornbread baked too long.

Not a green loving thing emerges.
Our children invade the sea.
Evolving fish
plot revolution
against seething ex-fish
& time is moving it on.

Verily
the power that churns the sea
is a solar delight
a celestial upheaval:
the moon is not the moon we think
but serves.

The moon is your face
in the window of the world
the power heart that pumps beneath
the blood that would splatter every whichway
(as from the bellies of cool slit fish)
coursing to its original destinations
watering insights
bathing our insides
washing the way clear for new origins.

It is inevitable
that we should come to these dark places
to these waters where the drowning
appears to take place &
where attitudes of the ignorant
—our former future selves—
appall us in our journeying forth.
Many's the throat I may have slashed
or angel betrayed
in lives past
out of indignation
thinking it might be one less ass
to contend with
in bringing the promiseland to this planet
here & now
once & for all who counted.

But the knife doubles back
& gets to the point
where environment becomes foul

or the mind has harbored so much pain
that it gives itself up
throws itself away
or collapses
wanting to die
wanting to have been dead
& absent

3

Be the mystic
& wage ultimate revolution,
be true to your self,
be what you always wanted
but be that.

No need to pack up
rush into hiding
& be teaching hypnotism in Harlem
advanced gun-running in Angola
Lima or Port-au-Prince
or be back on 12th Street
dealing in automatics
before the dramatic eye
of national educational television.

Be the taker by surprise
of CIA-subsidized marimba bands &
disconsolate hindu castaways,
be the avowed lover of
nothing-to-lose niggers
thru whom Ive returned to the scene of our crimes
because of whose endurance
& in whose care
I was first able to discern
the forcefulness of living love
magnetized at last
from its hidingplace:
the lie,
the not-for-real.

Be yourself
man
they always warned.
                              Find out

what you really are.
Be that!

4

> *I have busted my gut enough*
> *in this absurd horserace*
> *where the jockeys are thrown*
> *from their saddles*
> *and land among the spectators*
> —Nicanor Parra

Now that some layers have been peeled back
& I can see where dreams I acted out at 15
came true
I want nothing more than
the touch of that peace
the digging for which
has rocked me down thru months & years
of nothing doing
getting nowhere
drinking too much in
drowning too little out
desiring to be infinitely drunk
hiding up under the skirts of women
the soft skin
attracting
as it always does
the hard of seeing
the impossible to touch.
Now that I have walked along envying birds
the security of their placement in nature
& on moment's notice
glanced down toward the sea
on a schedule
that doesnt permit me
time to sit much out;
now that some crystalization of what living's about
has taken place
within
I'm content to settle
for nothing less
than the honey itself.

I have tasted the milk &
found it sour.

Heaven was never more delicious
to me: an earth eater
than when rhythmically presented
the April I met a stranger in a street
a mystic
a prophet
a seeker true enough
with no bullshit attached
who looked honestly into my eyes
& explained to me more than where I'd been
or would have to go;
he touched my trembling hand & hinted
what steps I might take to get there.
Now that I have retraced all the old roads
in this road show version of my past
Ive been putting on
for some time
now
I am ready
to fade out of show biz.

Now that I have risen from the long nap
it is again 7:35 pm
of what this morning
was a lucid new day.
Lights are shining from my window.
Outside
new men & women walk toward one another
in a nighttime field of energy.

Warmblooded &
a little confused
I move toward what I'm hoping is the light.

All my struggles have led me to this moment.

May all your struggles lead likewise toward peace.

Let the revolutions proceed!

JEANNE WAKATSUKI HOUSTON AND JAMES D. HOUSTON

On February 19, 1942, a little over two months after the bombing of Pearl Harbor, President Roosevelt signed Executive Order 9066, defining military areas in the United States and giving the green light for war-connected relocation of citizens within those areas. Thus began what John Hersey, in a commentary included in John Armour and Peter Wright's *Manzanar* (1988), later termed "the mass incarceration, on racial grounds alone," of over 110,000 West Coast Americans of Japanese descent. Uprooted from homes and jobs, they were taken to ten camps, two of which—Tule Lake in the north and Manzanar in the Owens Valley—were in California. Manzanar, a square-bordered 6,000 acres, was described by *Life* magazine in April 1942 as a "scenic spot of lonely loveliness," perhaps true enough to someone not held there involuntarily. This was the place to which young Jeanne Wakatsuki (b. 1934) was brought. Her account, written thirty years later with her husband, the novelist James D. Houston, reflects the almost incredible adaptability, tolerance, and even humor of the internees, and also the deep and rankling hurt of not being trusted simply because of one's ethnic background. The relocation may be an example of wartime hysteria (even Walter Lippman and William O. Douglas swallowed the alarmist notion of military danger on the West Coast), or an instance of simple racism, or both together. It remains an instructive mark on western and American history.

Chapter 4, from *Farewell to Manzanar* (1973)

A Common Master Plan

I don't remember what we ate that first morning. I know we stood for half an hour in cutting wind waiting to get our food. Then we took it back to the cubicle and ate huddled around the stove. Inside, it was warmer than when we left, because Woody was already making good his promise to Mama, tacking up some ends of lath he'd found, stuffing rolled paper around the door frame.

Trouble was, he had almost nothing to work with. Beyond this temporary weather stripping, there was little else he could do. Months went by, in fact, before our "home" changed much at all from what it was the day we moved in—bare floors, blanket partitions, one bulb in each compartment dangling from a roof beam, and open ceilings overhead so that mischievous boys like Ray and Kiyo could climb up into the rafters and peek into anyone's life.

The simple truth is the camp was no more ready for us when we got there than we were ready for it. We had only the dimmest ideas of what to expect. Most of the families, like us, had moved out from southern California with as much luggage as each person could carry. Some old men left Los Angeles wearing Hawaiian shirts and Panama hats and stepped off the bus at an altitude of 4000 feet, with nothing available but sagebrush and tarpaper to stop the April winds pouring down off the back side of the Sierras.

The War Department was in charge of all the camps at this point. They began to issue military surplus from the First World War—olive-drab knit caps, earmuffs, peacoats, canvas leggings. Later on, sewing machines were shipped in, and one barracks was turned into a clothing factory. An old seamstress took a peacoat of mine, tore the lining out, opened and flattened the sleeves, added a collar, put arm holes in and handed me back a beautiful cape. By fall dozens of seamstresses were working full-time transforming thousands of these old army clothes into capes, slacks and stylish coats. But until that factory got going and packages from friends outside began to fill out our wardrobes, warmth was more important than style. I couldn't help laughing at Mama walking around in army earmuffs and a pair of wide-cuffed, khaki-colored wool trousers several sizes too big for her. Japanese are generally smaller than Caucasians, and almost all these clothes were oversize. They flopped, they dangled, they hung.

It seems comical, looking back; we were a band of Charlie Chaplins marooned in the California desert. But at the time, it was pure chaos. That's the only way to describe it. The evacuation had been so hurriedly planned, the camps so hastily thrown together, nothing was completed when we got there, and almost nothing worked.

I was sick continually, with stomach cramps and diarrhea. At first it was from the shots they gave us for typhoid, in very heavy doses and in assembly-line fashion: swab, jab, swab, *Move along now*, swab, jab, swab, *Keep it moving*. That knocked all of us younger kids down at once, with fevers and vomiting. Later, it was the food that made us sick, young and old alike. The kitchens were too small and badly ventilated. Food would spoil from being left out too long. That summer, when the heat got fierce, it would spoil faster. The refrigeration kept breaking down. The cooks, in many cases, had never cooked before. Each block had to provide its own volunteers. Some were lucky and had a professional or two in their midst. But the first chef in our block had been a gardener all his life and suddenly found himself preparing three meals a day for 250 people.

"The Manzanar runs" became a condition of life, and you only hoped that when you rushed to the latrine, one would be in working order.

That first morning, on our way to the chow line, Mama and I tried to use the women's latrine in our block. The smell of it spoiled what little appetite we had. Outside, men were working in an open trench, up to their knees in muck—a common sight in the months to come. Inside, the floor was covered with excrement, and all twelve bowls were erupting like a row of tiny volcanoes.

Mama stopped a kimono-wrapped woman stepping past us with her sleeve pushed up against her nose and asked, "What do you do?"

"Try Block Twelve," the woman said, grimacing. "They have just finished repairing the pipes."

It was about two city blocks away. We followed her over there and found a line of women waiting in the wind outside the latrine. We had no choice but to join the line and wait with them.

Inside it was like all the other latrines. Each block was built to the same design, just as each of the ten camps, from California to Arkansas, was built to a common master plan. It was an open room, over a concrete slab. The sink was a long metal trough against one wall, with a row of spigots for hot and cold water. Down the center of the room twelve toilet bowls were arranged in six pairs, back to back, with no partitions. My mother was a very modest person, and this was going to be agony for her, sitting down in public, among strangers.

One old woman had already solved the problem for herself by dragging in a large cardboard carton. She set it up around one of the bowls, like a three-sided screen. OXYDOL was printed in large black letters down the front. I remember this well, because that was the soap we were issued for laundry; later on, the smell of it would permeate these rooms. The upended carton was about four feet high. The old woman behind it wasn't much taller. When she stood, only her head showed over the top.

She was about Granny's age. With great effort she was trying to fold the sides of the screen together. Mama happened to be at the head of the line now. As she approached the vacant bowl, she and the old woman bowed to each other from the waist. Mama then moved to help her with the carton, and the old woman said very graciously, in Japanese, "Would you like to use it?"

Happily, gratefully, Mama bowed again and said, "*Arigato*" (Thank you). "*Arigato gozaimas*" (Thank you very much). "I will return it to your barracks."

"Oh, no. It is not necessary. I will be glad to wait."

The old woman unfolded one side of the cardboard, while Mama opened the other; then she bowed again and scurried out the door.

Those big cartons were a common sight in the spring of 1942. Eventually sturdier partitions appeared, one or two at a time. The first were built of scrap lumber. Word would get around that Block such and such had partitions now, and Mama and my older sisters would walk halfway across the camp to use them. Even after every latrine in camp was screened, this quest for privacy continued. Many would wait until late at night. Ironically, because of this, midnight was often the most crowded time of all.

Like so many of the women there, Mama never did get used to the latrines. It was a humiliation she just learned to endure: *shikata ga nai*, this cannot be helped. She would quickly subordinate her own desires to those of the family or the community, because she knew cooperation was the only way to survive. At the same time she placed a high premium on personal privacy, respected it in others and insisted upon it for herself. Almost everyone at Manzanar had inherited this pair of traits from the generations before them who had learned to live in a small, crowded country like Japan. Because of the first they were able to take a desolate stretch of wasteland and gradually make it livable. But the entire situation there, especially in the beginning—the packed sleeping quarters, the communal mess halls, the open toilets—all this was an open insult to that other, private self, a slap in the face you were powerless to challenge.

EDWARD ABBEY

Writers about nature tend not to be funny. There is just too much sadness, for most, in the losses that have become our daily story. Whole species, forests, topsoil, quietness, simple space: all are declining in the massive erosion that, unfortunately, characterizes the twentieth century. But Edward Abbey (1927–1989), displaying a wolfish, enjoying grin, called out to his fellow environmentalists, "Joy, shipmates, Joy!" even as he described universal folly and despoliation. He often recommended that people of a green persuasion should get outside more frequently, affirm and enjoy this life more, literally keep their feet on the good ground. Abbey's ground was the desert Southwest, particularly the Colorado Plateau and the Utah canyon country, though as a Pennsylvania native he also maintained nostalgic allegiance to Appalachia. He had first seen the West on a hitchhiking expedition at age seventeen, in 1944, and was permanently marked by what he later called the "burnt, barren, bold, bright landscape" of Arizona, seen from an open boxcar door. That stretch of alliteration is a clue to Abbey's extravagance and playfulness, the undercurrent of wise humor that kept him sane (more or less sane, he would likely interject) in the face of accelerating events. The following selection is from *The Journey Home: Essays In Defense of the American West* (New York: E. P. Dutton, 1977).

"The Great American Desert," from *The Journey Home* (1977)

In my case it was love at first sight. This desert, all deserts, any desert. No matter where my head and feet may go, my heart and my entrails stay behind, here on the clean, true, comfortable rock, under the black sun of God's forsaken country. When I take on my next incarnation, my bones will remain bleaching nicely in a stone gulch under the rim of some faraway plateau, way out there in the back of beyond. An unrequited and excessive love, inhuman no doubt but painful anyhow, especially when I see my desert under attack. "The one death I cannot bear," said the Sonoran-Arizonan poet Richard Shelton. The kind of love that makes a man selfish, possessive, irritable. If you're thinking of a visit, my natural reaction is like a rattlesnake's—to warn you off. What I want to say goes something like this.

Survival Hint #1: Stay out of there. Don't go. Stay home and read a good book, this one for example. The Great American Desert is an awful place. People get hurt, get sick, get lost out there. Even if you survive, which is not certain, you will have a miserable time. The desert is for movies and God-intoxicated mystics, not for family recreation.

Let me enumerate the hazards. First the Walapai tiger, also known as conenose kissing bug. *Triatoma protracta* is a true bug, black as sin, and it flies through the night quiet as an assassin. It does not attack directly like a mosquito or deerfly, but alights at a discreet distance, undetected, and creeps upon you, its hairy little feet making not the slightest noise. The kissing bug is fond of warmth and like Dracula requires mammalian blood for sustenance. When it reaches you the bug crawls onto your skin so gently, so softly that unless your senses are hyperacute you feel nothing. Selecting a tender point, the bug slips its conical proboscis into your flesh, injecting a poisonous anesthetic. If you are asleep you will feel nothing. If you happen to be awake you may notice the faintest of pinpricks, hardly more than a brief ticklish sensation, which you will probably disregard. But the bug is already at work. Having numbed the nerves near the point of entry the bug proceeds (with a sigh of satisfaction, no doubt) to withdraw blood. When its belly is filled, it pulls out, backs off, and waddles away, so drunk and gorged it cannot fly.

At about this time the victim awakes, scratching at a furious itch. If you recognize the symptoms at once, you can sometimes find the bug in your vicinity and destroy it. But revenge will be your only satisfaction. Your night is ruined. If you are of average sensitivity to a kissing bug's poison, your entire body breaks out in hives, skin aflame from head to toe. Some people become seriously ill, in many cases requiring hospitalization. Others recover fully after five or six hours except for a hard and itchy swelling, which may endure for a week.

After the kissing bug, you should beware of rattlesnakes; we have half a dozen species, all offensive and dangerous, plus centipedes, millipedes, tarantulas, black widows, brown recluses, Gila monsters, the deadly poisonous coral snakes, and giant hairy desert scorpions. Plus an immense variety and near-infinite number of ants, midges, gnats, bloodsucking flies, and blood-guzzling mosquitoes. (You might think the desert would be spared at least mosquitoes? Not so. Peer in any water hole by day: swarming with mosquito larvae. Venture out on a summer's eve: The air vibrates with their mournful keening.) Finally, where the desert meets the sea, as on the coasts of Sonora and Baja California, we have the usual assortment of obnoxious marine life: sandflies, ghost crabs, stingrays, electric jellyfish, spiny sea urchins, man-eating sharks, and other creatures so distasteful one prefers not even to name them.

It has been said, and truly, that everything in the desert either stings, stabs, stinks, or sticks. You will find the flora here as venomous, hooked, barbed, thorny, prickly, needled, saw-toothed, hairy, stickered, mean, bitter, sharp, wiry, and fierce as the animals. Something about the desert inclines all living things to harshness and acerbity. The soft evolve out. Except for sleek and oily growths like the poison ivy—oh yes, indeed—that flourish in sinister profusion on the dank walls above the quicksand down in those corridors of gloom and labyrinthine monotony that men call canyons.

We come now to the third major hazard, which is sunshine. Too much of a good thing can be fatal. Sunstroke, heatstroke, and dehydration are common misfortunes in the bright American Southwest. If you can avoid the insects, reptiles, and arachnids, the cactus and the ivy, the smog of the southwestern cities, and the lung fungus of the desert valleys (carried by dust in the air), you cannot escape the desert sun. Too much exposure to it eventually causes, quite literally, not merely sunburn but skin cancer.

Much sun, little rain also means an arid climate. Compared with the high humidity of more hospitable regions, the dry heat of the desert seems at first not terribly uncomfortable—sometimes even pleasant. But that sensation of comfort is false, a deception, and therefore all the more dangerous, for it induces overexertion and an insufficient consumption of water, even when water is available. This leads to various internal complications, some immediate—sunstroke, for example—and some not apparent until much later. Mild but prolonged dehydration, continued over a span of months or years, leads to the crystallization of mineral solutions in the urinary tract, that is, to what urologists call urinary calculi or kidney stones. A disability common in all the world's arid regions. Kidney stones, in case you haven't met one, come in many shapes and sizes, from pellets smooth as BB shot to highly irregular calcifications resembling asteroids, Vietcong shrapnel, and crown-of-thorns starfish. Some of these objects may be "passed" naturally; others can be removed only by means of the Davis stone basket or by surgery. Me—I was lucky; I passed mine with only a groan, my forehead pressed against the wall of a pissoir in the rear of a Tucson bar that I cannot recommend.

You may be getting the impression by now that the desert is not the most suitable of environments for human habitation. Correct. Of all the Earth's climatic zones, excepting only the Antarctic, the deserts are the least inhabited, the least "developed," for reasons that should now be clear.

You may wish to ask, Yes, okay, but among North American deserts which is the *worst?* A good question—and I am happy to attempt to answer.

Geographers generally divide the North American desert—what was once termed "the Great American Desert"—into four distinct regions or subdeserts. These are the Sonoran Desert, which comprises southern Arizona, Baja California, and the state of Sonora in Mexico; the Chihuahuan Desert, which includes west Texas, southern New Mexico, and the states of Chihuahua and Coahuila in Mexico; the Mojave Desert, which includes southeastern California and small portions of Nevada, Utah, and Arizona; and the Great Basin Desert, which includes most of Utah and Nevada, northern Arizona, northwestern New Mexico, and much of Idaho and eastern Oregon.

Privately, I prefer my own categories. Up north in Utah somewhere is the canyon country—places like Zeke's Hole, Death Hollow, Pucker Pass, Buckskin Gulch, Nausea Crick, Wolf Hole, Mollie's Nipple, Dirty Devil River, Horse Canyon, Horseshoe Canyon, Lost Horse Canyon, Horsethief Canyon, and Horseshit Canyon, to name only the more classic places. Down in Arizona and Sonora there's the cactus country; if you have nothing better to do, you might take a look at High Tanks, Salome Creek, Tortilla Flat, Esperero ("Hoper") Canyon, Holy Joe Peak, Depression Canyon, Painted Cave, Hell Hole Canyon, Hell's Half Acre, Iceberg Canyon, Tiburon (Shark) Island, Pinacate Peak, Infernal Valley, Sykes Crater, Montezuma's Head, Gu Oidak, Kuakatch, Pisinimo, and Baboquivari Mountain, for example.

Then there's The Canyon. *The* Canyon. The Grand. That's one world. And North Rim—that's another. And Death Valley, still another, where I lived one winter near Furnace Creek and climbed the Funeral Mountains, tasted Badwater, looked into the Devil's Hole, hollered up Echo Canyon, searched for and never did find Seldom Seen Slim. Looked for *satori* near Vana, Nevada, and found a ghost town named Bonnie Claire. Never made it to Winnemucca. Drove through the Smoke Creek Desert and down through Big Pine and Lone Pine and home across the Panamints to Death Valley again—home sweet home that winter.

And which of these deserts is the worst? I find it hard to judge. They're all bad—not half bad but all bad. In the Sonoran Desert, Phoenix will get you if the sun, snakes, bugs, and arthropods don't. In the Mojave Desert, it's Las Vegas, more sickening by far than the Glauber's salt in the Death Valley sinkholes. Go to Chihuahua and you're liable to get busted in El Paso and sandbagged in Ciudad Juárez—where all old whores go to die. Up north in the Great Basin Desert, on the Plateau Province, in the canyon country, your heart will break, seeing the strip mines open up and the power plants rise where only cowboys and Indians and J. Wesley Powell ever roamed before.

Nevertheless, all is not lost; much remains, and I welcome the prospect of an army of lug-soled hiker's boots on the desert trails. To save what wilderness is left in the American Southwest—and in the American Southwest only the wilderness is worth saving—we are going to need all the recruits we can get. All the hands, heads, bodies, time, money, effort we can find. Presumably—and the Sierra Club, the Wilderness Society, the Friends of the Earth, the Audubon Society, the Defenders of Wildlife operate on this theory—those who learn to love what is spare, rough, wild, undeveloped, and unbroken will be willing to fight for it, will help resist the strip miners, highway builders, land developers, weapons testers, power producers, tree chainers, clear cutters, oil drillers, dam beavers, subdividers—the list goes on and on—before that zinc-hearted, termite-brained, squint-eyed, nearsighted, greedy crew succeeds in completely californicating what still survives of the Great American Desert.

So much for the Good Cause. Now what about desert hiking itself, you may ask. I'm glad you asked that question. I firmly believe that one should never—I repeated *never*—go out into that formidable wasteland of cactus, heat, serpents, rock, scrub, and thorn without careful planning, thorough and cautious preparation, and complete—never mind the expense!—*complete* equipment. My motto is: Be Prepared.

That is my belief and that is my motto. My practice, however, is a little different. I tend to go off in a more or less random direction myself, half-baked, half-assed, half-cocked, and half-ripped. Why? Well, because I have an indolent and melancholy nature and don't care to be bothered getting all those *things* together—all that bloody *gear*—maps, compass, binoculars, poncho, pup tent, shoes, first-aid kit, rope, flashlight, inspirational poetry, water, food—and because anyhow I approach nature with a certain surly ill-will, daring Her to make trouble. Later when I'm deep into Natural Bridges Natural Moneymint or Zion National Parkinglot or say General Shithead National Forest Land of Many Abuses why then, of course, when it's a bit late, then I may wish I had packed that something extra: matches perhaps, to mention one useful item, or maybe a spoon to eat my gruel with.

If I hike with another person it's usually the same; most of my friends have indolent and melancholy natures too. A cursed lot, all of them. I think of my comrade John De Puy, for example, sloping along for mile after mile like a goddamned camel—indefatigable—with those J. C. Penney hightops on his feet and that plastic pack on his back he got with five books of Green Stamps and nothing inside it but a sketchbook, some homemade jerky and a few cans of green chiles. Or Douglas Peacock, ex-Green Beret, just the opposite. Built like a buffalo, he loads a ninety-pound canvas pannier on his back at trailhead, loaded with guns, ammunition, bayonet, pitons and carabiners, cameras, field books, a 150-foot rope, geologist's sledge, rock samples, assay kit, field glasses, two gallons of water in steel canteens, jungle boots, a case of C-rations, rope hammock, pharmaceuticals in a pig-iron box, raincoat, overcoat, two-man mountain tent, Dutch oven, hibachi, shovel, ax, inflatable boat, and near the top of the load and distributed through side and back pockets, easily accessible, a case of beer. Not because he enjoys or needs all that weight—he may never get to the bottom of that cargo on a ten-day outing—but simply because Douglas uses his packbag for general storage both at home and on the trail and prefers not to have to rearrange everything from time to time merely for the purposes of a hike. Thus my friends De Puy and Peacock; you may wish to avoid such extremes.

A few tips on desert etiquette:

1. Carry a cooking stove, if you must cook. Do not burn desert wood, which is rare and beautiful and required ages for its creation (an ironwood tree lives for over 1,000 years and juniper almost as long).

2. If you must, out of need, build a fire, then for God's sake allow it to burn itself out before you leave—do not bury it, as Boy Scouts and Campfire Girls do, under a heap of mud or sand. Scatter the ashes; replace any rocks you may have used in constructing a fireplace; do all you can to obliterate the evidence that you camped here. (The Search & Rescue Team may be looking for you.)

3. Do not bury garbage—the wildlife will only dig it up again. Burn what will burn and pack out the rest. The same goes for toilet paper: Don't bury it, *burn it*.

4. Do not bathe in desert pools, natural tanks, *tinajas*, potholes. Drink what water you need, take what you need, and leave the rest for the next hiker and more important for the bees, birds, and animals—bighorn sheep, coyotes, lions, foxes, badgers, deer, wild pigs, wild horses—whose *lives* depend on that water.

5. Always remove and destroy survey stakes, flagging, advertising signboards, mining claim markers, animal traps, poisoned bait, seismic exploration geophones, and other such artifacts of industrialism. The men who put those things there are up to no good and it is our duty to confound them. Keep America Beautiful. Grow a Beard. Take a Bath. Burn a Billboard.

Anyway—why go into the desert? Really, why do it? That sun, roaring at you all day long. The fetid, tepid, vapid little water holes slowly evaporating under a scum of grease, full of cannibal beetles, spotted toads, horsehair worms, liver flukes, and down at the bottom, inevitably, the pale cadaver of a ten-inch centipede. Those pink rattlesnakes down in The Canyon, those diamondback monsters thick as a truck driver's wrist that lurk in shady places along the trail, those unpleasant solpugids and unnecessary Jerusalem crickets that scurry on dirty claws across your face at night. Why? The rain that comes down like lead shot and wrecks the trail, those sudden rockfalls of obscure origin that crash like thunder ten feet behind you in the heart of a dead-still afternoon. The ubiquitous buzzard, so patient—but only so patient. The sullen and hostile Indians, all on welfare. The ragweed, the tumbleweed, the Jimson weed, the snakeweed. The scorpion in your shoe at dawn. The dreary wind that blows all spring, the psychedelic Joshua trees waving their arms at you on moonlight nights. Sand in the soup du jour. Halazone tablets in your canteen. The barren hills that always go up, which is bad, or down, which is worse. Those canyons like catacombs with quicksand lapping at your crotch. Hollow, mummified horses with forelegs casually crossed, dead for ten years, leaning against the corner of a barbed-wire fence. Packhorses at night, iron-shod, clattering over the slickrock through your camp. The last tin of tuna, two flat tires, not enough water and a fortymile trek to Tule Well. An osprey on a cardón cactus, snatching the head off a living fish—always the best part first. The hawk sailing by at 200 feet, a squirming snake in its talons. Salt in the drinking water. Salt, selenium, arsenic, radon and radium in the water, in the gravel, in your bones. Water so hard it bends light, drills holes in rock and chokes up your radiator. Why go there? Those places with the hardcase names: Starvation Creek, Poverty Knoll, Hungry Valley, Bitter Springs, Last Chance Canyon, Dungeon Canyon, Whipsaw Flat, Dead Horse Point, Scorpion Flat, Dead Man Draw, Stinking Spring, Camino del Diablo, Jornado del Muerto . . . Death Valley.

Well then, why indeed go walking into the desert, that grim ground, that bleak and lonesome land where, as Genghis Khan said of India, "the heat is bad and the water makes men sick"?

Why the desert, when you could be strolling along the golden beaches of California? Camping by a stream of pure Rocky Mountain spring water in colorful Colorado? Loafing through a laurel slick in the misty hills of North Carolina? Or getting your head mashed in the greasy alley behind the Élysium Bar and Grill in Hoboken, New Jersey? Why the desert, given a world of such splendor and variety?

A friend and I took a walk around the base of a mountain up beyond Coconino County, Arizona. This was a mountain we'd been planning to circumambulate for years. Finally we put on our walking shoes and did it. About halfway around this mountain, on the third or fourth day, we paused for a while—two days—by the side of a stream, which the Navajos call Nasja because of the amber color of the water. (Caused perhaps by juniper roots—the water seems safe enough to drink.) On our second day there I walked down the stream, alone, to look at the canyon beyond. I entered the canyon and followed it for half the afternoon, for three or four miles, maybe, until it became a gorge so deep, narrow and dark, full of water and the inevitable quagmires of quicksand, that I turned around and looked for a way out. A route other than the way I'd come, which was crooked and uncomfortable and buried—I wanted to see what was up on top of this world. I found a sort of chimney flue on the east wall, which looked plausible, and sweated and cursed my way up through that until I reached a point where I could walk upright, like a human being. Another 300 feet of scrambling brought me to the rim of the canyon. No one, I felt certain, had ever before departed Nasja Canyon by that route.

But someone had. Near the summit I found an arrow sign, three feet long, formed of stones and pointing off into the north toward those same old purple vistas, so grand, immense, and mysterious, of more canyons, more mesas and plateaus, more mountains, more cloud-dappled sun-spangled leagues of desert sand and desert rock, under the same old wide and aching sky.

The arrow pointed into the north. But what was it pointing *at*? I looked at the sign closely and saw that those dark, desert-varnished stones had been in place for a long, long, time; they rested in compacted dust. They must have been there for a century at least. I followed the direction indicated and came promptly to the rim of another canyon and a drop-off straight down of a good 500 feet. Not that way, surely. Across this canyon was nothing of any unusual interest that I could see—only the familiar sun-blasted sandstone, a few scrubby clumps of blackbrush and prickly pear, a few acres of nothing where only a lizard could graze, surrounded by a few square miles of more nothingness interesting chiefly to horned toads. I returned to the arrow and checked again, this time with field glasses, looking away for as far as my aided eyes could see toward the north, for ten, twenty, forty miles into the distance. I studied the scene with care, looking for an ancient Indian ruin, a significant cairn, perhaps an abandoned mine, a hidden treasure of some inconceivable wealth, the mother of all mother lodes. . . .

But there was nothing out there. Nothing at all. Nothing but the desert. Nothing but the silent world.

That's why.

WALLACE STEGNER

The Mormons have been a major presence in the West, and from Richard Burton's time (*The City of the Saints*, 1862) to the present they haven't lacked for sympathetic outside observers. Over all this time, perhaps no writer has treated them so objectively, and with such friendly compassion, as has Wallace Stegner (1909–1993). In *Mormon Country* (1941) and *The Gathering of Zion* (1964), he paid tribute to their industry—pointing out that Brigham Young called into being over 300 western settlements, from Canada to Mexico, for example, between 1847 and 1877—and their sense of community while also recognizing their tendencies toward chauvinism and authoritarian rule. But Stegner's accomplishment is not simply a matter of balance: He felt for the Mormons humanly. One of the places his footloose father stayed in, rather longer than most of his stops, was Salt Lake City, at a time when Stegner was young and particularly needful of companionship and community. The Mormons gave him what he needed; he later wrote of Salt Lake City that it was the closest thing to a home town he'd had. In *Recapitulation*, which is a late sequel to the autobiographical masterpiece *The Big Rock Candy Mountain* (1943), he describes neighborhoods, friendships, relationships, Mormon family life, all within a lovingly detailed portrait of the Utah environment. In this selection, Stegner takes us and "Bruce Mason" back to a wedding at a ranch in the south-central part of the state, in country beautiful enough to be a national park, in a time that memory now makes almost purely sweet.

Part 2, Chapter 5, from *Recapitulation* (1979)

Like a curious dog, the camera comes hunting along the welted bank of a ditch. It is in no hurry. Moving close to the ground, it inspects close-to-the-ground details. It dwells on the slow, spinning surface of tea-colored water, it notes the dimpling tracks of skaters in the eddies, and the wakes that V down from rocks and clumps of half-drowned grass. It is not above spending a few seconds on a darning needle that sits on air for a moment and darts away a few feet to sit on other air. It wonders that a jimson weed is able to extract such rich dark foliage and such creamy trumpets of flowers from arid sand. It ruminates without comment on an old boot, curled and mummified, beside the path.

Now it arrives at a pole bridge, and above it a weir and the headworks of a branch ditch. The upper plank of the weir is raised, and water falls in a smooth curve over the lower one. The pool above is solid with watercress. Into the visual dream, stirred by some foot that the camera never discloses, and perceived by a nose for which there is no assignable body, rises the smell of mint.

The camera lifts its glance, and sees that all along the left is a cliff of cross-bedded sandstone, frozen dunes in whose base the wind has eroded caves. Men have improved them by building corrals around them, trapping for the use of stock shallow areas of shelter. Two corral-caves are open and empty. In a third, a mare stands hipshot above her sprawled sleeping colt. In a fourth, three calves lie chewing the cud. With the same unlocated nose that detected the mint, we know the smell of those caves: horse and cow dung both dry and fresh, the sun-dried reek of urine, dust, some residual odor of sage and juniper. The sun falls straight down; the band of shade in the caves is only eight or ten feet wide. Half buried in the pinkish sand is an Orange Crush bottle.

Poking along the cliff beyond the caves, the camera comes to a place where the face is vertical and stained with desert varnish. In this dark glazed surface primitive men have pecked the outlines of deer and bighorn sheep, which modern hands have reinforced with chalk. Below the chalked petroglyphs is a band of handprints in red ocher. A sun-steeped richness of life pervades these noon corrals, this quiet ditch, this billboard cliff. The fingers (though there are no fingers) feel how tepid-cool the water would be if one stooped to dip a hand in it.

The camera pans along the cliff, up it to its rounding rim, and with a gust as sudden as a wind that blows an umbrella inside out, we are looking high upward, away upward, to the rim of a level, lava-capped, spruce-spiked plateau. From a mile up, it looks down over this fertile desert. The interdependence is obvious without a caption. Up there is snow shed, summer range, a subalpine climate, recreation, coolness, relief. Up there is the source of this ditch that makes the desert live.

Withdrawing, the camera inspects the sod-roofed stable, two long haystacks, and the pole corrals that lie below the main ditch, with the branch ditch flowing past them. Beyond is an alfalfa field, intensely green. Out in the open valley, whitefaces are gleaning a stubble field, perhaps winter wheat, that ends at a barbed-wire fence. On the other side of the fence, a car tows a horizontal funnel of dust along a road, and beyond the road, another line of cliffs holds the valley in on the south. This is not rounded and domed and monolithic like the cliff on the north. It has been eroded into a line of gargoyles and hoodoos, all leaning southward.

The camera reasons that these are remnants of the outer shell of an enormous dome which wind and water have dissected to its salmon-pink heart, leaving the shell like a broken wall around the wilderness of stone inside. In there, the distance is hazed with transparent blue. It trembles with familiarity. Its cliffs and cameo buttes have been seen only moments ago. The mind gropes for identification, and finds it: The San Rafael Reef, leaning inward toward the waste of the San Rafael Swell. Robbers' Roost, Butch Cassidy's country. The camera surveys it with respect, withdraws to the safe ditch bank marked with the tracks of men and horses, and moves on until it is stopped by a fence made of slabs of ripple-marked sandstone set on end.

Path and ditch go through the fence; the pole gate is down. In the slabs to which gateposts have been bound by windings of baling wire (Mormon silk, says some amused folklorist at the dream's core) there are brown ribby shapes of fossil fish, some of them a foot long. Inside the gate is deep shade. We are looking into a half acre of big Fremont poplars that lean over a log ranch house and all but obscure the cliff behind. Through the grove, quicksilver bright, the ditch flows through grass that must be periodically flooded to keep it so green. Scattered and clustered through the grove are fifty or sixty people. They make a picture like a Renoir picnic or a Seurat promenade *sur l'herbe*, but different, special, simpler and homelier, quintessentially red-ledge Mormon.

The camera recognizes ranchers, farmers, dealers in alfalfa seed, coal miners from Helper or Sunnyside, beauticians from Price, schoolteachers from Castle Dale or Emery, rangers from the Manti-La Sal National Forest. Whoever they are, the women have been weathered by the same dry wind, and have bought their dresses from the same J. C. Penney store in Price, or from the ZCMI in Salt Lake at Conference time. Whatever trade the men practice, they all dress as cowboys, in boots, washed and ironed and faded Levi's, and shirts with yokes and snap buttons.

There are children of all ages, the boys small replicas of their fathers, the younger girls in white dresses with white stockings grass-stained at the knees. The yard has been raked and mown, but it is uneven, worn bare in spots, and already gathering a new drift of cottonwood fluff. Three old women sit in a swing lounge in the deepest shade. From a tree over by the cliff, an automobile tire has been hung on a lariat, and girl children are pushing each other in it. They swoop across the ditch, set feet against the cliff, and push out again, shrieking. Up the ditch, some boys throw a shepherd pup into the water. He crawls out dripping, yapping, and agog, and shakes himself on them. Yelling, they grab him and throw him in again. He loves it. He would happily drown, object of so much attention.

In this crowd the camera finds the city boy, Nola's young man, marked by his white corduroys and white buck shoes. The old women discuss him, girls eye him as they help set the long trestle tables near the house. He stands talking to Nola's father about cattle, and alfalfa, and grazing permits, and water rights. The camera understands that these subjects are not those on which he is prepared to be voluble, but he listens well, and he remembers enough from Saskatchewan and Montana to make an occasional sensible remark. When someone calls Nola's father away, the city boy falls into talk with her brother Buck. Their subject is bulldogging and roping and bronc riding, and here he does better, since he has an honest admiration for any athletic skill and is, moreover, much less wary than with the old man, who makes him nervous.

Soon the city boy and Buck go through the stone fence and on down to the stable. The old women watch them out of sight; the camera watches the old women. Then we pick up the two around the stable corner. Three others are there, sneaking cigarettes. The city boy offers Buck a Lucky and takes one himself. Buck winks and leans and pulls out of the manger a partly emptied fifth of unlabeled red-eye. It goes around until it comes to Bruce Mason, who declines, using his ulcer as an excuse. The others clearly do not understand about ulcers and look at him as if afraid he might be pious.

"I tell you, boy," Buck says, "you ain't gonna survive this struggle just on brute strength."

"Don't encourage him," another man says. "More he don't drink, more they is for us to. I dearly love a man that don't drink, myself."

The bottle goes around again. The next-to-last man, sensing shortage, takes it from his mouth, looks at it against the light, takes one more small sip—a tablespoonful—and regretfully passes it to Buck, who drains it and throws it over his shoulder without looking. It smashes against the log wall. "Who flang that?" a man asks. They laugh.

One of them leans around the corner to look. "About ready to start, up there, I guess."

"Maybe we better git back," Buck says, and steps on his cigarette. "Come on, boy, you're family."

He whacks Bruce on the shoulder and leaves his arm there as they walk together back to the sandstone fence and into the shade. The old women watch, noting the fraternal acceptance.

A sort of order is shaping out of the colored chaos under the poplars. Like particles in a kaleidoscope, people arrange themselves around a large genial man in white shirt and arm garters—the bishop—who pushes and pulls at the air, beckoning them in or moving them back. Women leave their work in the kitchen and at the tables and come over, untying apron strings and looking around for their children. The three men whom Bruce and Buck have left behind at the stable come up the slope and drape themselves warily on the sandstone fence at the very edge of things. Chatterers bore on into the growing quiet until they become aware and fall still. Women stoop and fiercely yank up their daughters' stockings and yank down their dresses. A loose aisle has formed, leading toward the kitchen door. The white-shirted bishop folds his arms and waits, smiling.

Heads turn like sunflowers, and the bride is at the kitchen door, in soft focus behind the screen. Her dress, greener than the grass, is unkind to her coloring, which is doubtful in any case because her brows are dark like Nola's and her hair, marcelled as rigid as tin, is newly blonded. Though she is weathered and not young, is really quite a homely woman with bony, too large features (that Southern Paiute inheritance?), the camera notes her resemblance to Nola. A stranger might think her Nola's mother. Her smile is tense.

She opens the screen and steps down onto the sandstone slab that serves as a doorstep. Coming after her, the groom lets the screen door slam, and winces at the noise, raising his narrow shoulders and grinning guiltily and drawing sympathetic laughter.

He is the only person there who wears a coat. He wears, in fact, a suit, black and ironed stiff. His boots, new, are outlined under the narrow legs of his pants. Through the collar of his checked cowboy shirt he has run a necktie from behind, so that in the opening where there would normally be a knot there is only a band of patterned silk. The ends of the tie must hang down his back, under his coat, like pigtails. The sun has reddened without tanning him. His hair is sandy and plastered down. His upper lip is cracked, and he keeps touching it with the tip of his tongue.

The screen opens again and Nola and Buck, maid of honor and best man, step down behind the bride and groom. Buck's maroon silk shirt glows against the gray logs like an exotic flower. Nola in a dress of soft yellow looks cool, serene, removed from all the stress of this marrying. The camera suffers a pang of pride and love, just looking at her.

Without intending to, she makes the bride and groom look like yokels. Her eyes go out over the crowd until they find Bruce. Then she smiles a small private smile, throws it like a rosebud, and as he catches it he is enveloped in blue static. She should be the bride here. Is. Will be. There is only one marriage scheduled, but there will be two honeymoons.

Buck has observed that smile, and who caught it. He says something to his sister out of the corner of his mouth, and she gives him an admonitory nudge with her shoulder, not looking at him, still smiling her inward smile.

The bishop nods, and the four on the doorstep, not unanimously, start forward. The bride turns her ankle in the rough grass and makes an exasperated, self-conscious grimace. In the front row of watchers a girl of twelve or so stands up with a gasp and a sob. The bride's daughter, even more tense than the bride. Promptly the woman above her wraps the girl in against her skirts. Pale, trapped, brimming, the girl watches as if at a hanging.

Her mother stops before the bishop, adjusts her feet in the grass, squares her shoulders, looks around helplessly for some place to lay her bouquet, and with abrupt decision hands it back to Nola. The bridegroom, tonguing his cracked lip, leans forward slightly and peeks down the front of his trousers.

"Darrell's nervous," the bishop says. Laughter, quickly hushed. Barely moving her lips, the bride says something, and the bishop nods. Aloud, he guesses comfortably that folks all seem to be here, they might as well get started.

A random puff of wind moves and dies in the high tops of the poplars. A watching woman bats cotton out of her face without taking her eyes off the drama before her. The camera strays past the principals, looks out from the shade across the glaring valley and sees the leaning reef of hoodoos and goblins, and away beyond, the Swell crawling with heat, the color of cliffs and canyons almost discharged in the steep light. The clouds in the visible arc of sky are rounded white above, flat below.

"Now, before we get down to the proceedings, let me remind you of what we were saying before," the bishop says. He speaks conversationally to the bride and groom, ignoring the spectators. "When you're married and settled down over there on the Minnie Maud, or for that matter if you should move anywhere else, whatever place you live in, become a real part of that place. Mmmmmmm? Dig in and work and belong in it and do your share."

They stand before him like culprits, wearing the look of good Mormons hearkening to counsel. The camera, meantime, interprets Bruce Mason's feelings. He looks upon his girl's sister and her husband-to-be as hicks. He feels superior to them and to everyone there unless perhaps Nola's father and brother. The father strikes him as a tough old bird with a gimlet eye, the brother as a good egg, skilled, worldly, and reckless. The rest are yokels. Yet he may not smile at these country Mormons, because they are her people, and she is loyal to them.

All her life she has been the darling of this tribe. Her sister mothered her, half a dozen aunties anxiously spoiled her. She was the one who could sit down at the piano, even as a little girl, and play by ear any tune you wanted to name. She was the one who would pick up a guitar, or an accordion, or whatever was lying around, and by suppertime be playing the thing. She was the one who went off to the university in Salt Lake. He has seen the fond and yearning looks they give her. Because of her, they deserve his politeness if not his respect.

He has also caught the women watching him, and seen their speculative eyes. How serious are those two? Is he good enough for her? Somebody said he isn't LDS. That's bad. But perhaps he could be brought to
receive the Word? He seems in other ways like a well-spoken, pleasant
young man.

An impostor, he knows that every single aspect of his background, if
it were known, would be a black mark against him, and their solidarity
makes him half envious. He feels how satisfying it would be to belong to
some tribe or family, and though he feels superior to this one, he does
not dismiss the notion of a not unfriendly alliance. Can he imagine being
married here himself—in this grove, before this shirt-sleeved bishop?
Would he bring his own family? His mother, yes, she could make contact
with anybody. Chet would be at home with the boys back of the stable.
But his father is unthinkable here. He belongs out in the Robbers' Roost,
not in this green and pious oasis.

"This marriage isn't just yours, you see," the Bishop is saying. "I'm
sure you both understand that. Other people have an interest in it, too.
Mmmm? The community has an interest in it because you'll be part of it,
and it has a right to expect you to live up to your obligations. The state
has an interest in it because it'll have you registered, all your records will
be there. And the Church has an interest in it because through it your
marriage is sanctified."

Around the edge of the bridegroom's hair, like a scalping scar, runs
a line of unsunburned white. This is probably the first time he has had
his hat off, except to sleep and get his hair cut, in weeks. The barber has
shaved his neck round. Down by the corrals a calf is bawling. The woman
with her arms around the bride's daughter frowns in annoyance, willing
the creature still.

"All right, then," the bishop says. "You understand all that. Now,
Darrell, you take Audrey by the right hand. Audrey, you take Darrell.
That's it. Now. By the authority in me vested as an Elder of the Church
of Jesus Christ of Latter-day Saints, I declare you man and wife."

It comes too quickly. Everyone is confused, including the principals.
They look uncertainly at the bishop, who has to motion Buck to step
forward with the ring. The bishop takes it from him and hands it to
Darrell, who fumbles and nearly drops it from his tonglike fingers, and
then has trouble shoving it over Audrey's knuckle.

"Darrell *is* nervous," the bishop says with a wide smile.

A black cat with its tail in the air walks around the corner of the house
and across the grass. Scare flares in the eyes of one of the watching
women, and with her skirts she tries to shoo it back. But her move is too
hesitant, inhibited by the occasion, and the cat comes on down the line,

rubbing against legs, watched by all, until a little girl stoops quickly and lifts it. Its hind legs and tail hang down, an inert weight, against the white confirmation dress.

The bride's daughter weeps steadily, copiously, not quite silently. The woman holding her makes an exasperated face and hands down a wadded handkerchief. The girl takes it, weeps, wipes.

"You may now kiss each other," the bishop says.

Violently the bride flings herself against the bridegroom's chest. The contrast between her worn vulnerability and Nola's composure confirms for Bruce Mason how far she has outgrown her origins. All around, those origins are wet-eyed.

Sheepishly the husband wraps his new wife around. Suspended, with drowning eyes, the daughter stares. It is a very swampy occasion. For relief, Bruce looks toward Nola, holding the bridal bouquet on her arm, but her eyes are for her sister, not for him.

The crowd stands, embarrassed and fulfilled. Nobody dares to break the tableau. Then Audrey pulls her homely wet face away from Darrell's Tom Mix shirt and cries accusingly, "Well, why don't somebody *say* something, instead of standin' there watchin' me cry!"

Laughter is sympathetic and relieved, inertia is broken. The daughter comes running and desperately clings to her mother's leg. Nola, then Buck, then their father, kiss the bride. The women kiss embarrassed Darrell, the men pump his hand. Two women quietly retrieve their aprons from behind the swing and, tying strings as they go, head for the kitchen.

"Look this way, Audrey," a woman says, and raises a camera. People fall back out of the line of fire. A man says, "It's too dark in the shade here, Ede. You won't get nothing," and the camera-woman says, "No, it ain't, I've got this *thing*."

Near her a half-grown boy, serious as a dynamiter's assistant, holds aloft a tray of flash powder. People back off further, respectful of advanced technology, while the bride assembles herself, dabs, blinks, laughs, grabs Darrell on one side and her daughter on the other, and freezes as stiff as the girl from whose head the crack shot shoots glass balls in a Wild West show.

"Wait!" Darrell says. He tears off his coat and rips the necktie out of his collar and tosses them to someone in the crowd. Cheers.

"Smile, now," the camerawoman says. "Say 'prunes.' "

She peers, squints, is on the brink. Prunes. Click, but no flash.

Uncertainly she looks up. "Didn't it go?"

Voices assure her that it didn't. She winds the film. The boy stares aggrievedly into his tray of flash powder. "Try it again."

Fixed smiles. Prunes. Click. Again no flash. "Why, what's the matter with the blame thing?" the camerawoman says.

Buck disconnects the flash boy, to the boy's disgust. "Try it over in the sun, where you don't need that contraption. Come on, Aud, get that lucerne-wrangler over here."

Bruce follows along, opening his camera. At the grove's edge the bride, with restrained violence, wipes her daughter's nose and hisses at her to stop her bawling. The three freeze again, then unfreeze while Buck waves his father into the picture.

"Where's Junior?" somebody asks.

"Hell," Buck says, "you won't get *him* in this." He looks down into the finder. "Hey, Aud, can't you laugh?"

"I'm *smiling*," Audrey says grimly.

Bruce, after a couple of frugal snapshots, saving his film for better things, comes up behind Nola and stabs her between the shoulder blades with his finger. She turns with a smile which his instinct tells him is too open. Those old women don't miss a thing. Yet he couldn't be happier. It thrills him to have her turn to him that way.

"I've got to go help with the food," she says a little breathlessly. "Save us places. Right at the end of the second table, there, by the ice-cream freezers."

"O.K. When do we start back?"

"They'd think it was funny if we didn't stay a while. They'll cut the cake right after we eat. Then I thought you and Buck and I might take a ride."

"All right. But don't forget we've both got to be back so we can get to work in the morning. Your aunties wouldn't want you driving late, without a chaperone."

They have drawn back against a tree, out of the crowd. Her eyes as she studies him are full of light, and promises, and secret understandings. "You devil. You've been down with Buck, sneaking drinks behind the stable. He came up smelling like a saloon."

"Not me. I copped a smoke, is all. I observe the Word of Wisdom."

"Yes, just the way the rest of them do." As if the answers to important questions were written on him, she studies him. "How's it going? I saw you talking to Dad."

"We had a good talk about alfalfa and peaches and whiteface cattle and I told him about my childhood in Saskatchewan. He thinks I'm a reformed cowboy."

"Reformed! How do you think the wedding went?"

"Fine. It got a little juicy there for a minute."

"Poor Audrey. She's scared."

"Scared why?"

"She was really in love with Elmo. She'll never get over him. But she needs somebody to help bring up the kids. It was no good when she was working in Price. That's a tough town."

"Darrell looks O.K."

"O.K. Not very exciting." Like a child with a secret she smiles at him. "Not like what I've got."

"You know something?"

"What?"

"You're a darling."

"Just you keep thinking so. Do *you* know something?"

"Probably."

"They like you. Buck thinks you're O.K. And Dad was leery about what I'd bring down, but he told me you're a very pleasant young fella."

"Isn't that kind of minimal? Didn't he find me exciting?"

They commune privately under their tree while the crowd mills and jabbers. Seriously she says, "How does it seem down here to you? Do you like it?"

"Like it? Sure, it's great."

"It's better than great. Would you like it if we could run the ranch sometime?"

"A reformed cowboy like me? Sure. Is there a chance?"

"I think Dad's about given up on Buck."

"What's the matter with Audrey and Darrell?"

"They've got all they can handle over on the Minnie Maud."

"I'm a heathen. Wouldn't that bother them?"

"Not for long. Anybody that's good enough for me is good enough for them."

"Ah," he says. "*Am* I good enough for you?"

Her light frown warns him: somebody heading their way. He looks, and it is one of the men who helped kill Buck's bottle. His Levi's have been shrunk to his skinny legs. He has ten inches of wrong-side lighter cloth turned up for a cuff around his boots.

"Well," Bruce says, "we'll have to see about that on the way back."

Her hand squeezes his arm, she turns and leaves him, moving with her incomparably physical, barefoot-woman's walk. The lean man arrives and props himself against the tree and breathes upon Bruce his most un-Mormon breath. His eye is on Darrell, growing more uninhibited now that the formalities are over and his coat and tie off. Audrey stands at his elbow, hooked to him like a gate to its post.

The lean man shakes his head. "Another good man gone wrong."

The camera wanders off among the million leaves of the grove, with only glitters of sun coming through them. Eventually it comes to rest on a length of railroad rail that hangs on a wire by the kitchen door. A hand bearing a tire iron comes into the picture and beats with vigor on the rail. Men stand up with alacrity, the old women rise from their swing, children come pouring from all directions. Bruce Mason reaches the end of the second table just in time to save the end place, and then the one to the right of it, from a twelve-year-old boy who, twice balked but hardly noticing what has balked him, promptly dives under the cloth and comes up on the other side next to the bride's daughter and two of her girl friends.

Women, Nola among them, make a procession from house to tables, bearing platters of fried chicken and corned elk, washbasins of potato salad, dishpans of hot biscuits, bowls of watermelon pickle, chokecherry jelly, pickled peaches and apricots. One stands by a milk can of lemonade, filling pitchers with a dipper. Close behind Bruce four ice-cream freezers, though covered with a yellow horse blanket, radiate cold.

Plates and platters go down the table, are emptied, are retrieved and carried back to the house for refilling. Eventually the procession slows. A woman sits down to eat, then another, only two or three anxious aunties standing ready for whatever need arises. Nola comes hurriedly to her seat, and Bruce stands up to tug her chair into place on the uneven ground. The bride's daughter watches, fascinated, this demonstration of big-city politesse.

On both sides of her, her girl friends are gnawing drumsticks and talking through them. One place down, the twelve-year-old is gobbling as if this might be his last chance for a square meal until the Fourth of July. For a minute the bride's daughter watches her friends with distaste and him with loathing. Unable to bear more, she leans around the girl next to her and says to him, "Eat with your fork!" Her eyes, seeking corroboration and approval, come around to Nola, who smiles, and Bruce, who winks. Conspiracy of good manners.

Now the feast is finished, the littered tables are abandoned. The freezers once filled with homemade peach ice-cream stand tilted and empty in their melting salt water, drawing flies. The drying shepherd pup is seeking out morsels under the tables. Audrey, with Darrell's hand guiding hers, has cut the cake, and girls have carefully wrapped their pieces with the intention of taking them home and sleeping on them.

There has been a lot of competitive pie-sampling: Elverna's apple, LaVon's peach, Aunt Vilate Chesnutt's coconut cream. Before the men and boys have quite finished with that, Audrey in a crowd of women and girls has thrown the bridal bouquet. But she has not given everybody a fair chance. She has grooved it like a three-and-nothing fast ball into Nola's hands.

Tearfully now she makes her way around family and friends, her bony face blurred with crying, and kisses each in turn, some several times, crying, "Oh, God love you, God love you!" She stands for a moment before Bruce, leans and kisses him quickly, says to him tensely, "I think it's great! You be good to her!" and goes on by. The crowd lines up before the rarely used front door, making an aisle from it to the sandstone fence, on the other side of which waits Darrell's pickup, the honeymoon vehicle. Buck, as best man, was supposed to guard it from pranksters, but instead has helped hang it with banners saying "Just married," and through the holes in its perforated solid-rubber rear tires he has helped string tin cans on baling wire. With his own hands he has tied a chunk of Limburger, imported from Salt Lake for the occasion and kept carefully hidden in the springhouse, to the exhaust manifold.

Now the run through showers of rice, the yelled good wishes, the pandemonium as the pickup jerks away with its wheels trailing tin cans. Men whoop, women scream, dogs bark, dust rises in clouds. Safely down past the stable, Darrell hops out and yanks the wires loose from the wheels and hops in again. Audrey is wadding the "Just married" banners in her hands. They start up, a wadded banner flies out, Darrell raises his clenched fist and pokes it at the sky. Their dust goes down the valley road toward some destination which Darrell has been too cagey to reveal even to his treacherous best man.

Dissolve. A moment of quiet. The dust settles.

It is not the newlyweds who drive down the valley and whose dust drifts southward across the reef. It is not early afternoon, but later, five or six o'clock. The light is growing flatter, the shadows are beginning to reach out from buttes and promontories. It is not a black pickup that the camera follows, but a gray Model A coupe with fender wells and a rear-bumper trunk, quite a snappy little heap. The two who ride in it, sitting close together in spite of the heat, are not sheepish or tearful, but young and glorified. The girl holds a bridal bouquet in her lap.

The dreaming eye follows their dust down to a junction, turns right with them up a long hill, passes the summit and swoops with them down the switchbacks on the other side. When the driver has to double-clutch and shift down on a steep turn, taking them smoothly around without so much as a minimum skid in the gravel, the girl hugging his arm hugs it tighter. "Good skinner," she says.

The camera loses them in a canyon and picks them up again as they top out at a great distance, buzzing along an elevated sagebrush plain above which rise the rounded shoulders of a higher plateau. Aspens are just leafing out on the high slopes, and in all the north-facing hollows there is snow. They drag their balloon of dust through little towns—Fremont, Loa, Bicknell—which seem to be inhabited exclusively by children on horseback who want to race. They round a corner under the colored cliffs of Thousand Lake Mountain, they pass through Torrey, they bore like a corkscrew into the rock along the Dirty Devil. On their left, the Capitol Reef rises. Its lower cliff is already in the shadow of the western wall; its domed white rim is still in light so brilliant that the eye squints against it.

The canyon widens and flattens. They are in a pocket of green among red cliffs. A dusty track turns off left. "Here," the girl says, and the driver swings the wheel. They bump down the ruts toward a grove of trees and stop against a ditch.

The leaves hang heavy, individual, heart-shaped, dark green, utterly still. The ditch runs clear knee-deep water. Across it, filling the bottom-land to the foot of the cliff, are spaced peach trees, braced and propped against the weight of ripening fruit. Just between cottonwoods and orchard is an old house of squared logs, doorless, its inside crammed with hay, a broken wagonwheel leaning against the jamb, a clutch of binder twine on a nail above the wheel. There is a dense, unnamed familiarity: we have known this place before.

Into the stillness that sifts down on them like feathers, a canyon wren drops its notes, musical as water. The ditch chuckles and guggles to itself under its banks. Down the canyon from the high plateaus, feeling its way toward the desert, comes the first stir of evening breeze.

The dreamer yearns and strains against an overwhelming sensibility. He is as susceptible as poor homely Audrey. He leans to kiss the girl beside him, but there is an encumbrance, and looking down, he sees with a shock that he is holding something alive and crippled, a big fierce scared bird that struggles against his hold and pecks his hands. In the enclosed car he can't let it go, and yet it struggles so powerfully that he has great trouble hanging on to it. Indecision rises toward panic. What will he do with the thing? Open the window and throw it out? Wring its neck? Cram it down between brake and gearshift and put his foot on it?

The girl's eyes are on him, full of growing aversion, and he is ashamed.

His shame awakens him, but he resists being awakened. With his knees under his chin he burrows back and down, wanting to pick up the dream where it was broken, deal with this buzzard or whatever it is, take that look off Nola's face and get on with the consummation he knows is coming.

But though his half-conscious mind can remember it, his unconscious refuses to dream it. Some censor forbids this movie. Dream and girl repudiate him, or he them. He finds that he can't evoke her face, much less her body, shivering and damp and goose-pimpled from their dip in the ditch, crowding against him, growing warmer, stopping her shivering, on the bedroll under the broken shadow of the cottonwoods. She blurs and evades him until in the end he lies quiet and lets her go.

The room hangs in its small-hours stillness above the stillness of the street. He feels bleak and old, done with, excluded and a failure, and is angry with himself for feeling so. For the dream, now that he has come fully awake, he neither wants nor believes. It lies to him about himself and it lies about the episode it pretends to recall. Some inferiority or self-doubt has been warping the facts in order to prove something. There was no repudiation then, and no failure. However fumbling and green he was, he was not unsuccessful, nor was Nola unwilling. The end of that initiation was not disappointment but a great grateful tenderness. Still the censor bans the rerun.

The trouble with the censor is that it knows too much. It has another, and much longer, and presumably far more important life to remember and keep under control. It is wary about accepting the illusion of wholeheartedness that would have to accompany this uncensored dream. It knows that the girl and first love are both victims, and so is the boy who took them joyriding. They cluster at the edge of consciousness like crosses erected by the roadside at the place of a fatal accident.

SAM SHEPARD

orn in Illinois, Sam Shepard (b. 1943) spent formative years on an avocado and sheep ranch in Duarte, California, at the foot of the San Gabriel Mountains about forty miles east of Los Angeles. After a year at the local junior college, where he went to study agricultural science, he migrated to New York City and, living a "starving artist" life, began writing one-act plays that soon developed an intense following on Off-Off-Broadway. These works, like his later, more ambitious dramas, are characterized by an unsettling inwardness, amounting to a laying-bare of characters' selves that renders them accessible to an audience in shared, no-barriers life. Using black humor, stock and stereotypical characters, the familiar idiom of pop culture, and occasionally violence, Shepard's plays deliver insight—and beyond that, unanswerable realization—into the psychological *thisness* of modern American life. He is particularly interested—as the dramas *Buried Child, Fool for Love*, and *True West* demonstrate—in depicting the tormenting gulf between American myths and American daily reality. Shepard has hit the national nerve accurately enough to have become both a popular favorite and one of the most highly regarded literary playwrights of his time. He has also worked successfully as a film actor, gaining an Academy Award nomination for his supporting role in *The Right Stuff* (1984). *True West* was first performed in San Francisco in 1980.

True West (1980)

Characters

AUSTIN: *early thirties, light blue sports shirt, light tan cardigan sweater, clean blue jeans, white tennis shoes*

LEE: *his older brother, early forties, filthy white t-shirt, tattered brown overcoat covered with dust, dark blue baggy suit pants from the Salvation Army, pink suede belt, pointed black forties dress shoes scuffed up, holes in the soles, no socks, no hat, long pronounced sideburns, "Gene Vincent" hairdo, two days' growth of beard, bad teeth*

SAUL KIMMER: *late forties, Hollywood producer, pink and white flower print sports shirt, white sports coat with matching polyester slacks, black and white loafers*

MOM: *early sixties, mother of the brothers, small woman, conservative white skirt and matching jacket, red shoulder bag, two pieces of matching red luggage*

SCENE: *All nine scenes take place on the same set; a kitchen and adjoining alcove of an older home in a Southern California suburb, about 40 miles east of Los Angeles. The kitchen takes up most of the playing area to stage left. The kitchen consists of a sink, upstage center, surrounded by counter space, a wall telephone, cupboards, and a small window just above it bordered by neat yellow curtains. Stage left of sink is a stove. Stage right, a refrigerator. The alcove adjoins the kitchen to stage right. There is no wall division or door to the alcove. It is open and easily accessible from the kitchen and defined only by the objects in it: a small round glass breakfast table mounted on white iron legs, two matching white iron chairs set across from each other. The two exterior walls of the alcove which prescribe a corner in the upstage right are composed of many small windows, beginning from a solid wall about three feet high and extending to the ceiling. The windows look out to bushes and citrus trees. The alcove is filled with all sorts of house plants in various pots, mostly Boston ferns hanging in planters at different levels. The floor of the alcove is composed of green synthetic grass.*

All entrances and exits are made stage left from the kitchen. There is no door. The actors simply go off and come onto the playing area.

NOTE ON SET AND COSTUME: *The set should be constructed realistically with no attempt to distort its dimensions, shapes, objects, or colors. No objects should be introduced which might draw special attention to themselves other than the props demanded by the script. If a stylistic "concept" is grafted onto the set design it will only serve to confuse the evolution of the characters' situation, which is the most important focus of the play.*

Likewise, the costumes should be exactly representative of who the characters are and not added onto for the sake of making a point to the audience.

NOTE ON SOUND: *The Coyote of Southern California has a distinct yapping, dog-like bark, similar to a Hyena. This yapping grows more intense and maniacal as the pack grows in numbers, which is usually the case when they lure and kill pets from suburban yards. The sense of growing frenzy in the pack should be felt in the background, particularly in Scenes 7 and 8. In any case, these Coyotes never make the long, mournful, solitary howl of the Hollywood stereotype.*

The sound of Crickets can speak for itself.

These sounds should also be treated realistically even though they sometimes grow in volume and numbers.

Act 1, Scene I

*Night. Sound of crickets in dark. Can-
dlelight appears in alcove, illuminating*
AUSTIN, *seated at glass table hunched
over a writing notebook, pen in hand,
cigarette burning in ashtray, cup of
coffee, typewriter on table, stacks of paper, candle burning on table.*

*Soft moonlight fills kitchen illumi-
nating* LEE, *beer in hand, six-pack on
counter behind him. He's leaning
against the sink, mildly drunk; takes a
slug of beer.*

LEE: So, Mom took off for Alaska,
huh?

AUSTIN: Yeah.

LEE: Sorta' left you in charge.

AUSTIN: Well, she knew I was coming down here so she offered me
the place.

LEE: You keepin' the plants watered?

AUSTIN: Yeah.

LEE: Keepin' the sink clean? She
don't like even a single tea leaf in
the sink ya' know.

AUSTIN: (*trying to concentrate on
writing*) Yeah, I know.

(*pause*)

LEE: She gonna' be up there a long
time?

AUSTIN: I don't know.

LEE: Kinda' nice for you, huh?
Whole place to yourself.

AUSTIN: Yeah, it's great.

LEE: Ya' got crickets anyway. Tons
a' crickets out there. (*looks around
kitchen*) Ya' got groceries? Coffee?

AUSTIN: (*looking up from writing*)
What?

LEE: You got coffee?

AUSTIN: Yeah.

LEE: At's good. (*short pause*) Real
coffee? From the bean?

AUSTIN: Yeah. You want some?

LEE: Naw. I brought some uh—(*motions to beer*)

AUSTIN: Help yourself to whatever's—(*motions to refrigerator*)

LEE: I will. Don't worry about me.
I'm not the one to worry about. I
mean I can uh—(*pause*) You always work by candlelight?

AUSTIN: No—uh—Not always.

LEE: Just sometimes?

AUSTIN: (*puts pen down, rubs his eyes*)
Yeah. Sometimes it's soothing.

LEE: Isn't that what the old guys
did?

AUSTIN: What old guys?

LEE: The Forefathers. You know.

AUSTIN: Forefathers?

LEE: Isn't that what they did? Candlelight burning into the night?
Cabins in the wilderness.

AUSTIN: (*rubs hand through his hair*)
I suppose.

LEE: I'm not botherin' you am
I? I mean I don't wanna break
into yer uh—concentration or
nothin'.

AUSTIN: No, it's all right.

LEE: That's good. I mean I realize
that yer line a' work demands a
lota' concentration.

AUSTIN: It's okay.

LEE: You probably think that I'm
not fully able to comprehend
somethin' like that, huh?

AUSTIN: Like what?

LEE: That stuff yer doin'. That art. You know. Whatever you call it.

AUSTIN: It's just a little research.

LEE: You may not know it but I did a little art myself once.

AUSTIN: You did?

LEE: Yeah! I did some a' that. I fooled around with it. No future in it.

AUSTIN: What'd you do?

LEE: Never mind what I did! Just never mind about that. (*pause*) It was ahead of its time.

(*pause*)

AUSTIN: So, you went out to see the old man, huh?

LEE: Yeah, I seen him.

AUSTIN: How's he doing?

LEE: Same. He's doin' just about the same.

AUSTIN: I was down there too, you know.

LEE: What d'ya' want, an award? You want some kinda' medal? You were down there. He told me all about you.

AUSTIN: What'd he say?

LEE: He told me. Don't worry.

(*pause*)

AUSTIN: Well—

LEE: You don't have to say nothin'.

AUSTIN: I wasn't.

LEE: Yeah, you were gonna' make somethin' up. Somethin' brilliant.

(*pause*)

AUSTIN: You going to be down here very long, Lee?

LEE: Might be. Depends on a few things.

AUSTIN: You got some friends down here?

LEE: (*laughs*) I know a few people. Yeah.

AUSTIN: Well, you can stay here as long as I'm here.

LEE: I don't need your permission do I?

AUSTIN: No.

LEE: I mean she's my mother too, right?

AUSTIN: Right.

LEE: She might've just as easily asked me to take care of her place as you.

AUSTIN: That's right.

LEE: I mean I know how to water plants.

(*long pause*)

AUSTIN: So you don't know how long you'll be staying then?

LEE: Depends mostly on houses, ya' know.

AUSTIN: Houses?

LEE: Yeah. Houses. Electric devices. Stuff like that. I gotta' make a little tour first.

(*short pause*)

AUSTIN: Lee, why don't you just try another neighborhood, all right?

LEE: (*laughs*) What'sa' matter with this neighborhood? This is a great neighborhood. Lush. Good class a' people. Not many dogs.

AUSTIN: Well, our uh—Our mother just happens to live here. That's all.

LEE: Nobody's gonna' know. All they know is somethin's missing.

That's all. She'll never even hear about it. Nobody's gonna' know.

AUSTIN: You're going to get picked up if you start walking around here at night.

LEE: Me? I'm gonna' git picked up? What about you? You stick out like a sore thumb. Look at you. You think yer regular lookin'?

AUSTIN: I've got too much to deal with here to be worrying about—

LEE: Yer not gonna' have to worry about me! I've been doin' all right without you. I haven't been anywhere near you for five years! Now isn't that true?

AUSTIN: Yeah.

LEE: So you don't have to worry about me. I'm a free agent.

AUSTIN: All right.

LEE: Now all I wanna' do is borrow yer car.

AUSTIN: No!

LEE: Just fer a day. One day.

AUSTIN: No!

LEE: I won't take it outside a twenty mile radius. I promise ya'. You can check the speedometer.

AUSTIN: You're not borrowing my car! That's all there is to it.

(*pause*)

LEE: Then I'll just take the damn thing.

AUSTIN: Lee, look—I don't want any trouble, all right?

LEE: That's a dumb line. That is a dumb fuckin' line. You git paid fer dreamin' up a line like that?

AUSTIN: Look, I can give you some money if you need money.

(LEE *suddenly lunges at* AUSTIN, *grabs him violently by the shirt and shakes him with tremendous power*)

LEE: Don't you say that to me! Don't you ever say that to me! (*just as suddenly he turns him loose, pushes him away and backs off*) You may be able to git away with that with the Old Man. Git him tanked up for a week! Buy him off with yer Hollywood blood money, but not me! I can git my own money my own way. Big money!

AUSTIN: I was just making an offer.

LEE: Yeah, well keep it to yourself!

(*long pause*)

Those are the most monotonous fuckin' crickets I ever heard in my life.

AUSTIN: I kinda' like the sound.

LEE: Yeah. Supposed to be able to tell the temperature by the number a' pulses. You believe that?

AUSTIN: The temperature?

LEE: Yeah. The air. How hot it is.

AUSTIN: How do you do that?

LEE: I don't know. Some woman told me that. She was a Botanist. So I believed her.

AUSTIN: Where'd you meet her?

LEE: What?

AUSTIN: The woman Botanist?

LEE: I met her on the desert. I been spendin' a lota' time on the desert.

AUSTIN: What were you doing out there?

LEE: (*pause, stares in space*) I forgit.

Had me a Pit Bull there for a while but I lost him.

AUSTIN: Pit Bull?

LEE: Fightin' dog. Damn I made some good money off that little dog. Real good money.

(*pause*)

AUSTIN: You could come up north with me, you know.

LEE: What's up there?

AUSTIN: My family.

LEE: Oh, that's right, you got the wife and kiddies now don't ya'. The house, the car, the whole slam. That's right.

AUSTIN: You could spend a couple days. See how you like it. I've got an extra room.

LEE: Too cold up there.

(*pause*)

AUSTIN: You want to sleep for a while?

LEE: (*pause, stares at* AUSTIN) I don't sleep.

(*lights to black*)

Scene 2

Morning. AUSTIN *is watering plants with a vaporizer,* LEE *sits at glass table in alcove drinking beer.*

LEE: I never realized the old lady was so security-minded.

AUSTIN: How do you mean?

LEE: Made a little tour this morning. She's got locks on everything. Locks and double-locks and chain locks and—What's she got that's so valuable?

AUSTIN: Antiques I guess. I don't know.

LEE: Antiques? Brought everything with her from the old place, huh. Just the same crap we always had around. Plates and spoons.

AUSTIN: I guess they have personal value to her.

LEE: Personal value. Yeah. Just a lota' junk. Most of it's phony anyway. Idaho decals. Now who in the hell wants to eat offa' plate with the State of Idaho starin' ya' in the face. Every time ya' take a bite ya' get to see a little bit more.

AUSTIN: Well it must mean something to her or she wouldn't save it.

LEE: Yeah, well personally I don't wann' be invaded by Idaho when I'm eatin'. When I'm eatin' I'm home. Ya' know what I'm sayin'? I'm not driftin', I'm home. I don't need my thoughts swept off to Idaho. I don't need that!

(*pause*)

AUSTIN: Did you go out last night?

LEE: Why?

AUSTIN: I thought I heard you go out.

LEE: Yeah, I went out. What about it?

AUSTIN: Just wondered.

LEE: Damn coyotes kept me awake.

AUSTIN: Oh yeah, I heard them. They must've killed somebody's dog or something.

LEE: Yappin' their fool heads off.

They don't yap like that on the desert. They howl. These are city coyotes here.

AUSTIN: Well, you don't sleep anyway do you?

(*pause,* LEE *stares at him*)

LEE: You're pretty smart aren't ya?

AUSTIN: How do you mean?

LEE: I mean you never had any more on the ball than I did. But here you are gettin' invited into prominent people's houses. Sittin' around talkin' like you know somethin'.

AUSTIN: They're not so prominent.

LEE: They're a helluva' lot more prominent than the houses I get invited into.

AUSTIN: Well you invite yourself.

LEE: That's right. I do. In fact I probably got a wider range a' choices than you do, come to think of it.

AUSTIN: I wouldn't doubt it.

LEE: In fact I been inside some pretty classy places in my time. And I never even went to an Ivy League school either.

AUSTIN: You want some breakfast or something?

LEE: Breakfast?

AUSTIN: Yeah. Don't you eat breakfast?

LEE: Look, don't worry about me pal. I can take care a' myself. You just go ahead as though I wasn't even here, all right?

(AUSTIN *goes into kitchen, makes coffee*)

AUSTIN: Where'd you walk to last night?

(*pause*)

LEE: I went up in the foothills there. Up in the San Gabriels. Heat was drivin' me crazy.

AUSTIN: Well, wasn't it hot out on the desert?

LEE: Different kinda' heat. Out there it's clean. Cools off at night. There's a nice little breeze.

AUSTIN: Where were you, the Mojave?

LEE: Yeah. The Mojave. That's right.

AUSTIN: I haven't been out there in years.

LEE: Out past Needles there.

AUSTIN: Oh yeah.

LEE: Up here it's different. This country's real different.

AUSTIN: Well, it's been built up.

LEE: Built up? Wiped out is more like it. I don't even hardly recognize it.

AUSTIN: Yeah. Foothills are the same though, aren't they?

LEE: Pretty much. It's funny goin' up in there. The smells and everything. Used to catch snakes up there, remember?

AUSTIN: You caught snakes.

LEE: Yeah. And you'd pretend you were Geronimo or some damn thing. You used to go right out to lunch.

AUSTIN: I enjoyed my imagination.

LEE: That what you call it? Looks like yer still enjoyin' it.

AUSTIN: So you just wandered around up there, huh?

LEE: Yeah. With a purpose.
AUSTIN: See any houses?

(*pause*)

LEE: Couple. Couple a' real nice ones. One of 'em didn't even have a dog. Walked right up and stuck my head in the window. Not a peep. Just a sweet kinda' surburban silence.
AUSTIN: What kind of a place was it?
LEE: Like a paradise. Kinda' place that sorta' kills ya' inside. Warm yellow lights. Mexican tile all around. Copper pots hangin' over the stove. Ya' know like they got in the magazines. Blonde people movin' in and outa' the rooms, talkin' to each other. (*pause*) Kinda' place you wish you sorta' grew up in, ya' know.
AUSTIN: That's the kind of place you wish you'd grown up in?
LEE: Yeah, why not?
AUSTIN: I thought you hated that kind of stuff.
LEE: Yeah, well you never knew too much about me did ya'?

(*pause*)

AUSTIN: Why'd you go out to the desert in the first place?
LEE: I was on my way to see the old man.
AUSTIN: You mean you just passed through there?
LEE: Yeah. That's right. Three months of passin' through.
AUSTIN: Three months?

LEE: Somethin' like that. Maybe more. Why?
AUSTIN: You lived on the Mojave for three months?
LEE: Yeah. What'sa' matter with that?
AUSTIN: By yourself?
LEE: Mostly. Had a couple a' visitors. Had that dog for a while.
AUSTIN: Didn't you miss people?
LEE: (*laughs*) People?
AUSTIN: Yeah. I mean I go crazy if I have to spend three nights in a motel by myself.
LEE: Yer not in a motel now.
AUSTIN: No, I know. But sometimes I have to stay in motels.
LEE: Well, they got people in motels don't they?
AUSTIN: Strangers.
LEE: Yer friendly aren't ya'? Aren't you the friendly type?

(*pause*)

AUSTIN: I'm going to have somebody coming by here later, Lee.
LEE: Ah! Lady friend?
AUSTIN: No, a producer.
LEE: Aha! What's he produce?
AUSTIN: Film. Movies. You know.
LEE: Oh, movies. Motion Pictures! A Big Wig huh?
AUSTIN: Yeah.
LEE: What's he comin' by here for?
AUSTIN: We have to talk about a project.
LEE: Whadya' mean, "a project"? What's "a project"?
AUSTIN: A script.
LEE: Oh. That's what yer doin' with all these papers?

AUSTIN: Yeah.

LEE: Well, what's the project about?

AUSTIN: We're uh—it's a period piece.

LEE: What's "a period piece"?

AUSTIN: Look, it doesn't matter. The main thing is we need to discuss this alone. I mean—

LEE: Oh, I get it. You want me outa' the picture.

AUSTIN: Not exactly. I just need to be alone with him for a couple of hours. So we can talk.

LEE: Yer afraid I'll embarrass ya' huh?

AUSTIN: I'm not afraid you'll embarrass me!

LEE: Well, I tell ya' what—Why don't you just gimme the keys to yer car and I'll be back here around six o'clock or so. That give ya' enough time?

AUSTIN: I'm not loaning you my car, Lee.

LEE: You want me to just git lost huh? Take a hike? Is that it? Pound the pavement for a few hours while you bullshit yer way into a million bucks.

AUSTIN: Look, it's going to be hard enough for me to face this character on my own without—

LEE: You don't know this guy?

AUSTIN: No I don't know—He's a producer. I mean I've been meeting with him for months but you never get to know a producer.

LEE: Yer tryin' to hustle him? Is that it?

AUSTIN: I'm not trying to hustle him! I'm trying to work out a deal! It's not easy.

LEE: What kinda' deal?

AUSTIN: Convince him it's a worthwhile story.

LEE: He's not convinced? How come he's comin' over here if he's not convinced? I'll convince him for ya'.

AUSTIN: You don't understand the way things work down here.

LEE: How do things work down here?

(pause)

AUSTIN: Look, if I loan you my car will you have it back here by six?

LEE: On the button. With a full tank a' gas.

AUSTIN: (digging in his pocket for keys) Forget about the gas.

LEE: Hey, these days gas is gold, old buddy.

(AUSTIN hands the keys to LEE)

You remember that car I used to loan you?

AUSTIN: Yeah.

LEE: Forty Ford. Flathead.

AUSTIN: Yeah.

LEE: Sucker hauled ass didn't it?

AUSTIN: Lee, it's not that I don't want to loan you my car—

LEE: You are loanin' me yer car.

(LEE gives AUSTIN a pat on the shoulder, pause)

AUSTIN: I know. I just wish—

LEE: What? You wish what?

AUSTIN: I don't know. I wish I wasn't—I wish I didn't have to be doing business down here. I'd like to just spend some time with you.

LEE: I thought it was "Art" you were doin'.

(LEE *moves across kitchen toward exit, tosses keys in his hand*)

AUSTIN: Try to get it back here by six, okay?

LEE: No sweat. Hey, ya' know, if that uh—story of yours doesn't go over with the guy—tell him I got a couple a' "projects" he might be interested in. Real commercial. Full a' suspense. True-to-life stuff.

(LEE *exits,* AUSTIN *stares after* LEE *then turns, goes to papers at table, leafs through pages, lights fade to black*)

Scene 3

Afternoon. Alcove, SAUL KIMMER *and* AUSTIN *seated across from each other at table.*

SAUL: Well, to tell you the truth Austin, I have never felt so confident about a project in quite a long time.

AUSTIN: Well, that's good to hear, Saul.

SAUL: I am absolutely convinced we can get this thing off the ground. I mean we'll have to make a sale to television and that means getting a major star. Somebody bankable. But I think we can do it. I really do.

AUSTIN: Don't you think we need a first draft before we approach a star?

SAUL: No, no, not at all. I don't think it's necessary. Maybe a brief synopsis. I don't want you to touch the typewriter until we have some seed money.

AUSTIN: That's fine with me.

SAUL: I mean it's a great story. Just the story alone. You've really managed to capture something this time.

AUSTIN: I'm glad you like it, Saul.

(LEE *enters abruptly into kitchen carrying a stolen television set, short pause*)

LEE: Aw shit, I'm sorry about that. I am really sorry Austin.

AUSTIN: (*standing*) That's all right.

LEE: (*moving toward them*) I mean I thought it was way past six already. You said to have it back here by six.

AUSTIN: We were just finishing up. (*to Saul*) This is my, uh—brother, Lee.

SAUL: (*standing*) Oh, I'm very happy to meet you.

(LEE *sets T.V. on sink counter, shakes hands with* SAUL)

LEE: I can't tell ya' how happy I am to meet you sir.

SAUL: Saul Kimmer.

LEE: Mr. Kipper.

SAUL: Kimmer.

AUSTIN: Lee's been living out on the desert and he just uh—

SAUL: Oh, that's terrific! (*to* LEE) Palm Springs?

LEE: Yeah. Yeah, right. Right around in that area. Near uh—Bob Hope Drive there.

SAUL: Oh I love it out there. I just love it. The air is wonderful.

LEE: Yeah. Sure is. Healthy.

SAUL: And the golf. I don't know if you play golf, but the golf is just about the best.

LEE: I play a lota' golf.

SAUL: Is that right?

LEE: Yeah. In fact I was hoping I'd run into somebody out here who played a little golf. I've been lookin' for a partner.

SAUL: Well, I uh—

AUSTIN: Lee's just down for a visit while our mother's in Alaska.

SAUL: Oh, your mother's in Alaska?

AUSTIN: Yes. She went up there on a little vacation. This is her place.

SAUL: I see. Well isn't that something. Alaska.

LEE: What kinda' handicap do ya' have, Mr. Kimmer?

SAUL: Oh I'm just a Sunday duffer really. You know.

LEE: That's good 'cause I haven't swung a club in months.

SAUL: Well we ought to get together sometime and have a little game. Austin, do you play?

(SAUL *mimes a Johnny Carson golf swing for* AUSTIN)

AUSTIN: No. I don't uh—I've watched it on T.V.

LEE: (*to* SAUL) How 'bout tomorrow morning? Bright and early. We could get out there and put in eighteen holes before breakfast.

SAUL: Well, I've got uh—I have several appointments—

LEE: No, I mean real early. Crack a'dawn. While the dew's still thick on the fairway.

SAUL: Sounds really great.

LEE: Austin could be our caddie.

SAUL: Now that's an idea. (*laughs*)

AUSTIN: I don't know the first thing about golf.

LEE: There's nothin' to it. Isn't that right, Saul? He'd pick it up in fifteen minutes.

SAUL: Sure. Doesn't take long. 'Course you have to play for years to find your true form. (*chuckles*)

LEE: (*to* AUSTIN) We'll give ya' a quick run-down on the club faces. The irons, the woods. Show ya' a couple pointers on the basic swing. Might even let ya' hit the ball a couple times. Whadya' think, Saul?

SAUL: Why not. I think it'd be great. I haven't had any exercise in weeks.

LEE: 'At's the spirit! We'll have a little orange juice right afterwards.

(*pause*)

SAUL: Orange juice?

LEE: Yeah! Vitamin C! Nothin' like a shot a' orange juice after a round a' golf. Hot shower. Snappin' towels at each others' privates. Real sense a' fraternity.

SAUL: (*smiles at* AUSTIN) Well, you make it sound very inviting, I must say. It really does sound great.

LEE: Then it's a date.

SAUL: Well, I'll call the country club and see if I can arrange something.

LEE: Great! Boy, I sure am sorry that I busted in on ya' all in the middle of yer meeting.

SAUL: Oh that's quite all right. We were just about finished anyway.

LEE: I can wait out in the other room if you want.

SAUL: No really—

LEE: Just got Austin's color T.V. back from the shop. I can watch a little amateur boxing now.

(LEE *and* AUSTIN *exchange looks*)

SAUL: Oh—Yes.

LEE: You don't fool around in Television, do you Saul?

SAUL: Uh—I have in the past. Produced some T.V. Specials. Network stuff. But it's mainly features now.

LEE: That's where the big money is, huh?

SAUL: Yes. That's right.

AUSTIN: Why don't I call you tomorrow, Saul and we'll get together. We can have lunch or something.

SAUL: That'd be terrific.

LEE: Right after the golf.

(*pause*)

SAUL: What?

LEE: You can have lunch right after the golf.

SAUL: Oh, right.

LEE: Austin was tellin' me that yer interested in stories.

SAUL: Well, we develop certain projects that we feel have commercial potential.

LEE: What kinda' stuff do ya' go in for?

SAUL: Oh, the usual. You know. Good love interest. Lost of action. (*chuckles at* AUSTIN)

LEE: Westerns?

SAUL: Sometimes.

AUSTIN: I'll give you a ring, Saul.

(AUSTIN *tries to move* SAUL *across the kitchen but* LEE *blocks their way*)

LEE: I got a Western that'd knock yer lights out.

SAUL: Oh really?

LEE: Yeah. Contemporary Western. Based on a true story. 'Course I'm not a writer like my brother here. I'm not a man of the pen.

SAUL: Well—

LEE: I mean I can tell ya' a story off the tongue but I can't put it down on paper. That don't make any difference though does it?

SAUL: No, not really.

LEE: I mean plenty a' guys have stories don't they? True-life stories. Musta' been a lota' movies made from real life.

SAUL: Yes. I suppose so.

LEE: I haven't seen a good Western since "Lonely Are the Brave." You remember that movie?

SAUL: No, I'm afraid I—

LEE: Kirk Douglas. Helluva movie. You remember that movie, Austin?

AUSTIN: Yes.

LEE: (*to* SAUL) The man dies for the love of a horse.

SAUL: Is that right.

LEE: Yeah. Ya' hear the horse screamin' at the end of it. Rain's comin' down. Horse is screamin'.

Then there's a shot. BLAM! Just a single shot like that. Then nothin' but the sound of rain. And Kirk Douglas is ridin' in the ambulance. Ridin' away from the scene of the accident. And when he hears that shot he knows that his horse has died. He knows. And you see his eyes. And his eyes die. Right inside his face. And then his eyes close. And you know that he's died too. You know that Kirk Douglas has died from the death of his horse.

SAUL: (*eyes* AUSTIN *nervously*) Well, it sounds like a great movie. I'm sorry I missed it.

LEE: Yeah, you shouldn't a' missed that one.

SAUL: I'll have to try to catch it some time. Arrange a screening or something. Well, Austin, I'll have to hit the freeway before rush hour.

AUSTIN: (*ushers him toward exit*) It's good seeing you, Saul.

(AUSTIN *and* SAUL *shake hands*)

LEE: So ya' think there's room for a real Western these days? A true-to-life Western?

SAUL: Well, I don't see why not. Why don't you uh—tell the story to Austin and have him write a little outline.

LEE: You'd take a look at it then?

SAUL: Yes. Sure. I'll give it a read-through. Always eager for new material. (*smiles at* AUSTIN)

LEE: That's great! You'd really read it then huh?

SAUL: It would just be my opinion of course.

LEE: That's all I want. Just an opinion. I happen to think it has a lota' possibilities.

SAUL: Well, it was great meeting you and I'll—

(SAUL *and* LEE *shake*)

LEE: I'll call you tomorrow about the golf.

SAUL: Oh. Yes, right.

LEE: Austin's got your number, right?

SAUL: Yes.

LEE: So long Saul. (*gives* SAUL *a pat on the back*)

(SAUL *exits,* AUSTIN *turns to* LEE, *looks at T.V. then back to* LEE)

AUSTIN: Give me the keys.

(AUSTIN *extends his hand toward* LEE, *doesn't move, just stares at* AUSTIN, *smiles, lights to black*)

Scene 4

Night. Coyotes in distance, fade, sound of typewriter in dark, crickets, candle-light in alcove, dim light in kitchen, lights reveal AUSTIN *at glass table typing,* LEE *sits across from him, foot on table, drinking beer and whiskey, the T.V. is still on sink counter,* AUSTIN *types for a while, then stops.*

LEE: All right, now read it back to me.

AUSTIN: I'm not reading it back to

you, Lee. You can read it when we're finished. I can't spend all night on this.

LEE: You got better things to do?

AUSTIN: Let's just go ahead. Now what happens when he leaves Texas?

LEE: Is he ready to leave Texas yet? I didn't know we were that far along. He's not ready to leave Texas.

AUSTIN: He's right at the border.

LEE: (*sitting up*) No, see this is one a' the crucial parts. Right here. (*taps paper with beer can*) We can't rush through this. He's not right at the border. He's a good fifty miles from the border. A lot can happen in fifty miles.

AUSTIN: It's only an outline. We're not writing an entire script now.

LEE: Well ya' can't leave things out even if it is an outline. It's one a' the most important parts. Ya' can't go leavin' it out.

AUSTIN: Okay, okay. Let's just—get it done.

LEE: All right. Now. He's in the truck and he's got his horse trailer and his horse.

AUSTIN: We've already established that.

LEE: And he sees this other guy comin' up behind him in another truck. And that truck is pullin' a gooseneck.

AUSTIN: What's a gooseneck?

LEE: Cattle trailer. You know the kind with a gooseneck, goes right down in the bed a' the pick-up.

AUSTIN: Oh. All right. (*types*)

LEE: It's important.

AUSTIN: Okay. I got it.

LEE: All these details are important.

(AUSTIN *types as they talk*)

AUSTIN: I've got it.

LEE: And this other guy's got his horse all saddled up in the back a' the gooseneck.

AUSTIN: Right.

LEE: So both these guys have got their horses right along with 'em, see.

AUSTIN: I understand.

LEE: Then this first guy suddenly realizes two things.

AUSTIN: The guy in front?

LEE: Right. The guy in front realizes two things almost at the same time. Simultaneous.

AUSTIN: What were the two things?

LEE: Number one, he realizes that the guy behind him is the husband of the woman he's been—

(LEE *makes gesture of screwing by pumping his arm*)

AUSTIN: (*sees* LEE'S *gesture*) Oh. Yeah.

LEE: And number two, he realizes he's in the middle of Tornado Country.

AUSTIN: What's "Tornado Country"?

LEE: Panhandle.

AUSTIN: Panhandle?

LEE: Sweetwater. Around in that area. Nothin'. Nowhere. And number three—

AUSTIN: I thought there was only two.

LEE: There's three. There's a third unforeseen realization.

AUSTIN: And what's that?

LEE: That he's runnin' outa' gas.

AUSTIN: (*stops typing*) Come on, Lee.

(AUSTIN *gets up, moves to kitchen, gets a glass of water*)

LEE: Whadya' mean, "come on"? That's what it is. Write it down! He's runnin' outa' gas.

AUSTIN: It's too—

LEE: What? It's too what? It's too real! That's what ya' mean isn't it? It's too much like real life!

AUSTIN: It's not like real life! It's not enough like real life. Things don't happen like that.

LEE: What! Men don't fuck other men's women?

AUSTIN: Yes. But they don't end up chasing each other across the Panhandle. Through "Tornado Country."

LEE: They do in this movie!

AUSTIN: And they don't have horses conveniently along with them when they run out of gas! And they don't run out of gas either!

LEE: These guys run outa' gas! This is my story and one a' these guys runs outa' gas!

AUSTIN: It's just a dumb excuse to get them into a chase scene. It's contrived.

LEE: It is a chase scene! It's already a chase scene. They been chasin' each other fer days.

AUSTIN: So now they're supposed to abandon their trucks, climb on their horses and chase each other into the mountains?

LEE: (*standing suddenly*) There aren't any mountains in the Panhandle! It's flat!

(LEE *turns violently toward windows in alcove and throws beer can at them*)

LEE: Goddamn these crickets! (*yells at crickets*) Shut up out there! (*pause, turns back toward table*) This place is like a fuckin' rest home here. How're you supposed to think!

AUSTIN: You wanna' take a break?

LEE: No, I don't wanna' take a break! I wanna' get this done! This is my last chance to get this done.

AUSTIN: (*moves back into alcove*) All right. Take it easy.

LEE: I'm gonna' be leavin' this area. I don't have time to mess around here.

AUSTIN: Where are you going?

LEE: Never mind where I'm goin'! That's got nothin' to do with you. I just gotta' get this done. I'm not like you. Hangin' around bein' a parasite offa' other fools. I gotta' do this thing and get out.

(*pause*)

AUSTIN: A parasite? Me?

LEE: Yeah, you!

AUSTIN: After you break into people's houses and take their televisions?

LEE: They don't need their televisions! I'm doin' them a service.

AUSTIN: Give me back my keys, Lee.

LEE: Not until you write this thing!

You're gonna' write this outline thing for me or that car's gonna' wind up in Arizona with a different paint job.

AUSTIN: You think you can force me to write this? I was doing you a favor.

LEE: Git off yer high horse will ya'! Favor! Big favor. Handin' down favors from the mountain top.

AUSTIN: Let's just write it, okay? Let's sit down and not get upset and see if we can just get through this.

(AUSTIN *sits at typewriter*)

(*long pause*)

LEE: Yer not gonna' even show it to him, are ya'?

AUSTIN: What?

LEE: This outline. You got no intention of showin' it to him. Yer just doin' this 'cause yer afraid a' me.

AUSTIN: You can show it to him yourself.

LEE: I will, boy! I'm gonna' read it to him on the golf course.

AUSTIN: And I'm not afraid of you either.

LEE: Then how come yer doin' it?

AUSTIN: (*pause*) So I can get my keys back.

(*pause as* LEE *takes keys out of his pocket slowly and throws them on table, long pause,* AUSTIN *stares at keys*)

LEE: There. Now you got yer keys back.

(AUSTIN *looks up at* LEE *but doesn't take keys*)

LEE: Go ahead. There's yer keys.

(AUSTIN *slowly takes keys off table and puts them back in his own pocket*)

Now what're you gonna' do? Kick me out?

AUSTIN: I'm not going to kick you out, Lee.

LEE: You couldn't kick me out, boy.

AUSTIN: I know.

LEE: So you can't even consider that one. (*pause*) You could call the police. That'd be the obvious thing.

AUSTIN: You're my brother.

LEE: That don't mean a thing. You go down to the L.A. Police Department there and ask them what kinda' people kill each other the most. What do you think they'd say?

AUSTIN: Who said anything about killing?

LEE: Family people. Brothers. Brothers-in-law. Cousins. Real American-type people. They kill each other in the heat mostly. In the Smog-Alerts. In the Brush Fire Season. Right about this time a' year.

AUSTIN: This isn't the same.

LEE: Oh no? What makes it different?

AUSTIN: We're not insane. We're not driven to acts of violence like that. Not over a dumb movie script. Now sit down.

(*long pause,* LEE *considers which way to go with it*)

LEE: Maybe not. (*he sits back down at table across from* AUSTIN) Maybe you're right. Maybe we're too intelligent, huh? (*pause*) We got our heads on our shoulders. One of us has even got a Ivy League diploma. Now that means somethin' don't it? Doesn't that mean somethin'?

AUSTIN: Look, I'll write this thing for you, Lee. I don't mind writing it. I just don't want to get all worked up about it. It's not worth it. Now, come on. Let's just get through it, okay?

LEE: Nah. I think there's easier money. Lotsa' places I could pick up thousands. Maybe millions. I don't need this shit. I could go up to Sacramento Valley and steal me a diesel. Ten thousand a week dismantling one a' those suckers. Ten thousand a week!

(LEE *opens another beer, puts his foot back up on table*)

AUSTIN: No, really, look, I'll write it out for you. I think it's a great idea.

LEE: Nah, you got yer own work to do. I don't wanna' interfere with yer life.

AUSTIN: I mean it'd be really fantastic if you could sell this. Turn it into a movie. I mean it.

(*pause*)

LEE: Ya' think so huh?

AUSTIN: Absolutely. You could really turn your life around, you know. Change things.

LEE: I could get me a house maybe.

AUSTIN: Sure you could get a house.

You could get a whole ranch if you wanted to.

LEE: (*laughs*) A ranch? I could get a ranch?

AUSTIN: 'Course you could. You know what a screenplay sells for these days?

LEE: No. What's it sell for?

AUSTIN: A lot. A whole lot of money.

LEE: Thousands?

AUSTIN: Yeah. Thousands.

LEE: Millions?

AUSTIN: Well—

LEE: We could get the old man outa' hock then.

AUSTIN: Maybe.

LEE: Maybe? Whadya' mean, maybe?

AUSTIN: I mean it might take more than money.

LEE: You were just tellin' me it'd change my whole life around. Why wouldn't it change his?

AUSTIN: He's different.

LEE: Oh, he's of a different ilk huh?

AUSTIN: He's not gonna' change. Let's leave the old man out of it.

LEE: That's right. He's not gonna' change but I will. I'll just turn myself right inside out. I could be just like you then, huh? Sittin' around dreamin' stuff up. Gettin' paid to dream. Ridin' back and forth on the freeway just dreamin' my fool head off.

AUSTIN: It's not all that easy.

LEE: It's not, huh?

AUSTIN: No. There's a lot of work involved.

LEE: What's the toughest part? Deciding whether to jog or play tennis?

(*long pause*)

AUSTIN: Well, look. You can stay here—do whatever you want to. Borrow the car. Come in and out. Doesn't matter to me. It's not my house. I'll help you write this thing or—not. Just let me know what you want. You tell me.

LEE: Oh. So now suddenly you're at my service. Is that it?

AUSTIN: What do you want to do Lee?

(*long pause,* LEE *stares at him then turns and dreams at windows*)

LEE: I tell ya' what I'd do if I still had that dog. Ya' wanna' know what I'd do?

AUSTIN: What?

LEE: Head out to Ventura. Cook up a little match. God that little dog could bear down. Lota' money in dog fightin'. Big money.

(*pause*)

AUSTIN: Why don't we try to see this through, Lee. Just for the hell of it. Maybe you've really got something here. What do you think?

(*pause,* LEE *considers*)

LEE: Maybe so. No harm in tryin' I guess. You think it's such a hot idea. Besides, I always wondered what'd be like to be you.

AUSTIN: You did?

LEE: Yeah, sure. I used to picture you walkin' around some campus with yer arms fulla' books. Blondes chasin' after ya'.

AUSTIN: Blondes? That's funny.

LEE: What's funny about it?

AUSTIN: Because I always used to picture you somewhere.

LEE: Where'd you picture me?

AUSTIN: Oh, I don't know. Different places. Adventures. You were always on some adventure.

LEE: Yeah.

AUSTIN: And I used to say to myself, "Lee's got the right idea. He's out there in the world and here I am. What am I doing?"

LEE: Well you were settin' yourself up for somethin'.

AUSTIN: I guess.

LEE: We better get started on this thing then.

AUSTIN: Okay.

(AUSTIN *sits up at typewriter, puts new paper in*)

LEE: Oh. Can I get the keys back before I forget?

(AUSTIN *hesitates*)

You said I could borrow the car if I wanted, right? Isn't that what you said?

AUSTIN: Yeah. Right.

(AUSTIN *takes keys out of his pocket, sets them on table,* LEE *takes keys slowly, plays with them in his hand*)

LEE: I could get a ranch, huh?

AUSTIN: Yeah. We have to write it first though.

LEE: Okay. Let's write it.

(lights start dimming slowly to end of scene as AUSTIN *types,* LEE *speaks)*

So they take off after each other straight into an endless black prairie. The sun is just comin' down and they can feel the night on their backs. What they don't know is that each one of 'em is afraid, see. Each one separately thinks that he's the only one that's afraid. And they keep ridin' like that straight into the night. Not knowing. And the one who's chasin' doesn't know where the other one is taking him. And the one who's being chased doesn't know where he's going.

(lights to black, typing stops in the dark, crickets fade)

Act 2, Scene 5

Morning. LEE *at the table in alcove with a set of golf clubs in a fancy leather bag,* AUSTIN *at sink washing a few dishes.*

AUSTIN: He really liked it, huh?
LEE: He wouldn't a' gave me these clubs if he didn't like it.
AUSTIN: He gave you the clubs?
LEE: Yeah. I told ya' he gave me the clubs. The bag too.
AUSTIN: I thought he just loaned them to you.
LEE: He said it was part a' the advance. A little gift like. Gesture of his good faith.

AUSTIN: He's giving you an advance?
LEE: Now what's so amazing about that? I told ya' it was a good story. You even said it was a good story.
AUSTIN: Well that is really incredible Lee. You know how many guys spend their whole lives down here trying to break into this business? Just trying to get in the door?
LEE: *(pulling clubs out of bag, testing them)* I got no idea. How many?

(pause)

AUSTIN: How much of an advance is he giving you?
LEE: Plenty. We were talkin' big money out there. Ninth hole is where I sealed the deal.
AUSTIN: He made a firm commitment?
LEE: Absolutely.
AUSTIN: Well, I know Saul and he doesn't fool around when he says he likes something.
LEE: I thought you said you didn't know him.
AUSTIN: Well, I'm familiar with his tastes.
LEE: I let him get two up on me goin' into the back nine. He was sure he had me cold. You shoulda' seen his face when I pulled out the old pitching wedge and plopped it pin-high, two feet from the cup. He 'bout shit his pants. "Where'd a guy like you ever learn how to play golf like that?" he says.

(LEE *laughs*, AUSTIN *stares at him*)

AUSTIN: 'Course there's no contract yet. Nothing's final until it's on paper.

LEE: It's final, all right. There's no way he's gonna's back out of it now. We gambled for it.

AUSTIN: Saul, gambled?

LEE: Yeah, sure. I mean he liked the outline already so he wasn't risking that much. I just guaranteed it with my short game.

(pause)

AUSTIN: Well, we should celebrate or something. I think Mom left a bottle of champagne in the refrigerator. We should have a little toast.

(AUSTIN *gets glasses from cupboard, goes to refrigerator, pulls out bottle of champagne*)

LEE: You shouldn't oughta' take her champagne, Austin. She's gonna miss that.

AUSTIN: Oh, she's not going to mind. She'd be glad we put it to good use. I'll get her another bottle. Besides, it's perfect for the occasion.

(pause)

LEE: Yer gonna' get a nice fee fer writin' the script a' course. Straight fee.

(AUSTIN *stops, stares at* LEE, *puts glasses and bottle on table, pause*)

AUSTIN: I'm writing the script?

LEE: That's what he said. Said we couldn't hire a better screenwriter in the whole town.

AUSTIN: But I'm already working on a script. I've got my own project. I don't have time to write two scripts.

LEE: No, he said he was gonna' drop that other one.

(pause)

AUSTIN: What? You mean mine? He's going to drop mine and do yours instead?

LEE: (*smiles*) Now look, Austin, it's jest beginner's luck ya' know. I mean I sank a fifty foot putt for this deal. No hard feelings.

(AUSTIN *goes to phone on wall, grabs it, starts dialing*)

He's not gonna' be in, Austin. Told me he wouldn't be in 'till late this afternoon.

AUSTIN: (*stays on phone, dialing, listens*) I can't believe this. I just can't believe it. Are you sure he said that? Why would he drop mine?

LEE: That's what he told me.

AUSTIN: He can't do that without telling me first. Without talking to me at least. He wouldn't just make a decision like that without talking to me!

LEE: Well I was kinda' surprised myself. But he was real enthusiastic about my story.

(AUSTIN *hangs up phone violently, paces*)

AUSTIN: What'd he say! Tell me everything he said!

LEE: I been tellin' ya'! He said he liked the story a whole lot. It was the first authentic Western to come along in a decade.

AUSTIN: He liked that story! Your story?

LEE: Yeah! What's so surprisin' about that?

AUSTIN: It's stupid! It's the dumbest story I ever heard in my life.

LEE: Hey, hold on! That's my story yer talkin' about!

AUSTIN: It's a bullshit story! It's idiotic. Two lamebrains chasing each other across Texas! Are you kidding? Who do you think's going to go see a film like that?

LEE: It's not a film! It's a movie. There's a big difference. That's somethin' Saul told me.

AUSTIN: Oh he did, huh?

LEE: Yeah, he said, "In this business we make movies, American movies. Leave the films to the French."

AUSTIN: So you got real intimate with old Saul huh? He started pouring forth his vast knowledge of Cinema.

LEE: I think he liked me a lot, to tell ya' the truth. I think he felt I was somebody he could confide in.

AUSTIN: What'd you do, beat him up or something?

LEE: (stands fast) Hey, I've about had it with the insults buddy! You think yer the only one in the brain department here? Yer the only one that can sit around and cook things up? There's other people got ideas too, ya' know!

AUSTIN: You must've done something. Threatened him or something. Now what'd you do Lee?

LEE: I convinced him!

(LEE makes sudden menacing lunge toward AUSTIN, wielding golf club above his head, stops himself, frozen moment, long pause, LEE lowers club)

AUSTIN: Oh, Jesus. You didn't hurt him did you?

(long silence, LEE sits back down at table)

Lee! Did you hurt him?

LEE: I didn't do nothin' to him! He liked my story. Pure and simple. He said it was the best story he's come across in a long, long time.

AUSTIN: That's what he told me about my story! That's the same thing he said to me.

LEE: Well, he musta' been lyin'. He musta' been lyin' to one of us anyway.

AUSTIN: You can't come into this town and start pushing people around. They're gonna' put you away!

LEE: I never pushed anybody around! I beat him fair and square. (pause) They can't touch me anyway. They can't put a finger on me. I'm gone. I can come in through the window and go out through the door. They never knew what hit 'em. You, yer stuck. Yer the one that's stuck.

Not me. So don't be warnin' me what to do in this town.

(*pause,* AUSTIN *crosses to table, sits at typewriter, rests*)

AUSTIN: Lee, come on, level with me will you? It doesn't make any sense that suddenly he'd throw my idea out the window. I've been talking to him for months. I've got too much at stake. Everything's riding on this project.

LEE: What's yer idea?

AUSTIN: It's just a simple love story.

LEE: What kinda' love story?

AUSTIN: (*stands, crosses into kitchen*) I'm not telling you!

LEE: Ha! 'Fraid I'll steal it huh? Competition's gettin' kinda' close to home isn't it?

AUSTIN: Where did Saul say he was going?

LEE: He was gonna' take my story to a couple studios.

AUSTIN: That's *my* outline you know! I wrote that outline! You've got no right to be peddling it around.

LEE: You weren't ready to take credit for it last night.

AUSTIN: Give me my keys!

LEE: What?

AUSTIN: The keys! I want my keys back!

LEE: Where you goin'?

AUSTIN: Just give me my keys! I gotta' take a drive. I gotta' get out of here for a while.

LEE: Where you gonna' go, Austin?

AUSTIN: (*pause*) I might just drive out to the desert for a while. I gotta' think.

LEE: You can think here just as good. This is the perfect setup for thinkin'. We got some writin' to do here, boy. Now let's just have us a little toast. Relax. We're partners now.

(LEE *pops the cork of the champagne bottle, pours two drinks as the lights fade to black*)

Scene 6

Afternoon. Lee *and* Saul *in kitchen,* Austin *in alcove*

LEE: Now you tell him. You tell him, Mr. Kipper.

SAUL: Kimmer.

LEE: Kimmer. You tell him what you told me. He don't believe me.

AUSTIN: I don't want to hear it.

SAUL: It's really not a big issue, Austin. I was simply amazed by your brother's story and—

AUSTIN: Amazed? You lost a bet! You gambled with my material!

SAUL: That's really beside the point, Austin. I'm ready to go all the way with your brother's story. I think it has a great deal of merit.

AUSTIN: I don't want to hear about it, okay? Go tell it to the executives! Tell it to somebody who's going to turn it into a package deal or something. A T.V. series. Don't tell it to me.

SAUL: But I want to continue with your project too, Austin. It's not

as though we can't do both.
We're big enough for that aren't
we?

AUSTIN: "We"? *I* can't do both! I
don't know about "we."

LEE: (*to* SAUL) See, what'd I tell ya'.
He's totally unsympathetic.

SAUL: Austin, there's no point in
our going to another screenwriter for this. It just doesn't
make sense. You're brothers. You
know each other. There's a familiarity with the material that just
wouldn't be possible otherwise.

AUSTIN: There's no familiarity with
the material! None! I don't know
what "Tornado Country" is. I
don't know what a "gooseneck"
is. And I don't want to know!
(*pointing to* LEE) He's a hustler!
He's a bigger hustler than you
are! If you can't see that, then—

LEE: (*to* AUSTIN) Hey, now hold on.
I didn't have to bring this bone
back to you, boy. I persuaded
Saul here that you were the right
man for the job. You don't have
to go throwin' up favors in my
face.

AUSTIN: Favors! I'm the one who
wrote the fuckin' outline! You
can't even spell.

SAUL: (*to* AUSTIN) Your brother told
me about the situation with your
father.

(*pause*)

AUSTIN: What? (*looks at* LEE)

SAUL: That's right. Now we have a
clear-cut deal here, Austin. We
have big studio money standing

behind this thing. Just on the basis of your outline.

AUSTIN: (*to* SAUL) What'd he tell
you about my father?

SAUL: Well—that he's destitute. He
needs money.

LEE: That's right. He does.

(AUSTIN *shakes his head, stares at
them both*)

AUSTIN: (*to* LEE) And this little as-
signment is supposed to go toward the old man? A charity project? Is that what this is? Did you
cook this up on the ninth green
too?

SAUL: It's a big slice, Austin.

AUSTIN: (*to* LEE) I gave him money!
I already gave him money. You
know that. He drank it all up!

LEE: This is a different deal here.

SAUL: We can set up a trust for your
father. A large sum of money. It
can be doled out to him in parcels
so he can't misuse it.

AUSTIN: Yeah, and who's doing the
doling?

SAUL: Your brother volunteered.

(AUSTIN *laughs*)

LEE: That's right. I'll make sure he
uses it for groceries.

AUSTIN: (*to* SAUL) I'm not doing this
script! I'm not writing this crap
for you or anybody else. You
can't blackmail me into it. You
can't threaten me into it. There's
no way I'm doing it. So just give
it up. Both of you.

(long pause)

SAUL: Well, that's it then. I mean this is an easy three hundred grand. Just for a first draft. It's incredible, Austin. We've got three different studios all trying to cut each other's throats to get this material. In one morning. That's how hot it is.

AUSTIN: Yeah, well you can afford to give me a percentage on the outline then. And you better get the genius here an agent before he gets burned.

LEE: Saul's gonna' be my agent. Isn't that right, Saul?

SAUL: That's right. *(to AUSTIN)* Your brother has really got something, Austin. I've been around too long not to recognize it. Raw talent.

AUSTIN: He's got a lota' balls is what he's got. He's taking you right down the river.

SAUL: Three hundred thousand, Austin. Just for a first draft. Now you've never been offered that kind of money before.

AUSTIN: I'm not writing it.

(pause)

SAUL: I see. Well—

LEE: We'll just go to another writer then. Right, Saul? Just hire us somebody with some enthusiasm. Somebody who can recognize the value of a good story.

SAUL: I'm sorry about this, Austin.

AUSTIN: Yeah.

SAUL: I mean I was hoping we could continue both things but now I don't see how it's possible.

AUSTIN: So you're dropping my idea altogether. Is that it? Just trade horses in midstream? After all these months of meetings.

SAUL: I wish there was another way.

AUSTIN: I've got everything riding on this, Saul. You know that. It's my only shot. If this falls through—

SAUL: I have to go with what my instincts tell me—

AUSTIN: Your instincts!

SAUL: My gut reaction.

AUSTIN: You lost! That's your gut reaction. You lost a gamble. Now you're trying to tell me you like his story? How could you possibly fall for that story? It's as phony as Hoppalong Cassidy. What do you see in it? I'm curious.

SAUL: It has the ring of truth, Austin.

AUSTIN: *(laughs)* Truth?

LEE: It is true.

SAUL: Something about the real West.

AUSTIN: Why? Because it's got horses? Because it's got grown men acting like little boys?

SAUL: Something about the land. Your brother is speaking from experience.

AUSTIN: So am I!

SAUL: But nobody's interested in love these days, Austin. Let's face it.

LEE: That's right.

AUSTIN: (*to* SAUL) He's been camped out on the desert for three months. Talking to cactus. What's he know about what people wanna' see on the screen! I drive on the freeway every day. I swallow the smog. I watch the news in color. I shop in the Safeway. I'm the one who's in touch! Not him!

SAUL: I Have to go now, Austin.

(SAUL *starts to leave*)

AUSTIN: There's no such thing as the West anymore! It's a dead issue! It's dried up, Saul, and so are you.

(SAUL *stops and turns to* AUSTIN)

SAUL: Maybe you're right. But I have to take the gamble, don't I?

AUSTIN: You're a fool to do this, Saul.

SAUL: I've always gone on my hunches. Always. And I've never been wrong. (*to* LEE) I'll talk to you tomorrow, Lee.

LEE: All right, Mr. Kimmer.

SAUL: Maybe we could have some lunch.

LEE: Fine with me. (*smiles at* AUSTIN)

SAUL: I'll give you a ring.

(SAUL *exits, lights to black as brothers look at each other from a distance*)

Scene 7

Night. Coyotes, crickets, sound of type-writer in dark, candlelight up on LEE *at typewriter struggling to type with* *one finger system,* AUSTIN *sits sprawled out on kitchen floor with whiskey bottle, drunk.*

AUSTIN: (*singing, from floor*)
"Red sails in the sunset
Way out on the blue
Please carry my loved one
Home safely to me

Red sails in the sunset—"

LEE: (*slams fist on table*) Hey! Knock it off will ya'! I'm tryin' to concentrate here.

AUSTIN: (*laughs*) You're tryin' to concentrate?

LEE: Yeah. That's right.

AUSTIN: Now you're tryin' to concentrate.

LEE: Between you, the coyotes and the crickets a thought don't have much of a chance.

AUSTIN: "Between me, the coyotes and the crickets." What a great title.

LEE: I don't need a title! I need a thought.

AUSTIN: (*laughs*) A thought! Here's a thought for ya'—

LEE: I'm not askin' fer yer thoughts! I got my own. I can do this thing on my own.

AUSTIN: You're going to write an entire script on your own?

LEE: That's right.

(*pause*)

AUSTIN: Here's a thought. Saul Kimmer—

LEE: Shut up will ya'!

AUSTIN: He thinks we're the same person.

LEE: Don't get cute.

AUSTIN: He does! He's lost his mind. Poor old Saul. (*giggles*) Thinks we're one and the same.

LEE: Why don't you ease up on that champagne.

AUSTIN: (*holding up bottle*) This isn't champagne anymore. We went through the champagne a long time ago. This is serious stuff. The days of champagne are long gone.

LEE: Well, go outside and drink it.

AUSTIN: I'm enjoying your company, Lee. For the first time since your arrival I am finally enjoying your company. And now you want me to go outside and drink alone?

LEE: That's right.

(*LEE reads through paper in typewriter, makes an erasure*)

AUSTIN: You think you'll make more progress if you're alone? You might drive yourself crazy.

LEE: I could have this thing done in a night if I had a little silence.

AUSTIN: Well you'd still have the crickets to contend with. The coyotes. The sounds of the Police Helicopters prowling above the neighborhood. Slashing their searchlights down through the streets. Hunting for the likes of you.

LEE: I'm a screenwriter now! I'm legitimate.

AUSTIN: (*laughing*) A screenwriter!

LEE: That's right. I'm on salary. That's more'n I can say for you. I got an advance coming.

AUSTIN: This is true. This is very true. An advance. (*pause*) Well, maybe I oughta' go out and try my hand at your trade. Since you're doing so good at mine.

LEE: Ha!

(*LEE attempts to type some more but gets the ribbon tangled up, starts trying to re-thread it as they continue talking*)

AUSTIN: Well why not? You don't think I've got what it takes to sneak into people's houses and steal their T.V.s?

LEE: You couldn't steal a toaster without losin' yer lunch.

(*AUSTIN stands with a struggle, supports himself by the sink*)

AUSTIN: You don't think I could sneak into somebody's house and steal a toaster?

LEE: Go take a shower or somethin' will ya!

(*LEE gets more tangled up with the typewriter ribbon, pulling it out of the machine as though it was fishing line*)

AUSTIN: You really don't think I could steal a crumby toaster? How much you wanna' bet I can't steal a toaster! How much? Go ahead! You're a gambler aren't you? Tell me how much yer willing to put on the line. Some part of your big advance? Oh, you haven't got that yet have you. I forgot.

LEE: All right. I'll bet you your car

that you can't steal a toaster without gettin' busted.

AUSTIN: You already got my car!

LEE: Okay, your house then.

AUSTIN: What're you gonna' give me! I'm not talkin' about my house and my car, I'm talkin' about what are you gonna' give me. You don't have nothin' to give me.

LEE: I'll give you—shared screen credit. How 'bout that? I'll have it put in the contract that this was written by the both of us.

AUSTIN: I don't want my name on that piece of shit! I want something of value. You got anything of value? You got any tidbits from the desert? Any Rattlesnake bones? I'm not a greedy man. Any little personal treasure will suffice.

LEE: I'm gonna' just kick yer ass out in a minute.

AUSTIN: Oh, so now you're gonna' kick me out! Now I'm the intruder. I'm the one who's invading your precious privacy.

LEE: I'm trying to do some screenwriting here!!

(LEE *stands, picks up typewriter, slams it down hard on table, pause, silence except for crickets*)

AUSTIN: Well, you got everything you need. You got plenty a' coffee? Groceries. You got a car. A contract. (*pause*) Might need a new typewriter ribbon but other than that you're pretty well fixed. I'll just leave ya' alone for a while.

(AUSTIN *tries to steady himself to leave,* LEE *makes a move toward him*)

LEE: Where you goin'?

AUSTIN: Don't worry about me. I'm not the one to worry about.

(AUSTIN *weaves toward exit, stops*)

LEE: What're you gonna' do? Just go wander out into the night?

AUSTIN: I'm gonna' make a little tour.

LEE: Why don't ya' just go to bed for Christ's sake. Yer makin' me sick.

AUSTIN: I can take care a' myself. Don't worry about me.

(AUSTIN *weaves badly in another attempt to exit, he crashes to the floor,* LEE *goes to him but remains standing*)

LEE: You want me to call your wife for ya' or something?

AUSTIN: (*from floor*) My wife?

LEE: Yeah. I mean maybe she can help ya' out. Talk to ya' or somethin'.

AUSTIN: (*struggles to stand again*) She's five hundred miles away. North. North of here. Up in the North country where things are calm. I don't need any help. I'm gonna' go outside and I'm gonna' steal a toaster. I'm gonna' steal some other stuff too. I might even commit bigger crimes. Bigger than you ever dreamed of. Crimes beyond the imagination!

(AUSTIN *manages to get himself vertical, tries to head for exit again*)

LEE: Just hang on a minute, Austin.

AUSTIN: Why? What for? You don't need my help, right? You got a handle on the project. Besides, I'm lookin' forward to the smell of the night. The bushes. Orange blossoms. Dust in the driveways. Rain bird sprinklers. Lights in people's houses. You're right about the lights, Lee. Everybody else is livin' the life. Indoors. Safe. This is a Paradise down here. You know that? We're livin' in a Paradise. We've forgotten about that.

LEE: You sound just like the old man now.

AUSTIN: Yeah, well we all sound alike when we're sloshed. We just sorta' echo each other.

LEE: Maybe if we could work on this together we could bring him back out here. Get him settled down some place.

(AUSTIN *turns violently toward* LEE, *takes a swing at him, misses and crashes to the floor again,* LEE *stays standing*)

AUSTIN: I don't want him out here! I've had it with him! I went all the way out there! I went out of my way. I gave him money and all he did was play Al Jolson records and spit at me! I gave him money!

(*pause*)

LEE: Just help me a little with the characters, all right? You know how to do it, Austin.

AUSTIN: (*on floor, laughs*) The characters!

LEE: Yeah. You know. The way they talk and stuff. I can hear it in my head but I can't get it down on paper.

AUSTIN: What characters?

LEE: The guys. The guys in the story.

AUSTIN: Those aren't characters.

LEE: Whatever you call 'em then. I need to write somethin' out.

AUSTIN: Those are illusions of characters.

LEE: I don't give a damn what ya' call 'em! You know what I'm talkin' about!

AUSTIN: Those are fantasies of a long lost boyhood.

LEE: I gotta' write somethin' out on paper!!

(*pause*)

AUSTIN: What for? Saul's gonna' get you a fancy screenwriter isn't he?

LEE: I wanna' do it myself!

AUSTIN: Then do it! Yer on your own now, old buddy. You bull-dogged yer way into contention. Now you gotta' carry it through.

LEE: I will but I need some advice. Just a couple a' things. Come on, Austin. Just help me get 'em talkin' right. It won't take much.

AUSTIN: Oh, now you're having a little doubt huh? What happened? The pressure's on, boy. This is it. You gotta' come up with it now. You don't come up with a winner on your first time out they just cut your head off.

They don't give you a second chance ya' know.

LEE: I got a good story! I know it's a good story. I just need a little help is all.

AUSTIN: Not from me. Not from yer little old brother. I'm retired.

LEE: You could save this thing for me, Austin. I'd give ya' half the money. I would. I only need half anyway. With this kinda' money I could be a long time down the road. I'd never bother ya' again. I promise. You'd never even see me again.

AUSTIN: (*still on floor*) You'd disappear?

LEE: I would for sure.

AUSTIN: Where would you disappear to?

LEE: That don't matter. I got plenty a' places.

AUSTIN: Nobody can disappear. The old man tried that. Look where it got him. He lost his teeth.

LEE: He never had any money.

AUSTIN: I don't mean that. I mean his teeth! His real teeth. First he lost his real teeth, then he lost his false teeth. You never knew that did ya'? He never confided in you.

LEE: Nah, I never knew that.

AUSTIN: You wanna' drink?

(AUSTIN *offers bottle to* LEE, LEE *takes it, sits down on kitchen floor with* AUSTIN, *they share the bottle*)

Yeah, he lost his real teeth one at a time. Woke up every morning with another tooth lying on the mattress. Finally, he decides he's gotta' get 'em all pulled out but he doesn't have any money. Middle of Arizona with no money and no insurance and every morning another tooth is lying on the mattress. (*takes a drink*) So what does he do?

LEE: I dunno'. I never knew about that.

AUSTIN: He begs the government. G.I. Bill or some damn thing. Some pension plan he remembers in the back of his head. And they send him out the money.

LEE: They did?

(*they keep trading the bottle between them, taking drinks*)

AUSTIN: Yeah. They send him the money but it's not enough money. Costs a lot to have all yer teeth yanked. They charge by the individual tooth, ya' know. I mean one tooth isn't equal to another tooth. Some are more expensive. Like the big ones in the back—

LEE: So what happened?

AUSTIN: So he locates a Mexican dentist in Juarez who'll do the whole thing for a song. And he takes off hitchhiking to the border.

LEE: Hitchhiking?

AUSTIN: Yeah. So how long you think it takes him to get to the border? A man his age.

LEE: I dunno.

AUSTIN: Eight days it takes him. Eight days in the rain and the sun and every day he's droppin' teeth on the blacktop and nobody'll pick him up 'cause his mouth's full a' blood.

(*pause, they drink*)

So finally he stumbles into the dentist. Dentist takes all his money and all his teeth. And there he is, in Mexico, with his gums sewed up and his pockets empty.

(*long silence,* AUSTIN *drinks*)

LEE: That's it?

AUSTIN: Then I go out to see him, see. I go out there and I take him out for a nice Chinese dinner. But he doesn't eat. All he wants to do is drink Martinis outa' plastic cups. And he takes his teeth out and lays 'em on the table 'cause he can't stand the feel of 'em. And we ask the waitress for one a' those doggie bags to take the Chop Suey home in. So he drops his teeth in the doggie bag along with the Chop Suey. And then we go out to hit all the bars up and down the highway. Says he wants to introduce me to all his buddies. And in one a' those bars, in one a' those bars up and down the highway, he left that doggie bag with his teeth laying in the Chop Suey.

LEE: You never found it?

AUSTIN: We went back but we never did find it. (*pause*) Now that's a true story. True to life.

(*they drink as lights fade to black*)

Scene 8

Very early morning, between night and day. No crickets, coyotes yapping feverishly in distance before light comes up, a small fire blazes up in the dark from alcove area, sound of LEE *smashing typewriter with a golf club, lights coming up,* LEE *seen smashing typewriter methodically then dropping pages of his script into a burning bowl set on the floor of alcove, flames leap up,* AUSTIN *has a whole bunch of stolen toasters lined up on the sink counter along with* LEE's *stolen T.V., the toasters are of a wide variety of models, mostly chrome,* AUSTIN *goes up and down the line of toasters, breathing on them and polishing them with a dish towel, both men are drunk, empty whiskey bottles and beer cans litter floor of kitchen, they share a half empty bottle on one of the chairs in the alcove,* LEE *keeps periodically taking deliberate ax-chops at the typewriter using a nine-iron as* AUSTIN *speaks, all of their mother's house plants are dead and drooping.*

AUSTIN: (*polishing toasters*) There's gonna' be a general lack of toast in the neighborhood this morning. Many, many unhappy, bewildered breakfast faces. I guess it's best not to even think of the victims. Not to even entertain it. Is that the right psychology?

LEE: (*pauses*) What?

AUSTIN: Is that the correct criminal psychology? Not to think of the victims?

LEE: What victims?

(LEE *takes another swipe at typewriter with nine-iron, adds pages to the fire*)

AUSTIN: The victims of crime. Of breaking and entering. I mean is it a prerequisite for a criminal not to have a conscience?

LEE: Ask a criminal.

(*pause,* LEE *stares at* AUSTIN)

What're you gonna' do with all those toasters? That's the dumbest thing I ever saw in my life.

AUSTIN: I've got hundreds of dollars worth of household appliances here. You may not realize that.

LEE: Yeah, and how many hundreds of dollars did you walk right past?

AUSTIN: It was toasters you challenged me to. Only toasters. I ignored every other temptation.

LEE: I never challenged you! That's no challenge. Anybody can steal a toaster.

(LEE *smashes typewriter again*)

AUSTIN: You don't have to take it out on my typewriter ya' know. It's not the machine's fault that you can't write. It's a sin to do that to a good machine.

LEE: A sin?

AUSTIN: When you consider all the writers who never even had a machine. Who would have given an eyeball for a good typewriter. Any typewriter.

(LEE *smashes typewriter again*)

AUSTIN: (*polishing toasters*) All the ones who wrote on matchbook covers. Paper bags. Toilet paper. Who had their writing destroyed by their jailers. Who persisted beyond all odds. Those writers would find it hard to understand your actions.

(LEE *comes down on typewriter with one final crushing blow of the nine-iron then collapses in one of the chairs, takes a drink from bottle, pause*)

AUSTIN: (*after pause*) Not to mention demolishing a perfectly good golf club. What about all the struggling golfers? What about Lee Trevino? What do you think he would've said when he was batting balls around with broomsticks at the age of nine. Impoverished.

(*pause*)

LEE: What time is it anyway?

AUSTIN: No idea. Time stands still when you're havin' fun.

LEE: Is it too late to call a woman? You know any women?

AUSTIN: I'm a married man.

LEE: I mean a local woman.

(AUSTIN *looks out at light through window above sink*)

AUSTIN: It's either too late or too early. You're the nature enthusiast. Can't you tell the time by the light in the sky? Orient yourself around the North Star or something?

LEE: I can't tell anything.

AUSTIN: Maybe you need a little breakfast. Some toast! How 'bout some toast?

(AUSTIN *goes to cupboard, pulls out loaf of bread and starts dropping slices into every toaster,* LEE *stays sitting, drinks, watches* AUSTIN)

LEE: I don't need toast. I need a woman.

AUSTIN: A woman isn't the answer. Never was.

LEE: I'm not talkin' about permanent. I'm talkin' about temporary.

AUSTIN: (*putting toast in toasters*) We'll just test the merits of these little demons. See which brands have a tendency to burn. See which one can produce a perfectly golden piece of fluffy toast.

LEE: How much gas you got in yer car?

AUSTIN: I haven't driven my car for days now. So I haven't had an opportunity to look at the gas gauge.

LEE: Take a guess. You think there's enough to get me to Bakersfield?

AUSTIN: Bakersfield? What's in Bakersfield?

LEE: Just never mind what's in Bakersfield! You think there's enough goddamn gas in the car!

AUSTIN: Sure.

LEE: Sure. You could care less, right. Let me run outa' gas on the Grapevine. You could give a shit.

AUSTIN: I'd say there was enough gas to get you just about anywhere, Lee. With your determination and guts.

LEE: What the hell time is it anyway?

(LEE *pulls out his wallet, starts going through dozens of small pieces of paper with phone numbers written on them, drops some on the floor, drops others in the fire*)

AUSTIN: Very early. This is the time of morning when the coyotes kill people's cocker spaniels. Did you hear them? That's what they were doing out there. Luring innocent pets away from their homes.

LEE: (*searching through his papers*) What's the area code for Bakersfield? You know?

AUSTIN: You could always call the operator.

LEE: I can't stand that voice they give ya'.

AUSTIN: What voice?

LEE: That voice that warns you that if you'd only tried harder to find the number in the phone book you wouldn't have to be calling the operator to begin with.

(LEE *gets up, holding a slip of paper from his wallet, stumbles toward phone on wall, yanks receiver, starts dialing*)

AUSTIN: Well I don't understand why you'd want to talk to anybody else anyway. I mean you can talk to me. I'm your brother.

LEE: (*dialing*) I wanna' talk to a woman. I haven't heard a woman's voice in a long time.

AUSTIN: Not since the Botanist?

LEE: What?

AUSTIN: Nothing. (*starts singing as he tends toast*)

> "Red sails in the sunset.
> Way out on the blue
> Please carry my loved one
> Home safely to me"

LEE: Hey, knock it off will ya'! This is long distance here.

AUSTIN: Bakersfield?

LEE: Yeah, Bakersfield. It's Kern County.

AUSTIN: Well, what County are *we* in?

LEE: You better get yourself a 7-Up, boy.

AUSTIN: One County's as good as another.

(AUSTIN *hums "Red Sails" softly as* LEE *talks on phone*)

LEE: (*to phone*) Yeah, operator look— first off I wanna' know the area code for Bakersfield. Right. Bakersfield! Okay. Good. Now I wanna' know if you can help me track somebody down. (*pause*) No, no I mean a phone number. Just a phone number. Okay. (*holds a piece of paper up and reads it*) Okay, the name is Melly Ferguson. Melly. (*pause*) I dunno'. Melly. Maybe. Yeah. Maybe Melanie. Yeah. Melanie Ferguson.

Okay. (*pause*) What? I can't hear ya' so good. Sounds like yer under the ocean. (*pause*) You got ten Melanie Fergusons? How could that be? Ten Melanie Fergusons in Bakersfield? Well gimme all of 'em then. (*pause*) What d'ya' mean? Gimmie all ten Melanie Fergusons! That's right. Just a second. (*to* AUSTIN) Gimme a pen.

AUSTIN: I don't have a pen.

LEE: Gimme a pencil then!

AUSTIN: I don't have a pencil.

LEE: (*to phone*) Just a second, operator. (*to* AUSTIN) Yer a writer and ya' don't have a pen or a pencil!

AUSTIN: I'm not a writer. You're a writer.

LEE: I'm on the phone here! Get me a pen or a pencil.

AUSTIN: I gotta' watch the toast.

LEE: (*to phone*) Hang on a second, operator.

(LEE *lets the phone drop then starts pulling all the drawers in the kitchen out on the floor and dumping the contents, searching for a pencil,* AUSTIN *watches him casually*)

LEE: (*crashing through drawers, throwing contents around kitchen*) This is the last time I try to live with people, boy! I can't believe it. Here I am! Here I am again in a desperate situation! This would never happen out on the desert. I would never be in this kinda' situation out on the desert. Isn't there a pen or a pencil in this house! Who lives in this house anyway!

AUSTIN: Our mother.

LEE: How come she don't have a pen or a pencil! She's a social person isn't she? Doesn't she have to make shopping lists? She's gotta' have a pencil. (*finds a pencil*) Aaha! (*he rushes back to phone, picks up receiver*) All right operator. Operator? Hey! Operator! Goddamnit!

(LEE *rips the phone off the wall and throws it down, goes back to chair and falls into it, drinks, long pause*)

AUSTIN: She hung up?

LEE: Yeah, she hung up. I knew she was gonna' hang up. I could hear it in her voice.

(LEE *starts going through his slips of paper again*)

AUSTIN: Well, you're probably better off staying here with me anyway. I'll take care of you.

LEE: I don't need takin' care of! Not by you anyway.

AUSTIN: Toast is almost ready.

(AUSTIN *starts buttering all the toast as it pops up*)

LEE: I don't want any toast!

(*long pause*)

AUSTIN: You gotta' eat something. Can't just drink. How long have we been drinking, anyway?

LEE: (*looking through slips of paper*) Maybe it was Fresno. What's the area code for Fresno? How could I have lost that number! She was beautiful.

(*pause*)

AUSTIN: Why don't you just forget about that, Lee. Forget about the woman.

LEE: She had green eyes. You know what green eyes do to me?

AUSTIN: I know but you're not gonna' get it on with her now anyway. It's dawn already. She's in Bakersfield for Christ's sake.

(*long pause,* LEE *considers the situation*)

LEE: Yeah. (*looks at windows*) It's dawn?

AUSTIN: Let's just have some toast and—

LEE: What is this bullshit with the toast anyway! You make it sound like salvation or something. I don't want any goddamn toast! How many times I gotta' tell ya'! (LEE *gets up, crosses upstage to windows in alcove, looks out,* AUSTIN *butters toast*)

AUSTIN: Well it is like salvation sort of. I mean the smell. I love the smell of toast. And the sun's coming up. It makes me feel like anything's possible. Ya' know?

LEE: (*back to* AUSTIN, *facing windows upstage*) So go to church why don't ya'.

AUSTIN: Like a beginning. I love beginnings.

LEE: Oh yeah. I've always been kinda' partial to endings myself.

AUSTIN: What if I come with you, Lee?

LEE: (*pause as* LEE *turns toward* AUSTIN) What?

AUSTIN: What if I come with you out to the desert?

LEE: Are you kiddin'?

AUSTIN: No. I'd just like to see what it's like.

LEE: You wouldn't last a day out there pal.

AUSTIN: That's what you said about the toasters. You said I couldn't steal a toaster either.

LEE: A toaster's got nothin' to do with the desert.

AUSTIN: I could make it, Lee. I'm not that helpless. I can cook.

LEE: Cook?

AUSTIN: I can.

LEE: So what! You can cook. Toast.

AUSTIN: I can make fires. I know how to get fresh water from condensation.

(AUSTIN *stacks buttered toast up in a tall stack on plate*)

(LEE *slams table*)

LEE: It's not somethin' you learn out of a Boy Scout handbook!

AUSTIN: Well how do you learn it then! How're you supposed to learn it!

(*pause*)

LEE: Ya' just learn it, that's all. Ya' learn it 'cause ya' have to learn it. You don't *have* to learn it.

AUSTIN: You could teach me.

LEE: (*stands*) What're you, crazy or somethin'? You went to college. Here, you are down here, rollin' in bucks. Floatin' up and down in elevators. And you wanna' learn how to live on the desert!

AUSTIN: I do, Lee. I really do. There's nothin' down here for me. There never was. When we were kids here it was different. There was a life here then. But now—I keep comin' down here thinkin' it's the fifties or somethin'. I keep finding myself getting off the freeway at familiar landmarks that turn out to be unfamiliar. On the way to appointments. Wandering down streets I thought I recognized that turn out to be replicas of streets I remember. Streets I misremember. Streets I can't tell if I lived on or saw in a postcard. Fields that don't even exist anymore.

LEE: There's no point cryin' about that now.

AUSTIN: There's nothin' real down here, Lee! Least of all me!

LEE: Well I can't save you from that!

AUSTIN: You can let me come with you.

LEE: No dice, pal.

AUSTIN: You could let me come with you, Lee!

LEE: Hey, do you actually think I chose to live out in the middle a' nowhere? Do ya'? Ya' think it's some kinda' philosophical decision I took or somethin'? I'm livin' out there 'cause I can't make it here! And yer bitchin' to me about all yer success!

AUSTIN: I'd cash it all in in a second. That's the truth.

LEE: (*pause, shakes his head*) I can't believe this.

AUSTIN: Let me go with you.

LEE: Stop sayin' that will ya'! Yer worse than a dog.

(AUSTIN *offers out the plate of neatly stacked toast to* LEE)

AUSTIN: You want some toast?

(LEE *suddenly explodes and knocks the plate out of* AUSTIN's *hand, toast goes flying, long frozen moment where it appears* LEE *might go all the way this time when* AUSTIN *breaks it by slowly lowering himself to his knees and begins gathering the scattered toast from the floor and stacking it back on the plate,* LEE *begins to circle* AUSTIN *in a slow, predatory way, crushing pieces of toast in his wake, no words for a while,* AUSTIN *keeps gathering toast, even the crushed pieces)*

LEE: Tell ya' what I'll do, little brother. I might just consider makin' you a deal. Little trade. (AUSTIN *continues gathering toast as* LEE *circles him through this)* You write me up this screenplay thing just like I tell ya'. I mean you can use all yer usual tricks and stuff. Yer fancy language. Yer artistic hocus pocus. But ya' gotta' write everything like I say. Every move. Every time they run outa' gas, they run outa' gas. Every time they wanna' jump on a horse, they do just that. If they wanna' stay in Texas, by God they'll stay in Texas! (*Keeps circling*) And you finish the whole thing up for me. Top to bottom. And you put my name on it. And

I own all the rights. And every dime goes in my pocket. You do that and I'll sure enough take ya' with me to the desert. (LEE *stops, pause, looks down at* AUSTIN) How's that sound?

(*pause as* AUSTIN *stands slowly holding plate of demolished toast, their faces are very close, pause)*

AUSTIN: It's a deal.

(LEE *stares straight into* AUSTIN's *eyes, then he slowly takes a piece of toast off the plate, raises it to his mouth and takes a huge crushing bite never taking his eyes off* AUSTIN's, *as* LEE *crunches into the toast the lights black out)*

Scene 9

Mid-day. No sound, blazing heat, the stage is ravaged; bottles, toasters, smashed typewriter, ripped out telephone, etc. All the debris from previous scene is now starkly visible in intense yellow light, the effect should be like a desert junkyard at high noon, the coolness of the preceding scenes is totally obliterated. AUSTIN *is seated at table in alcove, shirt open, pouring with sweat, hunched over a writing notebook, scribbling notes desperately with a ballpoint pen.* LEE *with no shirt, beer in hand, sweat pouring down his chest, is walking a slow circle around the table, picking his way through the objects, sometimes kicking them aside.*

LEE: (*as he walks*) All right, read it back to me. Read it back to me!

AUSTIN: (*scribbling at top speed*) Just a second.

LEE: Come on, come on! Just read what ya' got.

AUSTIN: I can't keep up! It's not the same as if I had a typewriter.

LEE: Just read what we got so far. Forget about the rest.

AUSTIN: All right. Let's see—okay— (*wipes sweat from his face, reads as* LEE *circles*) Luke says uh—

LEE: Luke?

AUSTIN: Yeah.

LEE: His name's Luke? All right, all right—we can change the names later. What's he say? Come on, come on.

AUSTIN: He says uh—(*reading*) "I told ya' you were a fool to follow me in here. I know this prairie like the back a' my hand."

LEE: No, no, no! That's not what I said. I never said that.

AUSTIN: That's what I wrote.

LEE: It's not what I said. I never said "like the back a' my hand." That's stupid. That's one a' those—whadya' call it? Whadya' call that?

AUSTIN: What?

LEE: Whadya' call it when somethin's been said a thousand times before. Whadya' call that?

AUSTIN: Um—a cliché?

LEE: Yeah. That's right. Cliché. That's what that is. A cliché. "The back a' my hand." That's stupid.

AUSTIN: That's what you said.

LEE: I never said that! And even if I did, that's where yer supposed to come in. That's where yer supposed to change it to somethin' better.

AUSTIN: Well how am I supposed to do that and write down what you say at the same time?

LEE: Ya' just do, that's all! You hear a stupid line you change it. That's yer job.

AUSTIN: All right. (*makes more notes*)

LEE: What're you changin' it to?

AUSTIN: I'm not changing it. I'm just trying to catch up.

LEE: Well change it! We gotta' change that, we can't leave that in there like that. ". . . the back a' my hand." That's dumb.

AUSTIN: (*stops writing, sits back*) All right.

LEE: (*pacing*) So what'll we change it to?

AUSTIN: Um—How 'bout—"I'm on intimate terms with this prairie."

LEE: (*to himself considering line as he walks*) "I'm on intimate terms with this prairie." Intimate terms, intimate terms. Intimate—that means like uh—sexual right?

AUSTIN: Well—yeah—or—

LEE: He's on sexual terms with the prairie? How dya' figure that?

AUSTIN: Well it doesn't necessarily have to mean sexual.

LEE: What's it mean then?

AUSTIN: It means uh—close—personal—

LEE: All right. How's it sound? Put it into the uh—the line there. Read it back. Let's see how it sounds. (*to himself*) "Intimate terms."

AUSTIN: (*scribbles in notebook*) Okay. It'd go something like this: (*reads*) "I told ya' you were a fool to follow me in here. I'm on intimate terms with this prairie."

LEE: That's good. I like that. That's real good.

AUSTIN: You do?

LEE: Yeah. Don't you?

AUSTIN: Sure.

LEE: Sounds original now. "Intimate terms." That's good. Okay. Now we're cookin! That has a real ring to it.

(AUSTIN *makes more notes,* LEE *walks around, pours beer on his arms and rubs it over his chest feeling good about the new progress, as he does this* MOM *enters unobtrusively down left with her luggage, she stops and stares at the scene still holding luggage as the two men continue, unaware of her presence,* AUSTIN *absorbed in his writing,* LEE *cooling himself off with beer*)

LEE: (*continues*) "He's on intimate terms with this prairie." Sounds real mysterious and kinda' threatening at the same time.

AUSTIN: (*writing rapidly*) Good.

LEE: Now—(LEE *turns and suddenly sees* MOM, *he stares at her for a while, she stares back,* AUSTIN *keeps writing feverishly, not noticing,* LEE *walks slowly over to* MOM *and takes a closer look, long pause*)

LEE: Mom?

(AUSTIN *looks up suddenly from his writing, sees* MOM, *stands quickly, long pause,* MOM *surveys the damage*)

AUSTIN: Mom. What're you doing back?

MOM: I'm back.

LEE: Here, lemme take those for ya.

(LEE *sets beer on counter then takes both her bags but doesn't know where to set them down in the sea of junk so he just keeps holding them*)

AUSTIN: I wasn't expecting you back so soon. I thought uh—How was Alaska?

MOM: Fine.

LEE: See any igloos?

MOM: No. Just glaciers.

AUSTIN: Cold huh?

MOM: What?

AUSTIN: It must've been cold up there?

MOM: Not really.

LEE: Musta' been colder than this here. I mean we're havin' a real scorcher here.

MOM: Oh? (*she looks at damage*)

LEE: Yeah. Must be in the hundreds.

AUSTIN: You wanna' take your coat off, Mom?

MOM: No. (*pause, she surveys space*) What happened in here?

AUSTIN: Oh um—Me and Lee were just sort of celebrating and uh—

MOM: Celebrating?

AUSTIN: Yeah. Uh—Lee sold a screenplay. A story, I mean.

MOM: Lee did?

AUSTIN: Yeah.

MOM: Not you?

AUSTIN: No. Him.

MOM: (*to* LEE) You sold a screen-play?

LEE: Yeah. That's right. We're just sorta' finishing it up right now. That's what we're doing here.

AUSTIN: Me and Lee are going out to the desert to live.

MOM: You and Lee?

AUSTIN: Yeah. I'm taking off with Lee.

MOM: (*she looks back and forth at each of them, pause*) You gonna go live with your father?

AUSTIN: No. We're going to a different desert Mom.

MOM: I see. Well, you'll probably wind up on the same desert sooner or later. What're all these toasters doing here?

AUSTIN: Well—we had kind of a contest.

MOM: Contest?

LEE: Yeah.

AUSTIN: Lee won.

MOM: Did you win a lot of money, Lee?

LEE: Well not yet. It's comin' in any day now.

MOM: (*to* LEE) What happened to your shirt?

LEE: Oh. I was sweatin' like a pig and I took it off.

(AUSTIN *grabs* LEE's *shirt off the table and tosses it to him,* LEE *sets down suitcases and puts his shirt on*)

MOM: Well it's one hell of a mess in here isn't it?

AUSTIN: Yeah, I'll clean it up for you. Mom. I just didn't know you were coming back so soon.

MOM: I didn't either.

AUSTIN: What happened?

MOM: Nothing. I just started missing all my plants.

(*she notices dead plants*)

AUSTIN: Oh.

MOM: Oh, they're all dead aren't they. (*she crosses toward them, examines them closely*) You didn't get a chance to water I guess.

AUSTIN: I was doing it and then Lee came and—

LEE: Yeah I just distracted him a whole lot here, Mom. It's not his fault.

(*pause, as* MOM *stares at plants*)

MOM: Oh well, one less thing to take care of I guess. (*turns toward brothers*) Oh, that reminds me— You boys will probably never guess who's in town. Try and guess.

(*long pause, brothers stare at her*)

AUSTIN: Whadya' mean, Mom?

MOM: Take a guess. Somebody very important has come to town. I read it, coming down on the Greyhound.

LEE: Somebody very important?

MOM: See if you can guess. You'll never guess.

AUSTIN: Mom—we're trying to uh— (*points to writing pad*)

MOM: Picasso. (*pause*) Picasso's in town. Isn't that incredible? Right now.

(*pause*)

AUSTIN: Picasso's dead, Mom.

MOM: No, he's not dead. He's visiting the museum. I read it on the bus. We have to go down there and see him.

AUSTIN: Mom—

MOM: This is the chance of a lifetime. Can you imagine? We could all go down and meet him. All three of us.

LEE: Uh—I don't think I'm really up fer meetin' anybody right now. I'm uh—What's his name?

MOM: Picasso! Picasso! You've never heard of Picasso? Austin, you've heard of Picasso.

AUSTIN: Mom, we're not going to have time.

MOM: It won't take long. We'll just hop in the car and go down there. An opportunity like this doesn't come along every day.

AUSTIN: We're gonna' be leavin' here, Mom!

(*pause*)

MOM: Oh.

LEE: Yeah.

(*pause*)

MOM: You're both leaving?

LEE: (*looks at* AUSTIN) Well we were thinkin' about that before but now I—

AUSTIN: No, we are! We're both leaving. We've got it all planned.

MOM: (*to* AUSTIN) Well you can't leave. You have a family.

AUSTIN: I'm leaving. I'm getting out of here.

LEE: (*to* MOM) I don't really think Austin's cut out for the desert do you?

MOM: No. He's not.

AUSTIN: I'm going with you, Lee!

MOM: He's too thin.

LEE: Yeah, he'd just burn up out there.

AUSTIN: (*to* LEE) We just gotta' finish this screenplay and then we're gonna take off. That's the plan. That's what you said. Come on, let's get back to work, Lee.

LEE: I can't work under these conditions here. It's too hot.

AUSTIN: Then we'll do it on the desert.

LEE: Don't be tellin' me what we're gonna do!

MOM: Don't shout in the house.

LEE: We're just gonna' have to postpone the whole deal.

AUSTIN: I can't postpone it! It's gone past postponing! I'm doing everything you said. I'm writing down exactly what you tell me.

LEE: Yeah, but you were right all along see. It is a dumb story. "Two lamebrains chasin' each other across Texas." That's what you said, right?

AUSTIN: I never said that.

(LEE *sneers in* AUSTIN's *face then turns to* MOM)

LEE: I'm gonna' just borrow some a' your antiques, Mom. You don't mind do ya'? Just a few plates and things. Silverware.

(LEE *starts going through all the cupboards in kitchen pulling out* plates and stacking them on counter as MOM and AUSTIN watch)

MOM: You don't have any utensils on the desert?

LEE: Nah, I'm fresh out.

AUSTIN: (to LEE) What're you doing?

MOM: Well some of those are very old. Bone China.

LEE: I'm tired of eatin' outa' my bare hands, ya' know. It's not civilized.

AUSTIN: (to LEE) What're you doing? We made a deal!

MOM: Couldn't you borrow the plastic ones instead? I have plenty of plastic ones.

LEE: (as he stacks plates) It's not the same. Plastic's not the same at all. What I need is somethin' authentic. Somethin' to keep me in touch. It's easy to get outa' touch out there. Don't worry I'll get em' back to ya'.

(AUSTIN rushes up to LEE, grabs him by shoulders)

AUSTIN: You can't just drop the whole thing, Lee!

(LEE turns, pushes AUSTIN in the chest knocking him backwards into the alcove, MOM watches numbly, LEE returns to collecting the plates, silverware, etc.)

MOM: You boys shouldn't fight in the house. Go outside and fight.

LEE: I'm not fightin'. I'm leavin'.

MOM: There's been enough damage done already.

LEE: (his back to AUSTIN and MOM, stacking dishes on counter) I'm clearin' outa' here once and for all. All this town does is drive a man insane. Look what it's done to Austin there. I'm not lettin' that happen to me. Sell myself down the river. No sir. I'd rather be a hundred miles from nowhere than let that happen to me.

(during this AUSTIN has picked up the ripped-out phone from the floor and wrapped the cord tightly around both his hands, he lunges at LEE whose back is still to him, wraps the cord around LEE's neck, plants a foot in LEE's back and pulls back on the cord, tightening it, LEE chokes desperately, can't speak and can't reach AUSTIN with his arms, AUSTIN keeps applying pressure on LEE's back with his foot, bending him into the sink, MOM watches)

AUSTIN: (tightening cord) You're not goin' anywhere! You're not takin' anything with you. You're not takin' my car! You're not takin' the dishes! You're not takin' anything! You're stayin' right here!

MOM: You'll have to stop fighting in the house. There's plenty of room outside to fight. You've got the whole outdoors to fight in.

(LEE tries to tear himself away, he crashes across the stage like an enraged bull dragging AUSTIN with him, he snorts and bellows but AUSTIN hangs on and manages to keep clear of LEE's attempts to grab him, they crash into the table, to

the floor, LEE *is face down thrash-*
ing wildly and choking, AUSTIN
pulls cord tighter, stands with one
foot planted on LEE's *back and the*
cord stretched taut)

AUSTIN: *(holding cord)* Gimme back
my keys, Lee! Take the keys out!
Take 'em out!

(LEE *desperately tries to dig in his*
pockets, searching for the car keys,
MOM *moves closer)*

MOM: *(calmly to* AUSTIN) You're not
killing him are you?
AUSTIN: I don't know. I don't know
if I'm killing him. I'm stopping
him. That's all. I'm just stopping
him.

(LEE *thrashes but* AUSTIN *is re-*
lentless)

MOM: You oughta' let him breathe
a little bit.
AUSTIN: Throw the keys out, Lee!

(LEE *finally gets keys out and*
throws them on floor but out of
AUSTIN's *reach,* AUSTIN *keeps*
pressure on cord, pulling LEE's
neck back, LEE *gets one hand to the*
cord but can't relieve the pressure)

Reach me those keys would ya',
Mom.
MOM: *(not moving)* Why are you do-
ing this to him?
AUSTIN: Reach me the keys!
MOM: Not until you stop choking
him.
AUSTIN: I can't stop choking him!
He'll kill me if I stop choking
him!

MOM: He won't kill you. He's your
brother.
AUSTIN: Just get me the keys would
ya'!

(pause. MOM *picks keys up off*
floor, hands them to AUSTIN)

AUSTIN: *(to* MOM) Thanks.
MOM: Will you let him go now?
AUSTIN: I don't know. He's not
gonna' let me get outa' here.
MOM: Well you can't kill him.
AUSTIN: I can kill him! I can easily
kill him. Right now. Right here.
All I gotta' do is just tighten up.
See? *(he tightens cord,* LEE *thrashes*
wildly, AUSTIN *releases pressure a*
little, maintaining control) Ya' see
that?
MOM: That's a savage thing to do.
AUSTIN: Yeah well don't tell me I
can't kill him because I can. I can
just twist. I can just keep twisting.
(AUSTIN *twists the cord tighter,* LEE
weakens, his breathing changes to a
short rasp)
MOM: Austin!

(AUSTIN *relieves pressure,* LEE
breathes easier but AUSTIN *keeps*
him under control)

AUSTIN: *(eyes on* LEE, *holding cord)*
I'm goin' to the desert. There's
nothing stopping me. I'm going
by myself to the desert.

(MOM *moving toward her lug-*
gage)

MOM: Well, I'm going to go check
into a motel. I can't stand this
anymore.
AUSTIN: Don't go yet!

(MOM *pauses*)

MOM: I can't stay here. This is worse than being homeless.

AUSTIN: I'll get everything fixed up for you, Mom. I promise. Just stay for a while.

MOM: (*picking up luggage*) You're going to the desert.

AUSTIN: Just wait!

(LEE *thrashes*, AUSTIN *subdues him*, MOM *watches holding luggage, pause*)

MOM: It was the worst feeling being up there. In Alaska. Staring out a window. I never felt so desperate before. That's why when I saw that article on Picasso I thought—

AUSTIN: Stay here, Mom. This is where you live.

(*she looks around the stage*)

MOM: I don't recognize it at all.

(*she exits with luggage*, AUSTIN *makes a move toward her but* LEE *starts to struggle and* AUSTIN *subdues him again with cord, pause*)

AUSTIN: (*holding cord*) Lee? I'll make ya' a deal. You let me get outa' here. Just let me get to my car. All right, Lee? Gimme a little headstart and I'll turn you loose. Just gimme a little headstart. All right?

(LEE *makes no response*, AUSTIN *slowly releases tension cord, still nothing from* LEE)

AUSTIN: Lee?

(LEE *is motionless*, AUSTIN *very slowly begins to stand, still keeping a tenuous hold on the cord and his eyes riveted to* LEE *for any sign of movement*, AUSTIN *slowly drops the cord and stands, he stares down at* LEE *who appears to be dead*)

AUSTIN: (*whispers*) Lee?

(*pause*, AUSTIN *considers, looks toward exit, back to* LEE, *then makes a small movement as if to leave. Instantly* LEE *is on his feet and moves toward exit, blocking* AUSTIN's *escape. They square off to each other, keeping a distance between them. Pause, a single coyote heard in distance, lights fade softly into moonlight, the figures of the brothers now appear to be caught in a vast desert-like landscape, they are very still but watchful for the next move, lights go slowly to black as the after-image of the brothers pulses in the dark, coyote fades*)

RUDOLFO ANAYA

To anyone with the notion that western American writing has boundaries, or has been defined, the work of Rudolfo Anaya (b. 1937) would be unsettling. His reach to the south, his magical-realist humor, and his sense of a worldwide fellahin connection all tend to blow away categories. He is a writer of a singularly unidentified consciousness, to whom any subject, any turn of events, would be, one thinks, genially welcomed. It is a mistake to think of him as a Chicano author definitively, though as much as anyone he has brought Mexican-American writing respect and a place in the new American canon. He is, again, a writer, period. In *A Chicano in China* (1986), he notices that the Chinese peasants remind him of his forebears on the hard-to-farm fields of eastern New Mexico. There is a look about them, and suddenly there comes to Anaya a perception of humanity all over the globe, working the soil, eating, having family life. This world gave birth to Antonio Marez of New Mexico, the young protagonist of Anaya's first novel, *Bless Me, Ultima* (1972), and presumably to Anaya as a writer. It is the "folk" world, traditional in its values but surprisingly free in the mind, willing to try anything on for size and see if it works.

"B. Traven Is Alive and Well in Cuernavaca," from *The Anaya Reader* (1984)

I didn't go to Mexico to find B. Traven. Why should I? I have enough to do writing my own fiction, so I go to Mexico to write, not to search out writers. B. Traven? you ask. Don't you remember *The Treasure of the Sierra Madre*? A real classic. They made a movie from the novel. I remember seeing it when I was kid. It was set in Mexico, and it had all the elements of a real adventure story. B. Traven was an adventurous man, traveled all over the world, then disappeared into Mexico and cut himself off from society. He gave no interviews and allowed few photographs. While he lived he remained unapproachable, anonymous to his public, a writer shrouded in mystery.

He's dead now, or they say he's dead. I think he's alive and well. At any rate, he has become something of an institution in Mexico, a man honored for his work. The cantineros and taxi drivers in Mexico City know about him as well as the cantineros of Spain knew Hemingway, or they claim to. I never mention I'm a writer when I'm in a cantina, because inevitably some aficionado will ask, "Do you know the work of B. Traven?" And from some dusty niche will appear a yellowed, thumb-worn novel by Traven. Thus if the cantinero knows his business, and they all do in Mexico, he is apt to say "Did you know that B. Traven used to drink here?" If you show the slightest interest, he will follow with, "Sure, he used to sit right over here. In this corner. . . ." And if you don't leave right then you will wind up hearing many stories about the mysterious B. Traven while buying many drinks for the local patrons.

Everybody reads his novels, on the buses, on street corners; if you look closely you'll spot one of his titles. One turned up for me, and that's how this story started. I was sitting in the train station in Juárez, waiting for the train to Cuernavaca, which would be an exciting title for this story except that there is no train to Cuernavaca. I was drinking beer to kill time, the erotic and sensitive Mexican time which is so different from the clean-packaged, well-kept time of the Americanos. Time in Mexico can be cruel and punishing, but it is never indifferent. It permeates everything, it changes reality. Einstein would have loved Mexico because there time and space are one. I stare more often into empty space when I'm in Mexico. The past seems to infuse the present, and in the brown, wrinkled faces of the old people one sees the presence of the past. In Mexico I like to walk the narrow streets of the cities and the smaller pueblos, wandering aimlessly, feeling the sunlight which is so distinctively Mexican, listening to the voices which call in the streets, peering into the dark eyes which are so secretive and proud. The Mexican people guard a secret. But in the end, one is never really lost in Mexico. All streets lead to a good cantina. All good stories start in a cantina.

At the train station, after I let the kids who hustle the tourists know that I didn't want chewing gum or cigarettes, and I didn't want my shoes shined, and I didn't want a woman at the moment, I was left alone to drink my beer. Luke-cold Dos Equis. I don't remember how long I had been there or how many Dos Equis I had finished when I glanced at the seat next to me and saw a book which turned out to be a B. Traven novel, old and used and obviously much read, but a novel nevertheless. What's so strange about finding a B. Traven novel in that dingy little corner of a bar in the Juárez train station? Nothing, unless you know that in Mexico one never finds anything. It is a country that doesn't waste anything, everything is recycled. Chevrolets run with patched up Ford engines and Chrysler transmissions, buses are kept together, and kept running, with baling wire and home-made parts, yesterday's Traven novel is the pulp on which tomorrow's Fuentes story will appear. Time recycles in Mexico. Time returns to the past, and the Christian finds himself dreaming of ancient Aztec rituals. He who does not believe that Quetzalcoatl will return to save Mexico has little faith.

So the novel was the first clue. Later there was Justino. "Who is Justino?" you want to know. Justino was the jardinero who cared for the garden of my friend, the friend who had invited me to stay at his home in Cuernavaca while I continued to write. The day after I arrived I was sitting in the sun, letting the fatigue of the long journey ooze away, thinking nothing, when Justino appeared on the scene. He had finished cleaning the swimming pool and was taking his morning break, so he sat in the shade of the orange tree and introduced himself. Right away I could tell that he would rather be a movie actor or an adventurer, a real free spirit. But things didn't work out for him. He got married, children appeared, he took a couple of mistresses, more children appeared, so he had to work to support his family. "A man is like a rooster," he said after we talked awhile, "the more chickens he has the happier he is." Then he asked me what I was going to do about a woman while I was there, and I told him I hadn't thought that far ahead, that I would be happy if I could just get a damned story going. This puzzled Justino, and I think for a few days it worried him. So on Saturday night he took me out for a few drinks and we wound up in some of the bordellos of Cuernavaca in the company of some of the most beautiful women in the world. Justino knew them all. They loved him, and he loved them.

I learned something more of the nature of this jardinero a few nights later when the heat and an irritating mosquito wouldn't let me sleep. I heard music from a radio, so I put on my pants and walked out into the Cuernavacan night, an oppressive, warm night heavy with the sweet perfume of the dama de la noche bushes which lined the wall of my friend's villa. From time to time I heard a dog cry in the distance, and I remembered that in Mexico many people die of rabies. Perhaps that is why the walls of the wealthy are always so high and the locks always secure. Or maybe it was because of the occasional gunshots that explode in the night. The news media tell us that Mexico is the most stable country in Latin America and, with the recent oil finds, the bankers and the oil men want to keep it that way. I sense, and many know, that in the dark the revolution does not sleep. It is a spirit kept at bay by the high fences and the locked gates, yet it prowls the heart of every man. "Oil will create a new revolution," Justino had told me, "but it's going to be for our people. Mexicans are tired of building gas stations for the Gringos from Gringolandia." I understood what he meant: there is much hunger in the country.

I lit a cigarette and walked toward my friend's car, which was parked in the driveway near the swimming pool. I approached quietly and peered in. On the back seat with his legs propped on the front seat-back and smoking a cigar sat Justino. Two big, luscious women sat on either side of him running their fingers through his hair and whispering in his ears. The doors were open to allow a breeze. He looked content. Sitting there he was that famous artist on his way to an afternoon reception in Mexico City, or he was a movie star on his way to the premiere of his most recent movie. Or perhaps it was Sunday and he was taking a Sunday drive in the country, towards Tepoztlán. And why shouldn't his two friends accompany him? I had to smile. Unnoticed I backed away and returned to my room. So there was quite a bit more than met the eye to this short, dark Indian from Ocosingo.

In the morning I asked my friend, "What do you know about Justino?"

"Justino? You mean Vitorino."

"Is that his real name?"

"Sometimes he calls himself Trinidad."

"Maybe his name is Justino Victorino Trinidad," I suggested.

"I don't know, don't care," my friend answered. "He told me he used to be a guide in the jungle. Who knows? The Mexican Indian has an incredible imagination. Really gifted people. He's a good jardinero, and that's what matters to me. It's difficult to get good jardineros, so I don't ask questions."

"Is he reliable?" I wondered aloud.

"As reliable as a ripe mango," my friend nodded.

I wondered how much he knew, so I pushed a little further. "And the radio at night?"

"Oh, that. I hope it doesn't bother you. Robberies and break-ins are increasing here in the colonia. Something we never used to have. Vitorino said that if he keeps the radio on low the sound keeps thieves away. A very good idea, don't you think?"

I nodded. A very good idea.

"And I sleep very soundly," my friend concluded, "so I never hear it."

The following night when I awakened and heard the soft sound of music from the radio and heard the splashing of water, I had only to look from my window to see Justino and his friends in the pool, swimming nude in the moonlight. They were joking and laughing softly as they splashed each other, being quiet so as not to awaken my friend, the patrón who slept so soundly. The women were beautiful. Brown skinned and glistening with water in the moonlight they reminded me of ancient Aztec maidens, swimming around Chac, their god of rain. They teased Justino, and he smiled as he floated on a rubber mattress in the middle of the pool, smoking his cigar, happy because they were happy. When he smiled the gold fleck of a filling glinted in the moonlight.

"¡Qué cabrón!" I laughed and closed my window.

Justino said a Mexican never lies. I believed him. If a Mexican says he will meet you at a certain time and place, he means he will meet you sometime at some place. Americans who retire in Mexico often complain of maids who swear they will come to work on a designated day, then don't show up. They did not lie, they knew they couldn't be at work, but they knew to tell the señora otherwise would make her sad or displease her, so they agree on a date so everyone would remain happy. What a beautiful aspect of character. It's a real virtue which Norteamericanos interpret as a fault in their character, because we are used to asserting ourselves on time and people. We feel secure and comfortable only when everything is neatly packaged in its proper time and place. We don't like the disorder of a free-flowing life.

Some day, I thought to myself, Justino will give a grand party in the sala of his patrón's home. His three wives, or his wife and two mistresses, and his dozens of children will be there. So will the women from the bordellos. He will preside over the feast, smoke his cigars, request his favorite beer-drinking songs from the mariachis, smile, tell stories and make sure everyone has a grand time. He will be dressed in a tuxedo, borrowed from the patrón's closet of course, and he will act gallant and show everyone that a man who has just come into sudden wealth should share it with his friends. And in the morning he will report to the patrón that something has to be done about the poor mice that are coming in out of the streets and eating everything in the house.

"I'll buy some poison," the patrón will suggest.

"No, no," Justino will shake his head, "a little music from the radio and a candle burning in the sala will do."

And he will be right.

I liked Justino. He was a rogue with class. We talked about the weather, the lateness of the rainy season, women, the role of oil in Mexican politics. Like other workers, he believed nothing was going to filter down to the campesinos. "We could all be real Mexican greasers with all that oil," he said, "but the politicians will keep it all."

"What about the United States?" I asked.

"Oh, I have traveled in the estados unidos to the north. It's a country that's going to the dogs in a worse way than Mexico. The thing I liked the most was your cornflakes."

"Cornflakes?"

"Sí. You can make really good cornflakes."

"And women?"

"Ah, you better keep your eyes open, my friend. Those gringas are going to change the world just like the Suecas changed Spain."

"For better or for worse?"

"Spain used to be a nice country," he winked.

We talked, we argued, we drifted from subject to subject. I learned from him. I had been there a week when he told the story which eventually led me to B. Traven. One day I was sitting under the orange tree reading the B. Traven novel I had found in the Juarez train station, keeping one eye on the ripe oranges which fell from time to time, my mind wandering as it worked to focus on a story so I could begin to write. After all, that's why I had come to Cuernavaca, to get some writing done, but nothing was coming, nothing. Justino wandered by and asked what I was reading and I replied it was an adventure story, a story of a man's search for the illusive pot of gold at the end of a make-believe rainbow. He nodded, thought awhile and gazed toward Popo, Popocatepetl, the towering volcano which lay to the south, shrouded in mist, waiting for the rains as we waited for the rains, sleeping, gazing at his female counterpart, Itza, who lay sleeping and guarding the valley of Cholula, there, where over four-hundred years ago Cortés showed his wrath and executed thousands of Cholulans.

"I am going on an adventure," he finally said and paused. "I think you might like to go with me."

I said nothing, but I put my book down and listened.

"I have been thinking about it for a long time, and now is the time to go. You see, it's like this. I grew up on the hacienda of Don Francisco Jimenez, it's to the south, just a day's drive on the carretera. In my village nobody likes Don Francisco, they fear and hate him. He has killed many men and he has taken their fortunes and buried them. He is a very rich man, muy rico. Many men have tried to kill him, but Don Francisco is like the devil, he kills them first."

I listened as I always listen, because one never knows when a word or phrase or an idea will be the seed from which a story sprouts, but at first there was nothing interesting. It sounded like the typical patrón-peón story I had heard so many times before. A man, the patrón, keeps the workers enslaved, in serfdom, and because he wields so much power soon stories are told about him and he begins to acquire super-human powers. He acquires a mystique, just like the divine right of old. The patrón wields a mean machete, like old King Arthur swung Excaliber. He chops off heads of dissenters and sits on top of the bones and skulls pyramid, the king of the mountain, the top macho.

"One day I was sent to look for lost cattle," Justino continued. "I rode back into the hills where I had never been. At the foot of a hill, near a ravine, I saw something move in the bush. I dismounted and moved forward quietly. I was afraid it might be bandidos who steal cattle, and if they saw me they would kill me. When I came near the place I heard a strange sound. Somebody was crying. My back shivered, just like a dog when he sniffs the devil at night. I thought I was going to see witches, brujas who like to go to those deserted places to dance for the devil, or la Llorona."

"La Llorona," I said aloud. My interest grew. I had been hearing Llorona stories since I was a kid, and I was always ready for one more. La Llorona was that archetypal woman of ancient legends who murdered her children then, repentant and demented, she has spent the rest of eternity searching for them.

"Sí, la Llorona. You know that poor woman used to drink a lot. She played around with men, and when she had babies she got rid of them by throwing them into la barranca. One day she realized what she had done and went crazy. She started crying and pulling her hair and running up and down the side of cliffs of the river looking for her children. It's a very sad story."

A new version, I thought, and yes, a sad story. And what of the men who made love to the woman who became la Llorona, I wondered? Did they ever cry for their children? It doesn't seem fair to have only her suffer, only her crying and doing penance. Perhaps a man should run with her, and in our legends we would call him "El Mero Chingón," he who screwed up everything. Then maybe the tale of love and passion and the insanity it can bring will be complete. Yes, I think someday I will write that story.

"What did you see?" I asked Justino.

"Something worse than la Llorona," he whispered.

To the south a wind mourned and moved the clouds off Popo's crown. The bald, snow-covered mountain thrust its power into the blue Mexican sky. The light glowed like liquid gold around the god's head. Popo was a god, an ancient god. Somewhere at his feet Justino's story had taken place.

"I moved closer, and when I parted the bushes I saw Don Francisco. He was sitting on a rock, and he was crying. From time to time he looked at the ravine in front of him, the hole seemed to slant into the earth. That pozo is called el Pozo de Mendoza. I had heard stories about it before, but I had never seen it. I looked into the pozo, and you wouldn't believe what I saw."

He waited, so I asked, "What?"

"Money! Huge piles of gold and silver coins! Necklaces and bracelets and crowns of gold, all loaded with all kinds of precious stones! Jewels! Diamonds! All sparkling in the sunlight that entered the hole. More money than I have ever seen! A fortune, my friend, a fortune which is still there, just waiting for two adventurers like us to take it!"

"Us? But what about Don Francisco? It's his land, his fortune."

"Ah," Justino smiled, "that's the strange thing about this fortune. Don Francisco can't touch it, that's why he was crying. You see, I stayed there, and watched him closely. Every time he stood up and started to walk into the pozo the money disappeared. He stretched out his hand to grab the gold, and poof, it was gone! That's why he was crying! He murdered all those people and hid their wealth in the pozo, but now he can't touch it. He is cursed."

"El Pozo de Mendoza," he said aloud. Something began to click in my mind. I smelled a story.

"Who was Mendoza?" I asked.

"He was a very rich man. Don Francisco killed him in a quarrel they had over some cattle. But Mendoza must have put a curse on Don Francisco before he died, because now Don Francisco can't get to the money."

"So Mendoza's ghost haunts old Don Francisco," I nodded.

"Many ghosts haunt him," Justino answered. "He has killed many men."

"And the fortune, the money. . . ."

He looked at me and his eyes were dark and piercing. "It's still there. Waiting for us!"

"But it disappears as one approaches it, you said so yourself. Perhaps it's only an hallucination."

Justino shook his head. "No, it's real gold and silver, not hallucination money. It disappears for Don Francisco because the curse is on him, but the curse is not on us." He smiled. He knew he had drawn me into his plot. "We didn't steal the money, so it won't disappear for us. And you are not connected with the place. You are innocent. I've thought very carefully about it, and now is the time to go. I can lower you into the pozo with a rope, in a few hours we can bring out the entire fortune. All we need is a car. You can borrow the patrón's car, he is your friend. But he must not know where we're going. We can be there and back in one day, one night." He nodded as if to assure me, then he turned and looked at the sky. "It will not rain today. It will not rain for a week. Now is the time to go."

He winked and returned to watering the grass and flowers of the jardín, a wild Pan among the bougainvillea and the roses, a man possessed by a dream. The gold was not for him, he told me the next day, it was for his women, he would buy them all gifts, bright dresses, and he would take them on vacation to the United States, he would educate his children, send them to the best colleges. I listened and the germ of the story cluttered my thoughts as I sat beneath the orange tree in the mornings. I couldn't write, nothing was coming, but I knew that there were elements for a good story in Justino's tale. In dreams I saw the lonely hacienda to the south. I saw the pathetic, tormented figure of Don Francisco as he cried over the fortune he couldn't touch. I saw the ghosts of the men he had killed, the lonely women who mourned over them and cursed the evil Don Francisco. In one dream I saw a man I took to be B. Traven, a grey-haired distinguished looking gentlemen who looked at me and nodded approvingly. "Yes, there's a story there, follow it, follow it. . . ."

In the meantime, other small and seemingly insignificant details came my way. During a luncheon at the home of my friend, a woman I did not know leaned toward me and asked me if I would like to meet the widow of B. Traven. The woman's hair was tinged orange, her complexion was ashen grey. I didn't know who she was or why she would mention B. Traven to me. How did she know Traven had come to haunt my thoughts? Was she a clue, which would help unravel the mystery? I didn't know, but I nodded. Yes, I would like to meet her. I had heard that Traven's widow, Rosa Elena, lived in Mexico City. But what would I ask her? What did I want to know? Would she know Traven's secret? Somehow he had learned that to keep his magic intact he had to keep away from the public. Like the fortune in the pozo, the magic feel for the story might disappear if unclean hands reached for it. I turned to look at the woman, but she was gone. I wandered to the terrrace to finish my beer. Justino sat beneath the orange tree. He yawned. I knew the literary talk bored him. He was eager to be on the way to el Pozo de Mendoza.

I was nervous, too, but I didn't know why. The tension for the story was there, but something was missing. Or perhaps it was just Justino's insistence that I decide whether I was going or not that drove me out of the house in the mornings. Time usually devoted to writing found me in a small cafe in the center of town. From there I could watch the shops open, watch the people cross the zócalo, the main square. I drank lots of coffee, I smoked a lot, I daydreamed, I wondered about the significance of the pozo, the fortune, Justino, the story I wanted to write about B. Traven. In one of these moods I saw a friend from whom I hadn't heard in years. Suddenly he was there, trekking across the square, dressed like an old rabbi, moss and green algae for a beard, and followed by a troop of very dignified Lacandones, Mayan Indians from Chiapas.

"Victor," I gasped, unsure if he was real or a part of the shadows which the sun created as it flooded the square with its light.

"I have no time to talk," he said as he stopped to munch on my pan dulce and sip my coffee. "I only want you to know, for purposes of your story, that I was in a Lacandonian village last month, and a Hollywood film crew descended from the sky. They came in helicopters. They set up tents near the village, and big-bosomed, bikined actresses emerged from them, tossed themselves on the cut trees which are the atrocity of the giant American lumber companies, and they cried while the director shot his film. Then they produced a grey-haired old man from one of the tents and took shots of him posing with the Indians. Herr Traven, the director called him."

He finished my coffee, nodded to his friends and they began to walk away.

"B. Traven?" I asked.

He turned. "No, an imposter, an actor. Be careful for imposters. Remember, even Traven used many disguises, many names!"

"Then he's alive and well?" I shouted. People around me turned to stare.

"His spirit is with us," were the last words I heard as they moved across the zócalo, a strange troop of near naked Lacandon Mayans and my friend the Guatemalan Jew, returning to the rain forest, returning to the primal, innocent land.

I slumped in my chair and looked at my empty cup. What did it mean? As their trees fall the Lacandones die. Betrayed as B. Traven was betrayed. Does each one of us also die as the trees fall in the dark depths of the Chiapas jungle? Far to the north, in Aztlán, it is the same where the earth is ripped open to expose and mine the yellow uranium. A few poets sing songs and stand in the way as the giant machines of the corporations rumble over the land and grind everything into dust. New holes are made in the earth, pozos full of curses, pozos with fortunes we cannot touch, should not touch. Oil, coal, uranium, from holes in the earth through which we suck the blood of the earth.

There were other incidents. A telephone call late one night, a voice with a German accent called my name, and when I answered the line went dead. A letter addressed to B. Traven came in the mail. It was dated March 26, 1969. My friend returned it to the post office. Justino grew more and more morose. He was under the orange tree and stared into space, my friend complained about the garden drying up. Justino looked at me and scowled. He did a little work then went back to daydreaming. Without the rains the garden withered. His heart was set on the adventure which lay at el pozo. Finally I said yes, dammit, why not, let's go, neither one of us is getting anything done here, and Justino cheering like a child, ran to prepare for the trip. But when I asked my friend for the weekend loan of the car he reminded me that we were invited to a tertulia, an afternoon reception, at the home of Señora Ana R. Many writers and artists would be there. It was in my honor, so I could meet the literati of Cuernavaca. I had to tell Justino I couldn't go.

Now it was I who grew morose. The story growing within would not let me sleep. I awakened in the night and looked out the window, hoping to see Justino and women bathing in the pool, enjoying themselves. But all was quiet. No radio played. The still night was warm and heavy. From time to time gunshots sounded in the dark, dogs barked, and the presence of a Mexico which never sleeps closed in on me.

Saturday morning dawned with a strange overcast. Perhaps the rains will come, I thought. In the afternoon I reluctantly accompanied my friend to the reception. I had not seen Justino all day, but I saw him at the gate as we drove out. He looked tired, as if he, too, had not slept. He wore the white shirt and baggy pants of a campesino. His straw hat cast a shadow over his eyes. I wondered if he had decided to go to the pozo alone. He didn't speak as we drove through the gate, he only nodded. When I looked back I saw him standing by the gate, looking after the car, and I had a vague, uneasy feeling that I had lost an opportunity.

The afternoon gathering was a pleasant affair, attended by a number of affectionate artists, critics, and writers who enjoyed the refreshing drinks which quenched the thirst.

But my mood drove me away from the crowd. I wandered around the terrace and found a foyer surrounded by green plants, huge fronds and ferns and flowering bougainvillea. I pushed the green aside and entered a quiet, very private alcove. The light was dim, the air was cool, a perfect place for contemplation. At first I thought I was alone, then I saw the man sitting in one of the wicker chairs next to a small, wrought iron table. He was an elderly white-haired gentlemen. His face showed he had lived a full life, yet he was still very distinguished in his manner and posture. His eyes shone brightly.

"Perdón," I apologized and turned to leave. I did not want to intrude.

"No, no, please," he motioned to the empty chair, "I've been waiting for you." He spoke English with a slight German accent. Or perhaps it was Norwegian, I couldn't tell the difference. "I can't take the literary gossip. I prefer the quiet."

I nodded and sat. He smiled and I felt at ease. I took the cigar he offered and we lit up. He began to talk and I listened. He was a writer also, but I had the good manners not to ask his titles. He talked about the changing Mexico, the change the new oil would bring, the lateness of the rains and how they affected the people and the land, and he talked about how important a woman was in a writer's life. He wanted to know about me, about the Chicanos of Aztlán, about our work. It was the workers, he said, who would change society. The artist learned from the worker. I talked, and sometime during the conversation I told him the name of the friend with whom I was staying. He laughed and wanted to know if Vitorino was still working for him.

"Do you know Justino?" I asked.

"Oh, yes, I know that old guide. I met him many years ago, when I first came to Mexico," he answered. "Justino knows the campesino very well. He and I traveled many places together, he in search of adventure, I in search of stories."

I thought the coincidence strange, so I gathered the courage and asked, "Did he ever tell you the story of the fortune at el Pozo de Mendoza?"

"Tell me?" the old man smiled. "I went there."

"With Justino?"

"Yes, I went with him. What a rogue he was in those days, but a good man. If I remember correctly I even wrote a story based on that adventure. Not a very good story. Never came to anything. But we had a grand time. People like Justino are the writer's source. We met interesting people and saw fabulous places, enough to last me a lifetime. We were supposed to be gone for one day, but we were gone nearly three years. You see, I wasn't interested in the pots of gold he kept saying were just over the next hill, I went because there was a story to write."

"Yes, that's what interested me," I agreed.

"A writer has to follow a story if it leads him to hell itself. That's our curse. Ay, and each one of us knows our own private hell."

I nodded. I felt relieved. I sat back to smoke the cigar and sip from my drink. Somewhere to the west the sun bronzed the evening sky. On a clear afternoon, Popo's crown would glow like fire.

"Yes," the old man continued, "a writer's job is to find and follow people like Justino. They're the source of life. The ones you have to keep away from are the dilettantes like the ones in there." He motioned in the general direction of the noise of the party. "I stay with people like Justino. They may be illiterate, but they understand our descent into the pozo of hell, and they understand us because they're willing to share the adventure with us. You seek fame and notoriety and you're dead as a writer."

I sat upright. I understood now what the pozo meant, why Justino had come into my life to tell me the story. It was clear. I rose quickly and shook the old man's hand. I turned and parted the palm leaves of the alcove. There, across the way, in one of the streets that led out of the maze of the town towards the south, I saw Justino. He was walking in the direction of Popo, and he was followed by women and children, a rag-tail army of adventurers, all happy, all singing. He looked up to where I stood on the terrace, and he smiled as he waved. He paused to light the stub of a cigar. The women turned, and the children turned, and all waved to me. Then they continued their walk, south, towards the foot of the volcano. They were going to the Pozo de Mendoza, to the place where the story originated.

I wanted to run after them, to join them in the glorious light which bathed the Cuernavaca valley and the majestic snow-covered head of Popo. The light was everywhere, a magnetic element which flowed from the clouds. I waved as Justino and his followers disappeared in the light. Then I turned to say something to the old man, but he was gone. I was alone in the alcove. Somewhere in the background I heard the tinkling of glasses and the laughter which came from the party, but that was not for me. I left the terrace and crossed the lawn, found the gate and walked down the street. The sound of Mexico filled the air. I felt light and happy. I wandered aimlessly through the curving, narrow streets, then I quickened my pace because suddenly the story was overflowing and I needed to write. I needed to get to my quiet room and write the story about B. Traven being alive and well in Cuernavaca.

GARY SNYDER

By far the most scholarly of the writers identified with the Beat Generation or the San Francisco Renaissance, Gary Snyder (b.1930) has for a half century made it his business to be well-informed about American Indian culture, Buddhist thought and practice, and ecology. Where professionals in the study of each of these fields may tend not to know much about the others, Snyder early on described a meaningful convergence and helped to create a synthesis that is now a recognizable reference in American life. The ingredients are set forth in remarkably well-finished interviews (see especially *The Real Work: Interviews and Talks, 1964–1979*, edited by Scott McLean), and in a body of essays including *The Practice of the Wild* (1990) and *A Place In Space* (1995). Snyder's poetic practice, with its valuation of community, Zen-or haiku-like compression of imagery, and environmental commitment, can be seen to derive from the same study. We see here a body of work with a distinct identity not to be limited to the 1960s, when Snyder first became nationally popular. Ekbert Faas, discussing Snyder's poems in *Towards a New American Poetics* (1978) spoke of images of "almost unearthly clarity and precision." The point is understood, of course, but it might be more in tune with this poet's philosophical position—his resolute departure from mainstream Western civilization's thought—to say instead, *"earthly."*

"Mid-August at Sourdough Mountain Lookout," from *Riprap and Cold Mountain Poems* (1965)

Down valley a smoke haze
Three days heat, after five days rain
Pitch glows on the fir-cones
Across rocks and meadows
Swarms of new flies.

I cannot remember things I once read
A few friends, but they are in cities.
Drinking cold snow-water from a tin cup
Looking down for miles
Through high still air.

"Marin-An," from *The Back Country* (1968)

sun breaks over the eucalyptus
grove below the wet pasture,
water's about hot,
I sit in the open window
& roll a smoke.

distant dogs bark, a pair of
cawing crows; the twang
of a pygmy nuthatch high in a pine—
from behind the cypress windrow
the mare moves up, grazing.

a soft continuous roar
comes out of the far valley
of the six-lane highway—thousands
and thousands of cars
driving men to work.

"Anasazi" from *Turtle Island* (1974)

Anasazi,
Anasazi,

tucked up in clefts in the cliffs
growing strict fields of corn and beans
sinking deeper and deeper in earth
up to your hips in Gods
        your head all turned to eagle-down
        & lightning for knees and elbows
your eyes full of pollen

        the smell of bats.
        the flavor of sandstone
        grit on the tongue.

        women
        birthing
at the foot of ladders in the dark.

trickling streams in hidden canyons
under the cold rolling desert

corn-basket   wide-eyed
   red baby
   rock lip home,

Anasazi

"Magpie's Song," from *Turtle Island* (1974)

Six A.M.,
Sat down on excavation gravel
by juniper and desert S.P. tracks
interstate 80 not far off
   between trucks
Coyotes—maybe three
     howling and yapping from a rise.

Magpie on a bough
Tipped his head and said,

> *"Here in the mind, brother*
> *Turquoise blue.*
> *I wouldn't fool you.*
> *Smell the breeze*
> *It came through all the trees*
> *No need to fear*
> *What's ahead*
> *Snow up on the hills west*
> *Will be there every year*
> *be at rest.*
> *A feather on the ground—*
> *The wind sound—*

Here in the Mind, Brother,
Turquoise Blue"

"True Night," from *Axe Handles* (1983)

Sheath of sleep in the black of the bed:
From outside this dream womb
Comes a clatter
Comes a clatter
And finally the mind rises up to a fact

Like a fish to a hook
A raccoon at the kitchen!
A falling of metal bowls,
    the clashing of jars,
    the avalanche of plates!
I snap alive to this ritual
Rise unsteady, find my feet,
Grab the stick, dash in the dark—
I'm a huge pounding demon
That roars at raccoons—
They whip round the corner,
A scratching sound tells me
    they've gone up a tree.

I stand at the base
Two young ones that perch on
Two dead stub limbs and
Peer down from both sides of the trunk:
    Roar, roar, I roar
    you awful raccoons, you wake me
    up nights, you ravage
    our kitchen

As I stay there then silent
The chill of the air on my nakedness
Starts off the skin
I am all alive to the night.
Bare foot shaping on gravel
Stick in the hand, forever.
Long streak of cloud giving way
To a milky thin light
Back of black pine bough,
The moon is still full,
Hillsides of Pine trees all
Whispering; crickets still cricketting
Faint in cold coves in the dark

I turn and walk slow
Back the path to the beds
With goosebumps and loose waving hair
In the night of milk-moonlit thin cloud glow
And black rustling pines
I feel like a dandelion head
Gone to seed

About to be blown all away
Or a sea anemone open and waving in
cool pearly water.

Fifty years old.
I still spend my time
Screwing nuts down on bolts.

At the shadow pool,
Children are sleeping,
And a lover I've lived with for years,
True night.
One cannot stay too long awake
In this dark.

Dusty feet, hair tangling,
I stoop and slip back to the
Sheath, for the sleep I still need,
For the waking that comes
Every day

With the dawn.

GRETEL EHRLICH

retel Ehrlich's (b. 1946) mid-1970s relocation from California to Wyoming, and the meanings she draws from the move, show that it is sometimes necessary now to go east to get to the West. The move was into a new job, different clothes, a new, rural lifestyle, and in the end a whole different outlook, that of a working, emplaced inhabitant. "For the first time I was able to take up residence on earth with no alibis, no self-promoting schemes," she writes. She began to pay intense attention to the weather, the land, the folkways of sheep ranching, the new kind of talk she was hearing. The spareness of the Wyoming landscape became a guiding metaphor: "Space has a spiritual equivalent and can heal what is divided and burdensome in us." As the following selection shows, she became a student of what Walter Prescott Webb and Wallace Stegner always argued was the decisive definer of the West: aridity. Like open space, aridity developed into a rich metaphor for Ehrlich, a teacher giving her new ideas, insights, connections. Learning how her new place worked, how it had to exist under the givens of climate and topography, she entered a new understanding of life at large. The title of a succeeding book of essays was *Islands, the Universe, Home* (1991).

"On Water," from *The Solace of Open Spaces* (1985)

Frank Hinckley, a neighboring rancher in his seventies, would rather irrigate than ride a horse. He started spreading water on his father's hay- and grainfields when he was nine, and his long-term enthusiasm for what's thought of disdainfully by cowboys as "farmers' work" is an example of how a discipline—a daily chore—can grow into a fidelity. When I saw Frank in May he was standing in a dry irrigation ditch looking toward the mountains. The orange tarp dams, hung like curtains from ten-foot-long poles, fluttered in the wind like prayer flags. In Wyoming we are supplicants, waiting all spring for the water to come down, for the snow pack to melt and fill the creeks from which we irrigate. Fall and spring rains amount to less than eight inches a year, while above our ranches, the mountains hold their snows like a secret: no one knows when they will melt or how fast. When the water does come, it floods through the state as if the peaks were silver pitchers tipped forward by mistake. When I looked in, the ditch water had begun dripping over Frank's feet. Then we heard a sound that might have been wind in a steep patch of pines. "Jumpin' Jesus, here it comes," he said, as a head of water, brown and foamy as beer, snaked toward us. He set five dams, digging the bright edges of plastic into silt. Water filled them the way wind fattens a sail, and from three notches cut in the ditch above each dam, water coursed out over a hundred acres of hayfield. When he finished, and the beadwork wetness had spread through the grass, he lowered himself to the ditch and rubbed his face with water.

A season of irrigating here lasts four months. Twenty, thirty, or as many as two hundred dams are changed every twelve hours, ditches are repaired and head gates adjusted to match the inconsistencies of water flow. By September it's over: all but the major Wyoming rivers dry up. Running water is so seasonal it's thought of as a mark on the calendar—a vague wet spot—rather than a geographical site. In May, June, July, and August, water is the sacristy at which we kneel; it equates time going by too fast.

Waiting for water is just one of the ways Wyoming ranchers find themselves at the mercy of weather. The hay they irrigate, for example, has to be cut when it's dry, but baled with a little dew on it to preserve the leaf. Three days after Frank's water came down, a storm dumped three feet of snow on his alfalfa and the creeks froze up again. His wife, "Mike," who grew up in the arid Powder River country, and I rode to the headwaters of our creeks. The elk we startled had been licking ice in a draw. A snow squall rose up from behind a bare ridge and engulfed us. We built a twig fire behind a rock to warm ourselves, then rode home. The creeks didn't thaw completely until June.

Despite the freak snow, April was the second driest in a century; in the lower elevations there had been no precipitation at all. Brisk winds forwarded thunderclouds into local skies—commuters from other states—but the streamers of rain they let down evaporated before touching us. All month farmers and ranchers burned their irrigation ditches to clear them of obstacles and weeds—optimistic that water would soon come. Shell Valley resembled a battlefield: lines of blue smoke banded every horizon and the cottonwoods that had caught fire by mistake, their outstretched branches blazing, looked human. April, the cruelest month, the month of dry storms.

Six years ago, when I lived on a large sheep ranch, a drought threatened. Every water hole on 100,000 acres of grazing land went dry. We hauled water in clumsy beet-harvest trucks forty miles to spring range, and when we emptied them into a circle of stock tanks, the sheep ran toward us. They pushed to get at the water, trampling lambs in the process, then drank it all in one collective gulp. Other Aprils have brought too much moisture in the form of deadly storms. When a ground blizzard hit one friend's herd in the flatter, eastern part of the state, he knew he had to keep his cattle drifting. If they hit a fence line and had to face the storm, snow would blow into their noses and they'd drown. "We cut wire all the way to Nebraska," he told me. During the same storm another cowboy found his cattle too late: they were buried in a draw under a fifteen-foot drift.

High water comes in June when the runoff peaks, and it's another bugaboo for the ranchers. The otherwise amiable thirty-foot-wide creeks swell and change courses so that when we cross them with livestock, the water is belly-deep or more. Cowboys in the 1800s who rode with the trail herds from Texas often worked in the big rivers on horseback for a week just to cross a thousand head of longhorn steers, losing half of them in the process. On a less-grand scale we have drownings and near drownings here each spring. When we crossed a creek this year the swift current toppled a horse and carried the rider under a log. A cowboy who happened to look back saw her head go under, dove in from horseback, and saved her. At Trapper Creek, where Owen Wister spent several summers in the 1920s and entertained Mr. Hemingway, a cloudburst slapped down on us like a black eye. Scraps of rainbow moved in vertical sweeps of rain that broke apart and disappeared behind a ridge. The creek flooded, taking out a house and a field of corn. We saw one resident walking in a flattened alfalfa field where the river had flowed briefly. "Want to go fishing?" he yelled to us as we rode by. The fish he was throwing into a white bucket were trout that had been "beached" by the flood.

Westerners are ambivalent about water because they've never seen what it can create except havoc and mud. They've never walked through a forest of wild orchids or witnessed the unfurling of five-foot-high ferns. "The only way I like my water is if there's whiskey in it," one rancher told me as we weaned calves in a driving rainstorm. That day we spent twelve hours on horseback in the rain. Despite protective layers of clothing: wool union suits, chaps, ankle-length yellow slickers, neck scarves and hats, we were drenched. Water drips off hat brims into your crotch; boots and gloves soak through. But to stay home out of the storm is deemed by some as a worse fate: "Hell, my wife had me cannin' beans for a week," one cowboy complained. "I'd rather drown like a muskrat out there."

Dryness is the common denominator in Wyoming. We're drenched more often in dust than in water; it is the scalpel and the suit of armor that make westerners what they are. Dry air presses a stockman's insides outward. The secret, inner self is worn not on the sleeve but in the skin. It's an unlubricated condition: there's not enough moisture in the air to keep the whole emotional machinery oiled and working. "What you see is what you get, but you have to learn to look to see all that's there," one young rancher told me. He was physically reckless when coming to see me or leaving. That was his way of saying he had and would miss me, and in the clean, broad sweeps of passion between us, there was no heaviness, no muddy residue. Cowboys have learned not to waste words from not having wasted water, as if verbosity would create a thirst too extreme to bear. If voices are raspy, it's because vocal cords are coated with dust. When I helped ship seven thousand head of steers one fall, the dust in the big, roomy sorting corrals churned as deeply and sensually as water. We wore scarves over our noses and mouths; the rest of our faces blackened with dirt so we looked like raccoons or coal miners. The westerner's face is stiff and dark red as jerky. It gives no clues beyond the discerning look that says, "You've been observed." Perhaps the too-early lines of aging that pull across these ranchers' necks are really cracks in a wall through which we might see the contradictory signs of their character: a complacency, a restlessness, a shy, boyish pride.

I knew a sheepherder who had the words "hard luck" tattooed across his knuckles. "That's for all the times I've been dry," he explained. "And when you've been as thirsty as I've been, you don't forget how something tastes." That's how he mapped out the big ranch he worked for: from thirst to thirst, whiskey to whiskey. To follow the water courses in Wyoming—seven rivers and a network of good-sized creeks—is to trace the history of settlement here. After a few bad winters the early ranchers quickly discovered the necessity of raising feed for livestock. Long strips of land on both sides of the creeks and rivers were grabbed up in the 1870s and '80s before Wyoming was a state. Land was cheap and relatively easy to accumulate, but control of water was crucial. The early ranches such as the Swan Land & Cattle Company, the Budd Ranch, the M-L, the Bug Ranch, and the Pitchfork took up land along the Chugwater, Green, Greybull, Big Horn, and Shoshone rivers. It was not long before feuds over water began. The old law of "full and undiminished flow" to those who owned land along a creek was changed to one that adjudicated and allocated water by the acre foot to specified pieces of land. By 1890 residents had to file claims for the right to use the water that flowed through their ranches. These rights were, and still are, awarded according to the date a ranch was established regardless of ownership changes. This solved the increasing problem of upstream-downstream disputes, enabling the first ranch established on a creek to maintain the first water right, regardless of how many newer settlements occurred upstream.

Land through which no water flowed posed another problem. Frank's father was one of the Mormon colonists sent by Brigham Young to settle and put under cultivation the arid Big Horn Basin. The twenty thousand acres they claimed were barren and waterless. To remedy this problem they dug a canal thirty-seven miles long, twenty-seven feet across, and sixteen feet deep by hand. The project took four years to complete. Along the way a huge boulder gave the canal diggers trouble: it couldn't be moved. As a last resort the Mormon men held hands around the rock and prayed. The next morning the boulder rolled out of the way.

Piousness was not always the rule. Feuds over water became venomous as the population of the state grew. Ditch riders—so called because they monitored on horseback the flow and use of water—often found themselves on the wrong end of an irrigating shovel. Frank remembers when the ditch rider in his district was hit over the head so hard by the rancher whose water he was turning off that he fell unconscious into the canal, floating on his back until he bumped into the next head gate.

With the completion of the canal, the Mormons built churches, schools, and houses communally, working in unison as if taking their cue from the water that snaked by them. "It was a socialistic sonofabitch from the beginning," Frank recalls, "a beautiful damned thing. These 'western individualists' forget how things got done around here and not so damned many years ago at that."

Frank is the opposite of the strapping, conservative western man. Sturdy, but small-boned, he has an awkward, knock-kneed gait that adds to his chronic amiability. Though he's made his life close to home, he has a natural, panoramic vision as if he had upped-periscope through the Basin's dust clouds and had a good look around. Frank's generosity runs like water: it follows the path of least resistance and, tumbling downhill, takes on a fullness so replete and indiscriminate as to sometimes appear absurd. "You can't cheat an honest man," he'll tell you and laugh at the paradox implied. His wide face and forehead indicate the breadth of his unruly fair-mindedness—one that includes not just local affections but the whole human community.

When Frank started irrigating there were no tarp dams. "We plugged up those ditches with any old thing we had—rags, bones, car parts, sod." Though he could afford to hire an irrigator now he prefers to do the work himself, and when I'm away he turns my water as well, then mows my lawn. "Irrigating is a contemptible damned job. I've been fighting water all my life. Mother Nature is a bitter old bitch, isn't she? But we have to have that challenge. We crave it and I'll be goddamned if I know why. I feel sorry for these damned rich ranchers with their pumps and sprinkler systems and gated pipe because they're missing out on something. When I go to change my water at dawn and just before dark, it's peaceful out there, away from everybody. I love the fragrances—grass growing, wild rose on the ditch bank—and hearing the damned old birds twittering away. How can we live without that?"

Two thousand years before the Sidon Canal was built in Wyoming, the Hohokam, a people who lived in what became Arizona, used digging sticks to channel water from the Salt and Gila rivers to dry land. Theirs was the most extensive irrigation system in aboriginal North America. Water was brought thirty miles to spread over fields of corn, beans, and pumpkins—crops inherited from tribes in South and Central America. "It's a primitive damned thing," Frank said about the business of using water. "The change from a digging stick to a shovel isn't much of an evolution. Playing with water is something all kids have done, whether it's in creeks or in front of fire hydrants. Maybe that's how agriculture got started in the first place."

Romans applied their insoluble cement to waterways as if it could arrest the flux and impermanence they knew water to signify. Of the fourteen aqueducts that brought water from mountains and lakes to Rome, several are still in use today. On a Roman latifundium—their equivalent of a ranch—they grew alfalfa, a hot-weather crop introduced by way of Persia and Greece around the fifth century B.C., and fed it to their horses as we do here. Feuds over water were common: Nero was reprimanded for bathing in the canal that carried the city's drinking water, the brothels tapped aqueducts on the sly until once the whole city went dry. The Empire's staying power began to collapse when the waterways fell into disrepair. Crops dried up and the water that had carried life to the great cities stagnated and became breeding grounds for mosquitoes until malaria, not water, flowed into the heart of Rome.

There is nothing in nature that can't be taken as a sign of both mortality and invigoration. Cascading water equates loss followed by loss, a momentum of things falling in the direction of death, then life. In Conrad's *Heart of Darkness*, the river is a redundancy flowing through rain forest, a channel of solitude, a solid thing, a trap. Hemingway's Big Two-Hearted River is the opposite: it's an accepting, restorative place. Water can stand for what is unconscious, instinctive, and sexual in us, for the creative swill in which we fish for ideas. It carries, weightlessly, the imponderable things in our lives: death and creation. We can drown in it or else stay buoyant, quench our thirst, stay alive.

In Navajo mythology, rain is the sun's sperm coming down. A Crow woman I met on a plane told me that. She wore a flowered dress, a man's wool jacket with a package of Vantages stuck in one pocket, and calf-high moccasins held together with two paper clips. "Traditional Crow think water is medicinal," she said as we flew over the Yellowstone River which runs through the tribal land where she lives. "The old tribal crier used to call out every morning for our people to drink all they could, to make water touch their bodies. 'Water is your body,' they used to say." Looking down on the seared landscape below, it wasn't difficult to understand the real and imagined potency of water. "All that would be a big death yard," she said with a sweep of her arm. That's how the drought would come: one sweep and all moisture would be banished. Bluebunch and June grass would wither. Elk and deer would trample sidehills into sand. Draws would fill up with dead horses and cows. Tucked under ledges of shale, dens of rattlesnakes would grow into city-states of snakes. The roots of trees would rise to the surface and flail through dust in search of water.

Everything in nature invites us constantly to be what we are. We are often like rivers: careless and forceful, timid and dangerous, lucid and muddied, eddying, gleaming, still. Lovers, farmers, and artists have one thing in common, at least—a fear of "dry spells," dormant periods in which we do no blooming, internal droughts only the waters of imagination and psychic release can civilize. All such matters are delicate of course. But a good irrigator knows this: too little water brings on the weeds while too much degrades the soil the way too much easy money can trivialize a person's initiative. In his journal Thoreau wrote, "A man's life should be as fresh as a river. It should be the same channel but a new water every instant."

This morning I walked the length of a narrow, dry wash. Slabs of stone, broken off in great squares, lay propped against the banks like blank mirrors. A sagebrush had drilled a hole through one of these rocks. The roots fanned out and down like hooked noses. Farther up, a quarry of red rock bore the fossilized marks of rippling water. Just yesterday, a cloudburst sent a skinny stream beneath these frozen undulations. Its passage carved the same kind of watery ridges into the sand at my feet. Even in this dry country, where internal and external droughts always threaten, water is self-registering no matter how ancient, recent, or brief.

LOUIS L'AMOUR

Fifteen-year-old Louis LaMoore (1908–1988) dropped out of school in Oklahoma in 1923 and embarked on a Jack London–like education in hard work, soaking up facts and skills in orchards, cattle ranches, mines, logging shows, dockyards, and even boxing rings across the American West. In World War II, he taught winter survival to Army recruits (the details in *Last of the Breed* are earned) and served in the European theater. His first novel as Louis L'Amour was *Westward the Tide* (1950); the fifties saw sixteen more novels, nearly all Westerns, with the historical romance *Sitka* (1957) an exception and an augury. In 1960, he began the first of his family sagas with *The Daybreakers*, a story of the Sacketts. There would be sixteen more Sackett-family romances, five about the Chantrys, and three about the Talons; L'Amour's plan, cut short by his death in 1988, was to write several more, dramatizing the entire history of the American frontier. For ambition and for attention to realistic detail, the self-taught L'Amour would be hard to equal among western historical novelists; for a certainty, no one approaches his mid-1990s figure of 225,000,000 copies in print. His hero in *Last of the Breed*, Joe Mack, is three-fourths American Indian, a test pilot captured by the Soviets and held near Lake Baikal whose only chance is to make his way across Siberia to the Pacific and then find a water way home. He is being chased by a Soviet master-tracker, but he is a more-than-master survivalist.

Chapter 16, from *Last of the Breed* (1986)

Their voices were stilled. Wind moaned around the eaves, and the fire crackled. A stick fell, sparks flew up. Joe Mack smelled the good smell of wood smoke and waited, ears straining for a breath of sound.

It came. A crunch of feet on the gravel outside. One man only. Joe Mack relaxed, watching the door, as they all were. The latch lifted. The new arrival stamped his feet to free them of mud before entering; then the door opened.

It was Yakov.

He carried no weapon. He came closer to the fire and took off his mittens, stretching his hands to the fire. "It is cold," he said, "cold."

His eyes found Joe Mack. "So? It is not easy, what you did. To come here, to find this place."

Nobody spoke, all seemed to be waiting for something. Joe Mack looked over at Baronas. "Should I go? If you have something to discuss—?"

"No. You are one of us now. Please stay."

Yakov looked up at Baronas, rubbing warmth into his hands. "It is no use. He is no longer in Nerchinsk. He was taken from the prison in the night." He poked a small stick into the fire. "We were too late," he spoke almost in a whisper, "too late!"

"But he lives?" Baronas asked.

"He lived then," Yakov said, "and when he was taken from the prison he was able to walk. I do not know where they have taken him. We must wait."

He glanced at Joe Mack. "They look for you. The job has been given to Alekhin."

"*Alekhin!*" Baronas exclaimed. "That is bad, bad!"

Yakov shrugged. "He is only a man."

Nobody spoke. Outside the wind whispered. Then Natalya asked, "Yakov? Have you eaten?"

He smiled. "Not today. Yesterday, a little."

"Sit where you are. I shall fix something."

"Meanwhile there is tea," Baronas said. Glancing at him, he said, "You must be tired."

Yakov indicated Joe Mack. "The country is alive because of him. You must be important."

Joe Mack shrugged, accepting a cup of tea for himself. "I have escaped. They do not like that."

Yakov thrust another stick into the fire. "You have not escaped. Siberia is a prison. It has walls of ice. Nobody escapes from Siberia."

"I shall."

"You are a good man in the forest," Yakov admitted. "You left no mark of your passing that I could see, but I am not Alekhin."

"He is good, then?"

"The master. No one is better, no one nearly so good. He is a ghost in the forest, and he can see where nothing is. No one has ever escaped him, no one."

There was talk between them then, but his few words were not enough. When they spoke slowly and directly to him, he could understand if the words were simple. Much he had learned from the miners' children returned to him, and Stephan Baronas was a patient teacher. But when they conversed among themselves, he could catch only a word from time to time. Yet it was warm and comfortable, and he did not wish to move.

The comfort was a danger. He must return to the chill of his own camp, where he would not be so much at his ease as here, where the very cold would serve to keep him alert.

Twenty-nine people, they had told him. He had met no more than half a dozen, and there was little moving about. He knew there was discussion of his presence and argument between those who feared the trouble he would attract and those who valued the meat he could contribute.

Joe Mack got to his feet. "I go," he said, and went out without looking back.

Outside in the dark the wind was raw and cold. The earth was frozen. It was unlikely anyone was watching at this hour and in the cold, but he was wary. When he arrived back at his camp in the rocky hideaway, he built a small fire and prepared his bed. He must make warmer clothing or he would freeze. Yet cold as it was, his health was good, and he lived on the meat he killed. It was a wild life he was living now, but a life to which he was born. He banked his fire and rolled in his bearskin and stared up at the rock overhead. Soon he must be going. He was a danger to them here. A little longer, to learn more of the language, just a little longer.

His eyes had closed, and now they opened again. Was that truly why he was staying on? Or was it that he needed people more than he had believed?

An icy wind whined through the trees, and a branch cracked in the cold. He pulled his bearskin snug about him and tried to hide his head from a trickle of wind from somewhere. He needed to warm the stone before sleeping, to warm it with his fire; this he must do before he slept at night. He reached an arm from the warmth of his bed to push another stick into the coals of his fire. He thought of the rocky cliffs along which he had traveled, of the rivers he must cross and the forests he must travel. And then he thought of Alekhin, the man tracker, of Alekhin who was out there somewhere, out there looking for sign, trying to find him.

He had believed they did not know where he was, but over the past weeks he had seen several parties of soldiers, searching. By chance? Or had he left some clue, some indication of his passing?

Alekhin was good. He must be doubly careful.

For two days he remained away from what he had come to think of as the village, but on the third day he killed a goral and took its meat to share.

He went to the house of Baronas, but there was no one there. Disappointed, he turned to go; then he added some fuel to the fire and left the meat he had brought. He walked away into the forest.

He was deep in the forest, walking on damp leaves among the birch trees and the larch, when he saw her.

She was standing in a natural aisle among the birch and the larch. Her hood was thrown back, and a vagrant shaft of sunlight touched her blond hair. She was, he realized, a beautiful woman. Not that it mattered to him. The days were passing into weeks, and soon he would be leaving.

She came down through the forest to meet him and paused a few feet away. "You have not been to see us."

"I built up your fire, and I left meat."

"Thank you. We found the meat and knew it was you." She paused. "We were not gone long." She hesitated again. "There was a meeting."

He waited, saying nothing. Somewhere, something stirred among the dead leaves.

"The meeting was about you. Peshkov wants you to leave. So does Rusinov. They are important men among us. My father spoke for you, and so did Yakov.

" 'Where would he go?' Yakov asked. 'It is the dead of winter.'

" 'No matter,' Peshkov argued. 'He is a danger to us all.'

" 'And we all eat meat he has killed,' my father said."

"I shall go soon."

"Where will you go? Where can you go?"

"Where I was when I came to you. I shall go back to the forest."

A wind rustled the leaves, a cold, cold wind. "My father says you may stay. It is not Peshkov who speaks for us." A last golden leaf from an aspen fell and lodged in her hair. Joe Mack looked away. She was a woman, this one.

"How are they here? Do they keep hunting even in the cold?"

She shrugged. "Usually, no. For you, maybe. This is Zamatev this time, and it is Alekhin. This has not happened before. I think there will be some hunting but not much. Men could die out there." She paused, considering it. "I think they will go to a few places. They will try to eliminate, to locate you. Then when spring comes, they will move."

She paused. "There was a woman in Aldan. It was she who was directing. I do not know her."

"A woman? What sort of woman?"

"Very attractive, someone said, but we do not know." She looked at him. "We have ways . . . I mean, sometimes we can find out such things. This woman was in Aldan where the furs were sold. The man with her we know. His name is Stegman. We know him. He is KGB, or he was. He has been assigned to Colonel Zamatev, so the woman no doubt works with him, too. They were using a helicopter."

He remembered the helicopter that had flown over him. The same one? It could be. Whoever was flying it had stopped to investigate that old building.

"At your meeting, what was decided?"

"You may stay, for the time being. Your meat has won you friends. It is very hard here in winter. In the warm times we can all get out and look for food. We plant. We gather in the forest. We do not do badly. In the winter it is very bad sometimes, and you brought us meat."

They walked down the dim path together. There were many deadfalls, often criss-crossed, black with damp. It was treacherous walking. His eyes were busy, watching, seeking. There were few animals in the thick forest. Usually they were found closer to the streams or near clearings or open meadows. The forest was dense and, even at midday, shadowed and dim. But the days were even shorter now, the nights long and bitterly cold.

"You must talk to Yakov. His mother was from the Tungus people. They are keepers of reindeer, great travelers and hunters. They still live much as they wish, and there are many of them northeast of here. You might meet them."

They walked on without talking. Stepping over a deadfall, her foot came down on another and slipped. She caught his arm and was astonished. "You are strong!"

"Where I lived there was much hard work, and then at school—do you know the decathlon? It requires all-around athletic skill. In college I won several meets, but lost out in the Olympic trials. I just wasn't good enough."

"Botev will go to Yakutsk soon. He will take furs."

"I shall have some. Is it not far?"

"We cannot go always to the same place, and Stegman and that woman were seen in Aldan, visiting the place there. It is a danger to return now."

"He will go alone?"

"No. Someone will go with him. They may not have to go all the way. Sometimes they meet with other trappers and trade their furs. We get less for them, but the risk is less, too."

They lingered, neither wishing to end the moment. A cold wind moaned in the larch and spruce. "Come to see us, Joe Mack. I want you to tell me of the cities and the women." She looked up at him. "I have been nowhere since I was a child. We hear so little here. Sometimes, on the Voice of America—"

Surprised, he asked, "You hear it *here*?"

"When we have batteries. There is no power. Yakov has been working on a waterwheel he hopes will generate power for us but it is far from complete."

"I am the wrong person to tell you of the cities." His eyes met hers and he shrugged. "I did not get around very much. Some of my people there drink too much, and I never wished to chance it."

She laughed, but without humor. "It is a problem here, too. We hear of efforts to convince people to drink less, but so far they have not succeeded."

"I know very little of Russia."

"My father says it has not changed. Russia now is the same as under the Tsars. As a nation, Russians have always been suspicious of outsiders. They have always lived outside the community of nations. What is happening now in Afghanistan began long ago. Read Kipling's *Kim* again and especially some of his short stories. Nor have they ever permitted free travel in their country or allowed their people to travel freely outside of Russia. Balzac had to meet his Polish mistress in Switzerland, as travel to France was not permitted for long periods."

"It is a pity. I have seen much beauty here, and I have seen little."

"The Kamchatka Peninsula is magnificent. There are volcanos, snow-covered peaks, waterfalls, and splendid forests. If it was possible, I think your people would come to see it. You are great travelers, I know."

She shivered. "It grows colder. We shall have a bad winter, I believe."

"They have not bothered you here?"

She shrugged. "We are far out of the way, and we do nothing to attract attention to ourselves. Wulff knows we exist, but our furs enrich him. Nevertheless, if we caused trouble he would have us all in prison or shot." She paused. "I think he only knows we exist, but does not know where and does not wish to know. Nor does he know who is here or how many.

"You see," she looked up at him again, "we are far from anywhere. No one travels this way. Someday—"

They walked on. "Is it true that everybody in America has an automobile?"

"Some families have two or three. A car is not considered a luxury, but a necessity. Many people drive many miles to work, and someone who does not drive a car or own one is a curiosity."

"And you?"

"I could fly a plane before I drove a car, and I would still rather fly. In the mountains where I grew up, there were no roads. Not close by, at least. My grandfather and my father did not want them, nor did they want visitors. When I left the mountains to go to school I lived with some Scottish relatives and rode in a car for the first time."

"Do Indians have cars?"

He chuckled. "The pickup has replaced the pony. I think every Indian has one, or if he does not own a pickup he soon will."

They paused again. "The way of life changes very rapidly in America. When cars became available, Americans began to travel even more, and at first there were tourist parks where they could stop at night and camp. Usually there was one building where there were showers and a place to cook. Then there were tourist courts where you could rent a room with a carport attached. That gave way to the motel, and now the motels are passing. Too many Americans are flying now, rather than driving. It used to be that there were filling stations on every corner and almost as many motels. Each year now there are fewer. I believe that soon there will be vast stretches in America where nobody travels but local people. It is faster to go by air."

"But you have railroads!"

"Of course, and for something less than one hundred years they were very important. They grow less so year by year."

Joe Mack did not go further. There was a restlessness in him that he felt was a warning. They parted there at the edge of the cluster of shelters, and she walked away without looking back. For a long moment he stood looking after her.

It was a grim life that faced her, a truly beautiful young woman condemned to live her life out in a forest, making do in a crude shelter, always in fear of discovery and what might follow. He had never been given to parties or even the essential affairs an officer was called upon to attend. He had gone, and he had known the effect he created, but he was happiest when far out in the woods or when flying alone and high in the sky. Yet thinking of Natalya he could see her in an evening gown at some of the balls or dinners he had attended. She was made for that world, not this.

He paused again when well back into the birch forest and looked carefully around. He must not be followed. And he must prepare, now, for an escape. Above all he must not settle down to a day-by-day existence here. True, this was the best sort of place he could find to ride out the winter, but he must be prepared to move, and quickly, at any time.

The search was on, and it would be a relentless search. Remembering Alekhin, he knew the man would be ruthless as well as persevering. And somewhere down the chain of days they would meet. Somewhere, somehow, he knew it would happen.

Man to man, face to face, and death for one or both.

Remembering Alekhin's cold, heavy-lidded eyes, he felt a chill.

DENISE CHÁVEZ

There is a certain yearning, learning, vulnerable quality to Denise Chávez's protagonists. Life seems to be new to them; cynicism has not set in, and they face
crucial moments with a rare, beautiful freshness. "My work is rooted in the
Southwest, in heat and dust, and reflects a world where love is as real as the land,"
Chavez (b. 1948) has said. "In this dry and seemingly harsh and empty world there
is much beauty to be found. That hope of the heart is what feeds me, my characters." A founding member of the National Institute of Chicana Writers, she has
written some twenty-five plays, performed her one-woman show, "Women in the
State of Grace," many times on stages across the country, and had her first novel,
Face of an Angel (1994), chosen as a Book-of-the-Month-Club selection. The collection of which "The Last of the Menu Girls" is the title story won the Puerto
del Sol Fiction Award, a significant Southwest regional honor, in 1986. Ms. Chávez
has written, "I feel, as a Chicana writer, that I am capturing the voice of so many
who have been voiceless for years." She was given the New Mexico Governor's
Award in Literature in 1995.

"The Last of the Menu Girls," from *The Last of the Menu Girls* (1987)

NAME: *Rocío Esquibel*
AGE: *Seventeen*
PREVIOUS EXPERIENCE WITH THE SICK AND DYING: *My Great Aunt Eutilia*
PRESENT EMPLOYMENT: *Work-study aide at Altavista Memorial*

I never wanted to be a nurse. My mother's aunt died in our house,
seventy-seven years old and crying in her metal crib: "Put a pillow on
the floor. I can jump," she cried. "Go on, let me jump. I want to get away
from here, far away."

Eutilia's mattress was covered with chipped clothlike sheaves of yellowed plastic. She wet herself, was a small child, undependable, helpless.
She was an old lady with a broken hip, dying without having gotten
down from that rented bed. Her blankets were sewn by my mother: cor-
duroy patches, bright yellows, blues and greens, and still she wanted to
jump!

"Turn her over, turn her over, turn her, wait a minute, wait—turn . . ."

Eutilia faced the wall. It was plastered white. The foamed, concrete turnings of some workman's trowel revealed daydreams: people's faces, white clouds, phantom pianos slowly playing half lost melodies, "Las Mañanitas," "Cielito Lindo," songs formulated in expectation, dissolved into confusion. Eutilia's blurred faces, far off tunes faded into the white walls, into jagged, broken waves.

I never wanted to be a nurse, ever. All that gore and blood and grief. I was not as squeamish as my sister Mercy, who could not stand to put her hands into a sinkful of dirty dishes filled with floating food—wet bread, stringy vegetables and bits of softened meat. Still, I didn't like the touch, the smells. How could I? When I touched my mother's feet, I looked away, held my nose with one hand, the other with finger laced along her toes, pulling and popping them into place. "It really helps my arthritis, baby—you don't know. Pull my toes, I'll give you a dollar, find my girdle, and I'll give you two. Ouch. Ouch. Not so hard. There, that's good. Look at my feet. You see the veins? Look at them. Aren't they ugly? And up here, look where I had the operations . . . ugly, they stripped them and still they hurt me."

She rubbed her battered flesh wistfully, placed a delicate and lovely hand on her right thigh. Mother said proudly, truthfully, "I still have lovely thighs."

PREVIOUS EXPERIENCE WITH THE SICK AND DYING: *Let me think . . .*

Great Aunt Eutilia came to live with us one summer and seven months later she died in my father's old study, the walls lined with books, whatever answers were there—unread.

Great Aunt Eutilia smelled like the mercilessly sick. At first, a vague, softened aroma of tiredness and spilled food. And later, the full-blown emptyings of the dying: gas, putrefaction and fetid lucidity. Her body poured out long, held-back odors. She wet her diapers and sheets and knocked over medicines and glasses of tepid water, leaving in the air an unpleasant smell.

I danced around her bed in my dreams, naked, smiling, jubilant. It was an exultant adolescent dance for my dying aunt. It was necessary, compulsive. It was a primitive dance, a full moon offering that led me slithering into her room with breasts naked and oily at thirteen . . .

No one home but me.

Led me to her room, my father's refuge, those halcyon days now that he was gone—and all that remained were dusty books, cast iron bookends, reminders of the spaces he filled. Down the steps I leaped into Eutilia's faded and foggy consciousness where I whirled and danced and sang: I am your flesh and my mother's flesh and you are . . . are . . . Eutilia stared at me. I turned away.

I danced around Eutilia's bed. I hugged the screen door, my breasts indented in the meshed wire. In the darkness Eutilia moaned, my body wet, her body dry. Steamy we were, and full of prayers.

Could I have absolved your dying by my life? Could I have lessened your agony with my spirit-filled dance in the deep darkness? The blue fan stirred, then whipped nonstop the solid air; little razors sliced through consciousness and prodded the sick and dying woman, whose whitened eyes screeched: Ay! Ay! Let me jump, put a pillow, I want to go away . . . let me . . . let me . . .

One day while playing "Cielito Lindo" on the piano in the living room, Eutilia got up and fell to the side of the piano stool. Her foot caught on the rug, "¡Ay! ¡Ay! ¡Ay! ¡Ay! Canta y no llores . . ."

All requests were silenced. Eutilia rested in her tattered hospital gown, having shredded it to pieces. She was surrounded by little white strips of raveled cloth. Uncle Toño, her babysitter, after watching the evening news, found her naked and in a bed of cloth. She stared at the ceiling, having played the piano far into the night. She listened to sounds coming from around the back of her head. Just listened. Just looked. Just shredded. Shredded the rented gown, shredded it. When the lady of the house returned and asked how was she, meaning, does she breathe, Toño answered, "Fine."

Christ on his crucifix! He'd never gone into the room to check on her. Later, when they found her, Toño cried, his cousin laughed. They hugged each other, then cried, then laughed, then cried. Eutilia's fingers never rested. They played beautiful tunes. She was a little girl in tatters in her metal bed with sideboards that went up and down, up and down . . .

The young girls danced they played they danced they filled out forms.

PREVIOUS EMPLOYMENT: *None.*

There was always a first job, as there was the first summer of the very first boyfriend. That was the summer of our first swamp cooler. The heat bore down and congealed sweat. It made rivulets trace the body's meridian and, before it stopped, was wiped away, never quite dismissed.

On the tops of the neighbors' houses old swamp coolers, with their jerky grating and droning moans, strained to ease the southern implacabilities. Whrr whrr cough whrr.

Regino Suárez climbed up and down the roof, first forgetting his hammer and then the cooler filter. His boy, Eliterio, stood at the bottom of the steps that led to the sun deck and squinted dumbly at the blazing sun. For several days Regino tramped over my dark purple bedroom. I had shut the curtains to both father and son and rested in violet contemplation of my first boyfriend.

Regino stomped his way to the other side of the house where Eutilia lay in her metal crib, trying to sleep, her weary eyes uncomprehending. The noise was upsetting, she could not play. The small blue fan wheezed freshness. Regino hammered and paced then climbed down. When lunchtime came, a carload of fat daughters drove Regino and the handsome son away.

If Eutilia could have read a book, it would have been the Bible, or maybe her novena to the Santo Niño de Atocha, he was her boy ...

PREVIOUS EXPERIENCE WITH THE SICK AND DYING:

This question reminds me of a story my mother told me about a very old woman, Doña Mercedes, who was dying of cancer. Doña Mercedes lived with her daughter, Corina, who was my mother's friend. The old woman lay in bed, day after day, moaning and crying softly, not actually crying out, but whimpering in a sad, hopeless way. "Don't move me," she begged when her daughter tried to change the sheets or bathe her. Every day this ordeal of maintenance became worse. It was a painful thing and full of dread for the old woman, the once fastidious and upright Doña Mercedes. She had been a lady, straight and imposing, and with a headful of rich dark hair. Her ancestors were from Spain. "You mustn't move me, Corina," Doña Mercedes pleaded, "never, please. Leave me alone, mi'jita," and so the daughter acquiesced. Cleaning around her tortured flesh and delicately wiping where they could, the two women attended to Doña Mercedes. She died in the daytime, as she had wanted.

When the young women went to lift the old lady from her death bed, they struggled to pull her from the sheets; and, when finally they turned her on her side, they saw huge gaping holes in her back where the cancer had eaten through the flesh. The sheets were stained, the bedsores lost in a red wash of bloody pus. Doña Mercedes' cancer had eaten its way through her back and onto those sheets. "Don't move me, please don't move me," she had cried.

The two young women stuffed piles of shredded disinfected rags soaked in Lysol into Doña Mercedes' chest cavity, filling it, and horrified, with cloths over their mouths, said the prayers for the dead. Everyone remembered her as tall and straight and very Spanish.

PRESENT EMPLOYMENT: Work-study aide at Altavista Memorial Hospital

I never wanted to be a nurse. Never. The smells. The pain. What was I to do then, working in a hospital, in that place of white women, whiter men with square faces? I had no skills. Once in the seventh grade I'd gotten a penmanship award. Swirling R's in boredom, the ABC's ad infinitum. Instead of dipping chocolate cones at the Dairy Queen next door to the hospital, I found myself a frightened girl in a black skirt and white blouse standing near the stairwell to the cafeteria.

I stared up at a painting of a dark-haired woman in a stiff nurse's cap and gray tunic, tending to men in old-fashioned service uniforms. There was a beauty in that woman's face whoever she was. I saw myself in her, helping all of mankind, forgetting and absolving all my own sick, my own dying, especially relatives, all of them so far away, removed. I never wanted to be like Great Aunt Eutilia, or Doña Mercedes with the holes in her back, or my mother, her scarred legs, her whitened thighs.

MR. SMITH

Mr. Smith sat at his desk surrounded by requisition forms. He looked up to me with glassy eyes like filmy paperweights.

MOTHER OF GOD, MR. SMITH WAS A WALL-EYED HUNCHBACK!

"Mr. Smith, I'm Rocío Esquibel, the work-study student from the university and I was sent down here to talk to you about my job."

"Down here, down here," he laughed, as if it were a private joke.

"Oh, yes, you must be the new girl. Menus," he mumbled. "Now just have a seat and we'll see what we can do. Would you like some iced tea?"

It was nine o'clock in the morning, too early for tea. "No, well, yes, that would be nice."

"It's good tea, everyone likes it. Here, I'll get you some." Mr. Smith got up, more hunchbacked than I'd imagined. He tiptoed out of the room whispering, "Tea, got to get this girl some tea."

There was a bit of the gruesome Golom in him, a bit of the twisted spider in the dark. Was I to work for this gnome? I wanted to rescue souls, not play attendant to this crippled, dried-up specimen, this cartilaginous insect with his misshapen head and eyes that peered out to me like the marbled eyes of statues one sees in museums. History preserves its freaks. God, was my job to do the same? No, never!

I faced Dietary Awards, Degrees in Food Management, menus for Low Salt and Fluids; the word Jello leaped out at every turn. I touched the walls. They were moist, never having seen the light.

In my dreams, Mr. Smith was encased in green Jello; his formaldehyde breath reminded me of other smells—decaying, saddened dead things; my great aunt, biology class in high school, my friend Dolores Casaus. Each of us held a tray with a dead frog pinned in place, served to us by a tall stoop-shouldered Viking turned farmer, our biology teacher

Mr. Franke, pink-eyed, half blind. Dolores and I cut into the chest cavity and explored that small universe of dead cold fibers. Dolores stopped at the frog's stomach, then squeezed out its last meal, a green mash, spinach-colored, a viscous fluid—that was all that remained in that miniaturized, unresponding organ, all that was left of potential life.

Before Eutilia died she ate a little, mostly drank juice through bent and dripping hospital straws. The straws littered the floor where she'd knocked them over in her wild frenzy to escape. "Dioooooooos," she cried in that shrill voice. "Dios mío, Diosito, por favor. Ay, I won't tell your mamá, just help me get away ... Diosito de mi vida ... Diosito de mi corazón ... agua, agua ... por favor, por favor ..."

Mr. Smith returned with my iced tea.

"Sugar?"

Sugar, yes, sugar. Lots of it. Was I to spend all summer in this smelly cage? What was I to do? What? And for whom? I had no business here. It was summertime and my life stretched out magically in front of me: there was my boyfriend, my freedom. Senior year had been the happiest of my life; was it to change?

"Anytime you want to come down and get a glass of tea, you go right ahead. We always have it on hand. Everyone likes my tea," he said with pride.

"About the job?" I asked.

Mr. Smith handed me a pile of green forms. They were menus.

In the center of the menu was listed the day of the week, and to the left and coming down in a neat order were the three meals, breakfast, lunch and dinner. Each menu had various choices for each meal.

LUNCH

☐ Salisbury Steak   ☐ Mashed potatoes and gravy
☐ Fish sticks   ☐ Macaroni and cheese
☐ Enchiladas   ☐ Broccoli and onions
☐ Rice almondine

Drinks   *Dessert*
☐ Coffee   ☐ Jello
☐ Tea   ☐ Carrot cake
☐ 7-Up   ☐ Ice Cream, vanilla
☐ Other

"Here you see a menu for Friday, listing the three meals. Let's take lunch. You have a choice of Salisbury steak, enchiladas, they're really good, Trini makes them, she's been working for me for twenty years. Her son George Jr. works for me, too, probably his kids one day." At this possibility, Mr. Smith laughed at himself. "Oh, and fish sticks. You a . . . ?"

"Our Lady of the Holy Scapular."

"Sometimes I'll get a menu back with a thank you written on the side. 'Thanks for the liver, it was real good,' or 'I haven't had rice pudding since I was a boy.' Makes me feel good to know we've made our patients happy."

Mr. Smith paused, reflecting on the positive aspects of his job.

"Mind you, these menus are only for people on regular diets, not everybody, but a lot of people. I take care of the other special diets, that doesn't concern you. I have a girl working for me now, Arlene Rutschman. You know . . ."

My mind raced forward, backward. Arlene Rutschman, the Arlene from Holy Scapular, Arlene of the soft voice, the limp mannerisms, the plain, too goodly face, Arlene, president of Our Lady's Sodality, in her white and navy blue beanie, her bobby socks and horn-rimmed glasses, the Arlene of the school dances with her perpetual escort, Bennie Lara, the toothy better-than-no-date date, the Arlene of the high grades, the muscular, yet turned-in legs, the curly unattractive hair, *that* Arlene, the dud?

"Yes, I know her."

"Good!"

"We went to school together."

"Wonderful!"

"She works here?"

"Oh, she's a nice girl. She'll help you, show you what to do, how to distribute the menus."

"Distribute the menus?"

"Now you just sit there, drink your tea and tell me about yourself."

This was the first of many conversations with Mr. Smith, the hunchbacked dietician, a man who was never anything but kind to me.

"Hey," he said proudly, "these are my kids. Norma and Bardwell. Norma's in Junior High, majoring in boys, and Bardwell is graduating from the Military Institute."

"Bardwell. That's an unusual name," I said as I stared at a series of 5 × 7's on Mr. Smith's desk.

"Bardwell, well, that was my father's name. Bardwell B. Smith. The Bard, they called him!" At this he chuckled to himself, myopically recalling his father, tracing with his strange eyes patterns of living flesh and bone.

"He used to recite."

The children looked fairly normal. Norma was slight, with a broad toothy smile. Bardwell, or Bobby, as he was called, was not unhandsome in his uniform, if it weren't for one ragged, splayed ear that slightly cupped forward, as if listening to something.

Mr. Smith's image was nowhere in sight. "Camera shy," he said. To the right of Mr. Smith's desk hung a plastic gold framed prayer beginning with the words: "Oh Lord of Pots and Pans." To the left, near a dried-out water-cooler was a sign, "Bless This Mess."

Over the weeks I began to know something of Mr. Smith's convoluted life, its anchorings. His wife and children came to life, and Mr. Smith acquired a name—Marion—and a vague disconcerting sexuality. It was upsetting for me to imagine him fathering Norma and Bardwell. I stared into the framed glossies full of disbelief. Who was Mrs. Smith? What was she like?

Eutilia never had any children. She'd been married to José Esparza, a good man, a handsome man. They ran a store in Agua Tibia. They prospered, until one day, early in the morning, about three A.M., several men from El Otro Lado called out to them in the house. "Don José, wake up! We need to buy supplies." Eutilia was afraid, said, "No, José, don't let them in." He told her, "Woman, what are we here for?" And she said, "But at this hour, José? At this hour?" Don José let them into the store. The two men came in carrying two sacks, one that was empty, and another that they said was full of money. They went through the store, picking out hats, clothing, tins of corned beef, and stuffing them into the empty sack. "So many things, José," Eutilia whispered, "*too* many things!" "Oh no," one man replied, "we have the money, don't you trust us, José?" "Cómo no, compadre," he replied easily. "We need the goods, don't be afraid, compadre." "Too many things, too many things," Eutilia sighed, huddled in the darkness in her robe. She was a small woman, with the body of a little girl. Eutilia looked at José, and it was then that they both knew. When the two men had loaded up, they turned to Don José, took out a gun, which was hidden in a sack, and said, "So sorry, compadre, but you know . . . stay there, don't follow us." Eutilia hugged the darkness, saying nothing for the longest time. José was a handsome man, but dumb.

The village children made fun of José Esparza, laughed at him and pinned notes and pieces of paper to his pants. "Tonto, tonto" and "I am a fool." He never saw these notes, wondered why they laughed.

"I've brought you a gift, a bag of rocks"; all fathers have said that to their children. Except Don José Esparza. He had no children, despite his looks. "At times a monkey can do better than a prince," la comadre Lucaya used to say to anyone who would listen.

The bodies of patients twisted and moaned and cried out, and cursed, but for the two of us in that basement world, all was quiet save for the occasional clinking of an iced tea glass and the sporadic sound of Mr. Smith clearing his throat.

"There's no hurry," Mr. Smith always said. "Now you just take your time. Always in a hurry. A young person like you."

ARLENE RUTSCHMAN

"You're so lucky that you can speak Spanish," Arlene intoned. She stood tiptoes, held her breath, then knocked gently on the patient's door. No sound. A swifter knock. "I could never remember what a turnip was," she said.

"Whatjawant?" a voice bellowed.

"I'm the menu girl; can I take your order?"

Arlene's high tremulous little girl's voice trailed off, "Good morning, Mr. Samaniego! What'll it be? No, it's not today you leave, tomorrow, after lunch. Your wife is coming to get you. So, what'll it be for your third-to-the-last meal? Now we got poached or fried eggs. Poached. P-o-a-c-h-e-d. That's like a little hard in the middle, but a little soft on the outside. Firm. No, not like scrambled. Different. Okay, you want scrambled. Juice? We got grape or orange. You like grape? Two grape. And some coffee, black."

A tall Anglo man, gaunt and yellowed like an old newspaper, his eyes rubbed black like an old raccoon's, ranged the hallway. The man talked quietly to himself and smoked numbers of cigarettes as he weaved between attendants with half-filled urinals and lugubrious I.V.'s. He reminded me of my father's friends, angular Anglos in their late fifties, men with names like Bud or Earl, men who owned garages or steak houses, men with firm hairy arms, clear blue eyes and tattoos from the war.

"That's Mr. Ellis, 206." Arlene whispered, "jaundice."

"Oh," I said, curiously contemptuous and nervous at the same time, unhappy and reeling from the phrase, 'I'm the menu girl!' How'd I ever manage to get such a dumb job? At least the Candy Stripers wore a cute uniform, and they got to do fun things like deliver flowers and candy.

"Here comes Mrs. Samaniego. The wife."

"Mr. Ellis's wife?" I said, with concern.

"No, Mr. Samaniego's wife, Donelda." Arlene pointed to a wizened and giggly old woman who was sneaking by the information desk, past the silver-haired volunteer, several squirmy grandchildren in tow. Visiting hours began at two P.M., but Donelda Samaniego had come early to beat the rush. From the hallway, Arlene and I heard loud smacks, much kidding and general merriment. The room smelled of tamales.

"Old Mr. Phillips in 304, that's the Medical Floor, he gets his cath at eleven, so don't go ask him about his menu then. It upsets his stomach."

Mrs. Daniels in 210 told Arlene weakly, "Honey, yes, you, honey, who's the other girl? Who is she? You'll just have to come back later, I don't feel good. I'm a dying woman, can't you see that?" When we came back an hour later, Mrs. Daniels was asleep, snoring loudly.

Mrs. Gustafson, a sad wet-eyed, well-dressed woman in her late sixties, dismissed us from the shade of drawn curtains as her husband, G. P. "Gus" Gustafson, the judge, took long and fitful naps only to wake up again, then go back to sleep, beginning once more his inexorable round of disappearances.

"Yesterday I weighed myself in the hall and I'm getting fat. Oh, and you're so thin."

"The hips," I said, "the hips."

"You know, you remind me of that painting," Arlene said, thoughtfully.

"Which?"

"Not which, who. The one in the stairwell. Florence Nightingale, she looks like you."

"That's who that is!"

"The eyes."

"She does?"

"The eyes."

"The eyes?"

"And the hair."

"The eyes and the hair? Maybe the hair, but not the eyes."

"Yes."

"I don't think so."

"Oh yes! Every time I look at it."

"Me?"

Arlene and I sat talking at our table in the cafeteria, that later was to become *my* table. It faced the dining room. From that vantage point I could see everything and not be seen.

We talked, two friends almost, if only she weren't so, so, little girlish with ribbons. Arlene was still dating Bennie and was majoring in either home ec or biology. They seemed the same in my mind: babies, menus and frogs. Loathsome, unpleasant things.

It was there, in the coolness of the cafeteria, in that respite from the green forms, at our special table, drinking tea, laughing with Arlene, that I, still shy, still judgmental, still wondering and still afraid, under the influence of caffeine, decided to stick it out. I would not quit the job.

"How's Mr. Prieto in 200?"

"He left yesterday, but he'll be coming back. He's dying."

"Did you see old Mr. Carter? They strapped him to the wheelchair finally."

"It was about time. He kept falling over."

"Mrs. Domínguez went to bland."

"She was doing so well."

"You think so? She couldn't hardly chew. She kept choking."

"And that grouch, what's her name, the head nurse, Stevens in 214 . . ."

"She's the head nurse? I didn't know that—god, I filled out her menu for her . . . she was sleeping and I . . . no wonder she was mad . . . how did I know she was the head nurse?"

"It's okay. She's going home or coming back, I can't remember which. Esperanza González is gonna be in charge."

"She was real mad."

"Forget it, it's okay."

"The woman will never forgive me, I'll lose my job," I sighed.

I walked home past the Dairy Queen. It took five minutes at the most. I stopped midway at the ditch's edge, where the earth rose and where there was a concrete embankment on which to sit. To some this was the quiet place, where neighborhood lovers met on summer nights to kiss, and where older couples paused between their evening walks to rest. It was also the talking place, where all the neighbor kids discussed life while eating hot fudge sundae with nuts. The bench was large; four could sit on it comfortably. It faced an open field in the middle of which stood a huge apricot tree. Lastly, the bench was a stopping place, the "throne," we called it. We took off hot shoes and dipped our cramped feet into the cool ditch water, as we sat facing the southern sun at the quiet talking place, at our thrones, not thinking anything, eyes closed, but sun. The great red velvet sun.

One night I dreamt of food, wading through hallways of food, inside some dark evil stomach. My boyfriend waved to me from the ditch's bank. I sat on the throne, ran alongside his car, a blue Ford, in which he sat, on clear plastic seat covers, with that hungry Church-of-Christ smile of his. He drove away, and when he returned, the car was small and I was too big to get inside.

Eutilia stirred. She was tired. She did not recognize anyone. I danced around the bed, crossed myself, en el nombre del padre, del hijo y del espíritu santo, crossed forehead, chin and breast, begged for forgiveness even as I danced.

And on waking, I remembered. *Nabos. Turnips.* But of course.

It seemed right to me to be working in a hospital, to be helping people, and yet: why was I only a menu girl? Once a menu was completed, another would take its place and the next day another. It was a never ending round of food and more food. I thought of Judge Gustafson.

When Arlene took a short vacation to the Luray Caverns, I became the official menu girl. That week was the happiest of my entire summer.

That week I fell in love.

ELIZABETH RAINEY

Elizabeth Rainey, Room 240, was in for a D and C. I didn't know what a D and C was, but I knew it was mysterious and to me, of course, this meant it had to do with sex. Elizabeth Rainey was propped up in bed with many pillows, a soft blue, homemade quilt at the foot of her bed. Her cheeks were flushed, her red lips quivering. She looked fragile, and yet her face betrayed a harsh indelicate bitterness. She wore a creme-colored gown on which her loose hair fell about her like a cape. She was a beautiful woman, full-bodied, with the translucent beauty certain women have in the midst of sorrow—clear and unadorned, her eyes bright with inexplicable and self-contained suffering.

She cried out to me rudely, as if I personally had offended her. "What do you want? Can't you see I want to be alone. Now close the door and go away! Go away!"

"I'm here to get your menu." I could not bring myself to say, I'm the menu girl.

"Go away, go away, I don't want anything. I don't want to eat. Close the door!"

Elizabeth Rainey pulled her face away from me and turned to the wall, and, with deep and self-punishing exasperation, grit her teeth, and from the depths of her self-loathing a small inarticulate cry escaped— "Oooooh."

I ran out, frightened by her pain, yet excited somehow. She was so beautiful and so alone. I wanted in my little girl's way to hold her, hold her tight and in my woman's way never to feel her pain, ever, whatever it was.

"Go away, go away," she said, her trembling mouth rimmed with pain, "go away!"

She didn't want to eat, told me to go away. How many people yelled to me to go away that summer, have yelled since then, countless people, of all ages, sick people, really sick people, dying people, people who were well and still rudely tied into their needs for privacy and space, affronted by these constant impositions from, of all people, the menu girl!

"Move over and move out, would you? Go away! Leave me alone!"

And yet, of everyone who told me to go away, it was this woman in her solitary anguish who touched me the most deeply. How could I, age seventeen, not knowing love, how could I presume to reach out to this young woman in her sorrow, touch her and say, "I know, I understand."

Instead, I shrank back into myself and trembled behind the door. I never went back into her room. How could I? It was too terrible a vision, for in her I saw myself, all life, all suffering. What I saw both chilled and burned me. I stood long in that darkened doorway, confused in the presence of human pain. I wanted to reach out . . . I wanted to . . . I wanted to . . . But *how?*

As long as I live I will carry Elizabeth Rainey's image with me: in a creme-colored gown she is propped up, her hair fanning pillows in a room full of deep sweet acrid and overspent flowers. Oh, I may have been that summer girl, but yes, I knew, I understood. I would have danced for her, Eutilia, had I but dared.

DOLORES CASAUS

Dolores of the frog entrails episode, who'd played my sister Ismene in the world literature class play, was now a nurse's aide on the surgical floor, changing sheets, giving enemas and taking rectal temperatures.

It was she who taught me how to take blood pressure, wrapping the cuff around the arm, counting the seconds and then multiplying beats. As a friend, she was rude, impudent, delightful; as an aide, most dedicated. One day for an experiment, with me as a guinea pig, she took the blood pressure of my right leg. That day I hobbled around the hospital, the leg cramped and weak. In high school Dolores had been my double, my confidante and the best Ouija board partner I ever had. When we set our fingers to the board, the dial raced and spun, flinging out letters— notes from the long dead, the crying out. Together we contacted la Llorona and would have unraveled *that* mystery if Sister Esperidiana hadn't caught us in the religion room during lunchtime communing with that distressed spirit who had so much to tell!

Dolores was engaged. She had a hope chest. She wasn't going to college because she had to work, and her two sisters-in-law, the Nurses González and González—Esperanza, male, and Bertha, female—were her supervisors.

As a favor to Dolores, González the Elder, Esperanza would often give her a left-over tray of "regular" food, the patient having checked out or on to other resting grounds. Usually I'd have gone home after the ritualistic glass of tea but one day, out of boredom perhaps, most likely out of curiosity, I hung around the surgical floor talking to Dolores, my only friend in all the hospital. I clung to her sense of wonder, her sense of the ludicrous, to her humor in the face of order, for even in that environment of restriction, I felt her still probing the whys and wherefores of science, looking for vestiges of irregularity with immense childlike curiosity.

The day of the left-over meal found Dolores and me in the laundry room, sandwiched between bins of feces-and urine-stained sheets to be laundered. There were also dripping urinals waiting to be washed. Hunched over a tray of fried chicken, mashed potatoes and gravy, lima beans and vanilla ice cream, we devoured crusty morsels of Mr. Smith's fried chicken breasts. The food was good. We fought over the ice cream. I resolved to try a few more meals before the summer ended, perhaps in a more pleasant atmosphere.

That day, I lingered at the hospital longer than usual. I helped Dolores with Francisca Pacheco, turning the old woman on her side as we fitted the sheet on the mattress. "Cuidado, no me toquen," she cried. When Dolores took her temperature rectally, I left the room, but returned just as quickly, ashamed of my timidity. I was always the passing menu girl, too afraid to linger, too unwilling to see, too busy with summer illusions. Every day I raced to finish the daily menus, punching in my time card, greeting the beginning of what I considered to be my *real* day outside those long and smelly corridors where food and illness intermingled, leaving a sweet thick air of exasperation in my lungs. The "ooooh" of Elizabeth Rainey's anxious flesh.

The "ay ay ay" of Great Aunt Eutilia's phantom cries awaited me in my father's room. On the wall the portrait of his hero Napoleon hung, shielded by white sheets. The sun was too bright that summer for delicate fading eyes, the heat too oppressive. The blue fan raced to bring freshness to that acrid tomb full of ghosts.

I walked home slowly, not stopping at the quiet place. Compadre Regino Suárez was on the roof. The cooler leaked. Impatient with Regino and his hearty wave, his habit of never doing any job thoroughly, I remembered that I'd forgotten my daily iced tea. The sun was hot. All I wanted was to rest in the cool darkness of my purple room.

The inside of the house smelled of burnt food and lemons. My mother had left something on the stove again. To counteract the burnt smell she'd placed lemons all over the house. Lemons filled ashtrays and bowls, they lay solidly on tables and rested in hot corners. I looked in the direction of Eutilia's room. Quiet. She was sleeping. She'd been dead five years but, still, the room was hers. She was sleeping peacefully. I smelled the cleansing bitterness of lemons.

MRS. DANIELS

When I entered rooms and saw sick, dying women in their forties, I always remembered room 210, Mrs. Daniels, the mother of my cousin's future wife.

Mrs. Daniels usually lay in bed, whimpering like a little dog, moaning to her husband, who always stood nearby, holding her hand, saying softly, "Now, Martha, Martha. The little girl only wants to get your order."

"Send her away, goddammit!"

On those days that Mr. Daniels was absent, Mrs. Daniels whined for me to go away. "Leave me alone, can't you see I'm dying?" she said and looked toward the wall. She looked so pale, sick, near death to me, but somehow I knew, not really having imagined death without the dying, not having felt the outrage and loathing, I knew and saw her outbursts for what they really were: deep hurts, deep distresses. I saw her need to release them, to fling them at others, dribbling pain/anguish/abuse, trickling away those vast torrential feelings of sorrow and hate and fear, letting them fall wherever they would, on whomever they might. I was her white wall. I was her whipping girl upon whom she spilled her darkened ashes. She cried out obscenely to me, sending me reeling from her room, that room of loathing and dread. That room anxious with worms.

Who of us has not heard the angry choked words of crying people, listened, not wanting to hear, then shut our ears, said enough, I don't want to. Who has not seen the fearful tear-streamed faces, known the blank eyes and felt the holding back, and, like smiling thoughtless children, said: "I was in the next room, I couldn't help hearing, I heard, I saw, you didn't know, did you? I know."

We rolled up the pain, assigned it a shelf, placed it in the hardened place, along with a certain self-congratulatory sense of wonder at the world's unfortunates like Mrs. Daniels. We were embarrassed to be alive.

JUAN MARIA/THE NOSE

"Cómo se dice when was the last time you had a bowel movement?" Nurse Luciano asked. She was from Yonkers, a bright newlywed. Erminia, the ward secretary, a tall thin horsey woman with a postured Juárez hairdo of exaggerated sausage ringlets, replied through chapped lips, "Oh, who cares, he's sleeping."

"He's from México, huh?" Luciano said with interest.

"An illegal alien," Rosario retorted. She was Erminia's sister, the superintendent's secretary, with the look of a badly scarred bulldog. She'd stopped by to invite Erminia to join her for lunch.

"So where'd it happen?" Luciano asked.

"At the Guadalajara Bar on Main Street," Erminia answered, moistening her purple lips nervously. It was a habit of hers.

"Hey, I remember when we used to walk home from school. You remember, Rocío?" Dolores asked. "We'd try to throw each other through the swinging doors. It was real noisy in there."

"Father O'Kelley said drink was the defilement of men, the undoing of staunch, god-fearing women," I said.

"Our father has one now and then," Rosario replied, "that doesn't mean anything. It's because he was one of those aliens."

"Those kind of problems are bad around here I heard," Luciano said, "people sneaking across the border and all."

"Hell, you don't know the half of it," Nurse González said as she came up to the desk where we all stood facing the hallway. "It's an epidemic."

"I don't know, my mother always had maids, and they were all real nice except the one who stole her wedding rings. We had to track her all the way to Piedras Negras and even then she wouldn't give them up," Erminia interjected.

"Still, it doesn't seem human the way they're treated at times."

"Some of them, they ain't human."

"Still, he was drunk, he wasn't full aware."

"Full aware, my ass," retorted Esperanza angrily, "he had enough money to buy booze. If that's not aware, I don't know what aware is. Ain't my goddam fault the bastard got into a fight and someone bit his nose off. Ain't *my* fault he's here and *we* gotta take care of him. Christ! If *that* isn't aware, I don't know what aware is!"

Esperanza González, head surgical floor nurse, the short but highly respected Esperanza of no esperanzas, the Esperanza of the short-bobbed hair, the husky deferential voice, the commands, the no-nonsense orders and briskness, Esperanza the future sister-in-law of Dolores, my only friend, Esperanza the dyke, who was later killed in a car accident on the way to somewhere, said: "Now get back to work all of you, we're just here to clean up the mess."

Later when Esperanza was killed my aunt said, "How nice. In the paper they called her lover her sister. How nice!"

"Hey, Erminia, lunch?" asked Rosario, almost sheepishly. "You hungry?"

"Coming, Rosario," yelled Erminia from the back office where she was getting her purse. "Coming!"

"God, I'm starving," Rosario said, "can you hear my stomach?"

"Go check Mr. Carter's cath, Dolores, will you?" said Esperanza in a softer tone.

"Well, I don't know, I just don't know," Luciano pondered. "It doesn't seem human, does it? I mean how in the world could anyone in their right mind bite off another person's nose? How? You know it, González, you're a tough rooster. If I didn't know you so well already, you'd scare the hell out of me. How long you been a nurse?"

"Too long, Luciano. Look, I ain't a new bride, that's liable to make a person soft. Me, I just clean up the mess."

"Luciano, what you know about people could be put on the head of a pin. You just leave these alien problems to those of us who were brought up around here and know what's going on. Me, I don't feel one bit sorry for that bastard," Esperanza said firmly. "Christ, Luciano, what do you expect, he don't speak no Engleesh!"

"His name is Juan María Mejía," I ventured.

Luciano laughed. Esperanza laughed. Dolores went off to Mrs. Carter's room, and Rosario chatted noisily with Erminia as they walked toward the cafeteria.

"Hey, Rosario," Luciano called out, "what happened to the rings?"

It was enchilada day. Trini was very busy.

Juan María the Nose was sleeping in the hallway; all the other beds were filled. His hospital gown was awry, the grey sheet folded through sleep-deadened limbs. His hands were tightly clenched. The hospital screen barely concealed his twisted private sleep of legs akimbo, moist armpits and groin. It was a sleep of sleeping off, of hard drunken wanderings, with dreams of a bar, dreams of a fight. He slept the way little boys sleep, carelessly half exposed. I stared at him.

Esperanza complained and muttered under her breath, railing at the Anglo sons of bitches and at all the lousy wetbacks, at everyone, male and female, goddamn them and their messes. Esperanza was dark and squat, pura india, tortured by her very face. Briskly, she ordered Dolores and now me about. I had graduated overnight, as if in a hazy dream, to assistant, but unofficial, ward secretary.

I stared across the hallway to Juan Maria the Nose. He faced the wall, a dangling I.V. at the foot of the bed. Esperanza Gońzález, R.N., looked at me.

"Well, and *who* are you?"

"I'm the menu, I mean, I *was* the menu . . ." stammered. "I'm helping Erminia."

"So get me some cigarettes. Camels. I'll pay you tomorrow when I get paid."

Yes, it was really González, male, who ran the hospital.

Arlene returned from the Luray Caverns with a stalactite charm bracelet for me. She announced to Mr. Smith and me that she'd gotten a job with an insurance company.

"I'll miss you, Rocío."

"Me, too, Arlene." God knows it was the truth. I'd come to depend on her, our talks over tea. No one ever complimented me like she did.

"You never get angry, do you?" she said admiringly.

"Rarely," I said. But inside, I was always angry.

"What do you want to do?"

"Want to do?"

"Yeah."

I want to be someone else, somewhere else, someone important and responsible and sexy. I want to be sexy.

"I don't know. I'm going to major in drama."

"You're sweet," she said. "Everyone likes you. It's in your nature. You're the Florence Nightingale of Altavista Memorial, that's it!"

"Oh God, Arlene, I don't want to be a nurse, *ever!* I can't take the smells. No one in our family can stand smells."

"You look like that painting. I always did think it looked like you . . ."

"You did?"

"Yeah."

"Come on, you're making me sick, Arlene."

"Everyone likes you."

"Well . . ."

"So keep in touch. I'll see you at the University."

"Home Ec?"

"Biology."

We hugged.

The weeks progressed. My hours at the hospital grew. I was allowed to check in patients, to take their blood pressures and temperatures. I flipped through the patients' charts, memorizing names, room numbers, types of diet. I fingered the doctors' reports with reverence. Perhaps someday I would begin to write in them as Erminia did: "2:15 P.M., Mrs. Daniels, pulse normal, temp normal, Dr. Blasse checked patient, treatment on schedule, medication given to quiet patient."

One day I received a call at the ward desk. It was Mr. Smith.

"Ms. Esquibel? Rocío? This is Mr. Smith, you know, down in the cafeteria."

"Yes, Mr. Smith! How are you? Is there anything I can do? Are you getting the menus okay? I'm leaving them on top of your desk."

"I've been talking to Nurse González, surgical; she says they need you there full time to fill in and could I do without you?"

"Oh, I can do both jobs; it doesn't take that long, Mr. Smith."

"No, we're going by a new system. Rather, it's the old system. The aides will take the menu orders like they used to before Arlene came. So, you come down and see me, Rocío, have a glass of iced tea. I never see you any more since you moved up in the world. Yeah, I guess you're the last of the menu girls."

The summer passed. June, July, August, my birth month. There were serious days, hurried admissions, feverish errands, quick notes jotted in the doctor's charts. I began to work Saturdays. In my eagerness to "advance," I unwittingly had created more work for myself, work I really wasn't skilled to do.

My heart reached out to every person, dragged itself through the hallways with the patients, cried when they did, laughed when they did. I had no business in the job. I was too emotional.

Now when I walked into a room I knew the patient's history, the cause of illness. I began to study individual cases with great attention, turning to a copy of *The Family Physician*, which had its place among my father's old books in his abandoned study.

Gone were the idle hours of sitting in the cafeteria, leisurely drinking iced tea, gone were the removed reflections of the outsider.

My walks home were measured, pensive. I hid in my room those long hot nights, nights full of wrestling, injured dreams. Nothing seemed enough.

Before I knew it, it was the end of August, close to that autumnal time of setting out. My new life was about to begin. I had made that awesome leap into myself that steamy summer of illness and dread—confronting at every turn, the flesh, its lingering cries.

"Ay, Ay, Ay, Ay, Canta y no llores! Porque cantando se alegran, Cielito Lindo, los corazones . . ." The little thin voice of an old woman sang from one of the back rooms. She pumped the gold pedals with fast furious and fervent feet, she smiled to the wall, its faces, she danced on the ceiling.

Let me jump.

"Goodbye, Dolores, it was fun."

"I'll miss you, Rocío! But you know, gotta save some money. I'll get back to school someday, maybe."

"What's wrong, Erminia? You mad?" I asked.

"I thought you were gonna stay and help me out here on the floor."

"Goddamn right!" complained Esperanza. "Someone told me this was your last day, so why didn't you tell me? Why'd I train you for, so you could leave us? To go to school? What for? So you can get those damned food stamps? It's a disgrace all those wetbacks and healthy college students getting our hard-earned tax money. Makes me sick. Christ!" Esperanza shook her head with disgust.

"Hey, Erminia, you tell Rosario goodbye for me and Mrs. Luciano, too," I said sadly.

"Yeah, okay. They'll be here tomorrow," she answered tonelessly. I wanted to believe she was sad.

"I gotta say goodbye to Mr. Smith," I said, as I moved away.

"Make him come up and get some sun," González snickered. "Hell no, better not, he might get sunstroke and who'd fix my fried chicken?"

I climbed down the steps to the basement, past the cafeteria, past my special table, and into Mr. Smith's office, where he sat, adding numbers.

"Miss Esquibel, Rocío!"

"This is my last day, Mr. Smith. I wanted to come down and thank you."

"I'm sorry about . . ."

"Oh no, it worked out all right. It's nothing."

Did I see, from the corner of my eye, a set of Friday's menus he himself was tabulating—Salisbury steak, macaroni and cheese . . .

"We'll miss you, Rocío. You were an excellent menu girl."

"It's been a wonderful summer."

"Do you want some tea?"

"No, I really don't have the time."

"I'll get . . ."

"No, thank you, Mr. Smith, I *really* have to go, but thanks. It's really good tea."

I extended my hand, and for the first time, we touched. Mr. Smith's eyes seemed fogged, distracted. He stood up and hobbled closer to my side. I took his grave cold hand, shook it softly, and turned to the moist walls. When I closed the door, I saw him in front of me, framed in paper, the darkness of that quiet room. Bless this mess.

Eutilia's voice echoed in the small room. Goodbye. Goodbye. And let me jump.

I turned away from the faces, the voices, now gone: Father O'Kelley, Elizabeth Rainey, Mrs. Luciano, Arlene Rutschman, Mrs. Daniels, Juan María the Nose, Mr. Samaniego and Donelda, his wife, their grandchildren, Mr. Carter, Earl Ellis, Dolores Casaus, Erminia and her sister, the bulldog. Esperanza González, Francisca Pacheco, Elweena Twinbaum, the silver-haired volunteer whose name I'd learned the week before I left Altavista Memorial. I'd made a list on a menu of all the people I'd worked with. To remember. It seemed right.

From the distance I heard Marion Smith's high voice: "Now you come back and see us!"

Above the stairs the painting of Florence Nightingale stared solidly into weary soldiers' eyes. Her look encompassed all the great unspeakable sufferings of every war. I thought of Arlene typing insurance premiums.

Farther away, from behind and around my head, I heard the irregular but joyful strains of "Cielito Lindo" played on a phantom piano by a disembodied but now peaceful voice that sang with great quivering emotion: De la sierra morena. Cielito Lindo . . . viene bajando . . .

Regino fixed the cooler. I started school. Later that year I was in a car accident. I crashed into a brick wall at the cemetery. I walked to Dolores' house, holding my bleeding face in my hands. Dolores and her father argued all the way to the hospital. I sat quietly in the back seat. It was a lovely morning. So clear. When I woke up I was on the surgical floor. Everyone knew me. I had so many flowers in the room I could hardly breathe. My older sister, Ronelia, thought I'd lost part of my nose in the accident and she returned to the cemetery to look for it. It wasn't there.

Mr. Smith came to see me once. I started to cry.

"Oh no, no, no, now don't you do that, Rocío. You want some tea?"

No one took my menu order. I guess that system had finally died out. I ate the food, whatever it was, walked the hallways in my gray hospital gown slit in the back, railed at the well-being of others, cursed myself for being so stupid. I only wanted to be taken home, down the street, past the quiet-talking place, a block away, near the Dairy Queen, to the darkness of my purple room.

It was time.

PREVIOUS EMPLOYMENT: Altavista Memorial Hospital
SUPERVISORS: Mr. Marion Smith, Dietician, and Miss Esperanza Gon-
zález, R.N., Surgical Floor.
DATES: June 1966 to August 1966
IN A FEW SENTENCES GIVE A BRIEF DESCRIPTION OF YOUR JOB: As Ward
Secretary, I was responsible for . . . let me think . . .

MAY SWENSON

ogan, Utah, in the 1920s and '30s was perhaps the quintessential Mormon village, in some ways a holdover from the century before. Wide, Norway-maple-lined streets, arranged in squares according to the Mormon plan, their gutters running with irrigation water; the town center surrounded by pastures, themselves bordered by what Wallace Stegner affectionately called "Mormon Trees"—Lombardy poplars. Shopkeepers along Main Street came out in the early morning and hosed down the sidewalks in front of their businesses. On a shoreline-bench of ancient Lake Bonneville stood the Mormon temple; on a slightly higher bench, the Utah State Agricultural College, where May Swenson's father taught. There was a quiet, removed, almost Brigadoon-like coherence to the place, something now quite gone from the West and America. May Swenson (1913–1989) naturally went to the home school, up the hill a half-block to campus, worked on the student literary magazine, and sometime in those years caught the poetic fire. A few years after graduation, she went to New York and for the rest of her life supported herself modestly by a succession of clerical and editorial jobs, devoting her real, deepest energy to her poems. Her work is marked by psychological insight, language play, intense attention to nature (she was a studious bird-watcher), and a strong, home-remembering sense of self and family.

"The Centaur," from *A Cage of Spines* (1958)

The summer that I was ten—
Can it be there was only one
summer that I was ten? It must

have been a long one then—
each day I'd go out to choose
a fresh horse from my stable

which was a willow grove
down by the old canal.
I'd go on my two bare feet.

But when, with my brother's jack-knife,
I had cut me a long limber horse
with a good thick knob for a head,

and peeled him slick and clean
except a few leaves for the tail,
and cinched my brother's belt

around his head for a rein,
I'd straddle and canter him fast
up the grass bank to the path,

trot along in the lovely dust
that talcumed over his hoofs,
hiding my toes, and turning

his feet to swift half-moons.
The willow knob with the strap
jouncing between my thighs

was the pommel and yet the poll
of my nickering pony's head.
My head and my neck were mine,

yet they were shaped like a horse.
My hair flopped to the side
like the mane of a horse in the wind.

My forelock swung in my eyes,
My neck arched and I snorted.
I shied and skittered and reared,

stopped and raised my knees,
pawed at the ground and quivered.
My teeth bared as we wheeled

and swished through the dust again.
I was the horse and the rider,
and the leather I slapped to his rump

spanked my own behind.
Doubled, my two hoofs beat
a gallop along the bank,

the wind twanged in my mane,
my mouth squared to the bit.
And yet I sat on my steed

quiet, negligent riding,
my toes standing the stirrups,
my thighs hugging his ribs.

At a walk we drew up to the porch.
I tethered him to a paling.
Dismounting, I smoothed my skirt

and entered the dusky hall.
My feet on the clean linoleum
left ghostly toes in the hall.

Where have you been? said my mother.
Been riding, I said from the sink,
and filled me a glass of water.

What's that in your pocket? she said.
Just my knife. It weighted my pocket
and stretched my dress awry.

Go tie back your hair, said my mother,
and *Why is your mouth all green?*
*Rob Roy, he pulled some clover
as we crossed the field,* I told her.

"The Poplar's Shadow," from *A Cage of Spines* (1958)

When I was little, when
the poplar was in leaf,
its shadow made a sheaf,
the quill of a great pen
dark upon the lawn
where I used to play.

Grown, and long away
into the city gone,
I see the pigeons print
a loop in air and, all
their wings reversing, fall
with silver undertint
like poplar leaves, their seams
in the wind blown.

Time's other side, shown
as a flipped coin, gleams
on city ground
when I see a pigeon's feather:
little and large together,
the poplar's shadow is found.

Staring at here,
and superposing then,
I wait for when.
What shapes will appear?
Will great birds swing
over me like gongs?
The poplar plume belongs
to what enormous wing?

"Camping in Madera Canyon," from *Nature: Poems Old and New* (1994)

We put up our tent while the dark closed in
and thickened, the road a black trough
winding the mountain down. Leaving the lantern
ready to light on the stone table,
we took our walk. The sky was a bloom
of sharp-petaled stars.

Walls of the woods, opaque and still,
gave no light or breath or echo, until,
faint and far, a string of small toots—
nine descending notes—the whiskered owl's
signal. A tense pause . . . then, his mate's
identical reply.

At the canyon's foot, we turned,
climbed back to camp, between tall walls
of silent dark. Snugged deep into our sacks,
so only noses felt the mountain chill,
we heard the owls once more. Farther from us,
but closer to each other. The pause, that linked
his motion with her seconding, grew longer
as we drowsed. Then, expectation frayed,
we forgot to listen, slept.

In a tent, first light tickles the skin
like a straw. Still freezing cold out there,
but we in our pouches sense the immense
volcano, sun, about to pour
gold lava over the mountain, upon us.
Wriggling out, we sleepily unhinge,

make scalding coffee, shivering, stand and sip;
tin rims burn our lips.

Daybirds wake, the woods are filling
with their rehearsal flutes and pluckings,
buzzes, scales and trills. Binoculars
dangling from our necks, we walk
down the morning road. Rooms of the woods
stand open. Glittering trunks
rise to a limitless loft of blue. New snow,
a delicate rebozo, drapes the peak that,
last night, stooped in heavy shadow.

Night hid this day. What sunrise may it be
the dark to? What wider light ripens to dawn
behind familiar light? As by encircling arms
our backs are warmed by the blessing sun,
all is revealed and brought to feature.
All but the owls. The Apaches believe
them ghosts of ancestors, who build their nests
of light with straws pulled from the sun.

The whiskered owls are here, close by,
in the tops of the pines, invisible and radiant,
as we, blind and numb, awaken—our just-born
eyes and ears, our feet that walk—
as brightness bathes the road.

CHARLES BOWDEN

Until Edward Abbey, American writing about nature (Thoreau excepted) was so earnest and plain that it was commonly left out of consideration as literature. Abbey's knowing wit, along with his digs at the genre itself, helped personalize nature writing and make it more interesting to sophisticated readers and critics. Now it is common for nature writers to project a literary identity and tell a personal story, and if natural-history exposition gets into the narrative, so much the better. One of the Arizonan Charles Bowden's (b. 1945?) contributions is his self-characterization along hard-boiled, Raymond Chandler–reminiscent lines, absolutely appropriate to the Sunbelt disarray he describes. As the area's population balloons, the water table drops precipitously (see Bowden's *Killing the Hidden Waters*, 1977), the scarce species head toward extinction, simple space and naturalness become rarer and rarer, pollution spreads both above and below ground, and the streets of once-mellow cities can become mean indeed. It takes an experienced journalist's eyes to look unblinkingly at all this, and an American idealist's heart to sustain passionate caring. Charles Bowden has stuck by his place in its travail. Of his twelve books, many, as he says, "are about the Southwest, or what is left of it." Frog Mountain is an Indian name for the massif just north of Tucson.

"Afterword," from *Frog Mountain Blues* (1987)

A couple of years after the publication of this book, I was asked to appear at a Forest Service hearing to discuss the merits of expanding a ski development in the Santa Catalina Mountains. Being a true believer in democracy and a child trained on Tom Paine and the Whisky Rebellion, I naturally attended this meeting. A local environmental organization had instigated my invitation under the mistaken notion that I knew the mountain. No one knows the mountain, and no one ever will. That is why I wrote a book about the range and why you read it. But we are all hungry to know a little more of the brooding rock pile we call the Catalinas because we need, to borrow that wonderful phrase of F. Scott Fitzgerald's, something commensurate with our capacity for wonder.

The brute facts of the hearing were simple: the ski development had existed on the mountain for decades, had never been planned, had grown willy-nilly by little increments and was now considered a given. In short, it typified our policies in the national forests and on all the other ground under our dominion. A couple of hundred people filled the auditorium—most of them waffle-stomping tree-huggers, but there was also a healthy contingent speaking for the life-sustaining powers of decent cognac, the spiritual value of fires in the ski lodge, the necessity of lycra clothing, the biological imperative of fornication in alpine chalets, and the importance of riding boards downhill on snow.

I was ushered up on the stage, where I sat with a SWAT team of Forest Service minions in civilian dress and bereft of their comical hats. The issue at hand was rather simple: whether to cut down some Douglas firs that were older than the European conquest of the Western Hemisphere in order to make yet one more ski run on the mountain. As I chatted with the earnest foresters, it soon became apparent to me that in their eyes the merits of this silvicide were beyond question. I had come armed with a quote by John Steinbeck, one plucked from his sad and yet joyous book, *The Log of the Sea of Cortez*. It was, I hoped, my silver bullet to slay the dragons of federal power. As I sat there bantering with the federal officials (who looked upon me as their long-lost pit bull), I glanced through my arsenal:

> Other animals may dig holes to live in; may weave nests or take possession of hollow trees. . . . They make little impression on the world. But the world is furrowed and cut, torn and blasted by man. Its flora has been swept away and changed; its mountains torn down by man; its flat lands littered by the debris of his living. . . . Physiological man does not require this paraphernalia to exist, but the whole man does. He is the only animal who lives outside of himself, whose drive is in external things—property, houses, money, concepts of power. . . . His house, his automobile are a part of him and a large part of him. This is beautifully demonstrated by a thing doctors know—that when a man loses his possessions a very common result is sexual impotence.
>
> Perhaps, it is all a part of the process of mutation and perhaps the mutation will see us done for. We have made our mark on the world, but we have really done nothing that the trees and creeping plants, ice and erosion, cannot remove in a fairly short time.

I suddenly realized that I had brought insufficient weaponry for the encounter. I was underarmed not because I faced crafty government warriors or savage downhill racers but because I was confronting a mind-set that was such a commonplace that anything I might say would appear at best insane, at worst the product of an illegal smile. I listened to official after official report on the proposed ski run, and they all pretty much said what I expected: the whacking of some big trees would have no effect on the mountain, or if it had any effect, it would be a good one. Though I am not noted as a psychic, I had slyly anticipated this line of reasoning.

When it comes to tinkering with the natural world, the defense underlying all proposed changes is simply that they will actually change nothing. It does not matter whether the instruments of our pleasure are chainsaws, dams, highways, toxic waste dumps, or houses. I had had a crash course in this Things Just Get Better and Better syndrome shortly after the publication of this book.

The book's tender and moderate thesis had been to blow up the only paved highway leading into the mountain and then leave the mountain alone to heal. The Forest Service, ever keen for public input, had taken heed of my thoughts and had enlarged the existing highway. They named a new lookout (complete with parking for our machines) Babat Toak, Frog Mountain. In addition to this contribution to the commonweal, the Forest Service in the ensuing years had seen to it that more trees had been cut, visitor usage had increased (can't stop people from coming, I'm told), key wildlife had wavered or declined, and the normal patterns of our vaunted stewardship had continued apace.

Eventually, my turn to speak came, and I will (to use the current namby-pamby usage) share with you what I said on that occasion:

I suspect my ideas here tonight will be dismissed by the Forest Service as simplistic, unrealistic, and some other icks. In fact, I'll save them the time and deliver the critique myself: I'll be told that the increasing numbers of people dictate more intensive use of the ski run area. Well, if numbers are the game, why not level the forest and put in a crack park or a casino?

And surely I'll be told about trade-offs—you give up this and get that. Trade-off has a crazed ring to me. It always sounds like the canyon that has been gutted, the stream polluted, or the tree that has been killed has actually just been traded off and is now happily playing Triple A ball for some team in San Diego.

Then there will be the argument of historic use—a rhetorical device that was a favorite of antebellum slaveholders. You'd think Father Eusebio Kino, S. J., had set up the lodge and was a downhill racer. Actually, the ski development was an idea in the forties and a fact in the fifties, and let's face it, it has turned out to be a less-than-great idea.

And then there will be the charge of elitism—I'm kind of curious how you bring this one into play to defend a downhill ski resort.

I suspect there will be charts, cost-benefit analyses, and a kind of bar tab toting up recreational user days. Where do they file recreational user nights—under wildlife?

Land of Many Uses is the slogan of the Forest Service. But so far as I can see, there is actually only one use: anything goes for one species, human beings. The picnic areas are not for the squirrels. The highway is not for the deer. The radio towers and observatories are not for the birds. The cabins in Summerhaven are not for the benefit of the creek. And the ski runs, ski lift, proposed alpine slide, maintenance building, parking lot, and observation deck (I always thought the Santa Catalina Mountains themselves were a pretty dandy observation deck)—well, none of these things are going to benefit the trees killed to make room for them. When black bears dropped in at the cabin slums of Summerhaven a while back, it became a problem story in the newspapers. What kind of national forest are we running where the existence of black bears is a problem and the existence of a bunch of cabins, ski runs, and a lodge is not?

It's hard for me not to wonder if I'm going a little insane or maybe still having afterflashes from my chemical indulgences in the sixties. When I was a kid my dad told me there would be hard times, but he never warned me I'd be dealing with a Forest Service that wondered whether parking lots, observation decks, and alpine slides were more important than the forest itself. Just why are we here tonight talking about ski runs on a mountain with little snow? Why are we considering expanding a ski resort by cutting down ancient trees in something we call a national forest? Did I miss something? Or should we just rename it the Coronado National Ski Run, or the Coronado National Cabin Center, or the Coronado National Lodge Saloon? Or the Coronado National Highway Department?

The Forest Service has been around a long time, and I'm sure that back in the days of Teddy Roosevelt I would have thought it was a great thing with a great mission. But now I think the agency needs somebody with a little bigger vision, someone who can sense that times are changing, a kind of Gandhi or Crazy Horse. If a bunch of Cold Warriors in the United States and the Soviet Union can change their ways and disarm their missiles and stop laying up kegs of poison gas in the cellar like fine wines, surely the Forest Service can change its concept of mission from being dedicated to the single use of the ground by Homo sapiens and start dealing with the things that actually live in the forest. We need true multiple use. A plan for use by the trees, by the spotted owls, the warblers. The black bear. The rocks. Especially the rocks.

We need to begin decommissioning things in the forest, just like we mothball and scuttle warships when peace arrives. Stopping this proposed ski run is a tiny first step, but with practice we can finally learn how to walk without falling on our faces. Little children learn to walk all the time—I've actually seen this happen. Look, I'll leave you with a simple rule that will make all these questions easy: Any proposal for a national forest that means there will be less national forest still standing in the end is a bad idea.

I realize now that, as is often the case in my efforts, I had given in to my besetting sin and was far too moderate that night. In fact, when I finished speaking and sat down to what I might modestly record as thunderous applause, the federal official next to me muttered, "You pandered to the audience." And I courteously replied, "You can bet your ass on that." I now agree with that official: I had pandered to the mob, and the time is past for pandering. The hour is growing late on this ball of dirt we call home, and I vow to cease to be The Panderer and to become The Rude Boy.

When I wrote *Frog Mountain Blues* I believed that if one taught people how to love something, they would become better people and better lovers. I still think this is true. After all, I have seen grown men and women love each other, and it is a very pretty sight. But I now know this goal is not sufficient. In the case of Frog Mountain and our national forests, we must become, alas, celibate lovers. It all goes to the heart of the Forest Service idea of multiple use, a vision that must have been constructed by a pimp, a madam, or some other kind of professional consultant. I'll spell out what this concept really means. The Forest Service hosts orgies, and because it must satisfy diverse appetites in our culture, it plans for all tastes: we have a room for those who like whips, a place for the leather freaks, a venue for those who have fetishes of the foot and whatnot, an arena for those who crave them at an unseemly young age, and so forth. Under the mask of language, we call these depraved habits mining, cattle raising, lumbering, hunting, fishing, and on and on. But just for an instant imagine you are a rock or a tree or a flower or an animal or soil. What does multiple use look like then? Well, it looks like a scheme for allowing Homo sapiens to have you in different ways. And when you have been had, it is not likely that you are going to be particularly grateful.

Besides, this ongoing federal orgy is not working. We are now bedeviled by a national debate over the cutting of old-growth forest, a debate that ignores the real point. What is old-growth forest? It is the forest that the Forest Service has never managed. It is the stuff that precedes our presence and our actions. It is natural. And if, after a century of silviculture, multiple use, and brilliant management of the national forests, we are finally coming with sharpened fangs for these shreds of old growth, it means we have failed by every criteria we can imagine. We want the old growth because our policy of cutting trees and then replanting the forests has not worked. If it had, why would we need to murder the old growth, the one part of the forest that owes nothing to our genius? If our management of the forests were sound, why do we have to reintroduce California condors? In fact, if we knew what we were doing in the forests, why are they filled with endangered species? If the Forest Service had been employed by what we call the private sector, it would have been given its pink slip long ago.

The obvious conclusion to this litany of failure is that we do not know what we are doing. Don't feel bad about this fact; no sane man or woman actually thinks he or she can understand an ecosystem, much less run one. I've been told this by foresters, wildlife biologists, and other toilers in the natural world. In fact, to introduce a bright note, there is a quiet revolt going on in our federal agencies. The old timber bulls, who looked at a tree and saw lumber or counted wildlife and babbled about harvesting them, are being replaced by men and women who think of ecosystems as intricate wholes, who are humble about their knowledge, ravenous to learn more, and restrained in their appetites. These new men and women will run our federal lands in the near future, and for that fact we should thank the Lord. However, like my former self, they tend to fall prey to the sin of moderation, and I wish to lead them from this crooked way to the straight and narrow path that winds upward toward salvation. I will be their Chuck the Baptist and briefly sketch a new, modest, and conservative program that will save our immortal souls and possibly some trees, animals, and plants: It is time, at the very least, to leave our national forests alone. Zero cutting for a generation or two or three. No more damn roads. Good-bye to the cows. Forget mining. Kiss *adiós* to the 4 × 4s, dirt bikes, Skidoos, and other hellcats. And if we need to commune with nature with our backpacks, binoculars, and rifles, why don't we create more nature instead of sacking what little has survived our tender mercies? If this creates unemployment, so be it. When a war ends, the soldiers have to find some other form of fun. The war against our forests must cease, and we must seek other ways of living our lives. Genocide, though a nifty blood sport, never promises a future. After all, the Romans eventually learned how to get through the day without feeding a few Christians to the lions. I'm sure that at first they missed the chomping of jaws, the blood running down the tawny chins, the tongues lapping, and the screams of horror, but they eventually detoxed from their thrills.

Frog Mountain is but a little fragment of our failure, and this failure is now a sin because we actually know better. Frog Mountain can be a little fragment of our penance and perhaps in time our new virtue. We are living in a time of global destruction, and we all know it. We all shrug and say, What can be done? It's too big for anyone to deal with. Well, I'll tell you what can be done. We will right this catastrophe one mountain at a time, one canyon at a time, one hill at a time. And we can begin with the Frog Mountains just outside all our doors, sierras that stare down to our actions in disbelief. We will cease to be moderate. We will say, "Nunca más. Never again." We will become conservative, and like all good conservatives, we will conserve. Every day at sundown we will make sure that we have added a little bit more life to the planet. We will literally expand the earth by letting other living things have a piece of it.

And if we do this, our hearts will sing, our sleep will be dreamless and full of joy. At the dawn our bodies will quicken, and Frog Mountain and her numerous global kin will look down upon us and no longer shudder.

Don't tell me this is impossible. I'll tell you what is really impossible: that we can continue to live and act the way we have in the past. Believe me, the problem is not that some spotted owl will perish or that ancient trees will die. The problem is that we will start dying in a big and clumsy way. We have already, I suspect, lost our souls. Next we will lose our lives. I'm an optimist. I believe our souls can be beckoned back and will once again inhabit our bodies. I keep a candle burning every day and every night of the year. I believe we can actually learn to live and let live. In fact, I know it. A bird told me so.

A person's life purpose is nothing more than to rediscover, through detours of art, or love, or passionate work, those one or two images in the presence of which his heart first opened.

—ALBERT CAMUS

I am by heritage half German. This is not a problem for me so long as I avoid the cooking, although I do have a weakness for parsnips, sauerkraut, and blutwurst. But long before I could ever scribble this page I vowed one very simple thing: I would never be a "good German," closing my eyes to the destruction. Never. I will always know the darkness on the edge of town, I will not deny this knowledge, and I will act on this knowledge or the gods may damn me to all their hells with my consent.

There is another matter I would like to dispatch swiftly: Don't ask me what's in it for you. We have been seduced by the bogus notion that self-interest is the only interesting thing, an idea that every faith denounces and mocks. You are going to die, I am going to die, and everything on the mountain is going to die. I don't know the master plan; they will not tell me. But I am certain that if we ask what's in it for us, we will never understand the answer when we are told. Not even if the message comes in words of one syllable, not even if the message comes in the fist of a storm or in the song of a stream.

It is time for you and me to set aside our childish ways. We have some years on us now, and all Homo sapiens, it is said, become conservative with time. So let's all get out of the closet and show the world what the conscience of a conservative really looks like. It will be painful standing suddenly in the glare of the sun, but it will be a new and beautiful sight. We will like it. And for the first time in a long time, we will be liked. Perhaps even loved.

AMY TAN

A my Tan (b. 1952) determined to try fiction writing, along with jazz piano lessons, as relief when in the 1980s her work as a freelance technical writer ballooned to some ninety hours per week. Her first work of fiction was a national bestseller.

The Joy Luck Club deals with complex challenges for coming through into maturity, in these trials ethnicity puts a special twist on the usual human, generational difficulties. Amy Tan, whose mother was a member of a Joy Luck Club, has affinity for minority characters with ambivalence about their family backgrounds, and in The Joy Luck Club and The Kitchen God's Wife (1991) presents young women whose search to "find" and understand their mothers, over the terrain of immigrant circumstances, becomes eventually a path to personal integration and self-understanding. She has said that writing The Joy Luck Club showed her "how very Chinese I was. And how much had stayed with me that I had tried to deny." The author Michael Dorris, himself no stranger to the perplexities of ethnic life and identity, wrote that The Joy Luck Club is the sort of book that "makes a difference, that alters the way we understand the world and ourselves. . . ."

"Rules of the Game," from *The Joy Luck Club* (1989)

I was six when my mother taught me the art of invisible strength. It was a strategy for winning arguments, respect from others, and eventually, though neither of us knew it at the time, chess games.

"Bite back your tongue," scolded my mother when I cried loudly, yanking her hand toward the store that sold bags of salted plums. At home, she said, "Wise guy, he not go against wind. In Chinese we say, Come from South, blow with wind—poom!—North will follow. Strongest wind cannot be seen."

The next week I bit back my tongue as we entered the store with the forbidden candies. When my mother finished her shopping, she quietly plucked a small bag of plums from the rack and put it on the counter with the rest of the items.

My mother imparted her daily truths so she could help my older brothers and me rise above our circumstances. We lived in San Francisco's Chinatown. Like most of the other Chinese children who played in the back alleys of restaurants and curio shops, I didn't think we were poor. My bowl was always full, three five-course meals every day, beginning with a soup full of mysterious things I didn't want to know the names of.

We lived on Waverly Place, in a warm, clean, two-bedroom flat that sat above a small Chinese bakery specializing in steamed pastries and dim sum. In the early morning, when the alley was still quiet, I could smell fragrant red beans as they were cooked down to a pasty sweetness. By daybreak, our flat was heavy with the odor of fried sesame balls and sweet curried chicken crescents. From my bed, I would listen as my father got ready for work, then locked the door behind him, one-two-three clicks.

At the end of our two-block alley was a small sandlot play-ground with swings and slides well-shined down the middle with use. The play area was bordered by wood-slat benches where old-country people sat cracking roasted watermelon seeds with their golden teeth and scattering the husks to an impatient gathering of gurgling pigeons. The best play-ground, however, was the dark alley itself. It was crammed with daily mysteries and adventures. My brothers and I would peer into the medicinal herb shop, watching old Li dole out onto a stiff sheet of white paper the right amount of insect shells, saffron-colored seeds, and pungent leaves for his ailing customers. It was said that he once cured a woman dying of an ancestral curse that had eluded the best of American doctors. Next to the pharmacy was a printer who specialized in gold-embossed wedding invitations and festive red banners.

Farther down the street was Ping Yuen Fish Market. The front window displayed a tank crowded with doomed fish and turtles struggling to gain footing on the slimy green-tiled sides. A hand-written sign informed tourists, "Within this store, is all for food, not for pet." Inside, the butchers with their blood-stained white smocks deftly gutted the fish while customers cried out their orders and shouted, "Give me your freshest," to which the butchers always protested, "All are freshest." On less crowded market days, we would inspect the crates of live frogs and crabs which we were warned not to poke, boxes of dried cuttlefish, and row upon row of iced prawns, squid, and slippery fish. The sanddabs made me shiver each time; their eyes lay on one flattened side and reminded me of my mother's story of a careless girl who ran into a crowded street and was crushed by a cab. "Was smash flat," reported my mother.

At the corner of the alley was Hong Sing's, a four-table café with a recessed stairwell in front that led to a door marked "Tradesmen." My brothers and I believed the bad people emerged from this door at night. Tourists never went to Hong Sing's, since the menu was printed only in Chinese. A Caucasian man with a big camera once posed me and my playmates in front of the restaurant. He had us move to the side of the picture window so the photo would capture the roasted duck with its head dangling from a juice-covered rope. After he took the picture, I told him he should go into Hong Sing's and eat dinner. When he smiled and asked me what they served, I shouted, "Guts and duck's feet and octopus gizzards!" Then I ran off with my friends, shrieking with laughter as we scampered across the alley and hid in the entryway grotto of the China Gem Company, my heart pounding with hope that he would chase us.

My mother named me after the street that we lived on: Waverly Place Jong, my official name for important American documents. But my family called me Meimei, "Little Sister." I was the youngest, the only daughter. Each morning before school, my mother would twist and yank on my thick black hair until she had formed two tightly wound pigtails. One day, as she struggled to weave a hard-toothed comb through my diso-bedient hair, I had a sly thought.

I asked her, "Ma, what is Chinese torture?" My mother shook her head. A bobby pin was wedged between her lips. She wetted her palm and smoothed the hair above my ear, then pushed the pin in so that it nicked sharply against my scalp.

"Who say this word?" she asked without a trace of knowing how wicked I was being. I shrugged my shoulders and said, "Some boy in my class said Chinese people do Chinese torture."

"Chinese people do many things," she said simply. "Chinese people do business, do medicine, do painting. Not lazy like American people. We do torture. Best torture."

My older brother Vincent was the one who actually got the chess set. We had gone to the annual Christmas party held at the First Chinese Baptist Church at the end of the alley. The missionary ladies had put together a Santa bag of gifts donated by members of another church. None of the gifts had names on them. There were separate sacks for boys and girls of different ages.

One of the Chinese parishioners had donned a Santa Claus costume and a stiff paper beard with cotton balls glued to it. I think the only children who thought he was the real thing were too young to know that Santa Claus was not Chinese. When my turn came up, the Santa man asked me how old I was. I thought it was a trick question; I was seven according to the American formula and eight by the Chinese calendar. I said I was born on March 17, 1951. That seemed to satisfy him. He then solemnly asked if I had been a very, very good girl this year and did I believe in Jesus Christ and obey my parents. I knew the only answer to that. I nodded back with equal solemnity.

Having watched the other children opening their gifts, I already knew that the big gifts were not necessarily the nicest ones. One girl my age got a large coloring book of biblical characters, while a less greedy girl who selected a smaller box received a glass vial of lavender toilet water. The sound of the box was also important. A ten-year-old boy had chosen a box that jangled when he shook it. It was a tin globe of the world with a slit for inserting money. He must have thought it was full of dimes and nickels, because when he saw that it had just ten pennies, his face fell with such undisguised disappointment that his mother slapped the side of his head and led him out of the church hall, apologizing to the crowd for her son who had such bad manners he couldn't appreciate such a fine gift.

As I peered into the sack, I quickly fingered the remaining presents, testing their weight, imagining what they contained. I chose a heavy, compact one that was wrapped in shiny silver foil and a red satin ribbon. It was a twelve-pack of Life Savers and I spent the rest of the party arranging and rearranging the candy tubes in the order of my favorites. My brother Winston chose wisely as well. His present turned out to be a box of intricate plastic parts; the instructions on the box proclaimed that when they were properly assembled he would have an authentic miniature replica of a World War II submarine.

Vincent got the chess set, which would have been a very decent present to get at a church Christmas party, except it was obviously used and, as we discovered later, it was missing a black pawn and a white knight. My mother graciously thanked the unknown benefactor, saying, "Too good. Cost too much." At which point, an old lady with fine white, wispy hair nodded toward our family and said with a whistling whisper, "Merry, merry Christmas."

When we got home, my mother told Vincent to throw the chess set away. "She not want it. We not want it," she said, tossing her head stiffly to the side with a tight, proud smile. My brothers had deaf ears. They were already lining up the chess pieces and reading from the dog-eared instruction book.

I watched Vincent and Winston play during Christmas week. The chess board seemed to hold elaborate secrets waiting to be untangled. The chessmen were more powerful than Old Li's magic herbs that cured ancestral curses. And my brothers wore such serious faces that I was sure something was at stake that was greater than avoiding the tradesmen's door to Hong Sing's.

"Let me! Let me!" I begged between games when one brother or the other would sit back with a deep sigh of relief and victory, the other annoyed, unable to let go of the outcome. Vincent at first refused to let me play, but when I offered my Life Savers as replacements for the buttons that filled in for the missing pieces, he relented. He chose the flavors: wild cherry for the black pawn and peppermint for the white knight. Winner could eat both.

As our mother sprinkled flour and rolled out small doughy circles for the steamed dumplings that would be our dinner that night, Vincent explained the rules, pointing to each piece. "You have sixteen pieces and so do I. One king and queen, two bishops, two knights, two castles, and eight pawns. The pawns can only move forward one step, except on the first move. Then they can move two. But they can only take men by moving crossways like this, except in the beginning, when you can move ahead and take another pawn."

"Why?" I asked as I moved my pawn. "Why can't they move more steps?"

"Because they're pawns," he said.

"But why do they go crossways to take other men. Why aren't there any women and children?"

"Why is the sky blue? Why must you always ask stupid questions?" asked Vincent. "This is a game. These are the rules. I didn't make them up. See. Here. In the book." He jabbed a page with a pawn in his hand. "Pawn. P-A-W-N. Pawn. Read it yourself."

My mother patted the flour off her hands. "Let me see book," she said quietly. She scanned the pages quickly, not reading the foreign English symbols, seeming to search deliberately for nothing in particular.

"This American rules," she concluded at last. "Every time people come out from foreign country, must know rules. You not know, judge say, Too bad, go back. They not telling you why so you can use their way go forward. They say, Don't know why, you find out yourself. But they knowing all the time. Better you take it, find out why yourself." She tossed her head back with a satisfied smile.

I found out about all the whys later. I read the rules and looked up all the big words in a dictionary. I borrowed books from the Chinatown library. I studied each chess piece, trying to absorb the power each contained.

I learned about opening moves and why it's important to control the center early on; the shortest distance between two points is straight down the middle. I learned about the middle game and why tactics between two adversaries are like clashing ideas; the one who plays better has the clearest plans for both attacking and getting out of traps. I learned why

it is essential in the endgame to have foresight, a mathematical understanding of all possible moves, and patience; all weaknesses and advantages become evident to a strong adversary and are obscured to a tiring
opponent. I discovered that for the whole game one must gather invisible
strengths and see the endgame before the game begins.

I also found out why I should never reveal "why" to others. A little
knowledge withheld is a great advantage one should store for future use.
That is the power of chess. It is a game of secrets in which one must show
and never tell.

I loved the secrets I found within the sixty-four black and white
squares. I carefully drew a handmade chessboard and pinned it to the
wall next to my bed, where at night I would stare for hours at imaginary
battles. Soon I no longer lost any games or Life Savers, but I lost my
adversaries. Winston and Vincent decided they were more interested in
roaming the streets after school in their Hopalong Cassidy cowboy hats.

On a cold spring afternoon, while walking home from school, I detoured
through the playground at the end of our alley. I saw a group of old men,
two seated across a folding table playing a game of chess, others smoking
pipes, eating peanuts, and watching. I ran home and grabbed Vincent's
chess set, which was bound in a cardboard box with rubber bands. I also
carefully selected two prized rolls of Life Savers. I came back to the park
and approached a man who was observing the game.

"Want to play?" I asked him. His face widened with surprise and he
grinned as he looked at the box under my arm.

"Little sister, been a long time since I play with dolls," he said, smiling
benevolently. I quickly put the box down next to him on the bench and
displayed my retort.

Lau Po, as he allowed me to call him, turned out to be a much better
player than my brothers. I lost many games and many Life Savers. But
over the weeks, with each diminishing roll of candies, I added new secrets. Lau Po gave me the names. The Double Attack from the East and
West Shores. Throwing Stones on the Drowning Man. The Sudden Meeting of the Clan. The Surprise from the Sleeping Guard. The Humble Servant Who Kills the King. Sand in the Eyes of Advancing Forces. A Double
Killing Without Blood.

There were also the fine points of chess etiquette. Keep captured men
in neat rows, as well-tended prisoners. Never announce "Check" with
vanity, lest someone with an unseen sword slit your throat. Never hurl
pieces into the sandbox after you have lost a game, because then you
must find them again, by yourself, after apologizing to all around you.

By the end of the summer, Lau Po had taught me all he knew, and I had become a better chess player.

A small weekend crowd of Chinese people and tourists would gather as I played and defeated my opponents one by one. My mother would join the crowds during these outdoor exhibition games. She sat proudly on the bench, telling my admirers with proper Chinese humility, "Is luck."

A man who watched me play in the park suggested that my mother allow me to play in local chess tournaments. My mother smiled graciously, an answer that meant nothing. I desperately wanted to go, but I bit back my tongue. I knew she would not let me play among strangers. So as we walked home I said in a small voice that I didn't want to play in the local tournament. They would have American rules. If I lost, I would bring shame on my family.

"Is shame you fall down nobody push you," said my mother.

During my first tournament, my mother sat with me in the front row as I waited for my turn. I frequently bounced my legs to unstick them from the cold metal seat of the folding chair. When my name was called, I leapt up. My mother unwrapped something in her lap. It was her *chang*, a small tablet of red jade which held the sun's fire. "Is luck," she whispered, and tucked it into my dress pocket. I turned to my opponent, a fifteen-year-old boy from Oakland. He looked at me, wrinkling his nose.

As I began to play, the boy disappeared, the color ran out of the room, and I saw only my white pieces and his black ones waiting on the other side. A light wind began blowing past my ears. It whispered secrets only I could hear.

"Blow from the South," it murmured. "The wind leaves no trail." I saw a clear path, the traps to avoid. The crowd rustled. "Shhh! Shhh!" said the corners of the room. The wind blew stronger. "Throw sand from the East to distract him." The knight came forward ready for the sacrifice. The wind hissed, louder and louder. "Blow, blow, blow. He cannot see. He is blind now. Make him lean away from the wind so he is easier to knock down."

"Check," I said, as the wind roared with laughter. The wind died down to little puffs, my own breath.

My mother placed my first trophy next to a new plastic chess set that the neighborhood Tao society had given to me. As she wiped each piece with a soft cloth, she said, "Next time win more, lose less."

"Ma, it's not how many pieces you lose," I said. "Sometimes you need to lose pieces to get ahead."

"Better to lose less, see if you really need."

At the next tournament, I won again, but it was my mother who wore the triumphant grin.

"Lost eight piece this time. Last time was eleven. What I tell you? Better off lose less!" I was annoyed, but I couldn't say anything.

I attended more tournaments, each one farther away from home. I won all games, in all divisions. The Chinese bakery downstairs from our flat displayed my growing collection of trophies in its window, amidst the dust-covered cakes that were never picked up. The day after I won an important regional tournament, the window encased a fresh sheet cake with whipped-cream frosting and red script saying, "Congratulations, Waverly Jong, Chinatown Chess Champion." Soon after that, a flower shop, headstone engraver, and funeral parlor offered to sponsor me in national tournaments. That's when my mother decided I no longer had to do the dishes. Winston and Vincent had to do my chores.

"Why does she get to play and we do all the work," complained Vincent.

"Is new American rules," said my mother. "Meimei play, squeeze all her brains out for win chess. You play, worth squeeze towel."

By my ninth birthday, I was a national chess champion. I was still some 429 points away from grand-master status, but I was touted as the Great American Hope, a child prodigy and a girl to boot. They ran a photo of me in *Life* magazine next to a quote in which Bobby Fischer said, "There will never be a woman grand master." "Your move, Bobby," said the caption.

The day they took the magazine picture I wore neatly plaited braids clipped with plastic barrettes trimmed with rhinestones. I was playing in a large high school auditorium that echoed with phlegmy coughs and the squeaky rubber knobs of chair legs sliding across freshly waxed wooden floors. Seated across from me was an American man, about the same age as Lau Po, maybe fifty. I remember that his sweaty brow seemed to weep at my every move. He wore a dark, malodorous suit. One of his pockets was stuffed with a great white kerchief on which he wiped his palm before sweeping his hand over the chosen chess piece with great flourish.

In my crisp pink-and-white dress with scratchy lace at the neck, one of two my mother had sewn for these special occasions, I would clasp my hands under my chin, the delicate points of my elbows poised lightly on the table in the manner my mother had shown me for posing for the press. I would swing my patent leather shoes back and forth like an impatient child riding on a school bus. Then I would pause, suck in my lips, twirl my chosen piece in midair as if undecided, and then firmly plant it in its new threatening place, with a triumphant smile thrown back at my opponent for good measure.

I no longer played in the alley of Waverly Place. I never visited the playground where the pigeons and old men gathered. I went to school, then directly home to learn new chess secrets, cleverly concealed advantages, more escape routes.

But I found it difficult to concentrate at home. My mother had a habit of standing over me while I plotted out my games. I think she thought of herself as my protective ally. Her lips would be sealed tight, and after each move I made, a soft "Hmmmmph" would escape from her nose.

"Ma, I can't practice when you stand there like that," I said one day. She retreated to the kitchen and made loud noises with the pots and pans. When the crashing stopped, I could see out of the corner of my eye that she was standing in the doorway. "Hmmmmph!" Only this one came out of her tight throat.

My parents made many concessions to allow me to practice. One time I complained that the bedroom I shared was so noisy that I couldn't think. Thereafter, my brothers slept in a bed in the living room facing the street. I said I couldn't finish my rice; my head didn't work right when my stomach was too full. I left the table with half-finished bowls and nobody complained. But there was one duty I couldn't avoid. I had to accompany my mother on Saturday market days when I had no tournament to play. My mother would proudly walk with me, visiting many shops, buying very little. "This my daughter Wave-ly Jong," she said to whoever looked her way.

One day, after we left a shop I said under my breath, "I wish you wouldn't do that, telling everybody I'm your daughter." My mother stopped walking. Crowds of people with heavy bags pushed past us on the sidewalk, bumping into first one shoulder, then another.

"Aiii-ya. So shame be with mother?" She grasped my hand even tighter as she glared at me.

I looked down. "It's not that, it's just so obvious. It's just so embarrassing."

"Embarrass you be my daughter?" Her voice was cracking with anger.

"That's not what I meant. That's not what I said."

"What you say?"

I knew it was a mistake to say anything more, but I heard my voice speaking. "Why do you have to use me to show off? If you want to show off, then why don't you learn to play chess."

My mother's eyes turned into dangerous black slits. She had no words for me, just sharp silence.

I felt the wind rushing around my hot ears. I jerked my hand out of my mother's tight grasp and spun around, knocking into an old woman. Her bag of groceries spilled to the ground.

"Aii-ya! Stupid girl!" my mother and the woman cried. Oranges and tin cans careened down the sidewalk. As my mother stooped to help the old woman pick up the escaping food, I took off.

I raced down the street, dashing between people, not looking back as my mother screamed shrilly, "Meimei! Meimei!" I fled down an alley, past dark curtained shops and merchants washing the grime off their windows. I sped into the sunlight, into a large street crowded with tourists examining trinkets and souvenirs. I ducked into another dark alley, down another street, up another alley. I ran until it hurt and I realized I had nowhere to go, that I was not running from anything. The alleys contained no escape routes.

My breath came out like angry smoke. It was cold. I sat down on an upturned plastic pail next to a stack of empty boxes, cupping my chin with my hands, thinking hard. I imagined my mother, first walking briskly down one street or another looking for me, then giving up and returning home to await my arrival. After two hours, I stood up on creaking legs and slowly walked home.

The alley was quiet and I could see the yellow lights shining from our flat like two tiger's eyes in the night. I climbed the sixteen steps to the door, advancing quietly up each so as not to make any warning sounds. I turned the knob; the door was locked. I heard a chair moving, quick steps, the locks turning—click! click! click!—and then the door opened.

"About time you got home," said Vincent. "Boy, are you in trouble."

He slid back to the dinner table. On a platter were the remains of a large fish, its fleshy head still connected to bones swimming upstream in vain escape. Standing there waiting for my punishment, I heard my mother speak in a dry voice.

"We not concerning this girl. This girl not have concerning for us."

Nobody looked at me. Bone chopsticks clinked against the insides of bowls being emptied into hungry mouths.

I walked into my room, closed the door, and lay down on my bed. The room was dark, the ceiling filled with shadows from the dinnertime lights of neighboring flats.

In my head, I saw a chessboard with sixty-four black and white squares. Opposite me was my opponent, two angry black slits. She wore a triumphant smile. "Strongest wind cannot be seen," she said.

Her black men advanced across the plane, slowly marching to each successive level as a single unit. My white pieces screamed as they scurried and fell off the board one by one. As her men drew closer to my edge, I felt myself growing light. I rose up into the air and flew out the window. Higher and higher, above the alley, over the tops of tiled roofs, where I was gathered up by the wind and pushed up toward the night sky until everything below me disappeared and I was alone.

I closed my eyes and pondered my next move.

TERRY TEMPEST WILLIAMS

erry Tempest Williams's (b. 1955) Utah family history goes back to the Mormon pioneers. Over the course of a century and a third, they and the other settlers of Utah had adjusted to the aridity of the Great Basin, building irrigation systems to distribute the snowmelt and not fearing to live and work on the flatland shores of the Great Salt Lake. In the early 1980s, after a series of extraordinarily heavy winters began to raise the lake level, the arrangement was nearly overturned. The rich, marshy, freshwater margins of the lake, home to dozens of bird and mammal species, were flooded by rising brine, and human industry was threatened. At this same time, Williams's mother Diane Tempest was diagnosed with cancer; the unstoppable progress of her disease inevitably joined in Williams's mind with the lakeside ecological calamity. Simultaneously, Williams was questioning other pillars of her life: the ethos of collection-oriented biology (as Naturalist-in-Residence at the Utah Museum of Natural History, she had an inside view of this), the patriarchal traditions of her religious background, and the trust in society and government that had, on a Utah-wide basis, facilitated open-air atomic bomb testing. (It was becoming increasingly apparent that the tests' fallout had something to do with the elevated cancer in Utah and in her family.) *Refuge* combines all these themes into a deep-going narrative of grief, growing insight, and passage.

"Snowy Plovers," from *Refuge* (1991)

lake level: 4209.10'

The day the pumps were turned on, the lake did an about-face on its own. Great Salt Lake is receding, having dropped more than two feet from last year's lake level high of 4211.85'.

Where the water has pulled back, the land looks as though it is recovering from a long illness. Barbed-wire fences act as strainers. Sheets of algae and rotting vegetation hang like handmade paper and bobs of tangled hair.

A "bomb catcher" is being built in the West Desert. It is the newest component of the West Desert Pumping Project.

The United States Air Force has disclosed information from their own environmental assessment report: although most bombs exploded on impact during training missions conducted since World War II, some did not. There is a fear that unexploded bombs, including some in watertight containers embedded in the salt flats might be dislodged by the pond water and float toward Great Salt Lake.

"Imagine a giant comb about eleven hundred feet long," says Brent S. Bingham, president of Bingham Engineering, Inc., the Salt Lake City company that has designed the bomb catcher. "It consists of twenty-two hundred fiberglass bars, five feet tall and six inches apart, that will span the spillway, preventing bombs from being carried into the lake by the stream of water pouring out of the new holding pond west of the Newfoundland Mountains."

Mr. Bingham told newspaper reporters today that no bombs have been seen floating in the pond, which is two and a half to three feet deep, but state officials don't want to take any chances.

Dee Hansen, Director of the Utah Department of Natural Resources says, "The bomb catcher is not for major bombs. It's for phosphorous bombs and different types of bombs in canvas bags . . . The Air Force experimented with a bunch of stuff out there. Most of it has probably deteriorated if it didn't explode. But the Air Force is pretty cautious, and we want them to be." He adds, "An explosive ordnance disposal unit from Hill Air Force Base inspected the corridor for the twelve-mile-long Newfoundland Dike before construction began. They found some unexploded ordnance in the area, which were retrieved."

All I can see are thousands upon thousands of tumbleweeds cartwheeling over the surface of the water, beating the floating bombs to the strainer.

The West Desert Pumping Project is one of thirteen engineering efforts nominated for the 1988 Outstanding Civil Engineering Achievement Award presented by the American Society of Civil Engineers.

"The award recognizes engineering projects that demonstrate the greatest engineering skills and represent the greatest contribution to civil engineering progress and mankind," said Sheila Brand, spokesperson for the society.

We had several calls at the museum today from people who wanted to know if there had been an earthquake. According to the seismology station on campus, there had been no tremors.

It turns out the rattling vibrations were in the air, not the ground.

Atmospheric shock waves were generated when the air force exploded twenty-five thousand pounds of munitions near Great Salt Lake at 2:30 P.M.

Airman First Class Jay Joerz, with Hill Air Force Base public affairs, said, "Munitions are disposed of on a regular basis at the test and training range just west of the lake. Weather conditions must have been just right for the shock wave to carry so far. Yesterday we had another twenty-five thousand-pound explosion and nobody noticed."

Snowy plovers have shown a 50 percent decline in abundance on the California, Oregon, and Washington coasts since the 1960s, due to the loss of coastal habitats. The National Audubon Society petitioned the U.S. Fish and Wildlife Service in March, 1988, to list the coastal population of the western snowy plover as a threatened species. The present population estimate for the western United States, excluding Utah, is ten thousand adult snowy plovers, rising to thirteen thousand individuals after breeding season. A knowledge of inland population numbers and distribution is essential to our understanding of the status of the species as a whole. That's why we are counting them in Utah.

I have been combing the salt flats north of Crocodile Mountain for them since early morning. So far, my count is zero.

Margy Halpin, a non-game biologist leading the survey for the Utah Division of Wildlife Resources, and I are walking parallel to each other, maybe a half-mile apart. The distance between us feels greater than it is because of the intense heat and glare of the alkaline terrain.

I walk slowly, following the western shoreline of Great Salt Lake. Clay bluffs along the water's edge resemble Normandy: they have eroded into fantastic shapes, alcoves, and tunnels from past wave action. There are no footprints here.

Windrows of brine flies and ladybug carcasses twist along the beach. Otherwise, it is littered with limestone chips, which clamor like coins when walked upon. The heat is brutal. I pause to dip my scarf in the lake and tie it back around my forehead.

I turn west away from the lake and walk back across the salt flats. Another hour passes. I see movement. Two snowy plovers skitter ahead. Margy also has them in view—we motion each other simultaneously waving with our right hands. If they were not dashing across the white-brocaded landscape, they would be impossible to see. They are perfectly camouflaged.

Margy and I join each other and sit on the salt to watch them. I have to squint through my binoculars to shut out the light reflecting off the flats. Heatwaves blur the plovers. They appear to be foraging on half-inch golden beetles. We pick up one of the insects close to us for a better examination of what the plovers are eating. The golden carapace is trans-lucent, gemlike. We set the creature back on its course, and it skeeters away.

Snowy plovers are the scribes of the salt flats. Their tracks are cursive writing, cabalistic messages for the bird-watcher who cares enough to follow their eccentric wanderings.

We spot two more adult plovers with chicks. Two chicks. Margy and I check with each other to make sure.

"Ku-wheet! Ku-wheet! Ku-wheet!"

On this day, their calls are the only dialogue in the desert.

The snowy plover is considered to be an uncommon summer resident around the shores of Great Salt Lake, so our total count of six on June 11, 1988, is no surprise. They are listed as common residents of Pyramid Lake in Nevada and Mono Lake in California. Long-term distribution records show that snowy plover populations rise as Great Salt Lake retreats. More habitat supports more birds.

What intrigues me about these tiny white birds with brown bands across their breasts is how they manage their lives in such a forbidding landscape. The only shade on the salt flats is the shadow they cast. There is little fresh water, if any. And their diet consists of insects indigenous to alkaline habitats—brine flies and beetles.

Fred Ryser explains, in *Birds of the Great Basin*, how this "wet food, even during the driest and hottest time of year, contains much water of succulence . . . with each mouthful of food, the plover drinks."

To cool off, the snowy plover stands in the salt water and lets the brackish water evaporate from its body.

Another question rises with the heat of the salt desert. Why don't their eggs bake?

Snowy plovers nest in shallow scrapes, open and exposed. Some plov-ers will use brine fly pupal carcasses for a nesting bed, and then line them with small pebbles and shells. Both male and female snowys incubate the eggs; on hot days, such as today, they trade places frequently, alternating from sitting to standing (not so unlike us). Parenting plovers have been seen to soak in salt water and, upon returning to their clutch of eggs, will ruffle their wet feathers, sprinkling the eggs with water. An average clutch size is three eggs. Research suggests half the broods in Utah might fledge two young.

Margy and I share drinks from her canteen. I have a throbbing head-ache, which tells me I have been ignoring my own need for water. I fear I may be suffering from heatstroke and begin to worry about getting home. Too much exposure.

Before walking back through shoulder-high greasewood, I take a quick swim in the lake. The silky waters of Great Salt Lake cool my parched skin, even though the salt burns. This offers a momentary reprieve from my nausea. I lick my swollen lips and am careful not to rub my eyes.

I catch up with Margy and follow her through the maze of greasewood. We hear rattles and stop. It is the driest sound on earth. We take another path and walk briskly toward Crocodile Mountain.

Driving home alone on the solitary dirt road that winds around the lake, I am struck with delirium. I stop the car. Nothing looks familiar. I get out and heave violently behind the sagebrush.

The next thing I remember is waking up in a dark motel room in Tremonton, Utah. I call Brooke to see if he can tell me what happened. He is not home. Snowy plovers come to mind. They can teach me how to survive.

November 15, 1988. Lettie Romney Dixon passed away at noon from lingering illness. My grandfather, Sanky, has not left her side for months. Last night, I sat with them all night long. He held her hand and I held his. Mother felt near. Death has become a familiar landscape. I can smell it.

We prepare my grandmother's body. Her tiny arms stiff around her chest are like chicken wings because of Parkinson's Disease. They have not been able to hold those she loved for years. This was the pain I could not embrace. Her blue eyes did. And now they are closed.

My uncle Don, from out of town, walks into the room. We hug. I see my mother's face in his and do not hear a word he says.

Once home, I split open a ripe pomegranate. Red juice trickles over my hand and spills on to my lap as I eat the tart, succulent seeds.

Mothers. Daughters. Granddaughters. The myth of Demeter and Persephone lives through us.

"This cannot be a coincidence, can it?" I ask my cousin Lynne, over the telephone. "Three women in one family unrelated by blood, all contract cancer within months of each other?"

"I have no idea, Terry. All I know is that my mother has breast cancer and her surgery is tomorrow."

"Is there a pattern here, Lynne, that we are not seeing?"

Lynne's voice breaks. "What I do know," she says, "is that I resent so much being asked of the women and so little being asked of the men." There is a long pause. "I'm scared, Terry. I'm scared for you and me."

"So am I. So am I."

Something is wrong and I can't figure it out—the egg collection at the Museum of Natural History. On first appearance, these clutches of eggs arranged in a nest of cotton move me. The size range and color differentiation is stunning, from the pink and brown splotching of a peregrine falcon's eggs to the perfectly white, perfectly round eggs of a great horned owl. And the smaller birds' eggs are individual works of art, canvases on calcium spheres—some spotted, some striped.

But when I hold one of these eggs, there is no gravity in my hand. A weightless shell. Life has literally been blown out through a pinhole.

It dawns on me, eggs are not meant to be seen. This collection is a sacrilege, the exposed medicine bundles of a tribe. These eggs are the hidden wealth of a species, tenderly guarded beneath the warm, bare brood patch of a female bird.

Secrets were housed inside these shells, enough avian lives to repopulate a marsh, even Bear River. But we have sacrificed them in the name of biology to substantiate the obvious, that we know where each bird comes from. These hollow eggs are our stockpile of evidence.

On my way home, I drop by to visit Mimi. She is painting on her easel in the dining room. She rinses her brushes and we sit in her turquoise study.

"What's on your mind?" she asks.

"Tell me what eggs symbolize?"

She runs her hand through her short gray hair. "For me, it is where life originates. In mythic times, the Cosmic Egg was believed to be held within the pelvis of the ancient Bird Goddess. Why do you ask?"

I describe my encounter with the egg collection at the museum, how disturbing it was.

"The hollow eggs translated into hollow wombs. The Earth is not well and neither are we. I saw the health of the planet as our own."

Mimi listened intently. She stood and turned sideways to switch on the lamp. It was dusk. I could not help but notice her distended belly, pregnant with tumor.

"It's all related," she said. "I feel certain."

"The total number of snowy plovers counted around Great Salt Lake was 487, with 26 young in 11 broods," I tell Mimi as we drive out to Stansbury Island. "Biologists figure we may have two thousand breeding pairs in Utah." She wanted to get out of the house for a change of view. Her strength is holding in spite of the cancer.

We had just seen four snowys scurrying between clumps of pickleweed.

Just outside Grantsville, thousands of Wilson's phalaropes and eared grebes were feeding in the median ponds adjacent to the freeway. No doubt a migratory stop.

In recognition of Great Salt Lake's critical role as a migrational mirror reflecting ducks, geese, swans, and shorebirds down for food and rest, the Western Hemisphere Shorebird Reserve Network has identified the lake as a crucial link in the chain of primary migratory, breeding, and wintering sites along the great shorebird flyways that extend from the arctic to the southern tip of South America.

By becoming part of the network, Great Salt Lake could gain international support for local conservation efforts and wetlands management. It has been nominated by the Utah Division of Wildlife Resources, the U.S. Fish and Wildlife Service, and Bureau of Land Management. And just recently, the Utah Division of Parks and Recreation, along with the Division of State Lands and Forestry, endorsed the nomination.

To qualify, a site must entertain in excess of 250,000 birds a year, or more than 30 percent of a species' flyway population.

Great Salt Lake qualifies. It hosts millions of birds in a season. Don Paul points out, however, that the lake qualifies on the basis of Wilson's phalaropes alone—flocks of 500,000 to 1,000,000 are not uncommon during July and August, when they are en route to South America.

The Western Hemisphere Reserve Shorebird Network has paired Great Salt Lake with Laguna Del Mar Chiquita, the salt lake in the Cordoba region of Argentina where the phalaropes winter. They are sister reserves.

"Think about one phalarope flying those distances," Mimi said, looking through her binoculars. "And then think about flocks of phalaropes, millions of individuals being driven on their collective journey. We go about our lives giving little thought, if any, to such miracles."

There is a chorus of wings navigating the planet. Twenty million shorebirds migrate through the United States each year to arctic breeding grounds in the spring and back to their wintering sites in South America. One bird may cover as many as fifteen thousand miles in a year.

Great Salt Lake is a refuge for these migrants. And there are certainly other strategic sites along the migratory path, essential to the health and well-being of those birds dependent upon wetlands. The Copper River Delta in Alaska, Canada's Bay of Fundy, Grays Harbor in Washington, the Cheyenne Bottoms of Kansas, and Delaware Bay in New Jersey are just a few of the oases that nurture hundreds of thousands of shorebirds.

Without these places of refuge, successful migrations would cease for millions of birds. None of these sites are secure. Conservation laws are only as strong as the people who support them. We look away and they are in danger of being overturned, compromised, and weakened.

Wetlands have a long history of being dredged, drained, and filled, or regarded as wastelands on the periphery of our towns. Already in Utah, there are those who envision a salt-free Great Salt Lake. A proposal has been drafted for the Utah State Legislature to introduce the concept of "Lake Wasatch." The Lake Wasatch Coalition would impound freshwater flowing into Great Salt Lake from the Bear, Weber, Ogden, and Jordan Rivers and other tributaries, by means of more than eighteen miles of inter-island dikes stretching through four counties between Interstate-80, Antelope Island, Fremont Island, and Promontory Point.

They see Lake Wasatch as fifty-two miles long and twelve and a half miles wide—three times the size of Lake Powell in southern Utah and northwest Arizona.

With 192 miles of shoreline, which unlike Lake Powell, is mostly under private ownership, there would be opportunities for unlimited lakeside development. Promotors already have plans for Antelope Island. They see it as an ideal site for a theme park with high-rise hotels and condominiums.

Lake Wasatch is a chamber of commerce dream. Finally, the Great Salt Lake would be worth something.

What about the birds?

Mimi turns to me, her legs outstretched on the sands of Half-Moon Bay.

"How do you place a value on inspiration? How do you quantify the wildness of birds, when for the most part, they lead secret and anonymous lives?"

WILLIAM KITTREDGE

If there is any single author whose work epitomizes the new western writing, gathering many of its threads and dramatizing its core vision, the writer would have to be William Kittredge (b. 1932). A native of little populated southeastern Oregon, Kittredge grew up on a large cattle ranch and inherited the tough-handed tradition of working and reworking the big land. In *Hole In the Sky* (1992) he describes his gradual growing-away from the tradition, a slow awakening to other possibilities both personal and ecological. He came to see the fields of his childhood in a new way. Leaving the ranch, doing graduate work in creative writing at the University of Iowa, and becoming a teacher at the University of Montana, Kittredge came into a very different life. In writing, his mentors were Raymond Carver and Richard Hugo. He, in turn, has been generous as a teacher, workshop director, and anthology editor, besides writing his own fiction (see *The Van Gogh Field and Other Stories*, 1978; and *We Are Not in This Together*, 1984), essays (most recently, *Who Owns the West?* 1996). He worked on the screenplay for *Heartland* (1979), and was an Associate Producer for *A River Runs Through It* (1992). A many-dimensioned talent who has earned a central position in western literature, Kittredge as much as anyone has sustained the native western self-awareness that Wallace Stegner hoped and believed would lead the region toward maturity.

"Reimagining Warner," from *Heart of the Land* (1994)

A scab-handed wandering child who rode off on old horses named Snip and Moon, I grew up with the constant thronging presence of animals. Herds of feral hogs inhabited the swampland tule beds where the water birds nested. Those hogs would eat the downy young of the Canada geese if they could, but never caught them so far as I knew.

Sandhill cranes danced their courtship dances in our meadows. The haying and feeding and the cowherding work couldn't have been done without the help of horses. We could only live the life we had with the help of horses.

All day Sunday sometimes in the summer my family would spread blankets by Deep Creek or Twenty-mile Creek and even us kids would catch all the rainbow trout we could stand.

Warner Valley was a hidden world, tucked against an enormous reach of Great Basin sagebrush and lava-rock desert in southeastern Oregon and northern Nevada. The landlocked waters flow down from the snowy mountains to the west but don't find a way out to the sea. They accumulate and evaporate in shallow lakes named Pelican, Crump, Hart, Stone Corral, and Bluejoint.

The late 1930s, when I was a child in that valley, were like the last years of the nineteenth century. What I want to get at is our isolation. We were thirty-six gravel-road miles over the Warner Mountains from the little lumbering and rancher town of Lakeview (maybe twenty-five hundred souls). Warner Valley was not on the route to anywhere.

The way in was the way out. The deserts to the east were traced with wagon-track roads over the salt-grass playas and around rimrocks from spring to spring, water hole to water hole, but nobody ever headed in that direction with the idea of going toward the future.

To the east lay deserts and more deserts. From a ridge above our buckaroo camp beside the desert spring at South Corral, we could see the long notched snowy ridge of Steens Mountain off in the eastern distances, high country where whores from Burns went in summer to camp with the sheepherders amid aspen trees at a place called Whorehouse Meadows, where nobody but wandering men ever went, men who would never be around when you needed them. And beyond, toward Idaho, there was more desert.

By the end of the Second World War my grandfather had got control of huge acreages in Warner, and my father was making serious progress at draining the swamplands. The spring of 1946 my grandfather traded off close to two hundred or so work teams for chicken feed. He replaced those horses with a fleet of John Deere tractors. Harness rotted in the barns until the barns were torn down.

I wonder if my father and his friends understood how irrevocably they were giving up what they seemed to care about more than anything when they talked of happiness, their lives in conjunction to the animals they worked with and hunted. I wonder why they acted like they didn't care.

Maybe they thought the animals were immortal. I recall those great teams of workhorses running the hayfields in summer before daybreak, their hooves echoing on the sod as we herded them toward the willow corral at some haycamp, the morning mists and how the boy I was knew at least enough to know he loved them and that this love was enough reason to revere everything in sight for another morning.

Those massive horses were like mirrors in which I could see my emotions reflected. If they loved this world, and they seemed to, with such satisfaction, on those mornings when our breaths fogged before us, so did I.

Soon after World War II electricity from Bonneville Power came to Warner, and telephones that sort of worked. The road over the mountains and down along Deep Creek was paved. Our work in the fields had in so many ways gone mechanical. Eventually we had television. Our isolation was dissolving.

About the time I watched the first Beatles telecast in the early 1960s, Chamber of Commerce gentlemen in Winnemucca got together with likeminded gentlemen from Lakeview, and decided it made great economic sense to punch a highway across the deserts between those two little cities. Think of the tourists.

The two-lane asphalt ran north from Winnemucca to Denio, then turned west to cross the million or so acres of rangeland we leased from the Bureau of Land Management, or BLM (we saw those acreages as ours, like we owned them: in those days we virtually did), over the escarpment called Dougherty Slide, across Guano Valley and down Greaser Canyon, and directly through our meadowlands in Warner Valley.

I recall going out to watch the highway-building as it proceeded, the self-important recklessness of those men at their work, the roaring of the D-8 Caterpillars and the clouds of dust rising behind the huge careening of the self-propelled scrapers, and being excited, sort of full up with pride because the great world was at last coming to us in Warner Valley. Not that it ever did. The flow of tourism across those deserts never amounted to much. But maybe it will, one of these days.

Enormous changes were sweeping the world. We didn't want to encounter hippies or free love or revolutionaries on the streets in Lakeview. Or so we said. But like anybody, we yearned to be in on the action.

We were delighted, one Fourth of July, to hear that the Hell's Angels motorcycle gang from Oakland had headed across the deserts north to Winnemucca on their way to a weekend of kicking ass in Lakeview, and that they had been turned back by a single deputy sheriff.

There had been the long string of lowriders coming on the two-lane blacktop across one of the great desert swales, and the deputy, all by himself, standing there by his Chevrolet. The deputy, a slight, balding man, had flagged down the leaders and they'd had a talk. "Nothing I can do about it," the deputy said, "but they're sighting in their deer rifles. These boys, they just mean to sit back there three hundred yards and just shoot you off them motorcycles. They won't apologize or anything. You fellows are way too far out in the country."

According to legend, the leaders of the Hell's Angels decided the deputy was right: they knew they were way too far out in the country, and they turned back. I never talked to anybody who knew if that story was true, but we loved it.

It was a story that told us we were not incapable of defending ourselves, or powerless in a nation we understood to be going on without us. We never doubted some of our southeastern Oregon boys would have shot those Hell's Angels off their bikes. Some places were still big and open enough to be safe.

During the great flood in December of 1964, when the Winnemucca-to-the-Sea highway acted like a dam across the valley, backing up water over four or five thousand acres, my brother Pat walked a D-7 out along the asphalt and cut the highway three or four times, deep cuts so the floodwaters could pour through and drain away north. What he liked best, Pat said, was socking that bulldozer blade down and ripping up that asphalt with the yellow lines painted on it. We were still our own people.

But even as huge and open to anything as southeastern Oregon may have seemed in those old days, it was also inhabited by spooks. In autumn of the same year the Winnemucca-to-the-Sea highway came across our meadowlands, I had our heavy equipment, our Carry-All scrapers and D-7 Caterpillars, at work on a great diversion canal we were cutting through three hundred yards of sage-covered sandhills at the south end of Warner, rerouting Twenty-mile Creek.

Soon we were turning up bone—human bones, lots of them. I recall a clear October afternoon and all those white bones scattered in the gravel, and my catskinners standing there beside their great idling machines, perplexed and unwilling to continue. Ah, hell, never mind, I said. Crank 'em up.

There was nothing to do but keep rolling. Maybe bones from an ancient Indian burial ground were sacred, but so was our work, more so, as I saw it. My catskinners threatened to quit. I told them I'd give them a ride to town, where I'd find plenty of men who would welcome the work. My catskinners didn't quit. I ducked my head so I couldn't see, and drove away.

If you are going to bake a cake, you must break some eggs. That was a theory we knew about. We thought we were doing God's work. We were cultivating, creating order, and what we liked to think of as a version of Paradise.

What a pleasure that work was, like art, always there, always in need of improving, doing. It's reassuring, so long as the work is not boring, to wake up and find your tools are still in the tunnel. You can lose a life in the work. People do. Oftentimes they are taken to be the best people, the real workers.

But we left, we quit, in a run of family trouble. I have been gone from farming and Warner for twenty-five years. People ask if I don't feel a great sense of loss, cut off from the valley and methods of my childhood. The answer is no.

Nothing much looks to have changed when I go back. The rimrock above the west side of the valley lies as black against the sunset light as it did when I was a child. The topography of my dreams, I like to think, is still intact.

But that's nonsense. We did great damage to the valley as we pursued our sweet impulse to create an agribusiness paradise. The rich peat ground began to go saline, the top layer just blew away. We drilled chemical fertilizers along with our barley seed, and sprayed with 24D Ethyl and Parathion (which killed even the songbirds). Where did the water birds go?

But the water birds can be thought of as part of the *charismatic megafauna*. Everybody worries about the water birds. Forms of life we didn't even know about were equally threatened.

Catostomus warnerensis, the Warner sucker, is endangered. So are eight other fish species in the region, seven plant species, and seven plant communities such as *Poptri/corsto-salix*, a riparian plant community centered on black cottonwood, red osier dogwood, and willow.

As a child I loved to duck down and wander animal trails through dense brush by the creeksides, where ring-necked Manchurian pheasants and egg-eating raccoons and stalking lynx cats traveled. I wonder about colonies of red osier dogwood and black cottonwood. I was maybe often among them, curled in the dry grass and sleeping in the sun as I shared in their defenselessness and didn't know it.

The way we built canals in our efforts to contain the wildness of the valley and regulate the ways of water to our own uses must have been close to absolutely destructive to the Warner sucker, a creature we would not have valued at all, slippery and useless, thus valueless. It's likely I sent my gang of four D-7 Caterpillar bulldozers to clean out the brush along stretches of creekside thick with red osier dogwood and black cottonwood.

Let in some light, let the grass grow, feed for the livestock, that was the theory. Maybe we didn't abandon those creatures in that valley, maybe we mostly destroyed them before we left. We did enormous damage to that valley in the thirty-some years that we were there. Countrysides like the Dordogne and Umbria and Tuscany, which have been farmed thousands of years, look to be less damaged. But maybe that's because the serious kill-off took place so long ago.

I love Warner as a child loves his homeland, and some sense of responsibility for what's there stays with me. Or maybe I'm just trying to feel good about myself.

But that's what we all want to do, isn't it? It's my theory that everyone yearns, as we did in Warner, plowing those swamps, with all that bulldozing, to make a positive effect in the world. But how?

How to keep from doing harm? Sometimes that seems to be the only question. But we have to act. To do so responsibly we must first examine our desires. What do we really want?

A few years ago I went to Warner with a couple of filmmakers from NBC. Some footage ran on the "Today" show. Sitting in an antique GMC pickup truck alongside a great reef of chemically contaminated cowshit which had been piled up outside the feedlot pens where our fattening cattle had existed like creatures in a machine, I found it in myself to say the valley should be given back to the birds, and turned into a wildlife refuge.

It was a way of saying good-bye. I was saying the biological health of the valley was more important to me than the well-being of the community of ranchers who lived there. I had gone to grade school with some of them. It was an act people living in Warner mostly understood as betrayal.

Some eggs were broken, but I had at last gotten myself to say what I believed. Around 1990, when I heard that our ranch in Warner, along with two others out in the deserts to the east, were for sale, and that The Nature Conservancy was interested, I was surprised by the degree to which I was moved and excited.

A huge expanse of territory, adjacent to and including our ranch, would be affected. The total area comprised 1,111,587 deeded and permitted acres in an intricate run of private, BLM, and state lands. This included:

1. the wetlands we farmed in south Warner (more than 20,000 irrigated acres belonging to the MC Ranch and close to 10,000 acres of floodplain in the valley leased from the state of Oregon—which could possibly be drained and farmed);
2. the wetlands of the Malheur National Wildlife Refuge (some 380,000 ducks, 19,000 geese, and 6,000 lesser sandhill cranes migrate through Warner and the Malheur);
3. Catlow Valley with its wetlands;

4. Guano Valley;
5. the Beatty Buttes;
6. Hart Mountain Wildlife Refuge (where a new management plan banning grazing for the next fifteen years has just been announced);
7. a 78,000-acre grazing allotment held by the MC Ranch on the Sheldon National Wildlife Refuge in northern Nevada;
8. alpine habitats on Steens Mountain, the largest fault-block mountain in North America, with alpine aspen groves and great glacial cirques 3,000 feet deep and 20 miles in length (an area often mentioned as a possible national park);
9. the alkaline playas, sand dunes, and desert saltbrush expanses of the Alvord Desert.

Maybe, I thought, this would be a second chance at paradise in my true heartland, an actual shot at reimagining desire.

What did I really want? A process, I think, everybody involved—ranchers and townspeople, conservationists—all taking part in that reimagining. I wanted them to each try defining the so-called land of their heart's desiring, the way they would have things if they were running the world. I wanted them to compare their versions of paradise, and notice again the ways we all want so many of the same things—like companionship in a community of people we respect and meaningful work.

Then I wanted them to get started on the painstaking work of developing a practical plan for making their visions of the right life come actual, a plan for using, restoring, and preserving the world in which I grew up. I liked to imagine some of the pumps and dikes and headgates would be torn out in Warner, and that some of the swamps would go back to tules. That's part of my idea of progress—re-create habitat for the water birds, and the tiny, less charismatic creatures. But nothing like that has happened.

Although they still maintain a strong presence in the high desert country of southeastern Oregon (a full-time staff person is assigned to the region, and they are negotiating on important parcels in Warner), The Nature Conservancy did not end up buying the MC Ranch, our old property in Warner Valley. Instead, the ranch was stripped of livestock and machinery, and sold to what I understand to be a consortium of local ranchers. I have no idea of their plans—they don't confide in me, the turncoat.

But the world is inevitably coming to Warner Valley. The BLM recently purchased several thousands of acres of prime hayland in north Warner, and included it in a special management unit in which no grazing is allowed. The idea of the federal government buying land and taking it out of production (out of the tax base) was unthinkable when I lived in Warner.

Other unthinkable ideas are blowing in the wind. In May 1991, a consortium of environmental groups led by the Oregon Natural Resources Council announced their plan for southeastern Oregon. It included the national park on Steens Mountain; three new national monuments; forty-seven wilderness areas totaling more than 5 million acres; expanding the Hart Mountain Refuge to include the wetlands in Warner Valley; a new national wildlife refuge at Lake Abert; wild and scenic river status for fifty-four streams totaling 835 miles, mostly creeks in the glacial cirques in the Steens and Pueblo mountains; and phasing out, over a ten-year period, all livestock grazing on federal lands designated as national park, preserve, wildlife refuge, wilderness, or wild and scenic river (about 5.9 million acres).

There's no use sighting in the scopes on deer rifles, not anymore. This invasion will not be frightened away. There is not a thing for the people in my old homeland to do but work out some accommodation with the thronging, invading world.

So many of our people, in the old days of the American West, came seeking a fold in time and actuality, a hideaway place where they and generations after them could be at home. Think of *familia*, place and hearth and home fire, the fishing creek where it falls out of the mountains, into the valley, and the Lombardy poplar beside the white house, and the orchard where the children ran in deep sweet clover under the blossoming apple trees. But that's my paradise, not yours.

We have taken the West for about all it has to give. We have lived like children, taking and taking for generations, and now that childhood is over.

It's time to give something back to the natural systems of order which have supported us, some care and tenderness, which is the most operative notion I think—tenderness. Our isolations are gone, in the West and everywhere. We need to give some time to the arts of cherishing the things we adore, before they simply vanish. Maybe it will be like learning a skill: how to live in paradise.

RICK BASS

With postmodernist philosophy and literary criticism, there has arisen a notion that "nature" as a concept is purely a cultural construct; and not too big a step beyond that position, a relativism about ground nature itself has become chic. Since humanity's effects are everywhere, there is nothing pristine to measure by, the thinking goes. Opponents of wildland protection have gleefully taken this relativism as gospel and used it against those remnants of the wild still more or less intact. All the talkers, however, may have forgotten one thing: the passion of a true defender. They will not know how to deal with Rick Bass (b. 1958), for whom the loss of wilderness is not just someone's *view*, one opinion among many. And wilderness isn't something you can draw a line around. No: It is the whole thing, and it is real. The decline of wild health is for Bass the great fact and definer of our times. His fiction and straight-ahead essays, done in intimate, conversational prose that gives rise somehow to soaring images, all grow within an overarching passion for wild nature. The center for Bass is the Yaak Valley of northwestern Montana, and the creative energy behind an outpouring of books clearly comes from this writer's love for place. Bass may be a kind of throwback in displaying a moral center in his work, but readers and critics have responded nevertheless, making him one of the most-praised contemporary American writers. "The Sky, the Stars, the Wilderness," the title story of a gathering of three novellas by Bass published in 1997, is as provocative a piece of writing about nature and human life as has been done in the West.

"Days of Heaven," from *In the Loyal Mountains* (1995)

Their plans were to develop the valley, and my plans were to stop them. There were just the two of them. The stockbroker, or stock analyst, had hired me as caretaker on his ranch here. He was from New York, a big man who drank too much. His name was Quentin, and he had a protruding belly and a small mustache and looked like a polar bear. The other one, a realtor from Billings, was named Zim. Zim had close-together eyes, pinpoints in his pasty, puffy face, like raisins set in dough. He wore new jeans and a western shirt with silver buttons and a metal belt buckle with a horse on it. In his new cowboy boots he walked in little steps with his toes pointed in.

The feeling I got from Quentin was that he was out here recovering from some kind of breakdown. And Zim—grinning, loose-necked, giggling, pointy-toe walking all the time, looking like an infant who'd just shit his diapers—Zim the predator, had just the piece of Big Sky Quentin needed. I'll go ahead and say it right now so nobody gets the wrong idea: I didn't like Zim.

It was going fast, the Big Sky was, Zim said. All sorts of famous people—celebrities—were vacationing here, moving here. "Brooke Shields," he said. "Rich people. I mean *really* rich people. You could sell them things. Say you owned the little store in this valley, the Mercantile. And say Michael Jackson—well, no, not him—say Kirk Douglas lives ten miles down the road. What's he going to do when he's having a party and realizes he doesn't have enough Dom Perignon? Who's he gonna call? He'll call your store, if you have such a service. Say the bottle costs seventy-five dollars. You'll sell it to him for a hundred. You'll deliver it, you'll drive that ten miles up the road to take it to him, and he'll be glad to pay that extra money.

"Bing-bang-bim-bam!" Zim said, snapping his fingers and rubbing his hands together, his raisin eyes glittering. His mouth was small, round, and pale, like an anus. "You've made twenty-five dollars," he said, and the mouth broke into a grin.

What's twenty-five dollars to a stock analyst? But I saw that Quentin was listening closely.

I've lived on this ranch for four years now. The guy who used to own it before Quentin was a predator too. A rough guy from Australia, he had put his life savings into building this mansion, this fortress, deep in the woods overlooking a big meadow. The mansion is three stories tall, rising into the trees like one of Tarzan's haunts.

The previous owner's name was Beauregard. All over the property he had constructed various outbuildings related to the dismemberment of his quarry: smokehouses with wire screening, to keep the other predators out, and butchering houses complete with long wooden tables, sinks, and high-intensity lamps over the tables for night work. There were even huge windmill-type hoists on the property, which were used to lift the animals—moose, bear, and elk, their heads and necks limp in death—up off the ground so their hides could first be stripped, leaving the meat revealed.

It had been Beauregard's life dream to be a hunting guide. He wanted rich people to pay him for killing a wild creature, one they could drag out of the woods and take home. Beauregard made a go of it for three years, before business went downhill and bad spirits set in and he got divorced. He had to put the place up for sale to make the alimony payments. The divorce settlement would in no way allow either of the parties to live in the mansion—it had to be both parties or none—and that's where I came in: to caretake the place until it was sold. They'd sunk too much money into the mansion to leave it sitting idle out there in the forest, and Beauregard went back east, to Washington, D.C., where he got a job doing something for the CIA—tracking fugitives was my guess, or maybe even killing them. His wife went to California with the kids.

Beauregard had been a mercenary for a while. He said the battles were usually fought at dawn and dusk, so sometimes in the middle of the day he'd been able to get away and go hunting. In the mansion, the dark, noble heads of long-ago beasts from all over the world—elephants, greater Thomson's gazelles, giant oryx—lined the walls of the rooms. There was a giant gleaming sailfish leaping over the headboard of my bed upstairs, and there were woodstoves and fireplaces, but no electricity. This place is so far into the middle of nowhere. After I took the caretaking position, the ex-wife sent postcards saying how much she enjoyed twenty-four-hour electricity and how she'd get up during the night and flick on a light switch, just for the hell of it.

I felt that I was taking advantage of Beauregard, moving into his castle while he slaved away in D.C. But I'm a bit of a killer myself, in some ways, if you get right down to it, and if Beauregard's hard luck was my good luck, well, I tried not to lose any sleep over it.

If anything, I gained sleep over it, especially in the summer. I'd get up kind of late, eight or nine o'clock, and fix breakfast, feed my dogs, then go out on the porch and sit in the rocking chair and look out over the valley or read. Around noon I'd pack a lunch and go for a walk. I'd take the dogs with me, and a book, and we'd start up the trail behind the house, following the creek through the larch and cedar forest to the waterfall. Deer moved quietly through the heavy timber. Pileated woodpeckers banged away on some of the dead trees, going at it like cannons. In that place the sun rarely made it to the ground, stopping instead on all the various levels of leaves. I'd get to the waterfall and swim—so cold!—with the dogs, and then they'd nap in some ferns while I sat on a rock and read some more.

In midafternoon I'd come home—it would be hot then, in the summer. The fields and meadows in front of the ranch smelled of wild strawberries, and I'd stop and pick some. By that time of day it would be too hot to do anything but take a nap, so that's what I'd do, upstairs on the big bed with all the windows open, with a fly buzzing faintly in one of the other rooms, one of the many empty rooms.

When it cooled down enough, around seven or eight in the evening, I'd wake up and take my fly rod over to the other side of the meadow. A spring creek wandered along the edge of it, and I'd catch a brook trout for supper. I'd keep just one. There were too many fish in the little creek and they were too easy to catch, so after an hour or two I'd get tired of catching them. I'd take the one fish back to the cabin and fry him for supper.

Then I'd have to decide whether to read some more or go for another walk or just sit on the porch with a drink in hand. Usually I chose that last option, and sometimes while I was out on the porch, a great gray owl came flying in from the woods. It was always a thrill to see it—that huge, wild, silent creature soaring over my front yard.

The great gray owl's a strange creature. It's immense, and so shy that it lives only in the oldest of the old-growth forests, among giant trees, as if to match its own great size against them. The owl sits very still for long stretches of time, watching for prey, until—so say the ornithologists—it believes it is invisible. A person or a deer can walk right up to it, and so secure is the bird in its invisibility that it will not move. Even if you're looking straight at it, it's convinced you can't see it.

My job, my only job, was to live in the mansion and keep intruders out. There had been a For Sale sign out front, but I took it down and hid it in the garage the first day.

After a couple of years, Beauregard, the real killer, did sell the property, and was out of the picture. Pointy-toed Zim got his 10 percent, I suppose—10 percent of $350,000; a third of a million for a place with no electricity!—but Quentin, the stock analyst, didn't buy it right away. He *said* he was going to buy it, within the first five minutes of seeing it. At that time, he took me aside and asked if I could stay on, and like a true predator I said, Hell yes. I didn't care who owned it as long as I got to stay there, as long as the owner lived far away and wasn't someone who would keep mucking up my life with a lot of visits.

Quentin didn't want to live here, or even visit; he just wanted to *own* it. He wanted to buy the place, but first he wanted to toy with Beauregard for a while, to try and drive the price down. He wanted to *flirt* with him, I think.

Myself, I would've been terrified to jack with Beauregard. The man had bullet holes in his arms and legs, and scars from various knife fights; he'd been in foreign prisons and had killed people. A bear had bitten him in the face, on one of his hunts, a bear he'd thought was dead.

Quentin and his consultant to the West, Zim, occasionally came out on "scouting trips" during the summer and fall they were buying the place. They'd show up unannounced with bags of groceries—Cheerios, Pop Tarts, hot dogs, cartons of Marlboros—and want to stay for the weekend, to "get a better feel for the place." I'd have to move my stuff—sleeping bag, frying pan, fishing rod—over to the guest house, which was spacious enough. I didn't mind that; I just didn't like the idea of having them around.

Once, while Quentin and Zim were walking in the woods, I looked inside one of their dumb sacks of groceries to see what they'd brought this time and a magazine fell out, a magazine with a picture of naked men on the cover. I mean, drooping penises and all, and the inside of the magazine was worse, with naked little boys and naked men on motorcycles.

None of the men or boys in the pictures were ever *doing* anything, they were never touching each other, but still the whole magazine—the part of it I looked at, anyway—was nothing but heinies and penises.

In my woods!

I'd see the two old boys sitting on the front porch, the lodge ablaze with light—those sapsuckers running *my* generator, *my* propane, far into the night, playing *my* Jimmy Buffett records, singing at the top of their lungs. Then finally they'd turn the lights off, shut the generator down, and go to bed.

Except Quentin would stay up a little longer. From the porch of the guest house at the other end of the meadow (my pups asleep at my feet), I could see Quentin moving through the lodge, lighting the gas lanterns, walking like a ghost. Then the sonofabitch would start having one of his fits.

He'd break things—plates, saucers, lanterns, windows, my things and Beauregard's things—though I suppose they were now his things, since the deal was in the works. I'd listen to the crashing of glass and watch Quentin's big, whirling polar-bear shape passing from room to room. Sometimes he had a pistol in his hand (they both carried nine-millimeter Blackhawks on their hips, like little cowboys), and he'd shoot holes in the ceiling and the walls.

I'd get tense there in the dark. This wasn't good for my peace of mind. My days of heaven—I'd gotten used to them, and I wanted to defend them and protect them, even if they weren't mine in the first place, even if I'd never owned them.

Then, in that low lamplight, I'd see Zim enter the room. Like an old queen, he'd put his arm around Quentin's big shoulders and lead him away to bed.

After one of their scouting trips the house stank of cigarettes, and I wouldn't sleep in the bed for weeks, for fear of germs; I'd sleep in one of the many guest rooms. Once I found some mouthwash spray under the bed and pictured the two of them lying there, spraying it into each other's mouths in the morning, before kissing . . .

I'm talking like a homophobe here. I don't think it's that at all. I think it was just that realtor. He was just turning a trick, was all.

I felt sorry for Quentin. It was strange how shy he was, how he always tried to cover up his destruction, smearing wood putty into the bullet holes and mopping the food off the ceiling—this fractured stock analyst doing domestic work. He offered me lame excuses the next day about the broken glass—"I was shooting at a bat," he'd say, "a bat came in the window"—and all the while Zim would be sitting on my porch, looking out at my valley with his boots propped up on the railing and smoking the cigarettes that would not kill him quick enough.

Once, in the middle of the day, as the three of us sat on the porch— Quentin asking me some questions about the valley, about how cold it got in the winter—we saw a coyote and her three pups go trotting across the meadow. Zim jumped up, seized a stick of firewood (*my* firewood!), and ran, in his dirty-diaper waddle, out into the field after them, waving the club like a madman. The mother coyote got two of the pups by the scruff and ran with them into the trees, but Zim got the third one, and stood over it, pounding, in the hot midday sun.

It's an old story, but it was a new one for me—how narrow the boundary is between invisibility and collusion. If you don't stop something yourself, if you don't singlehandedly step up and change things, then aren't you just as guilty?

I didn't say anything, not even when Zim came huffing back up to the porch, walking like a man who had just gone out to get the morning paper. There was blood speckled around the cuffs of his pants, and even then I said nothing. I did not want to lose my job. My love for this valley had me trapped.

We all three sat there like everything was the same—Zim breathing a bit more heavily, was all—and I thought I would be able to keep my allegiances secret, through my silence. But they knew whose side I was on. It had been *revealed* to them. It was as if they had infrared vision, as if they could see everywhere, and everything.

"Coyotes eat baby deer and livestock," said the raisin-eyed sonofabitch. "Remember," he said, addressing my silence, "it's not your ranch anymore. All you do is live here and keep the pipes from freezing." Zim glanced over at his soul mate. I thought how when Quentin had another crackup and lost this place, Zim would get the 10 percent again, and again and again each time.

Quentin's face was hard to read; I couldn't tell if he was angry with Zim or not. Everything about Quentin seemed hidden at that moment. How did they do it? How could the bastards be so good at camouflaging themselves when they had to?

I wanted to trick them. I wanted to hide and see them reveal their hearts. I wanted to watch them when they did not know I was watching, and see how they really were—beyond the fear and anger. I wanted to see what was at the bottom of their black fucking hearts.

Now Quentin blinked and turned calmly, still revealing no emotion, and gave his pronouncement. "If the coyotes eat the little deers, they should go," he said. "Hunters should be the only thing out here getting the little deers."

The woods felt the same when I went for my walks each time the two old boys departed. Yellow tanagers still flitted through the trees, flashing blazes of gold. Ravens quorked as they passed through the dark woods, as if to reassure me that they were still on my side, that I was still with nature, rather than without.

I slept late. I read. I hiked, I fished in the evenings. I saw the most spectacular sights. Northern lights kept me up until four in the morning some nights, coiling in red and green spirals across the sky, exploding in iridescent furls and banners. The northern lights never displayed themselves while the killers were there, and for that I was glad.

In the late mornings and early afternoons, I'd sit by the waterfall and eat my peanut butter and jelly sandwiches. I'd see the same magic sights: bull moose, their shovel antlers in velvet, stepping over fallen, rotting logs; calypso orchids sprouting along the trail, glistening and nodding. But it felt, too, as if the woods were a vessel, filling up with some substance of which the woods could hold only so much, and when the forest had absorbed all it could, when no more could be held, things would change.

Zim and Quentin came out only two or three times a year, for two or three days at a time. The rest of the time, heaven was mine, all those days of heaven. You wouldn't think they could hurt anything, visiting so infrequently. How little does it take to change—spoil—another thing? I'll tell you what I think: the cleaner and emptier a place is, the less it can take. It's like some crazy kind of paradox.

After a while, Zim came up with the idea of bulldozing the meadow across the way and building a lake, with sailboats and docks. He hooked Quentin into a deal with a log-house manufacturer in the southern part of the state who was going to put shiny new "El Supremo" homes around the lake. Zim was going to build a small hydro dam on the creek and bring electricity into the valley, which would automatically double real estate values, he said. He was going to run cattle in the woods, lots of cattle, and set up a little gold mining operation over on the north face of Mount Henry. The two boys had folders and folders of ideas. They just needed a little investment capital, they said.

It seemed there was nothing I could do. Anything short of killing Zim and Quentin would be a token act, a mere symbol. Before I figured that out, I sacrificed a tree, chopped down a big, wind-leaning larch so that it fell on top of the lodge, doing great damage while Zim and Quentin were upstairs. I wanted to show them what a money sink the ranch was and how dangerous it could be. I told them how beavers, forest beavers, had chewed down the tree, which had missed landing in their bedroom by only a few feet.

I know now that those razor-bastards knew everything. They could sense that I'd cut that tree, but for some reason they pretended to go along with my story. Quentin had me spend two days sawing the tree for firewood. "You're a good woodcutter," he said when I had the tree all sawed up and stacked. "I'll bet that's the thing you do best."

Before he could get the carpenters out to repair the damage to the lodge, a hard rain blew in and soaked some of my books. I figured there was nothing I could do. Anything I did to harm the land or their property would harm me.

Meanwhile the valley flowered. Summer stretched and yawned, and then it was gone. Quentin brought his children out early the second fall. Zim didn't make the trip, nor did I spy any of the skin magazines. The kids, two girls and a boy who was a younger version of Quentin, were okay for a day or two (the girls ran the generator and watched movies on the VCR the whole day long), but little Quentin was going to be trouble, I could tell. The first words out of his mouth when he arrived were "Can you shoot anything right now? Rabbits? Marmots?"

And sure enough, before two days went by he discovered that there were fish—delicate brook trout with polka-dotted, flashy, colorful sides and intelligent-looking gold-rimmed eyes—spawning on gravel beds in the shallow creek that ran through the meadow. What Quentin's son did after discovering the fish was to borrow his dad's shotgun and begin shooting them.

Little Quentin loaded, blasted away, reloaded. It was a pump-action twelve-gauge, like the ones used in big-city detective movies, and the motion was like masturbating—*jack-jack boom, jack-jack boom*. Little Quentin's sisters came running out, rolled up their pant legs, and waded into the stream.

Quentin sat on the porch with drink in hand and watched, smiling.

During the first week of November, while out walking—the skies frosty, flirting with snow—I heard ravens, and then noticed the smell of a new kill, and moved over in that direction.

The ravens took flight into the trees as I approached. Soon I saw the huge shape of what they'd been feasting on: a carcass of such immensity that I paused, frightened, even though it was obviously dead.

Actually it was two carcasses, bull moose, their antlers locked together from rut-combat. The rut had been over for a month, I knew, and I guessed they'd been attached like that for at least that long. One moose was long dead—two weeks?—but the other moose, though also dead, still had all his hide on him and wasn't even stiff. The ravens and coyotes had already done a pretty good job on the first moose, stripping what they could from him. His partner, his enemy, had thrashed and flailed about, I could tell—small trees and brush were leveled all around them—and I could see the swath, the direction from which they had come, floundering, fighting, to this final resting spot.

I went and borrowed a neighbor's draft horse. The moose that had just died wasn't so heavy—he'd lost a lot of weight during the month he'd been tied up with the other moose—and the other one was a ship of bones, mostly air.

Their antlers seemed to be welded together. I tied a rope around the newly dead moose's hind legs and got the horse to drag the cargo down through the forest and out into the front yard. I walked next to the horse, soothing him as he pulled his strange load. Ravens flew behind us, cawing at this theft. Some of them filtered down from the trees and landed on top of the newly dead moose's humped back and rode along, pecking at the hide, trying to find an opening. But the hide was too thick—they'd have to wait for the coyotes to open it—so they rode with me, like gypsies: I, the draft horse, the ravens, and the two dead moose moved like a giant serpent, snaking our way through the trees.

I hid the carcasses at the edge of the woods and then, on the other side of a small clearing, built a blind of branches and leaves where I could hide and watch over them.

I painted my face camouflage green and brown, settled into my blind, and waited.

The next day, like buffalo wolves from out of the mist, Quentin and Zim reappeared. I'd hidden my truck a couple of miles away and locked up the guest house so they'd think I was gone. I wanted to watch without being seen. I wanted to see them in the wild.

"What the shit!" Zim cried as he got out of his mongotire jeep, the one with the electric winch, electric windows, electric sunroof, and electric cattle prod. Ravens were swarming my trap, gorging, and coyotes darted in and out, tearing at that one moose's hide, trying to peel it back and reveal new flesh.

"Shitfire!" Zim cried, trotting across the yard. He hopped the buck-and-rail fence, his flabby ass caught momentarily astraddle the high bar. He ran into the woods, shooing away the ravens and coyotes. The ravens screamed and rose into the sky as if caught in a huge tornado, as if summoned. Some of the bolder ones descended and made passes at Zim's head, but he waved them away and shouted "Shitfire!" again. He approached, examined the newly dead moose, and said, "This meat's still good!"

That night Zim and Quentin worked by lantern, busy with butchering and skinning knives, hacking at the flesh with hatchets. I stayed in the bushes and watched. The hatchets made whacks when they hit flesh, and cracking sounds when they hit bone. I could hear the two men laughing. Zim reached over and smeared blood delicately on Quentin's cheeks, applying it like makeup, or medicine of some sort, and they paused, catching their breath from their mad chopping before going back to work. They ripped and sawed slabs of meat from the carcass and hooted, cheering each time they pulled off a leg.

They dragged the meat over the autumn-dead grass to the smoke-house, and cut off the head and antlers last, right before daylight.

I hiked out and got my truck, washed my face in a stream, and drove home.

They waved when they saw me come driving in. They were out on the porch having breakfast, all clean and freshly scrubbed. As I approached, I heard them talking as they always did, as normal as pie.

Zim was lecturing to Quentin, waving his arm at the meadow and preaching the catechism of development. "You could have a nice hunting lodge, send 'em all out into the woods on horses, with a yellow slicker and a gun. *Boom!* They're living the western experience. Then in the winter you could run just a regular guest lodge, like on *Newhart*. Make 'em pay for everything. They want to go cross-country skiing? Rent 'em. They want to race snowmobiles? Rent 'em. Charge 'em for taking a *piss*. Rich people don't mind."

I was just hanging back, shaky with anger. They finished their breakfast and went inside to plot, or watch VCR movies. I went over to the smokehouse and peered through the dusty windows. Blood dripped from the gleaming red hindquarters. They'd nailed the moose's head, with the antlers, to one of the walls, so that his blue-blind eyes stared down at his own corpse. There was a baseball cap perched on his antlers and a cigar stuck between his big lips.

I went up into the woods to cool off, but I knew I'd go back. I liked the job of caretaker, liked living at the edge of that meadow.

That evening, the three of us were out on the porch watching the end of the day come in. The days were getting shorter. Quentin and Zim were still pretending that none of the previous night's savagery had happened. It occurred to me that if they thought I had the power to stop them, they would have put my head in that smokehouse a long time ago.

Quentin, looking especially burned out, was slouched down in his chair. He had his back to the wall, bottle of rum in hand, and was gazing at the meadow, where his lake and his cabins with lights burning in each of them would someday sit. I was only hanging around to see what was what and to try to slow them down—to talk about those hard winters whenever I got the chance, and mention how unfriendly the people in the valley were. Which was true, but it was hard to convince Quentin of this, because every time he showed up, they got friendly.

"I'd like that a lot," Quentin said, his speech slurred. Earlier in the day I'd seen a coyote, or possibly a wolf, trot across the meadow alone, but I didn't point it out to anyone. Now, perched in the shadows on a falling-down fence, I saw the great gray owl, watching us, and I didn't point him out either. He'd come gliding in like a plane, ghostly gray, with his four-foot wingspan. I didn't know how they'd missed him. I hadn't seen the owl in a couple of weeks, and I'd been worried, but now I was uneasy that he was back, knowing that it would be nothing for a man like Zim to walk up to that owl with his cowboy pistol and put a bullet, point blank, into the bird's ear—the bird with his eyes set in his face, looking straight at you the way all predators do.

"I'd like that so much," Quentin said again—meaning Zim's idea of the lodge as a winter resort. He was wearing a gold chain around his neck with a little gold pistol dangling from it. He'd have to get rid of that necklace if he moved out here. It looked like something he might have gotten from a Cracker Jack box, but was doubtless real gold.

"It may sound corny," Quentin said, "but if I owned this valley, I'd let people from New York, from California, from wherever, come out here for Christmas and New Year's. I'd put a big sixty-foot Christmas tree in the middle of the road up by the Mercantile and the saloon, and string it with lights, and we'd all ride up there in a sleigh, Christmas Eve and New Year's Eve, and we'd sing carols, you know? It would be real small town and homey," he said. "Maybe corny, but that's what I'd do."

Zim nodded. "There's lonely people who would pay through the nose for something like that," he said.

We watched the dusk glide in over the meadow, cooling things off, blanketing the field's dull warmth. Mist rose from the field.

Quentin and Zim were waiting for money, and Quentin, especially, was still waiting for his nerves to calm. He'd owned the ranch for a full cycle of seasons, and still he wasn't well.

A little something—peace?—would do him good. I could see that Christmas tree all lit up. I could feel that sense of community, of new beginnings.

I wouldn't go to such a festivity. I'd stay back in the woods like the great gray owl. But I could see the attraction, could see Quentin's need for peace, how he had to have a place to start anew—though soon enough, I knew, he would keep on taking his percentage from that newness. Taking too much.

Around midnight, I knew, he'd start smashing things, and I couldn't blame him. Of course he wanted to come to the woods, too.

I didn't know if the woods would have him.

All I could do was wait. I sat very still, like that owl, and thought about where I could go next, after this place was gone. Maybe, I thought, if I sit very still, they will just go away.

BARBARA KINGSOLVER

arbara Kingsolver's second book, after her successful novel *The Bean Trees*
(1988), was a spirited piece of reportage based on interviews: *Holding the Line:
Women in the Great Arizona Mine Strike of 1983*. It describes the women, most
of them Latina, who stood in the picket lines when their miner husbands were
legally prevented from doing so, and it blasts the unfairness and discrimination
these women and their families were subjected to, both during the strike and in
ordinary working time. As outspoken and sympathetic as this book was, Kingsolver
(b. 1955) had more to say. She worked the women of the picket line into fiction,
later telling an interviewer that in "Why I Am a Danger to the Public," there were
"things that didn't quite happen but could have, and I sort of wish had." She
thoroughly inhabited "Vicki Morales," her protagonist, and let her enlarge upon
the documentary. "All my life I've been someone who just stands on the street
corner and yells about things that are wrong," Kingsolver continued. In *High Tide
in Tucson* (1995), her biological training joins with her social sense in a collection
of strong, environment-based essays. She has won several prizes for her work,
including a *Los Angeles Times* Book Award for Fiction and an Edward Abbey Eco-
fiction Award.

"Why I Am a Danger to the Public," from *Homeland and Other Stories* (1989)

Bueno, if I get backed into a corner I can just about raise up the dead. I'll
fight, sure. But I am no lady wrestler. If you could see me you would
know this thing is a *joke*—Tony, my oldest, is already taller than me, and
he's only eleven. So why are they so scared of me I have to be in jail? I'll
tell you.

Number one, this strike. There has never been one that turned so
many old friends *chingándose*, not here in Bolton. And you can't get away
from it because Ellington don't just run the mine, they own our houses,
the water we drink and the dirt in our shoes and pretty much the state
of New Mexico as I understand it. So if something is breathing, it's on
one side or the other. And in a town like this that matters because everybody you know some way, you go to the same church or they used to
babysit your kids, something. Nobody is a stranger.

My sister went down to Las Cruces New Mexico and got a job down there, but me, no. I stayed here and got married to Junior Morales. Junior was my one big mistake. But I like Bolton. From far away Bolton looks like some kind of all-colored junk that got swept up off the street after a big old party and stuffed down in the canyon. Our houses are all exactly alike, company houses, but people paint them yellow, purple, colors you wouldn't think a house could be. If you go down to the Big Dipper and come walking home *loca* you still know which one is yours. The copper mine is at the top of the canyon and the streets run straight uphill; some of them you can't drive up, you got to walk. There's steps. Oliver P. Snapp, that used to be the mailman for the west side, died of a heart attack one time right out there in his blue shorts. So the new mailman refuses to deliver to those houses; they have to pick up their mail at the P.O.

Now, this business with me and Vonda Fangham, I can't even tell you what got it started. I never had one thing in the world against her, no more than anybody else did. But this was around the fourth or fifth week so everybody knew by then who was striking and who was crossing. It don't take long to tell rats from cheese, and every night there was a big old fight in the Big Dipper. Somebody punching out his brother or his best friend. All that and no paycheck, can you imagine?

So it was a Saturday and there was just me and Corvallis Smith up at the picket line, setting in front of the picket shack passing the time of day. Corvallis is *un tipo*, he is real tall and lifts weights and wears his hair in those corn rows that hang down in the back with little pieces of aluminum foil on the ends. But good-looking in a certain way. I went out with Corvallis one time just so people would have something to talk about, and sure enough, they had me getting ready to have brown and black polka-dotted babies. All you got to do to get pregnant around here is have two beers with somebody in the Dipper, so watch out.

"What do you hear from Junior," he says. That's a joke; everybody says it including my friends. See, when Manuela wasn't hardly even born one minute and Tony still in diapers, Junior says, "Vicki, I can't find a corner to piss in around this town." He said there was jobs in Tucson and he would send a whole lot of money. Ha ha. That's how I got started up at Ellington. I was not going to support my kids in no little short skirt down at the Frosty King. That was eight years ago. I got started on the track gang, laying down rails for the cars that go into the pit, and now I am a crane operator. See, when Junior left I went up the hill and made such a rackus they had to hire me up there, hire me or shoot me, one.

"Oh, I hear from him about the same as I hear from Oliver P. Snapp," I say to Corvallis. That's the rest of the joke.

It was a real slow morning. Cecil Smoot was supposed to be on the

picket shift with us but he wasn't there yet. Cecil will show up late when
the Angel Gabriel calls the Judgment, saying he had to give his Datsun a
lube job.

"Well, looka here," says Corvallis. "Here come the ladies." There is
this club called Wives of Working Men, just started since the strike. Meaning Wives of Scabs. About six of them was coming up the hill all cram-
packed into Vonda Fangham's daddy's air-conditioned Lincoln. She pulls
the car right up next to where mine is at. My car is a Buick older than
both my two kids put together. It gets me where I have to go.

They set and look at us for one or two minutes. Out in that hot sun,
sticking to our T-shirts, and me in my work boots—I can't see no point
in treating it like a damn tea party—and Corvallis, he's an eyeful anyway.
All of a sudden the windows on the Lincoln all slide down. It has those
electric windows.

"Isn't this a ni-i-ice day," says one of them, Doreen Carter. Doreen
visited her sister in Laurel, Mississippi, for three weeks one time and now
she has an accent. "Bein' payday an' all," she says. Her husband is the
minister of Saint's Grace, which is scab headquarters. I quit going. I was
raised up to believe in God and the union, but listen, if it comes to pushing or shoving I know which one of the two is going to keep tires on the
car.

"Well, yes, it is a real nice day," another one of them says. They're all
fanning theirselves with something paper. I look, and Corvallis looks.
They're fanning theirselves with their husbands' paychecks.

I haven't had a paycheck since July. My son couldn't go to Morse with
his baseball team Friday night because they had to have three dollars for
supper at McDonald's. Three damn dollars.

The windows start to go back up and they're getting ready to drive
off, and I say, "Vonda Fangham, *vete al infierno*."

The windows whoosh back down.

"What did you say?" Vonda wants to know.

"I said, I'm surprised to see you in there with the scab ladies. I didn't
know you had went and got married to a yellow-spine scab just so somebody would let you in their club."

Well, Corvallis laughs at that. But Vonda just gives me this look. She
has a little sharp nose and yellow hair and teeth too big to fit behind her
lips. For some reason she was a big deal in high school, and it's not her
personality either. She was the queen of everything. Cheerleaders, drama
club, every school play they ever had, I think.

I stare at her right back, ready to make a day out of it if I have to.
The heat is rising up off that big blue hood like it's a lake all set to boil
over.

"What I said was, Vonda Fangham, you can go to hell."

"I can't hear a word you're saying," she says. "Trash can't talk."

"This trash can go to bed at night and know I haven't cheated nobody out of a living. You want to see trash, *chica*, you ought to come up here at the shift change and see what kind of shit rolls over that picket line."

Well, that shit I was talking about was their husbands, so up go the windows and off they fly. Vonda just about goes in the ditch trying to get that big car turned around.

To tell you the truth I knew Vonda was engaged to get married to Tommy Jones, a scab. People said, Well, at least now Vonda will be just Vonda Jones. That name Fangham is *feo*, and the family has this whole certain way of showing off. Her dad's store, Fangham Drugs, has the biggest sign in town, as if he has to advertise. As if somebody would forget it was there and drive fifty-one miles over the mountains to Morse to go to another drugstore.

I couldn't care less about Tommy and Vonda getting engaged, I was just hurt when he crossed the line. Tommy was a real good man, I used to think. He was not ashamed like most good-looking guys are to act decent once in a while. Me and him started out on the same track crew and he saved my butt one time covering the extra weight for me when I sprang my wrist. And he never acted like I owed him for it. Some guys, they would try to put the moves on me out by the slag pile. Shit, that was hell. And then I would be downtown in the drugstore and Carol Finch or somebody would go *huh-hmm*, clear her throat and roll her eyes, like, "Over here is what you want," looking at the condoms. Just because I'm up there with their husbands all day I am supposed to be screwing around. In all that mud, just think about it, in our steel toe boots that weigh around ten pounds, and our hard hats. And then the guys gave me shit too when I started training as a crane operator, saying a woman don't have no business taking up the good-paying jobs. You figure it out.

Tommy was different. He was a lone ranger. He didn't grow up here or have family, and in Bolton you can move in here and live for about fifty years and people still call you that fellow from El Paso, or wherever it was you come from. They say that's why he went in, that he was afraid if he lost his job he would lose Vonda too. But we all had something to lose.

That same day I come home and found Manuela and Tony in the closet. Like poor little kitties in there setting on the shoes. Tony was okay pretty much but Manuela was crying, screaming. I thought she would dig her eyes out.

Tony kept going, "They was up here looking for you!"

"Who was?" I asked him.

"Scab men," he said. "Clifford Owens and Mr. Alphonso and them police from out of town. The ones with the guns."

"The State Police?" I said. I couldn't believe it. "The State Police was up here? What did they want?"

"They wanted to know where you was at." Tony almost started to cry. "Mama, I didn't tell them."

"He didn't," Manuela said.

"Well, I was just up at the damn picket shack. Anybody could have found me if they wanted to." I could have swore I saw Owens's car go right by the picket shack, anyway.

"They kept on saying where was you at, and we didn't tell them. We said you hadn't done nothing."

"Well, you're right, I haven't done nothing. Why didn't you go over to Uncle Manny's? He's supposed to be watching you guys."

"We was scared to go outside!" Manuela screamed. She was jumping from one foot to the other and hugging herself. "They said they'd get us!"

"Tony, did they say that? Did they threaten you?"

"They said stay away from the picket rallies," Tony said. "The one with the gun said he seen us and took all our pitchers. He said, your mama's got too big a mouth for her own good."

At the last picket rally I was up on Lalo Ruiz's shoulders with a bull horn. I've had almost every office in my local, and sergeant-at-arms twice because the guys say I have no toleration for BS. They got one of those big old trophies down at the union hall that says on it "MEN OF COPPER," and one time Lalo says, "Vicki ain't no Man of Copper, she's a damn stick of *mesquite*. She might break but she sure as hell won't bend."

Well, I want my kids to know what this is about. When school starts, if some kid makes fun of their last-year's blue jeans and calls them trash I want them to hold their heads up. I take them to picket rallies so they'll know that. No law says you can't set up on nobody with a bull horn. They might have took my picture, though. I wouldn't be surprised.

"All I ever done was defend my union," I told the kids. "Even cops have to follow the laws, and it isn't no crime to defend your union. Your grandpapa done it and his papa and now me."

Well, my grandpapa one time got put on a railroad car like a cow, for being a Wobbly and a Mexican. My kids have heard that story a million times. He got dumped out in the desert someplace with no water or even a cloth for his head, and it took him two months to get back. All that time my granny and Tía Sonia thought he was dead.

I hugged Tony and Manuela and then we went and locked the door.

I had to pull up on it while they jimmied the latch because that damn door had not been locked one time in seven years.

What we thought about when we wanted to feel better was: What a God-awful mess they got up there in the mine. Most of those scabs was out-of-towners and didn't have no idea what end of the gun to shoot. I heard it took them about one month to figure out how to start the equipment. Before the walkout there was some parts switched around between my crane and a locomotive, but we didn't have to do that because the scabs tied up the cat's back legs all by theirselves. Laying pieces of track back-wards, running the conveyors too fast, I hate to think what else.

We even heard that one foreman, Willie Bunford, quit because of all the jackasses on the machinery, that he feared for his life. Willie Bunford used to be my foreman. He made fun of how I said his name, "Wee-lee!" so I called him Mr. Bunford. So I have an accent, so what. When I was first starting on the crane he said, "You aren't going to get PG now, are you, Miss Morales, after I wasted four weeks training you as an operator? I know how you Mexican gals love to have babies." I said, "Mr. Bunford, as far as this job goes you can consider me a man." So I had to stick to that. I couldn't call up and say I'm staying in bed today because of my monthly. Then what does he do but lay off two weeks with so-called whiplash from a car accident on Top Street when I saw the whole story: Winnie Hask backing into his car in front of the Big Dipper and him not in it. If a man can get whiplash from his car getting bashed in while he is drinking beer across the street, well, that's a new one.

So I didn't cry for no Willie Bunford. At least he had the sense to get out of there. None of those scabs knew how to run the oxygen machine, so we were waiting for the whole damn place to blow up. I said to the guys, Let's go sit on Bolt Mountain with some beer and watch the fireworks.

The first eviction I heard about was the Frank Mickliffs, up the street from me, and then Joe Gomez on Alameda. Ellington wanted to clear out some company houses for the new hires, but how they decided who to throw out we didn't know. Then Janie Marley found out from her friend that babysits for the sister-in-law of a scab that company men were driving scab wives around town letting them pick out whatever house they wanted. Like they're going shopping and we're the peaches getting squeezed.

Friday of that same week I was out on my front porch thinking about a cold beer, just thinking, though, because of no cash, and here come an

Ellington car. They slowed way, way down when they went by, then on up Church Street going about fifteen and then they come back. It was Vonda in there. She nodded her head at my house and the guy put something down on paper. They made a damn picture show out of it.

Oh, I was furious. I have been living in that house almost the whole time I worked for Ellington and it's all the home my kids ever had. It's a real good house. It's yellow. I have a big front porch where you can see just about everything, all of Bolton, and a railing so the kids won't fall over in the gulch, and a big yard. I keep it up nice, and my brother Manny being right next door helps out. I have this mother duck with her babies all lined up that the kids bought me at Fangham's for Mother's Day, and I planted marigolds in a circle around them. No way on this earth was I turning my house over to a scab.

The first thing I did was march over to Manny's house and knock on the door and walk in. "Manny," I say to him, "I don't want you mowing my yard anymore unless you feel like doing a favor for Miss Vonda." Manny is just pulling the pop top off a Coke and his mouth goes open at the same time; he just stares.

"Oh, no," he says.

"Oh, yes."

I went back over to my yard and Manny come hopping out putting on his shoes, to see what I'm going to do, I guess. He's my little brother but Mama always says "*Madre Santa*, Manuel, keep an eye on Vicki!" Well, what I was going to do was my own damn business. I pulled up the ducks, they have those metal things that poke in the ground, and then I pulled up the marigolds and threw them out on the sidewalk. If I had to get the neighbor kids to help make my house the ugliest one, I was ready to do it.

Well. The next morning I was standing in the kitchen drinking coffee, and Manny come through the door with this funny look on his face and says, "The tooth fairy has been to see you."

What in the world. I ran outside and there was *pink* petunias planted right in the circle where I already pulled up the marigolds. To think Vonda could sneak into my yard like a common thief and do a thing like that.

"Get the kids," I said. I went out and started pulling out petunias. I hate pink. And I hate how they smelled, they had these sticky roots. Manny woke up the kids and they come out and helped.

"This is fun, Mom," Tony said. He wiped his cheek and a line of dirt ran across like a scar. They were in their pajamas.

"Son, we're doing it for the union," I said. We threw them out on the sidewalk with the marigolds, to dry up and die.

After that I was scared to look out the window in the morning. God knows what Vonda might put in my yard, more flowers or one of those ugly pink flamingos they sell at Fangham's yard and garden department. I wouldn't put nothing past Vonda.

Whatever happened, we thought when the strike was over we would have our jobs. You could put up with high water and heck, thinking of that. It's like having a baby, you just grit your teeth and keep your eyes on the prize. But then Ellington started sending out termination notices saying, You will have no job to come back to whatsoever.

They would fire you for any excuse, mainly strike-related misconduct, which means nothing, you looked cross-eyed at a policeman or whatever. People got scared.

The national office of the union was no help; they said, To hell with it, boys, take the pay cut and go on back. I had a fit at the union meeting. I told them it's not the pay cut, it's what all else they would take if we give in. "Ellington would not have hired me in two million years if it wasn't for the union raising a rackus about all people are created equal," I said. "Or half of you either because they don't like cunts or coloreds." I'm not that big of a person but I was standing up in front, and when I cussed, they shut up. "If my papa had been a chickenshit like you guys, I would be down at the Frosty King tonight in a little short skirt," I said. "You bunch of no-goods would be on welfare and your kids pushing drugs to pay the rent." Some of the guys laughed, but some didn't.

Men get pissed off in this certain way, though, where they have to tear something up. Lalo said, "Well, hell, let's drive a truck over the plant gate and shut the damn mine down." And there they go, off and running, making plans to do it. Corvallis had a baseball cap on backwards and was sitting back with his arms crossed like, Honey, don't look at me. I could have killed him.

"Great, you guys, you do something cute like that and we're dead ducks," I said. "We don't have to do but one thing, wait it out."

"Till when?" Lalo wanted to know. "Till hell freezes?" He is kind of a short guy with about twelve tattoos on each arm.

"Till they get fed up with the scabs pissing around and want to get the mine running. If it comes down to busting heads, no way. Do you hear me? They'll have the National Guards in here."

I knew I was right. The Boots in this town, the cops, they're on Ellington payroll. I've seen strikes before. When I was ten years old I saw a cop get a Mexican man down on the ground and kick his face till blood ran out of his ear. You would think I was the only one in that room that was born and raised in Bolton.

Ellington was trying to get back up to full production. They had them working twelve-hour shifts and seven-day weeks like Abraham Lincoln had never freed the slaves. We started hearing about people getting hurt, but just rumors; it wasn't going to run in the paper. Ellington owns the paper.

The first I knew about it really was when Vonda come right to my house. I was running the vacuum cleaner and had the radio turned up all the way so I didn't hear her drive up. I just heard a knock on the door, and when I opened it: Vonda. Her skin looked like a flour tortilla. "What in the world," I said.

Her bracelets were going clack-clack-clack, she was shaking so hard. "I never thought I'd be coming to you," she said, like I was Dear Abby. "But something's happened to Tommy."

"Oh," I said. I had heard some real awful things: that a guy was pulled into a smelter furnace, and another guy got his legs run over on the tracks. I could picture Tommy either way, no legs or burnt up. We stood there a long time. Vonda looked like she might pass out. "Okay, come in," I told her. "Set down there and I'll get you a drink of water. Water is all we got around here." I stepped over the vacuum cleaner on the way to the kitchen. I wasn't going to put it away.

When I come back she was looking around the room all nervous, breathing like a bird. I turned down the radio.

"How are the kids?" she wanted to know, of all things.

"The kids are fine. Tell me what happened to Tommy."

"Something serious to do with his foot, that's all I know. Either cut off or half cut off, they won't tell me." She pulled this little hanky out of her purse and blew her nose. "They sent him to Morse in the helicopter ambulance, but they won't say what hospital because I'm not next of kin. He doesn't have any next of kin here, I *told* them that. I informed them I was the fiancée." She blew her nose again. "All they'll tell me is they don't want him in the Bolton hospital. I can't understand why."

"Because they don't want nobody to know about it," I told her. "They're covering up all the accidents."

"Well, why would they want to do that?"

"Vonda, excuse me please, but don't be stupid. They want to do that so we won't know how close we are to winning the strike."

Vonda took a little sip of water. She had on a yellow sun dress and her arms looked so skinny, like just bones with freckles. "Well, I know what you think of me," she finally said, "but for Tommy's sake maybe you can get the union to do something. Have an investigation so he'll at least get his compensation pay. I know you have a lot of influence on the union."

"I don't know if I do or not," I told her. I puffed my breath out and leaned my head back on the sofa. I pulled the bandana off my head and rubbed my hair in a circle. It's so easy to know what's right and so hard to do it.

"Vonda," I said, "I thought a lot of Tommy before all this shit. He helped me one time when I needed it real bad." She looked at me. She probably hated thinking of me and him being friends. "I'm sure Tommy knows he done the wrong thing," I said. "But it gets me how you people treat us like kitchen trash and then come running to the union as soon as you need help."

She picked up her glass and brushed at the water on the coffee table. I forgot napkins. "Yes, I see that now, and I'll try to make up for my mistake," she said.

Give me a break, Vonda, was what I was thinking. "Well, we'll see," I said. "There is a meeting coming up and I'll see what I can do. If you show up on the picket line tomorrow."

Vonda looked like she swallowed one of her ice cubes. She went over to the TV and picked up the kids' pictures one at a time, Manuela then Tony. Put them back down. Went over to the *armario* built by my grandpapa.

"What a nice little statue," she said.

"That's St. Joseph. Saint of people that work with their hands."

She turned around and looked at me. "I'm sorry about the house. I won't take your house. It wouldn't be right."

"I'm glad you feel that way, because I wasn't moving."

"Oh," she said.

"Vonda, I can remember when me and you were little girls and your daddy was already running the drugstore. You used to set up on a stool behind the counter and run the soda-water machine. You had a charm bracelet with everything in the world on it, poodle dogs and hearts and a real little pill box that opened."

Vonda smiled. "I don't have the foggiest idea what ever happened to that bracelet. Would you like it for your girl?"

I stared at her. "But you don't remember me, do you?"

"Well, I remember a whole lot of people coming in the store. You in particular, I guess not."

"I guess not," I said. "People my color was not allowed to go in there and set at the soda fountain. We had to get paper cups and take our drinks outside. Remember that? I used to think and *think* about why that was. I thought our germs must be so nasty they wouldn't wash off the glasses."

"Well, things have changed, haven't they?" Vonda said.

"Yeah." I put my feet up on the coffee table. It's my damn table. "Things changed because the UTU and the Machinists and my papa's union the Boilermakers took this whole fucking company town to court in 1973, that's why. This house right here was for whites only. And if there wasn't no union forcing Ellington to abide by the law, it still would be."

She was kind of looking out the window. She probably was thinking about what she was going to cook for supper.

"You think it wouldn't? You think Ellington would build a nice house for everybody if they could still put half of us in those falling-down shacks down by the river like I grew up in?"

"Well, you've been very kind to hear me out," she said. "I'll do what you want, tomorrow. Right now I'd better be on my way."

I went out on the porch and watched her go down the sidewalk— click click, on her little spike heels. Her ankles wobbled.

"Vonda," I yelled out after her, "don't wear high heels on the line tomorrow. For safety's sake."

She never turned around.

Next day the guys were making bets on Vonda showing up or not. The odds were not real good in her favor. I had to laugh, but myself I really thought she would. It was a huge picket line for the morning shift change. The Women's Auxiliary thought it would boost up the morale, which needed a kick in the butt or somebody would be busting down the plant gate. Corvallis told me that some guys had a meeting after the real meeting and planned it out. But I knew that if I kept showing up at the union meetings and standing on the table and jumping and hollering, they wouldn't do it. Sometimes guys will listen to a woman.

The sun was just coming up over the canyon and already it was a hot day. Cicada bugs buzzing in the *paloverdes* like damn rattlesnakes. Me and Janie Marley were talking about our kids; she has a boy one size down from Tony and we trade clothes around. All of a sudden Janie grabs my elbow and says, "Look who's here." It was Vonda getting out of the Lincoln. Not in high heels either. She had on a tennis outfit and plastic sunglasses and a baseball bat slung over her shoulder. She stopped a little ways from the line and was looking around, waiting for the Virgin Mary to come down, I guess, and save her. Nobody was collecting any bets.

"Come on, Vonda," I said. I took her by the arm and stood her between me and Janie. "I'm glad you made it." But she wasn't talking, just looking around a lot.

After a while I said, "We're not supposed to have bats up here. I know a guy that got his termination papers for carrying a crescent wrench in his back pocket. He had forgot it was even in there." I looked at Vonda to see if she was paying attention. "It was Rusty Cochran," I said, "you know him. He's up at your dad's every other day for a prescription. They had that baby with the hole in his heart."

But Vonda held on to the bat like it was the last man in the world and she got him. "I'm only doing this for Tommy," she says.

"Well, so what," I said. "I'm doing it for my kids. So they can eat."

She kept squinting her eyes down the highway.

A bunch of people started yelling, "Here come the ladies!" Some of the women from the Auxiliary were even saying it. And here come trouble. They were in Doreen's car, waving signs out the windows: "We Support Our Working Men" and other shit not worth repeating. Doreen was driving. She jerked right dead to a stop, right in front of us. She looked at Vonda and you would think she had broke both her hinges the way her mouth was hanging open, and Vonda looked back at Doreen, and the rest of us couldn't wait to see what was next.

Doreen took a U-turn and almost ran over Cecil Smoot, and they beat it back to town like bats out of hell. Ten minutes later here come her car back up the hill again. Only this time her husband Milton was driving, and three other men from Saint's Grace was all in there besides Doreen. Two of them are cops.

"I don't know what they're up to but we don't need you getting in trouble," I told Vonda. I took the bat away from her and put it over my shoulder. She looked real white, and I patted her arm and said, "Don't worry." I can't believe I did that, now. Looking back.

They pulled up in front of us again but they didn't get out, just all five of them stared and then they drove off, like whatever they come for they got.

That was yesterday. Last night I was washing the dishes and somebody come to the house. The kids were watching TV. I heard Tony slide the dead bolt over and then he yelled, "Mom, it's the Boot."

Before I can even put down a plate and get into the living room Larry Trevizo has pushed right by him into the house. I come out wiping my hands and see him there holding up his badge.

"Chief of Police, ma'am," he says, just like that, like I don't know who the hell he is. Like we didn't go through every grade of school together and go see *Suddenly Last Summer* one time in high school.

He says, "Mrs. Morales, I'm serving you with injunction papers."

"Oh, is that a fact," I say. "And may I ask what for?"

Tony already turned off the TV and is standing by me with his arms crossed, the meanest-looking damn eleven-year-old you ever hope to see in your life. All I can think of is the guys in the meeting, how they get so they just want to bust something in.

"Yes you may ask what for," Larry says, and starts to read, not looking any of us in the eye: "For being a danger to the public. Inciting a riot. Strike-related misconduct." And then real low he says something about Vonda Fangham and a baseball bat.

"What was that last thing?"

He clears his throat. "And for kidnapping Vonda Fangham and threatening her with a baseball bat. We got the affidavits."

"*Pa'fuera!*" I tell Larry Trevizo. I ordered him out of my house right then, told him if he wanted to see somebody get hurt with a baseball bat he could hang around my living room and find out. I trusted myself but not Tony. Larry got out of there.

The injunction papers said I was not to be in any public gathering of more than five people or I would be arrested. And what do you know, a squad of Boots was already lined up by the picket shack at the crack of dawn this morning with their hands on their sticks, just waiting. They knew I would be up there, I see that. They knew I would do just exactly all the right things. Like the guys say, Vicki might break but she don't bend.

They cuffed me and took me up to the jailhouse, which is in back of the Ellington main office, and took off my belt and my earrings so I wouldn't kill myself or escape. "With an earring?" I said. I was laughing. I could see this old rotten building through the office window; it used to be something or other but now there's chickens living in it. You could dig out of there with an earring; for sure. I said, "What's that over there, the Mexican jail? You better put me in there!"

I thought they would just book me and let me go like they did some other ones, before this. But no, I have to stay put. Five hundred thousand bond. I don't think this whole town could come up with that, not if they signed over every pink, purple, and blue house in Bolton.

It didn't hit me till right then about the guys wanting to tear into the plant. What they might do.

"Look, I got to get out by tonight," I told the cops. I don't know their names, it was some State Police I have never seen, seem like they just come up out of nowhere. I was getting edgy. "I have a union meeting and it's real important. Believe me, you don't want me to miss it."

They smiled. And then I got that terrible feeling you get when you see somebody has been looking you in the eye and smiling and setting a trap, and there you are in it like a damn rat.

What is going to happen I don't know. I'm keeping my ears open. I found out my kids are driving Manny to distraction—Tony told his social-studies class he would rather have a jailbird than a scab mom, and they sent him home with a note that he was causing a dangerous disturbance in class.

I also learned that Tommy Jones was not in any accident. He got called off his shift one day and was took to Morse in a helicopter with no explanation. They put him up at Howard Johnson's over there for five days, his meals and everything, just told him not to call nobody, and today he's back at work. They say he is all in one piece.

Well, I am too.

LINDA HOGAN

A Chickasaw poet, novelist, essayist, and teacher at the University of Colorado, Linda Hogan (b. 1947) has an almost casual, sudden, juxtaposing way of evoking unthought-of connections. It is as if the surface mentality, that which needs linear logic and proof, has been edited out, and we go directly to the spirit of things. The poetic kind of seeing is apparently seldom far from this writer's consciousness, resulting in some unusual images of interdependent life. In her 1990 novel, *Mean Spirit*, some Indians are sleeping outside their houses, in order to have fresh air in the hot summer nights of Oklahoma. "Near the marshland, tents of gauzy mosquito netting sloped down over the bony shoulders and hips of dreamers. A hand hung over the edge of a bed, fingers reaching down toward bluegrass that grew upward in fields. Given half a chance, the vines and leaves would have crept up the beds and overgrown the sleeping bodies of people." In "Creations," a trip to the Yucatan Peninsula becomes the vehicle for insights into the nature of nature and our place in it, insights that may appear dramatic or dreamy from the traditional perspective of mainstream Western civilization. Hogan's specialty, however, is to make the poetic feel utterly familiar, as real as daily life.

"Creations" from *Heart of the Land* (1994)

We were told by the Creator; This is your land. Keep it for me until I come back.
—THOMAS BANYACA, HOPI ELDER

We are traveling toward the end of land, to a place called Ría Celestún, Estuary of Heaven. It is a place where clouds are born. On some days they rise up above the river and follow water's path. On those days, from across the full length of the land, Río Esperanza, the River of Hope, can be seen as it is carried up into the sky. But today, the late morning clouds have formed further out, above the ocean.

It is the day after spring equinox, and as we near the ocean, whiteness is the dominant feature. Salt beds stretch out at water's edge. Beaches, made of sea-worn limestone and broken-down coral, are nearly blinding in the early spring light. Water, itself, wears the sun's light on its back, and near a road sign several young men are at work, throwing buckets of salt-dried fish into the bed of a pickup truck.

It has been a long, narrow road through the Yucatán. We have passed jungle, brush, and villages created from bone-colored limestone. A woman in an embroidered white huipil walks along the road carrying a bundle of firewood. Smoke from a household fire rises above the thatched roofs. Two boys with small rifles step into the forest in search of food. In spite of the appearance of abundance in the Yucatán, it is a world endangered, not only by deforestation but by other stresses to the environment, by the poverty some people's greed has created for others. It is a hungry place with dwindling resources.

In some villages, the few livestock—a single horse, a solitary cow— are bony of rib. People, too, in many towns, are thin with an evident hunger, a poverty that, as it grows, is left with little choice but to diminish the world about it.

Many of the people in and near Ría Celestún are new people. Previously, they were farmers of henequen, a plant used to make hemp rope, but since the introduction of plastic and nylon rope, the people have been relocated without consideration for what their presence would mean in this region, or how they would stretch a living out of the land. In order to build houses, swamps were filled in with garbage. There are sewage problems, contaminated water, and the cutting of trees has resulted in the destruction of watershed. With the close-in waters now overfished, the farmers turned fishermen are forced into the dangerous business of taking poorly equipped boats out to deeper waters in search of food. Subsistence, a thin daily scraping by of hunger and need, has taken its toll on the people and the land.

In geological history, as with that of the people, this is a place of rising and collapsing worlds. There is constant movement and transformation. Some are subtle changes—the way mangrove swamps create new soil, the way savannah grows from the fallen mangrove leaves—but most of the boundaries here are crossed in sudden and dramatic ways, the result of the elemental struggle between water and land, where a water-shaped cave collapses and new water surges to fill the sinkhole left behind, where water claims its edges from land, where swamp becomes ocean, ocean evaporates and leaves salt. The land itself bears witness to the way elements trade places: it is limestone that floated up from the sea, containing within it the delicate, complex forms of small animals from earlier times, snails, plants, creatures that were alive beneath water are still visible beneath the feet. To walk on this earth is to walk on a living past, on the open pages of history and geology.

Now even the dusty road we travel becomes something else as it disappears into the ocean at Celestún. It is a place of endings and of beginnings, full with the power of creation.

Holy Mother Earth, the trees and all nature, are witnesses of your thoughts
and deeds.

WINNEBAGO

For the Maya, time was born and had a name when the sky
                    didn't exist and the earth had not yet awakened.
The days set out from the east and started walking.
The first day produced from its entrails the sky and the earth.
The second day made the stairway for the rain to run down.
The cycles of the sea and the land, and the multitude of things,
                    were the work of the third day.
The fourth day willed the earth and the sky to tilt so that they
                    could meet.
The fifth day decided that everyone had to work.
The first light emanated from the sixth day.
In places where there was nothing, the seventh day put soil; the eighth
          plunged its hands and feet in the soil.
The ninth day created the nether worlds; the tenth earmarked for them
          those who had poison in their souls.
Inside the sun, the eleventh day modeled stone and tree.
It was the twelfth that made the wind. Wind blew, and it was called spirit
because there was no death in it.
The thirteenth day moistened the earth and kneaded the mud into
                    a body like ours.
Thus it is remembered in Yucatán.

EDUARDO GALEANO, Memory of Fire

Inside the people who grow out of any land, there is an understanding
of it, a remembering all the way back to origins, to when the gods first
shaped humans out of clay, back to when animals could speak with people, to when the sky and water were without form and all was shaped
by such words as "Let there be."

In nearly all creation accounts, life was called into being through language, thought, dreaming, or singing, acts of interior consciousness. For
the Maya, time itself is alive. In the beginning, the day set out walking
from the east and brought into being the world and all that inhabited it—
jaguar, turtle, deer, trees. It was all sacred.

Then there were the first humans, whose job it was to offer prayer,
tell stories, and remember the passage of time. Made of the clay of this
earth, the mud people of the first creation did not endure; when it rained,
their bodies grew soft and dissolved.

In the next creation, humans were lovingly carved of wood. These
prospered and multiplied. But in time, the wooden people forgot to give
praise to the gods and to nurture the land. They were hollow and without

compassion. They transformed the world to fit their own needs. They did not honor the sacred forms of life on earth and they began to destroy the land, to create their own dead future out of human arrogance and greed. Because of this, the world turned against them. In a world where everything was alive, the forms of life they had wronged took vengeance on them. There was black rain. The animals they harmed attacked them. The ruined waters turned against them and flooded their land.

In the final creation of mankind, the people were created from corn:

> And so then they put into words the creation,
> The shaping of our first mother
> And father.
> Only yellow corn
> And white corn were their bodies.
> Only food were the legs
> And arms of man.
> Those who were our first fathers
> Were the original men.
> Only food at the outset
> Were their bodies.
>
> QUICHÉ MAYA, *Popul Vuh*

At first, these care-taking, life-giving people made of corn, the substance of gods, saw what the gods saw. In order to make them more human, less god, some of that vision was taken away so there might be mystery, and the mystery of creation and of death inspired deep respect and awe for all of creation.

In most stories of genesis, unwritten laws of human conduct are taught at creation. For the Maya, too, the story of the hollow people is not only part of a beautiful and complex creation story, but a telling language, one that speaks against human estrangement from land and creation.

Emptiness and estrangement are deep wounds, strongly felt in the present time, as if we are living an incomplete creation. We have been split from what we could nurture, what could fill us. And we have been wounded by a dominating culture that has feared and hated the natural world, has not listened to the voice of the land, has not believed in the inner worlds of human dreaming and intuition, all things that have guided indigenous people since time stood up in the east and walked this world into existence. It is a world of maintained connection between self and land. The best hunters of the far north still find the location of their prey by dreaming. In *Maps and Dreams* by anthropologist Hugh Brody, one informant says, "Maybe you don't think this power is possible. Few people understand. The old-timers who were strong dreamers knew many things that are not easy to understand. . . . The fact that dream-hunting works has been proved many times." Maps of the land are revealed in dreams, and the direction of deer.

Like the wooden people, many of us in this time have lost the inner substance of our lives and have forgotten to give praise and remember the sacredness of all life. But in spite of this forgetting, there is still a part of everyone that is deep and intimate with the world. We remember it by feel. We experience it as a murmur in the night, a longing and restlessness we can't name, a yearning that tugs at us. For it is only recently, in earth time, that the severing of the connections between people and land have taken place. Something in our human blood is still searching for it, still listening, still remembering. Nicaraguan poet-priest Ernesto Cardenal wrote, "We have always wanted something beyond what we wanted." I have loved those words, how they speak to the longing place inside us that seeks to be whole and connected with the earth. This, too, is a place of beginning, the source of our living.

So also do we remember our ancestors and their lives deep in our bodily cells. In part, this deep, unspoken remembering is why I have come here, searching out my own beginnings, the thread of connection between old Maya cultures and my Chickasaw one. According to some of our oral traditions, a migration story of our tribe, we originated in this region, carved dugout canoes, and traveled to the southeast corner of what is now called Florida, the place of flowers. It's true, I have always felt a oneness with this Mexican land, but I know this call to origins is deeper, older, and stronger than I am, more even than culture and blood origins. Here, there is a feel for the mystery of our being in all ways, in earth and water. It is the same mystery that sends scientists in search for the beginning of the universe. We seek our origins as much as we seek our destinies.

And we desire to see the world intact, to step outside our emptiness and remember the strong currents that pass between humans and the rest of nature, currents that are the felt voice of land, heard in the cells of the body.

It is the same magnetic call that, since before human history, has brought the sea turtles to the beach of Celestún. The slow blood of the turtles hears it, turtles who have not been here since the original breaking of the egg that held them, who ran toward an ocean they did not know, who have lived their lives in the sea, then felt the call of land in deep memory and return to a place unseen. Forever, it seems, they have been swimming through blue waters in order to return, to lay their eggs in sun-warmed sand, and go back to the clear blue-green waters of their mothers in ancient journeys of creation and rituals of return.

The white shoreline stretches around us, wide and open. It is early for the endangered hawksbills and green turtles to be coming to land. Egg-laying usually begins in late April and early May. Because of the endangered status of the sea turtles, members of an organization called Pronatura will arrive to protect the turtles and the eggs. In this region in 1947, there were so many sea turtles that it was said forty thousand of them appeared on one beach to spawn. Now the hawksbills are the second most endangered species in the world. Today, despite the earliness of the season, there are tracks in the white sand, large tracks that have moved earth as if small tanks had emerged from the water and traveled a short distance up sand. Some of the tracks return, but others vanish, and where they end, there are human footprints.

In the traditional belief systems of native people, the terrestrial call is the voice of God, or of gods, the creative power that lives on earth, inside earth, in turtle, stone, and tree. Knowledge comes from, and is shaped by, observations and knowledge of the natural world and natural cycles.

In fact, the word "god," itself, in the dictionary definition, means to call, to invoke. Like creation, it is an act of language, as if the creator and the creation are one, the primal pull of land is the summoning thing.

It is significant that we explore the contrasts in belief systems. This exploration is meaningful, not only to the survival of the land, but in our terms of living with the land, our agreement with it, the conditions and natural laws set out at creation.

Sometimes beliefs are inventions of the mind. Sometimes they are inventions of the land. But how we interpret and live out our lives has to do with these belief systems, religious foundations, and the spiritual history we have learned.

From the European perspective, land and nature have been changed to fit human concepts, ideas, and abstractions.

The Western belief that God lives apart from earth is one that has taken us toward collective destruction. It is a belief narrow enough to forget the value of matter, the very thing that soul inhabits. It has created a people who are future-sighted only in a limited way, not in terms of taking care of the land for the future generations.

The Lakota knew that man's heart, away from nature, becomes hard; he knew that lack of respect for growing, living things soon led to lack of respect for humans, too.

—LUTHER STANDING BEAR

Reflecting on the destruction of the Americas, I can only think that the European invaders were threatened by the vast store of tribal knowledge, and by the land itself, so beautiful and unknown to them in its richness. Though they described it as "heaven" and "paradise," they set about destroying it. For the people described as gentle and generous, the genocide that began in the fifteenth century has been an ongoing process.

Not far from here is where Fray Diego de Landa, in the 1500s, tortured and killed the Maya people and burned their books in the alchemical drive of the Spanish to accumulate wealth, turn life into gold, and convert others to their own beliefs. They set into flames entire peoples, and centuries of remembered and recorded knowledge about the land. It is believed that there were considerable stores of knowledge in these people and in their books, not just history and sacred stories but medical knowledge, a math advanced enough to create the concept of zero, and a highly developed knowledge of astronomy that continues to surprise contemporary astronomers with its intelligence. It is certain that centuries of habitation on this land yielded more knowledge about the earth and its cycles than has been newly understood and recovered in the brief, troubled years that have since followed. And we are left to wonder if that ancient knowledge would help us in this time of threat, if the lost books held a clue to survival.

This burned and broken history is part of the story of the land. It is the narrative of the past we are still living by, a broken order that forgets to acknowledge the terrestrial intelligence at work here. But the memory of an older way remains, as if in the smallest human corner live the origins of the world, a way that remembers the earth is potent with life and its own divinity. This knowing is stored in the hearts and blood of the people and in the land. Fray de Landa, for one brief moment, acknowledged such life. He said of this land that it is "the country with the least earth that I have ever seen, since all of it is one living rock."

These words could have bridged a different connection, an understanding closer to the way indigenous people see the land, a life-sustaining way of being.

A rib of land separates ocean and barrier beach from the red-colored tidal estuary and wetlands area where the river runs toward larger waters. The river is so full of earth that it is red and shallow. In its marshy places, plants grow from its clay. There are places where freshwater underground rivers surge upward to create conditions that are unique to this place, and exist nowhere else.

There are a salt marsh, a tidal estuary, and mangrove swamps that contain one of the world's largest colonies of flamingos, birds named after flame, as if they belong, in part, to the next element of creation. This red estuary is alive and breathing, moving with embryonic clay and silt.

It is a place crucial not only to the flamingo colonies and waterfowl, but also to migratory birds from as far north as Maine, a connection that closes the miles, another boundary undone.

Traveling into this red water, we are surrounded by the many-rooted mangrove swamps. Mangroves are a part of creation and renewal in this land. Coastal plants, they live in the divide between land and water:

> The tides are always shifting things about among the mangrove roots. . . .
> Parts of it are neither land nor sea and so everything is moving from one element to another.
>
> Loren Eiseley, *Night Country*

They are a network of tangled roots and twisted branches. Both marine and terrestrial, they are boundary-bridgers that have created islands and continents. Consuming their own fallen leaves, they are nurturers in the ongoing formation of the world, makers of earth with a life-force strong enough to alter the visible face of their world, Rachel Carson said, a world "extending back into darkening swamps of its own creation."

The interior of the swamps is dark and filled with the intricate relationships of water with plant, animal, earth, sheltering small lives within them.

Mangroves are plants that reach out to grow, searching for water and mineral with a grasping kind of energy that can be felt. As they send their roots seeking outward, they move forward, leaving behind them the savannah that will become tropical forest. In turn, rainwater, flowing underground, will break through the forest, creating a cenote. No one knows the paths of these rivers; theirs is a vast underground network. It is only known where they rise. And in some of these sinkholes, or cenotes, are species of fish from one river system not found in other cenotes in the region.

The rain clouds have not yet reached us. Light shines through the leaves. A fish jumps. As we move forward, the path of our disturbance is lighter in color, like a vapor trail, behind us. Then it vanishes, unlike the paths we have left behind in other places. There is a dreaminess here where creation continues to happen all around us in time that is alive.

At the far edge of copper-colored water, a white egret steps through the shallows, an eye sharp for fish. On the other side of water's edge stands a solitary blue heron. Herons are fragile birds and it is not unusual for them to die from stress. I think of them when hearing that Hmong men, forced to leave their country and rootless in America, die of no apparent cause while they are sleeping. I understand the loss that leads to despair and to death. It has happened to us, and is happening to the land, the breaking of the heart of creation.

There is a poem that herons fly through. With rigid legs and boomerang wings, they fly beneath rolling clouds through a smoke-blue sky, flying toward dawn, flying without falling from heaven. The poet, Gertrud Kolmar, a woman who loved animals, died in Auschwitz, one of those lost by whatever other failures of the gods have made men hollow and capable of such crimes. But the holocaust began before her time. It began on this continent, with the genocide of tribal people, and with the ongoing war against the natural world. Here is a lesson, that what happens to people and what happens to the land is the same thing.

Shape, I think she meant by boomerang wings, although the boomerang is something more than that: it is something that returns. And there is great hope in return. Not just in returned time or history as the round cycles of the Maya worldview express, but in returned land and species; return is what we are banking on as we attempt to put back what we have disappeared, the songs of wolves in Yellowstone; the pale-edged wings of condors in California sky; the dark, thundering herds of buffalo to Indian country; the flamingos along the River of Hope. This colony, once diminished to five thousand birds in 1955, has increased its numbers to twenty-two thousand, according to Joann Andrews of Pronatura. This, and Ría Lagartos to the north, are the only wintering and nesting areas these flamingos have.

And then we see them, these returned flamingos, in their wintering ground, first as a red line along the darker water, red as volcanic fire breaking open from black rock, revealing its passionate inner light, fire from the center of earth's creative force, lit from within, each individual part of a more complex living whole.

For well over a mile, all along the shore, we see them, like dawn's red path stretched before us. It is almost too much for the eye to see, this great vision, the shimmering light of them. It's a vision so incredible and thick and numinous I know it will open inside my eyes in the moment before death when a lived life draws itself out one last time before closing forever and we are drawn to these birds the way fire pulls air into it. They are proof how far blood will travel to seek its beginning.

We sit, floating, and watch these lives with their grace and the black lines of their underwings. They are noisy. The birds at the outermost edges are aware of us. We are careful not to disturb them as they eat; at the end of winter, their mission here is to fill themselves. Already there are mating displays, though true nesting takes place to the north of here in Ría Lagartos, where they build and guard mud nests.

They are restless. One group begins to fly with a running start across water, red clouds rising across the thin red-brown skin of water as if water has come undone from itself, lost something to air where clouds, too, are born of water. Other groups are in water and onshore, long-necked, the rose-colored light coming from the marvelous feathers constructed of centuries of necessity and the love that life has for its many forms and expressions.

They are birds glorious and godly, and like us, are an ancient nation.

The clouds that were out at sea have moved east and now they reach us. Thunder breaks open the sky and it begins to rain a warm afternoon rain. We turn off the engine of the boat and pole into a shadowy corridor of mangroves until we reach a sheltered pool. A faint wind creaks the trees. Above us, in the branches, a termite nest is black and heavy. It is a splendid architecture wedged in the branches of a tree, one come to over time, a creation older than human presence on the earth by millions of years. The nest is a contained intelligence, made up of lives that work together with the mind of a single organism.

The word "termite" was given by Linnaeus and originally meant "end of life." That's how young and new our oldest knowledge is, because these, too, are old participants in creation, in beginnings. They break down wood, forming rich soil in a place that would otherwise be choked.

The overhead canopy of leaves shelters us. We watch the drops meet water, returning to their larger country, becoming it, recreating it out of themselves.

This is one of the places where an underground river has broken through the shelf of limestone and risen to the surface. It is called Ojo de Agua, Eye of Water. Looking into this eye, it seems to gaze back, and in that blue gaze are tiny fish. The water is one of earth's lanterns, the same blue of glacier light and of the earth from out in space. Beneath us, a larger fish eats algae off a fallen tree, long-legged insects move about the unclosed eye of water, the spring of light.

There is a second eye and we decide to crawl through roots and dark mud to find it. Frederico, the guide, is barefoot and barefoot is the only way to move here. As we pass through the tangles and intricacies, he offers me a hand and helps me through. His hand is strong and warm, but in spite of it, my foot slips off the convoluted roots. I think it is all right; I see the blue leaves resting on the water's floor, but it is a false bottom and my leg keeps going until both legs are in to the hip, my foot still slipping down, "To China," Frederico says, as I find a limb to grasp. Here again the boundaries did not hold. What looked like bottom was merely blue leaves and algae held up by a rising current of boundless water.

And here, where the underground river ends, other beginnings are fed, other species and creations. If it were time, instead of space, scholars would call it "Zero Date," that place where, as for the Maya, the end of one world is the beginning of another, the start of this cosmos, a point of this origin. As they interpret the world, time is alive and travels in a circle. There were other creations and worlds before the one we now inhabit; the cosmos has reformed itself.

For those who know only this one universe, to think of its origins is an overwhelming task. It means to think before time, before space, all the way back to the void that existed before creation. And with people of science as with those of religion, the universe in its cosmic birth originated from small and minute beginnings. There was nothing and then life came into existence. Stephen Hawking says, "It was possible for the entire universe to appear out of nothing," the place from which all things grew into a miraculous emergence.

And astronomer-physicist Chet Raymo says, "All beginnings wear their endings like dark shadows." And maybe they do. If endings are foreshadowed by their beginnings, or are in some way the same thing, it is important that we circle around and come back to look at our human myths and stories, not only the creation accounts but stories of the end. Unlike the cyclic nature of time for the Maya, the Western tradition of beliefs within a straight line of history leads to an apocalyptic end. And stories of the end, like those of beginning, tell something about the people who created them. These are prophecies believed to be God-inspired.

In her article "Extinction," Lynda Sexson writes:

> We are so accustomed to myths (sacred stories) of extinction, that we are not as practical at imagining that greater gap—continuation. . . . Would the earth or our existence on it be in such peril if we did not harbor a profound desire for extinction? *"They lie down, they cannot rise, they are extinguished, quenched like a wick,"* resonates Isaiah. The crisis of Western culture is ecological. The source of that crisis is in Western culture's own version of reality; the myth of the urge to eradicate: earth and images of earth, body and song.

Without deep reflection, we have taken on the story of endings, assumed the story of extinction, and have believed that it is the certain outcome of our presence here. This belief has brought us to a point of no return, to the near realization of that belief. And from this position, fear, bereavement, and denial keep us in the state of estrangement from our natural connection with the land.

Maybe we need new stories, new terms and conditions that are relevant to the love of land, a new narrative that would imagine another way, to learn the infinite mystery and movement at work in the world. And it would mean we become the corn people who are givers of praise and nurturers of creation, lovers of life. There must be nothing that gives us permission to let some lives pass from sight and disappear forever, no acceptance of an end, and we must remember that all places are places of creation.

Indian people cannot be the only ones who remember the agreement with the land, the sacred pact to honor and care for the life that, in turn, provides for us. We need to reach a hand back through time and a hand forward, stand at the zero point of creation to be certain that we do not create the absence of life, of any species, no matter how inconsequential they might appear to be.

Belief, it is good to remember, is built on old beliefs, overturned, in science and philosophy as well as in religion. We have held too tightly to what we think, believe. The act of belief itself is nothing. And has mighty consequences in the world around us.

It is a mistaken vision that has seen earth dead or lifeless, without intelligence. Everything tells us this. The divine is on earth, is earth itself. We need to expand our knowing, our understanding, and our vision. And in this, we need to consider the scale of human suffering, as well. The hunger and loss of humans, too, are crimes against creation.

At the beginning, there was nothing and then there was something and, except in theory, in mathematical terms, we have not been able to map it. Like the rivers, we only see where it surfaces with the same mystery of swimming turtles, early morning's new light, the limestone floor of sea that rose up to become land. Every piece fits and has its place, we learned from Darwin. And that fitting has grown infinitely more complex and intricate as our knowledge has increased. There is an integrity, a terrestrial intelligence at work. It's an intelligence far-reaching and beyond our comprehension. As Alan Lightman says: "Creation lies outside of physics."

The immeasurable *quality* of this world has depth and breadth we can't measure. Yet we know it's there, and we believe in it, the whole of it, to the outermost strands of infinity. Slowly, a piece at a time, it is revealed to us. Cosmologists now surmise there are other universes. So for us, creation is still growing, and as the story becomes larger, we become smaller. Perhaps that is why we shape belief around mystery.

And those of us who love the land are searching for a language to say it because sometimes words are the only bridge between us and all the rest, as in prayer and ceremony, as in the creation of the world.

We come from the land, the sky, from love and the body. From matter and creation. We are, life is, an equation we cannot form or shape, a mystery we can't trace in spite of our attempts to follow it back to its origin, to find out when life began, even in all our stories of when the universe came into being, how the first people emerged. It is a failure of human intelligence and compassion that doesn't wonder about, and love, the mystery of our lives and all the rest.

As Cardenal knew by those words about the want behind our wanting, we do not even have a language to speak words deep enough, strong enough to articulate what it is we truly desire. And this is just one hint of our limitations. The real alchemy of our being here is the finest of transformations and we do not know it. We are atoms that were other patterns and arrangements of form.

We do not know the secrets of stars. We do not know the true history of water. We do not know ourselves. We have forgotten that this land and every life form is a piece of God. It's a divine community, with the same forces of creation in the plants as in the people. All the lives around us are lives of gods. The sometimes long history of creation that shaped plankton, shaped horseshoe crabs. Everything is Maker; mangroves, termites, all are sources of one creation or another. Without respect and reverence for it, there is an absence of holiness, of any God.

All over the earth, faces of all living things are alike. Mother Earth has turned these faces out of the earth with tenderness.

—LUTHER STANDING BEAR

Men talk much of matter and energy, of the struggle for existence that molds the shape of life. These things exist, it is true; but more delicate, elusive, quicker than fins in water, is that mysterious principle known as organization, which leaves all other mysteries concerned with life stale and insignificant by comparison.... Like some dark and passing shadow within matter, it cups out the eyes' small windows or spaces the notes of a meadowlark's song in the interior of a mottled egg. That principle—I am beginning to suspect—was there before the living in the deeps of water....

If "dead" water has reared up this curious landscape ... it must be plain even to the most devoted materialist that the matter of which it speaks contains amazing, if not dreadful powers, and may not impossibly be, as Hardy has suggested, "but one mask of many worn by the Great Face behind."

Loren Eiseley, *Night Country*

The face of the land is our face, and that of all its creatures. To see whole is to see all the parts of the puzzle, some of which have not even been found, as there are still numerous animals and plants who have not been identified. Even here at Celestún there are faces still unseen. What grows here and what grows within us is the same.

We are at the end of a way of knowing, being, and believing, and many of us are searching for a deeper insight into earth as a living organism, a return to the old beliefs, now called new. Or we are at a beginning, an old understanding of the world, newly brought to mind. It's a new and ancient spirituality and this knowing is stored in the hearts and blood of the people and in the living rock.

Later, swimming, I see a silver circle of fish, swimming in a cluster. In this place are spectacular fish, deep blue ones, green and yellow, but I see these small fish, silver and swimming in their circle, and they are fascinating. All of them turn at one time and they still hold the circle together. They avoid me, moving away, and they are still round, their circle holds. They share a mind, the way termites do, share a common mission of survival, like all the faces turned out of the earth, all part of one face, the one mask of many worn by the Great Face behind.

> The lands around my dwelling
> Are more beautiful
> From the day
> When it is given me to see
> Faces I have never seen before.
> All is more beautiful,
> All is more beautiful.
> And life is thankfulness.
> These guests of mine.
> Make my house grand.
>   Eskimo Song

What does God look like? These fish, this water, this land.

GUIDE TO FURTHER READING

I. General Interpretations

The most influential broad-gauge assessment of the West's place in American life has been Frederick Jackson Turner's charitable essay, "The Significance of the Frontier in American History" (1894), which became the first chapter of *The Frontier in American History* (New York, 1920). Turner told readers that the opening to the West had been the boon of America by helping to instill freedom, democracy, and self-reliance. This positive historical reading dovetailed beautifully, as it happened, with the heroic image of the West projected in popular literature and in such triumphalist renderings as Theodore Roosevelt's *The Winning of the West* (4 vols., New York, 1894–1898). For many decades, the western past was described with confidence and satisfaction, though demurrers to the general contentment were voiced by the early-revisionist, realistic novelists discussed above (pages 8–11). As late as midcentury, when two major studies of the frontier appeared, the Turnerian frame of reference still prevailed. Henry Nash Smith's *Virgin Land* (Cambridge, Mass., 1950) and Walter Prescott Webb's *The Great Frontier* (Boston, 1952) were both founded on Turner, although Smith, in stressing the frontier as myth and symbol, and Webb, emphasizing the psychological distress of a postfrontier world, each achieved some perspective on the subject. (The "frontier" interpretation itself was slowly emerging as an item of study.)

In the 1960s, with the founding of the Western History Association and the Western Literature Association and their journals, the *Western Historical Quarterly* and *Western American Literature*, western studies came into improved academic standing. An opening in American and western self-consciousness, perhaps coincident with the Vietnam War and certain undeniable indications of environmental decline, occurred during this decade and encouraged scholars to take fresh looks at the western region and its literature. An early indicator of new life in western studies was Wallace Stegner's essay, "Born a Square" (1964), included in his collection *The Sound of Mountain Water* (New York, 1969). In this essay, Stegner made an "American Scholar"–like declaration of western values, and while not claiming complete exceptionalism, he did plead the case for western distinctiveness and importance. One of the first to take to the new western field analytically was Leslie Fiedler with *The Return of the Vanishing American* (New York, 1968), a treatment of western myths that is both sardonic

in its analysis of white depictions of the frontier and hopeful in its proposal that Indians were now returning to visibility. The first anthology of
western writing whose contents, in effect, protested against the longtime
dominance of the cowboy was J. Golden Taylor's *The Literature of the American West* (Boston, 1969). In the following year, John G. Cawelti's keen
analysis of the genre in *The Six-Gun Mystique* raised consciousness of the
Western to an entirely new level. Cawelti spoke from outside the mythos,
implicitly portraying the formula Western as an anodyne for cultural contradictions and incompletenesses, a fantasy through which Americans
could feel good about themselves and their history. Three years later,
Richard Slotkin published a profoundly revisionist, psychocultural study,
*Regeneration through Violence: The Mythology of the American Frontier, 1600–
1860* (Middleton, Conn., 1973), questioning not only Americans' literary
tendency toward self-justifying fantasy but, by implication, the very morality of the national character and behavior. Slotkin has followed *Regeneration* with two similarly unsettling analyses, *The Fatal Environment: The
Myth of the Frontier in the Age of Industrialization, 1800–1890* (New York,
1985), and *Gunfighter Nation: The Myth of the Frontier in Twentieth-Century
America* (New York, 1992).

The new environmental awareness of post–Earth Day America began
to emerge in western literary criticism in the 1970s. In William Everson's
Archetype West (Berkeley, 1976), ecological sensitivity fused with the author's spiritual awareness to form an early instance of the nature-based
criticism that is now widespread. In the first year of the next decade,
Frederick Turner's *Beyond Geography: The Western Spirit against the Wilderness* (New York, 1980) took attitudes toward the environment, as expressed in literature, to be primary indicators of the American psyche. All
these studies undermine not only received notions of history but, at a
deeper level, the very nature of the dominant American and western identity. And these analyses, cumulatively, had an effect—the ideological climate began to change. By 1986, for example, Henry Nash Smith looked
back on his own earlier work in "Symbol and Idea in *Virgin Land*" (in
Ideology and Classic American Literature, ed. Sacvan Bercovitch and Myra
Jehlen [New York, 1986]) and declared that it had suffered "to some extent
from Turner's tunnel vision," meaning, he explained, Turner's "refusal to
acknowledge the guilt intrinsic to the national errand into the wilderness." In the late '80s, broad revisions in historical thinking about the
West were appearing. Donald Worster's *Rivers of Empire: Water, Aridity
and the Growth of the American West* (New York, 1985), notable for ecological consciousness, and Patricia Nelson Limerick's *Legacy of Conquest: The
Unbroken Past of the American West* (New York, 1987) with its explicit sub-
version of earlier positive interpretations, are emerging as perhaps the

most influential examples of the "new western history." Both Worster and Limerick use literary sources, as does Slotkin, to create a broad, cross-disciplinary perspective on the West. Worster in particular, with his command of an ecological point of view, suggests something like a unified-field theory of western history. In the last ten years—a period of intense activity in western studies—significant general analyses foregrounding psychological and cultural issues have been offered by Jane Tompkins in *West of Everything: The Inner Life of Westerns* (New York, 1992); Richard White in *"It's Your Misfortune and None of My Own": A New History of the American West* (Norman, 1991); Forrest G. Robinson in *Having It Both Ways: Self-Subversion in Western Popular Classics* (Albuquerque, 1993); A. Carl Bredahl in *New Ground: Western American Narrative and the Literary Canon* (Chapel Hill, 1989); Arnold Krupat in *The Voice in the Margin: Native American Literature and the Canon* (Berkeley, 1989); and Wallace Stegner in a collection of essays titled *Where the Bluebird Sings to the Lemonade Springs* (New York, 1992). The frontier and western mythos has been opened up, dissected, and deconstructed. We have come very far from the projected psychological and cultural assurance of Frederick Jackson Turner's era.

II. Histories, Anthologies, and Collections of Critical Essays

A Literary History of the American West (eds. Thomas J. Lyon et al., Fort Worth, 1987), treating literature published before 1982, and its sequel, *Updating the Literary West* (eds. Thomas J. Lyon et al., Fort Worth, 1997), covering the period 1982 to 1997, are the most comprehensive historical and critical guides to western writing. A student who digests their 2384 pages and who also studied the 872 pages of *The Oxford History of the American West* (eds. Clyde A. Milner II, Carol O'Connor, and Martha A. Sandweiss, New York, 1994) will probably emerge with a good general feel for the region and its expression. More specifically focused histories and criticism serve as further treatment of areas outlined in these general histories. Some solid, influential, and usable books include: H. David Brumble's *American Indian Autobiography* (Berkeley, 1988); John R. Milton's *The Novel of the American West* (Lincoln, 1980); Roy W. Meyer's *The Middle Western Farm Novel in the Twentieth Century* (Lincoln, 1965); Louis Owens's *Other Destinies: Understanding the American Indian Novel* (Norman, 1992); Annette Kolodny's *The Land before Her: Fantasy and Experience of the American Frontiers, 1630–1860* (Chapel Hill, 1984); Christine Bold's *Selling the Wild West: Popular Western Fiction, 1860 to 1960* (Bloomington, 1987); and Vera Norwood and Janice Monk's *The Desert Is No Lady: Southwestern Landscapes in Women's Writing and Art* (New Haven, 1987).

There are also a number of well-edited western anthologies of recent publication, demonstrating the region's ascension to readers' awareness:

Writers of the Purple Sage: An Anthology of Recent Western Writing, ed. Russell Martin and Mark Barasch (New York, 1984), followed up by *New Writers of the Purple Sage*, ed. Russell Martin (New York, 1992); *The Interior Country: Stories of the Modern West*, eds. Alexander Blackburn, Craig Lesley, and Jill Landem (Athens, Ohio, 1987); *Prose and Poetry of the American West*, ed. James Work (Lincoln, 1990); *The Best of the West: An Anthology of Classic Writing from the American West*, ed. Tony Hillerman (New York, 1991); *The Portable Western Reader*, ed. William Kittredge (New York, 1997); *The Remembered Earth: An Anthology of Contemporary Native American Literature*, ed. Geary Hobson (Albuquerque, 1981); *Harper's Anthology of 20th Century Native American Poetry*, ed. Duane Niatum (San Francisco, 1988); *Coming to Light: Contemporary Translations of the Native Literatures of North America*, ed. Brian Swann (New York, 1994); *A Republic of Rivers: Three Centuries of Nature Writing from Alaska and the Yukon*, ed. John Murray (New York, 1990); *The Open Boat: Poems from Asian America*, ed. Garrett Karou Hongo (New York, 1993); *The Stories That Shape Us: Contemporary Women Write about the West*, eds. Teresa Jordan and James Hepworth (New York, 1995); *Circle of Women: An Anthology of Contemporary Western Women Writers*, eds. Mary Clearman Blew and Kim Barnes (New York, 1994); *She Won the West: An Anthology of Frontier Stories by Women*, eds. Marcia Muller and Bill Pronzini (New York, 1985); *Cuentos Chicanos: A Short Story Anthology*, eds. Rudolfo Anaya and Antonio Marquez (Albuquerque, 1984); and *Many Californias: Literature from the Golden State*, ed. Gerald Haslam (Reno, 1993). These collections have various amounts of apparatus, with Work's and Haslam's anthologies perhaps the most freshly and insightfully introduced, but all were apparently created by editors with a sense for what might make the West distinctive and what areas within western writing deserve greater attention.

Two encyclopedic tomes deserve mention for handiness and depth beyond the expected limits of such compendia: *Twentieth Century Western Writers*, ed. Geoff Sadler (2nd ed., Chicago and London, 1991), and *The New Encyclopedia of the American West*, ed. Howard Lamar (New Haven, 1998).

Notable collections of critical essays are: *Reading the West: New Essays on the Literature of the American West*, ed. Michael Kowalewski (New York, 1996); *The Frontier Experience and the American Dream*, eds. David Mogen, Mark Busby, and Paul Bryant (College Station, 1989); *Narrative Chance: Postmodern Discourse on Native American Indian Literatures*, ed. Gerald Vizenor (Albuquerque, 1989; Norman, 1993); *Reconstructing a Chicano/a Literary Heritage*, ed. Maria Herrera-Sobek (Tucson, 1998); *Fifty Western Writers*, eds. Fred Erisman and Richard Etulain (Westport, Conn., 1982); and

Speaking for the Generations: Native Writers on Writing, ed. Simon J. Ortiz (Tucson, 1998).

III. Oral Traditions, the Early Hispanic Southwest, and Individual Authors

Good, older sources on Native American oral literature include: *The Red Swan: Myths and Tales of the American Indians*, ed. John Bierhorst (New York, 1976); *Tales of the North American Indians*, ed. Stith Thompson (Bloomington, 1966 [originally published in 1929]); Paul Radin, *The Trickster: A Study in American Indian Mythology* (New York, 1956; reprint 1972); and *Traditional American Indian Literatures: Texts and Interpretations*, ed. Karl Kroeber (Lincoln, 1981). The collection edited by Brian Swann, cited on page 428 offers fresh readings. Access to the early southwestern and California writings by Spanish explorers and colonists was greatly facilitated by Professor Herbert Eugene Bolton in *Spanish Explorers in the Southern United States, 1528–1543* (New York, 1907); *Spanish Exploration in the Southwest, 1542–1706* (New York, 1930); and *Anza's California Expeditions* (Berkeley, 1930). Readers interested in Álvar Núñez Cabeza de Vaca— and he *is* interesting—will want to consult Haniel Long's *The Power within Us* (New York, 1944) and, for a modern translation, *The Account: Álvar Núñez Cabeza de Vaca's Relacion*, trans. Martin A. Favata and José B. Fernández (Houston, 1993). The record of the Dominguez-Escalante trek is available in an excellent edition in *The Dominguez-Escalante Journal: Their Expeditions through Colorado, Utah, Arizona, and New Mexico in 1776*, ed. Ted J. Warner, and trans. Fray Angelico Chavez (Provo, 1976). The one-volume rendering of Lewis and Clark's accounts edited by Bernard DeVoto in *The Journals of Lewis and Clark* (Boston, 1953) is splendid, but readers with access to a good library should see *Original Journals of the Lewis and Clark Expedition, 1804–1806*, ed. Reuben Gold Thwaites (8 vols., New York, 1904–1905). On Jedediah Smith, George R. Brooks's *The Southwest Expedition of Jedediah S. Smith: His Personal Account of the Journey to California, 1826–1827* (Glendale, Calif., 1977) is indispensable. Kenneth Spaulding edited the Astorian Robert Stuart's journal in *On the Oregon Trail; Robert Stuart's Journey of Discovery* (Norman, 1953), offering a more realistic version of events than Washington Irving had in *Astoria* (Philadelphia, 1836), which nevertheless ought to be consulted as a shaper of the image of the West. Early western travelers such as Thomas Nuttall, John Kirk Townsend, John Charles Fremont, Francis Parkman, and Howard Stansbury are treated informatively in various chapters in the Western Literature Association's *A Literary History of the American West* (Fort Worth, 1987). Readers interested in San Francisco as a literary center should consult *LHAW* also, but Franklin Walker's *San Francisco's Literary Frontier* (New York, 1939) and Nancy J. Peters's and Lawrence Ferlinghetti's *Literary San Francisco* (San Francisco, 1980) are the major sources on this city and its writers. Ida Rae Egli's *No Rooms of Their Own: Women Writers of Early California* (San Francisco: 1992) is also important.

In the last few decades, authors of popular western literature have come in for serious study. Among notable sources are G. Edward White's *The Eastern Establishment and the Western Experience: The West of Frederic Remington, Theodore Roosevelt and Owen Wister* (New Haven, 1968); Arthur G. Kimball's *Ace of Hearts: The Westerns of Zane Grey* (Fort Worth, 1993); *Shane: The Critical Edition*, ed. James Work (Lincoln, 1984); and Robert Gale's *Louis L'Amour* (New York, 1992).

The deepening of interest in John Muir may have begun with Albert Saijo's interesting essay, "Elders of the Tribe 2: John Muir (1838–1914)" in the summer 1973 issue of *Backpacker* magazine. Saijo argues that Muir should be taken seriously as a writer and thinker, as do Michael P. Cohen's *The Pathless Way: John Muir and American Wilderness* (Madison, 1984) and Frederick Turner's *Rediscovering America: John Muir in His Time and Ours* (New York, 1985). The great early naturalist-writers of the West, such as Enos Mills, Mary Austin, Aldo Leopold, Olaus Murie, Roy Bedicheck, and Joseph Wood Krutch, are treated in *LHAW*, in *Updating the Literary West* (Fort Worth, 1997), and in the monumental collection, *American Nature Writers* (2 vols., New York, 1996), edited by the scholar-writer John Elder.

Fruitful sources on the great western realists, each containing suggestions for further reading, include two studies by Donald Pizer, *Hamlin Garland's Early Work and Career* (Berkeley, 1960) and *The Novels of Frank Norris* (Bloomington, 1966); Earle Labor's *Jack London* (New York, 1974); Jackson Benson's *The True Adventures of John Steinbeck, Writer* (New York, 1984); Tillie Olsen's *Silences* (New York, 1978); Meridel LeSueur's *Harvest Song: Collected Essays and Stories* (Albuquerque, 1977); Robert F. Gish's *Frontier's End: The Life and Literature of Harvey Fergusson* (Lincoln, 1988); Joseph Flora's *Vardis Fisher* (New York, 1965); Thomas W. Ford's *A. B. Guthrie Jr.* (Boston, 1981); the work of Helen W. Stauffer on Mari Sandoz, including *Mari Sandoz, Story Catcher of the Plains* (Lincoln, 1982); an interview with Frederick Manfred conducted by John R. Milton and published in *South Dakota Review* 7 (Winter, 1969–1970); Max Westbrook's *Walter Van Tilburg Clark* (New York, 1969); Alexander Blackburn's *A Sunrise Brighter Still: The Visionary Novels of Frank Waters* (Athens, Ohio, 1991); Martin Bucco's collection, *Critical Essays on Sinclair Lewis* (Boston, 1986); Harold Simonson's *Prairies Within: The Tragic Trilogy of Ole Rølvaag* (Seattle, 1987); and Jackson Benson's *Wallace Stegner* (New York, 1996).

Willa Cather presents a special case as the most-studied western writer—for an indication, the chapter on her in *Updating the Literary West*

(1997) is entitled "The Cather Enterprise: The Last Dozen Years." Numerous book-length studies—notably Susan J. Rosowski's *The Voyage Perilous: Willa Cather's Romanticism* (Lincoln, 1986), Marilyn Arnold's *Willa Cather: A Reference Guide* (Boston, 1986), Sharon O'Brien's *Willa Cather: The Emerging Voice* (New York, 1987), James Woodress's *Willa Cather: A Literary Life* (Lincoln, 1987), and Edward Wagenknecht's *Willa Cather* (New York, 1993)—appeared in that period, as well as three volumes of the Willa Cather Scholarly Editions published by the University of Nebraska Press; three Library of America collections devoted to Cather's works; and three volumes of *Cather Studies* (1990, 1993, and 1996), scholarly essays edited by Susan J. Rosowski. An exhaustive bibliography on Cather would occupy many pages; interested readers wanting to keep up to date with this important writer, whose deceptively straightforward prose inspires some of the best western literary criticism, should consult the current listings in the journals *Western American Literature* and the *Willa Cather Pioneer Memorial Newsletter*.

Among studies of important western poets, Lucile F. Aly's *John G. Neihardt: A Critical Biography* (Amsterdam, 1959), Robert J. Brophy's *Robinson Jeffers: Myth, Ritual, and Symbol in His Narrative Poems* (Cleveland, 1973), Brophy's collection, *Robinson Jeffers: Dimensions of a Poet* (New York, 1995), James Karman's *Robinson Jeffers, Poet of California* (Brownsville, Ore., 1995), and current issues of *Jeffers Studies* should be consulted. The section on Gary Snyder in Ekbert Faas's *Towards a New American Poetics* (Santa Barbara, 1978) and Patrick D. Murphy's collection, *Critical Essays on Gary Snyder* (Boston, 1990), are rewarding. Those struck by William Stafford's poetic vision will enjoy his unusual guide, *Writing the Australian Crawl* (Ann Arbor, 1978), part of the University of Michigan's Poets on Poetry series.

Alan R. Velie's *Four American Indian Literary Masters: N. Scott Momaday, James Welch, Leslie Marmon Silko, and Gerald Vizenor* (Norman, 1982) is a good source, as are Charles L. Woodard's *Ancestral Voice: Conversations with N. Scott Momaday* (Lincoln, 1989), Per Seyersted's *Leslie Marmon Silko* (Boise, 1980), and Peter Wild's *James Welch* (Boise, 1983), the latter two being examples of Boise State University's useful pamphlet series Western Writers, edited by James H. Maguire. In addition, Momaday, Welch, Silko, and Vizenor, along with Louise Erdrich, Sherman Alexie, and Simon Ortiz (among other Indian writers) are treated edifyingly in *Updating the Literary West* (1997).

That volume also carries forward the growing critical interest in the literature of nature, in "Rocky Mountain Nature Writing," by Allison Bulsterbaum Wallace and Harry Crockett. The essay discusses Rick Bass, Douglas Peacock, David Quammen, C. L. Rawlins, Gretel Ehrlich, Ann

Zwinger, Jack Turner, David Petersen, and Terry Tempest Williams, among others. Readers interested in the green surge in American writing will want to consult the *American Nature Writing Newsletter* and the journal *ISLE (Interdisciplinary Studies in Literature and Environment)*. The most comprehensive and authoritative guide to the field is, again, John Elder's *American Nature Writers* (2 vols., New York, 1996).

IV. Bibliographies

The section titled "The West" in Clarence Gohdes and Sanford Marovitz's *Bibliographical Guide to the Study of the Literature of the U.S.A.* (5th ed., Durham, N.C., 1984) and Richard W. Etulain's *A Bibliographical Guide to the Study of Western American Literature* (2nd ed., Albuquerque, 1995) are still useful as starting points. The chapter bibliographies in *A Literary History of the American West, Updating the Literary West,* and *Fifty Western Writers: A Bio-bibliographical Sourcebook* (Westport, Conn., 1982) are also helpful, totaling hundreds of pages of good leads to authors and titles. *LHAW* also contains a master listing by George F. Day, entitled "Major Reference Sources on the West." The annual bibliography in the journal *Western American Literature,* published each February, is indispensable for anyone wanting to be right up to date. Finally, readers with access to the Internet will want to visit www.usu.edu/~westlit and http://www.sonic.net/~ghaslam/callit/. Both these websites have links to other, related sources.

CREDITS

INDEX

CPSIA information can be obtained
at www.ICGtesting.com
Printed in the USA
BVHW032200231121
622414BV00001B/2

9 780195 124613